BOOKS 7-9

SECRETS OF THE FAE

MELISSA A. CRAVEN
M. LYNN

Edited by Caitlin Haines

For the readers who've stuck out cliffhangers,
heart wrenching deaths, and tragic love to bring us here.

QUEENS OF THE FAE
BOOK SEVEN

FAE'S REBELLION

MELISSA A. CRAVEN
M. LYNN

MYRKUR KINGDOM
NORTHERN VATLANDS
FARGELSI KINGDOM
LOCH VILLANDI
SOUTHERN VATLANDS
ELDUR KING
DRAGUR FOREST
VINDUR CITY
ELDUR DE
LOCH LANGT

NORTH EASTERN KATELANDS
INGDOM
HUNTING LODGE
VALE OF STORMS
FIRE PLAINS
LDFAL
LENYA
GRIMA KINGDOM
MINES
THE BURNING SEA
VONDUR KINGDOM
R CITY
THE ROCKY SEAS OF LENYA
THE GRIMA SHOALS

CHAPTER I
TIERNEY

Tierney O'Shea wished she was human.

She wanted options. Freedom to make the kind of choices someone like her just didn't get.

Instead, she was a fae princess. An heir.

Okay, so it wasn't such a bad life. There were the parties. She loved those. And the copious amounts of food laid out at every meal. Tierney liked her food.

Except tonight, she couldn't stomach a single bite of the delicious roasted hen with her favorite crisped potatoes, spinach pies, and an assortment of cakes for dessert.

"Why aren't you eating, Tierney?" Her father's voice was gruff, but there was an edge of softness to it. That really described who he was as a fae, as a king. Most fae thought he was all stern tones and icy glares, but she knew the difference. Which was why she couldn't understand how he could be so uncaring as he played with his daughter's life.

"I seem to have lost my appetite, Father." Tierney stared at the roasted fowl on her plate, as if it too had betrayed her.

Her father released a long sigh. "You're being unreasonable."

"Me?" Her voice rose an octave.

"Here we go again," Toby, her twin, muttered under his breath. He wasn't turned off his food. No. Toby stuffed his face with all her favorites because *he* wasn't the heir to Iskalt. He had no worries weighing him down.

"Tierney." Her father's voice held a warning now. Lochlan O'Shea was not a man most fae trifled with, but his children were hardly most fae. His scowl would have sent anyone else running in the other direction. "You have duties to this kingdom, young lady."

"Duties," she scoffed. "Yes, Father, I've been learning about my *duties* for twenty years." Twenty years may have been an exaggeration. No one lectured babies on what it meant to rule a kingdom.

"Do you care nothing for the traditions of this family?"

"Traditions?" Her tone could get just as dangerous and cold as his. The two had matching tempers, and it tended to throw them into war with one another. She stood, tossing her serviette onto the table. "I think I'm finished for tonight."

Without looking back at her father, who was most likely seething, she strode from the huge dining hall. The royal family used to dine frequently with the court, but all that changed when her mother became queen. Now, only the family ate together in the great hall, reserving special occasions for dining with the rest of the court.

The Iskalt palace had felt even colder than normal the past month with her mother away on a royal visit to Eldur. There was a time when Tierney and her father understood each other, a time when she thought he'd move on from his ridiculous ideas about her future.

Eleven minutes. That was all that put her in this position.

She'd been born eleven minutes before Toby, making her the heir to her father's throne.

Sconces lit the stone walls as she passed tapestries depicting battles of generations past. There were newer ones illustrating the evil Queen Regan of Fargelsi with a young Uncle Griff at her side. The next one showed the battle for Myrkur and the two fae children who brought down the prison realm.

She stopped in front of that one, running her fingers over the soft threads, pausing on the face of the child she wasn't sure was part of her anymore.

"I miss you," she whispered. That girl had been bold. She'd been brave. Fearless.

But that was ten years ago, when she didn't have enough sense to fear the world. Now, as an adult, she had complete control over her magic, but not over anything else in her life.

"Seems like another lifetime, doesn't it?" Toby stepped up to her side, his eyes lifting to the two figures standing before a shimmering wall of magic sewn into the tapestries.

"Is Father angry?"

Toby was quiet for a long moment. "I don't …" He pushed out a breath. "I don't think he wants to do this to you any more than you want it done. But Dad and tradition have never parted ways."

She turned on her heel and took off down the hall to the one place she could hide. "I don't need you defending him."

Toby ran to catch up. "I'm not. It's just … he's trying to protect Iskalt."

She shoved through a door and stopped, turning to him. Around them, high cherry wood bookshelves rose all the way to the ceilings. It took a ladder to get to the very top, and she wondered how thick the layer of dust on those tomes would be. Very few fae entered the palace library these days.

Except her.

"Sometimes, I wish he'd protect his daughter." That had always been the battle within her father. Kingdom or family. Most of the time, he found a way to do what was best for both. All her life, he'd done whatever he could for her, but this was new territory for both of them, and it wasn't going well.

Tierney slumped into a padded, brown leather chair, throwing one leg over a rounded arm. "I know, Toby. Don't say it. I'm being a child."

Toby shrugged. "Well, I'm glad you can see your own faults."

She reached for the table beside the chair, where she'd left a stack of books, not caring which one she grabbed as she threw it at him. He ducked with a laugh.

"It's a good thing you're a future queen. You never have to become an archer with an aim like that."

She groaned. "Thanks for the reminder." Though, she was actually quite good with an arrow.

"I live to serve."

No, that was what she did. But she smiled despite herself. Every time she argued with her father—and it was frequently these days—she could count on Toby to make her feel better.

He slid into the chair next to her, sitting properly like a royal should. But these tiny rebellions—slouching in a chair, eating too much food, dancing a bit too enthusiastically at balls—they were all she had to fight this stuffy world.

She hadn't realized the door to the library was still partially open until she heard someone yelling in the hallway. "Where are my little heathens?"

Tierney shared a look with her brother, one that went from exasperation to excitement. They weren't little anymore, but that voice … they'd missed it.

They both jumped up from their chairs and dashed into the hall, jostling with each other to get to their mother first.

Brea Robinson was the most popular fae in all of Iskalt. The kingdom adored her and made them like their father even more for having married her.

"Mom." Tierney slammed into her mother, using the human term. Much of their lives were influenced by their mother's connection with the human realm. As Brea often said, you could take the fae out of the human realm, but you couldn't take the human realm out of the fae.

Brea was raised on a human farm, something that seemed exotic and exciting to Tierney.

Toby always said it sounded terrifying to grow up there, but there was something so exotic about the idea of living among humans and the strange form of magic they called technology. They still visited the farm often, and those were Tierney's favorite days, but they rarely ventured into the cities.

Toby joined the group hug, and their mother's long, dark hair spread over them as if it could shield them from the harsh realities of the world.

A throat cleared, and Tierney lifted her head to find two men watching them. The first was her father. He had a folder grasped in one hand and conflict in his eyes.

But the second… Toby broke away. "Logan."

Their mother laughed. "I stole him from Eldur for a visit."

Logan was the oldest Eldurian prince, and also Toby's…

"Can't you guys go to Toby's room or something?" Tierney shielded her eyes from their disgustingly adorable reunion, their kiss going on way too long.

It had been at least a few weeks since anyone had kissed her, and that was weeks too long. Still, there wasn't much behind those stolen kisses. Not like with Toby and Logan, who just belonged together.

"Absolutely not," Father said.

Their mother shot him a look, and he went quiet, as usual. She turned to her son. "Go catch up."

The two boys practically sprinted down the hall.

"Keep your door open!" she called after them.

Tierney looked more closely at her mother. She was travel weary but happy. Dust from the road dulled her black riding trousers, as if she'd come directly from the stables.

Father put an arm around her, giving her an adoring look.

Tierney turned away, hating all the affection she was constantly surrounded by. Toby got to be in love, even her parents … yet she had to choose her future husband or wife from a pre-approved list.

With a snort, she walked back into the library and shut the door.

Her parents didn't knock before they came in.

"I see nothing has improved in the time I've been gone." Her mother leaned against a shelf and crossed her arms over her chest.

Tierney and her father avoided each other's gazes.

Her mother sighed. "You two are so similar in your stubbornness; it's driving me absolutely bonkers."

Tierney glanced sideways and caught her father's lips twitching. Even after more than twenty years in the fae realm, her mother hadn't lost her human way of speaking.

"It's his fault." Tierney threw herself into a chair.

"I'm only trying to make this easier." Her father perched on the arm of the other chair.

"Easier? How is any of this easy? You want to choose my partner for me. It's not fair."

"It's how things have always been done for the heirs of Iskalt."

"Not for you." She shot him a glare, daring him to contradict her. "You loved Mom when you married her."

"You forget, Tia, when I met your mother, I was a prince without a kingdom. No one would have called me the future king when my throne had been stolen. I was lucky to fall in love with a fae princess. After I fought for my throne, I couldn't have kept it without your mother at my side. But even after all of that, if Brea had never come into my life, I too would have had to choose a partner from among fae royalty or the noble families of Iskalt. It just so happens that your royal peers are either related to you or are as close as your own siblings. Iskalt nobility is our only option."

"Nobility." She rolled her eyes. "What does that even mean?"

"It means they come from ancient lines—"

She cut him off. "And these *noble* families ... did they come to their rightful king's aid when he wanted to take back the kingdom? Or were they too busy scraping and bowing to save their—"

"Watch it."

She ignored him and continued. "No, it was the *fae* who marched with you. And yet, I'm not allowed to choose one of them." If she could, she'd marry one of her friends from the village. At least then, she would know she could stand them.

Or maybe Gulliver if he was of Iskalt. Too bad the court didn't recognize him as such as the adopted son of Prince Griffin O'Shea. That would have made her choice much easier.

Her father stood, pushing a hand through his hair, and gestured to his wife. "She's your daughter."

Tierney's mother smiled. "And, my dear douchey Loch, she also has a point."

"I know what douchey means now," Tierney mumbled, trying not to pout. Pouting was definitely not for a twenty-year-old woman. "Uncle Myles told me."

Her father cursed Uncle Myles under his breath, and her mother laughed.

"Well, Tia, your father knows how I feel about this whole selling my daughter to the highest bidder thing, but let's see what he's brought us, shall we?" She held her hand out for the folder. "Maybe we'll find a gem among the swine."

He didn't give it to her. "You've only just returned, Brea. You should rest. Go find the rest of the children. They've been begging me to tell them when you return."

Tierney rolled her eyes. She had way too many siblings now, but somehow, her mother made time for all of them while also helping to rule the kingdom and assist Aunt Alona with magic whenever Eldur was in need of it.

Brea shook her head. "Tia is the one who needs me now. Rest can wait, and none of the others are about to be paraded around like a cow at the county fair."

His brow furrowed like it always did when he didn't understand one of her human sayings. He'd long since stopped asking her to explain all of them.

She took the folder from him. "Now, go, husband. Your services are no longer needed."

That made Tierney laugh. She loved her mother, loved being around her.

He stood in stunned silence for a moment before turning and leaving the two women to their own devices.

"Men." Tierney's mother shook her head. "Can't live with them, can't lock them in a prison world that no longer exists."

Tierney laughed so hard the corners of her eyes watered. "Sorry about that."

"Yes, it is becoming quite a problem that my children tore down the prison boundary and saved us all." She sent her a wink and dropped into the chair beside her. "Now, shall we see what kind of fae your father thinks would make a good match for you? He's never had the best taste in, well … anything, so I'm a bit scared."

Tierney leaned over the arm of her chair to get a look at the first page in the file. The name jumped out at her. "Calton Riley? Really?"

"What's wrong with Calton?" her mother asked. "The Riley family isn't so bad. They've used their trade connections to import Eldur beans just so I can have something resembling coffee in the morning."

"Mom, I'm not marrying someone so you can keep having your strange, bitter drink. Can't you just go buy coffee in the human realm?"

"Well, yes, but that's not the point."

"Then, do you have a point?"

Her mother reached out and pinched her.

"Ow, what was that for?"

"You deserved it."

"You're deranged, woman."

Her mother put a hand over her heart, her eyes glassing over.

"What?"

"You sounded almost human. I'm so proud."

Tierney rolled her eyes. "You get proud over the oddest things. Anyway, Calton has perpetually bad breath."

"And how would you know that, young lady?"

Tierney's face went hot. "Lucky guess." In truth, Calton had been one of the few noble fae she'd ever given the time of day. Her mistake.

Her mother flipped to the next page. "Aisling Murphy? Isn't she the girl who followed you around for a fortnight a few years ago?"

"Don't remind me." Tierney had become friends with Aisling when she was seeing the girl's older sister, but it was Aisling who'd developed feelings for Tierney, not the older Murphy. She hadn't taken it well when Tierney turned her down.

On the next page was a name she knew well. "No, absolutely not." Veren Rhatigan. "Mom, I can't do this." If these were her options … She stared at the thick pile of papers left to go through. Many of the noble children of Iskalt who were around her age.

But Veren … he was the first fae to hurt her. She'd been sixteen and thought she was in love with him. It turned out he just wanted to be seen with the princess.

"Honey." Her mother closed the folder. "I didn't know he'd put Veren in there."

"No, I can't do any of it. Marrying someone I barely know, let alone like. Just the thought of it … this isn't okay." Her breath wheezed in her chest, and power buzzed along her skin. It had been a long time since she felt her magic weaving in and out of control, but in that moment, she couldn't reel it back in.

A blast of power exploded from her, striking a shelf and toppling it over backward. It hit the one behind it and they went down like dominoes.

Her mother could have stopped them with her own magic, but she just stood there, watching Tierney spin out of control.

"Mom," she cried.

Warm fingers slid into hers, guiding her back from the edge. "Breathe, Tia. Everything is going to be okay. Just breathe."

"I don't want to breathe!"

"I don't like it either, and I'll work on your father some more. I promise you I'll try, but Iskalt stands on tradition. This is expected."

Tears spilled from Tierney's eyes as she reached out, trying to grasp her magic and pull it back. "I don't care about tradition. This is my life. It should belong to me."

Her mother squeezed her hand. "I will make it my mission for you to have your great love. I don't know how, but I promise you'll get your love story."

Tierney's power recoiled so suddenly that she slammed back into the chair, all energy drained from her. A love story.

Her mother thought she didn't want to marry without being in love, but that wasn't it at all. Tierney didn't believe in love, not for her, not for the heir.

After Veren, she'd never be able to trust that anyone loved her for more than the crown she'd wear someday.

CHAPTER 2
TIERNEY

"Your father has been working tirelessly for months to make your birthday ball the event of the century." Tierney's mother placed a glittering tiara on her head.

"We both know that could be catastrophic. Dad's not exactly well known for his party planning." Tierney watched her mother in the mirror. Her mother fussed with her dress and its many layers of fabric that would make it nearly impossible to move in, much less dance. But it was so beautiful Tierney couldn't stop staring at it.

"The dress is a gift from Aunt Neeve and Uncle Myles." She brushed at the many flounces of fabric until they lay just right. "It's the latest Gelsi style."

"It's gorgeous." Tierney was almost afraid to move in it. The wide ballgown skirt billowed around her, cascading in yards of midnight blue fabric that sparkled in the light, giving the illusion of the night sky. Tiny live flowers grew up from the hem, with buds of ivory and silver that would bloom as she entered the ballroom. The vines were the palest green with streaks of gold, and golden leaves cupped the flowers.

The strapless bodice was the same midnight blue fabric trimmed in silver with an intricate neckline of flowers and vines that constantly changed from ivory to silver to a rosy pink and back again.

"Well, go on. Give us a turn." Rowena stepped away from the other maids that had come to help. Rowena was like family. She'd arrived with Aunt Alona and Uncle Finn and was quick to offer her assistance with the birthday girl. Not that this night wasn't for Toby too. A fact Tierney kept reminding everyone of, but they all seemed intent on making this birthday celebration all about her.

"I'm afraid I'll crush it if I move." Tierney made a hesitant circle to the oohs and aahs of everyone in the room. It wasn't as if she'd never worn a ballgown before. As a princess of Iskalt, she'd worn plenty. But this dress was different. This was a gown fit for a queen. A future queen.

She hated being the heir. She would be an old lady by the time she was ever crowned Queen of Iskalt. Her father wasn't *that* old. He would rule for years to come while Tierney lived her life waiting in the wings for the inevitable. The monarch perpetually on hold.

"Let's give the birthday girl a moment alone, shall we?" Her mom flashed her a wink as she shooed the maids out of the room. "You look so grown up, Tia." She forced a smile for her daughter. "But you'll always be my baby. My first baby."

"For eleven blissful minutes, I was an only child." Tierney turned toward her mother, her skirts rustling as she moved. Without a little magical assistance, the dress would weigh her down before she ever made it to the ballroom.

"You ready, darling?" Her mother fussed with her own understated ballgown. Neither woman was overly happy about the fancy clothes—no matter how beautiful they were. It was a chore to wear them.

"Sure." She gathered up her courage for the long evening ahead. Tonight, she had a role to play as Princess of Iskalt. A role she'd had years to perfect. "Here's hoping I don't tumble down the stairs with my skirts over my head."

"Not again." Her mother laughed.

"It was one time, and I was four." Tierney followed her mother out of the room, feeling about as un-princess-like as she ever had before. Part of her wanted to tell all of Iskalt where they could take their crown and shove it. But the other part remembered all the lessons from her father about what it meant to be the heir of Iskalt. She represented the future of their kingdom, and the fae loved her for it. Adored her. She owed it to them to respect her station.

"Toby will meet you at the top of the stairs in five minutes." Her mom squeezed her hand before she made her way down to the main floor toward her father. "Happy birthday, sweetheart!" she called over her shoulder.

Tierney took a deep breath, exhaling it slowly as she walked down the empty hallway to the grand staircase that led to the ballroom. The entire castle was decked out for the twins' birthday celebration. Shimmering flowers bloomed in pots, and icicles hung from doorways, glittering with light and magicked to remain frozen even as the hallways pulsed with warmth from the braziers burning in every available corner.

"Happy birthday, Tia." Toby joined her as he entered the hall from his suite. "You look beautiful."

"Happy birthday, Tobes." She reached to hug her twin. "And you look handsome in your suit. Want to trade outfits?" She looped her arm through his.

"Not even a little. There's no doubt about it, your wardrobe is way more intense than mine." He brushed a hand over his midnight blue silk vest adorned with silver and ivory blossoms in a similar style to her gown.

"You think we'll ever get old enough for them to stop putting us in twin clothes?" He escorted her down the wide hallway.

"Probably not." Tierney halted in front of the stately double doors that were the last remaining barrier between her and their father's court.

"Do me a favor, Tia?"

"Of course." She turned to her brother.

"Try to have fun tonight. We don't turn twenty every day."

She pursed her lips at him. "I can't make any promises."

"Dad's gone to a lot of trouble to make this a special night for you."

"I know, but it's not just my night. It's *ours*. I don't like eclipsing your birthday just because I'm the heir."

"You know that doesn't bother me. Never has."

"Well, it should. You're just as important as me."

"To you and our family, yes. Not to Iskalt. I am just the spare, with a serious lack of magic."

"Fine. I will try to enjoy the party." Tierney smoothed a nervous hand over her dress.

"You ready?"

She nodded, taking another deep breath as her brother tapped on the door to let the footmen know they were ready to make their grand entrance.

Tierney pasted on her princess smile and stepped through the double doors with Toby at her side.

"May I have this dance, your Royal Highness?" Yet another young nobleman bowed at the waist before Tierney. She thought she'd danced with everyone her age at least twice already, but they kept approaching her.

Toby leaned in and murmured in her ear. "Lord Kellen Sullivan, heir to the Duke of Kildare."

"Lord Kellen, how nice to see you again." Tierney accepted his hand. "What brings you all the way from Kildare?"

"Your Highness, of course." Kellen stood to his full height, towering over her. "I couldn't pass up the opportunity to attend your ball this evening."

"I'm flattered." She turned onto the dance floor, her skirts billowing around her as she sank into the graceful curtsy this particular dance demanded. As the quartet's melody increased, she rose and stepped toward her dance partner.

"You dance beautifully, your Highness."

"Oh, please call me Tia." That was her first test after meeting someone new. If he refused to call her Tia, she would excuse herself, and that would be the last she'd see of Lord Kellen this evening. Tierney had rules she expected her friends to follow. And those rules existed to help them feel comfortable treating her like a normal person.

"I do hate it when my friends insist on calling me 'your Lordship' every time I turn around." Kellen kept them moving with the music. He was a great dancer, but Tierney could already tell he was a bit too pompous for her tastes. "I prefer my closest friends call me Kildare." He whirled her into a graceful turn.

"Isn't that a little premature?" As the reigning Duke of Kildare, Kellen's father, was known simply as Kildare. Kellen was nothing more than a lord trying to make himself appear more important than he was.

"Father's an old man." Kellen shrugged. "Though, there is still time for me to pursue other, more impressive titles before the dukedom passes to me." Kellen gave her a knowing smile.

The only title that would surpass the one he would inherit would be prince ... or prince consort.

Tierney was relieved when the dance ended. Dropping his Lordship's hand, she made a quick escape.

"Your Royal Highness." A familiar breathless voice caught her off guard.

"Lady Siobhan? Is that you?" Tierney pulled the slim girl up from her deep curtsy to give her a warm hug. "I haven't seen you in ages."

"Father insisted we make the journey down from the northern mountains. We didn't want to miss your ball."

"I'm thrilled you came." Tierney led her old friend onto the dance floor. "You look lovely." She admired her rose gold silk gown, but she knew Siobhan wasn't comfortable in her finery. Just like Tierney, she was much more suited to the leathers she wore on horseback, with a sword in her hand. As the future Marchioness of Belmore Keep along the border of the Northern Vatlands, Siobhan was more warrior than lady. Her father, the Marquess of Belmore, was probably one of the most important men in the room tonight. It was his responsibility to guard the border between Iskalt and the Northern Vatlands, which also bordered Myrkur—once known as the prison realm.

"I'm afraid Father has grand ideas." Siobhan rested her hand at Tierney's waist for the dance. She was a marvelous dancer, probably from her years of training as a swordswoman. Tierney had always found Siobhan beautiful. She was slim but strong, with wide shoulders and lovely chestnut brown hair that normally fell to her waist in a mess of loose braids. Tonight, her hair was elaborately styled in a pile of curls on top of her head, pulled back from the russet skin of her cheeks.

"How so?" Tierney pulled her attention away from the feel of Siobhan's smooth shoulder under her hand.

"He has hopes we will 'rekindle' our friendship." Siobhan ducked her head, embarrassed.

"There is nothing to rekindle. We are still friends as we have always been." Though, there was no doubt Siobhan had grown up in the years since Tierney had last seen her. Just a few years older than the princess, Lady Siobhan's presence was the highlight of the ball in Tierney's mind. Yet, she found herself wondering where on her father's list the future marchioness fell.

"I believe he is hoping I will catch your eye amidst all the eligible young nobles here this evening."

"Eligible?" Tierney frowned.

"When father received the king's invitation, he was so thrilled that I would be included—"

Tierney tilted her head in question. "As my friend?"

"As a noblewoman … eligible for your hand."

"My hand?" Tierney stopped dancing. Grabbing Siobhan's arm, she led the lady through the crowded ballroom, avoiding cries of happy birthday and offers to dance with this son or that daughter.

"Are you well, your Highness?" Siobhan's brown eyes filled with concern. Her full lips parted in question.

"Tell me about this invitation your father received." Tierney's heart raced, and her palms began to sweat.

"It was just an invitation to your party, sent to the families of all the young eligible fae nobles of Iskalt. I was actually surprised to see it. Not that the king invited me and father, but that you agreed to it."

"Agreed to what?" Tierney's voice rose.

"Tonight isn't just about celebrating your birthday. It's meant to introduce you to potential suitors. I thought you knew."

"No. I did not." Tierney was going to murder her meddling father as soon as she could get her hands on him.

"I'm so sorry, Tia." Siobhan squeezed her hand. "I didn't realize."

"Please excuse me." Tierney stepped away from her friend, her eyes burning with angry tears. "Enjoy the party." She darted around the crowd, making her way toward the service entrance. She had to get out of this ballroom immediately before she screamed.

She slipped through the doors into the wide servant corridor and ducked behind a row of columns to lean against the cool stone wall.

"Going somewhere, Princess?" Something flat and rather fuzzy tapped against her forehead. She'd recognize that tail anywhere.

"Gullie?" She stepped from the shadows to find her favorite person in all the realms eating a pastry with a smear of icing on his nose.

"Happy birthday." Gulliver wrapped her in a warm, familiar embrace.

"I'm so glad you're here." She wanted to cry, but she had lots of practice keeping her emotions in check.

"What's wrong?" Gulliver pushed her back at arm's length and studied her. "That is not a happy face."

"I'm feeling quite murderous, actually. Tell me, are you on the list?" Tierney stepped away and crossed her arms over her chest.

"List? What list?" He frowned. "I'm here for the food and to hopefully steal you away from all the fancy fae at some point so we can actually celebrate your birthday like normal fae."

Tierney lunged toward him and wrapped her arms around him. "At least one of my friends knows what I really need. I'm glad you're here."

"You know I'm always here when you need me, Tia." Gulliver gave her an awkward pat on her shoulder. "Your dad's about to make a speech, so let's trot you back out there and let the court get their Tia time. Then, we'll sneak away with a few friends and have a real party."

"Promise?" She sniffed.

"Promise." He turned her toward the ballroom.

"It was a lot easier when we were ten, Gullie." She took his hand in hers. "Why can't we just stay ten forever?"

"Easier? You do remember we were saving the realm from a sadistic king when you were ten, right? Anyway, easy is boring. At least now, we get to make our own decisions."

"Speak for yourself." Tierney looped her arm through his as they made their way around the crowd toward the king and queen.

"Dad's about to make his speech." Toby sidled up beside her, Logan right next to him. Tierney slipped her free arm around Toby's, still gripping Gulliver's with her other.

"Ah, there she is." Lochlan turned his smile on his daughter, tapping his champagne glass to get the court's attention. "Ladies and gentlemen, twenty years ago today, our lovely Queen Brea delivered our very first princess and prince. Sometimes, I feared these two would never make it to adulthood." He paused for the laughter that swept through the room.

"Never has this castle seen such a pair. Thick as thieves from the moment they were born, and a handful we were ill prepared for." Lochlan smiled at his eldest children. "But your mother and I couldn't be prouder.

"To Prince Toby, the Ogre Killer, our second born. You bring us joy every day, son. And with your gentle spirit, you remind us to always have hope. We wish nothing but happiness and love in your near future. Happy birthday." The king lifted his glass, and the court echoed his birthday wishes.

Lochlan turned to Tierney next. "To Princess Tierney, our first-born and heir to the throne of Iskalt." Lochlan blinked and took a deep breath. "You make me so proud, Tia." His voice went gruff and hard like it did when he was trying to hide his emotions. "You have your mother's strength, and a fair bit of her stubbornness too."

Tierney didn't miss the way her mother elbowed him for that. She couldn't help her smile. As mad as she was with her father right now, she still loved him more than he could ever know.

"You are the future of Iskalt, my darling girl. And as long as you fight for Iskalt, we all know our home will be safe in your capable hands. None of us would be standing here now without you and your brother. I can only hope your future consort stands in this room with you tonight. Your union with a fae of our kingdom will ensure your reign after I am gone. And that man or woman is a lucky fae indeed, for my daughter's hand is a precious one I will not offer to just anyone. We wish you nothing but joy and happiness, my children. Happy birthday, Tia and Toby." The king lifted his glass again, and his court cheered him on.

But to Tierney, his speech, though heartfelt, was nothing more than a presentation of her eligibility. A reminder to all those fae from his stupid list that to win the great Princess Tierney's hand in marriage was a prize like none other.

Chapter 3
Tierney

"You okay?" Gulliver whispered in Tierney's ear. "Tia." When she didn't respond, he elbowed her.

Toby cast pitiful glances her way.

"You're so lucky," another voice said on a sigh.

Tierney turned to find her little sister, Kayleigh. At fourteen years old, she still had fantastical ideas about what it would be like to be the heir, to be the one forced to follow their father around.

"Kay," Toby warned.

She ignored him, as always. No one could ever stop Kayleigh once she'd started. "I mean, to have your pick of all these fae." She fanned her face. "They're all so handsome and beautiful." She didn't seem to recognize the anxiety pouring off her sister in waves as she stepped up beside her. "So, tell me, who is your favorite? Some of the younger siblings, who have no chance, are making bets with lemon drops from Gelsi, and you know I always have a craving for those."

Her eyes scanned the room, landing on a man walking toward them. She leaned in. "It's Veren Rhatigan, isn't it? He's perfect. I always liked him when he was trying to court you before, but you were *so* oblivious. I can't believe you denied him."

Finally, Tierney turned to her sister. "You don't know anything.

You're just a child." She hated being mean to any of her siblings, but if she didn't yell at someone, she was going to bring this entire castle down with the force of her magic. "Just stop. Stop!"

Kayleigh stared at her in shock, hurt filling her eyes.

Tierney didn't get the chance to apologize because Veren had reached them.

A hand slid into hers, and she looked down to find Gulliver holding on to her. He'd always known what she needed. Their decade-long friendship had bonded them for life. This would be so much easier if she could just marry him. But he wasn't an Iskaltian nobleman or a foreign prince. And she wasn't *in* love with him.

Veren wore a gorgeous suit of deep red with silver embroidery, the colors of the Rhatigan family crest. His inky black hair was parted on one side and slicked down. She found herself missing his usual messy curls, the ones she'd loved playing with as they lay in the snow beyond the palace.

Long lashes brushed against the delicate beauty of his cheeks as he bowed at the waist. "Princess."

She extended her hand, letting him press a soft kiss to it. Her heart still quickened at the sight of him, even after all these years, and it made her hate him more.

He straightened, his casual smirk appearing on his face. "I came over here to ask for the pleasure of a dance with you."

Tierney could feel all eyes on her. Everywhere she glanced, fae watched her, examining her every move. They expected her to dance with Veren, to fall madly in love with him like half the noble girls in the kingdom.

Her parents stood with Uncle Griff and Aunt Riona, who'd made the trip from Myrkur. A smile played on her father's lips as he noticed her standing with Veren.

Duke Rhatigan was one of his most powerful supporters. A union with their line would be good for Iskalt. But the thought of it, of sitting by while Veren flirted and more with all the girls in the villages, while he yearned for more and more power … He'd always sought her position.

It made her want to puke.

"I-I need to pee." It was a very un-princess-like thing to say, but at the moment, she didn't particularly care how a princess should act.

Turning on her heel, she left Veren standing there and hurried from the great hall into the bustling corridor. Servants rushed to and from the hall with trays of food and goblets of wine.

Tierney grabbed a goblet from one of the servants and ducked her head, practically sprinting across the palace to her library. Once she slammed the door shut behind her, she gulped the wine, wanting it to dull the ache in her head, her heart.

This was going to happen. Whether she was in agreement or not, she had to choose a spouse. Another sip. She had no choices. Tradition was a cruel mistress. She drained the rest of the wine as the door opened.

Whirling around, she was ready to tell whoever it was to leave her in peace. But when her eyes connected with Gulliver's, a sob left her throat.

He rushed forward and crushed her into a hug. "I followed you here; hope that's okay."

Her entire body shook. "This is wrong, Gullie. So wrong." She looked up at him, sure her face looked like a wreck with tears streaming down her cheeks. "Can't I just run away to Myrkur with you?"

He laughed. "Your parents love Griff, but they'd start a war to get you back if Myrkur was hiding their princess. I'm not sure King Hector would approve."

"You can just keep me under your bed or something. No one has to know."

"Like I did with the stray dog I found in the human realm that time?"

She rolled her eyes. Gulliver had always had a soft spot for creatures in distress. They were fifteen the first time Uncle Griff took them to the human realm voluntarily. Gulliver found a puppy near the farmhouse and hid it in his coat on the trip back.

Griff only found out when the dog peed in his favorite boots.

"I can be a stray dog."

Gulliver wiped tears from Tierney's face. "You're going to be queen one day. My best friend, the queen." He grinned. "You can't give that up because I want to be able to tell everyone who will listen that I'm friends with the Queen of Iskalt."

She pinched him. "You're so odd."

His tail wrapped around her and flicked. "Come on, Tia. We'll figure this out."

There was a tentative knock at the door before it opened, revealing Siobhan. She smiled sadly. "I wanted to make sure you hadn't jumped from the ramparts."

Siobhan was shoved to the side as Veren strode in. "And I still want my dance."

Tierney narrowed her eyes. "I don't want to dance with you. Me leaving you in the middle of the ballroom should have been a sign."

Veren's brow rose at her icy tone. "Ah, still holding our youthful dalliance against me, I see."

Gulliver stepped in front of her. "You're not wanted here." Out in the grand hall, they'd all had to be civil, but here in private, they could let Veren know what they really thought of him.

Siobhan pretended to be examining the bookshelf.

"It's no matter." Veren met Tierney's gaze with a shrewdness she'd always known he had. "My father has been in talks with yours for your hand over the last year."

All the breath rushed from her lungs. "He wouldn't." Her father promised she'd at least get to choose. Were the Rhatigans his backup if she refused? Tierney stumbled back, her butt hitting a bookshelf that had somehow been righted and fixed since the last time she stood there. A leather-bound book teetered and fell, hitting her shoulder on the way down. Its collision with the stone floor echoed throughout the room.

Tierney stared at the book, laying with pages bent and its broken spine pointed up toward the ceiling. She felt just as ruined, just as bent and cracked as that spine.

She would never forgive her father for this.

Power buzzed in her fingertips, rising with her anger. Iskaltian night magic twisted and contorted with Gelsi magic. If she said the words to unleash the Gelsi power, it would be amplified.

And yet, it was neither of those that rose to the surface. Nor was it the Eldurian magic that lay dormant inside her without the sun in the sky.

No, this power that sparked now was one she'd inherited from her father, well, technically the man she called uncle Griffin. And it gave her an idea.

"I have to get out of here," she whispered.

Gulliver looked back at her. "We can go outside. Maybe head down to the village and see if any of your friends are in the tavern."

"The tavern?" Veren sneered. "With common folk?"

Tierney shook her head. The village wasn't far enough. Wine clouded her thoughts, pushing a singular focus to the front of her mind. Everything else faded to a fuzzy hue.

She could do this, right?

Looking down at her hands, she knew the truth. She'd learned long ago she could accomplish anything she desired with her magic. Anything except escaping her fate.

"I need …" She sucked in a breath, meeting Gulliver's gaze and willing him to understand what she wasn't saying. "An escape. Just for a few days."

"Come visit Myrkur and …" His eyes widened, understanding showing on his face. "Tia, you can't."

"But what if I *can*?"

"You've never done it before on your own."

It was the truth. She'd always had her father or Uncle Griff with her. They'd refused to teach any of their kids how to use the O'Shea magic until they were older for fear they'd go to the human realm on a whim.

Like now.

Veren and Siobhan shared a look. "What are we missing?"

Tierney narrowed her eyes. "Nothing you need to concern yourself with. Go back to the party, Rhatigan."

"Tierney?" a voice called from down the corridor outside the library. It was her father.

"Now or never, Tia," she muttered to herself as her magic flooded to the tips of her fingers.

Gulliver yelled to stop her, but she barely heard him as a flash of light filled the room. She didn't have time to bask in the fact that she'd done it before jumping into the portal and picturing the familiar farm her mother owned in the human realm.

The library disappeared. Voices faded into the distance. And then, it was just her, lying on soft grass with the sun shining overhead. The eerie sensation of Iskalt magic fading one moment to be replaced by Eldurian magic the next wasn't something she'd ever get used to. When it was night in the fae realm, it was day here. The switch was so abrupt it sapped her energy.

Her entire body ached as she lifted her head. But she wasn't alone.

"Oh, no." Around her, the others stirred.

"Talk about a bad landing," Gulliver groaned.

Veren sat up in a rush, his eyes darting toward the old, rickety farmhouse. "Where are we?" He scrambled back. "What happened?"

Tierney sighed. She sometimes forgot trips to the human realm weren't normal for most fae.

Siobhan looked less frightened than Veren. There was a sense of awe on her face. "Is this the human world?"

Tierney pushed to her feet, her legs weak beneath her. "Yes."

She strode toward the old house, past the barn that looked like it should have probably been torn down.

The front steps creaked and cracked as she climbed them. The place never changed. It had been months since she'd been here last, but it was as familiar as her own rooms.

Reaching underneath the strange carpeting humans kept outside their front doors, she grasped the rusty key and pulled open the swinging door. The screen was long gone, leaving it just a useless piece of metal that got in the way. Her mother liked to keep the house looking run down to keep the humans away.

Unlocking the main door, she shoved it open, preparing for the musty smell that always assaulted her senses here.

She didn't have the energy to look around or explain to the others what was going on. She headed straight up the stairs and walked into her parents' bedroom and crawled onto the big bed, collapsing on the pile of weird soft animals that humans had a penchant for.

She didn't hear the others come in and barely felt Gulliver climb into bed beside her and pull her into his arms or Siobhan sitting on the other side, clasping her hand.

Instead, she felt a bone-deep weariness. A hopelessness she couldn't shake.

Back in Iskalt, the young nobles were probably still waiting for their prize to return to the ball—her birthday ball. It was a day to be celebrated, and all she wanted was to disappear.

Her entire life, Tierney had told herself she had to be strong. For her parents, for her siblings, for Iskalt. She was the princess who'd saved all four kingdoms when she was ten years old. Heroes didn't cry. They didn't sink into their best friend's arms and give in to the pain fracturing their hearts.

And they certainly didn't give up.

But she no longer felt like a hero.

Tierney O'Shea, the most powerful magic wielder in the fae realm, the only living fae with the magic of three kingdoms, very much wanted to be someone else.

Chapter 4
TIERNEY

"Tia, how did you do it?" Gulliver whispered after the others had fallen asleep. It seemed the trip through the portal had sapped their energy as well. All four lay on the big bed in her mother's room. Together, they were nothing but a pile of silk and wrinkled ballgowns.

"I don't know." Tierney shook her head. "Sheer willpower, maybe. I had to get out of there, and this was the only place I could think of where Dad wouldn't immediately come looking for me." Because Tierney had very little control over her O'Shea portal magic. With the immense power of three realms thrumming through her veins, it was as if her body couldn't handle a fourth.

"I jumped in after you just as the portal was closing." Gulliver turned to glance at Siobhan and Veren, fast asleep on the other side of the bed. "But how did they follow?"

"I must have pulled them in." Tierney's voice lowered to a soft whisper. She couldn't believe she had the strength to bring three fae along with her, when before, she'd struggled to keep a portal open long enough for one person—and that was with her father's help. "Desperate times lead to crazy feats of magic. We've seen that happen before."

"It will be okay, Tia." The tip of Gulliver's tail stroked along her arm. "Your father will never force you to marry someone you don't love. He might want you to *try* finding someone from his list, but if it doesn't work for you—if you can't be happy with any of the eligible Iskaltian nobles—then he will find another solution."

"The only other solution would be for me to marry a foreign prince or princess, and in case you forgot, I'm related to nearly everyone who can claim that title."

"Technically, you aren't related to Eldurian royalty. At least not by blood."

"That's just gross. I grew up with Darra and Logan. And Toby is totally going to marry Prince Logan. That leaves Princess Darra. She's been like my little sister. And all of the Gelsi royals are my cousins and as close as siblings. Unless King Hector has a kid my age that no one's told us about, I have to choose from the Iskaltian noble families."

"Well, Hector and his queen are expecting. You could just wait around for a bit." Gulliver chuckled when she scrunched up her face at him.

"I'm not going to marry someone twenty years younger." Tierney rolled toward him on the bed, careful not to wake the others. "It's too bad the Iskalt court ruled against making you a nobleman." As an Iskaltian prince, it was within Griffin's right to request a title for his adopted son, but because Gulliver was of Myrkur and Griffin himself took no role in the rule of Iskalt, the king's council decided not to give him a formal title.

He was known simply as Lord Gulliver O'Shea in name only. Which meant the council would never allow a marriage between him and their princess. That was probably why they ruled against a formal title in the first place. Even a decade later, fae were still hesitant to accept the Dark Fae. For all Gulliver had done to aid Iskalt and Eldur in the war against King Egan, the least he deserved was a title and some lands of his own. Perhaps once she was queen, she could rectify that mistake.

"And it's too bad we're not in love." Gulliver took her hand. "I'd marry you in a second if I thought we could be happy together, but we'd probably end up killing each other. There is something more for both of us. Out there ... somewhere. We just need to find it."

"If I was just plain old Tia, I'd say let's run away and go find our destinies." Tierney sighed. "But like it or not, I'm Princess Tierney, heir to the Iskaltian throne. Imprisoned by the circumstances of my birth." She grew quiet for a moment, her fingertips tracing the coil of Gulliver's tail around her arm.

"Eleven minutes. How did eleven little moments decide what my life would be?" Toby would have made a much better heir. The fae loved him, despite his lack of magic. He was smart, and his heart bled for Iskalt. He would have been a great king. If not for those eleven minutes.

"I don't have the words that will make you feel better." Gulliver pulled her closer so her head rested on his shoulder. "But I know you. You'll fight for a future of your own making. And I'll be there to make sure you get it."

"Thanks, Gullie." Tierney yawned.

"Rest. Everything will look better after a nap. I promise."

"Princess, wake up." Someone shook Tierney's shoulder. "Please, Princess, something terrible has happened."

Tierney's eyes snapped open. "What's the matter?" She sat up, the boning of her corset pinching her sides. "I'm up." She blinked in the bright sunlight streaming in through the windows. They'd slept through the night and into the next morning. So much for portaling home right away.

"Right. Human world." She wiped her eyes and turned to Siobhan, who had a stricken look on her face.

"I'm so sorry, your Highness. It seems the humans have taken your Dark Fae friend."

"Gullie?" Tierney shook her head, trying to make sense of her surroundings. Of all the ways to wake up, finding herself sprawled across a big bed with an ex-suitor and a potential suitor—if her father had his way—was not one she'd ever imagined.

"We didn't see it happen," Veren said. "We woke to find him gone."

"Gulliver has spent a lot of time in the human realm. He's probably just out looking for food." Tierney rolled out of bed and reached behind her to loosen her skirts. She had to get this dress off immediately.

"He went foraging?" Veren looked out the window at the overgrown pasture and broken-down fences. "I can't imagine he will find anything edible in this place."

"I need human clothes." Tierney crossed the room to the closet doors. Her mother kept the house stocked with plenty of clothes and supplies for her frequent trips into the human world. Sometimes, the queen just needed an afternoon mani-pedi, with a stopover at Starbucks for an iced latte, and a few hours with a smart phone, free Wi-Fi, and online shopping. Tierney used to go with her but hadn't accompanied her mom in a while. "I'm sure I still have clothes here that fit." She rummaged through the closet and came back with a pair of jeans and a t-shirt for herself and Siobhan. She thrust a pair of her father's jeans and a sweatshirt at Veren.

"Change into these. You'll be more comfortable." Tierney stepped into the hall, intending to go to the bathroom to change, but her skirts wouldn't fit through the smaller door.

"I will help you, Princess." Siobhan came to her aid. "Veren, turn around," she ordered, fumbling with the laces at Tierney's back.

Her skirts fell to the floor, and Tierney stepped out of their many layers. "That's better. That thing weighs more than I do." She rubbed her lower back, eager to get out of her petticoat and underthings.

Siobhan scowled at the tiny room. "I will act as your lady's maid, your Highness, but is there a larger room where I may assist you?"

Tierney turned her back on Siobhan. "Just loosen my laces, and I can take it from there."

"Right here in the hallway?"

"Yep." Tierney was about ten seconds away from tapping her foot in annoyance. Why did no one think she could manage to dress herself?

"Very well." Siobhan closed the bedroom door where Veren still stood staring at the wall. She returned and worked at the laces of Tierney's corset.

"Thank you. I've got it now." Tierney clutched her clothes to her chest and darted into the bathroom, locking the door behind her.

Siobhan knocked on the door. "Your Highness, please let me help you. It isn't proper for a princess to dress herself."

"Proper schmoper," Tierney muttered from the bathroom, shrugging out of her under garments and tossing the stupid fracking corset to the floor. "You know, most humans manage to dress themselves in their simple clothes. Why don't you give it a shot?" She tugged a peach-colored t-shirt over her head and glanced down at the front. It said, 'Apparently I have an *Attitude*.' A sarcastic gift from her mother.

"Where might I change, your Highness?" Siobhan asked.

Tierney slid into a pair of faded jeans, surprised to see they still fit. "Bedroom across the hall." She turned to the bathroom mirror and the monstrosity that was her hair. Pulling pins from the elaborate hairstyle she'd slept in, she moaned with relief, running her hands through her strawberry blond hair to work out all the tangles.

"WWBRD?" Tierney asked herself in the mirror. Her mother was so much better at this rebellion stuff. What would Brea Robinson do in this situation? If the king had annoyed the queen about something to the point where she was well and truly angry with him, she'd take a day for herself. She'd relax and think her thoughts, feel her emotions, and then return to have a civil conversation with her husband.

Tierney smiled at her reflection, so like her mother's, except for the blond hair that came from her grandparents. Griffin, the man who technically fathered her had much more red to his long strands than she did. "And that's usually when Mom gets her way." She bent to splash water on her face and retreated to the hallway, kicking the remnants of her ballgown as she went.

"These clothes are strangely comfortable," Siobhan said, staring down at her pink t-shirt that said, 'Castles, Shoes and Bibbidi-Bobbidi-Boo.' Tierney's mom always giggle-snorted over that shirt.

"Don't you look cute?" Tierney smiled. "Just like a little human."

"I am not a human, your Highness." With their arrival in the human realm, Siobhan had grown far too serious and proper, and Tierney wasn't about to sit through an entire day of 'your Highness this' and 'Princess that.'

"Let's pretend you are. Just for one day."

"You want me to pretend to be human, Princess?" Siobhan bent to retrieve Tierney's bodice and undergarments from the floor.

"No!" Tierney slapped her hand away, letting the clothes fall back to the floor. "Just for today, we are going to be sloppy, lazy humans. Okay? Where's Veren?" Tierney knocked on the bedroom door. "Have you changed?"

Veren cracked the door open. "I look hideous."

"Okay, but that's fine. Just come downstairs. We need to have a meeting." Tierney turned back toward the stairs to find Siobhan folding her petticoat.

"Seriously, stop that. Put it back on the floor and follow me." Tierney pointed at the aged hardwood floor. "Leave the mess."

"Okay, your Highness." Siobhan glanced up at the ceiling when Tierney flipped on the hall lights. She followed her down the stairs, staying close behind her, like she thought something was going to reach out and grab her from the walls.

Veren was quick to follow in the awful dad jeans that were too long and baggy for him.

She led them into the living room, grabbing the sheets that covered the couch. "Sit. Both of you." Tierney pointed to the couch, balling the sheets up and tossing them on the floor. She wasn't normally messy, but for once she planned to indulge herself.

"We're in the human realm, and it's still daylight."

Both fae nodded.

"That means we're stuck here until the moon rises and I can create a portal to take us home." That was the plan anyway. "Which means we have most of the day left to enjoy, and I intend to do just that." Tierney folded her arms over her chest. "So, I have a few rules I expect you to follow while we're guests in my mother's home."

More nods.

"Rule number one: no one is to utter the words *your Highness,* or *Princess,* or *Tierney*. Today, you will call me Tia. Rule number two: it's my birthday and I want to have a normal day, so see rule number one."

"You really want us to call you … Tia?" Veren asked. "That's such an odd thing for a royal princess to request. Even my closest friends don't dare to use my family nickname."

"Well, it's my only house rule." Tierney opened the cabinet doors, revealing the flat screen television. "Allow me to introduce you to my little friend, technology." She flipped the power button on the remote and returned to sit between Veren and Siobhan. "It's the human's form of magic, and it's incredible." Tierney flipped to Netflix and scrolled through the shows on her list, stopping on *Anne with an E.* "Prepare to have your minds blown." She clicked play and sat back to enjoy her favorite human pastime.

"What about Gulliver?" Siobhan whispered. "Shouldn't we be worried?"

"He'll be back soon, and he'll have snacks. Lots of snacks."

"Food?" Veren leaned forward, his eyes glued to the television. "What sort of things do the humans eat?"

"You'll see." Tierney leaned her head back against the cushions.

"This settee is like sitting on a cloud." Siobhan curled up beside her.

"Right?" Tierney smiled. If anyone had bothered to ask her what she wanted for her birthday, it would have looked a lot more like this than the epic ball she'd escaped from last night.

"I've heard about human magic." Veren stood and paced to the television, looking behind it. "But I've never seen it. It's magnificent, really, how they survive with their technology and gadgets and no real magic."

"Humans have all the best stuff," Gulliver called from the kitchen. "Right, Tia?"

"You betcha." She paused the show to help him with the bags of food. "What'd you bring me?"

Gulliver dropped his sunglasses and hat on the counter and started unloading bags. "I've got all the basics. Peperoni pizza for you, cheeseburgers for me, and Chinese and birthday cake for everyone."

"Cake?" Tierney squealed. "I love human cake!"

"I know, right?" Gulliver elbowed her. "I got plenty of Cokes and seltzer water too."

"Yes! I'm dying for a Coke. Let's eat while it's hot. I don't like using the microwave. I always get it too hot or not hot enough." Tierney pulled down plates and glasses from the cabinet and turned to help Gulliver lay out all the food. She looked up to find Siobhan and Veren staring at her.

"What?" She blinked at them.

"It's ... I've never seen a royal ... work. At least not in the kitchens." Veren shrugged. "It's an odd sight."

"Well, get over it." Tierney shoved a carton of dumplings at him. "Try one of these."

"What is it?" Veren scrunched his nose.

"It's the best food ever created. Trust me."

He took a tentative bite, and his eyes widened. "That is good, Princess."

Tierney snatched the dumpling back and took the carton from him. "What's my name?"

"Oh, um, T-Tia," he stuttered. "I forgot rule number one."

She returned the carton with his half-eaten dumpling. "Try it with the plum sauce. It's even better."

"You gave them rules?" Gulliver stacked his plate with dumplings, cheeseburgers, and sweet and sour chicken.

"Just two. The first is that no princess-related words are allowed in this house." Tierney grabbed a slice of pizza and loaded up on Chinese food and dumplings. She and Gulliver turned toward the living room to find Siobhan and Veren holding empty plates. "Eat up," Tierney said. "Go nuts, help yourself. Drinks are in the fridge."

"That's the big white box in the corner," Gulliver called over his shoulder. "Just pull the handle and grab a red can."

Tierney curled up in her spot on the couch, and Gulliver took his seat on the floor beside her.

"What are we watching?" He reached for the remote.

"*Anne with an E.*"

"Ugh, no way. Let's watch *Outlander* or *Game of Thrones*."

"We're watching *Anne*. It's my birthday party, so I get to pick the first show." She grabbed the remote from him just as Veren and Siobhan joined them, their plates piled high with all the different types of food Gulliver had foraged for them.

"This isn't a party, Tia." Gulliver shook his head. "It's an accidental portaling."

Tierney shrugged. "It's the kind of party I would have wanted if it were up to me."

Siobhan gave her a gentle pat on her shoulder. "I'd want the same if it were me."

"This meat sandwich thing is tasty." Veren leaned back on the sofa. "I wonder if our chef could make these. Father would love it."

"I like the thing with the red dots all over it." Siobhan took a big bite of pizza. "It's like nothing I've ever tasted."

"I told you, humans have the best food." Gulliver grinned.

"And the best shows." Tierney hit play and tucked into her snacks. This was exactly what she needed after the disaster of last night. And when it was over, she would have a serious talk with her father about his plans for her future.

CHAPTER 5
TIERNEY

"I wish we could stay a little longer." Tierney sat on the grass, facing the farmhouse as the sun sank lower in the sky. This place was just as much her home as the palace. Sure, she didn't get to come as often as she'd like, but there were no courtiers bowing, no crushing expectations, no one else to make happy but herself.

Gulliver lay beside her, his eyes focused on the sky. "You know, they've probably turned the entire kingdom upside down looking for you."

"You really think he's that worried about me?" Sometimes, she wondered. For the last year, ever since the announcement that she would have to choose a husband or a wife, her relationship with her father had been strained.

Gulliver turned onto his side. "I think he's probably more worried for what you're doing than *for* you."

"What's that supposed to mean?" She crossed her arms over her chest.

A laugh escaped his lips. "Just that he knows you can take care of yourself. But he also knows you tend to create trouble when you're cornered."

"That's not true."

He flopped onto his back again, a grin spreading across his lips. "You were thirteen the first time an argument with your mom sent you riding off to Myrkur—alone. Dad was so angry when you showed up."

Tierney shrugged. "I missed you."

"You wanted to irritate your parents."

"That too."

"Then, there was the time you accidentally blew a hole in the sheet of ice covering the lake after your dad said you couldn't come out to skate."

She groaned. "He made me sit in a council meeting all day." Tierney cringed at the memory. Her power had spiraled out of control, but she hadn't even tried to reel it back in. "Okay, fine. I might like creating trouble a little." Gulliver was right. Her father knew she'd turn up, eventually. She'd be in less trouble if it was sooner rather than later.

"I just don't get why he's pushing this on me now. The whole marriage thing ... it's not like I'm going to live a short human life. I have plenty of time to find someone I actually like."

"Because he thinks he might die." Veren's voice surprised her.

"What?" She peered up at him. She hadn't heard him crossing the yard to them.

A sigh pushed out of him, like explaining himself was overly taxing. Veren never did anything out of the goodness of his heart, but this time she wasn't sure what benefit he derived from offering up any information.

"I overheard my parents speaking. My father says yours is worried about something happening to him. And if it does, he doesn't want you to have to rule alone."

Tierney sat frozen for a long moment. Her dad was worried about dying? It made so much sense. His parents both died when he was a child, and it threw Iskalt into chaos. In the years after, many fae suffered and her father had to fight for his throne.

Stability was key.

And her father didn't think she was stable enough without someone tempering her. Of course he didn't. She'd never shown she could keep herself out of trouble. And now, this …

"We need to get home." She pushed to her feet. "Where's Siobhan?"

"Here." Siobhan ran down the porch steps. "I'm not really sure how we ended up in the human realm with you, Pr—Tia, but I'm glad I had the opportunity to see it this once."

"Speak for yourself." Veren scowled. "This place is creepy, and I'm going to need more than a few drinks to forget it all."

If Tierney ever needed a reminder of why her feelings for Veren were completely gone now, all she needed to do was listen to him speak.

"Well, we'll all be rid of each other soon." She'd probably be rid of everyone for a long time, banished to her rooms in the palace until she turned gray with age. Maybe she could run to Myrkur to live with her grandmother, Faolan. Griff wouldn't have to find out. He used to be fun, a rulebreaker like her. Now, he was way too concerned with doing the right thing.

Boring.

But Grandmother Faolan, she'd never been able to say no to Tierney. Or she could get Uncle Myles to smuggle her back to Gelsi. That might be more realistic. He had a soft spot for adventure, and making her father mad had always been his favorite hobby.

Gulliver's hand slid into hers. "Can you make a portal to get us back?"

She nodded. Easy, right? She'd created the one to get them here on her own. Portaling home should be a piece of delicious human cake. Licking her lips, she wished they hadn't eaten it all so she could bring a piece back to Toby.

Maybe then, he wouldn't be so irritated she didn't bring him along. She tried focusing her magic, picturing the castle of Iskalt, but she heard her twin's voice in her mind. *You took Veren Rhatigan and not me? Veren, really?*

He hated Veren even more than Tierney did.

She tried to quiet her mind, wishing Toby was here simply because he could do this without thinking. He didn't have Iskaltian magic or Eldurian magic. Instead, he amplified hers. She drew strength from him. But he'd mastered the O'Shea power in a way she couldn't when their uncle forced him to during the war.

Directing the portal would have been easy for him.

"My dad could do this when he was a kid." And yet, he hadn't spent the time teaching her. He'd been too worried she'd come here without permission. And he was probably right not to trust her.

But she wished he had now.

Drawing in a deep breath, she let the power flow down her arms, heat gathering in her hands. A sliver of light shown through a small portal, and she widened it.

"Let's go." She kept the image of the Iskaltian palace firmly in her mind as they all grasped hands.

The moment she entered the portal, she knew something was wrong. It didn't feel right. It bent and twisted instead of creating a straight line from one point to the next.

At the last moment, she screamed, "Everyone back! Get out of the portal!"

A weight fell away from her right hand, Siobhan's fingers sliding free.

The last thing she saw was Gulliver on her other side, fading from view.

The ground rushed up to meet Tierney, and at first, all she could see was the blinding sun. All she could hear was a high-pitched keening.

But she knew.

She knew she wasn't home.

"Gulliver," she called, her voice getting lost in the din that started materializing around her.

A heavy boot struck her side as a man ran over her, sword held high above his head.

Sword?

Warriors crowded around her as they hacked away at each other. She'd landed right in the middle of a battle. A horse reared up, almost coming down on top of her. She rolled out of the way and jumped to her feet.

A wave of dizziness crested over her, but she managed to swerve away from a brute of a man wearing blazing red armor she didn't recognize. An unfamiliar crest decorated his helmet.

"Gulliver!" she screamed, her voice raw in her throat. "Siobhan! Veren!" She ducked away from another soldier as she pushed through the heaving mass of bodies, none of her friends in sight. *Friend* might have been a stretch for Veren, but she'd even welcome his smug face right now.

The ground beneath her was packed dirt. No wonder it had hurt so much when she landed.

Quick on her feet, she dodged every attack coming her way. She had no armor, but she'd always thought it was more of a hinderance anyway.

Spotting a thin sword gripped in the stiff fingers of a dead man, she bent to pry it free, whirling around to block a soldier from running her through. Their swords clashed before Tierney danced out of the way.

She didn't know who was fighting, where she was, or which side she should be on. So, it was best not to hurt anyone. The sword was only for protection until she figured out what was going on.

All she knew was she'd screwed up. Badly. The portal brought her somewhere that wasn't Iskalt—she could tell by the scorching heat—and she didn't know where the others were.

But she was trained. As the future heir of Iskalt, she'd studied sword dancing since she was a child and had sparred with the King's Guard for years.

"You can do this, Tia," she muttered to herself, not letting the rising fear take over. "You don't get scared. It's okay."

A soldier with blood spattered across his face lumbered her way, slowed by the weight of his golden armor. Okay, so, two sides. Red and gold. Which noble families wore those colors in the fae realms?

Stumbling back, she tripped over a body on the ground and scrambled to her feet. Her would-be attacker lifted his sword, but before he could bring it down, the tip of a blade appeared in his chest. Shock covered his face, and blood gurgled from his mouth before he collapsed, face in the dirt.

Tierney lifted wide eyes to the man who'd killed him. He was tall, impossibly so. Clad in the red armor of the soldiers who appeared to be winning. Blood dotted his face, giving him a barbarous look. He'd lost his helmet, revealing a head coated in inky hair, as dark as the darkest night.

His blazing eyes met Tierney's for a brief moment before he turned on one heel and rejoined the fight.

"Okay," she murmured. "Guess I'm team red."

She rammed her shoulder into a man trying to block her way. Gulliver had to be here somewhere. She just needed to get to a better spot to see him.

Her Eldurian magic pulled at her, but something about it didn't feel right.

A blast came from behind her, and she turned to see a soldier with his hand held out in front of him. He'd just thrown an enemy high into the air and slammed him so hard into the ground it cratered.

Magic. It had to be. Okay, so, she was definitely in the fae realm and not the human world. That narrowed things considerably.

Movement at the edge of the battle caught her eye, and she took off running for the horse that had scampered free of the fray. The saddle dangled loosely to the side, the straps trailing in the dirt.

Carefully slicing through the other strap, she let it fall to the ground. The horse tried to rear up, but she gripped its mane. "Whoa there. It's okay. I won't hurt you." She brushed a calm hand, much calmer than she felt, down the horse's neck before pulling herself onto its back.

Shielding her eyes against the sun, she surveyed the battle. It was winding down, but there were only a few faces she wanted to see. "Gullie!" she tried calling again.

Panic clawed at her. What had she done? Did he not make it out of the human realm? Was he stuck in the portal? She'd never seen something like that happen, but that didn't mean it couldn't. If anything happened to him because of her, she'd never forgive herself.

Maybe he'd made it back to Iskalt.

But she knew in her heart he hadn't.

From atop the horse, she could see a nearby village surrounded by green forests and rolling hills. She knew where she was instantly. "Fargelsi." Relief flooded her, but it didn't last. Why was there fighting in Fargelsi? Who were these warriors? And why was it so hot? The temperatures felt more like Eldur.

So many questions flooded her mind at once, and she knew she wouldn't like a single answer.

In the distance, trees stretched as far as she could see, a vast forest that covered much of the kingdom all the way to the palace.

The palace! If she made it there, she'd be safe. Uncle Myles and Neeve could even be home from the ball if her father had used the portals. But she knew that was a false hope. They'd never leave Iskalt while she was missing, and they rarely used portals for simple travel. But Grandfather Brandon … he'd help her find the others.

Golden soldiers took off running as a horn sounded from the woods. "Retreat!" they yelled.

The others didn't follow. Instead, a cheer spread through the exhausted fighters. Some fell to their knees, others attended to injuries. And in the middle of them all was that man, the one who'd saved her. When his unblinking eyes settled on her, a chill raced up her spine.

This was a dangerous man.

A new refrain reached her ears as a few soldiers started chanting in celebration.

"The queen is dead!"

Horror clawed at her. The queen was dead. Neeve? Aunt Neeve was dead?

Chapter 6
Tierney

"The queen is dead!"

"The princess is dead!"

The soldiers swarming the battlefield cheered for their triumph over Fargelsi, but Tierney's magic sizzled at her fingertips, responding to the rage and fear she felt for the royals these rebels had slaughtered. She wanted to tear them apart with her magic for daring to destroy the peace the three kingdoms had fought so hard to attain. But her magic was stuck inside her, just out of reach.

Uncle Myles? All her cousins? They must have gotten wind of this battle and her father or uncle had portalled them through the human realm to get back so quickly. It would have taken them an entire day to reach the human realm and then wait for night to open a new portal to Gelsi.

Which princess had they managed to kill? What about her grandfather? All these questions raced through her mind as she searched the sea of soldiers for an officer. She needed to speak with their general. Immediately.

Her horse danced beneath her. She was afraid and eager for escape. "Shhh." Tierney smoothed a hand down her neck. "It's all right. I won't let anything happen to you."

She guided the horse through the aftermath of battle, sidestepping bodies clad in their strange colored armor. She couldn't recall a single noble house of Fargelsi who used either the deep red or golden armor. The noble houses usually carried a flag with their crest, and most used three colors to set them apart.

"You there, soldier!" Tierney shouted in her most commanding voice, urging her mount to follow the tall soldier who'd caught her eye. "Where is your general?"

The man in blood-splattered red armor looked her over, taking in her strange human clothes. "You best find your way home, girl. You don't belong here." He shrugged her off and turned to leave.

His accent was strangely formal for a mere soldier. He was likely the kind of higher-ranking officer she was looking for, so she followed him through the chaos, hoping he would lead her to the one in charge of this outlandish rebellion. How had they not heard of such unrest in Iskalt? Surely Aunt Neeve and Uncle Myles would have asked for help from their closest allies. They were family, and family helped each other in times like these.

Tierney shuddered at the sounds of the victorious army as they finished slaughtering their injured foes.

"I don't think I dismissed you, soldier." Tierney pursued him. "Excuse me, sir." She grabbed his shoulder, forcing him to face her. "I am Princess Tierney O'Shea of Iskalt, and I demand you take me to your leader this instant."

She couldn't get a good look at him with his helmet on and every inch of him covered in gore.

"I know of no such princess." The man lifted his visor, and Tierney sucked in a breath. It was the same man who had saved her just moments ago. It seemed he'd found his helmet.

"You will take me to your general. Someone has a lot of explaining to do. We do not abide such rebellion in the fae kingdoms. We've fought too hard for the peace we've attained."

The man scowled at her again. "We haven't known true peace in a lifetime. Are you injured, Miss?"

Tierney drew herself up to her full height, which was still head and shoulders beneath this soldier if she stood beside him. "You may address me as Princess Tierney or your Highness." She lifted her chin for emphasis, staring down her nose at him from her position on the horse's back.

"All right, Princess. Follow me." His voice was like fine silk. Smooth and rich, despite his evident exhaustion.

Tierney dismounted her horse to follow him on foot through the maze of soldiers. "Tell me, which princess has been killed?" Tierney scrambled to keep up with his longer stride. Her horse—as eager to leave this place as she was—followed.

"There's just the two left, isn't there? You guess which one."

Tierney stumbled. The shock of her cousins' deaths lanced through her, and she had to choke back her emotions. She would have time to mourn later. For the moment, she was a representative of Iskalt, a staunch ally of Fargelsi, and it was her job to take charge.

"And the queen?"

"Hung from the ramparts of her palace. A just punishment for all she's done." Her companion led her to the rear of the battlefield, where a sea of tents dotted the once green hills.

A sob escaped her as she imagined the awful sight of her sweet Aunt Neeve hanging like a convicted criminal. She was the best thing that had ever happened to Gelsi. The fae loved her. Tierney couldn't wrap her mind around this rebellion.

From the look of their camp, these men had been here for months.

"What are your grievances? I will take them to my father, and we will make this right for all those involved."

Her dark companion gave a snort of disgust. "Our king will make it right, girl."

"And who is your *king*?" If not Myles, then who could it be? There were no other claimants to the throne of Gelsi. Aunt Neeve and

Tierney's own mother were the only surviving relatives of the O'Rourkes along with their father.

"None of your concern." He led her to a large tent, but Tierney had spent enough time in war camps to know the tent he'd taken her to was not the general's.

"I don't need medical attention, soldier. I need to speak with your general." Tierney backed away from this man she couldn't afford to trust, putting her horse between them.

"What's wrong with this one?" A weary-looking older man wiped his hands on a filthy apron.

"She's not right in the head, healer. She's babbling nonsense about being a princess and demanding to see the general."

"She's certainly dressed strangely." The healer nodded. "Come on, dearie. We'll get you fixed up right as rain in no time." The man stretched out his arm to take Tierney's hand, but she stepped out of his grasp.

"I must speak to whomever is in charge of this army. The royal families of Iskalt and Eldur will not tolerate such rebellion."

"See, she speaks with such insolence," the soldier muttered to the healer. "I'm going to need you to take her off my hands."

"She's a few tarts short of a pastry dish, that one. But I've got a thousand injured soldiers to stitch up, Kier. I don't have time to deal with flights of fantasy. She's no harm to herself or you. Give her a place to rest, and I'll come up to see about her later."

"Must I?" the soldier grumbled.

"Afraid so, my boy." The healer chuckled and left them to return where he was needed.

"I can hear you, you know?" Tierney crossed her arms over her chest.

"This way, *Princess.*" He offered her his arm, but she refused.

"You will take me to your general," she insisted, "or I will go find him or her myself." She glanced around the encampment, looking for a larger tent with flags and lots of activity.

"Of course." The soldier gave her a curt bow. "Right this way, your Majesty." He held his hand up to point the way.

"It's your Highness. My father is his Majesty."

"Whatever you say, Highness." He turned down a row of tents, guiding her and her horse through a sea of bloodied men. It was odd not to see a single female soldier in sight.

"Where are your female soldiers?"

"Women soldiers?" He snorted a laugh. "Never heard of such nonsense."

"My father's army has as many female soldiers and officers as men. It's nothing to scoff at."

"Here we are." He arrived at a nondescript tent. "While you speak with the general, I will have someone see to your horse and perhaps find you some proper clothing. A lady shouldn't be seen wearing trousers. It isn't right for a princess or a laundress."

"Lead the way." Tierney lifted her chin, hoping he was truly taking her seriously now. This man had some strange ideas about women. Hopefully, his general was more refined.

The soldier tugged off his helmet, running a hand through his sweaty dark hair.

"Squire!" He snagged a young boy passing by leading a mount. "Take this horse to the stable yard for the lady here. She will have need of it to return to her castle once she has rested." There was a slight bite of sarcasm in his voice.

"Yes, my Lord." The boy accepted the coin the soldier offered and led her newly acquired horse away. The beautiful black mare protested, snorting and stomping.

"It's okay, friend. I'll see you again soon." Tierney whispered to the horse.

"What is your general's name?" She moved to follow the soldier.

"You will meet with him soon." He ducked into the tent, and she followed, blinking at the stark dim interior. A cot lined one side of the tent. A single stool and small table were the only other furnishings. This was not the tent of a general.

"I will not stay here, soldier. I must speak with—"

"The general, yes, I know." He rubbed a weary hand over the stubble along his jaw. "But the general is quite busy at the moment to speak with a mere woman. Rest here and I will bring him to you soon, but mind your tongue when I do."

"Bring him to me? Mind my tongue? Who do you think you are?" She glanced around the sparse accommodations. "I won't be so easily fooled, soldier. I know very well how to find a general in the aftermath of battle." Tierney took a step toward the tent flap.

"I suggest you do what you're told, girl." The soldier stepped in front of her. "No one has time for your nonsense right now." He turned to leave.

"How dare you?" Tierney tried to call on her magic, but it refused to answer in her rage.

"Corporal!" he shouted through the opening. "I need you to put two men on this tent. Make sure she doesn't go anywhere."

The young corporal nodded and pulled two of his men from their ranks. "Right away, sir."

"She's a little confused from the battle. The healer will come check on her soon. Do not let her leave. We will need to question her."

"Yes, sir!" The soldiers took up their posts at her tent, and her guide started to walk away.

"If you think you can dump me off on a couple of young privates, think again!" Tierney called from her prison cell. But a tent guarded by a couple of green soldiers were no match for Tierney O'Shea … if she could figure out why her magic refused to rise when she needed it most.

CHAPTER 7
TIERNEY

Tierney paced across the small tent, only taking a few steps before she had to turn around and go back the other way. Now that she'd had a moment to think, her hands shook with the memory of the sword in her grasp, the images she couldn't get out of her head of a sea of bodies lying among the crows.

It had been ten years since she'd seen any sort of battle, but even then, she hadn't been in the middle of it, forced to wield a sword and watch the light fade from an opponent's eyes.

She hadn't killed anyone, but she'd never forget the shocked widening of eyes or the cries of anguish.

"I need to get out of here," she whispered to herself.

She had to find a way out of Gelsi. If these rebels had truly taken over, she needed to go home and tell her father to gather the armies of Iskalt and Eldur. He and Aunt Alona would never allow it to stand.

Swallowing back a sob, she tried to rid her mind of the faces of her aunt and uncle, her cousins. They'd been at her birthday party that seemed like another lifetime now.

Uncle Myles would have hated traveling home through a portal.

They always made him sick, but perhaps Aunt Neeve had needed to return sooner. Had she heard of the rebellion?

Tierney's legs shook, but she couldn't stop moving, couldn't sit down. If she did, she'd probably break altogether.

She wasn't sure how long she'd waited when a commotion stirred outside the tent. A young soldier, no older than Toby, stuck his head in, giving her a sympathetic look before pulling back the flap and shoving someone forward.

His knees hit the dirt, and Tierney went into action immediately.

"Gullie?" She bent down to touch his shoulder, where his sleeve was ripped open. She drew back at the sight of the fresh wound snaking down his arm. A salve covered the torn skin, but it didn't make it look any less gruesome.

He gave her a weak smile. "I've been looking for you."

A sob threatened to bubble up, but she swallowed it back. "I thought I'd lost you." She lowered herself to her knees in front of him and pressed her forehead to his. "Are you okay?"

"I'll be fine, but Tia, what's going on?"

"I don't know. These fae … they've invaded Fargelsi, and I'm not sure why." Her voice lowered. "The royal family … they're gone, Gullie."

He lifted a hand to her cheek. "I know. I'm so sorry."

"What am I supposed to do? I need to get out of here, get to my father."

"Do you think you can portal us back to the human realm? We could try getting to Iskalt from there."

Fear raced through her, and she drew back. "You saw what happened last time. I can't control it. What if … Gullie, have you seen Siobhan or Veren?"

He shook his head. "I've just been looking for you since I dropped into the battle, but I didn't see them anywhere."

"I lost them." She sat back on her heels. She'd thought this type of situation was a myth, something her family used to scare their children from creating portals unless absolutely necessary. It was always harder to bring others along for the trip, but if they were somehow disconnected from the fae who opened the portal, they could end up anywhere.

Not for the first time, she wished Toby was here. He understood portal magic in a way even their father and uncle didn't. Since he was ten years old, Toby had the ability to take large groups of fae through his portals.

"What am I going to do?"

Gullie reached out and took her hand. At least he was here with her. She wasn't alone. He was her person. The friend who knew all her secrets. And now, she'd gotten him imprisoned by some awful rebel group.

"I'm sorry," she whispered. "This is all my fault."

Voices sounded outside the tent, one a deep growl. She couldn't help feeling like all hope of escape was quickly unraveling.

"You listen to me." Gulliver put a hand on the side of her head, his cat-like eyes locking onto hers. "This is not your doing. Do you hear me?"

She did, but only barely as she focused on the voices moving closer, the way her magic resisted as she tried to pull it forth. She was more powerful than any fae in Fargelsi. If she tried, she could tear the palace down stone by stone as her mother once had. And all these rebels would cry out for her to save them.

White-hot rage ripped through her. Anger so deep it cut a chasm into her chest. This could not happen in Fargelsi. She'd get revenge for her family.

But the magic that should have accompanied such a strong emotion didn't rise to the surface. Instead, it sank within her, hollowing her out until she bent over gasping.

"Tia?" Gulliver's voice held a note of panic. "What is it?"

She lifted her tear-stained face. "Something is wrong. I can't …" She struggled for breath. "There's nothing there."

"What do you—" His words cut off as an imposing man in

tarnished red armor pushed into the tent, stopping when he saw them clutching each other on the dirt floor.

His broad shoulders and terrifying height barely fit inside the tent. He had to duck his head to avoid hitting the top. He didn't wear a helmet, but the armor still reeked of battle, of blood and sweat. His gaze immediately went to Gulliver, to his strange eyes and even stranger tail.

Had he never seen a Myrkurian before?

"What are you?" His voice was low, deep.

Gulliver was used to scorn whenever he traveled outside his own kingdom. He pushed himself to his feet and straightened his shoulders. "I'm not a what. My name is Lord Gulliver O'Shea, son of Prince Griffin O'Shea, guardian of the Myrkurian Rift." That was what they'd taken to calling the portal into the human realm that couldn't be closed in the mountains of Myrkur.

"I know of no such village."

"Village?" Gulliver's voice rose an octave in rage. "We are not a—" Tierney stood and gripped his arm to shut him up. She was normally the blabber mouth, with her frequent outbursts, but she could recognize danger when she saw it.

And this man? He was dangerous, just like the one who'd brought her here.

"Garix," he called suddenly.

The young soldier appeared in the doorway. "Yes, General?"

General? So, this was the man who'd led this force against Fargelsi. Tierney made a mental note to make him pay for that. Just as soon as she could call on her power.

"Take this one to Borgan." He pointed to Gulliver.

"Borgan?" Tierney tried to keep hold of Gulliver, but the soldier pried her fingers free. "Who is Borgan?"

"Quiet, girl." The general backhanded her across the face, and she fell back, her jaw dropping open.

But quiet wasn't in her nature. "Gullie," she screamed. He gave her a helpless look as the young soldier locked chains around his wrists. "No! Let him go."

She tried to go after him when he was dragged from the tent, but the general grabbed her roughly by the shoulders and shoved her further inside.

She wouldn't let him scare her into obedience. "I'll come for you, Gullie." She could no longer see him, but she had to believe he could hear her. "I'll find you, and we'll burn this rebellion to the ground." Her chest heaved; tears burned the corners of her eyes. And still, her power wouldn't come. She could feel it just out of reach, but that was no use to her now.

"I'm going to kill you," she growled, focusing on the general.

He crossed his arms, the joints of his armor creaking with the movement. "I don't know why the king wanted me to see to you." His eyes blazed. "But he wants answers from you. Your friend will serve as incentive."

"There is no king in Fargelsi except Myles Merrick."

"The only king I know is King Dagnan, and you'd do well to remember his name, girl."

"Why?"

"Because his son is the only reason you and that boy are still alive. It seems one of his soldiers witnessed your arrival in what he called a flash of light."

"My portal?" Her jaw tightened. "It's just magic."

"Where's your totem?" He held out a hand.

"My what?"

"Your crystal."

"I don't understand."

His fingers curled in. "No worries. You will be searched. You're surrounded by the red soldiers of Vondur, the best warriors in Lenya. There is no escape."

Vondur? Lenya? Tierney couldn't breathe. These were places she'd only read about in the books at the library of Aghadoon. Places that weren't supposed to exist any longer—if they ever had. "That's not possible."

He seemed to misunderstand her statement. "I assure you it is. We have all the capabilities we need to keep an insurgent girl from leaving. I don't know what the Grima court is paying you to infiltrate us, but they are in hiding now. Collecting won't be an easy feat."

He thought she was a spy? That was ridiculous. All she wanted was to find her friends and make her way home.

The general's gaze burned into her, studying her, as if trying to make a decision. "I've been told you are to go with the troops back to the palace of Vondur. You may be of use to the crown yet." He turned on his heel. "Prepare yourself. We are not Grima. Our prisoners always walk." With that, he left her alone in the tent once more.

She sank to the cot, her entire body shaking. Touching a finger to her cheek, she could already tell a bruise was forming. But that was the least of her worries.

In Iskalt, there were legends about kingdoms that once existed across the fire plains, the Eastern Vatlands bordering Eldur. No fae could cross the fire plains without succumbing to such intense heat it scorched the skin right from their bones while the air cooked their lungs in their chests.

Rivers of lava were said to flow freely from the many volcanoes.

The realm beyond was called Lenya, and it consisted of two kingdoms. Vondur and Grima. The dark kingdom and the light kingdom.

And Tierney just had to be taken by Vondur, known in the legends for their ruthlessness and cruelty.

Those golden warriors they cut down … they were the peace seekers, the ones who fought for the good of Lenya—or so the legends said.

None of this could possibly be true. The sob that had been trying to escape since she was first thrown into the tent pushed out of her. But it wasn't for this strange world her misguided portal had taken her to or the fact that she'd probably never make it out.

She wasn't in Fargelsi. Aunt Neeve's body wasn't hanging from the ramparts. Her cousins and their father were still alive and probably tucked away safely in Iskalt.

Even in the midst of the terror clinging to her every thought, relief washed over her like a soothing balm.

She thought of her mom, taken to a world she'd known nothing about when she was even younger than Tierney was now. And she'd fought, she'd adapted, she'd survived.

That was what their family was.

Survivors.

She'd find a way to Gullie. She'd seek out Siobhan and Veren. And she'd fight to get them home.

CHAPTER 8
TIERNEY

Tierney couldn't imagine how she'd ever thought this place was Fargelsi.

Fargelsi was beautiful. Beautiful and deceptively dangerous.

This place … Lenya was just dangerous.

After a two-day march from the battlefield, their small party had been attacked three times by rogue brigands. Keir's soldiers had slaughtered their attackers every time.

Lieutenant Keir, the man who'd saved her from the point of a sword and then imprisoned her, was an absolute misogynist *turd,* as her mother would have called him. And a brutal leader. His men followed his orders to the letter, not out of respect but out of fear.

"I can walk with the others, you know." Tierney squirmed against the ropes binding her hands to Keir's saddle. When he made her ride with him, he'd insisted she ride sidesaddle like a proper lady, despite her *inappropriate* clothes.

"You ruined any chance of that the moment you tried to free my captives our first day on the trail." His silky-smooth voice was like poison in her ear.

Tierney sat up straight, refusing to lean against him any more than she had to. "You could at least let me ride my own horse." She glanced back behind them, trying to get a glimpse of Gulliver. "The poor thing is scared to death back there with the pack animals."

"Nice try. Your mongrel friend is well under guard. You'll see him again once we make camp for the night."

"He isn't a mongrel. He is Lord Gulliver of Myrkur, son of Prince Griffin of Iskalt." She chanced another look at the contingent of soldiers behind them, She needed to know where Gulliver was and how he was doing. If they had any hope of escaping this awful place, they couldn't lose sight of each other. Once Tierney regained control of her power, they were going through the first portal she could manage. Any place was better than this … barbaric world.

"If he's the son of a prince, that would make him a prince, would it not? Or does it not work that way in *your* world?"

"You are infuriating." Tierney tugged at her restraints again. It had been that way for two days. Keir refused to believe her story about accidentally portalling into Lenya from the human world. He scoffed when she explained her homeland was on the other side of the fire plains. He couldn't seem to fathom what a portal was and insisted no one could travel across the burning lands and live to tell about it.

"And you are equally infuriating with your incessant *talking*. Didn't anyone ever tell you females should be seen and not heard?"

"No, actually." Tierney bristled at his tone. "Because in my world, women are equal to men in every way. If you expect me to fall in line with your meek and mild females, then you have some catching up to do."

"Do all your women backtalk their men?" Keir groaned, rubbing his gloved hand across his brow. "It's a wonder any of you get anything done."

"Well, if you don't want to listen to me talk, put me on a horse at the back of the line and I'll leave you in peace."

"There is no such thing as peace in this land. Now, be quiet, woman."

"Ugh! I seriously hate you." Tierney wanted to scratch his eyes out. Never in her life had she been so disrespected.

Keir just grunted at her like the barbarian he was.

"When will we arrive at the king's palace?" she asked simply because she wanted the last word.

"Soon."

"Very well." She fell quiet, watching the harsh landscape slip past as they made their way along the narrow trail bordering an angry river. The waters churned and frothed over boulders and the remnants of rockslides.

The forest that grew up around the river was like none Tierney had ever seen. Massive trees sprouted from the rocky ground, thrusting toward the skies like the tall buildings she had seen in human cities. Some of the tree trunks were so big it would take a dozen or more men holding hands to encircle the behemoths.

Tierney felt tiny and inconsequential next to such giants that blocked out the sun, leaving them in near darkness.

The soldiers behind them started to grow excited as they traveled along a tree-lined pathway with six massive trees on either side of the trail. A landmark they seemed to recognize.

Tierney squinted in the sudden rush of sunlight as they branched off to another narrow trail beside the river. The trail led down at a stark incline, and Tierney clutched the saddle horn as best she could with her restraints.

"The horse knows how to travel this terrain. You won't fall." Keir took hold of her waist, keeping her from shifting in the saddle.

"You should tell your king that your roads are seriously lacking. This is little more than a goat path."

"Our king is busy fighting a war."

The giant trees began to thin, and the ground grew rockier, the river more chaotic. Huge mountains lay scattered in the distance. Nothing but black boulders and gray rock formations lay between them and the mountains now.

"What is your war all about?" Tierney stared ahead at a rather odd-looking boulder.

"The courts of Vondur and Grima have been at war for a generation."

"Over what?"

"Royal matters." Kier sighed.

"Is that …?" Tierney's voice trailed off. "Is that a giant sword sticking up from the ground? With hands?" She pointed to the odd gray rocks.

"Ruins, Princess. These are the ruins of Nikandur. That sword is all that remains of a statue of the king's great-great-grandfather, who once guarded the city gates. The black stones are charred remains of our greatest buildings. This city was the crowning jewel of Vondur, and the Grima queen laid waste to it. Killing our soldiers was bad enough, but she slaughtered women and children in their beds and burned the city down around their still warm bodies. Then, she salted the ground so that nothing would ever thrive here again."

"So your king hung her from the walls of her own castle?" Tierney shook her head in disgust. "Her fae will retaliate, and your war will never end."

"She deserved far worse than such a clean end."

Tierney flinched at the sound of howling, much too close for her comfort.

"We must hurry across the wasteland before nightfall. We don't want to tempt the wolfhounds from their dens." Keir nudged his horse into a faster pace.

Tierney didn't want to tempt them either. She didn't want to know what kind of predators called the giant forest home.

They continued to follow the raging river across the city of ruins. As a princess, she'd seen some of the most beautiful cities in the three fae realms, and even the enormous human cities, but nothing as glorious as this city must surely have been. She found herself wishing she could have seen it before its destruction.

As the sun began to sink along the horizon and the cries of the wolfhounds surrounded them, Keir brought their horse to a stop and dismounted among a ruin of granite columns as tall as some of the giant trees they'd seen in the forest.

"We are stopping?" Tierney glanced around the barren rocky ground, cringing at the howls in the distance.

"We must make camp before nightfall." Kier cut her restraints and lifted her from the saddle.

"What about the wolfhounds?"

"They won't bother us down by the river."

"The river?" Tierney turned toward the water, far below where they now stood. "We're going all the way down there?"

"The wolfhounds won't brave the stairs."

"Stairs?"

Kier removed the last of the rope binding her hands, and Tierney immediately rubbed where the ropes had chaffed.

"Duncan!" Kier ignored her and called for one of his men.

The big brute of a man grunted his reply.

"See to camp and secure our captives for the night." And with that, Kier left her with Duncan. His great hulk and lack of manners terrified her.

"Go." He pointed to the edge of the cliff, calling for the rear guard to bring the other captives. Tierney's heart thrummed in her chest when she caught sight of Gulliver. His nose was caked in dried blood, and his hands were bound with shackles that linked him with the other captives, but he seemed okay.

"Move, girl," Duncan barked.

"*Where?*" Tierney crept toward the drop off, except it wasn't a drop off. It was a set of steep stairs carved into the cliffside. They reminded her more of a ladder than actual steps. One wrong move and she'd fall right over the cliff. "I'm not going down those. Have you lost your mind?" She took several steps back from the edge.

"Stairs or wolfhounds?" He glared back at her with his dark eyes. Duncan seemed to be a man of few words.

"Stairs it is." Tierney shuffled forward, trying to decide if it would be easier to go down backwards like a ladder since there was no railing to hold on to.

"You don't want to go down that way," Duncan finally spoke a full sentence. "You won't make it to the bottom."

To her horror, tears welled up in her eyes, and she thought she was going to be sick. There must be a thousand steps down to the riverbed. Choking back her fear, she sat down, dangling her legs over the cliff edge, and secured her footing on the top steps before she stood up again.

Vertigo threatened to send her sailing right over the cliff.

"Move. We don't want to be stuck on the stairs after sunset."

Tierney nodded and stepped down, her legs shaking beneath her. The steps were hardly big enough even for her small feet. She couldn't imagine how some of the larger men would make it. And if anyone behind her fell, they would all go down.

Taking a deep breath, Tierney focused on the next step and then the one after that. After the first hundred, it got a little easier as the stairs switched back and she finally had part of the cliff side to lean against.

Her legs burned, and her back ached. She didn't even want to think about climbing back up in the morning.

Tierney clutched the rough cliffside as she descended the last hundred stairs. All she wanted was to reach the solid flat ground below and go to sleep on a rock. But as she neared the bottom, a putrid briny scent filled her nose.

"Ugh, what is that awful smell?"

"The canyon bottom is a salt lick." Duncan pressed her forward. "The wildlife comes from all over to enjoy the salt on the opposite bank. Easy hunting from this side."

The river ran smooth as glass just beyond a sickly gray-looking beach. It was shallow enough here to ford the river on horseback.

"Will we go across in the morning? Or back up?"

"Across."

Tierney was relieved to hear that. She took the last few steps quickly and collapsed on the nearest flat boulder. Duncan walked past her like the descent hadn't taxed him in the least. He started barking orders to set up camp for the night.

With the sheer cliff rising up on three sides and the river on the fourth, escape was unlikely. And Tierney was too tired to even consider it now. She and Gulliver would have to come up with a plan soon. She wanted to get away from Keir and his men well before they reached the palace of the Vondurian king.

"Gullie!" Tierney's heart lifted at the sight of her best friend. He made it down the last of the steps, looking haggard and exhausted. He and the other captives had walked the entire journey. She had little to complain about by comparison.

She lunged for him, wrapping him in a tight embrace to the gasps of the other captives. "Are you okay?" She searched him over for any sign of permanent damage.

"Fine. Just tired and hungry." His eyes drooped with fatigue.

"Girl, get a hold of yourself." Keir's smoothly cultured voice made her cringe. "It isn't seemly to throw yourself at a man in such a public way."

"Throw myself?" She snorted. "Gulliver is my friend; there is nothing unseemly about that." She grabbed Gulliver's hand and tried to lead him to the rock she'd been sitting on.

"Prisoners go with Duncan," Kier snapped, and one of his soldiers tugged on the chains linking the captives together.

"What will you do with them?" Tierney hugged herself in the cool evening breeze.

"They are prisoners of war. They are bound for the king's dungeons."

"What about Gullie? He isn't a prisoner of war. We were just in the wrong place at the wrong time."

"He is an abomination."

"He is Dark Fae. That doesn't make him an abomination just because he's different from you. Trust me, nothing good will ever come from discriminating against a group of fae whose only crime is they look different."

"He will not be harmed, but he cannot go free." Keir shoved her forward, leading her to the campfire already burning bright. With a last glance at Gulliver and his fellow captives tethered to a petrified tree near the cliff face, she reluctantly went with Keir to sit beside the warm fire.

"What are you doing?" Tierney tried to pull her hands away from Keir.

"You think I'm going to let you roam free to go lie with your mongrel?" He wrapped a rope around her wrists, leashing her to an iron stake in the ground.

She tugged on her restraints in frustration. "You are a pig."

"You will stay by my side while we are at camp. You will eat when I eat, and you will sleep when I sleep. And you will be silent."

Tierney glowered at him, thinking she would be better off with the other prisoners.

Chapter 9
TIERNEY

"Filthy jerks." Tierney scowled at the soldiers who sat nearby, skinning the huge animal they'd hunted before she even woke. It was enormous and vaguely deer-like, but the meat held an intense gamey odor that put her off her breakfast. What sort of game did they have in this kingdom? The truth was, the legends said very little about Lenya other than mentioning its existence. She didn't know about the constant wars or what type of fae lived here.

She didn't even know if they had magic or if her mind had been playing tricks on her in the heat of battle.

Blood stained the rocks where the carcass lay. Back home, when she and Toby returned from hunts, one of the servants would string up their kills to drain them before butchering them. It was a much longer process than could be done in a single morning.

"We have an entire unit to feed." Keir sat sharpening his sword. He didn't look up. "They were out at dawn in search of a fianna."

"Fianna?"

For once, he didn't chastise her for speaking. "The animal. Smaller beasts wouldn't do, and we don't like to butcher any of the horses while we need them to travel."

She stared at him, at his penetrating beauty that hid the hideous soul, her jaw dropping open. "You wouldn't." Horse? In Iskalt, they'd never think of such a thing.

"I don't know what your life is like, girl, but here in Lenya, we do what we must to survive." He grunted and examined his gleaming blade, the conversation effectively over.

When a soldier brought her a piece of meat that had been charred over the morning fire, she ate it, grateful it wasn't as gamey as it smelled when freshly butchered.

The more time she spent with Keir, the more she missed the harsh general. At least his disdain had been so obvious she could see the hit coming before it happened. But he'd been left in charge of the castle they'd captured.

Keir hadn't hurt her, not physically, but his scorn burned slowly, and too much exposure would lead to her doing something stupid.

Like trying to kill him.

Her eyes fell on the knife that lay at his side. She could lunge for it and drive it right into his heart before he even noticed she'd moved. Even with her non-responsive magic, she had power. She was trained to be lethal, to protect herself by any means necessary. Judging by the view this man held for females, he wouldn't see it coming until it was too late.

Many fae relied solely on magic, but her mom had grown up human with no knowledge of her power. She knew what it was like to be helpless and refused to let her daughter ever feel the same.

Even now, surrounded by enemies, Tierney didn't feel helpless. She wouldn't be a victim of her circumstances.

But she had to be smart. If she acted now, Keir's men would be on her so fast she'd never even get to say goodbye to Gullie. He may have been the one in chains, but she was every bit the prisoner he was.

"Why am I not with the other prisoners?" she asked.

Keir set his sword aside and reached for his dagger to hone its blade. She didn't think he was going to answer, and she waited for harsh words about a woman daring to ask questions. This kingdom was seriously messed up.

"We do not put women in the dungeons."

Her eyes narrowed. "Truly? That's nice, considering you obviously value us with all your rules."

A sigh echoed from his lips. "Our women are why we fight, why we risk our lives. We must protect them."

"As long as we remain quiet, dutiful, and modest."

"We all have roles to play, girl." He pushed to his feet, sliding his knife into his belt. Picking up his sword, he sheathed it. "Now, I am done answering questions. Today, you will not speak." He untied her from the stake, yanking the ropes.

"Jerk," she muttered. "And my name is Tia, not girl."

He gave no indication he heard her as he pulled her toward a horse that had been saddled and readied for him.

Without waiting for Tierney's approval, Keir gripped her waist and lifted her into the saddle. She crossed her arms, looking longingly at the river. Yesterday's sweat still coated her skin. They could have at least allowed her a quick bath in the cool water.

She looked around at the filthy soldiers, many of whom still had blood on their clothing. None of them had bathed either.

"Sir." Duncan walked up and inclined his head. "The prisoners are ready to leave."

At his words, Tierney strained to get a look at them, hoping they'd been given some of the meat. No one had eaten the day before, and the prisoners most likely had to walk again.

Gulliver stood behind the horse he was tied to, his shoulders hunched. His energetic tail now hung lifeless behind him. He lifted his eyes to hers, connected for a moment. They were cut off from each other when Keir climbed up behind her, blocking Gulliver from view.

"Best forget about him." Keir nudged his horse toward the river. "I guarantee the dungeons will make him forget about you."

She didn't give him the dignity of a response. He didn't know

Gulliver or how much they meant to each other. Whatever this war in Lenya was, she was sure they'd experienced much worse.

"Move out," Keir called as his horse's hooves hit the water. It was shallow here, reaching halfway up the animal's flanks.

Tierney's boots dipped into the water, and she worried about Gulliver. He wasn't the best swimmer.

Wherever Veren and Siobhan were, she just hoped it was better than this.

They made it across the wide river without incident, and a breath rushed out of her.

Throughout the day, every time she tried to speak, Keir cut her off with a dark look, one that stole the words from her lips. She remembered the way he'd been in battle, hacking through golden soldiers like a beast. He'd saved her life, but for what?

For this?

Her parents must be so worried. When they made camp for the night, she took a moment to close her eyes and picture the snowy fields of Iskalt. She'd sometimes complained about the cold, about her duties as the crown princess. But if she could go home right now, she'd marry whomever her father chose. She'd attend every council meeting, perform every royal duty.

If it meant she could hug her mom, talk to her siblings, make peace with her father ... she'd do just about anything.

Tears hung in her lashes, and she blinked them away, not wanting Keir to see any kind of weakness he could exploit. Thoughts of her family were for her alone. He could take her voice, remove her dignity, but the love she had for Iskalt and everyone there was something that would always be with her.

That night, they made camp in a series of caves. Unable to drive a stake into the ground, Keir tied the other end of her rope to his ankle, forcing her to sleep close to him. Every time she closed her eyes, she imagined how all of this would end.

With her friends dead.

And Tierney ... she wasn't sure what would happen to her.

Sleep eluded her, and as the soldiers roused at first light, she found herself hoping they'd hunt, that they'd take the life of some poor animal so the emptiness in her stomach could be filled.

Except a horse. No matter how hungry she was, she'd refuse to eat that.

When Keir woke, he looked as if he'd had a comfortable sleep in a four-poster feather bed. There were no bags under his eyes, no puffiness marring his beautiful, if dirty, olive skin.

And his hair remained perfectly smooth, without so much as a tangle, even after the battle and days on horseback.

It wasn't fair.

For a moment, as he surveyed the cave, the ever-present anger was gone from his eyes, and he looked just like any fae, the kind she might have gravitated toward in Iskalt.

But then, he seemed to remember who he was. His eyes narrowed and settled on her, sending a shiver down her spine.

This is a man who could slit my throat and not feel an ounce of guilt, she reminded herself. The rules were different here. Though they might look the same, these fae were not her people.

Duncan walked toward them, his steps echoing off the stone walls. "Sir, we are ready to move."

Keir stood and issued a few commands before bending to untie the rope from his ankle. The other end burned against Tierney's wrists, and she knew there'd be a mark by the time she was free of it.

Scrambling to her feet, she looked to where the soldiers stood by their horses beyond the mouth of the cave. "Wait ... isn't anyone going to hunt? We need to eat."

Keir tugged her behind him into the morning light. "Our food stores are gone, and there will be nothing to hunt this close to the fire plains."

She swallowed, hoping she'd heard him wrong. "Did you say we are nearing the fire plains?"

The scowl he sent her said he would not repeat himself.

She knew of the fire plains of Eldur in the northeastern Vatlands. But few fae ever ventured near the lands that burned with a fire so hot none other compared. The last remaining village along the border had been destroyed long ago by the ever-rising temperatures. Could these be the same fire plains?

Again, she had to ride side saddle, but this time, her stomach was empty and her hope was slowly slipping away. She hadn't seen Gulliver this morning, but she could hear Duncan yelling for the prisoners to keep up.

The heat intensified throughout the day, and all signs of water disappeared. Here, the vegetation was dry, sparse—very much like the deserts of Eldur. They left the trees behind, venturing out onto a long road, with nothing in sight except the endless distance.

Sweat pooled on her skin as the sun beat down on them, and then she saw the fires. They wouldn't venture too close to the border of the fire plains, but craggy mountains rose in the distance, smoke pouring from their flat peaks.

Volcanoes.

They were surrounded by rolling hills, bare of any grasses or plant life. Iridescent flames seemed to dance along the horizon like a mirage. Nothing survived the fire plains. Not plants. Not animals. Definitely not fae.

Any last hope she'd held on to drifted away, lost in the boiling lava she imagined inside those dark basins.

If she never recovered her magic, the only way home was across that sweltering land.

She collapsed in on herself, exhausted from the constant need to keep calm, to show no vulnerability. She wanted her mom, her frozen lakes, and obnoxious noble suitors.

Keeping her focus solely on remaining in the saddle, she didn't look at the fire plains again, didn't imagine what existed beyond those hills in a far-off place that couldn't be reached.

It hurt too much.

Night had fallen by the time they slowed their journey. The horses were exhausted, but to stop so close to the fire plains would make for a very uncomfortable rest. Once they put the belching volcanoes and smoldering fires behind them, the air cooled considerably, turning from an unbearable heat to a more tolerable warmth.

Tierney barely had the energy to hold her head up when she realized they'd stopped in the shadow of a massive structure. She couldn't see much in the darkness, but she could make out tall spires, a watch tower, and the walls of a courtyard as they passed through a fortified gate.

Keir jumped down and lifted her from the saddle. She stumbled when her feet hit the ground, weak from days of travel, lack of food, and the emotions draining her.

Yet, the soldier she'd ridden with, who'd faced some of the same things, looked like he'd just been out for a simple ride.

A group of boys ran from the stables. One of them took hold of Keir's horse.

Keir drew a dagger, and Tierney waited. This was it, the moment he'd waited for to do away with the useless prisoner his general had forced on him. He stepped closer, his fingers curling around the hilt.

And then, he slipped the knife under the ropes and cut right through them. They dropped away from her, and she felt instant relief before it was replaced with guilt. In her turmoil, she'd forgotten Gulliver. Where was he?

Turning, she searched the courtyard, but he wasn't there. The dungeons. That's where they said the other prisoners would end up.

A young woman ran toward them before dropping into a curtsy.

"You may speak." Keir looked down at the woman, but she kept her eyes on her feet.

"I was told there is a young female prisoner, who is to be taken to a room."

"Good." He shoved Tierney toward the maid. "She's no longer my problem. Take her to the east rooms." He turned hard eyes on Tierney. "They lock from the outside. Two guards will take up their posts there before you even arrive." With that, he walked away and started issuing orders to the boys taking care of the horses.

The maid straightened and lifted her eyes, clicking her tongue as she took in Tierney's appearance. "Well, you must be hungry. And you need a bath. My name is Ariella. Follow me."

Tierney did as she was told, the entire time trying to figure out why the woman's personality had made a complete change as soon as Keir walked away.

CHAPTER 10
TIERNEY

Keir hadn't lied. Tierney paced across the wide expanse of her rooms in the east wing. Two menacing guards stood vigil at her door the moment she arrived with the maid.

Wrapping her arms around her middle, Tierney's frantic pacing increased as her mind whirled with a thousand things at once.

"Take off those filthy clothes, Miss." Ariella took the last steaming bucket of water from another servant and poured it into a shining brass tub. In all her life, Tierney had never seen a fae heat water before filling a tub. In Gelsi and Iskalt, they had magical means of heating their water, and in Eldur they had deep bathing pools that filled themselves.

Tierney's skin crawled with an itch she couldn't scratch. It had happened slowly. A distant tingling as she entered the grand palace of Vondur. As she followed the young maid through the palace, up the stairs and down long corridors, the tingling had grown into an unpleasant burn.

It was her magic returning! Tierney could feel it rushing through her veins, just out of reach, but it was there. She needed to get rid of the maid, with her incessant chatter, and focus on touching her magic. Then, maybe she could start planning their escape. She just needed to figure out how to enter the dungeons, break Gullie out, and get out of the palace, all without alerting anyone. Piece of cake.

"Miss?" Ariella broke through Tierney's thoughts. "Your bath is ready."

"Yes. Thank you. You may call me Tia." She watched the young woman, who was obviously trained as a lady's maid. If Tierney was to be a prisoner, why would they have given her a maid to care for her needs?

She was probably reporting to Keir, sent here to watch her every move. Tierney needed to befriend this girl. Maybe she would prove to be helpful. Tierney reached for her grubby t-shirt, lifting it over her head. She'd worn it since leaving her mother's childhood home in the human realm. That felt like a lifetime ago.

"Oh my, that wouldn't be proper, Miss." Ariella made a tsking noise at her. "My, but you have the strangest clothes." She took the shirt from Tierney's hands, frowning at it.

"I'd like to keep them if that's okay." Tierney quickly shed her jeans. "I could use the bathwater after I wash to clean my clothes." Not that Tierney even knew how to wash her clothes. She just knew offering to do her own chores was likely the best way to befriend the maid.

"Nonsense, dearie. I'll get them washed up for you." She folded the dirty clothes and added Tierney's underthings to the pile.

"This looks heavenly, thank you so much." Tierney slipped into the floral scented bathwater with a moan of pleasure. After so many days traveling with Keir and his men, she would never again take baths for granted. "What is that scent?" Tierney lifted a shriveled flower petal from the water. "It's almost like vanilla, but more floral."

"That's the Queen of the Night blossom." Ariella dipped a scrub brush into the hot water as Tierney leaned back against the tub. "It blooms only one night a year, near the fire plains. The perfume will make your skin soft and smooth. All the ladies at court use the night blossom in their bathwater."

"How do you know I'm a lady?" Tierney closed her eyes as Ariella scrubbed at her nails to clean them of dirt.

"You have the look about you, underneath all this dirt and grime. And you didn't bat an eyelash about taking your clothes off or letting me scrub your hands. You're used to having a lady's maid. Though, I think you do just fine on your own too."

"You're very observant, Ariella."

"'Tis the lot of a maid, my Lady." She moved to scrub Tierney's feet. "It helps when you can anticipate what your lady needs before she has to ask."

"I don't know how much attending I'll need as a prisoner of the king."

"I've been told to keep you comfortable, so you've no need to fear for your safety, my Lady."

"Please call me Tia. It would make me happy if you did." Tierney already liked the young maid, though it was odd to see how different she was in private than how she was when there was a man around. Even when the guards were present, Ariella fell silent as a mouse.

"Very well, Tia." Ariella stood up. "Enjoy your soak. I'll be back in a snap with some proper clothes for you, and I've sent to the kitchens for your dinner."

"Thank you, again, Ariella." Tierney watched her go. The moment the door closed behind her, Tierney sat forward, rinsing the soap from her shoulders. Here in Vondur, they didn't seem to have magic. She'd witnessed nothing remotely magical in her time with Keir since the battle. If she could reach her own power, that would give her an advantage her foes wouldn't see coming. As isolated as they were in this region of the fae realms, they might not know anything of true power.

But Tierney had to be much more careful than most fae. She'd made it clear she was a princess of Iskalt, though Keir didn't seem to believe her. But she had to operate as though he and his fae knew more of her land than they let on. She couldn't afford for them to discover she was one of the most powerful fae ever born, with the power of Iskalt, Eldur, and Fargelsi running through her veins. Particularly when that magic wasn't cooperating. Even now, she could feel it just out of her reach.

Gelsi power came more naturally to her. She'd used the ancient language of Gelsi nearly all her life. She'd only had use of her Eldurian and Iskaltian inheritance for the few years since she came of age.

Glancing out the nearest window, the sun still shone in the sky. Dusk would be upon them soon, and she would have access to all sides of her magic.

"*Hita,*" Tierney whispered the word that would reheat her tepid bathwater. Nothing happened.

She set her palm open on the edge of the tub and took a deep breath. "*Ljos.*" Her power sparked along the surface of her palm, but the simple spell failed to illuminate her hand with light.

Frustrated, Tierney stood up, letting the cooling water stream down her body before she stepped from the tub and wrapped herself in a linen sheet Ariella had left.

She moved to stand in front of the fireplace mantel, where a row of elaborately carved candles stood in a silver candelabra. Taking another deep breath, she reached within herself, searching for the place where her magic resided. Focusing on her intentions, the creepy, crawly sensation danced under her skin, making her shiver.

"*Dóiteán,*" she murmured the word for fire, focusing on the candle wick like she was a Gelsi toddler, learning her first spell. The wick ignited for a brief moment before flickering out.

A gasp sounded behind her, and she turned to see Ariella, her face as pale as the wall behind her.

"Where is your totem?" she demanded, two spots of color flushing her cheeks as she marched across the room, grabbing Tierney's hands, searching her frantically until she snatched the sheet from her body.

"Ariella? What is your problem?" Tierney tried to cover herself.

"Where is your totem? I was told you had none." Her eyes blazed with anger and confusion, and something that struck Tierney as … envy.

"I don't know what you mean." Tierney had an overwhelming feeling that she had just made a big mistake.

"Your crystal, my Lady." Ariella held her hand out, as if Tierney had something concealed on her person, though she stood there stark naked and shivering.

"Crystal?" She shook her head, holding her arms up. "I have no crystal."

"I saw you use it to light the candle. Give it to me. A lady such as yourself has no need of magic."

"Magic?" Tierney turned her gaze back to the candle, realizing her mistake. "It must have been a trick of the light. I have no totem to wield such magic. I wouldn't know what to do with one even if I had it." That was truth enough. Tierney had read about magical totems in the Aghadoon library. Her fae had no use for such things, but there were records of a type of crystal used in ancient times to carve totems that would give one magic for a time. They looked like small figurines or statues, or sometimes amulets worn as jewelry. Was that the kind of magic the fae of Vondur knew?

Ariella relaxed, nodding. "Of course, my Lady. Please forgive me." She dipped into a low curtsy before she placed a fine silk robe over Tierney's shoulders.

"Think nothing of it," Tierney murmured, her mind spinning with the possibilities. She walked woodenly over to the vanity stool where Ariella ran a comb through her wet hair and proceeded to braid it.

She would have to be careful with her magic. She couldn't risk letting that happen again, but Tierney needed to practice. Something about this land suppressed her magic, but she was strong. Reconnecting with her power was her only hope. Unless she could get her hands on a totem. Perhaps it would amplify her weaker power?

"Ariella, how might I schedule an audience with the king. I know

I'm technically a prisoner, but I would like to speak with him. Perhaps we could negotiate a truce."

The maid hummed as she finished braiding Tierney's hair. "I'm afraid the king has gone, my Lady. He won't be back for a while. Though, I wouldn't hold out much hope that he would agree to meet with a prisoner even if he was in residence."

"Could you get a message to Keir then? I should like to see him at his earliest convenience."

"I'll try." Ariella set the comb on the vanity and moved to dab lotion on Tierney's hands and arms. She frowned as she massaged the lotion into her skin. "I don't know what things are like where you come from." She sighed. "But you must understand, the men of Vondur palace are preoccupied with war and protecting their women and children from the Grima court. After so many years of war and destruction, resources are limited, and it's our job to make their lives easier. Keir works hard to do the king's bidding, particularly while the king is away. I can't imagine he would abide the summons of a female captive."

"I'm definitely not used to being treated like a nuisance or decoration," Tierney muttered just as her stomach gave a loud rumble.

"You must be starving. I will go see about your supper." She set the lotion back on the vanity table and wiped her hands on her apron.

"Captive." Tierney sighed as she glanced at her surroundings after Ariella left the enormous room. Her accommodations were fit for more than a captive, that was for sure. Her toes curled into the rich, plush carpet in the softest shade of pink. All the furnishings were made of dark woods edged in silver. The fireplace was large enough to stand in, and the windows were solid sheets of glass, with pristine views of the lush landscape beyond the palace walls. Silver candlesticks and trinkets covered every available surface. At the opposite end of the long room, a circular bed rested on a raised platform with silvery gray sheets and blankets. The pillows were the same pale pink as the carpet. A huge but uncomfortable-looking gray silk settee occupied the wall under the largest window, and heavy velvet drapes in pale shades of plum and rose hung from the ceiling to pool gracefully on the floor.

"Here we are, my Lady." Ariella swept back into the room with a tray covered in a silver domed lid. "Tonight, we have roasted fianna with honey glazed root vegetables and fresh baked bread. There is a shortage on butter and salt, but I hope you find it to your liking." She set the tray on the low table in front of the settee and poured murky water into a fine crystal goblet.

"I'm hungry enough to eat whatever's on that plate." Tierney stood, tightening the belt of her robe, and crossed the room to attack her meager meal. It looked like something she might have eaten on the trail with Keir and his men after a successful hunt. The water left something to be desired. She wasn't overly fond of the deer-like creature they seemed to have an abundance of in Vondur, but it was food. And this time, the fianna at least looked like it had been prepared by someone who knew what herbs were.

"Is there any tea?" she asked hopefully.

"Only at breakfast. We are on rations, even at the king's table, and especially with our prisoners."

"I see." Tierney tucked into her meal without complaint. The fianna was succulent and juicy with a hint of rosemary and another type of herb she couldn't place. There wasn't much honey in the honey glazed root vegetables, which tasted earthy and a bit tough. And the brown bread was dry, but it filled her stomach, and the only real complaint she had was that there wasn't more of it.

She was hesitant to drink the water, but if she was going to get out of this mess, she needed her strength, and that meant staying hydrated.

"What happens tomorrow?" Tierney used the last of her bread to mop up whatever juices were left on her plate.

"What do you mean?" Ariella cleared the plate from the table and poured her another glass of water.

"Where will I be taken?"

"I'm afraid this room will be the only thing of Vondur you will get to see, my Lady. You are a captive of the king. The only reason you've been given this room is because you are female and an obvious noblewoman of breeding. Otherwise, you would have been taken to the dungeons with the other prisoners."

"Surely there will be some allowances for fresh air or reading to pass the time?"

"You will find a few books on the shelf here in your room, but that is all you're allowed. I'll be back in the morning with your breakfast. I'll have more clothes for you then."

Tierney nodded. "I suppose that will have to do." She lifted her chin, refusing to let the maid see how terrified she was of never leaving this room again.

Chapter II
Tierney

A rattling at the door had Tierney shooting up in bed. It wasn't the first time.

This foreign palace was noisy. She could hear every step of the guards stomping down the halls on their patrols, the howl of wolfhounds out in the woods.

Shadows danced across the room, where silver moonlight streamed in the sliver between the thick curtains.

"You're okay, Tia," she whispered to herself. "You're alive, unharmed, and you're going to get out of here."

She'd taken to talking to herself in the four days since she'd arrived at the palace. The only person she'd seen was Ariella, and the maid hadn't been as keen on talking as that first time. She seemed almost … scared. Maybe it was the display of magic, small as it was.

Clutching the thick duvet to her chest, Tierney glanced around the dark room, taking in the still unfamiliar furniture, the door that no longer rattled.

The fire in the hearth had waned, but she suspected it had only been lit for comfort, a small piece of mercy from the maid. Because Vondur didn't exactly have a chill in the air. It was too close to the fire plains for that.

Tierney squeezed her eyes shut and slid farther down in bed. She was burning up underneath the covers, but without them she felt too exposed. To this place and these desperate feelings that had expanded inside her chest with each passing day.

Despite the early signs of hope, her magic hadn't grown any stronger than when she almost lit the candle. Every time she tried to pull on it, it sparked to life before slowly fading. Like something outside of her drew it close but wasn't strong enough to sustain it.

Crystals. Ariella had mentioned crystals. There'd been a single mention of them in the Aghadoon library. Of course, Tierney hadn't read every book there. That would have been impossible. But after the battle ten years ago, she'd taken to studying there, spending time with her grandfather, Brandon, and aiding in his quest to find all the dangerous material and destroy it. The library was the source of all fae magic. When a spell or a type of power was destroyed there, it disappeared forever.

But it was the histories more than the unusual spells that interested her the most.

It was actually Veren who found the book that talked of the ancients using crystals before discovering how to harness other kinds of power. Back when he'd pretended to enjoy her company, he'd sat beside her at the long oaken table inside the musty library in the always moving village and feigned interest.

Images of Veren flashed through her mind, and it made her think of Siobhan. Where were they? Were they okay?

Rattling sounded in the room again, but this time, it didn't come from the door. Instead, a picture frame containing a portrait of a very old, very pale man started to shake. Tierney rubbed her eyes, thinking she'd imagined it shifting to the side.

But then, a single flame appeared. A candle.

Her gaze traveled from the flame, up the arm of its bearer. It was a young woman, maybe only a few years younger than Tierney herself. An orange glow flickered across olive skin and glossy black hair that was pulled into a single braid stretching down her back.

Tierney eyed her warily, but the girl didn't speak. She stepped forward, and the portrait slid back into place.

Then, as if the bubble of silence popped. She laughed. The sound seemed so wrong in Tierney's prison cell that she thought whoever this was must have been mad.

"Well, I haven't used *that* tunnel in a while." She patted her nightgown, brushing a hand over the fabric. "It was rather dusty in there. I'm sure if Ariella saw me now, she'd have something to say about my midnight wanderings."

Tierney said nothing, she just stared.

"Oh, come now, I heard you had quite the tongue on you."

From whom? Pushing the covers down and sitting up, Tierney crossed her arms over her chest.

The girl laughed again. "Well, okay then, I guess I'll do the talking. That's more like me anyway. Just ask my father." She threw herself onto the settee across the room and leaned forward, plucking the last roll from Tierney's dinner tray Ariella had never come to collect. "I'm starving. I had to eat dinner with a group of noblemen today in my father's absence, and I never get to actually eat when I'm with them. I'm too busy trying to take dainty bites that are so small I barely taste anything."

She bit a giant chunk of the roll, chewed, and sighed. "Mara, our cook, makes the best bread. It's all the fresh butter she sneaks in. Just don't tell anyone she uses more than rations allow. She'll skin me alive." She finished the roll and picked at the plate Tierney had hardly touched.

Tierney was so confused that words failed her, an unusual occurrence.

"I have to say," the girl went on, her mouth full, "I'm sort of disappointed. Keir told me you had fire, and all I see is a girl, who is just like all the other women I meet. Meek, quiet."

Tierney, meek? She'd already gotten the sense the women here were a product of their suppression. "Who are you?" she demanded finally. And how did she know Keir?

"Oh, didn't I introduce myself?" She chuckled. "You must think I'm just some crazed woman who wanders the unused palace tunnels in the middle of the night."

"Well, the crazed part, yeah."

"Yeah?" The girl's smile widened. "Is that one of those human words?" She squealed. "Keir told me you had an outlandish story of coming here from the human realm. He didn't believe you, but he's never had an imagination. I'm not sure what to think. The human world could be accessible. I've just never met anyone who has actually faced a human before."

The girl still hadn't told Tierney her name, but Tierney found herself relaxing slightly. There was something so … unthreatening in her curious gaze. "My mother was raised there."

Her eyes lit up. "How incredible. I have so many questions."

Tierney rubbed her eyes. "What hour is it?"

"I don't really know. My mind was too active to rest."

"You don't say." Tierney sighed. "I ask again, who in the kingdoms are you?"

"Oh." She brought a hand to her mouth with a giggle. "I do tend to go off on a ramble once in a while."

Tierney suspected it was more often than that.

"My name is Eavha. You're Tierney O'Shea from Iskalt. I've heard the legends about the other fae kingdoms, but I never imagined they were true. This is the best thing to happen to me in a long time."

"Well, I'm glad my imprisonment is such a joy for *you.*" Tierney leaned back against the headboard. "Can I go back to sleep please?"

"Absolutely not." Eavha jumped from the settee and crossed the room to sit on the corner of the bed uninvited. Moonlight highlighted her soft yellow sleeping gown that reached her ankles. "We have so much to discuss."

"Like how you got past the guards into my rooms."

She waved a hand. "I've been secreting myself around this palace since I was a child, avoiding my father and brother's watchful gazes."

"Your father?"

"I didn't mention him? I'm sorry. Sometimes I forget myself. He's the king." She pushed on without stopping. "See, there are these tunnels that few fae use anymore, but you were put in this specific room for a reason. I imagine someone thought they might need to visit you without anyone knowing. But I don't think they meant it to be me."

Tierney's mind twisted and turned with this new information. This girl who talked too much, ate like she'd never been fed, and skulked around dusty tunnels was a princess?

Tierney could only think of one thing to say. "You do know I'm a prisoner here, right?"

Eavha blinked at her, her mouth popping open. "Well, I guess you are correct."

"No one will use the tunnels to visit me. They will come to interrogate me. My best friend is sitting in the dungeons on orders from your father."

The young princess pursed her lips. "I didn't—"

"What? Realize we aren't just two princesses catching up?"

"I'm sorry. My questions were rude. Ariella is always telling me I need to better mind my mouth." She picked at the duvet, averting her eyes. "I would help you if I could. The tunnels within the walls will only get you so far without a key."

Tierney's irritation faded. She remembered what it was like to be a lonely princess. Even though she'd had siblings, she'd always felt like she carried the weight of Iskalt on her own.

"It's fine," she found herself saying. "I know what it's like to have an overbearing father. Mine once locked up a boy for an entire week after he broke my heart. I'd had to bring a chandelier crashing to the ground with my magic to get his attention."

Her eyes widened. "You used magic on your own father? Did he whip you for it?"

Tierney's brow furrowed. Her father would never hurt her … unless she included him trying to marry her off. "No. And really, he'd put the boy in one of our most extravagant guest rooms, with all the luxuries he'd wanted. The chandelier was a bit of an overreaction."

Eavha released a breath. "I wish I could bring a chandelier down, but the crystals here are not for women." She scooted closer and dropped her voice. "Ariella mentioned the flame …"

Tierney closed her eyes with a sigh. "Does she tell you everything?"

"Of course. She's my Lady's maid."

That was a surprise. "Then, why is she caring for me?"

"That was my idea. We don't exactly have extra maids lying around here. War time and all. Many of our staff have left to go take care of their villages as all the men leave for battle. And I absolutely couldn't have another princess stay here without a maid, even if you are a prisoner from a kingdom no one believes in." She was sad for a moment before her mood immediately changed, and a smile returned to her lips. "Can you show me?"

"Show you?" Tierney could hardly follow the conversation, and she wasn't sure this girl truly believe she was from another kingdom.

Eavha nodded. "The magic. It's just … I've never seen anyone do it without a crystal. And since women don't have access to crystals, I've never seen a woman use the power at all."

"I …" She'd been about to tell her she couldn't, but Eavha's hopeful face stopped her. "I can try." She reached a hand out for Eavha's candle and blew out the flame, plunging them into darkness.

Drawing every bit of power she could from inside her, Tierney pictured a flame. It should have been easy with the Iskalt magic that now rose to life with the moon. Yet, nothing happened. She tried again, triumph surging through her when a tiny flame flickered to life.

Eavha gasped. "That was the most amazing act I've ever witnessed."

Tierney flopped back, that bit of magic exhausting her more than it should have. As if her hold on it slowly faded away, the flame grew smaller and smaller until it winked out completely.

Neither girl spoke at first. Then, Eavha laughed. "Well, it's the dark for us now."

Footsteps sounded in the hall, and Eavha dove off the bed onto the floor as the door opened.

A gruff voice cut through the dark, "Is everything okay in here, prisoner?"

Tierney pretended to just be waking up. She rubbed her eyes and took a moment to respond. "Yes. I'd appreciate it if you didn't burst into my room without warning."

She could almost feel his scowl. "Every room in this palace belongs to the king. Watch what you say, woman. Another man would strike you for such speak."

Tierney rolled her eyes, knowing he couldn't see her.

But it seemed Eavha wasn't so calm. She jumped from where she was hiding. "Declan Connel, you will not speak in such a way to my new friend."

Something warmed in Tierney at the term friend. Few girls had ever considered her such.

The soldier, presumably this Declan, stared at her in shock for a moment before glancing into the hall and shutting the door. To Tierney's surprise, he didn't chastise Eavha for her speech. "What are you doing here, Eavha?"

Hmm, not princess? Interesting.

"That's not really any of your business." They spoke as if Tierney was no longer there.

Declan's long strides carried him across the room. He wore a fraying uniform that Tierney imagined looked rather raggedy in the daylight. "You're lucky I was assigned to guard the prisoner tonight."

"She has a name."

His eyes narrowed in the dark. "You shouldn't be in here. Your father would … wait, how did you get past me?" He paused, his scowl deepening as he released a curse. "The tunnels. Eavha, you know how dangerous they are."

"Only if you don't know your way around."

Tierney didn't know what they meant about the tunnels or how they could be dangerous, but she saw the way they focused on each other. There was a familiarity there.

Declan scrubbed a hand across his face like this wasn't the first time they'd had this conversation. He reached out to grab her arm, but she pushed him away. "Stop."

"Eavha." His voice softened. "You know you can't visit a prisoner."

"Of course I can."

"If your father finds out I knew you were here …"

Tierney didn't need to see Eavha's face to assume it had paled. "I didn't know it was you out there."

"And it would be okay for him to hang one of my comrades?"

Hang? What kind of place was this?

Eavha ran a hand down his arm. "I'm sorry. I'll be careful, I promise."

A sigh pushed past his lips. "You do have a knack for evading trouble."

"Please just let me have this." Tierney didn't know why it was so important to Eavha to talk to her. "If my father finds out, I'll tell him Keir asked me to gather information from the prisoner—gain her trust and secrets. You know I'm good at that."

He pushed a hand through his hair and looked away. Tierney waited for him to say no, to say he didn't want anyone's fate in the hands of that grumpy soldier. But he didn't. "Fine."

A smile broke across Eavha's face, and she pressed a kiss to Declan's cheek. He backed away quickly.

"Go back to your rooms." He leveled one more glance her way and yanked open the door to take up his position in the hall again.

Tierney hardly breathed until the door was closed.

"That was close." Eavha laughed.

She'd lost her mind. "What if Keir tells the king the truth?"

Eavha shook her head. "He'd never do that. Declan is like a brother to him. He'd do anything to protect his men."

"And you? Why would that jerk lie to his king for you?" Something about this didn't make sense.

Eavha met her gaze in the dark. "Because that jerk is my brother."

Her brother.

Keir was the prince.

CHAPTER 12
KEIR

Keir stood behind his father's throne, waiting for the arrival of the king with the other members of the Vondur court. It was his job to govern the court in his father's absence—Keir's least favorite task as the son of a king.

Turlach Dagnan assumed the throne of Vondur more than a decade ago, yet Keir still didn't think of himself as a prince. It was difficult to accept the role when everyone knew it wasn't one that would last. There was no guarantee he would ever be king. Natural succession was rare in Vondur. The king could be usurped at any time.

Keir remembered the day his father had killed the former king and taken his throne for himself, believing he could do a better job—and he had. Vondur had fared well enough under his rule, but Turlach wasn't of a mind to end the war. He enjoyed the power and bloodshed too much. He wanted to take the throne of Grima as well. With the death of its queen, he was one step closer.

Rumor had it, the young Princess Bronagh was now Queen of Grima. She didn't stand a chance against Turlach. A loud knock shook Keir from his thoughts.

"His Majesty, King Turlach Dagnan has returned!" the court herald announced as the double doors of the throne room creaked open. Like everything within the palace walls, the throne room was grand, with deep purple carpets and golden surfaces. The throne itself was an enormous totem, carved from the crystal that gave them power—though, its power was long depleted. Everything in the room was old. Outdated and well used. The castellan and his staff did a marvelous job of keeping the richly appointed rooms looking just as they once had, giving the illusion that the kingdom of Vondur was a wealthy one. The truth was, every silver candlestick and golden furnishing was older than the oldest living Vondurian. And a great many of those fine things were fakes, the genuine silver and gold melted long ago for coin used to purchase necessities for the war.

Keir squared his shoulders and met his father's gaze as he entered the throne room.

"Leave us," the king ordered as he sat upon his throne, looking weary from his campaign to the eastern border of Grima. The battle there had not fared as well as the one Keir had led against the Grima queen from the western border nearest her palace. Just as the king predicted, the queen had divided her forces, sending the greatest of her army to meet the Vondur king, leaving Keir to face the remaining Grima soldiers.

King Turlach waited for the room to clear before he spoke.

"She is truly dead?" the king asked, not bothering to turn to face his son.

Keir stepped from behind the opaque crystal throne. "I gave the order myself. She hangs from her own ramparts." Keir had done what he had to for his kingdom, but he took no pleasure in it. Not like his father.

"Well done, my son." Turlach laughed at the demise of his foe. "The woman finally got what she deserved."

"Many of my men fell, Father." Keir hung his head. "We lost more men than we'd anticipated. Coupled with your dead from the eastern front, we've suffered an incredible loss."

The king waved off his concerns, a grin lighting up his face. "What does it matter when we've won the battle? We will take Grima soon, my son. I will have a united kingdom under our rule. Just like we've always planned."

Keir had no such plan. Those were his father's dreams. Keir dreamed of a world where he no longer had to fear what the inevitable death of his father would bring for Eavha and himself, should he be forced to fight for his right to rule.

"We must strike while the Grima are scattered and unorganized. You will ride out with your men at first light and hunt down the dispersed soldiers along the border while they're still confused over the death of their queen."

"We received word that Princess Bronagh has assumed the throne." Keir stood before his father now. He agreed that now was the time to act swiftly and with purpose, but that was where his thoughts deviated from his father's. If he had it his way, he would offer a peace treaty to the young queen and bring an end to this magic-forsaken war. But his father would never offer peace when there was still fighting to be had.

"I will lead an attack against the little chit before she has a chance to listen to her elders." The king was already planning his next battle.

"There's been another development." Keir pulled him out of his strategic plans.

"You may speak freely, my son." Turlach nodded, giving him his undivided attention.

Keir sighed. He and his father might not see eye to eye on anything, but he never doubted he had his father's love and respect. That made it difficult to go against his wishes.

"We have a captive staying in the east wing. A young woman I encountered in the midst of battle."

"A woman?" Turlach frowned. "Why go to the trouble of bringing her back to the palace? Why not slit her throat and be done with it?"

"She is not from Grima."

"She is ours, then? Why keep her captive?"

"She is not of Vondur either." Keir stood with his hands clasped behind his back. He still didn't believe her outlandish stories, but she was clearly not from either fae kingdom.

"You are saying she is human?" The king sat up straight, his attention fully on his son with this startling news.

"She is clearly fae, yet she holds foreign ideas and knows nothing of our war. I thought she could be of use."

"What is her story?" The king's eyes narrowed. He was quickly losing his father's interest.

"She claims to be a princess from a land called Iskalt."

"Iskalt?" Turlach leaned forward. "The land across the fire plains?"

"I do not know what she is playing at, or if her mind is befuddled, but I thought it prudent to bring her here for questioning."

The king nodded. "Yes. You did the right thing. Does she have magic?"

"Not that she has demonstrated."

"Have you tried giving her a small totem to see how she responds? I can't imagine a female would be able to do much with the weakest of our functioning crystals."

"She has strange ideas about women. And she is very confused and concerned for her mongrel friend in the dungeons."

"Mongrel?"

Keir nodded. "A strange fae fellow with a tail and eyes like a feral cat."

"You don't say?" The king seemed intrigued by the man known as Gulliver. "I shall have to consult my histories on this. We will question this princess and her mongrel once we have a better idea of where they came from."

As king, Turlach had access to the King's Library, a small room which contained all the knowledge of the previous kings and queens of Vondur and Grima. Keir had often dreamed of having such knowledge for himself. To truly understand why they were fighting this awful war. It couldn't just be about control of their magical resources. There had to be more to it than that.

The crystals that allowed them to perform magic were in short supply. Once, the lands were rich with the resource on both sides of the border, but now, only one active mine remained—right on the border—and the two kingdoms fought for control of it. In the end, one kingdom would reign supreme, and one would lose their magic forever.

Unless they came to an agreement over the use of their finite resources. An agreement King Turlach would never entertain.

"Have you restricted her to her rooms?"

"Yes, Father. She is confined to the eastern guest suite."

"You didn't put her in the prison quarters?"

"She is a lady, my King. I thought it best to give her some comforts."

"Keep her there, but restrict her diet. She is not to bathe or read. As she grows more uncomfortable, I will question her myself."

"She is a reasonable woman. I think we could accomplish a great deal just by talking to her as we would an envoy of a friendly kingdom—were there such a thing."

"You're too soft, Keir," the king grumbled. "This woman is probably a Grima spy. It is war time. It's best to make her as uncomfortable as possible and then get to the root of why she is here rather than waste time with unnecessary niceties."

"I disagree." Keir normally tried to avoid arguing with his father, but his plan for Tierney would surely backfire. The more uncomfortable Tierney was, the more she would argue. They needed her comfortable and cooperative. To do otherwise would put her on guard.

"It is not for you to—"

"Father, you're home!" Eavha came charging into the throne room, a disgruntled looking Declan limping behind her.

"I apologize, your Majesty. She kicked me." He hobbled on one foot.

"Eavha, we've talked about your kicking," Keir tried to chastise his sister, though he was no good at it. "You're at least a decade too old to be kicking fae."

"I wouldn't have to kick if Declan wasn't irritating." Eavha rushed up to hug their father.

"Eavha, we will make a lady of you someday." The king chuckled. His only soft spot was for his daughter, and she knew it.

"I'm afraid I must borrow Keir. It's an emergency," Eavha said in a rush.

"What's wrong?" the king asked.

"Sheba is missing!" Tears welled in the princess's eyes. "I can't find her anywhere in the palace. I'm afraid she's wandering the grounds again, and Keir is the only one who can ever find her."

"But I thought—" Declan started to speak, but Eavha stamped her foot down on his injured leg, and he bent over to catch his breath.

The king saw none of this, of course. Nor did he realize she was lying.

"Go help your sister find that cat of hers." The king dismissed him. "We will continue this discussion after dinner."

"Thank you, Father!" Eavha walked toward him, reached up on her tiptoes, and kissed his cheek before she ushered Declan and Keir out of the throne room.

As they turned the corner toward the main gardens, Sheba sat waiting, licking her giant paws and thumping her sleek tail. The big spotted mountain cat was Eavha's best friend, but she hated everyone else in the palace.

"There you are, Sheba! I've been looking all over for you!"

"Does she think we buy that story?" Declan stood with his arms crossed over his wide chest, watching the princess scratch the big cat behind the furry tuft of her ears.

"She knows better. What are you playing at, Eavha?"

"Oh fine." She dropped her hands back to her sides, and Sheba nosed at her fingers, licking them with her barbed tongue. "You were headed for that same old argument with Father, and I thought it best to dispel the tension with a fake emergency."

Declan sighed. "I'm going back to my post. You can take over Eavha duty."

"I am not a duty," Eavha called after him. "And certainly not yours, Declan!"

"Come on." Keir rolled his eyes. "I'll take you back to your rooms." He draped an arm over her shoulders.

"I don't want to go back to my rooms. My rooms are boring, and there's no one to talk to. I swear, my day to day isn't much better than poor Tierney's."

Of course she'd broken into Tierney's rooms. Keir wiped a weary hand over his face. "What do you know of our captive lady?"

"She's wonderful!" Eavha beamed at him. "It's like having a real friend. Though, we do need to keep Father from making her life any more miserable than it already is. The poor dear is bored to death. You know I can find out more about her and what has brought her here than either you or Father ever could. She trusts me. At least, I think she does, though she still refuses to tell me how her magic works without a totem."

Keir stopped walking. "She has magic?"

"Oh dear, I wasn't supposed to say that." Eavha groaned, covering her mouth with her hand. "Don't go in there raging at her, Keir. She's not going to tell you anything unless you speak to her like an actual person. Do not treat her like a simple-minded fae because she is nothing of the sort."

Keir ignored his sister's babble. "Her magic works without a totem? No crystal at all?"

"It was the most marvelous thing I've ever seen. To think, a woman using magic!"

"I will be cautious when I speak with her next, but you must promise me you will not visit her anymore. She could be a threat, Eavha. I mean it."

"Of course, dear brother. I understand." She linked her arm though his.

Keir shook his head. "I wonder why I don't believe you."

CHAPTER 13
TIERNEY

Tierney paced the length of the room like a feral animal desperate to break free of its cage. Somewhere in this palace, Gullie could be in an actual cage, and she was still here in these elaborate rooms. It wasn't fair.

Being a woman in this kingdom was obviously a bad thing, but it had also saved her.

She stopped and stared at the tray of food Ariella had brought her way too early this morning. It sat untouched near the settee on the ornate table that looked like it had been carved from some kind of turquoise crystal. Fragile, yet strong.

Her stomach folded in on itself, begging for something to fill it. But she couldn't fathom gorging herself on rich foods when her friends possibly had nothing. So, for another day, she didn't eat.

Edging closer to the table, she examined it, wondering if this was the kind of crystal Eavha mentioned. Lowering herself to the settee, she bent forward and wrapped her fingers around one of the legs. Closing her eyes, she tried to force magic to flow from the table into her hand.

This was ridiculous. Ridiculous and stupid. Tables didn't have magic.

The bits of power she'd managed to grab hold of ebbed away, and she leaned back with a huff. It was useless.

The door opened without a knock, and Ariella bustled in, stopping when she took in the full tray of food, the untouched tea. Putting her hands on her hips, she frowned. "And just how is starving yourself going to help anyone?"

"It won't." Tierney felt like a child, but being stuck in this room was slowly stealing all her sensibilities, and she just wanted someone to fight with. If Toby were here, he'd oblige. Even Gulliver would pretend irritation with her just to make her happy. "But it makes me feel better."

Ariella sighed, more resignation than anger. Such a disappointment. "Well, no one can force food into your throat. Though, I will be a twinge sad when you fall faint and eventually die from your idiocy. Such a willful girl, I'll claim at the funeral no one here will throw for you. And then, we'll all go on with our lives as if no prisoner had ever taken up residence in the east wing."

"Well …" Tierney crossed her arms. "That was mean."

"Just honest." She curtsied, adding a sarcastic afterthought, "My lady."

Tierney would have liked this maid under other circumstances. In a way, she reminded her of her mother. "What are you doing here anyway? Don't you have a princess to attend to?"

"Eavha is out riding with her cat, Sheba."

The only cats Tierney had ever seen were in the human realm. Uncle Myles once took her to his parents' farm, where they had a family of them living in the barn. "Cats don't ride."

Ariella gave her a pointed look. "And fae do not have magic without crystals."

Oh, so she hadn't forgotten. "Fair point."

"Besides," she busied herself making Tierney's bed, pressing out every last wrinkle, "I never said Sheba was riding. She simply runs beside the horse. It is good exercise."

Tierney needed to stop trying to understand anything in this kingdom. The small cats she remembered from the barn couldn't have kept up with a horse. "So, when Eavha is busy, you get to bother unwanted prisoners?"

"Oh, I assure you, as soon as the king learns of your origins, you will not be unwanted."

Great, just what she desired. A king who wouldn't let her leave. Keir's father. She wasn't sure why she felt so betrayed by a man who'd done nothing but tie her up and haul her back to this palace. He hadn't owed her the truth of who he was any more than she owed him her truths.

Ariella straightened the room, humming to herself. Before she left, she stopped in front of Tierney. "If you're determined to starve yourself, would you like me to take the tray?"

"Yes, thank you."

"Well, would you look at that. The princess has some manners, after all."

Before Tierney could respond, there was a heavy knock on the solid door. Ariella went to open it, stepping back immediately and dropping into a curtsy, her eyes trained on the ground as if she was afraid to look up. "Your Highness." Her voice was small, weak.

Keir's fierce gaze went right over her head, not even acknowledging the maid. "We need to have a conversation."

Tierney rose to her feet, a retort on the tip of her tongue. But Ariella's hurried exit caught her attention. One moment, the woman was chastising Tierney, and the next, she was simpering and flustered.

She closed the door after her, trapping Tierney in with an angry-looking prince. Narrowing her eyes, she took in his immaculate uniform, much more well-kept than the guards at her door. Silver buttons dotted the front of the deep red jacket. He had to be blazing hot in that thing.

Turning her back on him, she returned to sit on the settee, crossing her legs at the ankle like a good little princess. "What do you want, *Prince*?" Disdain dripped off the last word.

"I could have you whipped for that tone."

"Oh, right, because that's what you Lenyans do to women."

He was quiet for a moment before he spoke again, his voice low. "Some here do, yes, but I never ..." He blew out a frustrated breath. "I meant because you were a prisoner."

Something in his words told her to believe him, but she didn't trust herself at the moment. Standing, she whirled toward him. "If I'm a prisoner, take me to the dungeons. Please." Then, at least, she could be with Gullie.

Confusion flashed across his face before the expression hardened. "No."

"You're insufferable," she spat. She'd wanted someone to fight with, right? He'd come at the perfect time.

He seemed unruffled as he rubbed the front of his jacket. "Frequently."

"I hate you."

"You were meant to."

Ire raged through her. She wanted to break a leg off the table and stab it right into his heart. Her magic surged, the most powerful surge she'd felt since she arrived.

"So, Eavha was right." He looked down at her hands, which now had tiny flames licking across her skin, his eyes wide. As quickly as they came, they petered out. Why was fire the only magic she could seem to conjure?

"Of course." She clutched her hands together. "Your sister was your spy." She shouldn't have expected any different.

"You lied."

"Oh, I'm so sorry. Did you expect my every secret, my every desire, as you were tying me to stakes in the ground?"

She didn't see it coming. She told herself he just caught her off guard, and that was why she couldn't fight him. Keir rushed her, forcing her backward so she almost tripped over her own feet until her back hit the wall. He towered over her, his expression dark. "Do not play with me, girl."

"Play would imply this is fun." She lifted her chin, determined not to let him frighten her. Or at least, determined not to let him see how much he frightened her.

"Where does your magic come from?" he growled.

She lifted one shoulder in a shrug. "Oh, a little here and a little there."

His large hands gripped her upper arms, squeezing so hard it sent a shock of pain through her. "Do you have a crystal?"

"Maybe." She winced from the pain.

"You're impossible." He released her, shoving away from the wall.

"Frequently." She took great joy in throwing his word back at him.

His scowl told her he didn't appreciate it. Win.

But he wasn't the only angry one here. Now, it was her turn to put on her righteous pants. She stepped toward him, jabbing one finger into his chest. "I'm not the only one who lied, *Lieutenant*."

"I am a Lieutenant. That was not a lie."

"Right. The prince is just out there in the middle of battles, risking his own neck."

"I don't know how things are done in your kingdom, Princess, but here we fight with our soldiers."

It was the same in Iskalt. She frowned. Her parents had been right beside the rest of their fae ten years ago when they fought the Myrkurian king. "Fine. Princes can fight. But it doesn't change the fact that not a single person called you a prince on our journey."

"That title means little when crowns are not inherited."

Tierney had never heard of such a thing, and she wanted to know more, but she didn't want her curiosity to show.

He pushed out a breath. "I'm told you're not eating."

As if in protest, her stomach made a loud sound, like it was gnawing on itself. Her jaw clenched. "And I won't. Not until you take me to my friend."

"What do you want with the mongrel anyway?"

She slapped him before she even realized she'd raised her hand.

"You take that back. Gulliver is more noble than you could ever hope to be." She met his gaze. "You want to know about my magic?" It was the only bargaining chip she had. "I want to see him."

"Not possible."

"Then, my information stays hidden. I don't care what else you do to me. I've already lost my home, my family, my best friend. There's no hope of returning to Iskalt." She did her best to keep her voice from wavering. "I don't have anything else for you to take from me."

"There's always something more." His words were said on a breath, his eyes smiling with a thousand, a million different colors.

"I hate you," she whispered.

"Good." He turned away. "That will make everything I have to do so much easier."

Silence followed him when he left. Silence and a distinct lack of hope. His last words held a darkness she knew this kingdom was capable of. What would they do to her? To Gulliver?

Her legs felt suddenly weak beneath her, and she made it to the bed before collapsing face first, messing up Ariella's carefully pressed sheets. Every word she'd said to Keir was the truth. She had nothing left. Nothing except her determination, and that had slowly started to erode, breaking off piece by piece.

She needed her brother. He'd always been the strong one, the twin born without true magic. He had two powers. The first was an innate ability to master the O'Shea portal magic. He'd never have gotten himself into this type of trouble.

And the second … he made her power stronger, bigger. With him, she could have found a way to gain control over it once more.

But that wasn't the only reason she needed him. Other than Gullie, Toby was the fae who knew her best, the one who'd always say what she needed to hear.

She could imagine his voice in her head. *Stay strong, Tia. You will find a way.*

"But what if I can't, Toby?" Tears dampened the feather pillow beneath her face. "What if I'm not enough without you?"

She'd never been just Tierney. She was always part of a set, a twin, a part of the balance of power.

And now, she was alone.

The door banged open once more, and Keir stopped on the threshold as he took her in.

Tierney lifted her head, embarrassment flooding her at the wetness of her face, the flush of her cheeks. "What?"

His brow furrowed before he smoothed his expression. "I had one more thing to say to you."

"Can't you see I'm in the middle of feeling sorry for myself? A real prince would come back another time."

He stepped into the room. "It's a good thing no one considers the children of the king real royals." He stared at her for a long moment.

"Just say it, Keir!" She hadn't used his name since before she knew who he truly was. "Tell me. Tierney, we've decided to cut off your head. Tierney, I'm madly in love with you and want you to become my future queen."

His expression remained calm, neutral, and it only infuriated her more. "I will not marry." He cocked his head. "How many times must I tell you I will not inherit the throne? When the next king rises, he will want me dead for fear of a challenge. Any wife of mine would have to suffer constant pursuit."

Tierney threw her hands up. "Oh my gosh, it was a joke!"

He scratched his chin. "Have you done something that warrants an execution?"

"You insufferable ..." She caught a mild twitching of his lips. "You're making fun of me."

"I only returned to warn you."

"Warn me?" She sat up straighter. "Of what?"

"My father." He drew in a deep breath. "He will most likely visit you, and he won't be as kind as I have been."

"Kind?" She snorted. "Right."

He frowned. "You'll be better off telling him everything, even if it will endanger your friend in the dungeons."

Her teeth ground together as she thought of all the things she could tell them about Gulliver. That he was Dark Fae. That all Dark Fae had a defensive magic that would protect him to an extent.

That she would kill anyone who laid a hand on him.

"Some of us, Prince, do not betray others to save ourselves."

He gave a weary sigh. "I knew you'd say that."

"Then, why bother to issue your warning?"

"Because, prisoner, I'd hoped you were more intelligent than you were brave."

She scooted from the bed and stood to face him. "It's called love. Not bravery. It's not brave to protect the fae we love. We can't allow ourselves to do anything less."

He studied her for a moment longer before turning on his heel and walking from the room.

It left her wondering what kind of kingdom this truly was if they did not fight for each other.

What else was there to fight for?

Chapter 14
Tierney

"You must eat something, my Lady." Ariella stamped her foot impatiently. "It's been nearly four days, and you've hardly taken a bite."

"I refuse." Tierney sat against the arm of the settee with her feet up, staring out the window. She was listless, her mind wandering from one thing to the next with little interest in her surroundings.

"I promise you, starving yourself will not help your situation. You will face the king soon, and trust me, you will need your strength for that."

"Did you know the fire plains are made up of an untold number of active volcanos?" Tierney stared at the cloudy horizon, imagining she could just make out the smoke from the Eastern Vatlands that stood between her and her family. "The lands around them flow with lava. What manages to grow there burns with a fire so hot it's almost transparent. One might wander into the flames and never realize it until it was too late. That is, if they hadn't expired from the extreme temperatures, lack of clean water, and lava pools." Tierney twisted a lock of her unwashed hair around her finger.

"Of course," Ariella said. "Everyone knows nothing survives the burning lands." She lifted the domed lid covering the cold breakfast

Tierney had left ignored from earlier this morning. When Ariella arrived with her afternoon meal, she was surprised so many hours had escaped without her notice.

"Shame to let this go to waste." The maid scowled at the congealed bowl of porridge and the shriveled slices of fruit. "There are thousands of Vondurians who would see this as a feast." She replaced the breakfast tray with her noon meal.

Tierney ignored her. She'd given up trying to use her magic. Four days ago, she'd finally grasped hold of it, but she could barely light a candle with it. The smallest tasks left her exhausted.

That was when she lost her appetite.

She gave up on her magic not long after. It was hopeless. She had two means of escape: her portal magic and the fire plains. Neither were a viable option. All that was left was to accept that this war-torn kingdom was her home now. Her prison.

"At least drink some tea. I bartered with the cook for the tea and a bit of honey for you. It's a shame to let it go to waste."

Tierney nodded, feeling almost interested in the idea of a nice hot cup of tea, like she used to share with her mother in front of the fire.

She barely heard Ariella's chatter about the goings on in the palace as she watched the maid pour hot water over tea leaves, adding a drizzle of honey to the mug before handing it to Tierney.

The steaming warmth felt good against her hands.

Tierney took a sip, letting the herbal fragrance fill her nose, and then she spewed the mouthful of tea across the settee. "Ugh, that's dreadful." She choked, looking for anything that might get the bitter taste out of her mouth. "Are you trying to poison me?" She reached for the glass of water Ariella handed her.

"Haven't you ever had gentian tea?"

Tierney fanned her face as a warm flush stole across her skin and her tongue burned. "Never heard of it." Her voice came out in a harsh rasp. "What is it? Acid?"

"Gentian tea is the finest in all of Vondur. It is a bitter herb, known for its healing properties."

"I imagine it's an acquired taste." Tierney's eyes burned, and she let out a chuckle. "One I don't think I'll be trying again. Though, I do thank you for thinking of me. I think you're the only non-prisoner on this side of the fire plains who cares if I live or die."

Ariella frowned at the full mug of what Tierney was certain was an expensive Vondurian delicacy.

"Why don't you sit and enjoy the rest of this *tea*?"

"Oh, but I couldn't, my Lady." Ariella continued to stare at the tea with a longing look that reminded her of the way her mother looked at a cup of Eldur brew.

"Tell you what," Tierney reached for the fresh tray of food, "if you sit and enjoy that tea, I'll eat something." The truth of the matter was, Tierney had to get something in her mouth to chase away the bitter aftertaste of that disgusting drink.

"Are you sure you don't want it?" Ariella asked.

"Positive. Sit." She picked up a flat disk of soft bread and a slice of cheese. There was an assortment of vegetables as well.

"Add some pickled peppers and onions to that and fold the bread around it. It's delicious." Ariella sank down on the other end of the settee and put her feet up on the table.

Tierney paused and gave her a look. "As delicious as that tea?"

The maid smiled. "No surprises this time. I promise."

She set her flat bread and cheese on the tray and added long strips of bright red peppers and onions, rolling it up in a little package. Taking a tentative bite, dozens of flavors burst on her tongue. "Oh, that is ..." She stopped herself. "Not bad." She chewed and swallowed. And that was when the heat hit her. "Hot!" She choked again, and her face flushed bright red. She lunged for the glass of water, but the heat faded quickly, and her stomach rumbled for more.

"Oh my. The food here is going to be the death of me."

"Hot?" Ariella laughed. "Don't ever eat the purple peppers if you think the red ones are too spicy." She rested her head back and sipped her bitter acid tea.

Tierney turned as the door to her prison chamber creaked open and four guards entered, flanking a fifth who carried himself in a familiar way. Dark hair, cool gaze. He could only be one man. Keir's father. The king.

"Do I see a maid and a prisoner drinking tea with their feet on my table?" His voice was as cold as his gaze.

Ariella scrambled up from her seat, sloshing hot tea across her hands. She sank into a deep curtsy, keeping her head down.

"It is my fault." Tierney rose slowly from her seat, as if it were a throne. "I made her."

"You speak without permission, woman." The king's eyes snapped to hers.

"I do not ask permission to speak, *King*. I am and will always be a representative of my homeland. A *royal* representative. I do not abide by your archaic customs." She lifted her chin, fully aware that she was not getting off to a good start with Keir's father.

"You may address me as King Turlach or your Majesty, and only when I have addressed you first." He turned back to Ariella, still stooped in her bow. "Maid, leave us. The castellan will deal with your insolence later."

"Your Majesty," Ariella whispered, dipping her head again before she rose and scrambled from the room.

"And *you* may address me as Princess Tierney or your *Royal* Highness." Tierney sank back to her seat, gesturing for the king to take the stiff-backed chair opposite her.

"You, a woman, profess to be the heir of your mythical kingdom?" He sat in the chair, his unwavering gaze never leaving hers. Compared to his father, Keir's gruff countenance was like that of a hyper puppy, eager to please its master.

"Iskalt is no myth. My father is King Lochlan O'Shea, and my mother is Queen Brea Cahill O'Shea, daughter of the Queen of Eldur." And of a Fargelsian king, but no one here needed to know

Tierney held the magic of three kingdoms. Not when that magic was currently lukewarm in her veins.

"The fabled kingdoms of ancient myth." His tone mocked her, but his eyes said he wanted to believe her words.

"As fabled and ancient as the stories of the mythical kingdoms of Lenya, yet here we are." Tierney spread her hands wide.

"Where is your kingdom?" The king steepled his fingers under his chin.

"Beyond the fire plains and the frothing seas to the north."

The king leaned forward. "You mean to tell me you traveled across the burning plains?"

"No." Tierney offered no further explanation.

"Then you arrived by means of magic? Where is your totem?" He glanced around the room as if she'd left her magical talisman on display.

"I lost it. I arrived here with my dearest friend by accident, but somewhere in the … transition, I dropped my totem." The lie came easily to her lips. She could not afford for this man to learn of her immense magic. Not that her magic did her any good in this place. It did not escape Tierney O'Shea that she could be used as a weapon against this man's enemies. Against her own fae if he was to learn her secrets.

"Search the room." Turlach gave the order to his men without a glance in their direction.

"That is unnecessary." Tierney watched as they ripped through the room, tearing blankets from her bed, tossing the mattress, and emptying drawers. "I haven't a single possession in this room. You will accomplish nothing beyond destroying your own property and making a mess." She sat regally upon her makeshift throne, watching the soldiers ransack her room. It made no difference to her. She had nothing to hide.

"You were seen performing magic," the king continued. "I would know how."

She shrugged. "I know nothing of magic without the use of a crystal, of which I have none, as you will soon see."

"If what you say is true and you hale from Iskalt, you do not need crystals to wield your magic."

"That is absurd. Everyone needs an object of power to perform magic." Tierney met his cruel gaze. She would not falter. No matter what he did to her.

With a nod to his men, the king rose from his chair as if to leave, but Tierney knew his show of strength was not over yet. She stood to remain on even ground with Turlach.

Hands seized her and ripped the back of her dress from neck to waist. Tierney refused to react, though her heart thundered in her chest. The king's men held her arms in a bruising grasp that would leave marks.

The king circled her, taking his time to get to the point. "You will tell me of your magic—how it works and what you can accomplish with it."

"I have told you all I know." Tierney followed him with her eyes. "I am but a woman, unskilled in the art of magic. What little magic I can wield using a totem comes at great cost to me physically. My only worth as a princess of Iskalt is what I will bring my kingdom upon my marriage."

The king released a buckle from his belt, revealing a small statue sheathed like a dagger at his hip. Carved from turquoise crystal tipped with orange streaks, it sparkled like a prism in his hand. The figure was a rudimentary female form, as if the artist had put little effort into its shape.

So, this was a totem. The substance that gave those of Lenya their magic. Tierney steadied her breath, unsure what the king had planned for her. Whatever it was, it wouldn't be good.

"I do not believe you." The king held the totem in his hand, his thumb wrapped around the center of the figure. He circled behind her, his hand raised as if to strike.

Fire erupted along the exposed skin of her back. Power, like the lash of a whip, raked down her spine, and she bit back a scream, refusing to let him see her pain.

"There are many more where that came from, my dear princess. I shall ask you once more. Tell me of your magic and how it works without the use of a totem."

Tierney's legs trembled beneath her, but she forced herself to speak calmly, as if she didn't feel like her skin had been ripped open. "I've told you. Like your fae, our magic only works with the crystals. Same as yours." She recognized the crystal, having seen the grounds of all four kingdoms near home littered with them. There were even more deep within the various mines throughout the known lands. In Myrkur, they called them fire opals for their predominately orange color, and they were valuable to the Dark Fae as a gemstone. But they brought no magical advantages to them, at least not to her knowledge.

Pain blossomed across her back without warning. It seemed the king's magic held no noticeable precursor. It was simply pain unlike any she'd ever known. In all of Tierney's life, she'd suffered adversity, survived wars and kidnappings, but no one had ever raised a hand against her. Even when Callum O'Shea had kidnapped her and Toby, he'd treated them both with the respect their station demanded.

Ten lashes threatened to send her to her knees before he returned to stand in front of her. Tears burned her eyes, but she didn't let them fall.

"As King of Vondur, I have access to historical records no other living soul has seen. Not even my son. Great histories of a once-united Lenya and the mythical lands across the fire plains. I suggest you amend your answers and tell me how you crossed the burning lands. If you are truly the heir of Iskalt, you would be privy to such knowledge."

Tierney's eyes widened in surprise. Does he know a way across the fire plains? "I don't have anything to add." She glared at him, daring him to strike her again.

He approached her, his tall form towering over her as he lifted a hand to trace a thumb across her cheek. "Perhaps a few more days without food will convince you."

He lashed out with his magic once more, striking a blow across her face, splitting the skin like a knife through cooked meat. Blood oozed down her face, staining the collar of her dress.

"Do as you must." She managed a delicate shrug of her shoulders.

"Torrin, see to the lady's comforts." The king snapped his fingers, and three of his four men followed, leaving the head of his guard behind.

Clutching the remnants of her dress, Tierney managed to stay on her feet as the man made his way wordlessly around the room removing the books, all traces of food, and any water or wine. Without a word, he locked the door to the washroom, leaving her with nothing but a chamber pot and a giant mess.

Tierney sank to her knees after he'd gone. The only thought in her mind was that she needed to see whatever information the king had concerning the histories of the four kingdoms.

CHAPTER 15
TIERNEY

Tierney clutched at the shreds of her torn dress as she stood in front of the looking glass, her entire body shaking. *I will not cry,* she thought. Not for that man. In her time, she'd met cruelty head on, but it was nothing like the pure inhumanity in Turlach's eyes. He hadn't taken pleasure from her pain. It was more that he didn't care what he did to her.

And maybe that was more dangerous.

"You won't defeat me, you ugly piece of—" She stopped herself as she reached up and dabbed a finger along the cut on her face. Blood stained her skin. Her blood. The blood of a princess, heir to a throne, more powerful than these fae could possibly imagine.

If she ever gained full use of her power again, the king and all those around him would be sorry for the day they ever imprisoned her.

The old portrait on the far wall shuddered, and Tierney held the dress to her chest tighter, not releasing a breath until Eavha appeared. If Tierney had access to the keys that allowed entrance into the tunnels, she'd escape and find a way to save Gulliver. Instead, she stood here shaking as the princess rushed toward her.

"Tia."

Tierney stepped back. This girl was the daughter of the man who'd done this to her, and the pain was too fresh.

"What did he do?" Eavha breathed as she blinked back tears. "I'm so sorry."

Tierney still didn't speak. She could almost hear the crack of a lash against her back, though there'd been no sound, only the piercing pain where her skin split open.

"You have to understand something," Eavha said in a rush, "my father is trying to hold on to his throne."

Rage twisted through her. "By any means necessary? And that's okay with you?" Her voice was rough, full of unadulterated ire.

"No, of course not." Eavha bit her lip. "Turn around."

Tierney had no energy to argue, and she knew she was the princess' prisoner as much as her father's. That was the way of royals.

Eavha sucked in a breath. "Oh, Tia."

Tierney turned back to face her. "You can run back to your father and tell him I will never reveal anything that puts my fae at risk." She knew it had to be Eavha who'd told Keir about her magic, but that shouldn't have surprised her.

"My father didn't send me here."

"So, you're not trying to gain my trust in order to learn my secrets?"

"Well, I did suggest that, yes. But it was only because I knew the alternative would be … well … this." She wiped a tear from her cheek.

How dare she cry when Tierney was the one with stripes across her skin and pain sizzling like the hottest fire of the fire plains? "You can go now. Your plan has failed. I will never trust any fae in Lenya." The only fae she could trust on this side of the fire plains was in the dungeons.

"No, wait. I swear, my father didn't send me this time. Ariella came and informed me he'd appeared in your rooms. I …" She twisted her long hair over one shoulder. "I was scared for you."

"I'm alive. You've done your duty acting like you're different from your family. Please don't sneak in here again."

"You don't understand." She reached for Tierney's arm. "I'm not only here to check in on you."

The door opened, and a guard stepped through. Tierney yanked free of Eavha and backed away.

"It's okay." Eavha's voice held a plea.

The guard removed his helmet, and Tierney recognized him as the one who'd found Eavha in here before.

Everything crashed in on Tierney all at once. The king's arrival. His guards standing at attention as he brutalized her. The knowledge it would all happen again.

Her legs grew weak beneath her, whether from shock or blood loss, she did not know. The last thing she remembered was strong hands catching her before she could hit the ground.

Warmth enveloped Tierney. Water sizzled and bubbled around her. Was she being boiled alive? She was, wasn't she? Her first reaction was that it felt nice. Maybe it wasn't such a bad way to go.

"I think she's waking up," a hushed voice seemed to echo from everywhere all at once.

"Keep her feet on the bottom," another said.

Tierney's heavy eyelids peeled open to find she was staring up at the high ceiling of a dim cavern. Two torches hung along the wall nearby, and the very stone seemed to shimmer and move where the firelight flickered against it.

Energy buzzed along her skin, not unlike what she felt when she called on her magic, though a much-diminished form.

"Where am I?" She got her feet under her in the water, her toes sinking into what felt like a sandy bottom.

"These are the healing baths," Eavha said.

Tierney turned toward her voice, noticing the other girl was submerged in the water in her dress. "H-how did I get out of my rooms?"

She didn't know where her torn dress had gone, but she still wore her underclothes, thank small mercies for that.

"With help." Declan sat on the edge of the pool of water, his legs dangling in. The bottoms of his pants were wet where he'd pushed them above his knees, but the rest of him was still dry. "And just so you know, I could be killed for this. Or lose my friendship with Keir."

"Glad to know my brother ranks up there with your life." Eavha shook her head.

Tierney had to ask, "Then, why did you help me?"

He shrugged. "Eavha asked me to."

She thought of his answer as she ran a hand over the top of the roiling water. Everywhere it touched her skin, it seemed to infuse strength into her, and there was no more pain.

Eavha touched her back gently. "I got most of the blood off, but your clothes are a lost cause, I'm afraid." Tierney didn't care about her clothes. "Do you feel the sand at the bottom?"

Tierney nodded, shifting her feet to dig them in further.

"It's made up of crushed crystals. They've long since lost the ability to give us magic, but their healing powers are not diminished. Most of the kingdom has so few crystals they can't use them for such purposes anymore, but these baths have been here for a long time. Only royals have access because they lose some of their effectiveness with each use."

Tierney couldn't wrap her mind around anything Eavha was saying.

"All this bubbling, the swirling of the water, that's the crystals. The water is reacting to their presence. Just like each stone of this palace does."

"What do you mean?"

"Crystals have been infused into the very walls. There was a time long ago when the palace itself was a totem. But a totem's power is not infinite. It can only contain so much magic."

Tierney locked every bit of information she could away, knowing it all might be useful when she had to make her move. "So, the fae of Lenya constantly need new crystals for totems?"

She nodded. "That's why the war has been continuing for so long. The kingdom that controls the crystals controls Lenya."

"Eavha," Declan warned, "that's enough."

Eavha glared at him. "Don't speak to me that way."

Tierney expected him to snap back at her for her insolence as a woman. She'd seen enough of their low status to know that was what should happen. Instead, Declan pushed out a frustrated breath and got to his feet. "This woman is a prisoner. One you've already risked both our necks trying to help. She does not need to know anything about Lenya when she refuses to reveal what your father wishes to know."

"Maybe if my father had just asked her instead of shredding her back, she wouldn't hate us so much." She wiped tears away furiously.

She was wrong. Tierney would hate them regardless of her treatment for the simple fact that she was a prisoner. They kept her from Gullie, from trying to find the others and get home.

Eavha pulled herself from the massive pool, water dripping from her clothes to the stones at her feet. Every drop that hit swirled together, moving in a way water definitely didn't move.

Was it the crystal in the stones interacting with the water this time?

It was beautiful, mesmerizing. Declan took a torch from the wall, and when he stepped away from the pool, it illuminated the cavern, which was much larger than Tierney had thought. The span of water stretched across the vast space. High walls of rough rock and dark bricks speckled with white that shimmered in the light surrounded them.

"We need to get her back," Declan said, not looking at either girl.

"Without being seen." Eavha nodded before turning to Tierney. "Do you think you can walk?"

Tierney stretched her limbs, testing for pain. It was amazing. Truly. "Yes."

"Good," Declan grunted. "I don't want to carry you again." He started off toward the far wall.

Tierney climbed from the water. "I can see how he and Keir are friends."

Eavha retrieved the second torch. "He's not usually like this, but Declan doesn't like to go against his orders."

"Right, he's loyal to the king." She clenched her jaw.

"No, I don't think he is, actually. But he is loyal to Keir."

And Keir was the one who'd kept her prisoner.

Across the cavern were the entrances to three tunnels. Tierney didn't have the energy for any more long explanations, and she stumbled over her own feet as they entered one of them.

Eavha laughed. "The healing baths do not come without a price. You will need plenty of rest. They have drained your body of energy, using it to piece you back together. Trust me, you're about to have the best sleep of your life."

"Trust you," Tierney scoffed, low enough so Eavha couldn't hear her. "Right." She wouldn't make that mistake. Back home, she'd learned the only fae one could trust when times were hard were their family and Gulliver.

She dragged a hand along the bricks as they smoothed out. The shimmering grew fainter, and she guessed that meant they were getting closer to the main palace. Their footsteps echoed off the stone floor, and tiny rocks and dust fell from above.

They reached Declan as he put an arm out to stop them. They'd come to a dead end, but sounds could be heard on the other side.

"This tunnel doesn't connect to the one in your rooms," Eavha whispered.

"Then, where does it go?"

The king's voice crept into their hiding place. "Torrin, inform Keir to prepare the troops. We've had word that the little Grima princess is gathering her forces for an attack. She will try to recover her palace, and I won't allow it to slip from my grasp."

"Sir?"

"My son and I will both lead the men. I'm leaving you in charge here to defend the castle with the guard."

"Sir, if you're wrong and the Grima come here instead, the palace guard won't be suited for an attack."

"Are you saying my instincts are wrong?"

Torrin responded quickly, "No, your Majesty. You're right. They will want to recapture the Grima palace. We will be fine here. I won't let you down."

"See that you don't."

She shook off everything they'd heard, tried to push down the relief she felt at the thought of both Keir and his father leaving. Because a more pressing issue faced her. They had to be kidding her. The tunnel let out into the king's own quarters? This wouldn't end well.

"How did you get me into the tunnel?" she whispered.

"He was meeting with an advisor in the throne room." Eavha looked from Tierney to Declan. "He wasn't supposed to be back so soon."

Then, "Your Majesty?"

"Yes, Captain?"

"You're needed at the south tower."

Tierney released a long breath. He was leaving. As soon as they heard the door shut, Eavha and Declan pressed their hands against the stone and pushed. Something clicked, and the wall shifted, moving inward until there was a small gap to squeeze through.

"Let's go." Eavha went first to make sure no one else was in there. She was the only one who could plausibly explain her presence.

Declan shoved Tierney forward, and she stumbled into the king's opulent chambers. Red velvet carpet was soft under her bare feet. She'd completely forgotten she wore nothing but her underclothes. And yet, she couldn't seem to care.

The room was a shrine to the crystals. Totems sat on every surface, carved into rudimentary women, fearful warriors, one-eyed eagles, crooked stars, and so much more. They called to Tierney, each and every one of them. But she didn't go near.

"Most of these no longer hold any magic." Eavha fingered a carved dog that had no tail. "Most fae in Lenya only use magic when absolutely necessary to preserve the resource, but according to my father, the king has no need to hold back." She sounded sad.

"This is great and all," Declan said, "but we need to get out of here if we want to keep our heads."

He was right. Checking the corridor, Declan motioned for them to follow him. They managed to make it through the palace, ducking into alcoves when they heard footsteps or voices. Tierney didn't understand it, but she felt a tingling in her fingertips every time she needed to hide, like the palace itself was protecting her.

It was probably just her imagination.

They reached the room she'd been kept in to find no guard outside. That wasn't a surprise since Declan was on duty. But the door was slightly open, and she knew without a doubt it hadn't been that way when they left.

Preparing herself, Tierney stepped inside before Declan and Eavha could stop her. They'd done something incredibly kind today, and she refused to let them bear the consequences.

A man stood at the window. Somehow, since she'd been gone, it had turned to night. He looked out over the darkened palace grounds, probably basking in what his family controlled.

Keir clasped his hands behind his back. "And just where have you been?"

Chapter 16
KEIR

Keir prided himself on rarely losing his temper. It was one of the reasons he was an effective leader in battle. He was always calm, always in control of himself. But right now, as he stared at his reflection in the window, all he could think of was how much he wanted to wring her neck.

He saw Tierney lift her chin in the reflection, a clear sign she wasn't going to cower like she assumed he wanted. But she didn't know him, didn't know that as much as he struggled to believe a word she said, he respected the not-so-quiet strength in her.

He'd been raised to believe women wanted to be subservient, that it was their role to bow to the whims of men. Eavha had certainly never acted as such, but she was his sister and a princess. Certain liberties were afforded her.

A prisoner? Her audacity astounded him.

"I was taking a bath." She folded her arms across her chest.

"A bath?" He turned on his heel, ready to call her on the lie. She had a sunken tub right in these rooms. But then, he noticed her clothes, or lack of clothes. She wore sopping wet, white linen under-things. A red splotch stained the front, but it wasn't until she turned to see Eavha walk in that he saw the rest.

Angry red lines striped across her back. A bath. Eavha had taken her for a bath. The healing waters. He had so many questions, but only one escaped his lips. "Who did this to you?"

He hadn't ordered for her to be harmed. It wasn't how he dealt with prisoners. Intimidation was not an effective interrogation tactic, and the thought of someone raising a hand to this strong-willed woman shook him.

"Who do you think?" Her legs trembled beneath her, and Eavha grabbed her arm.

"She needs to rest, Keir. If you're done yelling at her, can you please leave?"

He was about to ask where Declan had been when he should have stood at his post and prevented them from leaving, but he didn't have to. Declan could never deny Eavha's requests, no matter how foolhardy.

Eavha helped Tierney to the bed. "We'll get you new clothes when you wake. For now, get under the covers and strip off your wet things. I promise my brother will leave." She glared at him.

The fight faded from Tierney's eyes, and he recognized the exhaustion. There'd been many times in his life he'd sank into the healing baths. The days following were always a blur of sleep and cloudy thoughts.

Keir averted his eyes as she slipped into bed and stripped underneath the covers. "Yes, I will go. Eavha, follow me."

He stormed into the hall, jabbing one finger at Declan, who stood beside the door. "You two, stand there."

They stood side by side, one a loyal soldier and the other a willful princess.

Keir paced in front of them, keeping his voice low so they weren't overheard. "What were you two thinking?"

"Keir," Eavha started, "we had to."

"No," he stopped, "you didn't. Do you realize if someone else had been the one to find her gone, you both could have faced execution? It's treason to go against the wishes of the king."

Declan hung his head. "I know, your Highness. I'm sorry." If he was using formal titles, Declan really was ashamed of himself.

Keir pushed a hand through his hair. "I don't blame you, Declan." He gave his sister a pointed look.

She huffed out a breath. "That's right, and I would do it again. You didn't see her, Keir. How could Father …" Her breath quivered. "She was so hurt, covered in blood."

Keir closed his eyes, not wanting them to see the rage building in them. Not for his sister and his friend, not even the prisoner. Every bit of anger he had inside of him had one target. His father.

It had been ten years since his father won the crown in the combat known as the Comhrac. Kings were not chosen, nor were they decided by birth. In Vondur, the successor was the man who killed the sitting king. It took a ruthless sort of fae to seek a throne. But he'd hoped there was some nobility left in his father, a nobility he'd watched ebb away over the years of war that tore this kingdom apart.

"Eavha." He sighed. "It is now up to you to make sure our prisoner does not reveal the existence of the healing baths to those outside these walls."

Eavha nodded. "I trust her."

She was naive. Tierney wasn't a friend; she wasn't even of Lenya if her story was to be believed. There was no trust to be had. But was she truly an enemy?

That was yet to be seen.

A guard walked up to them, stopping to bow. "Your Highness."

"Yarro." Keir inclined his head.

Soldier Yarro turned to Declan. "I'm here to relieve you for the night."

"Good." Keir pointed to Eavha. "You, go get some sleep. Declan, come with me."

There was a visit he'd been putting off, but he needed answers. There was no better time to visit the dungeons than the dead of night when few would see the prince coming or going.

Declan didn't ask where they were headed. He knew better than to question Keir, especially when he was in a dark mood.

They reached the western wing of the palace, where a spiral staircase led down into the depths. Torches lined the walls, and the steps grew narrower the farther down they went.

There were no crystals embedded into the stones of the expansive dungeons. It was the one place in the palace that had been built to keep magic out.

Keir lay a hand over the totem he wore on a leather strap around his neck. It was a simple hollow circle. He'd never been one for elaborate carvings. His magic warmed underneath his skin, but he didn't use it. He rarely unleashed the power, wanting to preserve his totem as long as he could.

The air underground was musky with the scent of unwashed bodies and damp mold. He tried to avoid breathing through his nose as he passed the guards, giving them curt nods.

He led Declan through the maze of cells that mostly held Grima prisoners no one knew what to do with. They couldn't release them to return to their new queen, but Keir had convinced his father to halt prisoner executions at least for a while. He'd told him there was no point to the killings if the Grima fae were not there to witness them.

In a cell buried in the far reaches of the dungeons was a lone fae —if one could call him that. Keir still did not know what kind of creature this was with his tail and strange feline eyes. He slept on his side, murmuring to himself every few seconds.

"I'd heard rumors from your men." Declan's eyes widened. "But I did not believe them to be true. What is he?"

"*He* is fae." The voice came from the pitiful creature on the ground. "Dark Fae, to be exact."

Keir had never heard of a Dark Fae.

The boy opened his eyes and sat up. His tail curled around his leg, flicking in agitation like it had a mind of its own.

Declan backed away, but Keir was determined to get answers. "From where do you hail?"

The boy's eyes narrowed almost to slits. "Myrkur. Does that answer satisfy you, Lieutenant?"

"He is the prince," Declan snapped. "You will speak to him with respect, prisoner."

A harsh laugh barked out of the young fae. "I'll bet Tia was overjoyed when you told her. She does love a good liar. Oh wait, no, she loves to expose a good liar." He scooted forward into the dim torchlight, and Keir sucked in a breath. Bruises marred his face, stretching from brow to jawline. He moved like a fae in great pain, one who'd been through a lot.

And the anger was back.

This was not how Vondur treated prisoners.

"Where is Tierney?" he asked, his fingers closing around the bars. "Is she okay?"

Keir had come here to get answers, not give them, but he found himself nodding. The fae sat back in relief.

"Declan," Keir bit out, "go talk to the guards and find out what has been done to this prisoner."

Declan hurried off, like he couldn't get away fast enough.

"This prisoner has a name." The fae winced as he stretched his legs out in front of him. "It's Gulliver."

"Gulliver," he tried out the name. "How odd."

"Odd? How about you get lost traveling through a portal from the human realm and end up in the dungeons of a kingdom that shouldn't exist. Then, you tell me about odd."

Portals. Human realm. It all seemed so very unbelievable. And yet …

Keir knew how to get the truth. All of it. It was one of the skills he'd honed his magic to do. Clutching his totem, he drew on its power to fuel his own, surging it toward Gulliver, preparing to pull out his secrets. He hadn't been able to bring himself to invade Tierney in such a way, and even now, it felt wrong.

But he had no other choice.

His magic crashed against an invisible wall before retreating into Keir with such force it knocked him back against the stone wall. He struggled to catch his breath. "What … what just happened?"

A satisfied smirk appeared on Gulliver's busted lips. "Guess some things still work in this kingdom."

Keir didn't know what he meant by that. It was almost like the fae before him had a resistance to magic.

"You know," Gulliver's voice was rough as he shifted, and pain flashed across his face, "if you have questions, you could always just ask me."

Ask? Was it really that simple?

"Have a seat in my comfortable home." Gulliver pointed to the stones at Keir's feet.

"I'm not sitting on the ground." Keir didn't understand this fae at all. He was obviously in pain, yet he was offering up answers.

"If you want me to talk to you, princeling, you'll get your butt a bit dirty. Go on. I swear, no one will know you got off your high horse for a few minutes."

With a sigh, Keir lowered himself to the dirty ground, disgust curling through him. "Tell me," he started, "what are you and Tierney after?" They had to have a motive for being here, for coming to Vondur.

Gulliver rolled his eyes, a sneer on his lips. "Pay attention. We don't wish to be here at all. All we want is to go home."

"To Iskalt?"

"For her. Myrkur for me. My adoptive father works for the king."

"Are you two betrothed?"

"Me and my father?"

Keir scowled. "Tierney."

"Tierney and my father? Gross. They're blood relatives. I don't know about Lenya, but in the four kingdoms, we don't allow such unions."

Keir rubbed his eyes. This boy was impossible. "Are you and Tierney betrothed?"

"Oh, that. Well, no. She was supposed to choose a betrothed at the ball, but that got sort of interrupted when we ran away to the human realm and then got lost on the way back. It was a whole thing, with her father forcing her into marriage since she was the heir and needed to start having cold Iskalt babies. But her mother wasn't completely okay with it. You see, she was raised as a human before finding out she was really a changeling, a fae. She and Alona were exchanged at birth, and—"

"Gulliver." Did this kid ever shut up? He reminded Keir of Eavha in a less endearing way. "I don't need the full history of Tierney's parents."

"Right." He nodded. "But it really is very interesting."

"What kind of magic does Tierney have?"

Gulliver shrugged. "All kinds. Iskaltian, Eldurian, Fargelsian. She has the O'Shea magic, though I'm not sure that counts since she's so bad at it. That's how we ended up here."

Keir didn't know what any of that meant. This was getting him nowhere. "Is she powerful?"

"If by powerful you mean, did she bring down the prison world wall when she was ten years old? Yeah, I'd say she is."

What was a prison world wall?

Footsteps neared them, echoing off the dark walls. Declan stopped a good distance from the cell. "Keir?"

Keir pushed to his feet and joined Declan. "What did you learn?"

"The king's men have visited Gulliver daily."

"And my father?"

"He hasn't come. The guards told me the fae doesn't scream. They hear the impact, the beatings, but he doesn't make a sound. They think he's crazed."

Keir shifted his eyes to Gulliver, who sat with a contented smile on his face, despite the pain he must be in. After everything he'd told him, Keir thought he might be crazed too.

"There's something else."

"What is it?"

Declan shifted to his other foot. "One of the guards heard a rumor there'll be orders coming to march from the palace."

Keir snapped his eyes to his friend's. "Who will be marching?"

"Everyone. You, your father, the troops. Only the guard will remain. I didn't get a chance to tell you, but when Eavha, Tierney, and I were coming back from the baths, we, ah, heard your father. I can confirm all this as true. The king thinks the Grima troops will try to take their palace back."

"And he'd rather expose our stronghold than lose theirs?" He glanced back at Gulliver, who seemed to be talking to himself. In all the answers he'd given Keir, all the many words he'd said, not a single one of them was of use. Keir couldn't help wondering if that was by design.

Had this fae lost his mind, or was he smart enough to know exactly what it was he did?

But there was no time. Not when the palace was going to be exposed by an overzealous king and there was nothing he could do but march out.

Chapter 17
TIERNEY

The sound of a horn crashed through Tierney's dreams, and she thrashed in bed. Flashes of a battle long past haunted the endless night. No, only endless in her dreams of a world without sun. The prison realm. Before they'd pushed the darkness from its lands, its fae lived in a perpetual void.

A king, now buried in the ground, appeared before her. Egan. He came for her, wanting her power, needing everything she was, craving it. But she wasn't alone. Not this time.

She felt him, the little boy who could give her the strength she needed to do what was necessary. Toby.

And then, it was all ripped away, and she was falling farther into a dark abyss, where nothing lived, nothing existed. And the horn still sounded.

"Tia!" A soft voice called to her, and she grasped for it, holding on. "Tia, wake up."

Her eyes snapped open. She wasn't in the prison realm, but once again, she wasn't free. The Vondurian room that served as her gilded cage rose up around her in the dark of night.

"Tia." Small hands shook her, and she looked up into the face of a princess who could've been her friend in a different life.

"What is it?" Rubbing sleep from her eyes, she sat up. "The few hours of sleep I manage are the only times my situation isn't hopeless, so this better be good." It was only then she noticed the wild look in Eavha's eyes. She appeared to have dressed in a hurry this morning, with her shirt untucked from her ... were those pants? Tierney had never seen her fellow princess in pants before.

Eavha drew in a breath and ran a hand along the braid that draped over one shoulder. "I ... I think the palace is being attacked."

Well, that was one way to wake a girl up. "What makes you think that?" It was then Tierney heard it again. The horn cut through any doubt. Eavha didn't think the palace was being attacked. She knew. "Okay, calm down. This place can withstand a siege, right? I've seen part of your army. It's not small."

"Not usually, no. But my father and Keir took most of the troops to defend the captured Grima palace from attack. They left a day ago."

No wonder he hadn't visited her. "Well, that's unfortunate." Tierney tried to remain calm, remain reasonable. But all she could think of was another time, another war, one that had threatened to take everything from her. She thought of Toby, missing in the Eldurian streets as she searched for him, frantically calling his name. She'd found him stuck beneath a dead ogre. "I need to get dressed." She scooted from the bed and hurried to dig through clothes in her armoire, looking for the only non-dress she knew was in there.

The jeans she'd worn through the portal.

Ariella had washed them and put them away just as she'd promised. Sliding them up her legs made Tierney feel a bit of home for the first time. Jeans weren't normal dress in Iskalt, but her mother had favored them when she didn't need to look the part of queen.

Closing her eyes for a brief moment, Tierney tried to call on the strength thoughts of her mother brought forth. Memories of her siblings and father. Then, she turned to Eavha. "We can't stay in this room while the palace is under attack." She wouldn't wait for unknown soldiers to rush the halls, killing all those within. If she had a chance of survival, it was helping those who'd kept her a prisoner but hadn't yet chosen to kill her. Trust the enemy you know, and all that.

Eavha smiled for the first time. "It's a good thing your guards were called to the wall then."

Tierney was quick to pull on a simple tunic and boots. "I need a weapon, Eavha."

"We'll find some. Come on." They burst out into the corridor to be immediately swallowed by a rush of servants and families hurrying by. "They'll be headed to the inner keep. It was built to protect women and children. That's where I was ordered to go."

"But you came to me."

One of her shoulders lifted in a shrug. "Well, something told me you'd be the one female fae in this palace who wouldn't let them force her into hiding."

"You guessed right." Tierney clenched her jaw and shoved past a scared woman who was yelling orders. "In Iskalt, those who can fight don't hide." It didn't matter if one was a woman, a young warrior, a grandma, a donkey. The choice of whether to fight or not was theirs. "I've been trained for this." All her years of sparring with her father and brothers came back to her. She'd bested all of them, save her father.

He wasn't one to show emotion, but he'd been proud.

Tierney gripped Eavha's arm. "Come on, Princess. Let's go make your brother mad." When he returned and found she'd encouraged Eavha into the fight, he'd probably want to be rid of Tierney. But that wasn't the only reason she ran against the flow of fae headed toward the inner keep. This was the first time in many weeks she could actually do something, take action.

Eavha took the lead, weaving through corridors. The flow of frightened fae slowed the farther from the inner keep they got until there was no one else in the halls at all.

"Siege protocol would make the palace guard line the top wall,"

Eavha explained, slightly out of breath. "That's where we'll be able to help."

"And the soldiers we don't have? Where would they be?"

"Preparing for a breach of the palace. Our gates have been in disrepair for years. It won't take more than a few days for the Grima forces to get through them. Ideally, we'd have troops inside the courtyard waiting for the battle."

"Great." Well, if this was the way she went down, it wouldn't be without a fight.

They ran out into the courtyard, but it was silent save for the neighs from the stables nearby. Straw littered the ground and belongings had been strewn about, dropped as fae ran for their lives into the palace.

Eavha bent to pick up a carved wooden horse, a child's toy. "Those from the nearest villages fled here in advance of the attack."

The horn sounded again, and Eavha let the toy fall from her fingers, her eyes drifting to the far wall. Tierney followed her gaze to the pitiful line of guards who stood at the ready with their bows. It wouldn't be enough. Not even by half.

Tierney spotted the tower that looked like it led to the wall and started running that way, without asking Eavha if it was right. Inside, a spiral stone staircase led up into the dank darkness.

They thundered up the steps and out onto the wide battlement at the top of the outer wall. A stone ledge rose halfway up Tierney's chest with notches for hidden archers to man their stations.

She scanned the tree line in the distance, seeing not a single torch in the night. "Where are they?"

"Coming." Eavha's eyes were fixed on the black horizon. "We received warning from the outer villages of their approach."

"What do you think you're doing?" Tierney knew that voice. She cursed silently and turned to Torrin as he stalked toward them. He ignored Tierney completely and yanked Eavha toward him roughly. "Princess, you need to leave."

She didn't respond, and Tierney saw her start to waver, the acquiescence in her eyes.

"That's enough." Tierney clamped a hand on Torrin's arm. "Let her go."

He released his grip, but only to backhand Tierney She stumbled toward the edge of the battlement, righting herself at the last moment, fire bursting through her veins. If only she had her magic, he'd regret touching her.

Then, the faintest light appeared among the trees, a single star moving toward them. As it grew larger, it was joined by others. The Grima army didn't try to conceal themselves. They didn't have to, Tierney realized, since they'd lured the main Vondurian force away from the palace.

Torrin turned away from the girls, almost like he forgot they were there entirely. "Archers! Ready your arrows."

Eavha edged close to Tierney. "Our best archers went with Keir." There was fear in her voice for the first time. She was finally starting to see this coming battle as Tierney had from the start.

Impossible.

The archers lit the tips of their arrows.

"Fire," Torrin screamed.

The enemy troops were still too far for the arrows to reach them, but Tierney quickly realized that wasn't their target. The sliver of moonlight reflected off a glistening trench that had been drenched despite the lack of rain.

The ground was wet.

Taking a few silent steps, Tierney joined the guards at the ledge. She ignored their hateful stares, the disdain they managed to show her before watching their arrows arc through the sky, raining down fire from above. They missed.

Eavha was right. These guards were hopeless. Days ago, Keir and his father took every last trained archer with them. Either that or Vondur didn't train their warriors in archery at all.

"For the sake of magic." Tierney ripped the bow from the guard nearest her.

"You can't—"

Before he could finish his protest, she nocked the arrow, lit the tip in the nearest torch, and fired. It sailed with perfect aim, and she sent another following and then one farther down the trench. They hit in quick succession, a fire erupting, spreading from one end to the other. A barrier.

One that wouldn't protect them for long. As soon as the flames burned out or brave Grima warriors decided to jump the trench, Tierney worried this palace had nothing left to protect it.

No army. No unbreachable walls.

Maybe it was for the best. Maybe those fae down there would set her free, would allow her to figure out a way home. But then, a hand closed around hers, and she realized what would happen if this palace fell. When Vondur took the Grima palace, they'd killed both the queen and the eldest princess.

Eavha would die if they reached her. Tierney squeezed her hand before two guards ripped them apart.

"Get the women off the wall," Torrin yelled.

Tierney kicked and bucked against the man who had an arm across her throat. "Let me go, you big fae oaf." She almost called him an ogre, but she knew a few ogres, and they had more brain cells than all of the Vondurian guard.

He clamped a hand over her mouth, and she didn't hesitate before biting down so hard she drew blood. He pulled back with a roar, and she spit out the taste of his dirty hand, the copper tang of his blood. He'd lose a lot more than that when the golden warriors of Grima reached him.

Tierney's magic rose from the depths, wanting to save her, wanting to show these men what she could do. They'd regret ever touching her. And yet, it didn't release, it didn't obey.

She stared at the guard, her chest heaving.

Torrin shoved him out of the way and faced Eavha, who was still struggling against her own guard. "Princess, your father will hear of this insolence. We don't have time for it when a Grima force is marching on us."

"Then, stop," she spat. "Let me fight, and you won't have to waste time trying to force me to the inner keep."

"That's impossible."

"The only thing that's impossible," Tierney started, "is you keeping your head on your shoulders once one of those Grima chooses to separate it."

His face reddened, but he kept his composure and ignored her. "Kent, release the princess. If she and her foreign pet want to get themselves killed, allow them to stay."

Tierney was no longer listening because her eyes caught on a crystal carved into the figure of a knife that hung from Torrin's neck. If any of the fae here were to be believed about the crystals, she had to get her hands on it.

Torrin turned to the approaching forces, visible as the fire lit up the night. They stretched from trench to tree line, an endless sea of fae ready to fight.

"Kent," Torrin grunted.

"Yes, sir?"

"Get a message to the king. Tell him we are under siege."

"Y-you want me to leave the palace, sir?" Fear tinged his voice. "There's an army out there."

"Then, send a page boy if you're too afraid. You'll find the king on the eastern road toward the Grima border. Go. That's an order."

"We're really staying?" Eavha whispered. "That's … a lot of soldiers."

Tierney shrugged. "Try being in a dark realm with a wall of magic separating you from the army that's on your side." She focused on the coming force. "This, Eavha, is easy."

To that, Eavha had nothing to say. And Tierney … she prepared to fight for her life in a kingdom every bit as separated from her home as Myrkur had once been.

If she died here, would her family ever know what became of her?

"Father, we must make camp soon. We're losing daylight quickly." Keir's horse struggled to keep up with the intense pace the king had set for most of the afternoon. Their soldiers were weary and needed rest before they could be asked to continue riding for several more days.

"Plenty of time to make camp in the evening." The king rarely listened to the advice of his council, much less his son's, but they were running out of time. The Vondurian palace sat near the burning lands. Turlach was used to a lingering light in the distant sky long after the sun had set, but they had left Vondur behind more than a day ago. Deep into the countryside, the king's men would not have the light of the fire plains to guide them this night.

"We are approaching the border of Grima. If we expect our men to fight in a few days' time, they will need plenty of rest each night."

"*Our* men?" The king's voice grew annoyed.

"The king's men, of course, your Majesty," Keir corrected himself, using the groveling tone the king preferred.

"We will ride hard for another hour, then you may set up camp." Turlach urged his mount into a faster pace.

At this rate, they would be lucky to arrive at the Grima palace with even a shred of energy left to fight. But that was where Turlach and his son disagreed. Keir preferred to fight with well-rested soldiers, eager for battle, so that more might survive to tell tales of their success back home among their village taverns. The king merely wanted to win. To him, it did not matter how many lives such a win would cost.

Swearing under his breath, Keir coerced his horse to follow. The men could handle one more hour.

Except, it was two hours before the king agreed to stop for the night.

"You three, set up my tent." King Turlach dismounted his horse and handed him off to a young soldier to care for, in addition to his own weary mount. "I'll have my supper once the hunters return with fresh game." He sauntered off into the woods to relieve himself.

"All right, men, the light is fading quickly!" Keir turned his horse to issue orders. "Make do with what you need for tonight. We will leave at dawn." There wouldn't be time for the luxury of tents and warm beds. They would get by with bedrolls beside campfires and full bellies. It wouldn't be the best sleep, but it would be better than nothing.

Keir continued to make rounds well after dark, circling back to the king's tent to find him fast asleep. At least someone would be fresh and battle-ready tomorrow. Keir shook his head in disgust, lugging his bedroll and pack to join his small company of soldiers.

"Hungry?" Declan stood by the fire, scraping the bottom of the stew pot.

Keir's stomach gave an angry rumble to answer his best friend's question. "Did I miss dinner?"

"Don't worry, I saved your share." Declan offered a bowl of venison stew and a hunk of hard bread. It was a thousand times better than a supper of hard tack and cheese would have been.

"Thanks." Keir sank down to the ground beside the fire. The other soldiers under his command were busy sharpening their swords, trading battle stories, and passing around a bottle of spirits to keep them warm.

Using a heel of bread as a spoon, Keir shoveled the warm stew into his mouth. It was thin and watery but with chunks of meat, potatoes, and carrots, along with a few unidentifiable ingredients, picked up along the trail. He had zero complaints.

Declan groaned as he lowered himself to the ground beside Keir. "Some of the men question the coming battle."

"As do I. But we must abide by our king's orders." He might not agree with his father's way of ruling, but Keir would support him publicly if for no other reason than he wanted to keep his head firmly attached to his shoulders.

"That's a diplomatic answer if I've ever heard one." Declan crumbled dried bearberry leaves into his pipe and used an ember from the fire to light it. "The Grima queen is no more. Her young daughter is trying to pick up the pieces of their kingdom. Kind of feels like kicking a puppy when she's already down."

"The king wishes to bring the Grima to heel." Keir sopped up the last of his stew with the hard bread and stuffed it into his mouth so he wouldn't have to talk anymore. Declan was right, the Grima were already beat. Without their queen, they would fall apart. The young girl-queen was about the same age as Eavha. She'd never be strong enough to hold her kingdom together. This battle was just a final show of power before the King of Vondur took all of Lenya for himself. It was a good thing too. The king's army was short on soldiers.

Keir still didn't know how he felt about a united Lenya under his father's rule.

"Better get some sleep, Deck. We've got another long day of riding tomorrow, and I don't want to have to save your neck by the time we finally reach Grima." Keir grabbed his bedroll and found a piece of ground near the fire to make a bed for the night.

Declan snorted, puffing on his pipe. "You've got that backwards, my friend. It is I who will be saving your neck."

Keir lay back and grinned up at the night sky. They'd exchanged those words in the days before every battle they'd faced together. It usually ended up being fairly even on the number of times they saved each other. Still, there was no one else Keir would rather go into battle with than his best friend.

Keir's eyes snapped open at the sound of hooves thundering through camp. He was a light sleeper, and it wasn't unusual for their sentries to come and go at all hours of the night, but something told Keir this was urgent. He rolled over and crawled out of his bedroll. It was still the dead of night. He hadn't slept long.

"Your Highness?" A young boy slid off the back of his lathering horse. A horse Keir recognized from the palace stables. "Is that you, Prince Keir?"

"Don't call me Highness." He hated the title he hadn't earned. "What message do you bring?"

The boy trembled in fright and swayed on his feet with fatigue.

"It's a siege, my Lord." The boy's voice wavered. "The Grima. They've surrounded the palace, and we have little protection. One of the king's guards sent me himself." The boy's chest puffed up with importance. "He said I was to tell you the Grima prince leads the army for his new queen."

"Prince?" Keir frowned at the boy. "Prince Donal, you mean? Isn't he just a boy?"

"He's about my age, my Lord."

The page couldn't be more than thirteen or fourteen at best. "Well done, young man. Go find the camp cook and tell him I said you're to be fed and given a comfortable bed for the remainder of the night." Keir clapped the boy's shoulder and set out to deliver the message to the king. They would have to turn back for home immediately. The Vondur palace could not withstand a siege. Even one led by a child.

"No." The king poured himself a drink, returning to the comfort of his bed while his soldiers slept on the cold, hard ground.

"No? What do you mean no?" Keir took a step forward before he reigned in his temper and remembered who he faced. "Your Majesty, forgive me. I am merely worried for the princess."

"Torrin will protect Eavha." My father rolled onto his side and settled the blankets around him. Even at war, he traveled with all his comforts.

"Who will protect the fae who cannot protect themselves?"

"I cannot think of everyone when I've nearly reached my goal. Leave me with this nonsense. I will not hear any more of the child-prince, who thinks to knock on my door with threats he is ill prepared to handle. He will never breach our walls with Torrin in charge. We will deal with the matter after we take control of Grima once and for all."

"As you wish, your Majesty." Keir turned on his heel, keeping his temper in check until he reached his men. Keir was a lieutenant commander in his Majesty's army, with a contingent of soldiers who were loyal to him. They'd fought together as boys, and those who had survived relied on each other.

Keir could not … would not leave his sister, nor their fae, under Torrin's protection when a Grima army stood on their doorstep.

"Declan." Keir nudged his oldest friend with the toe of his boot.

"What? I'm awake." He shot up from his bedroll, rubbing the sleep from his eyes. "Who needs killing?" He stared up at Keir, still half asleep.

"No one … yet. Wake the men, we're leaving." Keir stooped to pack up his belongings.

"Leaving? So soon?" He scrubbed a hand over his thick stubble.

"The Grima prince lays siege to our home."

"Donal?" Declan scowled. "Isn't he still crawling around the nursery, drooling on himself?"

"Apparently, they grow up fast in Grima when their mothers and sisters are executed." Keir pinched the strap around his bedroll and tossed his pack over his shoulder. "My father refuses to abandon his endeavors here, so we will return to make sure Eavha and our fae are protected."

Declan was on his feet the moment he heard Eavha's name. She was as much a sister to him as she was to Keir.

"I take it we do not have the king's permission to return?" Declan saw to his own belongings.

"Does that matter?" Keir glanced back at him over the glowing embers of their campfire.

"No." He moved to wake the others.

Keir stared back at his father's tent, his royal banners blowing in the breeze. His search for power would cost more Vondurian lives. Too many. He was a strong king, who ruled with an iron will, but he was not good for the fae. He cared little for them. It was one thing to risk the lives of soldiers who knew what they were getting into. It was another to risk the lives of hardworking fae who couldn't face a siege on their own. Someone had to protect them, and it wouldn't occur to Torrin to think of them.

And if that meant angering the king, so be it. He would still win his battle without Keir's men. But maybe Keir could prevent another battle at home. One they couldn't afford to lose. Maybe he could keep Eavha safe. And Tierney too.

CHAPTER 19

TIERNEY

Tierney clutched the young Vondurian princess's hand, gathering her bearings as guards ran along the battlements to prepare for the siege. The fire had bought them a little time, but it wouldn't last long with the strong winds bending and dampening the flames.

"It's going to be okay, Eavha. Your father will bring his army soon." Tierney was hardly aware of what she said. Her mind was moving at a rapid pace. The odds were not good that this would go in the Vondurians' favor. Given the fact that King Turlach was responsible for the death of the Grima queen and her eldest daughter and heir, the Grima had a lot to fight for and nothing to lose.

Eavha shook her head, her dark hair bouncing. "Father will be halfway to the Grima shores by now. It could take days for him to return once the message reaches him—*if* the message reaches him. And he isn't likely to leave his campaign when he's so close to claiming all of Lenya."

Tierney's heart plummeted to her stomach. The Vondurians were vastly outnumbered and the palace ill prepared for siege. Tierney's mind filled with thoughts of her training. As heir to Iskalt, she'd studied all manners of war tactics. Not to mention, she had plenty of first-hand experience in battle. If the Grima prince took the Vondurian palace, it could change the tide of the war. Tierney watched the eager young princess and made up her mind.

"Prepare the pitch," Torrin barked, marching along the battlements, issuing orders to the palace guard. Archers manned their stations along the wall with few remaining soldiers to guard the fae inside the inner sanctum of the palace.

"Sir, we do not have pitch." A castle steward trembled before the man in charge. "What little we had was given to the Brenandi village for repairs. The heat from the plains leaves cracks in their walls."

"What do you mean we don't have pitch?" Torrin glowered at him. "Go make some."

"There isn't time." Tierney stepped forward. "It takes days to gather enough resin to use for pitch."

"What do you know of it, prisoner?" Torrin sneered at her. "I haven't time for women's prattle."

"Sand!" Tierney glanced down at the inner courtyard, where the ground was pale and soft, with few green things growing. It reminded her of the desert sands of Eldur. Eldur, where they sometimes used heated sand rather than boiling pitch—at least that was something useful she'd remembered from her history lessons. Sand was something they had plenty of in Eldur.

Torrin was already ignoring her, but Tierney ran after him.

"Dig up the courtyard, and heat the sand until it's hotter than pitch." She jogged to keep up with him, dragging Eavha behind her. "It will accomplish the same thing, and it will stay hotter longer. It just won't ignite, but we have plenty of sand if we heat it round the clock."

"How do you know this?" Torrin's eyes scanned the Grima army below. Already, they prepared their battering rams. It would take a monumental effort to break through the castle walls, but they had enough men to accomplish the feat. The king's guard had to be ready with a means of defense.

"I have studied the art of war," Tierney snapped. "Do it. And protect what men you have if you want any hope of surviving long enough for your army to arrive."

Torrin gave a grunt of approval. "See to the sand, boy." He sent the steward on his way. "And be quick about it!"

The big man marched along the walls, calling to his men to arm themselves and prepare for the Grima archers.

"You must see to the fae inside." Tierney marched after him, keeping a firm grip on Eavha's hand. She didn't intend to let the young princess out of her sight.

Torrin halted, taking stock of the weapons the castle stewards brought up from the armory. Among the single bin of swords and knives lay a bag of crystal totems. Tierney grabbed a small sword that should suit her and strapped it around her waist, shoving a pair of daggers at Eavha. And when no one was looking, she grabbed a totem, tucking it into her dress. She had no need for it, but it could come in handy later.

"Put those back," Torrin growled. "The soldiers who can actually wield those weapons need them more than you do." He started passing out totems to his officers, barking more orders to use their limited magic wisely. "Shields only, men. Save your stores for later."

"Trust me, I know how to use a sword." Tierney adjusted the hilt of a dagger in the princess's hand, showing her how to hold it properly. "Stick the sharp end into anyone who comes at you and ask questions later." She tucked the second blade into Eavha's belt. "Do not let go of that."

By the time she turned her attention back on Torrin, he was across the wall, shouting orders to the Vondurian archers and soldiers prepping the trebuchets with whatever they had available.

"We have to see to those inside the palace." Tierney put herself between Torrin and the archers. "You need to give the order to put the staff on siege rations. Immediately."

"This will be over soon." Torrin brushed past her.

"You won't have time once this begins, and we need to make sure the provisions we have will last as long as possible. You don't know how long they will cut us off from supplies. Their numbers are greater, and they will surround the castle. What we have on hand has to last us. If everyone gets an equal but limited share, our odds of not starving will increase dramatically."

"The food goes to my men. The fae inside can go hungry for all I care. Now, leave me. I am a busy man."

Disgusted, Tierney let him go on about his preparations.

"What will we do, Tia?" Eavha twisted her free hand into the fabric of her pants in a helpless gesture.

"You are going to go inside and give the orders to put the whole castle on rations. The bulk of the food will go to the soldiers, but every man, woman, and child inside will get half rations until further notice. When you're done, come back to the wall and find me. Wherever Torrin is, I'll not be far behind. I don't trust him."

"You want me to go b-by myself?" Eavha's lips trembled.

"You can do this." Tierney grabbed her shoulders and smiled when the young princess lifted her chin in determination. "Take this." She pressed the small totem into Eavha's hand.

"What? No, I couldn't." Eavha flinched away from the statue as if burned.

"You might need it. I would feel better if you had an extra layer of protection.

She shook her head, staring at the totem in Tierney's hand. "I don't know how."

"You don't know how to use your magic?" Tierney was appalled.

"Only men wield magic in Vondur." Her eyes grew wide with fear. "The serving class are given weak stores of magic meant for cleaning and such, but ladies of the court … wouldn't dream of taking magic from the men."

Tierney let out a very un-ladylike noise of disgust. "When all this is over, you and I are going to have a long talk." She tucked the totem into her bodice. It might not help her reach her own magic, but anything could prove useful at this point.

"Go quickly." Tierney gave the young princess a gentle push toward the inner sanctum. She would be much safer inside, but Tierney understood the need to play her part.

Turning back to the wall, all the blood drained from Tierney's face as she took in the army below. The soldiers in golden armor just kept coming, surrounding the palace on all sides. If King Turlach didn't show up soon, they would never survive.

She stood out of the way, observing the choices Torrin had made thus far. He had too few soldiers manning the trebuchets. Those would be vital to their defense of the wall. In normal circumstances, he would be correct in the way he had placed his men, but these were not normal circumstances. He did not have enough men to take shifts at the wall. More soldiers at the trebuchets now meant they could fire more frequently, keeping the enemy from swarming the walls and allowing more time for their archers to be effective in picking off those who did make it to the wall. They had to manage their time well, but Torrin was trying to make an impressive show of force he couldn't possibly sustain for more than a few hours. This was all wrong, and he was about to lead them into slaughter.

Tierney hurried off after him. "What are you doing?" She stood with her hand on the hilt of her sword. "You don't have enough men for shifts. What will you do when they grow too weary to fight?" She wasn't above humiliating him in front of his men to prove her point.

"The siege will not last through the night," Torrin growled his words at her. "Not when a pup barely off his mother's breast is leading them."

"That boy has vengeance on his mind. I fought my first battle when I was ten years old. Do not underestimate his youth."

Torrin lunged his big bulk at Tierney's small frame, but she didn't flinch. She'd dealt with ogres twice his size in Myrkur. "You interrupt me one more time and I'll send you to the dungeons with your mongrel."

"Gullie," Tierney whispered. How had she forgotten him? Would he be safe in the dungeons?

"Torrin McIvar?" a shrill voice broke through Tierney's worries. Gulliver would have to manage on his own. The siege was upon them now.

"Boy prince," Torrin shouted back, his voice magically amplified. "Go back home to your little queen while you still have a chance."

Tierney found a place under the crenellations to shield herself when the arrows began to fly.

"I've come to return something your prince left at my castle." The boy sat tall and proud in his saddle. He would not back down. Tierney recognized the determination on his young face. And he had the men to back him up.

Even now, a line of ballista rolled forward to stand between the castle and the young prince, who meant to seize it.

Tierney ducked as the first projectile came soaring over the wall. Barely a breath later, a thick bolt shot through it, spearing it to the stone wall just over Torrin's head. The bolt glistened with the glittering substance Tierney was becoming familiar with. Magic.

The projectile was a head. A rotting one, oozing with gore and maggots. Tierney's stomach roiled at the gruesome sight. She'd seen some awful things in the war with Myrkur, but this was a new level of disgusting. She heaved, lunging to her feet to empty her stomach over the wall.

Laughter rang out among the Grima soldiers.

"I've come to return this general to your king," the boy called, sounding more like a jaded man than the child he was. He couldn't be more than fourteen.

"What's happening?" Eavha approached Tierney, stooped below the crenellations.

Tierney wrapped an arm around the girl, grateful she'd made it back with her dagger still clutched in her hand.

"It seems the Grima prince has returned the Vondurian general your brother left in charge."

"What does that mean?"

"It means the Grima have taken their palace back, and now they are here to take your father's."

"Can they do that?" Her eyes widened in fear.

"Yes, they can." Tierney peered over the wall to see what might be coming next. "He's preparing his archers. We need a shield." Tierney couldn't remember seeing another soldier with a shield.

"They use magic for shields," Eavha explained.

"Stay as close to the walls as you can once they open fire."

"You think they will?"

"This is war, Princess. No one is bluffing here." She thought of her beautiful—mostly ceremonial—armor back home. She'd give anything to have that protection now.

Torrin was busy trading insults with the Grima prince, and Tierney took the opportunity to search her surroundings for anything that might offer them shelter from the archers.

She eyed the bin of weapons the stewards had brought from the armory. It lay empty and on its side now, just big enough for two young women to cower under if worse came to worst.

Tierney scrambled across the wall, stooping low until she reached the bin. To her surprise, Eavha stayed right behind her. Together, they dragged the wooden bin back to their spot along the wall.

"What's this for?" Eavha asked.

Tierney ignored her, elated at the discovery of a square lid inside the bin. It was heavier than a shield, but she could lift it easily enough. A loop of rope attached to the lid on either side, creating handles. She just needed something to connect the two.

"Sorry about this, but my shirt is already torn." Crouching low, Tierney ripped several lengths of fabric from Eavha's long tunic. Quickly braiding them together to make a short rope, she used it to make a handle for her makeshift shield. Slipping her arm through the handle, she tested it, lifting her arm up to shield herself behind the wooden lid.

"That'll do." She crouched back down beside Eavha. "If things get out of control, I want you to climb into the bin and hide."

Eavha nodded. "What can I do until then? I want to be useful."

Tierney searched for something the princess could help with. A group of stewards were making fires to heat the mounds of sand they'd brought up from the courtyard.

"Here!" She waved a steward over. "Give us a fire and plenty of sand, we will man this portion of the wall."

"Madame, you—"

Tierney cut him off with a glare. "Do it, soldier. We may speak softly and take regular baths, but that doesn't make us simpering imbeciles. Set up the vat, and be on your way." Tierney rested her hand on her sword.

"Of course, er, ma'am." The steward bolted off to do her bidding.

"You *have* to teach me how to do that." Eavha blew out a breath, tucking sweaty strands of hair behind her delicately pointed ears.

"It's like we have to work twice as hard as any man to be taken seriously around here." Tierney sank back into a crouch against the wall, feeling better now that she had a semblance of a plan.

Torrin paced the wall just beside them, a large totem gripped in his fist. Tierney could just make out the telltale shimmer of magic that marked the use of the unusual Lenyan power. He'd shielded himself but left his soldiers to fend for themselves. The pecking order was clear. Men of status or rank wielded magic. The rest were cannon fodder.

Vats of sand stood over fires at regular intervals along the wall. The stewards worked hard to keep the fires going, bringing in carts of sand to dump at every station along the wall.

The air grew warm as the sun moved toward the horizon. It would take time for the fires to heat the sand. Time for the siege engines to take their places. Time still for archers and lancers to take their places. One thing about siege that was worse than battle was the waiting. Sieges were boring ... until they weren't.

Tierney peered over the wall, looking for the battering rams. The

Grima had felled several trees and were now preparing them to use against the gates. It was a rudimentary method that would work without the aid of magic that was such a limited resource in this realm.

"They aren't building a structure over their battering ram." Tierney smiled. If they didn't have magical shields either, she would hate to be down there once the sand grew hot enough to use.

"Why would they?" Eavha asked.

"To protect themselves from the burning pitch we don't have. They must believe we aren't prepared." Tierney smiled again. "It will be a big surprise to them when a scalding hot sandstorm rains down on their heads." She let out a nervous breath. War was hard work and even harder on the nerves. Tierney hadn't felt like this in ages. She couldn't say she'd missed the feeling.

"You aren't from Lenya; how do you know these things?" Eavha wiped her sweaty hands on her pants.

"A castle is a castle." Tierney clenched her shield, ready to fling it up over their heads the moment she heard the unmistakable sound of arrows flying through the air. "They're all defended the same way. Doesn't matter what kingdom you happen to be defending at the time."

"When this is over, you must tell me all about this kingdom you come from, where a woman can wield magic and rule her kingdom and lead an army to defend her castle. Even the Grima queen, who remained reagent after her king died, was unable to defend her crown."

"You got it, Eavha." Tierney lifted her shield just as a storm of arrows rained down around them.

The two princesses watched as the opposing armies exchanged several volleys of arrows. It had the makings of a long siege.

Their vat of sand smoldered and sizzled over the fire. It was ready.

A loud thud shook the stone beneath them.

"What was that?" Eavha's eyes widened in alarm. "Is the wall coming apart under our feet?"

"It's the battering ram." Tierney no sooner explained when a metal hook landed between them.

A scream escaped Eavha, and she scrambled back as the hook found its mark and the rope grew taut against the stone.

"They're trying to scale the wall." Tierney peeked over the side to see a line of men climbing at various stages along the wall. "Time for the sand. Come with me."

The two women worked together to fill a basin with hot sand, using thick leather gloves to protect their hands. "You lift that side. I'll lift this one," Tierney instructed, dropping her shield as they hefted the smoking basin to the wall. They aimed carefully and dumped the hot sand, letting it rain down on the soldiers below.

Tierney cringed as their screams reached them, and they fell from the wall. "Quickly, before anyone tries again."

Eavha huffed as they refilled the basin and made quick work of the second load. The bulk of the smoking sand landed on the soldier's chainmail covered torso, cooking him where he lay struggling on the ground.

"Oh, I think I'm going to be sick." Eavha sank down against the wall, sweat dripping from her brow.

Tierney moved to refill the vat over the fire with fresh sand the stewards had dumped behind the fire. They had to be careful to keep their sand as hot as they could. They could not run out or they would be in trouble.

"You okay?" Tierney sank down on shaky legs beside the princess.

Eavha nodded. "I can do this."

"If I have to leave you at any point, keep the vat filled and keep our section of the wall free of enemy soldiers. If they overwhelm you, use your daggers to knock them off the wall. If that doesn't work, run. Get inside the bin before anyone sees you. If that fails, come find me or retreat into the sanctum. The stewards will bring water. Make sure you stay hydrated. The fires will consume your energy."

Eavha nodded again. "I'll be okay. I can do this," she repeated, as if to convince herself. But in the next breath, her eyes widened. "Duck!" She pressed Tierney back against the wall, and Tierney lifted her makeshift shield.

A shimmering ballista bolt shot over their heads, crashing through Torrin's shield magic, ripping into his shoulder. Blood and gore sprayed the wall behind him, and he sank to the ground like a dead weight. Bone and sinew lay exposed from his shoulder.

"Blast!" Tierney groaned as the Vondurian soldiers crowded around their leader. "Don't rip it out!" She shot forward before one of the idiot men could remove the bolt from his shoulder. "He'll bleed to death."

The bolt was as long as her arm and nearly as thick. "It's too close to his heart. He needs a healer. Take him inside the palace."

"Lord Torrin is our commander. We take orders from him." A soldier stooped over their fallen leader. Tierney crouched down to avoid the next wave of arrows too.

"Does the man look like he's in any shape to lead?" Torrin stared wild-eyed, and his skin faded to an ashen gray. His eyes rolled to the back of his head, and he passed out from the pain. She didn't want to say it, but unless their healer was particularly gifted, he wasn't going to make it.

"Eavha." Tierney waved her over. "Can you escort Torrin to the healers and make sure they know he needs immediate attention?"

Eavha nodded. "You three pick him up. Follow me." She didn't wait for them to question her orders. Tierney smiled when the soldiers obeyed, lifting the huge hulk of a man from the battlements.

"Who is next in charge?" Tierney asked the remaining soldiers. They just looked at each other, shrugging. She ran a hand through her sweaty hair. Torrin was already third in command after Keir and the king. The hierarchy probably wasn't clear for the fourth man in charge.

"Sergeant Murphy, maybe," one of the men offered.

"And where is he?" she demanded.

"Not sure, ma'am."

"All right. I need someone to man the sand pit here." She nodded toward her station, and two young boys picked up where she and Eavha had left off.

"You four any good with the trebuchet?" She turned to a group of slightly older boys, likely only a year or two younger than her.

Heads nodded, staring at her in confusion.

Tierney took a quick look below, scanning the current conditions. The Grima prince had moved back to the rear of his army, letting his officers take command. They were pressing forward, their golden armor gleaming in the light. She couldn't let them gain any more ground.

Just as she was about to return to her scattered group of soldiers, a familiar form caught her eye. He didn't wear the Grima armor, and he held his sword like an Iskalt soldier. No. More like a nobleman.

"Veren!" She caught his eye for a brief moment before he fell back into the ranks of enemy soldiers. Her heart raced, and her pulse pounded in her head. Veren was here! Did that mean Siobhan was somewhere in Lenya as well?

Snapping her fingers, she set her mind back on the siege and the four soldiers awaiting her orders. "Go join the ballista contingent. Tell your officers manning the engines I want burning projectiles in the air after the next volley. They're gaining ground, and I want to drive them back." It was time Tierney took this siege in hand. She would not risk Veren's life or anyone else's. She knew how to keep a tight rein on the proceedings so it didn't escalate to an all-out battle.

"We don't have pitch, ma'am."

"Wrap your boulders in burlap soaked in lantern oil. They'll burn long enough to get the job done. The rest of you will deliver messages."

"We don't take orders from a female." One of the boys stood up, probably intending to return to wherever he was stationed, but he never got another word out. An arrow pierced his throat, and he fell over the wall.

"Would anyone else like to argue, or can we all try to survive?" Several heads bobbed, and a few shoulders shrugged. "Would anyone else like to take command here and report to your king upon his return?"

No one volunteered. "Very well, then, I am assuming command. Listen up for my orders, I'm only going to say this once."

Chapter 20
KEIR

Keir's father was wrong.

The young Grima prince was not as green as they'd assumed. He rode atop a giant gray stallion that had gold woven into its braided mane. It was an elegant war beast, not one fit for a young pup about to see his first battle.

Donal's back was tall as he rode among his guards. Guards clad in the golden armor Keir had become accustomed to seeing across the battlefield. The golden warriors of Grima were fierce, well-trained by a man none would question as the best fighter in all of Lenya. Daniel Branderson.

Keir had come across him before. He surveyed the back of the Grima army from his place among the trees, finding the old man. There were women with the men, the armor not hiding their gender. It was so very different from Vondur, where they would never allow their women to fight.

And maybe that was the problem. Lenya would never see peace while the only similarity between the two kingdoms was their desire for more magic.

Keir bowed his head and touched the totem at his neck. His magic roared to life, and he straightened from his crouch. "Okay, let's go." Motioning for the few loyal men who'd followed him in disobeying the king, he started running, using sparse power from the crystal to cover any sound.

The Grima prince was not among his soldiers, and that was the only thing that would keep him alive.

With Declan on his right and Ferrand on his left, Keir crept past the tree line, using the tall grasses to mask their movements. He took a brief moment to let his eyes fall on the now-visible palace gates, breathing a sigh of relief that they remained standing after more than two days of siege.

That wouldn't last.

Streaks of what looked like sand stained the high walls, burned into the stone, where it had been used in lieu of pitch they probably didn't have. Bodies littered the ground, some with arrows piercing their skin. A siege was long. It was messy and painful. They could destroy entire kingdoms.

This could go on for weeks, months. Keir couldn't let that happen.

Reaching out with his power, Keir put pressure on the rear of Donal's horse. Molding the magic, squeezing it from the crystal, Keir pulled it back and brought it down with a forceful crack.

The horse reared back, throwing the prince from his golden saddle. "Go," Donal yelled. "Don't let him get away. That's my horse." He picked himself up off the ground, rubbing his lower back. "That's an order!"

His guards looked at each other helplessly.

"I'll be fine. There's an entire army between me and the palace."

With that, the three guards took off after the horse.

Donal looked around as if searching for something. "I know my horse didn't just throw me out of the blue." He straightened his uniform. "Show yourself."

Keir looked down at his crystal, wondering if he should use its last bit of magic to restrain the prince. He'd felt the totem draining for days, and knew it needed replaced from the crown's dwindling store of crystals. But there was nothing to do about that now.

Despite a protest from Declan, Keir stepped into view.

To Donal's credit, he hid his surprise. "Prince Keir. How is it you ended up behind my army?" The tone was conversational, and it reminded Keir of years long past when he'd come across Donal and his oldest sister hiding in a Vondurian village. Keir had helped them escape before his father could find them.

Keir didn't answer his question, instead hardening his jaw. "I need you to come with me, Donal."

"Ah, so no formalities then. Thank the magic." He held out his wrists. "It appears I am your prisoner. It's all well and good. My generals can lead this army better with me out of the way."

Keir and Declan shared a look. Ferrand stepped forward, ready to take the prince prisoner, but Keir stopped him. "What game are you playing, Donal?"

"Oh, no game." He gave them a boyish grin. "I just do what I'm told. It is the life of a prince, is it not? My sister gets all the glory, and I am but a distraction."

"A distraction?" Keir stepped closer, his voice so low it was nearly a growl. "A distraction from what?"

He shrugged. "Go on. Do your abducting. I do not owe you any information. You will not get past my army, so you won't have me for long. Don't worry, I'll make sure they deal with you swiftly."

Keir wasn't sure how to take this kid seriously. The last time he'd seen him, Donal was only eight years old. Now, he was nearly a man, but he was still talking in circles. Even back then, he knew how to use words to manipulate.

Drawing on his totem, Keir wrapped his magic around Donal's wrists, his ankles. It was stronger than any chains and snaked up to cover his mouth. Donal didn't fight it. He didn't squirm when Declan hauled him over his shoulder nor when they ran back into the trees, where they'd left the rest of their men with the horses.

"What now?" Declan asked as he maneuvered Donal onto a saddle.

Keir wasn't sure this was the right thing to do, but he didn't know what else could possibly get the attention of the Grima force.

"Now, we fight."

The sun sat high in the sky, bringing with it the noonday heat by the time Keir rode out of the trees, his men flanking him to form one long line that probably looked quite pitiful to the army before them.

Until they saw their prince.

A volley of arrows arced through the sky, most missing their targets entirely. Soldiers crashed against the walls, pushing and prodding each other out of the way. It was chaos at the front and calm at the back, as most sieges were.

They may have expected the Vondurian forces to ride from the gates and break their lines. But Grima didn't know all the troops had marched out before the attack. The prince said he was a distraction, and Keir assumed he meant while the Grima queen fortified her palace.

But the distraction didn't work if the king didn't actually care about the fae inside those walls.

Keir halted as those soldiers out of range of burning sand or arrows turned to see what was happening. Donal sat astride Declan's horse, his back ramrod straight and magic keeping him in the saddle. Magic that wouldn't last much longer if Keir didn't get his hands on a new crystal soon.

He touched a hand to his throat to amplify his voice. "Torrin, tell your men to stand down."

Arrows continued to fly.

"I have the Grima prince." He cleared his throat. "This siege is over." He'd thought this through and came to a decision.

Lenya had few traditions, even less that were rooted in history.

But there was one ... an ancient tradition that was now mostly used to determine the succession of Vondurian kings. Even so, he knew Grima royals would not be able to say no.

The Comhrac.

No honorable man in Lenya refused the challenge of the Comhrac. To do so was a failure, one that the fae would never forget.

Daniel Branderson walked toward the line of Vondurian soldiers. He wore no gold armor, instead sporting a black leather chest piece and chain mail. Pushing back his mail hood, he fixed Keir with a disappointed frown.

There was a time when the old sword master was his teacher. But that was before he'd betrayed the kingdom to Grima. "Mo Chara Tine, what is it you do?" His worried gaze landed on the silent prince, the one held by magic.

Mo Chara Tine. It was like these years hadn't passed. *My fire friend.* It was what Daniel had called him as a kid. He said it was because there was a fire burning within Keir.

Keir looked straight ahead, refusing to meet his eyes. "What I must."

Daniel's disapproval sank into him, and anger raced through Keir. This man had no right to judge him after defecting to Grima. One of the first lessons Daniel taught was that the crystals were a gift, that their magic ought not to be used on another being.

Still not looking at him, Keir urged his horse forward. His fading magic continued to amplify his voice. "Vondurians, you have done well. But it is now time for me to end this. I have the Grima prince." He directed his words to the crowd of exhausted soldiers. "I will slit his throat if anyone so much as steps toward me."

He kept riding forward, his men falling in behind him. The soldiers parted, their eyes on the prince. They'd lost so much in the past few years, as had Keir and his fae. He could see it in their eyes.

"I have a proposal for Prince Donal of Grima. One I make before his fae, before my own." He nodded to Declan.

Declan slid down from his horse, dragging Donal with him.

Keir reeled his magic back in, releasing the prince from its bonds. Declan held him in place.

Dropping to the ground, Keir straightened and drew his sword. For the first time, there was real fear in Donal's eyes. Keir's heart pounded as he tried to remember every last part of the ritual, how to bind it with magic.

He lifted his sword, ready to strike. With one swift movement, he brought it in a slow arc until the tip hit the ground and drove into it.

When Keir let go, an audible gasp sounded. The Grima warriors had realized what he was doing.

As had Donal. He tried to step back, but Declan held him in place.

Keir wrapped his fingers around his totem, eking the bits of remaining power from it to fuel his magic. "Prince Donal Hugh of the land of Grima, I challenge you to face me in the Comhrac." Magic surged down his arm as he put a hand on the hilt of the sword.

Resignation came then because Donal knew he had no choice. Few knew the words of the Comhrac. Most combats were not magically bound. But the royals had been educated in their magic.

Donal knew if he refused the challenge, he would die anyway.

With a nod, he touched the hilt. "Let it be done."

Cheers rang from the battlements, and for a moment, Keir thought he saw his sister and … Tierney. That was when he realized he wasn't imagining it. They were there.

If he made it out of this alive, he was going to kill Torrin.

Declan walked beside him as he made his way among Grima soldiers he'd fought and tried to kill in many battles. They looked no different from him save for their golden armor. And their prince …

Keir hated the idea of fighting one so young, but he hated the idea of letting this siege continue more.

He unbuttoned his uniform jacket, sliding it down his arms and handing it to Declan. For once, he wished he had his armor. And he hated armor.

"You sure about this?" Declan asked, folding the jacket over his arm.

"I'm sure I need to save the fae inside that palace."

Donal picked the spot their combat would take place. It was a wide-open area, out of range of the palace archers and out of view of the Vondurian fae. Grima warriors surrounded them in a circle, save for one friendly space where Keir's men stood at the ready, prepared to protect him.

Donal took a sword from one of his men and arced it through the air with the type of skill Keir recognized. They'd both been trained by the same sword master, after all.

Daniel, he noticed, stood back from the others.

Declan handed Keir his sword, and Keir ran one finger down the ornate blade. It had been made for battle, for spilling blood. Except this time, Keir took no pleasure in the act.

"Do you have a second?" Donal asked.

Keir gestured to Declan. "Declan will back me."

Declan nodded.

"Veren," Donal called. "Where is Veren?"

There was murmuring among his men before a young soldier stepped forward. He did not wear the golden armor of the others, but his eyes were wild, in need of a fight. He held a long broadsword that had seen better days.

Donal nodded to him. "Veren Rhatigan will be my second."

A low ranking soldier? Keir wasn't going to argue, but this wouldn't go well for the prince.

The magic bound them to this place, this combat. It would only lessen when he spoke the words to end it. That or his death.

This was Lenya. It was dark and bloody, but both men only wanted to save the lives of their fae.

They circled each other, swords held aloft. Keir wouldn't make the first move. Daniel taught him to make the enemy come to him.

It seemed he had taught Donal differently because the prince lunged forward, his sword slicing through air, hoping to meet skin.

Keir ducked and rolled, bringing his sword up to block the next move.

He jumped to his feet, still waiting, still showing his patience. Donal would tire himself out first, and then all Keir had to do was clean up.

He moved on his toes for quickness, agility, always keeping one step ahead of Donal.

Donal ran at him, and Keir met him blade for blade, kicking a foot out to connect with his stomach and drive him back. "The old man taught me too, young prince."

"Oh yes, he told me." He twisted, pivoting on one heel to drive Keir back with a slash. "The student who never listened to him."

"Anyone who demands blind obedience does not want you to better yourself." Keir shoved Donal into one of the soldiers nearby. "They want you to better them."

Donal pushed away from his man. "Says the prince issuing the Comhrac. One of us must die here. And it won't be me." He lunged forward so quickly Keir almost failed to deflect the blow. Their swords crashed together with a loud clang.

Each move they made was met by equal force. Keir managed to nick Donal's arm, drawing blood, and Donal sliced through Keir's shirt, coming dangerously close to his chest.

Exhaustion weighed on Keir, but just like in battle, he couldn't stop. Wouldn't stop. Everything was his fault. If he'd disobeyed his father earlier, if he'd stayed here with his troops, how many lives could have been saved?

This had to end.

All smiles and jokes were gone from Donal, and he became a dangerous predator, determination in his gaze.

Fury raked through Keir, driving him, turning every move into a flurry of vicious attacks. This prince thought he could attack the palace without repercussions. That fury turned to a new target. Himself. He'd captured the Grima palace and hadn't expected the retaliation.

This was his reward.

His men had hung this boy prince's mother from the ramparts, killed his sister.

They alternated between grunts and growls in the endless fight, neither wanting to give up or give in, neither willing to lose. Pain exploded in his side as Donal's blade pierced him, slicing him open like he was made of nothing but butter.

Warm blood seeped into his shirt, and he stumbled back, his sword coming down. Donal stood across from him, chest heaving.

Pressing a hand to his side, Keir grimaced. This wasn't over. With a heave of effort and anger, he ran at the prince. Donal lifted his sword to fight off the attack, and Keir swept a leg out to drive him onto his rear. His sword clattered to the dirt as Keir's opened a gash from shoulder to elbow.

Donal cried out, a whimper following close behind.

This was how it had to end. Keir raised his sword over his head, ready to have his just due. He swallowed down the bile threatening to rise as the Comhrac magic urged him on. The sword came down swiftly, but before it could split Donal in two, another blocked it.

His second, Veren, wasted no time. He leaped over Donal, catching Keir by surprise. Shoving him back, he forced his sword into the flesh of Keir's stomach.

And then, Declan was there. He took a running start and tackled Veren to the ground.

The very earth beneath them shook as Keir fell to his knees, pulling the sword out as he did. Blood gushed from the wound. A mortal wound.

The ground continued to shake until both Declan and Veren were thrown back, ejected from the battle. Neither Keir nor Donal had called for their seconds and the magic had rules.

Keir crawled toward Donal, his blood staining the ground. He still had his fingers weakly gripping his sword, but it was enough. Donal writhed in pain, rocking back and forth where he lay.

This could still end in victory.

Keir lifted his sword once again, ready to kill the young prince and win the Comhrac. The crowd faded away, and in his mind, he saw another battle. One that ended in a queen and her daughter murdered.

It wasn't what he'd wanted. Burned villages. Hoarded resources. Starving fae. Dead warriors. But it was what he'd gotten.

"Déantar é," he whispered. It is done.

The magic that had kept them fighting pulled back, and Keir dropped his sword. "The siege is over, Donal. I am sparing your life, but make no mistake, I have won this Comhrac. You must leave my lands by nightfall. If I face you again in battle, I will not be so kind. A life for a life."

Donal lifted his head. "You think this absolves you of murdering my sister and mother?" He spat toward where Keir kneeled in the grass. "Worthless Vondurian." He was no longer the manipulatively charming young man. Now, he was real.

"Finally." Keir's head grew fuzzy, and his body tilted forward before he righted himself. "Now, you sound like a prince."

Keir was only vaguely aware of someone helping him to his feet. All he could focus on was the feel of blood seeping from his wounds, the way it weakened him with each passing moment.

There was a feeling of finality as the large, mostly intact gates opened to admit him. A feeling that while he'd saved them, he'd doomed himself.

Keir's knees buckled, and he slipped out of Declan's grasp, his legs crumpling beneath him. He faintly heard his name as his head hit the ground, but it faded away along with everything else.

Chapter 21
Tierney

Tierney sprinted from the battlements, where she'd watched Keir fight for his kingdom. His actions reminded her so much of her father, the way they both would do anything for their fae. Why hadn't she seen it before?

Lenya was not as barbarous as she'd thought. These fae weren't war-hungry men looking for their next kill. They were just trying to survive a war none of them started.

Still shaken from days spent under the threat of arrows, watching the men around her fall, she could hardly breathe. But the Grima soldiers were retreating. Because of Keir.

It didn't escape her notice only a small force returned with him, not the whole of the army. But that hadn't mattered. He'd still beaten them.

She didn't understand the customs of Lenya, why a prince who had the upper hand in a siege would agree to a battle with the one who didn't. Maybe it was honor, maybe it was ego or magic, but they'd both saved a lot of lives.

Keir stumbled through the gates. It was then she saw the blood. It covered him, seeping through his clothes.

She saw the moment realization hit him. His legs wobbled, and it was like seeing a giant building crumble from the inside out.

"Keir," she cried as he fell forward into the dirt. Jumping over the trench where the castle page boys were still digging for sand, she reached his side and immediately checked for a pulse.

"He's still alive." That realization she'd seen in his eyes, Keir knew he was going to die. Not on her watch. "Somebody help me get him up."

Then, Declan was there. "We have to get him to the healing pool."

She nodded. Of course. If he made it there alive, the power of the crystals would heal him. "Let's go."

A hand clamped down on her shoulder. "You're not going anywhere, prisoner." Torrin's voice was low in her ear. Tierney looked up at him, at the way he seemed to tilt as he stood, yet there was no sign of the injury.

He'd taken a forbidden trip to the healing pools himself. That was the only explanation. Exhaustion weighed on him, that much was obvious, but it didn't diminish his sneer.

Eavha reached them, crouching down next to her brother. "Is he going to be okay?"

Tierney tried to jerk away from Torrin. "Yes, he will be if this big oaf lets me go."

"Not on your life." He turned to his weary and beaten men, who watched the scene unfold. "Snyder, Cormichal, take the prisoner back to her room."

Neither of the men moved.

Torrin eyed them angrily. "Teris, take hold of the prisoner."

Again, no one stepped forward. Tierney was too focused on Keir's labored breathing to give much thought to the men around her, to their refusal to make her a prisoner once more.

"Sir," one of the guards said, his voice betraying his exhaustion, "you were hurt."

"I'm okay now."

The guards shared a confused look. "Tierney is the reason many of us are still alive."

She lifted her eyes at that. Sure, she'd taken over when Torrin was injured, but she hadn't saved anyone, not really. Every guard she saw met her eyes, something that wouldn't have happened before the siege.

Torrin pulled her arm back, and pain shot through her. She clenched her teeth to keep from crying out.

"She did nothing but disobey my orders." His grip tightened. "Fine, I will take her myself."

She wanted to fight him, to turned him into ash with the magic she couldn't reach. But she was so tired. She hadn't slept in days, and thinking about one's inevitable death drained all mental energy.

Yet, she was alive. That would have to be enough for now.

Torrin shoved her toward the palace.

"Declan," she yelled, "get him to the pools. Keep him alive." Without Keir, she worried this kingdom would fall into tyranny. It wasn't her kingdom, and she shouldn't care, but then she pictured Eavha and all the women who refused to speak out of turn.

It didn't escape her notice the king hadn't returned with his son.

The last glimpse she had of Keir was when Declan and another soldier lifted him, his head falling against his chest, his eyes closed.

Live, she pleaded silently. *Please live.*

Torrin dragged her through the silent halls. Those in the inner keep hadn't yet come into the light. It was all Tierney could do to stay on her feet as she stumbled along the stone floors.

Everything from the last few days hit her. Ducking arrows. The screams as they poured burning sand over the walls. The Grima hadn't yet breached the palace walls, but it wouldn't have taken them much longer.

Yet, here she was. Alive and uninjured.

The palace was a blur of stone and tapestries until they reached the familiar room, her prison cell. Torrin shoved her inside, sparing her one final seething look before slamming the door.

She listened to the sound of grinding metal as it was locked from the outside.

Turning, she saw the room through new eyes—battle-tested eyes. Ten years ago, her magic saved the fae kingdoms and human realm alike. But it was not something she'd earned, something she'd deserved. The power inside her had been simply the effect of having the blood of three kingdoms running through her veins.

But here, over the last few days, she'd proven herself in a new way. She'd kept the Grima from the walls of the palace with a knowledge and skill that had nothing to do with magic. It was only her.

Stumbling toward the bed, she collapsed onto it. One image wouldn't leave her. Veren, standing among the golden warriors. He'd looked like he belonged with them, like they accepted him. She had to find him, to find Siobhan. It was her fault they were here, that they were in a war for kingdoms that weren't their own.

As her eyes fluttered shut, she made a silent promise that if she ever made it out of here, she'd go in search of him.

Tierney didn't know what was going on outside her room. She imagined the palace was being put back to rights after the siege that ended sooner than any of them expected.

It had been two days since Torrin threw her back into her prison, two days since she'd spoken to another soul. Her food was brought by a guard, who did not speak to her, though his eyes told her he wanted to.

Not even Ariella was allowed to see her. She'd cleaned up as best she could from the siege, but she still felt those days crawling over her skin.

On the second day, she woke to yelling outside her room.

"I am the princess," Eavha yelled, sounding very unlike the young woman who had been raised in a kingdom where women were taught not to speak, not to get angry. "You will do as I say."

"I'm sorry, Highness," a man's voice said softly. "Orders from Torrin."

"Torrin is not in charge of this palace."

"In the absence of the king and the prince, he is."

"Tia!" she yelled.

Tierney scrambled to press herself against the door. "Eavha." She peered through a crack to see Eavha struggling against the guards.

"They've blocked me off from any of the rooms that would prove useful to you."

The tunnels. They were keeping her away from any of the tunnels. Torrin probably didn't know where they all went, but if he was the right hand of the king, he'd know where they all began.

"It's okay," Tierney called back. "I'm okay. Keir?"

"He's alive, but he hasn't woken up since Declan got him into the healing baths."

"He will, Eavha. I know it."

Eavha's expression tightened, and she stopped fighting the guard. "And when he does, I will tell him how you protected his palace. Then, Torrin will pay." She shoved away from the guard and stalked down the corridor.

Tierney collapsed against the door, a tear escaping her eye. This wasn't supposed to be her life. If she hadn't run from the ball, she'd be at home right now in the arms of her mom, watching Toby and Logan act sickeningly cute. Playing with Kayleigh and Ciarra.

But her family wasn't here, and she had to be strong for them.

Tierney was in bed staring up at her ceiling when a rattling sound came from the entrance to the tunnels. She sat up, wondering how Eavha had managed to get into her room. If Tierney knew how to navigate the labyrinth, she'd use them to get out of this room.

But it wasn't Eavha who appeared. The door opened, and Ariella came through, her kind face transforming into a scowl as she surveyed the room.

Empty food trays were scattered over various surfaces. The bedding was twisted on the end of the bed. There were articles of clothing strewn along the floor. Tierney had hardly left the bed, let alone kept her space tidy.

"You're already locked in here, Tia. You really needed to make it worse?" She started stacking dishes. They'd fed her basic fare, just enough to keep her alive.

"Ariella." Tierney crawled to the end of the bed. "What are you doing here? How—"

"Well, that awful Torrin has men following Eavha. They report her every action. She asked me to come here."

"And you—"

"Were stupid enough to agree? Apparently. Now, tell me why you have forsaken bathing." She scrunched her nose. "This room reeks, and I'm sure you don't smell much better."

"I ..." Tierney twisted her hands together. "I'm not really sure how to, um, prepare the bath." Even if she'd been brought clean water, she didn't know which oils went in, how to scent it.

Ariella sighed. "And if anyone doubted your noble blood, they wouldn't now. I will make sure you get clean water that is already prepared. All you have to do is dump it into the basin."

"Thank you."

"Oh, dear, it's not for you. It's for the good of all Vondur. We already face the stench of the burning pyres after the siege. No one needs to be subjected to your particular odor as well."

"How is Keir?" Tierney didn't want to discuss herself, not when she had no news of what was happening outside these walls.

"Resting." She smiled. "But he will recover fully from his injuries." She stopped cleaning enough to focus a contemplative gaze on Tierney. "There are rumors about our prisoner in the palace halls."

"Rumors?" She'd faced rumors before, none of them good. Drawing her legs up, she hugged her knees to her chest.

Ariella bent to pick up the filthy jeans Tierney had worn during the siege. "I do not understand this garment, but that is of no matter. Yes, soldiers and maids alike are speaking of you. Those who were on the walls during the siege use hushed tones to talk of how you, a woman, took command and kept the Grima force at bay."

Her face heated. "I just gave some advice."

"Dear, if it had just been advice, Torrin wouldn't have forbidden his men from speaking your name."

Tierney's eyes widened. That was … extreme.

"Yes, it seems like you were quite the challenge to his authority. Those most loyal to him, of course, talk of your insolence and how you only impeded his command and almost caused the palace to fall."

"That's ridiculous. He'd have had to do something for me to impede him."

"Well, wherever the truth lies, it is probably best it remain hidden until the prince wakes."

Tierney wasn't sure why she believed the maid. Keir was the man who'd put her here, the one keeping Gulliver in the dungeons. Yet, the moment she'd seen him ride forward with the Grima prince in his grasp, everything shifted.

He'd returned without his father to save the kingdom. He'd risked his own life.

And then, he'd let his enemy live. He'd let Veren live.

She'd known then that whatever her future in Vondur, her fate rested solely with Keir.

Chapter 22
KEIR

"Stupid idiot men." The angry voice pulled Keir from the fog of too much sleep, but he couldn't seem to make his eyes work. Loud thumping and stomping footsteps continued to draw him from the fog.

"How any of them manage to accomplish a single thing is beyond me. If they aren't starting wars, they're getting themselves injured in the Comhrac, of all the stupid, asinine things to do."

Someone punched the pillow under his head and rearranged the blankets around his aching body.

Keir's mind began to catch up to current events, and his eyes finally fluttered open, though he wished they hadn't. Blazing sunlight streamed into the room, setting his head throbbing with shooting daggers of pain.

"Too bright," he managed to croak the words through his dry throat and cracked lips. "How long have I been out?" He tried to sit up.

"Lay back, you fool; you're going to injure yourself all over again." Eavha gently pushed him back on the bed, worry and a bit of anger flashing in her eyes. "You almost got yourself killed." She pinched his shoulder.

"Ouch."

She pinched him again. "Did you ever think what might happen if you died, sacrificing yourself to the Comhrac like that? Did you stop to think what would happen to me without your protection? You think father wouldn't sell me off to the highest bidding old fart he could find?" She pinched him again. "Answer me."

"Stop pinching me, Eavha. Tell me how long I've been out."

"Five days. If it weren't for the healing pools, you'd have died." She reached out to pinch him again, but he moved out of her reach.

"Father won't like that." Keir laid his head back against the pillows. "The healing powers diminish with every use. It's only meant for the reigning king."

"I don't care." Eavha fell into the chair beside his bed. "Just let him say one word about it, and I'll have plenty to say to him." She folded her arms over her chest, her eyes losing some of the fire in them. "How are you feeling?"

"Like I've been blown apart and stitched back together." Keir rubbed his chest, feeling the still-healing wounds under thick bandages. "Where did you find such a sharp tongue? I seemed to have misplaced my sweet little sister."

Some of the spark returned to her eyes. "She's gone. Get used to it."

"Tierney's been a bad influence on you." Keir tried again to sit up, and Eavha rushed to his side to help him, stuffing more pillows behind his back. "Tell me what's happening. Has father returned?"

"No. We've had no word from him, though it's likely if we did, Torrin wouldn't bother to tell me." Eavha stood to pour him a glass of watered wine. "After the Comhrac, Prince Donal withdrew his army and we brought you to the healing pools. While I was gone, Torrin seized control." She helped him sip from the glass.

"He's third in command. It's his responsibility." Keir coughed and took another drink. "Wait. You said he seized control? I heard he was injured. Who was in charge while he was with the healers? Captain Murphy?"

Eavha shook her head, a small smile on her face. "Tierney took command."

"Tierney? A woman can't lead an army!" At least, not any woman he'd ever met. He supposed if anyone could, it would be Tierney.

"Oh, but she did, brother. And it was the most glorious thing I have ever seen." Stars shone in Eavha's eyes. "When Torrin fell, she stepped in. She took charge." Eavha slapped a fist in her hand and stood to pace. "And she knew exactly what to do and when to do it. And Keir, the men! They *listened* to her. They *obeyed* her orders. I've never seen anyone—man or woman—command such respect."

"Where did you hear all of this nonsense? I've told you not to listen to palace gossip. It's always exaggerated."

"I saw it with my own two eyes." Eavha turned toward him. "I worked right beside her for two whole days up on the wall. Until Torrin dragged himself from his bed and turned into a tyrant."

"You did *what*?" Keir flung the blankets aside. Clearly, he needed to return to his responsibilities if such insanity had taken root in the palace.

Eavha pushed him back onto the bed and tucked the blankets in around him. His teeth chattered, and just that little activity wiped him out.

"While Tierney took command, I manned the sand pit beside her."

"You did no such thing. You couldn't have handled such physical labor." He couldn't imagine his sister carrying around heavy loads of heated sand when the heaviest thing she'd ever lifted was her silver hairbrush that once belonged to Mother.

"I can, and I did. For nearly two days. I've never been so tired in my life, nor have I ever felt like anything I did mattered as much as what I did up on that wall. Keir, you have no idea. It was exhausting and terrifying, but never once have I felt so … *alive*."

"I'm going to kill her." Keir tried to roll to the edge of the bed, but a wave of nausea hit him. "As soon as I can get out of this bed, I'm going to kill her. She broke my little sister."

"No, Keir. She inspired me." She sank down onto the chair beside his bed. "And then, Torrin came and ruined it all." She leaned against the chair with a frustrated look on her face.

"He'll see to returning order." Keir's eyelids felt heavy. Like he needed a short nap, and then he could get up and go back to his duties. Just a quick nap.

"He's lost his mind." Eavha shook her head. "He has the whole palace on lockdown. Even the servants are on edge, and he won't let me see Tierney. He has her locked in her rooms. Me too, but I've been sneaking in here. Declan has been looking the other way."

"Torrin has locked you in your rooms? For nearly a week? Why?"

"Because I am guilty of treason for helping our soldiers through the siege. And for supporting Tierney."

"I need to find out where Father is. I don't like what I'm hearing." If he were honest with himself, he didn't want to think about how Torrin might be treating Tierney. Not many Vondurian men would forgive brashness from a woman, and he was beginning to think that wasn't right. "Help me out of this bed."

"You sure you aren't going to fall over once you're on your feet?" She gave Keir a skeptical look.

"Not if you help me to the throne room. If that fool thinks he can make a play for power, he's more of an idiot than I thought."

"You don't think Torrin will try to challenge Father, do you?" Eavha pushed the blankets aside and helped Keir sit up on the edge of the bed.

The room started to spin, and he closed his eyes for a moment. "I think he's waiting to see how Father's campaign against Grima went, but he could be positioning himself right now to seize the throne for himself if the king failed."

"No one will support him. He isn't of noble birth." Eavha shook her head.

"Where is my totem?"

"Torrin took it when they brought you in here after the healing baths. He said they were in short supply and he might need it."

"He can't be trusted." Keir tried to stand on his own, but Eavha leaned forward to drop his arm around her shoulders.

"I can't confront him like this. I need a totem to give me strength."

"Tierney! She stole one when no one was looking. She thought I could use it."

"She doesn't understand our ways. It's not that you aren't allowed to use magic. It's just in such short supply … and we've been at war for so long." But even to his own ears, the excuses sounded weak. He'd never stopped to consider what his sister would do if she was suddenly left without protection. He didn't like the idea that she would be defenseless. In her position, she should have magic. She should be taught to use it as a last resort.

"We'll go to her rooms through the tunnels."

"Torrin has all the entrances guarded." Eavha guided him across the room to the door.

"Wait. Torrin doesn't know of all the tunnel entrances."

"Is there another way into the east rooms?" Eavha struggled under his weight already. They had to move quickly.

"Through Mother's rooms."

"We can reach Mother's old rooms from here, but how do they connect to the east wing?" She turned them toward the concealed door in the wall that would lead them to the tunnels within the palace walls.

"There's another entrance there. Behind the mirror."

Eavha nodded. "Let's go."

It took them twice as long to reach Tierney in the east wing, and Keir was sweating and shivering by the time he leaned against the door to her room.

"Who's there?" Her voice sounded harsh. Like she hadn't used it in a long while. "Is that you, Ariella?"

"It's us." Eavha stepped into the room through the secret opening in the wall. Keir stumbled in behind her.

"Keir." Tierney rushed to help Eavha lead him to the settee.

"Do you still have it?" Eavha asked. "The totem? He needs it to give him the strength to deal with Torrin. He's still weak from his injuries."

"*He* can speak for himself." Keir wiped a hand over his sweaty face.

"I have it." Tierney crossed the room to her bed, reaching for a pack she'd stuffed under the mattress. "Not that it's the least bit useful to me." She searched through the contents, pulling out a small crystal figure of a bird.

"Is it enough?" Eavha asked.

Keir's fist closed around it and clarity rushed through his mind. It wasn't the strongest of totems, but it was full of magic. "It will do." He took a deep breath, letting the power of the crystal fortify him.

"Has the king returned?" Tierney asked.

"That's what we're about to find out." Keir stood up, feeling stronger by the minute.

"We?" Eavha asked, and Keir nodded.

"Stick close to me. Both of you." Keir crossed the room and opened the door to the hall.

"Get back inside, prisoner!" the guard ordered.

Keir raised his brows, and the man took several steps back. "Your Highness, I did not realize you were in there. The tunnels have all been guarded on Lord Torrin's orders."

"Lord?" Keir raised his brow again. "The last I checked the Captain of the King's Guard was not a nobleman."

"Right, of course, your Highness." The guard bowed and stepped aside.

"Come." Keir beckoned for Eavha and Tierney to follow him.

"But sir." The other guard stepped between him and Tierney. "We are under orders to keep the prisoner here."

"And as second in command of his Majesty's army, I am relieving you of your duty. You are dismissed, soldier. Or has my father's throne been usurped while I've been recovering from my injuries?"

"Of course not, Prince Keir." The first guard stepped in. "We are happy to follow your orders, sir."

Keir pinned them with a glare before he turned, making his way along the corridor to the throne room with Eavha and Tierney on his heels.

He wasn't in any way ready for another Comhrac, but if Torrin pushed him too far, Keir would challenge him before this day was out.

Charging past the soldiers standing guard at the throne room doors, Keir didn't wait to be announced.

"Who dares to interrupt while I meet with my officers?" Torrin—dressed in the finery of a nobleman—turned toward the entry. His face paled behind his thick black beard when he saw Keir with the princess and the prisoner at his side.

"*Your* officers?" Keir approached the king's war table where the officers in residence stood gathered around the inlaid map of Lenya. Torrin had placed figures representing the king's army at various stations along the Grima border.

"Prince Keir." Torrin swallowed. "I have been told you are still not well."

"I am well enough to relieve you of your command." Keir took his place at the table, at the right hand of the king, who had not yet returned.

"I am happy to continue leading the men until you've made a full recovery, sir." Torrin gave a curt nod. It wasn't a sign of the deepest respect, but it was a sign that he accepted Keir's position of authority.

"All is well with my health, Torrin. Unless we have a problem we need to discuss, then I suggest you take a seat." Keir eyed the chair meant for the Captain of the Guard, letting out a breath when Torrin lowered himself to the seat.

"Your Highness," Captain Murphy said, "it is good to see you recovered."

"Tell me, what news of my father?" Keir gestured for the men to sit as he remained standing.

"His Majesty's campaign against the Grima army has not been a success," Murphy explained. "We expect his return at any moment."

"And our losses?" Keir knew it would be bad, but he braced himself for the news.

"We took a grave loss of life, sir," Murphy continued. "More than a thousand souls."

Keir hung his head at the news. "So much bloodshed. Was it at least worth it?"

"I am afraid not, sir. The Grima have regained control of their palace, and the young Queen Bronagh remains on her throne. Prince Donal has led his men to a series of victories none here anticipated.

"We will continue to take stock of our situation today and wait for the king's return on the morrow."

"And what of the prisoner?" Torrin spoke for the first time. "She will be punished for her transgressions."

"Which are?" Keir gave him a level look.

"She usurped my authority in the midst of battle."

"I have heard direct accounts of the events that would say otherwise."

"She must be punished." Torrin hammered a fist against the table. "She overstepped in every possible way."

"And we will hear what she has to say." Keir took his seat. "But I will not allow her or anyone under the care of King Turlach—be they guest or prisoner—be treated poorly."

"His Majesty the King has returned," the court herald announced a moment before the doors of the throne room crashed open and King Turlach charged into the room, looking as fierce as ever.

"There he is." The king dropped into the chair beside Keir. "My son, the deserter." Rumpled and weary, the king was covered in grime from the lost battle and his time on the road back from the border. He propped his feet up on the table and called for wine.

"Torrin, I'd like a report."

"Father, I would prefer to give you a full report in private." Keir attempted to salvage the moment, but the king held up his hand in dismissal.

"Father, you must listen to Keir." Eavha rushed forward, and Keir closed his eyes. This was not going well, and he'd nearly drained the totem in his hand just trying to stay conscious.

"Eavha? What on earth are you doing here?" The king gaped at the princess.

"Please, we have so much to tell you. There was a siege, and it was awful, but Tierney—"

"I don't believe you were asked about the prisoner, daughter." The king dismissed her protests. "Keir, take your sister back to her rooms. She's clearly not feeling like herself. And get that prisoner out of my throne room. We will deal with her tomorrow once and for all."

Keir's shoulders slumped in defeat. As ever, his father had impeccable timing. One more hour and he would have had things squared away with Torrin and the king's officers. One more hour and he would have been ready to face his father with the truth.

CHAPTER 23
TIERNEY

Tierney didn't know what was happening in the palace or why every guard who took up his position seemed on edge. Ariella was allowed to see her now that Keir had recovered, but the maid had reverted to her quiet and morose demeanor, almost like she was scared of something.

She entered the room carrying a silver tea tray, just like she had every morning.

Tierney jumped off the settee to face her. "Do you have news of Keir or Eavha?" Neither had been to see her in days, not since the king returned.

Other than her best friend in the dungeons, they were only a few fae in this palace she sort-of trusted. She wasn't sure when she'd realized she wanted to trust Keir, but it had come slowly and completely unexpected. Yet, he wasn't here.

Ariella set the tray down on the table and wiped a tired hand over her face. "They have been otherwise occupied."

"What does that mean? What are they doing?" She'd thought her actions in the siege might earn her a release from this prison, allow her to attempt to find her friends and return home to the familiar ice fields of Iskalt. For so long, she'd wanted adventure, craved doing anything other than sitting in on her father's meetings, dealing with issues of the kingdom.

Now, she'd give anything for the boredom of life as a princess, for her only problem to be choosing which of the kingdom's noble sons or daughters would make her a match. How frivolous she must have appeared to those who knew true struggles.

How frivolous she now appeared to herself.

Ariella hadn't answered her question before she walked toward the washroom. "The king has requested you be bathed."

"Like a prized hound." She scowled. "How kind."

"Kind is not a word his Majesty believes in."

Tierney stepped into the washroom as Ariella filled the tub with tepid water. "Then, what does he believe in?" Everyone had principals, especially royals. Concepts they lived and ruled by. Ideas they would die for.

Ariella paused, her hand inside a bowl of crushed petals. "Power."

One word. It sent a shiver down Tierney's spine. She'd seen what the quest for power did to the fae seeking it. King Egan of Myrkur had nearly destroyed three kingdoms in his search for power.

Ariella let the petals flutter into the water and gestured for Tierney to undress. For once, she didn't argue with the woman.

Slipping off the loose tunic and trousers she wore—more for their familiarity than actual comfort—she stepped into the cooling water. Even as a prisoner, she enjoyed comforts most in Lenya couldn't imagine. She'd seen enough, heard enough to know that.

Yet, as she sank into the water, she could do nothing but pity herself.

Her father's voice came to her mind. *True power is not about magic, Tia; it is being willing to make the hard choices.* He'd been talking about his desire for her to marry, to have an heir and secure the throne for another generation. But the words were still true now.

The difference between the powerful and the weak was in caring for the kingdom over oneself. That was what made the crown. When the fae of a kingdom were loyal to their ruler out of love instead of fear, it was stronger than any magic.

She sank lower. "King Turlach will never have true power."

Ariella finally met her gaze. "There is a price that comes with becoming the king of Vondur."

"The Comhrac." In the days since the battle, she'd asked everyone she could of the true meaning of what had happened between Keir and the Grima prince.

She nodded. "The throne can only be won through death. It breeds a certain darkness that is hard to overcome."

Tierney scrubbed her skin, taking care not to wet her hair as she studied Ariella. She hadn't noticed before how haggard the woman looked. Dark circles rimmed her sunken eyes. Deep lines creased her forehead. Something wasn't right.

A sigh pushed past the maid's lips. "Dear, you can dress on your own today. I have laid out clothes I think the king will approve."

The king. Her clothes. The bath. She sat up, sloshing water over the side. "I'm to see the king?"

She nodded. "I must be off to attend to my other duties." She hurried away so quickly Tierney didn't have time to call her back.

Standing, she let rivulets of water drip from her body before stepping out. A trail of bathwater followed her as she walked farther into her room. On the bed was a dress she hadn't seen before. It was plain, the only colors white and brown. The neckline would reach all the way to her throat and the hem to the floor.

It was a dress meant to hide a woman's form, meant to make her unremarkable, just another fae.

Tierney narrowed her eyes. She was a princess. Turning away from the hideous dress, she dug through her few articles of clothing. She was standing in her underclothes when the entrance to the tunnels opened.

It was too late to cover herself, but she released a breath when Eavha appeared.

"You're not dressed."

"Have you seen what I've been given?" Complaining about a dress was stupid in the grand scheme of things. She was a prisoner and shouldn't expect to be treated as anything else. But she needed to hold on to her irritations, to remind herself who she truly was.

Eavha eyed the dress with distaste. "Well, you may as well put it on." When Tierney didn't move, the younger princess sighed. "It wasn't my father who sent this. This has Keir written all over it. He wants you to appear unthreatening, repentant."

"Repentant? For what?"

Eavha picked up the dress and handed it to her. "Torrin has my father's ear more than my brother right now. I don't think I've ever seen Keir scared before."

She swallowed. "I'm not sure what he should have to fear. I'm no threat. I just want to go home."

Eavha put a hand on her arm. "I didn't say he was scared of you, but *for* you ... that's a different matter."

The words sent a chill through her. The cold prince who'd taken her prisoner was worried? His castle was attacked, and he was scared for her. "I don't see why he should care what happens to me." She slid the dress over her head. She wore no corset, nothing to enhance her figure.

"Keir doesn't like anyone to know, but he actually cares about fae. There are so many things wrong here in Vondur, and sometimes it's as if he's the only one trying to do anything about it. My father ... Torrin ... they have no desire to end this war that has taken so many lives. Keir wants peace."

"And what does peace have to do with me?"

Eavha worked with nimble fingers on the buttons along the back of Tierney's dress. "Well, you may be the key."

"How so?"

"If you told us more about the new Grima queen ..."

Tierney turned, batting Eavha's hands away. "Wait ... what makes you think I know anything of Grima?" Dread curled in her gut. The one friend she thought she'd made in Lenya believed she'd lied about where she came from.

Eavha hesitated. "I truly wanted to believe your tall tale at first, but how is it possible anything exists beyond the fire plains? I cannot explain your peculiar magic, but no one can travel around or across the burning lands. Clearly, you aren't of Vondur, so you must hail from Grima. There is no other possibility."

Tierney had no response, no words that could rid her of the anger and hurt welling within. She had to get out of Vondur, to fae who didn't think so ill of her. Backing away from Eavha, she turned when the door banged open.

Two guards walked in, their heavy-booted steps echoing off the walls. "Prisoner," one of them said, "we have been ordered to take you to the courtyard."

The other bowed his head to Eavha. "Princess, your presence is requested as well. You must go ahead of us."

In Iskalt, a guard never would have dared to give Tierney orders. Yet, Eavha only nodded and walked past them, averting her eyes from Tierney as she did.

Tierney didn't have time to think of anything she'd said because the guards gripped her arms, dragging her into the hall. She wore no shoes, and the smooth stone was cool against her feet.

Her teeth ground together, but she didn't fight. Now was not the time.

Sunlight poured through the entrance to the courtyard, and as Tierney's eyes adjusted to the light, she could make out a crowd. It must have been the entirety of the king's court waiting in the heat for some event.

Torrin marched toward them, and the guards stopped. Declan came on his heels.

"I will handle her from here," Declan said.

Torrin practically growled. "You will do no such thing, soldier. Go join your puppy prince. He has more use for you."

Declan's eyes blazed with anger as he turned to Torrin, ready for a fight. "He is your prince. You will speak of him with respect."

"That title holds no true power." True power. Fae like Torrin would never understand the meaning.

Tierney surveyed the nervous faces in the courtyard. None of them knew why they were here. But then, she caught sight of the king emerging from one of the corridors, Keir two steps behind. Something big was happening, and she had a feeling it wouldn't be good.

"Your king will speak." One of the king's guards shouted above the crowd, cutting off Declan and Torrin's argument.

The courtyard quieted. Tierney tried to catch Keir's eye, but he was looking out over the gathered fae, seemingly just as confused as she was.

"You have made me proud," the king began. "While I was away defending our kingdom, you kept an army of Grima barbarians from our gates."

A hesitant cheer wound through the crowd.

The king went on, "I wish I had been here to defend the palace with you, but my soldiers were attacked. We fought many battles, lost many lives, and were unable to return. It is why I sent my son to relieve you of the siege."

The noise was louder at the mention of Keir, but Tierney's jaw clenched. He hadn't sent Keir. Keir disobeyed orders to return and saved every single person in this palace.

"This war has continued for too long, but I am lucky to have good fae surrounding me, good leaders. Torrin led you in battle. His actions have earned him great rewards, and we should all be grateful for his clear mind in the heat of the fight."

Wrong. And wrong again. Tierney wanted to punch Torrin's smug face as a smattering of lukewarm applause filtered through the air. As if reading her mind, he reached for her forearm, clenching it tightly.

There was no mention of Keir or his actions to end the siege.

The king's voice grew somber. "We've lost many great lives in these battles, but all is not lost. We will have our revenge."

Something about this wasn't right. The fact she'd been dragged here to witness a nothing speech. How the captain of the guard was the one holding her in his grasp.

And then, she saw him. Across the courtyard, hunched over, with bruises stretching the length of his bare chest, was Gulliver. Her heart leaped into her throat, and tears stung the back of her eyes.

No, no, this wasn't okay. Neither of them should be here.

She'd lost track of the king's words until he mentioned her by name. "She calls herself Tierney O'Shea, Princess of Iskalt. I am here to tell you Iskalt is a kingdom from old children's stories. One that does not exist. We have recently received a message telling us our prisoners are Grima spies."

The crowd gasped, but it was nothing compared to the way Keir's head jerked up in surprise. He took a step forward, saying something to his father. The king shoved him back with a scathing look.

"It is true, fellow Vondurians. We do not know how long they were among us before we managed to capture them."

Yeah, because Gulliver would have had an easy time concealing himself.

Rage seethed through her, and the crowd shifted, putting distance between them and her. Even guards who'd started looking toward her with sympathy after her actions in the siege angled themselves away.

"The Grima queen is said to value these spies. We will show her what it costs to attack Vondur. In two days' time, our prisoners will face execution, and their heads will be our gift to Grima."

Tierney couldn't breathe. She'd physically stopped as noise rang in her ears, making no more sense to her. Those words … execution. Execution. Gulliver met her gaze across the courtyard, more resignation than panic in his eyes.

He'd known all along it would come to this.

It seemed she was the only one deluding herself.

Someone screamed, a high-pitched keening Tierney would hear in her dreams. Eavha.

But she didn't have the energy for anyone else or for any thought save for a single realization.

She would never see her home again.

Chapter 24

TIERNEY

Tierney couldn't sleep with that single word running through her mind. Execution. Death. Hers.

She hadn't cried, hadn't screamed or ranted. It didn't seem real.

Moonlight cast shadows across her room, shadows that had been her biggest fear as a child. When she was young, she'd dreamed of a man coming to save her. She hadn't known it was Uncle Griff at the time or that her Uncle Griff was her biological father. His memory had been forgotten by the prison magic.

But he'd shown up, and yes, he'd saved her.

This time, there was no one to stop this, no one to change the wheels of fate.

Worse than her own demise was thinking of Gulliver standing under the hangman's noose, his tail as lifeless as it had been today. He shouldn't even be here, but he'd trusted her, trusted in her magic.

Magic that couldn't save either of them now.

If this was one of the human stories her mother liked to tell her of magical places that weren't unlike the fae realm, her power would return just when she needed it most.

But this wasn't a story, it was her life. Or rather, the end of her life.

She'd spent the hours after returning from the king's speech searching for a way into the tunnels, promising herself she'd escape and find her way to the dungeons to save Gulliver. But it had been no use. The door remained solidly shut, and she hadn't figured out how to force it open. Before long, she'd collapsed onto her bed, unable to make herself move again.

Tierney stared at her hands in the dark, wondering how they looked so weak when they'd once held immense magic.

"I'm sorry," she whispered, wishing the words could reach Iskalt, where her family, her twin, would never know what became of her. They wouldn't imagine she'd ended up in a fabled kingdom under the thumb of a ruthless king.

"What are you sorry for?" Keir's voice cut through the dark, and Tierney sat up so quickly her head swam. He stood near the entrance of the tunnel shrouded in darkness.

"What are you doing here?" She pulled the covers up to her chin as if that would shield her from this man.

His steps were the only sound other than the steady thumping of her heart, the rasp of her rushed breath. He stopped when he reached the settee and pushed a hand through his thick hair. "I'm not really sure." He paced across the rug, unable to stand still.

"It's the middle of the night, Keir." She didn't have the energy for this. "I need to be well rested to face my execution two days hence."

"Tierney." His voice was hoarse, as if he'd been using it often and loudly. "I won't let this happen to you. Give me time. I can convince my father to change his mind."

She very much doubted that. "Time is the one thing I don't have. Didn't you hear him?"

She crawled from the bed, aware of how her nightgown curved over her, leaving her in a state no man should see her in. Well, no honorable man. In Iskalt, she'd preferred the ... other-than-honorable sort.

Keir took a step back, his breath quickening.

Ignoring him, Tierney lit a candle and carried it toward the table in front of the settee. She set it down and lowered herself. "If I'm to be up, I will not be in the dark." She settled back against the cushions.

Keir returned to his pacing, one hand tugging at the collar of his uniform. "I just need to make him see …"

There was one thing Tierney didn't understand. "See what?" She cocked her head. "Why do you care, Keir? It would be easier for you if I was to die."

"Because it isn't right," he burst out. "You and I both know you're no Grima spy."

"Are you so sure about that?"

"I've known it since the moment you appeared in battle. My father knows it too. We've both heard the accounts of the men who saw your portal. He knows of your magic, the kind that requires no totem. If you could show it to the fae—"

"Then, your father would find a way to explain it away with crystals. No one will believe anything I say."

He shoved a hand through his hair again. "He's just punishing me."

"You?" Anger rose in her. "I'm to be killed, but you're the one being punished? Typical Vondurian male logic. It is the man who is the center of all things."

"I didn't mean …" He blew out a breath and dropped onto the settee, leaving ample space between them. "My father knows I … respect you."

"That's an odd way to say you'd like to bed me, Prince."

He looked as if she'd slapped him. "If I wanted to bed you, you'd know."

"Would I now?" She stood. "Good to know."

"You're a woman."

"Great observation." She whirled around, her hands on her hips as she glared at him. "Next, are you going to tell me Gullie has a tail?"

"No, I mean you're a woman who breaks all traditions of Vondur. You've taught my sister a new way to be, and I don't …" He paused. "I don't think it's a bad thing."

"Yeah, well, in my kingdom, we do not care what parts lie between a fae's legs. We certainly wouldn't execute someone for defying orders and saving a palace."

"That's not why—"

"Don't be an idiot. Of course that's why I'm to die. I challenged how things are done. It does not matter how many lives I save or what good I do. In the end, it only matters that I'm not someone who can be controlled. Tell me that's not true."

They were both silent for a long moment before Keir reached out, his fingers grazing Tierney's, sending a tantalizing shiver across her skin, down her spine. One finger hooked with hers, and he tugged her closer. "Come, sit. I do not want to be your enemy. Tell me who you are."

She swallowed back a sob as she returned to her seat. Her arm brushed against Keir's, and she closed her eyes, willing the tears at bay. "I've told you who I am. My father is the king of Iskalt."

"You are a princess, but that is not all. Answer me this, are you a threat to my fae?"

She opened her eyes, fixing him with an intense gaze. "Never. Keir, I don't want to be a threat to anyone. I just want to save my friends and go home."

"Your friends." He nodded, thinking.

"Friends might be a bit complicated for what the others are. Gulliver is my favorite person in all the realms, though, other than my twin brother."

"You have a brother?"

"A few of them. And two sisters. Plus, a million cousins, who are like siblings."

He broke eye contact, looking away, as if it hurt too much to see her, to find out she was more than he'd known. That there were fae missing her, hoping for her return.

"Then, there's Veren." She smiled at the relief she'd felt seeing him among the Grima soldiers. It was a piece of information she couldn't share with Keir. "My father wanted me to marry him, but Veren would make a terrible prince consort. He takes nothing seriously. He's not a friend, exactly, but it's my fault he's here, and I'm responsible for him."

A pretty face appeared in her mind, the one friend she didn't know the whereabouts of. "And Siobhan … she's kind. Too good for what I've done to her."

"I think it's honorable you want to save them all."

She shook her head. "Honorable would have been never endangering them in the first place."

"You cannot prevent danger."

"You don't know what you're talking about."

"Tia, I have led more men to their deaths in battle than I can count. Each of them weighs on me, but I never for one second believed I could save them all."

"You could end the war." There was a challenge in her voice.

"Not while my father is king."

"Then, maybe he shouldn't be king." She got to her feet, needing space.

Keir didn't give it to her, following her around to the other side of the settee. "Be careful of what you speak."

A harsh laugh burst out of her. "Why? I am to die regardless of the words that leave my lips. You say you will try to save me, but I'm like your soldiers, Keir. You can't prevent this while war still rages on." Not only war with Grima, but a deeper battle. One within Vondur itself between what was right and what was desirable.

Keir's fist crashed into a table, sending the chipped china on an empty tea tray scattering. The pot tipped over the edge, shattering as it hit the ground.

Tierney stared at it, letting the silence cover them. Whatever she thought of Keir, he wasn't strong enough for what he'd been given, not strong enough for his fae. "You're going to fail them."

He didn't respond, his eyes still on the broken china.

"These fae you're so worried about? Every day sitting in this palace, you fail them. They deserve better than a king sending them to be slaughtered on the front lines."

When he returned his gaze to hers, there was a burning desperation in his eyes. "And you have no war in Iskalt? Your father doesn't send men to die?"

"Men *and* women fight for their homes, but it is not this endless cycle. We have had peace in the four kingdoms since the day I ..." She clamped her lips shut. Revealing the extent of the power she possessed would be a mistake.

"Since you what?"

Well, she only had two days left to make mistakes. She wouldn't be Tierney O'Shea if she didn't take advantage. Lifting her chin, she stared at him with steel in her eyes. "I destroyed the prison magic."

"Prison magic ..."

Of course he wouldn't understand. "You and your father wanted to know how powerful I am? If we were in Iskalt, if my magic had not failed me, I could turn this kingdom inside out. I'd defeat all enemies single handedly. The power of Iskalt, Eldur, *and* Fargelsi runs in my veins. I was ten years old the first time I helped bring a king to his knees.

"So, tell me, Prince, why did you come here tonight? Was it so I'd absolve you of any wrongdoing? Tell you the best thing for your kingdom is to stand by your father and be loyal to his mindless pursuit of power? Are you sorry for what will be done to me?"

"I ... I don't know."

She pressed her lips into a grim smile and nodded. "Well, that's not good enough. Loyalty out of fear is no loyalty at all. It is only fear. You're scared to want power; you're scared to be something other than a bloodied soldier running from battle to battle. And in my last days, I have no use for fear."

"Tierney ..."

"I think it's best if you leave."

"If that is what you wish." He stopped at the entrance to the tunnels. "For what it's worth, I will try to save you."

Too bad it wasn't worth anything at all.

The door shut, leaving her alone once more. The sob she'd held on to pushed out of her, shaking her entire body. Tears hung in her lashes, and when she blinked, they dampened her cheeks.

Her knees weakened, and she slid to the floor next to the broken porcelain. Maybe the tea pot was her. Once it shattered, it could not be rebuilt.

And Tierney had been shattered the moment her portal brought her to these dangerous lands, the moment she lost her friends and condemned them to this place.

Everything that was coming for her was her own doing.

She hadn't lied to Keir about having no time for fear. Bone deep exhaustion overcame every emotion. She was tired of living like this, tired of suspicion and abuse. Tired of not knowing what came next.

An ending loomed near, but at least she could see it coming.

CHAPTER 25
KEIR

I think it's best if you leave.

Back in his room, Keir stared at himself in the mirror over the basin in his washroom, contemplating the most confusing princess he'd ever known. He'd admired her strength and force of will, but in the face of her execution, her will seemed to be failing her now. But Keir wasn't ready to give up. Not yet.

Splashing his face with cool water, he left his sparse rooms. Even as a prince of the realm, he had very little in the ways of luxurious comforts. Those were spared only for the king and the public areas of the palace.

The hour was early, and not even the maids were found going about their work in the dark corridors. The sun had yet to lighten the skies, but they could not afford to waste magic to light the halls at this hour. Keir hadn't slept at all. He spent the whole night trying to think of a way to talk his father out of the executions. It was ludicrous to think Tierney and her friend were Grima spies.

Keir quickened his pace, his footsteps echoing along the marble floors. The king's rooms were just down the hall from Keir's, and the guards were snoozing at their post. Using the barest hint of magic from the totem he'd acquired from Tierney, he quieted his steps and slipped into his father's rooms, closing the door silently behind him.

The king already sat at his enormous desk, which occupied the center of the room he'd converted from a sitting room to a private study. Even at this early hour, he was busy writing instructions for his officers to carry out. Vondur was now losing this war, and Turlach would resort to any means necessary to turn the tide back in his favor.

"I am busy, my son." The king didn't spare him a glance.

"I will be quick then, sire." Keir approached his father's white oak desk, resting his hands behind his back as a soldier would. "I believe the prisoner is who she says she is."

"Of course you do." Turlach continued to write his missives, his quill scratching across parchment.

"Too many things don't add up about this woman's sudden appearance in our land. Multiple witnesses saw her and her friend appear out of an icy blue light right on the battlefield. That coupled with their strange clothes and a myriad of other clues … She simply cannot be of Lenya. I am certain of it. As certain as I am that if she is executed, Vondur will pay dearly for her loss. I do not know how she came to be here, but we must tread carefully, Father."

The king set his quill aside, sprinkling a fine dust of sand across the ink to dry any excess. "You think you know more than I?" He arched a brow at his son. "I am the king, dear boy. I have access to information you could not imagine. You have nothing to worry about regarding the girl. She is but a girl, after all."

"But she is innocent."

"What does that matter?"

"What does that *matter*?" Keir stared at his father, aghast. "You *know*. You know she's not a Grima spy."

"I don't care what she is; she isn't of Vondur, and that is all that matters. Her execution is a means to an end. Something to refocus the fae's attention." Turlach folded his instructions, sealed the letter with a blob of red wax, and pressed his signet ring into the seal.

Tierney was nothing more than a pawn used to distract the Vondurians from the mess their king had made of this war. "And the fact that her father is a great king of a land we've only heard of in stories means nothing to you? A king with magic we cannot underestimate."

"Unless the man can travel across the burning lands or sail beyond the great storm, he can do nothing to avenge his daughter."

"You are a fool." The words left Keir's mouth before he could think better of it.

"And you are a child. A child who needs to listen to his betters." The king stood, still in his silk dressing robe. "Deserters fled the battle at the border. I would have you hunt them down and execute them as traitors."

How like the king to change the subject when the conversation displeased him.

"When we have lost more soldiers than we can afford, you'd have me slaughter more?" Keir stared at the king in disgust. "Has it occurred to you that they deserted you because they do not trust you to protect them? That you would throw them at the Grima soldiers like swine before the butcher."

"I demand loyalty. And I will have it." Turlach sorted through his missives, handing one to Keir. "You will find a list of their names here. I expect you to leave today. You have eight days to see to your task."

"Your timing is impeccable as ever, Father." Keir took the list. He would figure out what to do about that later.

"When you return after the executions, we will ride for the mines at Laous."

"The reserves?" Laous was the last remaining crystal mine in all of Vondur. Most believed it to be empty, like all the other mines in Lenya. "You would strip it of the only power we have left?"

He knew without asking that was exactly what his father intended. The Laous mines were the most valuable asset in all of Vondur. Set aside as an emergency reserve, the mines were abandoned more than a century ago when the then king declared them vital to the future of Vondur. No other king since had dared to reverse his orders.

"Magic is in short supply, but it is time to overpower the Grima royals once and for all. I will have a united Lenya under my rule. If I have to kill every last royal and noble in the Grima palace, then so be it. I will need magic to accomplish such a feat."

"And when you deplete our magical reserves, then what?" Keir had always known his father was power hungry. Any man who sought the crown for himself was. But he had never realized how little King Turlach cared for the fae he professed to rule. A king should be a benevolent ruler. Firm and unyielding as a monarch, but above all, he should put his fae first. Turlach would never be a true king as long as he thought only of himself.

"There is more than enough power left in Vondur for one king. And there will be no use for magic once we have peace. The remaining mines along the Grima border will be guarded more carefully in the future once they are firmly in my grasp. When I have won the war, I will declare a new reserve, and all will be well throughout our united Lenya."

"You will take magic from the fae at large and horde it for yourself like the tyrant you are."

"Watch your words, my son. I am your king. Just because you are a prince of Vondur doesn't mean you have any real power. Magic is not meant for the masses. It has brought us nothing but war."

Turlach was the worst sort of ruler. The kind who believed he was on the side of right, that his wants and needs surpassed all others. He would destroy them all in his quest for power.

Keir stuffed his orders from the king into his coat pocket. He would not be leaving just yet, but the king didn't need to know that.

"Where are we going?" Declan met him outside the king's chambers and directed him away from the other guards. "I know you're not going to let that innocent woman go to the gallows for nothing. So, what's our plan?"

"We're going to the dungeons." Keir turned a corner into the west wing, and together they took the winding steps down into the darkness.

"And what are we going to do when we get there?" Declan pressed for more answers, but Keir's mind was still trying to formulate a plan.

"I want to talk to the strange fae creature Tierney calls Gulliver."

"Again?" Declan groaned. "I find him ... disturbing."

"It's his feline eyes." Keir frowned. "They are unsettling."

As they approached the dungeon gates, the guards waved them through. Not many were at their posts this early in the morning.

"My Lord, how may we serve you?" A young guard gave him a deep, exaggerated bow. Just what Keir was hoping for. The young, eager, yet untested soldiers always drew the night watch.

"I need to question the spy." Keir reached for the ring of keys the boy kept around his bony wrist.

"Of course, sir. Right this way." He tucked the keys under his filthy shirtsleeve and guided them into the deepest part of the dungeons. "He was making the other prisoners nervous, so we moved him way back here. He seems more at home in the dark. Strange fellow but pleasant enough if you treat him with a bit of conversation and bring him his breakfast on time."

"We meet again." Gulliver's voice was rough with disuse.

Keir lifted a torch down from the wall so he could see the young man clearly.

"You're dismissed, soldier." Declan jerked his head at the guard.

"Thank you, sir." He left them and returned to his post.

"Fine bit of thievery, if I do say so." Gulliver climbed to his feet. "And I'm a master at such things, so I should know."

"What is he talking about?" Keir looked at Declan.

"I don't believe these belong to you, do they?" The flat end of

Gulliver's tail slipped into Declan's coat pocket, lifting a ring of keys. Declan staggered back away from the tail, snatching at the keys and tucking them back in his pocket.

"I didn't even tell you to do that." Keir grinned at his friend.

Declan shrugged. "I figured we'd need them."

"And what need do you have of me?" Gulliver's thin hands wrapped around the bars of his cell.

"Tell me again how you came to be here. The full truth, and use fewer words than last time." Keir crossed his arms over his chest. If he was even thinking about defying his father, he needed to know it was for good reason.

Gulliver mimicked his posture, his eyes drooping with fatigue. "At Tia's birthday ball, things did not go … pleasantly for her. She never wanted a big party. I'm her best friend, so naturally I was with her, along with two other friends, who just happened to be there with us. She wanted an escape. Somewhere her father wouldn't look right away. Tia's a powerful magician, but she's terrible at controlling her O'Shea magic—the ability to open portals into the human realm. So, we went there. That's where her mother grew up, so we stayed at the house there and had a small party for her with just a few friends."

Gulliver sighed, running a hand over his grimy hair. "The next evening, something went wrong when she opened a portal to take us back to Iskalt. It felt strange when we entered, but it was too late. We ended up here instead, right in the midst of your battle. I was captured right away, and Tia was with you, but I don't know what happened to our friends. I can only assume they're also here in Lenya somewhere."

"You say she has powerful magic yet it does not work here." Keir wanted to get to the bottom of this so he could help her, but she didn't trust him fully.

"If she hasn't used it yet, it's because she can't." Gulliver affirmed.

"Why can't she use her magic?" Declan asked. "It doesn't make any sense."

"Something is blocking her," Gulliver said.

"What about your magic?" Keir asked. "You were able to repel my power. Why can you use yours if she can't use hers."

"I have no magic to speak of. Not like you're thinking. I have defensive magic, meaning others' power will not work on me. It's part of my basic anatomy—or that's what Tia's mom claims. She's the one who grew up in the human world, so she knows all about science stuff."

"He's babbling again." Declan scowled. "I don't like it when he babbles."

"I don't like it when you interrupt my sleep, but here we are." Gulliver glared at him. "Are we done now? I'd like to go back to contemplating my impending execution now."

"You're coming with us." Keir nodded to Declan. "Let him out."

"Why would you help me?" Gulliver frowned.

"Because I need you."

CHAPTER 26
TIERNEY

"What does the daughter of Lochlan and Brea O'Shea have that no one else has?" Tierney paced across her room, wringing her hands together. "I have the magic of three kingdoms running through my veins." She balled her hands into fists as she paced. "Fat lot of good that does me now."

She hadn't slept at all. Her emotions ran the gamut between giving up and plotting to overthrow the king. At the moment, she was contemplating ways to challenge the king to the Comhrac. She could totally kick his butt and then take his crown. Maybe then, she could find a way home.

She was Tierney O'Shea, after all. And the O'Sheas did not give up.

"Think Tia! There has to be a way out of this." This was not how she met her end. Not after all she'd been through.

"It's just another challenge." She lifted her chin and squared her shoulders. "I have been trained by the greatest tactical minds of the age. I don't need magic. I can overcome that misogynist nit-wit of a king, find my friends, and go *home*."

"That's a great idea. Let's do that." Gulliver stepped through the secret door to the tunnels, and Tierney nearly fainted with relief.

"Gullie!" She raced to fling her arms around him.

He smelled awful, and he looked even worse, but she was so happy to see him. His thin arms wrapped around her waist, and his tail thumped against her back.

"I missed you." She pressed her forehead against his.

"That's great, but we don't have time for this. The castle will be swarming with guards and servants soon." Keir dropped a bag onto the floor.

"What's happening?" Tierney looked at him in confusion.

"It's not safe for you here. You and Gulliver are leaving Vondur as quickly as possible. Declan will escort you."

Tierney gaped at him. "It's not *safe*? Are you new?" She tilted her head at him. "And what, you're going to help me escape now? The same man who brought me here in the first place?" Something snapped inside her, and her fist slammed into Keir's too pretty face. "You think you could have figured that out *weeks* ago?" Her arm drew back for another punch, but Declan grabbed her from behind.

"Save that feisty spirit for the escape."

"Was that entirely necessary?" Keir dabbed at the blood trickling from his nose.

"You really want me to answer that?" Tierney growled, shrugging Declan off.

"Gulliver, you need to clean up." Declan nodded toward the washroom. "We need you to blend in with the servants. Though, that might be harder than it sounds given that tail of yours has a mind of its own. Not to mention the eyes."

"I'm used to blending in." Gulliver scooped up the set of clothes Keir offered him and marched into the washroom to fill the basin with cool water from the pitcher. "Too bad Tia can't just portal us out of here."

"How about you offer some feasible solutions, Gullie?" Tierney wasn't in the mood for any more what ifs and if onlys. She didn't have magic, but that didn't mean she wasn't capable of getting them out of this now that they had a means of escape.

"I have a dress for you. One of Eavha's. I think it will fit." Keir set the bag on her bed and started searching through the contents.

"No, that won't be enough." Tierney shook her head. "Your father will expect something like this. Especially once word reaches him of Gulliver's disappearance from the dungeons. He's going to be looking for a woman traveling with a man with strange eyes." Tierney eyed the prince's clothes.

"You can't be serious?" Keir frowned at her, smoothing a hand over his brocade jacket.

His clothes were simple but fine enough. Not too princely or outlandish. They were the perfect disguise if a little wrinkled and too big.

Tierney searched through the bag, finding another dress for her but nothing else. "You can wear this back to your rooms." She handed him her robe.

"I can't tell if she's serious." Keir looked to Gulliver for help.

"She's serious." He shut the washroom door behind him.

"I'll wear your clothes and braid my hair like a man's." She looked around the room. "Declan can give me his hat."

"She's mental." Declan looked positively scandalized.

"Chop-chop, boys." Tierney clapped her hands together. "Let's get over the fact that women can indeed wear pants and dress like a man and the world as we know it will not come to an end."

"No one would suspect her." Keir shrugged. "But what do we do about the fit?"

"How much time do we have?" Tierney glanced through the window at the sky that was just beginning to lighten.

"Not much." Keir shed his jacket. "This is going to swallow you whole."

Tierney marched to the mantle for Ariella's sewing kit she'd left there. "I'll do what I can to make it work."

She tried the jacket on. The shoulders were too large, but there wasn't much she could do about that. The sleeves were too long, but she used Ariella's scissors to cut them and folded them up, sewing a quick seam to keep them in place." Tierney was awful at needlepoint, but she'd seen the seamstresses work often enough that she could at least mimic their work.

She couldn't do anything about the length either, but she gathered some of the excess fabric in the back and secured it with several stitches to hold it together. She was butchering the job, but she didn't need it to look finely tailored. She just needed it to pass for fitting.

After altering the pants in the same way and adding a belt and one of her own shirts, she examined herself in the mirror over the wash basin.

"She still looks like a woman," Declan declared.

Tierney frowned, releasing a few notches in her belt to hide her figure behind the bulk of her clothes. Buttoning the jacket and placing Declan's hat over her strawberry blond hair, she turned around.

"Better?"

"You still have obvious girl parts from the waist up." Gulliver shook the water from his hair, slicking it back into a tail at the nape of his neck. "Can you not hide those things?"

Tierney glared at him and snatched up a sheet from the bed, folding it into a square. She stuffed it down her front, securing it with her belt to help fill out her torso to be more like a man's.

"That's … actually not bad." Declan gave a nod of approval. "Just don't look straight at anyone we meet. You're too pretty to be a man."

"Thanks. Can we go now?" Tierney glanced around the room for anything she didn't want to leave behind. With Gulliver here, that was all that mattered.

"Declan will lead you through the tunnels and out through the servants' quarters to the stables." Keir paced nervously, wiping his hands on the silk robe he was wearing over his underclothes. At any other time, she would have laughed her head off at the prince wearing the floral wrap.

"Once I change clothes, I will create a distraction to buy you some time to reach Brenandi village. I don't know where you'll go from there, but I wish you good speed and good luck." He clearly wanted to say more but shook his head, passing a totem and a key to Declan, and left through the tunnel door.

They waited several long agonizing minutes until they heard Keir return to speak with the guards after he'd gone to his rooms to change. Declan waved them into the tunnels.

Tierney felt a sense of winding down a large spiral funnel as they rushed through narrow tunnels, forever turning right and sloping downward. The air grew damp and fetid, and they'd gone down so many twists and turns she'd never find her way out again.

"This way," Declan whispered, peeking through a crack in the wall. He produced a key for the door. An ancient-looking key—it even looked as though it were made of bone. "The stables are just across the courtyard. Keir will have horses waiting for us. We have to move fast, but we can't call notice to ourselves."

Tierney nodded, her heart in her throat. After weeks of being cooped up in her prison room, she was eager to be on her way. She grabbed Gulliver's hand and gave it a squeeze. In his servant's clothes, with his tail tucked away, he looked like any other Vondurian. Except for the cat eyes, of course.

"Let's go." Declan stepped into the humid morning. The sky smoldered with the fires of the burning lands. The sun wouldn't be too far behind.

Tierney reminded herself to take long, purposeful strides like a man, keeping her head down. Few soldiers were about this early, and true to his word, three horses waited for them in the stable yard, along with a young stable boy.

"Mr. Declan, sir, I have your horses ready." The boy led a proud chestnut mare forward.

"That's a good lad." Declan turned to help Tierney into the

saddle, but she shook her head, taking the reins and mounting the horse on her own. She was itching to gallop far away from this place.

Gulliver scrambled up on his horse, and they turned toward the palace road.

"Ho there, soldier!" Guards flooded the yard from the stables, like they knew they would be here.

Tierney tilted the brim of her hat down, hoping to conceal her face.

"What have we here?" A familiar grating voice sent a dagger of fear through her heart. "Going somewhere, Declan?"

"Torrin." Declan's shoulders fell. "Just escorting this young man and his servant to Fangar village. He's my cousin, actually. Taking him to visit my mother."

"And does this young man have a name?" Torrin stepped forward, grabbing Tierney's horse. "Blast!" Torrin released the bridle like it burned him, waving his hand and swearing.

"Go, Tia!" Declan shouted, gripping the totem in his hand.

Tierney slammed her heels into her horse's flanks, Gulliver right behind her.

She took the stable yard gate at a leap and charged down the palace road, glancing over her shoulder to make sure Gullie was with her.

"Hurry, Gullie!" she cried, pulling on her reins in the next moment to skid to a halt. Soldiers barred the road. Guiding her horse to turn, her heart thundered in her chest. They were surrounded. The palace guard were everywhere.

"I'm so sorry, Gullie. This is all my fault." Tears burned her eyes, and her magic pulsed just out of reach.

Gulliver pulled up beside her. "It's okay, Tia. None of this is your fault." He grabbed her hand as the soldiers closed in on them.

"We're going to die because I was mad at my father for wanting the best for me." She hung her head, utterly defeated.

CHAPTER 27
TIERNEY

Tierney had been in danger before. She probably should have feared for her life many times, but somehow, she'd always believed everything would turn out all right. She'd had faith her parents or her uncles would show up to save her, save the day.

Like the day she'd been flirting with the village boy in Iskalt, the one who'd gotten too rough. The magic that blasted out of her had been too strong, and she'd injured him. When his friends turned on her, she ran, not wanting to level the entire village with her power.

Then, Uncle Griff had been there. All he'd needed to do was give them one intimidating look, and they left her alone. She'd cried in his arms, and he'd whispered that she should have flattened them all, something her father never would have approved of.

But this time, there was no Uncle Griff to save the day. Uncle Myles wasn't here to make her laugh and forget just for a moment. Uncle Finn couldn't wrap her in one of his warm hugs and tell her it was all going to work out.

This time, her prison cell was in the dungeons as she waited. And waited. But she wasn't alone. Gulliver, sporting a new cut, where they'd smacked him across the face, sat next to her, his hand in hers. Neither spoke.

And Declan. Sweet, Vondurian Declan, best friend of the prince, protector of the young princess he didn't know was in love with him … he sat with his back against the bars. The guards hadn't handled him as roughly as Gulliver and Tierney, but he'd been put in here all the same.

Once again, it was because of her.

Tierney leaned her head on Gulliver's shoulder. "I'm sorry, Gullie. For all of this."

He didn't respond for a long moment before he rested his head on hers. "I made the choice to follow you when I knew your portal magic was erratic."

"But—"

"No, Tierney, from the moment I met you, I knew I had to be with you for all the adventures you had, and there have been so many. I don't regret it. I don't regret you."

"But if it weren't for me, you'd be home in Myrkur right now."

"Without you, I'd be there without my favorite fae in any of the realms."

She tilted her head to look up at him. "Really?"

"I would stand with you through anything. I love you."

A smile parted her lips. "If this is you telling me you're *in* love with me, you may have to let me giggle a bit before you kiss me."

"I'm not going to kiss you."

"Are you sure? You looked like you were definitely going to kiss me."

He tucked her closer to his side. "I hate you."

She curled into him. "I love you too. Just as long as you don't kiss me."

A sigh escaped his lips. "Trust me, that would be gross."

Tears stung her eyes as she laughed through the mix of emotions. "I think you're gross too. Glad we cleared that up." Gross because he was her brother, nearly as close to her as her twin. Sometimes, she thought Gulliver was another part of her soul that had been put in a second fae. When he was with her, she was complete.

In the hours since their failed escape attempt, neither Keir nor Eavha had been to visit them in the dungeons. Tierney assumed it was because the king kept them away. She'd seen the way they were with Declan. The three of them were a set just like her, Toby, and Gulliver.

"Declan?" she said softly.

He lifted his head, no emotion showing on his face. "Yeah?"

"Thank you." She cleared her throat. "For trying to help us. I'm sorry you ended up here because of it."

His expression turned sad. "This shouldn't be happening to you. Keir does not believe you're spies, and I trust him. Too many innocent fae have died. If we do not do the honorable thing when we have the chance, then we have no honor. I'd rather die with honor than live without."

Die … Tierney didn't believe they'd kill Declan. He was one of them. As soon as she and Gulliver were gone, he'd be released to resume his duties. She was sure of it.

Heavy steps echoed down the long, narrow hall encased in stone before six guards stopped at their cell. The one in front, Torrin, didn't try to hide his pleasure as he said, "We've come to take the prisoners."

"No." Tierney gripped Gulliver more tightly. "We're supposed to have one more day."

Torrin cocked his head and smiled. "Change of plans, *Princess.*" He said her title with a sneer, like it was a joke. Sticking the rusted key into the lock, he yanked open the bars, and guards flooded the cell, ripping her from Gulliver. She held tight to his hand as another guard pulled him from the floor, shoving him against the wall.

"Gullie," she cried as her hand slipped and only their fingers hooked around each other. A tear tracked down her face. Her fingers disconnected from her best friend's. Her legs threatened to give out beneath her.

It was happening. It was real.

With two guards holding her up, she managed to get her feet under her and stumble down the dank corridor, up the narrow stairs, and into the palace. It was eerily quiet save for Gulliver's heavy breathing behind her, the guards' armor rattling as they walked.

Tierney's pulse pounded in her skull. *Thump. Thump.* Her heart was going to explode right out of her. This was her moment. There was no hope left.

Thump. Thump.

Out in the courtyard, the sun shone hot overhead, and she closed her eyes, letting the warmth wash across her face. Noise pushed in at her, a crowd come to see the execution of the spies in their midst.

The sun's warmth vanished as a shadow loomed overhead.

It wasn't until her eyes fluttered open and she took in her surroundings that she saw the gallows waiting for them. Erected sometime during the night, it was rudimentary, basic, but she guessed it didn't take much to hang someone by their neck.

That was when she noticed ... there were three nooses hanging. Three. Oh no. She jerked around, ignoring the pain of her arm twisting as the guard held it tightly.

Declan was there, also restrained, his gaze finding hers in confirmation. He'd known this was the consequence. She was being called a Grima spy, but he was a traitor who helped Grima spies. A large man with boulder-like shoulders spat on Declan as they passed through the crowd.

So soon after the siege, to help anyone from Grima was worse to them than actually being the enemy.

Tierney wanted to reach out to Declan, to squeeze his hand and find some way to help him. But she couldn't. Instead, she met his gaze unflinchingly, trying to communicate with her eyes how sorry she was.

Declan issued one deep nod. He'd made peace with this during those long hours in the cell. She'd had days and still couldn't come to terms with it.

It was then that she decided she'd be like him in the end. Strong. Unyielding. These fae would not take her dignity as well as her life.

Lifting her chin, Tierney straightened her spine and looked ahead toward the gallows. The three ropes swayed slightly in the breeze. A hooded man stood behind them, his hands clasped in front of him, his feet shoulder width apart. Waiting.

For them.

The guards jerked her forward, shoving through the crowd cheering for her demise. She didn't fight them. She would not show them her fear. There were six steps leading to the top of the platform, and she took each with the care of a princess.

If she were truly treated as a princess, she'd never face the noose. At least, not among the four kingdoms. Back when executions happened, nobles received the blessing of a quick beheading. A slow hanging death was reserved for commoners, as unfair as that was.

This king was sending a message.

Tierney was not who she claimed, but truly a common fae from Grima. If she had been, maybe she wouldn't be in this situation.

The guard shoved her onto the platform and positioned her in front of the far noose, the one directly in front of a crying Eavha. She stood at the back of the courtyard nearest the palace doors, but Tierney couldn't miss her or the way her own heart clenched at the sight of the closest thing she had to a friend in Vondur.

Go, she secretly urged her. *You shouldn't see this.* The Vondurian princess remained where she was, her eyes shifting from Tierney to Declan, who now stood behind the third noose.

Tierney searched the courtyard for Keir, wanting to see his stern face once more, to take him in and remember the arrogant soldier who'd saved her in the battle when she first arrived. The one with mesmerizing eyes and a stubborn personality. She'd hated him and respected him. Wanted him and fought with him.

Now, in her last moments, he wasn't even here.

She didn't know if he just hadn't been able to face Declan's death or if he really was as cold as he liked to appear, but his absence was like a knife twisting in her gut.

Stretching a hand out, Tierney tried to reach Gulliver. It wasn't until he lifted a hand toward hers that their fingers connected.

"You and me, Tia," he said, tears dampening his cheeks.

She was sure her face glistened as much, if not more, than his. "Always."

Their eyes locked, never straying from one another. Over his shoulder, she saw Declan, face forward, eyes on the crowd. He had no tears, no regret on his face.

But she and Gulliver couldn't claim that strength as they clutched each other. His cat-like eyes were as wide as she'd ever seen them, and they shone with tears.

She never expected this adventure to end in such a way. Even through all these weeks as a prisoner, she'd always expected to find a way home.

Searching inside herself, she let the remnants of her magic calm her and found a spark of something she didn't recognize at first, something she hadn't felt in a long time. Recognition.

"Toby," she whispered to herself. She felt her brother. It was just the faintest hint of him, like she was sitting across the palace of Iskalt in her rooms and caught the barest whiff of the cook's winter berry tarts as they baked. Just enough to know they were there.

Her magic sparked at the recognition, but not enough to do more than warm her already hot skin. It hit her then, why her magic didn't work. She was too far from Toby. Her mom called him her battery, a human term, because he supercharged her power. But did he make it work in the first place?

She hadn't lost it. Something about the fire plains cut her off from her twin and his influence.

She was about to die, and yet a smile curved her lips. If she'd made it home, her power would have returned. Knowing it hadn't failed her was some comfort in overcoming the dread inside. At least when she died, she'd have both Gulliver and her brother with her. Holding on to the spark of Toby she felt, she gave Gulliver a calm smile. "We've got this."

His eyes stayed on hers until a hood was thrown over his head, cutting off their connection. The hangman pried their hands apart before dropping a hood down on her head.

The entire world went black.

Her blood rushed in her ears, making her think of the ocean, the raging seas on the shores of Iskalt, both dangerous and magnificent. She kept that image in her head as the noose settled down around her neck and the unforgivable heat of the sun warmed her face. She thought of her home as a hand slid the knot tight until the fibers scraped her skin.

"Iskalt." She sighed, the words only for her. "I'm home in Iskalt." Soon, she'd see the grandmother she never knew, the one she was named after. And her father's father would be waiting for her.

"Please." The word was inaudible. "Take me back to Iskalt." She pictured her room with the giant four-poster bed and the massive hearth that roared with constant fire. The chill of the morning air as she sat in her sleeping gown, drinking tea in front of the flames.

Skating on the frozen lake. Walking through the village. Kissing boys in secret hideouts. Laughing with her siblings. Hugging her mom.

The way her father smiled when he was proud of her and supported her when she failed.

She'd sought adventure, trouble, failing to see she'd had everything right there at home.

Tears slipped from her eyes as she waited for the push that would send her off the platform, waited for the weight of her body to drag her down. If she was lucky, the fall would snap her neck.

"I'm sorry, Dad." She shouldn't have run, shouldn't have been so harsh with him.

A presence stepped up behind her, but he didn't push. Not yet.

Instead, a familiar voice rang out. "Today, we punish Grima for their crimes against Vondur," the king said. "The loss of life is never to be taken lightly, but I will always do what I must to protect this kingdom, to protect my fae."

The crowd was stunningly silent.

"I hereby condemn Tierney O'Shea to death by hanging alongside her accomplices Gulliver and Declan. Let us hope their souls find the peace they have not allowed us."

A hand gripped Tierney's shoulder, and she closed her eyes despite the darkness already surrounding her. Her feet stumbled forward on the platform, her toes hitting the edge. It was time.

"Stop the executions!"

Keir.

All the breath rushed out of Tierney. Keir had come.

"What is the meaning of this?" the king demanded.

A confused chatter came from the crowd, but the hand on her pulled back.

She didn't know what was happening as the din grew louder, but then Keir spoke again over the noise. "There will be no executions today, Father."

"And on what authority do you give such an order?"

"When a challenge is issued, all matters of the kingdom must stop until it has been satisfied."

"A challenge?"

"The Comhrac."

Tierney strained to hear every word, knowing the king could not turn down a nobleman contesting his crown. He would have to fight.

"And who dares to invoke the Comhrac against me?" Turlach seethed.

Keir didn't answer at first, and Tierney could see him in her mind standing tall above the crowd, not cowering to his father as he uttered the one simple word that would decide her fate.

"Me."

CHAPTER 28
KEIR

The king sneered from his spot high up on the dais, turning his attention to the crowd that had gathered in the courtyard to witness the executions. He would have them all believe he wasn't rattled by the prince's challenge, but Keir knew his father. He could see the uncertainty in his eyes.

King Turlach was a renowned swordsman from his days before staking his claim for the throne. He was still feared across all of Lenya, but he was older now. His time as king had softened him physically. Keir was the better swordsman, and his father knew it.

"You dare challenge your own father for the throne of Vondur?" Turlach sat back on his make-shift throne, an expression of mild boredom on his battle-scarred face.

Keir lifted his sword high, clutching the totem that hung from his neck. The magic swirled around him, empowering his voice. "I challenge you, King Turlock Dagnan, to the *King's* Comhrac." He brought his sword down in a powerful arc, letting the blade scrape across the stones at his feet as he spoke the binding words to begin the challenge.

"You dare? Why?" The king's face paled in the sunlight, showing the first signs of surprise that his son would invoke the magic to bind them to the laws of the King's Comhrac. There was no escaping the duel now.

"You have left me no choice, Father. This is the only way to save three innocent lives today. If that means the crown of Vondur falls to me, then so be it." Keir walked slowly along the aisle made by the guard through the crowd. He couldn't spare a glance for Tierney or Declan—even Gulliver—with the hangman's noose around their necks. A tremble wracked his body. There was no alternative. He refused to let his best friend die for a lie meant to make his father look better in the eyes of his fae. Not when the king cared nothing for those fae.

"Are you sure about this?" Turlach asked. "The King's Comhrac is a fight to the death. You won't be able to back out this time."

Keir nodded, thinking of his duel with the Grima prince. That Comhrac was different. In Vondur, when challenging a reigning monarch for his throne, the only way out was through death. "I am." He took a steadying breath, feeling more certain about his decision. King Turlach would never be a good king. Keir had never wanted the crown for himself. He wasn't a ruler. But if he could bring an end to this war and help move his fae forward, maybe he was the right man for the job.

"Very well. Name your terms." The king nodded to his stewards, who moved to clear the center of the courtyard. The noblemen of the court mingled with the commoners around the edges of the space, soft murmurings echoing in the silence.

"Should I win, I will earn the crown of Vondur like all kings before me." Keir couldn't believe he was doing this. "Should I lose, then the victor will honor my final wish as the magic of the King's Comhrac demands."

"And what is this final wish?" The king mocked him with his tone, but Kier continued.

"Release the prisoners Declan, Tierney, and Gulliver. Declan will be allowed to go his own way, unhindered, taking his family with him. Tierney and Gulliver will be allowed to find their way home to

Iskalt by any means available to this crown or that of Grima. It will be on you, King Turlach, to abide by the laws of the King's Comhrac."

"And if this fabled land doesn't exist?" Turlach's brow rose to mock him again.

"It does, but should they be unable to find a way across the fire plains, Tierney and Gulliver shall take refuge wherever they choose, and no harm shall come to them."

"They are Grima spies. You would have me let them go free?"

"These are my terms. The magic of the King's Comhrac is binding."

"Very well."

The king's scribe, working furiously to record the proceedings, raised his hand. "Challenger Keir Dagnan, who do you charge with the duty of carrying out your final wishes?"

"My sister. Princess Eavha Dagnan shall oversee the release of these prisoners should I fail today." Keir shared a look with his sister. She lifted her chin, even as tears rolled down her cheeks. She would be equal to the task.

"You must choose a man of this court." The king shook his head. "It is not our way to put such burdens on a young lady."

"It may be our tradition, but it is not against our laws. I stand firm in my decision to entrust Princess Eavha Dagnan with the task." She was the only one the king would not punish.

"I accept." Eavha's voice rang out strong and clear. "I wish you success this day, but should you fall, I will see your final wishes fulfilled."

Her words were binding. Said for all here to bear witness, the rules of the Comhrac were adhered to on Keir's side.

The king stepped down from the dais, facing the crowd. "I accept your terms, son, though it saddens me greatly that my own children would turn against me."

"You've given us little choice, Father." Keir bowed his head to show how much the decision weighed on him. "Name your terms."

"Should I win, I will remain King of Vondur and obey the terms of the Comhrac to the best of my ability." Turlach turned scorching eyes on his son. "Should I lose, my son, Keir Dagnan, will become king and fulfill my final wish. I require you to carry on in my stead to bring all of Lenya under one rule. You will see the task done, and the war will end with a united Lenya."

Keir gave a deep bow to his father. "It will be as you wish."

"The terms are satisfied," the scribe announced. "Each party will name their second."

"Torrin will fight as my second." The king gestured to the Captain of the King's Guard. His eyes filled with triumph, as if by choosing first, he'd taken the one swordsman Keir would have chosen for himself.

"And who will be your second, Prince Keir?" the scribe asked.

"I will ask Tierney O'Shea to fight as my second."

Excited murmurs swept across the courtyard.

"You cannot choose a woman." The scribe's face grew an angry red. "You must choose someone schooled in the art of swordplay."

"I believe your words are the exact law." Keir stood with his hands clasped behind his back. "The law does not say the second in a King's Comhrac must be male, but a fae trained for such duels."

"A woman of Lenya would never be trained as such," the scribe argued.

"If someone will take this foul hood off my head, I could answer for myself." Tierney struggled against the guard restraining her on the gallows.

"As she has claimed since the moment she came to Vondur, Princess Tierney O'Shea is not of Lenya." Keir nodded to the guard to remove the hood.

The guard hesitated until the king nodded his approval.

Tierney took a gulp of fresh air, her face flushed with the heat of the day and the stress of her situation. "I am heir to the throne of Iskalt. I have been trained by the best swordsmen—and women—of the four kingdoms. I will accept the role as second to Prince Keir in this challenge, but I have a question for the prince. Why me? Why not one of the men you've fought beside all your life?"

"Because if I lose, I will not have a Vondurian soldier forfeit his life as well." Keir spared a look for Declan, the one he would have chosen as his second in any other duel to the death.

"It seems you have thought of everything." The smile that spread across Tierney's face would have frightened him if she were not on his side. "Someone hand me a sword, and let's get on with it."

Keir had spent most of the night devising this plan. Should he win or lose, those he cared for would walk away from the gallows protected by the terms of their custom. It was Eavha's responsibility to see to that, and he knew she would never let him down. Now, he just needed to defeat his father and take his throne. Whatever happened after that … he'd cross that bridge when he got there.

Tierney stumbled down from the gallows, her legs shaking beneath her.

The palace stewards brought in an array of dueling weapons, buying Keir and Tierney a moment to choose their weapons and devise a plan. Keir would use his own sword, but Tierney would need something her smaller hands could wield.

"Are you sure about this?" Keir pulled her toward the table. "I'm betting my life on your word that you can actually use one of these things."

"You can count on it." Tierney lifted a slim sword with a blade nearly her full height. She tested the weight and balance of the weapon, moving with graceful steps. The tension left Keir's shoulders, and he relaxed, trusting by her posture with the sword that she indeed knew what she was doing.

"Will I have to fight him?"

"The king?" Keir shook his head. "Not likely. Unless he kills me or injures me in an illegal move. If he breaks the rules, then you can avenge me."

"And Torrin?"

He nodded. "You may take action against Torrin if he interferes. He may only step in to defend the king if I break the rules."

"And what are the rules?" Tierney strapped the sword to her belt. Her calm demeanor set Keir at ease. He'd made the right decision.

"Same as any fair fight." Keir lifted his sword from its scabbard at his hip, letting it fall back in place. "He cannot attack me when my back is turned. He cannot deliver a killing blow if I have been unarmed. And he absolutely cannot use magic."

Tierney nodded. "It must be an honorable fight to the death so there can be no question of the victor's win."

"Exactly. Your job is to watch my father and Torrin for any dishonorable behaviors and interfere when necessary."

Tierney placed her hand on his shoulder. "You can count on me to watch your back while you do what you must."

"I am about to face my father in a battle to the death, and I don't even know if it's the right thing to do for our fae." Keir searched her face for absolution and found it shining within the depths of her eyes.

"A just ruler puts their fae first above all things. That is what you are doing today."

"What would you do in my situation?" Keir grasped her hand with his trembling one.

"I would make the same choice you have made."

He nodded, finding solace in her words.

"Challenger, please take your position along with your second," Sergeant Murphy announced. As second in command of the king's guard, he would oversee the King's Comhrac.

Keir rested a hand along Tierney's lower back. "You will stand opposite Torrin."

"Good luck." Tierney crossed the makeshift arena to take her place on the sidelines.

Keir took position at the center of the ring of spectators, his back to his father's.

"You will relinquish your totems." Sergeant Murphy moved to

stand before them. "In a King's Comhrac, no magic is allowed." Keir removed the ebbing totem from around his neck, letting it fall into Murphy's outstretched hand. There were slightly differently rules when the prize was a crown.

"Any last words, son?" the king taunted.

The prince sighed, feeling the weight of his choices pressing down on him. Yet he believed in what he was about to do. "As a child, I only wanted your approval. For so long, I wished for you to be a better father. As a man, I just wish you had been a better king so I would not have to bear the burden of your crown. You have failed me. You have failed your daughter, and you have failed Lenya."

"And you will pay for your insolence with your life," Turlach's voice took on an angry edge.

"At my command, you will take five paces and turn to face your opponent." Sergeant Murphy stood on the dais to address the duelers. "This will be an honorable duel, gentlemen. You each know the rules. Every man, woman, and child in all of Lenya know the rules and expects you to abide by them. Today, you fight for the right and the honor to rule Vondur."

Keir bowed to the fae as was the custom, yet his father refused.

He has no honor. Keir rested a hand on the pommel of his sword, waiting for Murphy to give the command.

"Return to your stance, Torrin." The sound of a sword leaving its scabbard rang around the nearly silent courtyard. Tierney stood firmly with her sword pointed at Torrin's chest. "The duel has not begun. I suggest you step outside the circle and lower your weapon until such a time as it is needed."

Torrin gave her a scathing glare before he took three steps back.

"You will await the command, Captain." Murphy stood to his full height. "Or I will ask the king to appoint another as second."

Torrin gave a curt nod, returning his sword to his scabbard.

Sergeant Murphy gave one final look around the small arena. "Begin!" His voice echoed across the stones, and Keir took his first step forward, counting off his steps along with Murphy.

"Behind you!" Tierney shouted, and Keir turned on his fourth step to find the king nearly upon him. Keir snatched his sword from his hip just in time to block the first blow.

"Order!" Murphy snarled over the crowd's excitement. "Seconds, you may enter the fray at will to protect your champion according to the rules."

"What is a Comhrac without a little rule breaking?" A wicked smile crept across Torrin's face.

The prince retreated into himself, blocking out the roar of the crowd. He trusted Tierney to do the job he'd given her and to take care of herself. She was the fiercest woman he'd ever known, and he knew she was up to the task. He also knew he could trust Sergeant Murphy to do the right thing as well. He would keep this duel under control.

Keir needed only to fight. He was a career soldier. That was what he was born to do. He gave his father the lead, meeting him blow for blow. Turlach was a strong man when he was in his prime, and he was still stronger than most men his age. But Keir was the better swordsman. His blade moved to block and parry as he fought defensively. The king would put on a show, bringing the offense, driving them around the ring.

Occasionally, he heard a snarl from Tierney or the clang of swords that were not his or his father's. The shrieks of the court and the murmuring of the commoners sounded like a distant storm rumbling on the horizon.

The king stumbled, sinking down on his knee. A lesser man would have gone in for the kill, despite the rules, but Kier was better than that. He stepped back, taking a deep breath. With a growl of irritation, Turlach surged to his feet, his great sword arcing toward Keir with all his strength.

Keir stepped aside, dancing just out of reach. As the king began to grow weary, Keir transitioned from defensive steps into a more aggressive strike, driving his father back across the ring and around in circles. Sweat poured down Turlach's face, but he kept up with his son, matching his pace.

Keir's arms grew heavy, and he began to sweat like his father. For every two steps Keir gained, he lost one. The king was better than he'd anticipated. The years of leading battles yet not fighting in the thick of them had not softened the king as much as Keir had believed.

He needed to end this. Soon, before he ran the risk of losing. Moving faster, he managed to gain the upper hand, driving the king back to the center of the ring. With a quick flick of his sword, he drew first blood, slicing Turlach's forearm with a deep cut.

With blood gushing from his wound, Turlach was forced to move his sword to his left hand, putting him at a disadvantage. Dark blood stained the ground, red rivulets running between the tiny stones.

Torrin took up his place beside the king. For a brief moment, Keir fought them both, but a streak of strawberry blonde hair moved between him and Torrin, pushing him back from the king and the prince.

At any other time, Keir would have taken a moment to marvel at the sight of Tierney O'Shea battling Torrin like a seasoned soldier on the battlefield, but he was losing ground again and had to focus on the immediate threat.

"This is your own doing, son." Turlach lumbered toward him, the heavy weight of his broadsword crashing down on Keir's slimmer blade. The force of the blow nearly knocked the sword from his hand, and he was forced to take another step back. "I would have made you my heir after we won the war against the Grima."

"That is not our way," Keir spat out the words, losing more ground.

"I was going to change our traditions. Once Lenya was united under my rule, we would have built a dynasty upon the ruins of Grima."

"Then, this is your doing." Keir panted. "You crave too much power, and it will be your undoing. I would rather that be by my own hand than at the expense of too many lives we cannot afford to lose. Our fae matter, Father. But to you, they are nothing but bodies to throw at the walls of Grima."

"Power is everything." Turlach's voice echoed unnaturally. His movements became more fluid, and his blows landed with more accuracy. It was as if he'd received an influx of energy and stamina.

Keir saw the telltale signs that the king was using magic, though he had relinquished his totem at the onset of the duel.

He couldn't keep up with his father's renewed attacks. His own movements slowed, and he struggled to lift his arm. That was when he saw it. The small glow of crystal embedded into the pommel of the king's sword. It was barely noticeable, but a totem's power wasn't about its size but the potency of the crystal itself. In another age, the pure crystal totems were smaller, with untold magical reserves within their depths. They were nothing like the lesser totems they relied on today. But his father was king. He had access to powerful things left to him by the previous kings of Vondur.

Turlach intended to win this fight, even if he had to cheat to do it.

Keir stumbled, and Tierney rushed forward, her sword at the ready. He held his hand out to her, sending her back to the sidelines.

"You were right about one thing, my son." The king surged ahead, shoving the point of his sword through his son's chest, giving it a cruel twist before he pulled back. "You will have to take this crown off my cold dead body before it will ever be yours."

Glee filled Turlach's eyes, clearly expecting the fight to be over, but Keir refused to give in to his injuries. He stood tall, clutching his chest with his free hand, he brought his sword down with all the strength he could muster.

"If that is what it takes." Keir lunged for his father, using the momentum of his body to land the final blow. The king's eyes flashed with surprise and grew cold an instant later as his head parted ways with his body.

King Turlach's head rolled across the floor, and his body fell forward with a loud thump that echoed in the silence of the yard.

Keir stumbled to his knees, clutching the gushing wound in his chest.

"The terms of the King's Comhrac have been met. Long live King Keir!" Sergeant Murphy's voice rang in his ears. Gasping for breath, Keir couldn't look away from his father's dead eyes.

Something heavy settled on his brow, along with an enormous weight of responsibility. He was King of Vondur. His vision tunneled, his eyes landing on his sister for a single moment before his world went black.

"Take him to the healers."

"He is our king now, take him to the healing pools."

"Back up." Tierney shoved through the crowd around Keir, heedless of her own injuries. Her hair hung limp where it escaped her braid, and her arms felt useless and heavy, but it was over. Yet, she feared saving three lives had cost Keir far too much.

"Give him room to breathe!" Blood trickled down her face from the gaping wound Torrin had given her. Her face was numb to the pain, but the ugly wound would likely scar her for life.

"Back up!" Tierney pushed and shoved. The lords and ladies of the Vondurian court were all too eager to help their new king, to ingratiate themselves, but if they didn't give him some air, they were going to smother him.

"That's enough!" She roared, drawing her sword and pointing it at the circle of worried faces. "I said. Back. Away. From the king." She brandished her blade in a wide arc, pushing the nobles back.

"Keir?" Eavha scrambled to his side, her face streaked with tears. Her hands fluttered over his pale face. His chest moved with labored breath, and his wounds oozed too much blood. Declan came to sit with his friend, cradling his head in his lap at the princess's side.

"Put pressure on the wound," Tierney instructed Eavha, casting her eyes around the dusty courtyard.

In the chaotic moments after Turlach's death, Torrin had fought his way through the crowd toward the open front gates where the king's guards barred him from leaving.

"Sergeant Murphy, please take Captain Torrin into custody until the king decides his fate."

"It would be my greatest pleasure, Princess." Murphy gave her a courtly bow.

"Please consider yourself Captain of the Guard for the moment. As second in command, you will replace Torrin until the king is well."

Tierney didn't wait for his reply. There was too much to do to ensure a peaceful transition of power within this volatile kingdom.

"Tia!" Gulliver ran toward her, his arms still bound behind him, but someone had at least removed the hood from his head.

"Gullie!" She used her sword to cut through the bindings and fell into his arms, so grateful for what Keir had done to save their lives.

"Are you okay?" His arms wrapped around her, and she nodded.

"I just really want to go home."

"Me too. But at least we aren't dead."

She laughed at the understatement. "Stay with me. I have to see to the situation, but I don't want you out of my sight."

"Fae here really don't like my tail." Gulliver's ever errant tail wrapped around her arm. "I think they'd hang me for that alone."

"We need Keir to recover." Tierney led them toward the dais to check on Keir. "He is the only one who believes we are who we say we are. He's our key to getting home."

She crouched beside Keir, relieved to see some color returning to his face as his eyelids fluttered open.

"Rest, brother." Eavha brushed her fingertips over his face. "We will take you to the healing pools." She looked to Tierney for guidance.

"Right, I need four men to help carry his Majesty." Tierney, still holding her sword at the crowd, pulled several strong looking men to help Declan and Eavha with the king.

"No." Keir groaned. "Not the pools. Call the healers."

Tierney stooped beside him, studying his wound. Turlach's sword pierced his chest just under his breastbone. He likely missed the heart, but Tierney knew nothing of the healing arts. "You've lost a lot of blood, Keir," she murmured so as not to alarm the court. "The pools would be best."

"They'll also put me out of commission for several days if not longer. I can't afford that much time." His eyes clouded with pain, but he was lucid. Were she in his shoes, she would want the same.

Tierney nodded. He must establish his rule immediately. He would have to deal with the pain.

"We need to move him to his rooms," Tierney spoke softly to Eavha. "Can you summon the healers?"

She nodded, rising from her perch on the dais steps. "I'll see to his care. Can you dispatch this mob?"

"I'll do what I can."

Eavha stood tall, clearing her throat to get their attention. "Ladies and gentlemen of the court, the king is injured but all will be well soon. I will personally see to his care. In the king's absence, Princess Tierney will see to your needs. She has the full support of my brother's reign. Treat her as you would him."

Eavha and Declan swept into the palace, leading the way for the men carrying the injured king.

"Please be patient." Tierney stood on the dais as exhaustion began to sink into her bones. "We will bring you news of the king's health as soon as possible. I would ask the servants to please return to your duties. Ladies and gentlemen of the court, you may return to your individual pursuits."

Tierney nodded to the crowd of onlookers, leaving them to their gossip and speculation. Taking Gulliver's hand in hers, she set off across the courtyard to the palace doors. "Captain Murphy, a word?" Tierney approached the seasoned soldier.

"Of course, Princess." He left a furious Torrin with six of his men.

"We must see to King Turlach's ... remains." The severed head and bleeding body was a gruesome sight at the center of the courtyard.

"I have already called for my men to deal with the remains; they will be here shortly. As the customs of the Comhrac demand, Turlach will receive a funeral of state befitting a king of Vondur."

"Thank you." Tierney's shoulders drooped with her exhaustion.

"Thank *you*." Murphy bowed deeply. "I have never seen a woman fight so fiercely. I am honored to have witnessed your role as the king's second. Honored and impressed beyond words."

"That was nothing." Gulliver laughed. "You should see her when she's really mad."

Tierney smiled, nudging her best friend with her elbow. "Perhaps Vondur will learn that its females are more capable than your custom dictates."

"Perhaps we have been overzealous to protect the ladies of our kingdom when it seems we should have been teaching them to protect themselves."

"Wise words." Tierney smiled. "I would like to see how he is doing; may I leave you in charge here?"

"You have no need to worry, Princess Tierney. My men and I will keep order until the king is well."

Tierney breathed a sigh of relief.

"Let's get out of here." Gulliver guided her down the hall to the doors leading to the royal residence. "The sooner that king is well, the sooner we can get back to Iskalt."

Tierney just hoped it would be that easy.

They found their way to Keir's rooms, and Tierney was surprised to see him sitting up in bed, his chest bare. The livid arc of the entry wound grew an angry red around fresh stitches. The healers were busy mixing up a poultice to ward off infection.

Eavha and Declan sat on either side of him. Eavha trying to get him to drink a medicinal tea, Declan regaling him with a recap of the duel, focusing on Tierney's efforts to keep Torrin from cheating.

"How is he doing?" Tierney asked one of the healers working a mixture of herbs into a fine paste under a large pestle.

"He has lost a lot of blood, but he will recover. All thanks to you, my Lady." The healer bowed, a bright smile on her face. It seemed much of the court was happy with the outcome of the King's Comhrac.

Gulliver stayed with the healers, asking them to see to Tierney's injuries when they were done with the king. She approached the bed. Keir looked every inch the king, but a sad one.

Gulliver came to stand beside her, wrapping his tail around her wrist so the flat leaf-shaped tip rested against her palm.

"I owe you a debt of gratitude." Keir's voice grated in his throat, and Eavha pressed another cup of tea into his hands.

"As do we." Gulliver gave a bow. "I thank you for saving our lives, even though you do not know me."

"It was enough that you were Tierney's greatest friend and an innocent." Keir bowed his head in return. "I could not let my father use you like that."

Tierney moved to sit beside him when Eavha stood. Gulliver followed her as if afraid to leave her side. "Are you okay? How do you feel?" She took his hand in hers.

"Like I was skewered." Keir lifted a brow in faint amusement. "You are free to leave whenever you like. Neither you nor Gulliver are prisoners of Vondur. Though, if you decide to stay, I will help you find your missing friends and a way for you to return to your home."

"I don't know if such a way exists, but I'd sure like to try," Tierney said softly.

"It is the least my fae can do to repay you for all you have done. Both during the siege and today. I could not have survived the Comhrac without you. Vondur owes you a great debt, Princess

Tierney O'Shea." He moved to stroke her cheek along the open wound. "I would have my healers see to this immediately."

Exhaustion engulfed her like a cloud. All she wanted was a bath, something for the pain, and a long rest in a comfortable bed.

Chapter 30
TIERNEY

Tierney stepped out of the washroom into the room that had once been her prison cell. She was anxious to put everything behind her.

"Jeans, really?" Gulliver stared at her human attire. "Shouldn't we be blending in, not standing out?"

"I don't give a crap." Tierney stuffed the few belongings she wanted to take with her into a bag. A change of clothes and some provisions for the road. By this time tomorrow, the Vondur palace would be far behind them. "We've got a long road ahead of us, and I intend to be comfortable. If I never see another dress, it will be too soon." She packed a pair of trousers, a spare tunic, and the t-shirt she wore upon her arrival in Lenya.

"I will be glad to leave this place." Gulliver echoed her thoughts. "Your prison cell was a lot nicer than mine, but the experience wasn't one either of us needs to have again." Gulliver tucked in his tail, shoving a hat over his head to hide his feline eyes.

"What?" He looked at her. "Is my Dark Fae showing?" He looked behind him trying to see if his tail had escaped.

"That's just it." She scowled. "I don't want to see you hide your

Dark Fae features. It's who you are, Gullie. And you're beautiful just the way you are."

"I agree." He flashed a smile. "But while we're on this side of the fire plains, I'm not going to risk freaking anyone out." He tossed his bag over his shoulder. "Are you ready?" He held his palm out to her.

Tierney grabbed her best friend's hand. "Let's blow this popsicle stand."

"Do you even know what that means?" He snorted.

"Nope, but my mom says it." She shrugged, ignoring the shooting pain through her heart. She needed to see her mother again. If only to tell her how amazing she was. She understood Brea Cahill O'Shea in a way she never had before. She couldn't imagine what it must have been like for the girl who'd thought she was human to be swept away to a fae land full of magic—one at war no less.

"You're leaving?" Eavha stepped into the room from the secret tunnel entrance. "You can't, Tia. We need you." She crossed the room.

"We have friends who need us." Tierney took the princess' hands in hers. "We don't know if they are well or imprisoned like we were. We have to find them before we can go home."

"Keir has promised to help. He will send out a delegation to Grima to find your friends."

"That's exactly the kind of thing that will stir up trouble between the kingdoms again. Keir needs to focus on establishing his rule and negotiating peace with the Grima queen. The relationship between the kingdoms of Lenya is still too rocky."

"And he will need your help developing new relationships. My brother needs advisors who can think beyond the confines of our customs and the rivalry with the Grima court. He needs you."

"Keir will do fine without me. As will you." She squeezed Eavha's hands. "I need you to wait until tomorrow to tell him we've left." Tierney wasn't so sure he would let them leave—not that he would imprison them. She feared he would talk her out of it. "Give him this." She lifted a sealed letter from her bag and handed it to the princess.

"You won't say goodbye?" Eavha's eyes filled with tears.

"If we are able to return with our friends before we leave for home, we will. I would like to see you all again."

Eavha threw her arms around Tierney. "I wish you all the best. Please keep me informed of your progress. I want to know the moment you're reunited with your friends."

"I will. I promise." Tierney hugged her back. "You remind me of my little sisters. I'm anxious to see them again, but I will miss you."

Eavha turned to Gulliver. "Take good care of her."

Gulliver snorted a laugh. "I can guarantee you that will go the other way. But I will do my best, Princess." He gave her a deep bow.

"Do you have everything you need?" Eavha asked, stalling the inevitable goodbye. "Provisions? Clothing, horses?"

"I've asked Captain Murphy to provide horses. Discretely of course," Gulliver explained.

"We'd best be on our way before the day grows too hot to travel." Tierney gave her one last hug.

"Take this!" Eavha called out. She ripped something over her head and pressed it into Tierney's hands. "I know you can't use the magic of the crystals, but keep it close, you may find need of it. It's very valuable. Keir gave it to me from the royal treasury. Apparently, Father wasn't the only king to horde power for himself."

Tierney's eyes widened at the sight of the pure crystal. The orange stone shone bright in the light streaming in through the windows, with only a faint streaking of the turquoise color she'd come to recognize from the weaker crystals most Vondurian magic wielders used. This was no ordinary totem. Vast stores of magic pulsed within the stone no bigger than her thumb. It was then she realized the crystals that were plentiful all across the four kingdoms—the ones Myrkurians called fire opals for their orange color—contained the most potent magic.

"Declan and Keir are teaching me magic." Eavha beamed a smile at them. "I'm no good at it, but I'm trying."

"Keep trying new things, Princess." Gulliver winked. "It suits you."

"I will never forget your kindness." Tierney lifted the priceless necklace over her head, tucking the stone under her tunic. She would guard it with her life, even if it proved to be nothing more than a souvenir of her time in Vondur.

Taking to the tunnels, Tierney and Gulliver made their way through the winding narrow passages down into the inner workings of the palace to the door leading to the stable yard. Gulliver was convinced he could pick the lock.

Tierney waited patiently as he worked it with the tip of his tail, lifting the tumblers and sliding the door open. She would never again take her magic for granted. Her time in Vondur, cut off from the magic she'd had for most of her life, forced her to see how difficult life could be without it. If she ever got it back, she would treasure it always.

"Your poor tail is all crooked." Tierney eyed the tip of Gulliver's tail before he tucked it away. "Does it hurt?"

"It will flatten out again. It might be bruised, but I'd risk losing it altogether if it got us out of this place." They stepped into the sunlight, the heat of the day already intense at this early hour.

Captain Murphy waited for them with two horses saddled with camp provisions. It all felt eerily similar to the last time she was here when the king's guard swarmed them and she first realized she would likely not escape her impending execution. It felt like an age had passed since then, though it was but a few days.

"Are you sure you don't want an escort?" Murphy asked. "I know you're perfectly capable, Princess, but it would be my honor to take you to the Grima border at the very least."

"You have far more important work to do, Captain." Tierney mounted her horse. "We will do just fine with the maps and the gear you've provided." She and Gulliver had studied the maps and decided on their route into Grima. Their first goal was to reunite with Veren since they knew he was with the queen's guard. From there, they would look for clues of Siobhan's whereabouts.

Tierney didn't know when or if she would ever reach Iskalt again, but for the moment, she was glad to be the architect of her own destiny again.

"I have one more provision for you." The captain removed a package from his jacket. A golden medallion flashed in the sunlight as he handed it to Gulliver.

"If you are stopped by the Vondurian militia or the king's guard anywhere within our borders, show them my seal." He nodded to the medallion. "No one will attempt to keep you for questioning should they find your Dark Fae features alarming, Master Gulliver."

"Thank you, Captain." Tierney could hug him for thinking of Gulliver's safety.

"The papers are forgeries." He passed the package to Tierney. "Keep them hidden on this side of the border. There is a patent of nobility there, claiming you are the great-granddaughter of an elderly Grima nobleman who recently passed. It will give you a level of status within the Grima court, but not enough to warrant scrutiny."

"You've thought of everything." Tierney beamed at the captain. An enormous weight lifted from her shoulders.

"My king will be sad to hear you've left us, but he would want me to pave the way for your journey." He backed away from their mounts. "Take the southern road until you see the smoke of the fire plains on all sides, save the east. There is a small village there, where you will find an inn. Ask for Madame Maeve, she will see to your comforts."

"Thank you, Captain." Gulliver nodded, nudging his mount forward. "We are grateful."

"It is the least Vondur can do for you both." Murphy waved and Tierney turned her mount toward the southern road, eager to be one step closer to home.

Fires illuminated the skies well after the sun sank below the horizon. Smoke churned on all sides of the road that had faded into a dead end.

Tierney and Gulliver, unused to the smoke of the fire plains, had tied scraps of fabric over their faces to shield them from the plumes of black smoke.

Tierney stood along the edge of the road, facing west. Her eyes burned with the brilliance of the fires, smoldering with a vibrant red heat so intense, even from this distance, that her skin scorched and her lungs burned. But she couldn't look away. Something pulled her toward the fire plains. A force so strong she thought if she gave into it, she would wander right into the lava fields to her death.

"Home is that way." Tierney pointed into the depths of the hottest fires. She could just make out a shimmering river of lava in the distance.

"How will we ever make it across that?" Gulliver's tail hung lifeless behind him.

Tierney closed her eyes, reaching for the magic she knew was still inside her, somewhere buried deep. She couldn't have lost it so completely. She could feel it pulsing just beyond her reach.

The ground trembled beneath them, and Tierney reached for Gulliver's hand, hanging onto her horse's reins to steady her.

"Shhh, it's okay, girl," Tierney crooned. "It's just a bit of an earthquake somewhere out there."

"It's a volcano." Gulliver pointed to a streak of red-hot lava shooting into the sky. A moment later, another mountain belched a cloud of ash and smoke.

"It's the Vatlands," she muttered under her breath, bracing herself as the ground continued to shake beneath her.

"You're just now realizing that?" Gulliver gave her a worried look. "We're on the other side of the Eastern Vatlands."

"I know." She waved his concerns away. "Look at all the seismic activity here, Gullie."

"I'm aware," he said dryly.

She turned to him. "Do you think that's what has me cut off from my magic? All the volcanos and earthquakes are disrupting whatever connects me to Toby and makes my magic work on the other side of the fire plains?"

Gulliver frowned. "It's a feasible theory."

"Which means, unless we can figure out how to travel through that—"

"Or around it. Over it, maybe. Not under it." Gulliver shook his head, muttering to himself.

"Then, we're stuck here forever." Tierney's eyes burned with unshed tears. Tears she refused to let fall. It might be hopeless, but she wasn't ready to give up yet.

Turning her horse away from the churning smoke, ash, and fire, she led them down the southern road to the village Captain Murphy told them about. "First, we rest and eat a decent meal. Then, we find Veren."

"Hopefully, he'll know what happened to Siobhan." Gulliver sighed, tucking his tail back under his clothes to shield his Dark Fae features before they entered the village.

"Maybe one of them will have their magic and we can figure out our way home from the Grima shores." Tierney didn't spare a last glance toward home. She wasn't defeated. Not yet.

EPILOGUE
TOBY

Toby O'Shea stared at the fiery lands he'd never laid eyes on before. He'd learned of the Eastern Vatlands of Eldur. He'd studied the maps and traveled close enough to the fire plains to feel the heat but never this close.

"What do you see, Toby?" His mother stepped close behind him, resting her hands on his shoulders tense with his emotions.

He had not felt the presence of his sister in months. Not since the night of her birthday ball when she sought refuge in the human realm along with three of her friends who hadn't been seen since either.

"Is it your sister? Has she pulled you here?" their father asked, standing on Toby's other side. The king's voice strained with the stress her absence had caused him.

Their father had looked for Tierney in the human realm, finding the evidence of a birthday party Toby hadn't been invited to. It stung that she would leave him behind, but when the crown princess of Iskalt failed to return days later, he knew something terrible had happened. Tierney O'Shea was no longer in the human realm. He would sense her if she was.

In all the time since, Toby had thrown himself into finding her, using the limited magic he had to reach for their twin bond. The bond they'd shared all their lives.

At first, he couldn't find their bond at all. But as the days and weeks passed, he studied his every emotion and thought, deciphering his from his sister's. Hers were weaker, hardly noticeable, but they were there. He had known when she was happy. When she was afraid or lonely.

And then, a week ago, he'd experienced her fear. The terror so great, he could feel the hangman's noose around his own throat. Her fear turned into determination. She was happier now. She was free.

Toby pointed at the pools of lava in the distance, with their billowing black smoke. "She's on the other side."

The story continues in
Fae's Refuge: Queens of the Fae Book Eight.
Turn the page to dive in.

QUEENS OF THE FAE
BOOK EIGHT

FAE'S REFUGE

MELISSA A. CRAVEN
M. LYNN

MYRKUR KINGDOM
NORTHERN VATLANDS
FARGELSI KINGDOM
LOCH VILLANDI
SOUTHERN VATLANDS
ELDUR KIN
DRAGUR FOREST
VINDUR CITY
ELDUR
LOCH LANGT

NORTH EASTERN KAT LANDS
NGDOM
HUNTING LODGE
VALE OF STORMS
FIRE PLAINS
TAL
LENYA
ORIMA KINGDOM
THE BURNING SEA
MINES
VONDUR KINGDOM
CITY
THE ROCKY SEAS OF LENYA
THE GRIMA SHOALS

She couldn't stop moving.

Siobhan McGowan had never been in the human realm before. Not until a few weeks ago, when she entered a portal unwillingly. Princess Tierney hadn't meant to do it, she was certain of that. They'd known each other since they were little girls running around the palace together. Her friend would never intentionally hurt anyone.

But her magic was a different matter. The princess was powerful and sometimes she didn't know her own strength.

Exhaustion warred with her need to get home as she let herself take a brief break on the grassy hilltop of the Irish countryside. That was what a human had told her this place was called. Ireland. It was beautiful, with lush rolling hills, grazing sheep, and steep cliffs that dropped off into turbulent seas. Yet, there was also a starkness to the landscape, one that soothed her. It reminded Siobhan of her home among the rocky mountains of Iskalt.

In her weary state, she wasn't sure she could have handled brilliant blue skies or a blazing sun. The gray day suited her.

She lay back in the grass, wishing she could close her eyes for just a moment, but now was not the time. She'd come so far, and she was almost there. She could rest when she was home. After she'd delivered her message to the king and queen.

In the human lands, there was only one place to enter the fae realm without portal magic.

The rift.

That was what the people of Myrkur called the delicate tear in the veil between their lands and the human realm. Ten years ago, during the war for the prison realm, the Dark Fae king tried to conquer the human world, spilling the darkness of Myrkur through the rift. Now, all that remained to remind them of that time was something Siobhan wasn't even sure she could find.

But she wouldn't give up. She had to get home, had to find out what happened to Tierney, Gulliver, and Veren.

With a deep sigh, she heaved her tired limbs up to continue toward the clearing where the invisible fae village of Aghadoon once stood. At least, that was what she'd heard in the years since the war. She hadn't known that was where she was headed at first. She only knew she could sense the tear, like her home was calling to her. Not with words. She hadn't gone completely insane. But the air buzzed with an energy that pulled at her. It dared her to search the queen's old farmhouse until she found a collection of what humans used for money. It then tugged her across the sea, using all modes of human transportation. At first, it was overwhelming. Then, exhilarating. She'd always had a secret interest in all things human. She'd even studied the basics of the human world with their flying contraptions and fast ships, but it was so different than she'd expected.

Siobhan would pay Queen Brea back if she ever managed to return to Iskalt. For all she knew, she was wandering into the middle of an unfamiliar land with no hope of finding the passage between the worlds, one that wasn't supposed to be visible on this side. But the pull was stronger here. She could feel it pulsing in her veins, calling her home. She didn't want to think about what would happen if she couldn't find it.

Every night, she replayed what happened in the portal in her mind. One moment, she'd gripped Tierney so tightly she swore they'd never part, and the next, an unseen power slammed into Siobhan's chest, forcing her back out of the portal.

The impact when she'd landed in front of the farmhouse had stolen her breath, but it took her a few moments to realize something had gone very wrong, that she wasn't home in Iskalt.

And that she was alone.

She only hoped she would find Tierney the moment she arrived in Iskalt and everything would be all right again. It was what kept her going.

"My father will be happy with these new revelations," she mumbled to herself, thinking of how much he hoped she and Tierney would find their way to each other. Talking to herself was a new hobby. It gave her something to hear other than the wind in her ears.

It wasn't until the reality of her situation sank in that she realized she truly had hoped the princess would choose her, that they could be happy together. Tierney O'Shea was special, at least Siobhan thought so. The princess cared about other fae, and she showed it in her every action. There was no one braver … or more reckless. If the king truly forced her to marry an Iskaltian noble, Siobhan vowed she would make herself the best candidate for her hand.

"Who are you kidding, Siobhan?" she muttered as she trudged up the next hillside. She would prove no match for the likes of Veren Rhatigan, with his courtly charm and handsome face. Not when she was so utterly … rough around the edges. That was what most thought of her. She'd been raised to be her father's heir. The keeper of the mountain boundary between Iskalt and the Northern Vatlands—a wild country few could navigate. She would be the Marchioness of Belmore Keep one day. A noble title, but she would always be more comfortable in the saddle than as a lady, curtsying at the right times and saying all the right things. Most fae her age never tried to see past her well-worn leathers or the sword she was rarely without. She might be more warrior than lady, but she was still a prominent member of the noble class, and that alone made her suitable for their future queen's hand in marriage.

"I'll just have to try harder," she vowed. "One more hill." She clenched her fists as she gave herself a pep talk. Her legs ached, and a sheen of sweat and grime coated her normally matte brown skin.

Thankful for the strange human clothes instead of the dress she'd worn to Tierney's ball, she pushed through the burn. Her trousers were made from some kind of black fabric that stretched and moved with each step, and the large shirt hung off one shoulder and let air move underneath it to cool her.

Loose dark curls escaped her bun, sticking to the back of her neck, and she pushed them off to get some relief.

And then, she reached it—the top of the hill, where she could see over the land to the sea. A vast plain stretched across the valley. The rift was close, she could feel her homeland, like an old friend calling to her. She wasn't sure what she'd expected to see, but it certainly wasn't this.

It wasn't nothing.

Yet, there was no sign of the always moving village that once inhabited these lands, no sign in the sky directing her where she needed to go.

It was a blank canvas of green grass, waiting to be filled with color and hope. But she had no more hope to give.

Siobhan dropped to the ground, exhaustion finally winning out. The impact reverberated up her spine. She'd been so sure it was here, that this was the way home. She could still feel it tingling under her skin, that overwhelming sensation that home was just within reach. But maybe she'd put too much hope into a feeling when she had too little to go on.

If she'd been smart, she would have stayed at the farmhouse and waited for someone to come find her. They would have eventually. But Queen Brea was said to only visit her old home once or twice a year—that the people knew of. She'd tried to be patient, but after a few days the inactivity drove her mad. Siobhan needed to know if Tierney and Gulliver were okay. Veren too, she supposed.

She curled her legs up, hugging her knees to her chest. Tears fell from her eyes, tracking through the sweat and dirt on her face. "Tierney, please be okay."

Anger swept through her. Anger at this realm, at the magic that got her here, at the stupid rift between worlds that had given her so much hope. How had she thought she could find an invisible tear in the sky? Something no one in the human realm was supposed to be able to spot.

Her heart ached, but it was the familiar ache that led her here, the one she'd taken as a lead rope guiding her to where she needed to be.

"No. I'm done listening to invisible forces." Done listening to magic.

The ache grew, squeezing her heart until she gasped and clutched her chest. She bent over, trying to breathe. Pain seared through her chest, and she got to her knees. "Please." Whatever it was had to stop. It had to let her go.

Lifting her eyes to the horizon, she noticed the sky growing dimmer. The clouds blocked out the brilliant colors she'd seen so many times on her journey, but there was no mistaking the setting sun. Was the moon already above her, hidden by the clouds?

A drop of rain hit her cheek, and the rope around her heart pulled tighter. A scream ripped from her lips. It was like her magic was trying to shred her from the inside out, drag her heart right through her chest.

Siobhan managed to get to her feet. She started down the hill, her steps faltering as she stumbled and righted herself. The pain eased up the slightest bit, and she picked up the pace.

More rain broke free of the clouds, washing the human realm from her skin, cleansing her of everything these last weeks had put her through. Physical and emotional.

By the time she made it to the clearing, the pain was back to a dull ache and her clothes were drenched.

Her eyes darted around the open space, looking for anything, everything. Yet, it was empty, save for the rocks and sparse grass underneath her feet, the drops of water hitting her cheeks. An eerie silence surrounded her, only punctuated by the rain pounding into the ground.

"Why am I here if this won't get me home?" she screamed, knowing there was no one there to answer her.

She snatched a rock from the ground, wishing she had something to break. Instead, she threw it as hard as she could. As it arced through the sky, she realized it hadn't made her feel any better.

She pivoted so she could look for shelter for the night and figure out what was next in the morning. Then, she stopped and looked back to where the rock she'd thrown should have hit the ground. It wasn't there.

Her legs too tired to run anymore, she stumbled toward where it had vanished, and that was when she noticed it. There was a space in the air the rain couldn't pass through. Instead, it looked as if someone held a bucket, collecting it before it could hit the ground.

"The rift," she whispered, inching closer.

Fear gripped her, and she hesitated, her heart kicking into high gear. It pounded so fast it drowned out the rain, drowned out the human world entirely. What if the rift sent her to some other unknown place? Like Tierney's magic, what if, somehow, it rejected her, spitting her back out?

What then?

Closing her eyes, she tilted her face to the rain as her magic grew stronger inside her. Full night would be upon her in no time, she could feel it. She asked herself what Tierney would do, but she knew the answer without thinking. She'd jump in with both feet, fear never even crossing her mind.

But Siobhan was not Tierney O'Shea.

She thought of her father, alone without her there at the too-large Bellmore Keep. He was most likely beside himself with worry. "I'm coming home, Father," she whispered, opening her eyes. She was a warrior. She knew what it meant to be brave in the face of danger.

With a deep breath, she reached a hand out, following the rain in its descent into the void. Her fingers disappeared from view, and the first thing she felt was warmth. It enveloped her hand, beckoning her closer, urging her to let herself disappear into another world.

Taking a step, she let more of her arm fade into the rift. The smell hit her, and she smiled. There was something distinctly sweet about the fae realm—a scent she couldn't attribute to anything else. The scent of magic, as comforting as freshly baked bread, as sweet as Gelsi berry pie, though she wouldn't dare eat that.

A smile curved her lips, and she took one last step. The drumming of the rain disappeared, and sunlight nearly blinded her as she fell the rest of the way, thudding into the hard earth between two giant boulders.

The ache in her heart disappeared completely, but now her back screamed in agony. The mountains of Myrkur did not soften the impact like the thick grass at the farmhouse or even the packed snow of Iskalt.

Rolling onto her side, she groaned.

But she'd made it. She knew it for certain the moment she was through. Maybe not home in Iskalt, but this was her world.

Water hit her face, and she realized the rain was still falling through the rift. She shifted out of the way, basking in the warmth of the sun. A shiver raced up her spine as the chill from her drenched clothes sank in. But they would dry, and everything would be okay.

A laugh bubbled out of her. And then another, until she couldn't stop. She wanted to kiss the ground, to dance in honor of the magic that showed her the way. But she would do neither of those things. Despite her current appearance, in this world, Siobhan was of noble birth.

So, she picked herself up, rubbing a sore spot on her back before straightening her shoulders. She just had to find someone in Myrkur who could help her, who'd sell her a horse in return for a great reward from her father.

The distinct flap of a Dark Fae's wings rent the air. Maybe she wouldn't have to search one out.

Siobhan looked to the skies, finally spotting the brilliant color of the fae's wings highlighted by the sun. She had tattoos stretching across dark skin and leather armor.

Siobhan had seen her before. Riona. Tierney's aunt. She heaved a sigh of relief.

Before she could call out to her, a line of guards rushed into the mountain gap, their heavy armor clanging together.

Griffin O'Shea marched forward and lifted his visor, revealing pale skin, a shock of auburn hair, and intense violet eyes, magic sparking in their depths.

Something wasn't right here.

She opened her mouth to speak, but she didn't get the chance.

Riona landed next to her husband, her wings folding in.

"As guardians of the rift, we do not allow passage here from the human realm." No recognition showed in his eyes, but why would it? She'd never actually met the fabled warrior. Griffin turned to his soldiers. "Arrest her."

It was odd to see snow-capped mountains outside her bedroom window after so much time among the sweltering temperatures of Vondur. The Grima "palace" sat among the mountains near the rocky coast, far enough from the fire plains that they experienced the seasons.

The sight of snow never failed to send a pang of longing through Tierney O'Shea. Part of her wanted to hike up to the mountaintops just to feel something familiar, but Lord Cormac Agnew—the man who would have everyone believe he was regent over Queen Bronagh—assured her she would die before she ever reached the peaks of those mountains. Between the sheer altitude and freezing temperatures, the heights of Grima were a trial.

Tierney still struggled to think of this place as a palace. It was lovely, and comfortable in the extreme, but it reminded her of the hunting lodge her family owned in the farthest reaches of Iskalt. Grand enough, certainly, but it was an odd sort of kingdom here in Grima, where rolling green hills and valleys spanned jagged coastlines and rocky seas few ships could navigate stretched as far as the eye could see. The mountainous terrain to the north faded back into the fire plains and were nearly impassable, from what she'd learned.

The same fire plains that trapped Tierney from returning home from Vondur, trapped her here in Grima as well, and it seemed the mountains and treacherous seas were equally determined to keep her from finding safe passage home.

"Stop sighing, Tia." Gulliver brought her a cup of the rich, hot beverage that reminded her of hot chocolate from the human realm. Nowhere else in all the fae realms had she ever experienced anything as wonderful as chocolate. Her mother would be all too eager to trade powerful crystals for cartloads of this stuff.

"I miss home." Tierney moved to sit on the plush settee at the center of the common room she shared with Gulliver. A cheery fire burned in the massive fireplace, and stuffed heads of every kind of antlered creature in all of Grima hung on the walls, staring down at her in judgment.

"Me too, but I could get used to that view and this sweet milky heaven in a cup." He sipped his chocoah. "And the beds, Tia. The beds here are like sleeping on little fluffy clouds."

Tierney smiled. It was wonderful to be back with her best friend in a place of relative safety. But they were wasting time waiting for the queen to return from her survey of the army at the border between Grima and Vondur.

She still couldn't believe how welcoming the people of Grima were the moment she and Gulliver came to the palace asking to see Veren. Lord Cormac knew all about how they'd arrived in Lenya through the portal by mistake. He threw the doors open wide and welcomed them inside to await the queen's return.

It seemed Veren had ingratiated himself to the Grima general on the battlefield, and then later to the queen herself. Tierney had no doubt his charm had saved his life, though she knew firsthand how false that charm could be.

"I could love it here." Tierney sipped her chocoah, dipping a scone into the sweetness at the bottom. "If I could go home whenever I wanted, Grima would be the best vacation spot in all the fae kingdoms."

"And Vondur ranks dead last on that list." Gulliver flopped down beside her, putting his feet up on a fluffy footstool.

"We should probably clean up." Tierney set her empty cup aside. Their common room looked like a battle had come through. Discarded clothes and books lay everywhere.

"It's weird they don't have the usual servants here." Gulliver sighed. "That's the best part about being a guest in a palace; I don't have to see to my own laundry."

"We don't have to do our laundry now, Gullie." Tierney shook her head at her lazy friend. "We just have to send it down for laundering with the morning maids."

"This palace has weird rules," he grumbled, snatching up the suit coat he'd discarded after last night's formal dinner with the queen's uncle.

"It's not weird; it's just different." She folded up her stained overcoat, where she'd spilled wine on it at a luncheon picnic a few days prior. "I kind of like it." There were servants but none dedicated to a single royal or noble—not even the queen herself. Instead, there were maids, valets, pages, and any number of servant roles Tierney was accustomed to, but they served everyone in their small corners of the palace. The lady's maid who helped Tierney dress for formal functions also attended three other ladies staying in guest rooms along this corridor. It was efficient and left Tierney and Gulliver to care for themselves in most things they could easily manage on their own.

"Leave your dirty clothes in the closet at the front door, and the scullery maids will see to it in the morning." Tierney returned to her room to pick up a few more articles of clothing that needed washing.

They had been treated well upon their arrival at the Grima palace. Everything they could need to live as nobles had been provided. But Tierney liked how independent it felt to see to her own household chores. She drew her bath, washed and dried her hair, and even swept the floors herself. No one fussed over her or treated her like a helpless princess.

She liked the system here so much that if she ever made it home, she just might talk her father into making a similar arrangement in Iskalt.

"What do we do with books we've finished?" Gulliver peeked his head into her room, a stack of books in his hands. "Do I have to take them back to the library? Because I'm not sure I could find it again without a map." The lodge was a rambling structure, but it was an odd one. Where the palace in Iskalt was made up of many floors with grand staircases and towers, the Grima palace was all one level with vast rooms and hallways scattered across the rocky terrain. Endless corridors lined with windows overlooking cliffs, waterfalls, and cool mountain lakes provided some of the most beautiful scenery Tierney had ever seen. But it was easy to get lost without an escort.

"Leave the books in the hall by the door, and the page boy will return them for you." Tierney stripped the sheets off her bed and set them aside for the maids to take to the laundress. She shook out a fresh set and went about making her bed. She found the task a fun novelty.

"You're such a weirdo, Tia."

"How very human of you." She glared at him. "Uncle Myles teach you that one?"

"Of course. He's where I get all the best human-isms." Gulliver stuffed half a pastry in his mouth.

An urgent knock sounded at the door to their suite. "Princess Tierney?"

The familiar voice nearly brought tears to her eyes.

"Veren?" She dropped her sheets and ran back to the common room at the sound of his Iskalt brogue.

"Your Highness." Veren crossed the room, taking a knee before her. "It is good to see you, though I wish it were under better circumstances. Lord Cormac has just told us of your arrival. You've been trapped in Vondur all this time?"

"I think you got the better deal." Gulliver clapped him on the back. "But we're glad to see you are well and not lost in a portal somewhere."

Tierney pulled Veren up from his formal bow and threw her arms around him. In the past, they had a complicated relationship, going from kind of liking each other to severe disdain, but she was overjoyed to see him now. "I'm so happy you're safe." She hugged him tightly, pulling back to look at him. "What have you heard of Siobhan? Is she here with you?"

"No. When I came through the portal, I was alone. I lost sight of you and Gulliver, as well as Siobhan, before I landed right in the center of a raging battle. There was no time to look for you. I barely managed to keep my head on my shoulders before I fell in with General Haggerty of the Grima forces."

"Hello?" A soft voice called their attention away from their bittersweet reunion. A small, young woman entered the room dressed in fine silks befitting the royal court here in Grima. Tierney took her for another noblewoman at first, but she recognized the young man behind her. Prince Donal of Grima. The tiny girl must be the new queen.

"Your Majesty, please come meet my friends." Veren beamed at the unassuming queen.

The girl approached Tierney and took her hands. "It's a pleasure to meet a princess of another realm. An heir, no less. It's an oddity in Lenya for a woman to inherit the throne, yet here we are." Her clear blue eyes filled with sadness, and Tierney could imagine she was thinking of the mother and sister she had lost so recently. This morose girl had never expected to be a queen, yet she'd taken on the responsibility far beyond her years. She couldn't be more than eighteen years old.

"It's lovely to meet you, Bronagh." Tierney gave a nod to acknowledge the queen's higher ranking, but as Tierney was a Royal Highness herself, she didn't owe the young queen more than that.

Prince Donal joined them. "We welcome you to Grima. You may take refuge here for as long as you would like to stay."

The young royals struck Tierney as old souls, far more mature than they should have been at such an age. They reminded her of her younger brothers and sisters.

"I would like to hear of your trials in Vondur if you would be willing to share your experiences there." Bronagh gripped Tierney's hand. "I apologize on behalf of all of Lenya for your rough treatment at the hands of their barbarian king. I fear their newest king will be worse than his predecessor."

"Thank you." Tierney winced at the mention of Keir, but she accepted the queen's kindness.

"I must leave you for now, but please join us tonight for dinner. An informal affair. Just my brother and me and our uncle. We are eager to help you find your way home, though I remain uncertain how helpful we will be."

"Your kindness is much appreciated, Bronagh." Tierney followed the royals to the door. "We look forward to this evening and a chance to bring Grima and Iskalt together as loyal friends."

Tia closed the door behind the queen and her brother. She wasn't certain which way the wind would blow here in Grima, but it had to be better than Vondur.

The moment they were alone, Veren turned to Tierney, panic in his eyes. "Do not tell Donal you fought Grima during the siege." He walked past her and threw himself on the plush settee, all the formal tones and niceties upon first seeing her gone.

"Yes." Tierney crossed her arms. "That was my first thought. I'd just go to the prince and tell him how many of his men I killed." She rolled her eyes. "Glad we're past that strange, you-being-nice-to-me thing."

"I'm always nice, Princess." He winked.

A snort sounded from behind her. "Oh, don't mind me," Gulliver said. "I'm sure you're relieved I'm alive as well, great and noble Veren. No need to say it."

Tierney bit back a smile. Gulliver had always hated Veren. He was even more protective of her than she was of herself. But Veren hardly knew Gullie, and he certainly didn't know the depths of the hatred born out of loyalty.

"Who are you again?" Veren asked. "Oh, right. The Dark Fae." The way he said it set Tierney's nerves on edge.

"I'm so glad we came all the way across this foreign kingdom to find you." She smiled sweetly, sarcasm dripping from every word.

Veren grinned, his brilliant white teeth flashing. "I've got to say, it was quite the shock to catch sight of you during the battle. The Grima soldiers have told me how Vondur views their women. Then again, maybe the Vondurians were just trying to get you killed."

Gulliver lowered himself to the settee, purposefully bumping Veren. Veren shoved him out of the way.

This wasn't going to help anyone. With a sigh, Tierney walked into the sitting area and faced them. "Okay, boys, this isn't going to get us anywhere. We need to make a plan."

"A plan?" Veren asked.

"To get home."

"Ah, yes, home. The place where both your parents and my own are bent on making their children marry."

Staring down at him, she narrowed her eyes. "I thought you *wanted* to marry me."

A harsh laugh burst out of him. "For my family, maybe. But do you really think I wanted to live the rest of my days with a wife who hates me?"

"I don't hate you. I …" Her shoulders dropped. "Okay, maybe I did. But it was your fault."

"Here we go."

"I'm serious. You led me on just so you could be seen with the princess."

His brow creased, but he paused before responding. "I didn't have a choice."

She saw it then, the truth in his eyes. None of them had ever had a choice. His family played with his life just as her father had with hers. Making a quick decision she hoped she wouldn't regret, she stuck a hand out. "Truce?"

He didn't take it.

"Come on, Rhatigan. We're stuck here in this kingdom, separated from our own by deadly fire plains and raging seas. Siobhan is still missing. You, me, Gullie ... all we have is each other. Take my stupid hand."

One corner of his lips twitched before he reached out and slid his fingers into hers. "Fine, truce."

"Good." She pulled her arm back quickly and sat in the chair across from the two boys. A wooden table rested between them. Unlike the palace of Vondur, Grima's luxury wasn't built on crystals that had long ago lost their magic. It made her wonder what was different here. She hadn't seen anyone yet who even wore a totem.

"Okay." Gullie leaned forward, resting his elbows on his knees. "So, how do we get home?"

Veren looked from one to the other as if trying to make some decision. Tierney could practically see the wheels turning in his head. After what felt like an eternity, he stood. "Come with me."

Tierney ran to catch up with him as he pulled open the door. "Where are we going?"

"Do you have to know everything all the time?"

"Yes."

He pushed out a breath in exasperation. "The docks."

"Wait, this place has docks?" Tierney would never stop being amazed at the expansiveness of the Grima palace.

"Of course it does, we're on the sea."

She didn't miss the possessive "we're," but she ignored it. If Veren wanted to pretend he was one of these fae, she wouldn't stop him. "Iskalt is on the sea, and we don't have docks. It's more like one dock. And it's hidden so smugglers can pretend my father doesn't know what they're bringing into his kingdom."

"The king knows and doesn't stop them?" Gulliver looked sideways at her, his eyes wide.

"No. It's funny. Not all trade reaches the furthest villages in Iskalt, but smugglers have ways normal traders don't. So, he thinks it's good for the people to—"

"Will you two shut up?" Veren shook his head. "No one cares about Iskalt trade."

Tierney leaned closer to Gulliver and dropped her voice. "He's just salty because it cuts into his father's profits."

"Salty?" Gulliver asked.

"Yeah, isn't that a great word? Mom told me it means mad or—"

"Obnoxious," Veren cut in.

"No, actually, I was going to say vexed."

"I mean you're obnoxious."

She'd been called worse. With a shrug, she started whistling, the sound echoing off the stone walls.

Veren practically growled, but she didn't stop.

Gulliver joined her, the two whistling one of Iskalt's more famed drinking songs, one a princess like her had no business knowing. She could picture her dad's flushed cheeks now. And if she sang the bawdy words ... a giggle escaped her.

Veren, leading them through a series of halls where servants greeted him by name, gave her a skeptical look. "Has she gone mad?" he asked Gulliver.

Gulliver grinned. "Oh, dear Veren, Tierney has always been mad."

That brought another laugh out of her before she kept on whistling. It felt good to be with Gulliver, even Veren, to be free. There were no guards keeping tabs on her, no sneaking through tunnels. She got to go outside and feel the sun on her face. And a part of her believed maybe they could even find a way home.

Yet, she hadn't stopped thinking about the fae she left behind in Vondur. Was Keir wilting under the weight of the crown? Had Eavha found her voice? Would Declan recover from his king almost executing him?

Not to mention that Keir had to kill his own father.

She hadn't been able to get out of there fast enough when she was free, and she'd hardly said proper goodbyes, but something told her she'd see them all again.

Tierney hadn't been paying attention to the long and winding walk. Before she knew it, Veren led her through two heavy iron doors onto a wide landing at the top of a cliff. "I thought we were going to the docks."

He shot a grin back over his shoulder. "We are. They're down there." He pointed to the edge of the cliff. "Hope you're not scared of heights, Princess."

Gulliver gripped her hand, his fingers squeezing tight. She wasn't scared of heights. Her best friend, on the other hand ...

There was a steep wooden staircase built right into the face of the cliff, stretching far down below to where she presumed the docks were. Footsteps sounded, coming up the steps, and she slid out of the way to let a broad-shouldered man carrying a pile of broken wood pass.

"Morning, Lord Rhatigan." He nodded.

"Chasten." Veren returned the gesture. "How does our project proceed?"

"Very well. We should be ready within the month."

"Excellent. Tell Ania I wish her well in the last weeks of her pregnancy."

The man brightened. "I will. Thank you, my Lord." He hefted his load higher and continued down a path that skirted the palace, disappearing into a valley of boulders.

"Who are you and what have you done with the Veren we know and loathe?" Tierney had never known him to care about anyone but himself.

He pushed a hand through his hair and gave her one last look before beginning his descent.

Tierney had no choice but to follow him. Gullie came cautiously behind. The steps were slick, and they had to take each one slowly.

Tierney chanced a glance back at Gulliver to find his face had paled and he clutched the rock face.

None of them spoke until they made it safely to the bottom, where a series of docks spread out before them. Tierney had never seen anything like it. Wooden walkways stretched out over the water to bobbing fishing vessels, their sails billowing in the wind as they bobbed.

The creak of lines pulling tight, of wooden hulls scraping against the docks, filled the salt-laden air. Tierney lifted her eyes to the brilliant sun above. She inhaled deeply, drawing in the fresh, chilly air. This was what peace felt like.

The dark seas were calm save for the gentle rolling waves, much different from the stormy seas separating Iskalt from Eldur.

"I know," Veren said. "The ocean here is so different from the frozen seas along our shores."

For a moment, they really were in this together. "What have you become here, Veren?" she asked, her voice soft. It was more curiosity than anything that had her wanting, needing, to know.

He studied her for a moment. "When the Grima found me as they were retreating from battle, they were just desperate for soldiers. They'd lost a lot of men and women fighting the Vondurians. They asked few questions at first, but then the prince …" He shook his head and turned to walk across the crisscrossing walkways.

"The prince what?" She gripped his arm.

"I saved his life. When we were running from battle. After that, he felt indebted to me. It earned me the respect of my fellow soldiers. Many of these servants, shipbuilders, fought side by side with me. Here in Grima, even those not in the army fight for their kingdom. When you face death with others, it brings you rather close."

Tierney had so many questions, but something caught her eye—a ship she didn't see until a fishing vessel pushed away from the docks to sail out. Sitting at the far end was the most beautiful boat she'd ever set eyes on.

Her feet took her that way without direction. When she reached it, her eyes skated up the smooth, dark hull, painted with the golden Grima crest. This was no mere fishing trolley.

Veren stepped up beside her. “This is what I wanted to show you. It’s my project.”

Tierney didn’t take her eyes off it. “Why are you building a ship?”

“He wants to sail home across the sea.” Gulliver’s voice was low, quiet. “Don’t you?”

Veren swallowed. “Think about it. There is no way across the fire plains. They are more dangerous than any of the other vatlands. The only way to Iskalt is around them.”

But he didn’t know. He couldn’t. If he did, he’d certainly never imagine such a journey.

Tearing her eyes from the ship, she turned and shook her head. “It can’t be done.” There was no use hoping for the impossible. She started back toward the stairs she never wanted to traverse again.

Veren ran after her. “You can’t just come here and tear down what I’ve been working on since I arrived and then leave with no explanation.”

“You need to show him the map.” Gulliver huffed, trying to keep up with their fast pace.

He was right.

“What map?” Veren asked.

Tierney climbed the stairs with slightly less caution than she’d descended them, just wanting to get back to her rooms and find the map. She yanked open the door, still marveling at how she could do it herself. In Iskalt, doors were opened by guards.

She stopped in the middle of the hall, and Gullie crashed into her, sending them both stumbling forward. A maid swerved out of their way to avoid the collision, and Veren mumbled something under his breath.

Righting herself, Tierney turned hard eyes on him. “I will never find my way back to our rooms. You lead.”

He did so without argument. The palace twisted in so many different directions it made her head spin.

The moment she stepped into her rooms, she hurried toward the table beside the bed, where she'd put her few belongings, including a folded parchment.

"I got this in Vondur." She unfolded it and pressed it flat, revealing a map of Lenya that included the fire plains and the seas on both sides. "Honestly, I didn't think it would be too useful since we had no way to sail the seas anyway. But now …"

"What am I seeing?" Veren leaned closer.

Tierney pointed to a spot on the map. "The southern seas are shallow and rocky. The Vondurians have limited coastline and even more limited seas for fishing. The way through is treacherous, and few have ventured beyond sight of the mainland. I was told no ship can navigate the rocky shoals. Countless vessels have crashed and broken apart against the rocks."

"I get it. What about the northern sea?" He pointed north, presumably where Iskalt's shores should be.

"That's more of an unknown, but what is known is right there in the center." She pointed to the swirling mass on the map. "The maelstrom lies beyond the Vale of Storms, a dangerous corridor, where no one dares to sail. No one survives the Vale long enough to reach the maelstrom."

"That's the thing, Tierney," Veren said. "This ship we're building, it's made to withstand anything. There has never been one like it. It will be a rough journey, but it's our only way home."

"We don't even know for certain if Iskalt is on the other side of those seas." Tierney let out an anxious breath. "We don't know how far it is. Even if we made it past such dangerous obstacles, we'd be sailing blind with no way to navigate whatever lies beyond the farthest reaches of this map."

He backed up, scrubbing a hand over his face. "We have to try."

"We'll find another way. Maybe my magic will return, and …"

"No, the people of Grima don't have that kind of time."

Tierney froze. Something in his voice was very wrong.

Gulliver came to her rescue. "What do you mean?"

"The fire plains." Desperation leaked into his voice. "They're expanding."

"Ex—"

He cut her off. "They're encroaching on Grima, and we don't know how to stop it."

CHAPTER 4
KEIR

She left without saying goodbye. Keir lifted his sword, using the hilt to shield his face and deflect his opponent's blade. Steel crashed, and Keir's temper flared as he surged forward, putting all his strength into the downward arc of his weapon.

He couldn't get her off his mind. A woman traveling alone—well, with a Dark Fae man who probably wouldn't offer her the best protection—it just wasn't safe. Though, Tierney O'Shea wasn't just any woman.

Keir lunged forward, his knee bent as he leaned into the formations he could do in his sleep. Lifting his shield to block, he let his sword drop down toward his rival, grazing his arm with the sharp bite of the blade. The man howled and hobbled back, but Keir barely heard him over the din of his thoughts.

She'd left weeks ago, but he still couldn't sleep, worrying if Tierney had made it to the Grima palace. Had they welcomed her as a guest or as an enemy? Keir didn't trust them.

Yet, he understood her need to find her friends. To leave the place that had imprisoned her and nearly executed her and her closest friend in the world. In her shoes, he would have fled Vondur as soon as possible.

Still, the thought of her in enemy territory plagued his mind. More than anything, he wanted to see the end of this war. An end to the devastation, hunger, and bloodshed his people suffered. He wasn't sure he would ever see those of Grima as anything other than the enemy, but for Tierney, Vondur was the enemy. At least until he'd done the unthinkable to protect her. To give her the chance to find her friends and a way home.

His opponent was weakening. Keir took a step back to brace his footing, letting the stupid man come to him.

"I grow weary of this." Keir met the man's charge, springing forward at the last moment. Hot blood rushed down Keir's leg, but it was just a scratch; he had his opponent right where he wanted him. He ran his sword into the man's shoulder where it met his thick neck, but he didn't stop there. With the force of his momentum, Keir's blade sank into the man's torso, through his heart and lungs, and down into his bowels, until hilt met cold, dead skin.

The man sank to his knees, blood gurgling from his mouth. Keir braced his foot against the dead man's chest, pulling his sword free and letting him fall to the floor. Again.

Barely sweating this time, Keir turned to the silent onlookers. "Would anyone else care to challenge their king to the Comhrac today?" He wiped his blade against his leathers, returning it to the scabbard at his hip.

With a deep breath, he stepped up onto the dais, returning to his throne. A throne he never wanted, though he would not change anything even if he could.

Keir still remembered long ago when his father had first challenged his predecessor and won the crown of Vondur for himself. Keir was just a boy then, but in the early days of his rule, King Turlach received many challenges. Yet, Keir could not remember there being quite so many.

It was nearly every day now. One nobleman or another stepped forward, speaking the binding words of the King's Comhrac that inevitably ended with their deaths at Keir's hands.

He was so tired of killing his own men, but his court was restless. Murmurings of his perceived weakness still spread. It wasn't that Keir himself was weak. There was a growing pile of bodies to prove that was not the case. It was his desire to feed and care for the common folk of Vondur that led his court to believing he was weak.

Some thought him a fool for taking surplus food from the army to feed the poor villagers who were starving. It wasn't a permanent solution, but it was a necessary one. He had every intention of caring for both the army and the common folk with long-term solutions that would make everyone happy. If his noblemen would stop challenging him long enough to allow him the time to make such changes.

The Vondurian court knew what was coming though. It was only a matter of time before they would be taxed to make up the difference. In Keir's mind, it shouldn't be a tax at all but a gift of common decency to see their kinsmen well cared for.

Such a gift would trickle down from the wealthiest noble house to the poorest of souls eking out a living along the fire plains. Pride. Pride in their country and their fellow Vondurians. That was the future Keir wanted. One where soldiers earned a fair wage to care for their families. Where they joined the army as a viable career and a way to proudly serve their people. Where armies no longer marched to foreign lands to wage a war no one would ever win.

But Keir wasn't sure he was the right man to inspire such a future. Not when he couldn't even sway the court to his side. Right now, everyone wanted something from him and he couldn't seem to get his feet under him long enough to make his next move and secure his rule.

But he refused to die at the end of a sword in the King's Comhrac.

Even now, his court still stared at him, taking in the bloodstains on the carpets and the fresh blood still streaming from his leg.

"Your Majesty." One of the stewards bravely stepped forward. "We should get you to the healing pools."

“Bah.” Keir waved him away. “I’ll not waste the power on a scratch. I’ll be fine.” He stood, his head swimming for a moment before Declan stepped forward to offer his shoulder to lean on.

“I’ll see the king to his rooms. Get this place cleaned up.” He scowled at the familiar faces, probably wondering which one would challenge the king tomorrow.

Keir made it out of the throne room under his own steam but was grateful for Declan’s presence the moment the door shut behind him.

“You’ve got to stop these fights.”

“I do what I must.” Keir leaned on Declan as they made their way along the corridors to Keir’s quarters. The same ones he’d always occupied.

His sister insisted he move into the king’s rooms, but it still felt strange to think of his father’s domain as his now.

“I would say congratulations,” Declan eased him down into a chair in front of the cold fireplace in his rooms, “but I don’t want to get yelled at again.” He leaned down and ripped open Keir’s pant leg to reveal his injury.

“It is never cause for celebration to kill my own men.” Keir winced at the sight of his leg.

“That is hardly a scratch, Keir.” Eavha entered the room and rushed to his side, her giant cat trailing behind. “I’ll fetch the healer.”

Keir grabbed her and pulled her back. “Don’t. The last thing I need is for anyone to think I’ve been injured enough to call the healer. There’ll be ten challengers tomorrow. Just … stitch it up and put a bandage on it if you must.”

Sheba let out a low growl, telling Keir to unhand his mistress. He obeyed.

Eavha glared at Keir. “You want me to stitch your leg?” Her face grew pale in the dim afternoon light streaming in through the windows. The skies were smoke-filled today as the winds blew in from the fire plains.

“It can’t be all that different from your endless embroidery.”

"Listen to him." Eavha stood, sharing a look with Declan. "He's lost his mind."

Declan shrugged and glanced back at Keir. "We could do it. It's just a few stitches."

"Fetch your sewing, Eavha." Keir reached for a bottle on the table at his side.

"Oh, very well." She rushed to the secret door that had connected their rooms since childhood. "Find him something to bite down on. I'll be right back. And get those boots off him while I'm gone."

Keir took a long pull on the bottle, wishing for something much stronger than watered wine. "She's gotten bossy, hasn't she?"

"I blame Tierney." Declan crouched down beside him, tugging on his boots. "And that pet of hers. It's quite territorial, isn't it?" He sighed. "That's going to take at least twelve stitches, Keir. You have any whiskey?"

Keir shook his head. "Get my belt, would you?" He gestured toward the chest of drawers in the corner opposite his bed.

Eavha returned a moment later, this time alone. Her hands were full of bottles and her latest embroidery project.

"Let's get this over with." She moved to set her things on the table beside Keir's chair. "Move." She shoved his feet off the footstool and sat down.

"Ouch, I'm injured here." Keir scowled at her.

"Stop whining." Eavha poured wine on her hands and into a basin, sloshing some along the wound that ran from his knee down to his calf. Shoving the bottle into Keir's hands, she picked up a long, sharp needle. "Drink that, it's stronger."

Her hands trembled as she threaded a needle.

"Relax. I can handle it." Keir took another gulp of crisp wine from the wineskin she'd brought with her. He wouldn't ask how she got it. The wine was for the men. Women her age drank tea.

"The thread is blue." Declan snorted.

"It's all I have." Eavha bent over Keir's leg and stabbed the needle through his skin without warning.

He sucked in a breath, stuffing the leather strap of his belt between his teeth, and urged her to keep going. Better to get it done quickly.

"Neat stitch work," Declan murmured over her. "She's pretty good at this."

Keir gripped the arms of his chair until he thought he might crush it under his hands, his teeth grinding into the leather strap.

"You can breathe now." Eavha tied off the thread and cut it. And then, she balled up her fist and punched his arm.

"Ouch, what was that for?" Keir clutched his arm.

"For making me do that. It was gross." She rinsed her hands in warm water and reached for a small jar she'd brought with her. "I don't know how much this will help, but I asked Ariella for something to aid with pain and infection. I told her it was for a hangnail for me."

"She'll know who it's really for," Declan said in a worried tone.

"She won't say anything. I trust her." Eavha dabbed the poultice mixture over Keir's leg.

"That feels good." Keir took a steady breath. "It's numbing the pain."

"Thank the heavens." She blew a sweaty strand of hair from her face and slathered a thick layer of the stuff over the wound and then wrapped it with a strip of fabric from one of Keir's old shirts.

"We have got to stop these challenges." Eavha patted her brother's shoulder, letting him find solace in the wineskin. She looked to Declan, worry creasing her brow. "He can't keep this up much longer."

"I don't know how to stop it. It's not unusual for a new king to receive the challenge of the Comhrac." Declan ran a hand through his unruly hair. "But the court always settles down in the end."

"Except, my court isn't settling down." Keir turned to the only two people he could trust, a smile tugging at his mouth. "At this rate, I won't be king much longer."

Chapter 5
Tierney

Tierney would never get enough of this palace with its winding halls, friendly servants, and even guards who smiled. There was a love for their kingdom in their eyes, but through it all, she could sense a weariness. They'd been through a lot. Losing their palace and hiding in the woods before taking it back. Fighting many battles for their lives.

And they didn't believe they'd find relief any time soon.

This morning, Tierney woke before Gulliver, avoiding him in favor of exploring on her own. She loved her friend, but he'd grown cautious since the war, despite growing up a thief. Now, he never wanted to do anything to disappoint Griff or others protecting him. Never wanted to go where they weren't supposed to or ask intrusive questions. She had no such qualms.

The freedom of movement here reminded her of her palace. Her mother insisted the guards always remain at an unobtrusive distance. She didn't want to feel watched and wanted the fae of Iskalt to access her should they need to. It was one of the many reasons she was such a beloved queen.

Tierney wanted to be just like her when it came time to take the throne. Respected, but most of all loved. Not only by simpering nobles seeking position but by the average fae who had nothing to gain from an immense loyalty.

She had long lost any sort of direction and found herself in a colder part of the palace. It didn't take much for her to realize why. A lengthy corridor stretched in front of her with doors lining both sides. They were open, allowing the wind to tunnel through the small space.

A blast of that wind struck Tierney, and she closed her eyes, savoring the feel. It wasn't nearly as cold as Iskalt, but the departure from the heat of Vondur still felt like it brought her closer to home.

A slow rain drizzled down, making a steady rhythm as it hit the stones. She walked forward, stopping in one of the open arched doorways, her breath stuttering. Enclosed on all sides by the walls of the palace was a garden, beautiful in its vastness. A winding path was framed with twisted bushes that looked like they were reaching toward the palace. Yellow and white flowering buds hung from their branches.

Color stretched in every direction. Pinks and blues and purples. It was like someone had captured a rainbow and managed to harness its power. Tierney had never seen anything quite like it.

Unable to resist, she stepped outside, ignoring the raindrops hitting her softly curled hair. The air smelled of fresh rain and roses, a heady scent that had her stopping to inhale deeper.

Before she could go farther, a man stepped into her path. It took her a moment to see his uniform and realize he was a guard. "No one is allowed into the queen's gardens."

Oh! She'd wandered into the royal quarters. Her cheeks heated. If anyone did that in Iskalt, her father would throw them from the balcony. Only, there were no balconies here.

"I'm sorry; I must have gotten lost." She smiled, trying to keep the royal tone from her voice. "It's such a large palace, and I'm a new maid. Can you direct me to the kitchens?"

His face softened. "Just don't find yourself this way again. The kitchens are—"

"Tarrow," a subdued feminine voice called from behind him. "Let her pass."

The guard, Tarrow, she presumed, gave Tierney a skeptical look, but he stepped aside. Behind him on the path was Queen Bronagh, her hands clasped together in front of her waist.

"Your Majesty." Tierney knew the best way to get home was to ingratiate herself with this family.

The queen seemed not to notice the rain dampening her pale blue gown. She had no expression on her face as she studied Tierney. Tierney's first impression of Bronagh had been that she was a sweet, but quiet girl, and she was starting to wonder if it was more than that.

Finally, the queen nodded. "Would you sit with me, Princess?" She gestured across the garden, where a small white gazebo sat perched among vining plants that crawled up the pillars. It would be a shield from the rain, at least, and Tierney wasn't ready to leave the garden behind.

Silently, she followed Bronagh toward the wooden benches in the gazebo and then sat facing her. Neither girl spoke for a long moment. Tierney drummed her fingers on the edge of the bench. She wasn't someone who got nervous or anxious, but there was something ethereal about this girl.

She was younger than Tierney, but there was no youth to her. Instead, she looked like she'd lived a hundred years, with wise eyes and a contemplative nature.

"I am told you fought my brother in the siege of Vondur."

Those words stopped Tierney's lungs from expanding. Her pulse pounded in her head, and a response popped out before she could stop it. "Veren wasn't supposed to mention that."

For the first time, the queen smiled, her lips barely moving. "In his short time here, Veren has become a trusted friend. He thought I deserved the facts and knew I would not hold it against you."

"You don't?"

"Tierney." She dropped her eyes, the first crack to her confidence showing. "We all do what we must to survive. If you had not joined the fight, you wouldn't be sitting here with me now."

"And that's a good thing?" She hadn't been sure. In a way, it felt like she had nothing to offer these fae who'd been so good to her.

"I believe it is." Bonagh pressed her hands into the skirt of her dress. "Tell me of Iskalt." She paused. "Please."

"Iskalt? Veren can tell you everything."

"I want to hear about it from you."

Tierney had avoided the topic of Iskalt in Vondur. Any talk of her home could have led to secrets she hadn't been ready to reveal. Not to Keir, nor anyone else there. Not while she was a prisoner. The king had hurt her for her silence.

But that king is dead, she reminded herself. And something about Bronagh made Tierney want to trust her, to have faith that she could truly help.

Tierney closed her eyes, picturing home. "We have fields of snow, icy winds colder than you've experienced in your life. There's a vast lake that rages and seethes. Life in Iskalt is hard." For so long, she'd wanted out. A smile curved her lips. "But the fae are wonderful. My family ... I would live in the coldest reaches of the kingdom just to see them again."

She opened her eyes and tears hung in her lashes.

Bronagh leaned forward, looking like she had absorbed every word. "You miss them very much ... your family."

Tierney nodded.

"I do too."

For just a moment, they were the same, both separated from those they loved. Tierney by the fire plains, and Bronagh by death. "I'm sorry about your mother and your sister."

"Me too. But they were ..." She sighed. "They wanted us to continue this war. Donal and I tried to convince them to stop advancing their forces; we tried to put an end to all of this. And now, it is just us two and our uncle."

"You can still end it."

"I'm afraid it's not as simple as that anymore. The Vondurians … they're a bloodthirsty lot. They will not stop until they have destroyed what is left of us and united Lenya under one crown. I will not let my fae become part of that barbaric culture. They deserve better." Anger flashed in her eyes, the first deep emotion Tierney had seen out of her.

"They do," Tierney agreed. "But I think you underestimate the new king. Keir is a good man."

"Vondur does not breed good men."

She thought of Keir, of Declan. And then of those like Torrin. "You're wrong. I have seen it firsthand. Keir is not like his father. He can be reasoned with, bargained with. You have to—"

"Enough." Bronagh didn't raise her voice, but she didn't have to. The word held command. "I did not invite you to sit with me to defend our enemy. We will deal with the Vondurian king when we must. For now, I need you to tell me about the crystals."

"Crystals?"

"In Iskalt. Veren tells me the crystals we so desperately seek are abundant in your kingdom."

Tierney had guessed as much when she first held a Vondurian totem. It was made from crystals similar to the fire opals Myrkurians used for trade. In Iskalt, they had no use for the crystals except as exquisite decoration. There was a table in her father's study made entirely of fire opal that probably could have powered half the people in the palace of Grima for a long while.

But what would it mean for Iskalt if she revealed the truth?

Bronagh sighed. "I understand your hesitation. You have to protect your fae just as I have to protect mine. But my kingdom will die if we can no longer gain access to our power. We must keep the fire plains from engulfing us."

Tierney looked into her clear eyes, sensing a sincerity in their depths. She didn't know if this was the right thing, but she drew in a deep breath. "Yes, we have crystals. The opals … they are in most areas of Iskalt, hidden beneath layers of ice and snow. Most of what is accessible has been gifted to us from the other three kingdoms. My father and his allies have access to enough crystal for every man, woman, and child in all of Lenya."

The rain came heavier than before, drumming on the roof of the gazebo and momentarily distracting Tierney from her thoughts. This made little sense. How could the key to saving Lenya exist in Iskalt? A land they once believed was a myth.

Was that why she was here? Did something pull her where she was needed? Did her magic bring her here for a purpose? She'd always had a deep need to save people like when her brother was kidnapped or when the poor souls in the prison realm needed a way out.

But those were her people. Here, she was in a land that wasn't supposed to exist. Yet, something had happened in that portal to land her right in the middle of a dispute tearing two kingdoms apart.

"So," Tierney rubbed her hands up her arms, wishing she could call on her power to warm her, "you're telling me the key to saving Grima may lie in my kingdom, but I have to ask, what does that mean for Vondur?"

Bronagh slumped, letting her queenly façade fade, and she suddenly looked years younger, almost her age. "I can only think of my people right now. We have no more options, and we're running out of time."

And then, it hit her. "So, the boat Veren is building … you aren't allowing it just to get us home. You—"

"Plan to come with you, yes."

They expected her to take them to Iskalt with nothing but the stars to guide them. With the roiling, rocky seas in one direction and an impassable maelstrom in the other, it was a death sentence.

Setting foot on that ship would likely mean never returning. "This is why you welcomed us into the palace."

The queen shook her head. "We welcomed you because an enemy of Vondur is a friend of ours. Yes, we ask for your help, but you are also welcome to stay here whether you agree or not."

But she wasn't an enemy of Vondur. At least, she didn't think she was. Keir was king now. She might not know what that meant for her or for the Vondurian fae, but it had to be better than before.

She wished she could ask his advice now, ask him what he knew of this Grima queen. Reality hit her a few days ago. She missed him. The man who'd kept her prisoner and then fought to free her. She missed their arguments, the way his eyes blazed when she annoyed him.

And yet, she sat here with his enemy, discussing a deal to provide them with magic … if it was even possible.

Even if it was dangerous, shouldn't she try any means to get home? She rubbed the back of her neck and gazed up into the rafters of the gazebo. A spider web caught her attention, and she watched a tiny fly try to free itself. That was her. She was the fly caught in a web. No matter what choice she made, she would always be stuck, trapped.

She was no longer a prisoner, but this was not her home. Not her war. But was it her responsibility to intervene?

A breath pushed past her lips, and she let her eyes drift down to the queen's. "I will try to help you save Grima, but you have to make me a promise."

"I will do anything within my capabilities."

"It can't just be Grima. You must try to save all of Lenya."

A lightness entered her eyes, and she straightened her spine, sitting once again like the prim woman she was. "Veren was right about you."

"What did he say?"

"That you could be my greatest ally because you will always do what is right."

She thought of Keir and how she'd left after everything he'd done for her.

Not always. Sometimes, I do what is easiest.

CHAPTER 6
KEIR

Keir slid the kerchief off his face, wiping the sweat from his brow. This close to the burning lands, the smoke nearly obscured the sky. His men were weary from marching in this heat, choking on the smoke they weren't used to breathing.

"It's a wonder anything can live here." Declan coughed, pulling his mount up beside Keir's. "That people choose this place as their home astounds me."

"I don't think there's much choice involved." Keir sipped cool water from a waterskin. "But when you don't have anything, you do the best you can with what you've got."

"I wonder if your court came on campaign with you, if they could witness these conditions for themselves, they'd understand why you've made the choices you have since taking the throne."

"They would still see what they want to see." Keir dismounted on the outskirts of the village, where his army camped. He couldn't stand another day among his court. He was a soldier and would never be comfortable among the nobility. A campaign to review his army was exactly what he needed. Maybe he could get things done away from all the simpering of court nobles trying to win his favor and the endless challenges from those who thought they could do a better job.

And if the reports could be trusted, his troops were growing by leaps and bounds in the last weeks. Keir would like to know where these magical new soldiers had appeared. His generals wanted him to believe the influx of recruits was due to the loyalty the new king inspired among his people. That kind of ego boost might have worked for his father, but not for Keir. Soldiers didn't appear out of thin air just when he needed them most.

"Identify yourselves!" Sentries swarmed the dusty plain, riding out to stop Keir from entering camp.

"Your king need not identify himself," Declan shouted back, stepping in front of Keir and waving several of his guards forward.

"Step aside soldiers." Keir moved through the crowd. "I am here to speak with your general." The sentry glanced at the standard his guard carried, clearly uncertain of who their king was. "I am Keir Dagnan, son of Turlach Dagnan. Your new king." He glared at the soldiers, weary from his travels and the pressure of ruling a kingdom. "Surely you've heard of the King's Comhrac even way out here?"

"Of course, your Majesty." The sentry stepped aside. "Right this way. I apologize for the hesitation, sire. It's only that I didn't recognize you." The other sentries trotted ahead to clear the way. They were an eager lot, young and likely untested in battle.

Keir marched through the camp with his guard, trying to act like a king, but he didn't know what that entailed. So, he did the only thing he could do and acted like his father.

Ignoring the sea of unfamiliar faces, he stood tall, keeping a blank expression on his face. Kings didn't speak to lowly soldiers. But for all of his indifference, Keir didn't miss anything. The camp was poorly equipped. It reeked, and there wasn't a soldier in sight who was more than sixteen years old.

Not waiting for his escort to the general's headquarters, Keir stopped at a tent where several boys worked to start a fire. They bickered among themselves while another attempted to put together a meal of thin stew with root vegetables, wild onions, and a few unidentifiable chunks of meat. Three others sat by, sharpening their swords.

"Where is your totem?" Keir asked, crouching down beside the cold fire pit.

"Bugger off." One of the boys swiped at his forehead, not bothering to look up.

Declan stepped forward to chastise him, but Keir lifted a hand to stall him.

"You haven't been taught to start fires with your totem?"

"Don't have one." Another shrugged, trying to strike two rocks together to create a spark. "Lieutenant Briggs won't let us get an ember from a different fire till we prove we can make one with nothing."

"All soldiers have to learn to make fire this way. I take it you lot haven't earned a totem yet?"

"Wouldn't know how to use one if we did," another offered. He was the youngest of them all.

"How old are you, soldier?" Keir asked.

"Old enough, sir." He squared his shoulders and lifted his chin.

"Humor me." Keir hid his smile.

"Eleven, but I'm a good shot. At least, with a slingshot." He glanced down at the sword that was too long for his height.

"Of course you are." Keir reached into his bag, retrieving a pair of rough stones he probably didn't need anymore. "Try these." He handed the quartz to the slightly older boys still trying to start a fire. "You'll always get a better spark with quartz."

He spent a few more minutes asking the boys some questions about how they came to be in the army and teaching them a few tricks to get their camp squared away for the night. They were more than just green; they'd had no training at all.

"Why join the army at such a young age? Where are your

parents?" Keir asked the most talkative of the bunch, the one adding small branches to the fire they'd finally coaxed to life.

"No parents, most of us. Our fathers and brothers died in the war, and our mothers and sisters are starving. Nothing left to do but join up and send half our wages home to feed the little ones."

"Aren't you afraid of dying in battle?" Keir moved to stir the pot of stew, adding a few herbs from his stores to bring some flavor to the meal. He frowned at the dry brown bread the boys passed around. It was full of weevils they picked out. Keir was no stranger to roughing it when times were bad, but these boys had no place fighting a war when they weren't yet grown.

The youngest shrugged, stuffing a piece of bread in his mouth. "Dying in battle's better than dying with an empty belly. Nowhere else to go."

As the days passed since he'd killed his father, Keir wanted the throne less and less. But the responsibility had fallen to him. He refused to lead an army of starving children when there was enough food in Vondur to feed everyone. It was the least he owed those families who had sacrificed their fathers and brothers in a war for power they would never grasp for themselves.

Keir stood, anger leaving his chest tight and his fists clenched. "Where is your general?" He turned to the sentry who had escorted him into camp.

"We've sent a messenger, sire. He's busy carrying out a punishment." The sentry trembled at the look on Keir's face.

"Take me to him, soldier." He left the boys with his own supplies. Things he'd carried from one battle to the next for more years than he cared to think about. He wouldn't need them now.

As they walked along a dusty path through the tents, the familiar sounds of camp life set him at ease. This felt more like home than the palace ever had. But the unmistakable sound of a strap against flesh stoked Keir's anger. The strap was part of being a soldier. Even Keir had received his fair share of lashes and had the scars to prove it.

"This is what we do to deserters." The gruff voice reminded Keir of his father. As the lash struck the boy's back, Keir winced. The boy couldn't have been more than fourteen. Just a skinny runt with his ribs showing, but he took his punishment, sucking back his tears.

The general reared back to strike again, landing the blow with the force used to whip a full-grown, seasoned soldier. "Your duty is to serve your king!" The general's face flushed red with rage. As he moved to strike again, Keir stepped in, yanking the whip from the man's grasp.

"How dare you!" The general turned his anger on Keir. "I am a general in his Majesty's army; who do you think you are to defy me?"

Keir ignored him, throwing the whip to the ground. "Release this boy." He turned to the sentry, who rushed forward to remove the restraints tethering the young man to the whipping post. "Take him to the healer."

"I give the orders around here." The general blustered.

"And I am your king." Keir turned his cold gaze on the stupid man who wasn't fit to lead a flock of sheep, let alone an army.

The general sputtered for a moment before he collected himself. "I see the news is true then. We have a new king. I beg your pardon, your Majesty." He attempted a courtly bow. "I was just punishing a deserter."

"All I see is a young, frightened boy who shouldn't even be here." Keir glowered, dangerously close to drawing his sword.

"Perhaps your Majesty would accompany me to my tent, where we may speak in private?" He gestured toward the grand tent at the center of the camp. No doubt it was fit for a king.

"No need. Why have you inflated your numbers, reporting an influx of recruits who aren't fit to wield their father's pitchforks, much less a sword?"

"They still need some proper training."

"They are children. How many ten and eleven year olds here do you expect to make it through their first battle against Grima?"

Keir's voice rang out around the silent camp. "Or do you wish to throw them at the front line, hoping your seasoned soldiers can win this war?"

The general's face turned a darker shade of red, his mustache trembling as he spoke. "With all due respect, sire, I have only followed orders."

"Whose orders?"

"Your father's. I beg your pardon if I've missed any orders that have come directly from you since your rise to the throne."

"My father gave orders to recruit orphaned children?" Not even Turlach was that despicable.

"With most Vondurian soldiers already dead, sire, where do you expect your new soldiers to come from?"

"You have new orders, General. Send the boys home." Keir turned to leave before he did something he would regret.

"If I'm to do that, I'll not have an army to lead, your Majesty."

Keir whirled around, closing the distance between himself and the battle-scarred man who stood head and shoulders beneath him. "You are relieved of your command. You will gather your belongings and leave my camp immediately."

"You can't do that. Who will train these men?" The man blustered, and his face grew so red Keir thought his head might explode right off his shoulders.

"Declan Connel, you've been promoted to Commander. Please have your men escort this man to his tent to clear his belongings."

"What, now, your Majesty? Me?" Declan lunged forward. "Commander?"

"Yes. I need someone I can trust to make sure this isn't happening anywhere else. You have command of all the Vondurian troops. See to it these boys are sent somewhere safe. Somewhere that isn't here."

Keir ignored the outraged ranting of the former general, leaving Declan to clean up this mess while he continued surveying his troops.

"You three, you heard the king. Get this disgrace out of my sight,"

Declan barked orders to those standing around, sending half those present scrambling to get back to work.

Keir walked slowly along the path, relieved to see a company of seasoned soldiers sitting around their fires along the perimeter of the camp. The young ones didn't yet realize the worst part of camp life was the center.

"Have you taken leave of your senses?" Declan charged down the path to catch up with him. "Me, Commander of your entire army?"

"You're the best man for the job."

"I'm just a soldier in the king's guard. I never even thought about becoming an officer."

"You don't want it?" Keir turned to face his best friend. "Commander pays a lot better than the king's guard."

"It's also a nobleman's position. And in case you forgot, I'm a commoner. You expect your other generals to defer to me?" Declan's eyes were wild with uncertainty, flashing from one corner of the camp to the next, as if their conversation was somehow taboo.

"I do. Lesser men have risen to greater rank with minimal effort. No one deserves this more than you, Deck."

"I don't know what to say." He raked a hand through his sweaty hair.

Keir shrugged. "The job comes with a lot of responsibility. I expect loyalty and your best efforts. You will lead my army, but you will also take your place among my court. And when the time comes, you'll marry some nobleman's daughter … or sister. And you'll be happy." Keir clapped his stunned friend on the back.

"*Marry*?" Declan shook his head. "I can't process what you just said right now. We need to talk about these boys. They need their pay, Keir. If you send them away, half of them have nowhere to go and no prospects for paid work. They'll starve on the streets of this poor village. These kids need what little pay they get to feed their families."

"You're not suggesting we let them fight?"

"Of course not. I don't know what the answer is, but sending them home isn't it."

Keir nodded. "Get me an accurate count of how many actual soldiers there are here. And a count of all the boys under the age of sixteen. We'll figure out what to do with them once we know how many we're dealing with. Maybe we can train them to be squires and stable boys. And if that doesn't work, we'll take them with us and place them in the king's guard.

"And after I deal with that piece of garbage calling himself a general, you and I need to have a long talk about what comes next."

Declan nodded. "I'll have orders ready to send out by first light."

"May I escort you to dinner?" Gulliver offered Tierney his arm.

"Almost ready." Tierney smoothed a hand over the dark blue skirt of her dress. It reminded her of the elaborate gown she'd worn for her birthday ball. A much simpler version. Rather than the wide, cumbersome skirts Iskaltian and Gelsi nobles preferred, Tierney's simple dress fell to the floor without the hassle of layers and layers of petticoats and dress forms that weighed more than she did.

"You look fine." Gulliver held the door open for her so they could join the other nobles making their way to the great hall for the evening meal. "I'm starving."

"You're always starving, yet you never die." She adjusted the silver belt at her hips, studying her appearance in the mirror. It was to be a formal affair tonight. But formal attire in Grima seemed more like everyday wear to Tierney. Even some of her day dresses at home would be considered too fancy and frivolous among the Grima court.

"I like the fashion here." She tugged on the long sleeve of her dress, clipping a silver broach at her throat. "Their clothes are lovely, with beautiful fabrics, but so comfortable." She tucked her strawberry blond hair behind her pointed ears and retrieved her clutch.

"They do seem to value comfort and economy in all things." Gulliver took her hand as they left their suite. His attire was nothing more than trousers, a dress shirt, and a soft suede waistcoat.

Several other nobles who called the palace home already filled the corridors, heading to the great hall and the queen's summons for a celebratory dinner.

Tierney expected a large crowd of guests, but the great hall was much smaller than the dining hall they normally attended for their meals.

"Princess Tierney O'Shea and Lord Gulliver O'Shea," the herald announced their arrival. A footman escorted them to the high table to dine with the queen and her brother. Their uncle, Lord Cormac, was absent.

Tierney was surprised to find herself seated next to the queen in a place of honor. Gulliver sat beside Prince Donal, who immediately captured his attention with questions about Myrkur. Tierney vaguely wondered if there was a bit of a divide-and-conquer maneuver happening at the formal dining table.

Like most things in Grima, the table was simple yet elegant. Fine linens covered the long table, with sleek goblets filled with the strange pale wine favored by the court. It was delicious, crisp, and fruity, and nothing like the rich dark wines of Iskalt.

Simple white china dishes trimmed in silver adorned the table, along with fresh-cut flowers from the queen's gardens. In Iskalt, the tables at such gatherings were so elaborate Tierney often struggled to see over the flower arrangements to the person seated opposite her.

There was something non-threatening about the way the Grima court operated. It was refreshing. Yet, Tierney had trouble trusting it. The queen might be young, but she was cunning. Odd for a girl who'd grown up with an older sister meant to inherit the throne had she survived the day their mother was murdered by the Vondurian soldiers.

"Good evening, Queen Bronagh." Tierney dipped her head toward the monarch. "I trust you are in fine spirits this evening. The court seems delighted with the impromptu dinner."

"It is good for the morale of the people to see their queen carrying on in the wake of so much tragedy."

"It's a shame our young queen hasn't had time to properly mourn her family." An older gentleman lifted his glass. Tierney recognized him as the swordmaster who had accompanied the prince at the siege.

At Tierney's look of confusion, Bronagh explained, "In Grima, royals do not mourn during a time of war. I will grieve for my sister and mother once Vondur has been defeated."

"Here, here." The swordmaster raised his cup to the queen. "To the defeat of our enemies."

Cries of agreement rang out around the table.

"What news of the front, Daniel?" another gentleman of the court asked.

Tierney supposed the topic of any conversation among the court would center on the war with Vondur, but she was torn. She was a guest here, yet she didn't think of Keir, now the King of Vondur, as an enemy. He was a good man. The only reason she sat here now, drawing breath, was due to his actions at the King's Comhrac.

"The front has been quiet since the murder of their king," the swordmaster answered.

"Such a barbaric custom they have." The man, Lord Fitzgerald, if she remembered correctly, shook his head in disgust. "What is known of this new king?"

"He is King Turlach's son, Keir Dagnan," Tierney replied. "He is an honorable man."

"There is no such thing as an honorable Vondurian." Queen Bronagh patted Tierney's hand, as if she was a child speaking out of turn at the dinner table.

"I'll remind you, King Keir challenged your own Prince Donal to the Comhrac. Yet, when he won the fight, Keir allowed Donal to live, going against the traditions of your people and theirs. The siege at the Vondur palace could have lasted months before it turned into a full-fledged battle. But Keir, acting as he did that day, saved hundreds of lives."

"Pardon me, Princess Tierney," Donal turned a curious gaze on her, "but it sounds as if you would defend the Vondurians at our table. A table where you sit as an honored guest of our queen."

"I am a royal of Iskalt. I hold no sway in the disputes of Lenya. I am but an impartial observer. And as that observer, I can't help but think that if both sides of this war could set aside generations of hate and betrayal, you might be surprised to see that you both want the same things."

"And what is that, Princess?" Donal's cold gaze sent a shiver down her spine. The boy might be young, but he was intimidating—at least, in his palace.

"Peace." Tierney turned to the queen to give her reply. "A thriving, united Lenya, where all have access to the power, and more importantly, all have full bellies when they go to sleep at night, not worrying about what fresh terrors the morning might bring."

"You speak of fantasies, Princess." Lord Fitzgerald sipped his wine. "None here shall fall under the rule of the barbarians across the border."

Tierney tilted her cup against her lips, taking a cool sip to fortify herself. With a smile, she ignored the lords and ladies around the table, focusing her attention on the silent little queen, who was still trying to find her voice among her court.

"I grew up in Iskalt. Our neighbors were the kingdoms of Eldur and Fargelsi. Each vastly different from the other. In generations past, Fargelsi was our enemy. My mother and father fought a long, brutal war to bring peace to our three kingdoms.

"When I was a young girl, we fought another war against the kingdom of Myrkur, which was unknown to us, much like those of

Lenya here beyond the fire plains." Tierney dropped her gaze to her lap. "It was a difficult time. I was a small child, but I fought. My twin brother and I were pawns the Dark King of Myrkur thought to use to gain power." She took another sip of wine. "He is dead now, and his people are free."

Tierney turned her gaze to settle on each member of the court seated around the long table. "It took four kingdoms and two wars to find peace, but we did it. Our people are happy. They have access to power, knowledge of how to use that power, food is plentiful, and every single Iskaltian, Eldurian, Fargelsian, and Myrkurian, down to the last child, has a voice in our world. I would wish the same for all of Lenya. It breaks my heart to see good fae, on both sides, suffer when they don't have to."

A hushed silence fell as each fae present looked at their queen for her reaction to Tierney's words.

"Ah." A smile erupted across the queen's face. "The duck has arrived."

At her signal, servants flooded the dining room with platters of roasted duck and dishes Tierney couldn't identify.

"Prince Donal has provided our feast tonight." She smiled at her brother. "I am happy to see your hunting has been plentiful, brother."

"It is my pleasure, your Majesty." Donal sat back to allow the servers to fill his plate. "I hope all will enjoy the bounties of Grima this evening." He lifted his glass to the queen, and the others followed his lead.

"You might want to keep your thoughts to yourself, Tia." Gulliver flopped onto the settee back in their common room. "I like my neck where it is, thank you." Rubbing his full belly, he shot her a deeply satisfied smile. "They do have great food here. Far better than the Vondurian dungeons."

"So, you're saying I shouldn't think of Vondur as anything but the enemy?" Tierney shed her intricate silvery belt and broach, her temper flaring at the absolute farce that dinner was.

"Didn't say that." Gulliver patted his belly again. "Just remarking on the tasty food and the … chilly reception your speech got from the queen. Maybe we should just stay out of it and focus on getting home."

"They're all just so stubborn." She tossed her jewelry onto the table and sat beside Gulliver. "That duck was delicious, wasn't it?"

"Pretty sure I took down a whole bird myself."

"How are we ever going to get out of here, Gullie?" Frustration brought tears to her eyes. Part of her just wanted to go home. And the other part wanted to help these warring kingdoms find peace.

"Did you mean it?" The gentle voice sounded behind them, and they both jumped to turn in their seats, peeking over the back of the settee to find the queen in their rooms.

"Um, hello, Queen Bronagh." Tierney leaped to her feet. "What, um, brings you to our rooms?" Tierney patted her hair, making sure it wasn't a mess.

"Did you mean it?" Bronagh lifted her chin, meeting Tierney's bewildered look with a fierce one of her own.

"Mean what?"

"The words you didn't say between the pretty words you did. You think this new king of Vondur can be trusted? Do you truly believe he wants the same things I do?"

"Without a doubt." Tierney didn't pause to consider her answer. She didn't know Keir well, but she'd witnessed his actions often enough to understand what kind of man he was and what he wanted for his people.

"The young Dagnan's reputation in battle is worse than his father's." Bronagh crossed to the sitting area and collapsed onto a chair with a weary sigh.

Tierney returned to her seat, leaning toward the queen. She always seemed so poised and collected, if a little too quiet. Tierney suspected the girl's silence was more about her shrewdly listening and watching than being intimidated by her position. She might never have expected to be queen, but she'd been trained for the role.

Tierney knew what that was like. She also knew what it was like to have a thousand opinions thrown at her, never knowing which she could trust.

"Did you know I was charged as a Grima spy you sent to infiltrate the Vondurian court?"

Bronagh lifted a brow in surprise. "I did not."

"Turlach used me to turn his court's attention away from his recent failures in battle and on to something juicier for them to gossip about. I found myself standing on the gallows beside my best friend and a brave Vondurian soldier—an innocent man. The executioner's hood was placed over my head, the rope around my neck."

"He would dare execute a foreign royal without the benefit of a trial? With a common hanging, no less?" Bronagh leaned forward, her elbows resting on her knees.

Tierney mimicked her posture. "He claimed there was no such land as Iskalt; therefore, I was nothing but a common spy."

"And he believed I was some kind of abomination." Gulliver grimaced.

"Ignorant beasts, all of them." Bronagh shook her head. "How did you escape?"

"We didn't. That was the moment Keir Dagnan challenged his father to the Comhrac. He is king now simply because he was trying to save our lives."

CHAPTER 8
KEIR

Keir lost track of his days. All he knew was they were long and longer. Provisioning troops, dealing with petty squabbles at court, preparing for whatever Grima sent for them next.

At least the constant onslaught of Comhrac challenges had ceased, his nobles finally realizing they would not win. Not when their king was determined to help his people. He couldn't do that if he was dead.

But how did one help the people of a war-torn kingdom? As the prince, he'd led armies to battle, but he'd never considered the true toll the war took on the villages, on the children of those he'd served with.

Lowering himself into a seat at the table in the informal dining room, he rested his head in his hands and let his body relax for just a moment. He'd carried so much tension since the moment he realized what he'd have to do to stop his father.

He could still see it. That fight, the way betrayal shone in the man's eyes when he breathed his last breath. But he'd saved her. Tierney. He'd saved Declan. It had been the right thing to do, but right was never easy.

"Your Majesty?" Lord Robert entered the room, and Keir looked up into his kind face, relieved the aged man was the first to arrive.

He stood. "Lord Robert, I wasn't sure you would attend my summons." He held out a hand, but the man didn't take it. Instead, he bowed, as was fitting.

"I wasn't sure I would either, to be honest. When I left this palace, I vowed never to return." Lord Robert had been a trusted ally of Keir's father when he became king, but the relationship turned when he refused to send the young men from the village on his lands to fight for the crown.

"I'm glad you did. Please have a seat." Keir returned to his chair, his posture no longer relaxed. As a child, Lord Robert was like an uncle to him. Now, he was another fae who had to be convinced of Keir's sincerity.

A silence stretched between them before Keir spoke. "I am forming a council."

"In the small hall?" The man lifted one brow.

Keir's lips twitched. "When my father abolished the council years ago, he had the council chambers turned into a library. I will find a better place, but I prefer to look into a fae's eyes when I'm speaking to determine his motives. This table suits that endeavor."

Lord Robert nodded. "Sensible. And what are my motives, your Majesty?"

"I do not need to look at you to know that. Not unless you have changed in the last many years."

"Change is for the winds."

"Then, your motives are clear. You do not approve of our war with Grima."

Lord Robert folded his hands on the table. "You say *our* as if it belongs to all in Vondur. I make no claim on the blood your men shed."

"Ah, but it still belongs to you," Keir said. "You cannot escape what is happening. This kingdom suffers, and no speck of dirt will be unaffected."

A long sigh left Lord Robert, and he seemed to age right there in his seat. "What of you, your Majesty? I did not come here to learn that those I've protected will suffer. I want to know what you plan to do to stop it."

That was the question, wasn't it? Keir let loose a smile. "I plan to end the war, of course."

Lord Robert looked like he wanted to respond, but they were interrupted when the door opened and a guard allowed a handful of other nobles into the room. Keir invited many of his father's allies to join this council meeting, as well as those who'd opposed him. But that wasn't going to be the most difficult part.

"Lord Garnet." Keir smiled at the rotund man who'd never had a kind word for him. Yet, now that Keir was king, the fae had to keep his mouth shut.

"Your Majesty," he muttered with a stiff bow.

"Did we hear you say you plan to end the war?" Lord Osterian asked, his face bright. "Music to my ears, sire."

"It's preposterous is what it is." Lord Garnet's face went red. "With all due respect, sire, do you really think Grima will agree to end to war while the remaining crystals are in our possession?"

He didn't have an answer for that. Grima was an unknown, but they couldn't go on letting the men of this kingdom die. It would destroy Vondur faster than Grima could.

What would Tierney do? She was a strong-willed princess. He couldn't imagine her not involving herself in matters of the kingdom, and she'd been to war. How would she deal with unruly nobles? An enemy kingdom who kept coming?

Shouting ensued, one side of the table bickering with the other, and Keir had no interest in being the arbitrator.

When the door opened once more, they stopped.

Declan walked in, each step rigid like that of a soldier marching to war. He bowed. "Sorry I'm late, your Majesty."

Lord Garnet shot from his chair, one finger pointed at Declan. "Absolutely not. Your Majesty, this man is a commoner. The king's council has always been seated with noblemen. It's bad enough you have made him commander of your army, but I will not stand for this council's work to be tainted by a simple mind."

Declan looked ready to bolt, but Keir shot him a look that made him stay put. After a stunned silence, Keir fixed his eyes on the blustering lord. "The only mind that is simple is one that cannot see value in a diversity of voices. Declan, sit down. If I'm not getting out of this, neither are you."

No one argued after that. Well, about Declan anyway. The truth was, Keir didn't only want him there for solidarity. He respected the tactical brilliance Declan had gained from years in the guard. None of these pompous fools would last five seconds in a battle with the golden warriors.

Just when he thought they'd gotten through the rough edges of this first meeting, the door opened again. He expected to see a servant bringing tea, but instead, Eavha stood in the doorway.

None of the nobles noticed her at first, but Declan's alarmed gaze met Keir's. Keir valued his sister's council, he always had, and he realized how wrong so many of the Vondurian traditions regarding women were. After the war, he vowed to make changes. But he hadn't wanted his sister to face the cruelty these men would inflict upon her.

But she stepped into the room with a flinty gaze, looking as if she was ready for the fight, and he realized he was wrong. It shouldn't have been his decision at all.

For a moment, pride warmed him. Pride and gratitude. Because, in the rigid righteousness of her shoulders, he saw Tierney. In the newfound confidence his sister showed, he recognized the foreign princess' influence.

Sensing his distraction, the noblemen around the table followed the king's gaze, finding the same courageous woman he saw.

Lord Osterian blinked rapidly before turning to Keir. "I'm sorry, your Majesty. I kept my mouth shut when you invited a commoner to join us, but this is highly unusual. Women cannot advise a king."

"Your Highness," Lord Garnet grunted, eying Eavha like a leech. "Go fetch a servant and tell them we require refreshments, my dear."

Eavha's face tightened, but her voice was sugary sweet. "I am a princess, my Lord, not your errand girl. I'd be happy to point you in the direction of the kitchens, though. Some warm biscuits would make this meeting so much more pleasant, don't you think?" And then, she walked right to the empty chair beside Lord Garnet and sat down.

Keir stared at her in awe, wondering how he hadn't seen this side of her all these years. He thought that was the end of it, but then Sheba strolled in, her teeth flashing with a growl. Just what he needed. He gave his sister an irritated glance. No one could quite control the cat except for Eavha, but she chose not to. Sheba prowled around the table, getting too close to a few of the nobles who seemed to be holding their breath, before settling behind Eavha. She laid down and began licking her giant paws.

Keir cleared his throat, needing to get this meeting back on track. "I meant what I said before. It is past time we value all Vondurians and the talents they possess." He looked from Declan to Eavha to a smiling Lord Robert.

Only Lord Garnet still seemed to be struggling, the others silenced by Sheba's presence. "But—"

Keir had to put an end to this. He stood, slamming his hands down on the wooden table and leaning over it. "My sister fought in the siege. When the Grimian warriors were at our gates, she and Tierney O'Shea stood alongside my men atop the walls as arrows rained down on them. Let me ask, Lord Garnet, where were you?" Not a single nobleman had ridden to the palace with their personal guard to fight. Not. One. But Eavha was there.

"Colluding with a prisoner, a Grima spy no less, is not exactly a point in her favor."

A low growl ripped from Keir's throat before he calmed himself, replacing the anger with the cool mask of a king and sliding back into his seat. "As this is our first meeting of the council, I must make a few things clear. First, the prisoner was no spy. Tia—Tierney, that is—is a friend of Vondur. Should she return, she is to be treated as such."

He didn't expect to see Tierney again, but a king could hope.

"Second, the commander and the princess are my two closest advisors. I trust them above all others. If you want influence with the crown, you must heed them." He searched each face, looking into their eyes for any sign of dissension. But even Lord Garnet looked thoroughly shamed.

"My father disbanded the council to consolidate power, but if we are to do right by our kingdom, I believe power must be shared. Not only among those seated here but with the villagers, the soldiers. I am not my father. You would do well to remember that."

He bit back the harsh words he wanted to say and instead settled for, "And last, I do not care about your bloodlines or the wealth of your lands. The only thing that matters to me is that you have Vondur's best interests at heart. I think you do. Despite your outdated notions of tradition, the men …and woman … gathered here can find a way to bring Lenya peace. And we won't stop until we do."

Keir realized the air in the room had changed. There were no more arguments, no more heated looks or seething tempers. Even the blasted cat seemed to stare at him in approval. It was a start.

Keir was the last to leave the council chamber, and he found Lord Robert waiting for him outside the door.

"Well," Keir started, "do you regret coming?"

Lord Robert put a hand on his shoulder, not something anyone typically did with a king. "Keir, your father would disapprove of everything that happened in that meeting."

He nodded. He'd be disappointed in a lot.

Lord Robert's weathered face stretched into a kind smile. "You are going to be a great king." He bowed. "I am here for whatever it is you need. Your vision is mine now."

Keir swallowed back a mountain of emotions. "Thank you, my Lord."

Lord Robert winked before turning and walking down the corridor.

His stomach grumbling, Keir headed toward the great hall in search of lunch. He'd almost reached it when Eavha accosted him, hugging him from behind.

"You were perfect," she squealed.

Keir glanced toward the guards, who were trying not to watch, and then into the great hall, where the nobles were sure to see them soon. With a groan, he pulled Eavha away from him and led her out of sight. "Are you trying to undo all the credibility I've just gained with my new council?"

She bit her lip, trying not to laugh. "I was just so excited for you. I mean, you were all, 'me king, you stupid nobles,' and it was the coolest thing I've ever seen."

He scrubbed a hand across his face. "Well, can you contain your excitement a bit?"

"Not really. It's a flaw."

He couldn't help the laugh that escaped. "You're incorrigible."

"Most of the time, yes." Her smile fell the smallest bit. "She'd have been proud of you too."

"Eavha, Mom has been gone since you were—"

"I'm not talking about Mom. I didn't know her enough to know what would make her proud. But Tierney, I think if she saw you in that council meeting, she'd have kissed you."

Warmth crept up his neck. "Honestly, I don't know where you get such notions."

"Aw, your cheeks are red. That's adorable."

"Eavha, stop." He searched the hall. "Where is Sheba? Don't tell me she's skulking around the kitchens again."

"Oh, no. I had her follow Lord Garnet out to the stables." She dropped her voice. "Has there been any news?"

He shook his head. They'd had no word of Tierney since she left, and he tried to forget about her, about the moment he learned the fate his father handed her. She was strange, with her constant babble and sarcasm. He hadn't realized how much he enjoyed her company until she was gone.

Even though most of their time together had been spent fighting.

Eavha watched him too closely, and he looked away.

"She's gone."

"I know." Her shoulders dropped. "It's just … she was my friend, the first woman who made me believe … I don't know. She just made me believe."

"Are you two coming to eat?" Declan joined them, eyes flicking from brother to sister.

Eavha stared at Keir for a moment longer before sliding an arm through Declan's. "Come on, Deck. From one unwanted council member to another, let's go make them uncomfortable by sitting at the high table." A table reserved for the king and his closest noblemen. No commoners. No women.

Declan gave Keir a helpless look before Eavha dragged him off.

But Keir was no longer hungry. He turned, walking back the way he'd come, knowing there was work to do. He'd decided to become king when he challenged his father to the Comhrac. Now, he had to prove he was worthy.

"Still abed, are we?" Some unknown—soon to be murdered—person zoomed around Tierney's bedroom.

"Wa's happening?" Tierney rolled over. "'M 'sleep. Come back later."

"Princesses don't lie in like spoiled courtiers. Not when there's work to be done." The curtains parted and blazing sunshine streamed across Tierney's bed. The bed she was still trying to figure out how to take home with her.

"This princess is on vacation." She ducked her head under the covers. "Be gone. Before I put the guard on you."

"You say the funniest things." The servant ripped the covers off the bed, and Tierney contemplated a beheading. That would teach this idiot not to interrupt her sleep. Not when she hadn't had more than a few hours' rest.

"Come on." The girl clapped her hands, her voice too bright and chipper for such an ungodly hour.

Tierney sat up, her normally smooth, silky hair a pile of tangles hanging in her face. "Go." She swiped at her brow. "Away. Now." She lifted her gaze, rubbing her eyes to clear the cobwebs away.

"Queen Bronagh?" She gaped at the girl, blinking her bleary eyes.

"What's happening? Why are you in my room in the middle of the night?"

"It's morning, and we have much to do. Come, come. Get out of bed. We have a plan to devise."

"We do?" Tierney slid her feet to the floor, still confused. "What plan?" She reached for her dressing robe, contemplating regicide.

"I've been awake all night thinking, and I'll need your help to make it happen."

Tierney stood, shrugging into her robe as she crossed the room. Without a word, she opened the door, gesturing for the queen to exit ahead of her.

"We don't have a lot of time—"

Tierney held up her hand to stall the queen's next words. "Make me some tea. Strong, black tea. I will join you in five minutes." She slammed the door in Bronagh's face.

Shuffling to her vanity, she sat, running a brush through her hair. It was morning, all right. The sun shone just over the horizon, but she'd wager the entire court was still in bed at this hour after the long evening of celebration.

Smoothing her hair back in a simple bun and straightening her dressing gown, Tierney couldn't fathom what the queen wanted from her.

Splashing some water on her face from the basin, she shook the last vestiges of sleep from her fuzzy mind and went to join the Grima queen.

"And she'd better have that tea." Tierney yanked on the door to the common room, not in the mood for a meeting in diplomacy.

"Not a morning person, are you?" Bronagh sat on the settee. Tierney could have sworn they'd just left it an hour ago, but the queen brought tea and pastries, so she overlooked it.

"Nope." Tierney went for the steaming teapot, eager to get something warm in her belly. After a snack and a chat with the queen, she was going right back to bed.

Tierney took a big bite of a crusty lemon scone.

"I need you to teach me how to be a lady's maid," the queen blurted ... and Tierney promptly choked on her laughter.

She pounded on her chest, coughing. "You need me to do what?"

"Teach me to be a maid." Bronagh lifted a dainty pastry to her mouth.

"You're going to need to use more words. If you expect *me* to teach *you* to be a maid, we are in trouble."

"I would meet this Keir Dagnan for myself."

"And ... you want to be his maid?" Tierney took a deep sip of the scalding hot tea, hoping it would clear her head so the queen's words might make some actual sense.

"I would like to return to the Vondurian court with you. Not as Queen Bronagh, but as a member of your household. Someone who would go unnoticed."

"Okay. Why?" She set her scone and teacup on the edge of the table.

"I have great respect for everything you said last night. I want a united Lenya. I want all people of our two kingdoms to have the things they need." Bronagh stood up, twisting her hands as she paced. "This war needs to end. You say King Keir wants peace. I would like to observe him for myself before I attempt negotiations with him—negotiations my court would never approve."

"You want to infiltrate the palace so you can observe the king for yourself?" Tierney's mind chugged along, trying to keep up. "I can ... sort of get that."

"My uncle wishes to rule as regent." She whirled around. "He thinks I am too young and need further training before I can rule on my own."

"You have more strength of will than you would have your court believe." Tierney sat back, studying the shrewd young woman before her.

"I do not make big decisions. I keep my council small, with only those I trust implicitly, while I continue to establish my authority.

But make no mistake, Princess Tierney, I am queen here, and I will rule Grima until the day I die."

"How would you explain your absence?" Tierney asked. For a girl with a tenuous grasp on her throne, leaving seemed like a bad idea.

"I will go on campaign, visiting the villages and my troops. I'll leave Donal and my uncle in charge. My brother is young, but I trust him to keep the nobles in line."

"You would risk leaving at such a precarious time in your reign?"

Bronagh stopped her pacing. "To finally bring an end to this war, I would risk far more."

"You want to make the right decisions for your people." Tierney nodded. "I can respect that."

"Then, you will help me?"

"I will do what I can." Tierney didn't want to think about returning to the place where she was almost executed. She didn't want to think about seeing Keir again. "But if you want to masquerade as a maid, then we're going to need help. And possibly a miracle or two."

"She wants to do what?" Veren blinked rapidly in the bright sunshine.

It was ungodly hot for the Grima region, yet they were traveling down the mountain roads to the sea.

"You heard me." Tierney patted her horse's vibrant red mane. "She wants to see for herself what the Vondurian king is like."

"It's out of the question." Veren trotted his mount up to her side, nudging between Tierney and Gulliver.

"That's what I said." Gulliver munched on a bright red fruit filled with succulent seeds. "She's got a few too many bats in the belfry, that one. I'd rather stay here for the rest of my life than go back to Vondur, but nobody ever asks me."

"We're going," Tierney said. "And who are you two to be making decisions for a queen?" She nudged her horse forward along the road. "The queen has a mind to make decisions for her people based on her own experiences with the new king. We're going to support that."

"But … how? How does she expect to slip into the enemy's palace undetected?" Veren scoffed. "She's a queen. That's like expecting you to suddenly become a milkmaid among the Gelsi villagers. They'd know you for a royal without ever having seen your face before."

"She's going as a maid of my household." Tierney lifted her face into the slight breeze, searching for some relief from this oppressive heat. She hadn't experienced such temperatures since leaving Vondur.

"A maid?" Veren pulled his horse to a stop. "Have you both lost your minds?"

"I'd go with yes." Gulliver tossed the remains of his fruit down before the horses, letting them search for the plump seeds.

"The queen's lady's maid is her best friend. They grew up together, so Bronagh trusts her. She's working with the queen as we speak, training her to pass as a maid."

"The woman has never placed a cube of sugar into her own teacup, but you think she'll be able to make and serve tea to others?" Veren's face clouded with worry. He seemed to care for the young queen's welfare. "She's going to get herself killed."

"That's why you're coming with us."

"Us?" Gulliver snorted. "I'm staying right here, thanks. Those people put me in a dungeon and starved me to within an inch of my life. I won't give them a second chance."

"Keir wouldn't let anything happen to you, Gullie. And Veren won't let anything happen to Bronagh."

"And who's going to watch out for you?" Gulliver's tail swished behind him in agitation. "Don't say you can take care of yourself; we all know that. But you're going to need someone watching your back."

"Which is why you will brave the Vondurian palace at my side." Tierney turned her bright smile on her best friend.

"I swear, Tia O'Shea, if I find myself at the end of a rope for a second time, I'm never speaking to you again."

"So, we're in agreement then? We will return to Vondur on some pretense or another, bringing Bronagh with us to see for herself what kind of man Keir Dagnan is."

"Just one question, Tia." Gulliver turned in his saddle to meet her gaze. "How does this help us get home? How does it help us find Siobhan?"

Tierney sighed, looking at the dusty fields ahead of them. "I don't know, Gullie. First, I need to see how the fire plains are encroaching on Grima. I think that's the key to our next steps."

"See for yourself." Veren pointed across the dry, lifeless field as he nudged his mount forward, leaving the main road.

"This close to the palace already?" Tierney shielded her eyes from the bright sun glaring off the packed earth.

"When I first arrived in Grima, I rode with Prince Donal past these fields." Veren dismounted his horse, moving to stand beside Tierney, who remained mounted. "Just a few short months ago, that was a verdant green expanse, full of life. And over there." He pointed to a spot where the air shimmered and swayed as the heat rose from the ground. "That was a village. And not your average poor farming community either. It was a thriving village with a strong economy. Shops lined the streets and fields of every color spread into the distance. It's gone now."

"Where did it all go?" Gulliver squinted, trying to see the remnants of the village that once stood here.

"It's been swallowed up by the fire plains."

"It doesn't look like the plains." Tierney turned her horse in a circle, looking for the scorched earth, the lava pools, and the billowing smoke she associated with the burning lands.

"It started with the rising temperatures," Veren explained. "Then, a season of poor crops, lack of rain. Small things at first—or so I'm told. Then, the residents complained their water supplies had gone foul. Ponds and streams turned warm and then hot with the taste of sulfur. When the fires started, homes and businesses closest to the rising temperatures began to smolder, bursting into flames before anything could be done to salvage the buildings. Within a matter of weeks, there was nothing left. The families lost everything. Their livelihood. Their crops, livestock. Everything."

Veren pointed to a post in the ground just a few yards from the road. "Last week, the ground was green up to that post. Now, everything from there to the road is dying. It won't be long before the spread takes out the next village. Grima is in danger, Tierney." Veren settled wide eyes on her. "And I don't know how to stop it."

"All of Lenya is in danger." Tierney steered her horse back to the road. "And with both kingdoms at each other's throats, it might be up to us to find a solution."

"Just perfect." Gulliver groaned. "Why is it always us?"

"What did you do to her?" Prince Tobias ran past the guards stationed near the front of the Iskalt palace before Siobhan could even dismount.

Siobhan's relief at seeing the familiar face almost overcame her grief at still not knowing where his sister was. Almost.

Griffin slid from his horse. "Good to see you too, nephew."

Tobias crossed his arms, and he looked so much like Tierney in that moment Siobhan had to blink back tears. "It would have been good to see you before you took an Iskaltian noblewoman as prisoner."

"We didn't hold her prisoner." Griffin sounded tired from the journey, tired and sad. He hadn't asked for specifics of what happened in the portal once she told him she didn't know where Tierney was. He said Lochlan should be the first to know the full story.

"But you did arrest her."

Riona jumped down, landing with grace on the snow-packed ground. "Does it always have to be so blasted cold here?"

"Yes," Tobias and Siobhan said simultaneously.

From the moment they entered the ice kingdom, Siobhan knew she was home. As the gooseflesh rose on her arms and a shiver raced down her spine, she looked away. It wouldn't do to have any of them see her tears.

Two boys ran toward them and bowed to Tobias. "We've come to take care of the horses. The king sent us." Another young man followed behind, and Siobhan recognized him as the prince of Eldur, Tobias' suitor.

Tobias eyed the younger boys. "You're not needed. My uncle can care for his own horses after the trouble he caused."

The Eldurian prince snorted. "That was what your mother said."

Stepping to the side of her horse, Tobias looked up at Siobhan like she held all the answers he so desperately needed. "Come, let me help you down."

She slid a leg over the saddle and let her feet drop to the ground with Tobias' hands at her waist. He wasn't the twin she wanted to see, but he had Tierney's smile as he gave her a soft look.

"Let's get you inside." He wrapped a protective arm around her shoulders and led her away from a grumbling Griffin and a stoic Riona. They'd refused to bring guards with them, saying this was a family affair. But Siobhan was not part of that family, and she just wanted to go home to see her father.

"Give her some room to breathe, Tobes," Logan said. "You're suffocating her."

Siobhan had never been so grateful for a simple request before. The moment Tobias released her, she drew in a long breath and listened to the rapid pounding of her heart.

It wasn't her first time in the Iskaltian palace. There were royal balls and dinners, plays and musicals. But Tobias wasn't leading her to the grand hall or any of the other public places. This corridor wound up to the royal family's wing.

"So …" Tobias didn't sound like he was sure he should speak. "Griff didn't hurt you, did he? He's not so bad, but really, he can be quite pigheaded sometimes."

"Pigheaded, your Highness?" The momentary confusion was a welcome distraction. "Like, a fae who has a pig's head? Is that a type of Dark Fae in Myrkur?"

He stifled a laugh. "No, um, my mom says it to my father quite often. It's like … well, actually I'm not sure what it means. I just know she says it when he's being particularly insufferable."

"Well, then I guess Griffin and Riona both had pig heads at first. Then, I explained who I was and they immediately began preparations for our journey to Iskalt."

Tobias nodded. "We received word days ago and have been awaiting your arrival. Griffin explained everything in the letter. You came through the rift after my sister left you in the human world?"

"I'm not sure that is quite accurate." Tierney leaving her implied choice, and she got the feeling Tierney didn't have control over anything that happened.

"Oh, of course. I didn't mean it like that. But Tia shouldn't have taken you to the human realm."

"Toby," Logan warned.

"What?" Tobias looked back at his prince. "I love my sister, but she was reckless, and now she's across the fire plains in a land we know little about. I'm allowed to be angry. I'm allowed to hate her just a bit for being gone." His chest heaved with anger, and his eyes grew wild with frustration.

In his calm greeting, Siobhan hadn't realized how much the prince was hurting, but she could see it now in the tension he carried in his shoulders, the way his eyes wouldn't focus.

What he'd said didn't register until that moment. "Wait, across the fire plains? How do you know this?" Her heart swelled at hearing Tierney was alive.

"Maybe we should save explanations for when we've all gathered." Queen Brea stood in the doorway of the royal suites, looking as regal as Siobhan had always found her. The pale blue dress was embroidered with what looked like icicles. Her long hair was swept up into an unusual hairstyle, pulled back from her face with some kind of lace holding it in a high tail at the back of her head.

"Siobhan." She gave her a kind smile. "We are so glad you've returned, dear. Come, let's get you warm. Your father is on his way, and he will be brought up as soon as he arrives."

Siobhan's shoulders sagged in relief, and a soft sob escaped her lips. It was over. All this time alone, traveling through a world she didn't know, her arrest in Myrkur, the journey here upon learning Tierney hadn't returned ... it all came crashing down around her.

"Oh, honey." The queen pulled her into a tight hug. "You're safe now."

Siobhan's body shook. Under normal circumstances, she'd never let the royal family see her in such a state, but right now, she just needed a mother. Even if said mother was the queen.

"Come near the fire." She led Siobhan into a grand sitting room with plush velvet carpeting and soft white drapes. Two settees faced each other in front of the black opal hearth. They were the toughest gems in the fae realm, and it was a welcome sight seeing the familiarity in Iskalt.

Siobhan sat before the queen, something that was considered poor manners, but all she could think of was thawing her frozen limbs. She held them toward the warmth, and it snaked over her skin, coiling in her belly.

"Here." Queen Brea handed her a cup of tea before turning to her son. "Where is your uncle?"

"I made him take the horses to the stables." He shrugged.

"I knew you were my son." Brea ruffled his hair. "Your siblings?"

"Kayleigh is keeping everyone occupied in the nursery, so we won't be interrupted."

"Good, good. Now, we must wait for—"

"I'm here." King Lochlan walked in, his steps heavy and firm.

"Us too." Griffin followed him, looking like he'd gone a few rounds with a bull.

"What happened to you?" Lochlan asked.

Griffin sent Toby a pointed look. "Horse kicked me, and I landed in the hay."

Lochlan looked from his brother to his son with a sigh. "Tia isn't here so you become her?"

Toby's satisfied smile dropped. "If I do, will you make me marry an Iskaltian noble too?"

Siobhan winced at the vitriol in his tone, and she noticed both Griffin and Riona do the same. She'd never truly considered what this marriage arrangement would mean for Tierney. When Siobhan's father broached the topic of making her an eligible choice for the princess, Siobhan agreed, but she'd been half in love with Tierney already.

And if she'd said no? Her father would have accepted that.

The queen sat beside Siobhan and reached for her hand. "It's best not to get involved." There was sadness in her voice.

Lochlan walked to the tea cart and poured himself a cup. Then, he pulled out a flask and tipped it against the cup.

Griffin snatched the flask from him and didn't bother with the tea, drinking whatever was inside it straight. He grimaced, but he didn't stop.

"Okay." Brea brought everyone to attention. "Here's what will happen. I want to know every tiny detail about what happened to my girl. So, you boys will not get in the way. Toby, you'll stop blaming your father for the next hour. Griffin, you will listen to someone other than yourself. And Loch, you will not take whatever is said and go running into danger." Her eyes fell on Riona. "You just … do you, Ri."

Riona nodded. "I don't know how to do anything else."

"Siobhan, start at the beginning." She patted Siobhan's hand. "Please."

"Well, none of us planned on going with Tia to the human realm. At least, Veren and I didn't. Gulliver jumped into the portal after her, but it sort of just pulled us in."

Tobias pursed his lips. "It must have been too powerful. Tierney has never been good at holding back, and with portals, everything needs to be precise."

"The human realm was … different. But we were enjoying ourselves, eating odd food and watching a box with strange portraits that moved."

"A television," both Brea and Lochlan said at once.

Lochlan smiled. "Tierney loves the television. When she was younger, she wanted me to figure out how to make one work in our world, but that is magic we do not possess."

Siobhan went on to tell them about the rest of their time in the human realm, the party they'd thrown Tierney, how they'd planned to come home.

"We knew staying there wasn't right when fae would worry about us here."

Brea covered her mouth with her hand. "We checked the farmhouse, but it wasn't until a few days after she'd disappeared, when we figured out she hadn't just gone to Myrkur with Gulliver. It wouldn't have been the first time she left and didn't send word for days. When we saw the remnants of the party, we started to worry."

"Yeah," Tobias said. "No one ever feels good about Tierney opening portals. It's like the one thing she's terrible at."

"And what happened next?" Lochlan perched on the arm of a settee, tipping his teacup against his lips.

Siobhan twisted her hands together and stared at her lap. "She opened the portal. We all held on to each other, not wanting to be separated, but something pulled us apart. I lost consciousness, and when I woke, I was back in the human realm. Alone. From there, I made my way to the rift. It was this pull I couldn't ignore. I considered waiting for someone to find me, but the magic… I'd never felt anything like it."

Lochlan rubbed the back of his neck and met his brother's gaze. "Is it possible?"

"I don't know." Griffin shook his head. "It shouldn't be, but the O'Shea magic still has so many unknowns."

"Care to share with the class?" Brea nudged her husband.

Lochlan was quiet for a moment, thinking. "A portal is like a road. It goes from one point to another. In our case, from our world to the human world and back, depending on where you direct it to. It should not let anyone off that road until they've reached the final destination."

"I still don't understand."

"Siobhan began journeying down that road with Tierney and the others," Griffin explained. "But the portal let her off. Whatever Tierney did, however she crafted the portal, it seems she created one with … branches."

"Branches?" Brea scrubbed a hand over her face. "You're saying my daughter created a portal and led four people in, but something went wrong and the portal spit them all out in different places?"

"I wouldn't say spit …" Lochlan muttered. "But essentially, yes. Her magic is strong, Brea. We've always known this. Strong and sometimes erratic. This time, it may have been too strong even for the portal."

A stunned silence filled the room. Too strong for a portal.

"So, Tierney, Gulliver, and Veren could all be in different places?" Tobias asked, reaching for Logan's hand.

"Toby …" Siobhan couldn't wrap her head around any of this. "You said she's across the fire plains. How do you know?"

"I can feel her. Just enough to know she's alive. She's too far for me to feel her magic, to amplify it, but something in me just knows that she's okay and she's trying to get home to us."

There was a knock on the door, and Riona went to open it. After a moment, Siobhan heard her father's voice. "Where's my daughter?"

She jumped from the settee and sprinted across the ornate sitting room, caring nothing for propriety. Not now. Her father caught her as she crashed against him and folded her into his arms.

"My girl," he whispered. "My girl."

Her tears dampened his shirt as his familiar smell of cherry pipe tobacco invaded her senses.

He brushed her hair away from her face and looked down at her. "You're really here."

She nodded. "I'm home, Father. I made it home."

"Yes, you did." He smiled before his expression hardened and he looked over her head. "I'm taking my daughter to our estate. She's done here."

"Lord Belmore." Brea stood. "We were speaking to her about Tierney, and—"

"No, it has been enough for today. She is exhausted, and this ordeal has been long and drawn out. I must leave this palace before I say what I wish to say."

"Father—"

"No, Siobhan, you do not owe them more."

Didn't he get that she wanted to help? "Father!" Her brusque tone had his surprised eyes finding hers. "You have a pig's head."

"Excuse me?"

"What happened to me is not his Majesty's fault, nor is it even the princess'. It was a mistake—sure, a large one—but there was no ill intent. We must work together to find the others."

"But you—"

"No. They're my friends, Father." Friends. She'd never truly used that word before. "And I will do anything in my power to bring them home." She turned to the royals seated before the roaring flames. Respect shone in their eyes. "What do we know about the fire plains?"

"Only that it is impossible to survive a journey across them," Lochlan said.

Brea nodded. "Impossible is a state of mind. I want to hear solutions, not problems."

Siobhan met Tobias' gaze and gave him a small nod, a promise. They would bring his sister home.

"I still think this is the worst idea you've ever had." Gulliver trotted his horse up between Tierney and Queen Bronagh. He tugged his hood down low over his eyes as they traveled the long dusty road that would soon take them into Vondurian territory.

"It wasn't my idea," Tierney said, chewing on her bottom lip.

"I know. I'm just saying there is no way either of you could ever pass for a credible maid. Not without weeks of training. A few days learning how to make tea isn't going to fool anyone who's ever had an actual maid. Not even Keir."

"We couldn't waste any more time, Gullie." Tierney cast a wary glance around them, looking for danger around every corner. "We'll keep working on Bronagh's training as we travel. See." Tierney nodded toward the Grima Queen. "She's working on her slouching right now."

"It will be fine, Gulliver." Bronagh made an effort to shrug off her queenly posture. "I only need a few days to observe the king from the shadows.

"She looks like a maid." Tierney admired the effort of the queen's maid. In a borrowed dress and her hair in a simple bun with a white cap over her head, she did look the part. As long as she didn't speak, most wouldn't give her much notice.

"She sounds like a queen." Veren rode up beside them.

"We have time to teach her some slang."

"Yeah, and what kind of slang do you know?" Gulliver asked.

"Human slang." Tierney's shoulders drooped.

"Exactly. And when Keir finds out we've brought the enemy into his court, we're all going to hang." Gulliver rubbed his throat absently.

Tierney balled her hand into a fist to keep herself from doing the same. The feel of the hangman's noose around her neck was not something she would ever forget.

"How close are we to the border?" Bronagh asked.

"We will reach Vondur lands by late afternoon." Veren studied his map with a frown. "I believe this road leads to a lesser traveled route that will allow us to slip past the border guards undetected. I studied all possible routes with Prince Donal before we left." He returned the map to his saddle bags. "He assures me this is the best way to reach the palace without risking the king's guard."

Tierney's stomach twisted into knots at the thought of facing the king's soldiers. Though King Keir had released her, the general assumption among Vondurian soldiers was that she was the hated Grima spy. She'd rather not run the risk of discovery out here on the road.

As they approached the border, Veren rode ahead to scout the way. A voice inside Tierney's mind screamed *Abort! Abort!* Her horse danced under her in response to her mounting tension.

"It will be okay, Tia." Bronagh's hand reached out to grasp hers. "You've assured me time and again that Keir is a different sort of king."

"And he is." Tierney nodded. "However, while there are several people I'd love to see again, I can't help but think of all the others who wished me dead."

"As much as I don't want to see anyone of Vondur ever again," Gulliver muttered, "it's been weeks since we left. Time enough for Keir to have established his rule. He won't let any harm come to you again."

"Let's hope." She let out a breath but still didn't feel any better about what they were doing.

"Ride!" Veren came charging back up the road, kicking up a storm of dust behind him.

"What's happening?" Bronagh turned toward him.

"I don't need to be told twice." Gulliver reached for the queen's reins and urged her mount to follow his away from the Vondurian border. "Come on, Tia!"

Just as they pulled into an all-out gallop the way they'd come, Tierney reared her horse back from the king's guard blocking their retreat.

"The bloody sneaks came up behind us!" Gulliver growled, his eyes scanning their surroundings looking for a way out.

"Get the mongrel!" The captain in charge barked out orders to his men. "The king has promised a high price for his head. And he'll pay handsomely for the Grima spy and her consorts too."

"Run, Gullie!" Tierney dug her heels into her horse's flanks and turned off the road, guiding her mount through the short, scrubby brush, heading for the cover of the forest. Casting a glance over her shoulder, she saw her friends following her lead. She had to find a way out. If Keir was searching for them, whatever awaited them at the palace wouldn't be good.

"This cannot happen again."

"Tia, watch out!" Veren shouted, and she turned a moment too late. Her horse skidded to a halt in front of a line of grubby, half-starved-looking soldiers. Circling back around, the other soldiers swarmed her.

"Gullie!" Tierney sobbed at the sight of her best friend lying on the ground with a soldier's foot on his back while another tied his hands behind him. "Stop! You can't treat him like that!"

"The king will decide what to do with the mongrel."

"Don't call him that." Veren struggled against the soldiers holding him. "Leave her alone!" He kicked out at the soldier pushing Bronagh to her knees beside Gulliver.

"Come on, *Princess*." The captain lunged toward Tierney, grabbing for her reins. "You might have escaped the hangman's noose once, but it won't happen again."

"The king released us," Tierney argued, kicking the captain's chin so his head snapped back, and he spit out a gob of blood.

"Get her off that horse."

Dirty hands and arms wrapped around her, dragging her off her horse and tossing her in a heap on the ground. She groaned and curled into a ball when the captain landed a brutal kick to her stomach.

"Tierney is the Crown Princess of Iskalt," Veren shouted, struggling anew against his captors. "You will treat her as such!"

"I know nothing of any land called Iskalt." The man spit on the ground. "You're in Vondur now, and we don't take kindly to Grima spies."

Tia tucked into a ball to avoid the kicks and bruising punches that raked across her torso and arms. Scrunching her face up, she closed her eyes and held her breath to avoid choking on the dust and grime.

"Welcome back, *Princess*." A torrent of spit rained down on her.

Why did I think I could return here and it would be different this time?

CHAPTER 12
KEIR

"We need to fortify the north wall of the palace." Keir glanced up at the crumbling stone damaged in the siege. His father hadn't bothered to do a survey of their defenses after everything that happened.

He really had to stop thinking about his father. None of this was about him.

"Sire?" The young builder who'd been tasked with recording the king's desires gave him a questioning look.

"Sorry, moving on. Let's go have a look at the battlements." He headed for the far tower and the spiral staircase within. In his mind, he saw Tierney and Eavha running up these steps to join the fight. He saw his men arguing with them, but the women winning.

With a sigh, he trudged up the stairs. Had he failed Eavha? She was on his council now, but something wasn't altogether right. This morning, he'd asked her to accompany him on this task, but she'd made up an excuse about needing to air out her rooms—a job Ariella should have done for her.

And then, when he stopped by her rooms to see how she was

progressing, she wasn't there and the windows were firmly shut, leaving the space as closed in as ever.

She'd lied.

He reached the top of the walls, where a line of guards stood ready for any threat that could come from all directions. He'd had to bolster the palace guard with men from his troops, and not all of them were particularly good at the standing still part.

Keir took note of the few who squirmed and whispered amongst themselves while the others went rigid at the presence of the king, standing at attention. The chatterers were young, probably from a village unit that had never received a visit from the king.

"Your Majesty." The nearest guard turned and bowed. Keir recognized him as Colin, a man who'd worked in the palace for many years. "I think you'll find everything in order up here. Most of the damages during the siege occurred at the gates."

Keir nodded. "Those will be taken care of, and—" He stopped when he caught sight of movement near the tree line. He wasn't the only one.

"Guards!" Colin barked. "At the ready." Every third man raised a bow, preparing an assault on whomever traveled those woods.

Riders appeared, waving the king's standard high. As they neared in the blazing afternoon sun, Colin ordered, "Stand down; they're our scouts."

In the middle of the group rode two women, but Keir couldn't make out their faces. If they brought prisoners, he had to know why. Why else would women ride with them? He hadn't yet allowed them to join the scouting parties in search of Grima troops.

"It's the Grima spy," a guard shouted.

Keir stepped forward, gripping the wall. Despite his own words, he knew there was only one person his men would call the Grima spy. Her blond hair came into view first. There was no mistaking it. The way she rode the horse like a Vondurian warrior, one leg to either side, the lithe movement of her body as the group trotted toward the castle.

"Open the gates," Keir yelled. He took off running down the stairs and out into the courtyard. The gates opened with an agonizing slowness, and he waited. The scouting party thundered through, pulling to a stop.

There was no doubt in his mind now. In the time since they'd been separated, he often wondered if she'd survived, if she'd made it to safety. With every decision he made as king, he asked himself what she would think. His entire life changed because he chose to save her, chose to believe she was who she claimed to be.

And now, she sat atop a horse just feet from him.

Keir lifted his gaze, skating it up the horse's flanks to Tierney's strong, trouser-clad legs. Up over her capable hands until he finally reached the scowl she directed his way. Her face was dirty and bruised. She looked like she'd been through war and back since he'd last seen her.

"Your Majesty." One of the scouts slid from his horse, but Keir paid him no mind.

Tierney jumped down with the grace of a seasoned fighter. She still wasn't smiling, but her eyes connected with his, anger swirling in their depths.

He'd missed that anger.

She strode forward to greet him, causing a stir behind her that she would dare approach the king without permission.

Keir opened his mouth to speak, but he didn't get a word out before Tierney's fist slammed into his jaw sending a sharp pain through him.

"Despicable," she growled and shoved him hard, forcing him to take several steps back. "Unconscionable."

"Tierney ..."

Guards gripped her arms, pulling her away. She didn't struggle, and her gaze remained burning into his. "You were supposed to be different, and yet here I am, once again taken captive by your men. My friends treated like animals."

"I didn't ..."

"Sire," Colin said. "Want us to escort her to a cell?"

"What? Absolutely not." He straightened. "Release her at once."

The guards looked at each other, as if not sure they should obey their own king. "Sire—"

"That was an order." Keir's voice took on a hard edge.

They released Tierney, and thankfully she didn't lunge forward again. Instead, she turned to check on one of her companions perched atop another mount. "Are you okay?" Her voice was low, soft.

The woman nodded but did not speak.

"Gullie? Veren?"

They both gave her an affirmative answer, so she turned back to Keir. "Why, Keir? You let me go. I came back for a reason, but I didn't get the chance to do it on my terms because you instructed your scouts to seize us."

"I didn't—"

"Tierney?" A shriek pierced the courtyard. Eavha sprinted toward the other princess, barreling into her. "I didn't think I'd ever see you again."

Tierney hugged her back just as tightly, something Keir couldn't help smiling at. The smile fell when he noticed what his sister was wearing. She was clad in leather armor not suitable for a day spent in the palace.

"I only wish I could have returned under my own volition." Tierney held her at arm's length.

"What do you mean?" Eavha asked. "What did Keir do now?"

He tried to object, but the girls ignored him.

"He had us arrested again."

Eavha gasped. "He wouldn't."

"Not if he was intelligent, no."

Eavha turned, her eyes narrowed. "I'm disappointed in you, brother. Just because Tierney chose to go to Grima does not make her the enemy."

"I—"

"You can't jump to conclusions just to suit your mood." She looked sideways at Tierney. "You would not believe it, but I think he's even more morose since becoming king."

"Not possible." Tierney shook her head.

"I wouldn't have thought so either."

"I'm right here, you know." Keir let loose a scowl that would've frightened the hardest of Grima's golden warriors. Neither girl reacted.

He couldn't help noticing the eyes on them from the guards and the travel weary scouts. "I will handle our visitors. Return to your posts." When none of them moved, he clapped his hands once to get their attention. "Now, soldiers."

Guards dispersed, and scouts led their horses toward the stables, leaving Keir standing face to face with two annoyed princesses, a woman he didn't recognize, a tall man, and Gulliver. They all stared at him with accusation in their eyes.

Keir rubbed the back of his neck. "No one is a prisoner, but maybe we should talk inside." He turned on his heel, knowing they'd follow him.

Eavha chattered incessantly through the halls, telling Tierney of all the palace gossip he didn't know existed. He tried not to listen, but the moment he caught his own name, he couldn't help it.

"Most people are okay with Keir being king and think he'll protect us," Eavha whispered. "But some of the women are still preparing."

Preparing how? He didn't get an answer because they arrived at the very same rooms Tierney inhabited before.

Pushing open the door, he gestured for them to enter.

When Tierney passed him, she looked up. "Will I be able to leave this time, your Majesty?" There was a bite to her tone, and he realized how much he'd missed that.

Very few fae challenged him. Most feared he might order their punishment if they spoke out of turn. It was how his father had ruled.

Once they were all inside, he closed the door. Before any of them could throw out further accusations, he spoke hard and firm. "Let me make one thing clear. I ordered no one to apprehend you. I will be questioning the captain who brought you in as soon as I leave here. He will be punished for acting in my name without orders to do so. I speak true, Tierney, when I say you and yours are always welcome in Vondur."

Tierney lowered herself to the settee, perching on the edge, and crossed her arms.

"Who are you?" Eavha asked. She was eying the tall man like he was a river running through the bone-dry desert.

The man smiled, clearly enjoying the princess' attention. "Lord Rhatigan." He lifted Eavha's hand, pressing a kiss to the back of it. "Heir to the Duchy of Rhatigan, at your service."

Tierney made a gagging sound. "The duke is his father. This is just Veren." She stood and crossed the room, grabbing Eavha's arm and pulling her away. "Don't let the good looks fool you. He's a snake." She sent him a smile.

Veren winked. "We'll see if you still think so once I've won your hand."

Keir's throat tightened. "That friend you were seeking … he is your betrothed?" He was glad she'd found him, but the idea of …

A harsh laugh barked out of Tierney. "He wishes. If we ever find Siobhan, I'm choosing her. At least I can stand to be around her."

One of her friends was still missing? Keir studied the way she tried and failed to smile, the sadness in her eyes. His heart twisted at her pain.

Her expression returned to neutral, all traces of emotion gone. "This is Yvonne." She gestured to the small woman trying to make herself unobtrusive.

"She's a maid I took a liking to. I brought her with us to attend to me while we are here."

Keir nodded. "Eavha, please take Yvonne to Ariella. She'll show her where she will stay in the servants' quarters."

"But Keir—"

"Please just do as I say for once."

With a huff, she led Yvonne from the room, leaving Keir with Tierney, Veren, and Gulliver. Veren circled the room, picking up every item he could and examining them. "Wow, you really do build everything out of depleted crystals. Donal was right."

"Donal?" Keir's eyes snapped to the other man. "Just how close were you to the royal family of Grima?"

Tierney sent him a sharp look.

Veren shrugged. "I heard a few speeches. Vondurians are evil, blah blah blah. Lenya isn't my kingdom, so I don't really care about your wars."

Keir didn't like Veren already, and he definitely didn't trust him. He'd have to assign a guard to keep an eye on him. For now, he turned away, intent on ignoring him and focusing on the woman he never thought he'd see again.

Tierney looked road-weary and a little worse for the wear but strong. Despite the tangles in her hair, the smudges of dirt on her face, she drew her shoulders back and held her head high. He wondered if she had a weapon hidden on her or if the scouts had completely disarmed her.

He had so many questions. Questions a king needed to ask a fae returning from an enemy court, but the words didn't come. Instead, he gave her a self-deprecating smile. "Eavha won't listen to a word I say since you left."

Tierney laughed and relaxed back onto the settee. "I don't think she ever really listened to you before that. She just didn't voice her disagreements." Her eyes slid shut.

"You're probably right." He sat on the other end of the settee, keeping a respectable distance between them. "I invited her to sit on my council."

Tierney opened one eye. "And how did that go?"

"She was pleased. Some of my nobles had issues with it. But in order for us to move forward, we must change. No good comes from remaining stuck in antiquated notions."

"I seem to remember a prince who believed in those antiquated notions."

"Just as the kingdom evolves, so do I."

Her lips twitched. "I yelled at you in front of your men."

He nodded. "I noticed that."

"I'm not sorry."

"I would not presume to believe you are." Keir felt her nearness, the way she seemed to radiate with life. "But, Tierney, this time is different. I promise you are my welcome guest and will be treated as such as long as I am king. What you endured before … I cannot begin to express how—"

"Please don't apologize."

"But it is necessary."

A sigh breathed out of her. "Necessary is boring. Just tell me I deserved it because I probably did. Own your actions, your Majesty. I was a foreigner who arrived out of the sky in the middle of your battle. Don't be disingenuous and tell me you wish you'd reacted differently."

"What a strange world we live in."

"Especially when you consider we've now gone the last few minutes without yelling at one another."

Keir stared at her, at the way her face softened when she grew more tired, how sweet she could appear even when delivering the harshest of remarks. She lifted one brow, and he cleared his throat, getting to his feet. "I have some things I must attend to. I'll send Ariella to get you three something to eat. Feel free to leave this room. My castle is your castle, but please alert me to any trouble you encounter."

With one final glance at where Veren and Gullie lounged on the bed and then to Tierney, he turned on his heel and forced himself to walk away.

She was back. The woman who got him into this situation, the one that made him realize his fae deserved a better king.

He didn't know how long she would stay, or why she'd come at all, but at least he knew now what became of her. And that was enough. For the moment.

CHAPTER 13
KEIR

Tell me I deserved it.

She'd wanted to believe Keir was justified in his actions, that the wrong he'd committed was for a reason. Yet, he knew the truth. What he'd done to her and her friend was unconscionable. He'd acted just as his father would have.

When Tierney first appeared at the end of the battle, Keir had only wanted to get home. He hadn't considered who she might really be, that maybe she wasn't the spy he'd assumed she was.

And even once he began to realize how wrong he was, he hadn't let her go. There had been so many opportunities, and still, he'd obeyed his father. Choosing the easy route over what was right.

Turning over in bed, Keir kicked the blanket tangled around his legs. Sleep was a fruitless pursuit tonight. His mind wouldn't quiet, not when he saw her every time he closed his eyes.

Tierney was a princess in her own right. Heir to her own kingdom. He didn't know how he'd ever questioned it. The way she held herself with authority, the fierceness in her eyes. She wasn't of Lenya, and soon, she would have to find a way home. But she'd changed him, changed his sister, changed Vondur.

And there was no going back to what they were before.

Rubbing his eyes, he sat up in the dark. It took a while to adjust and be able to see the table carved from totems that had long lost their magic, the walls glittering with fragments of crystals.

Even as a child, before his father became king, he'd thought the palace was a magical place. But now, he needed to get out of these walls. Sliding from the bed, he retrieved a tunic from his wardrobe and pulled it on over his chest—a chest that should have been criss-crossed with scars from all the wounds he'd suffered in battle. Most warriors of Vondur, who still lived, suffered from the remnants, the reminders of the war.

But not the king. For only he had access to the healing baths. It didn't feel right that so many should die while he hoarded such life-saving magic for himself.

Stuffing his feet into his boots, he laced them up and pulled open the door. He'd hardly stepped into the hall before running into Declan, the commander giving him a formal bow.

"Stop that." Keir scowled.

Declan's voice was low to keep from being overheard. "We must keep up appearances, your Majesty. I am your commander now."

"Yes, but you're still my friend, and I'll not have you bowing every time you see me."

"As you wish." The stubborn man lowered himself to one knee. "Is this better?"

Keir sighed. "Being king is hard enough without you making a mockery of it."

"I would never mock, your Majesty." His lips twitched.

"Just get up, Deck."

Declan rose to his feet. "I thought I'd have to wake you tonight."

"That would imply I ever went to sleep." Keir started down the corridor.

"You need your rest, Keir."

"Thanks for that. Why were you coming to see me in the middle of the night?" He stopped, realizing if it couldn't wait until morning, it must be serious.

"I just returned from the troops at the border. There have been no sightings of the golden warriors of late, but something is amiss in Grima."

"What do you mean?"

"We received intel that the queen has left the palace."

Keir froze. "And where would she go?" The palace was the safest place for her. She would know that as well as everyone else.

Declan shrugged. "No one seems to know. There are rumors she is on campaign, visiting some of the far reaches of Grima to solidify her reign, but no one has actually seen her."

A string of curses flew from Keir's lips. If the queen left the palace, she was preparing for something. "Keep the troops on high alert for anything out of the ordinary. I don't want us to be caught unawares."

Footsteps neared them, and Keir looked up to find the maid who'd arrived with Tierney. Her face reddened.

"I'm sorry, your Majesty," she stammered, dipping into an awkward curtsy. It looked like she'd done very few of them in her life. "I didn't mean to interrupt. My lady is up on the walls, and I was returning to fetch a cloak for her."

"That's quite all right, Yvonne." Keir stepped aside. "You can continue on your way."

She scurried off on her errand, and Declan chuckled. "Who was that?"

"Tierney's maid."

His eyes widened. "Tierney is back?"

Keir clapped him on the shoulder. "You missed a lot today. I'm sure you'll learn it all in the morning, but you need your rest and I need some air."

"That air wouldn't happen to be atop the walls, would it?"

Keir ignored him and changed direction, heading for the courtyard. Once outside, he searched the grounds, nodding to a few guards. When he tilted his head back, he caught sight of a lone figure sitting atop the wall silhouetted by the silver light of the moon.

His guards kept their distance from her, and he wondered if they were frightened. Honestly, she scared him a bit. Her lack of restraint, the way she did whatever it was she wanted to do. Even men in Vondur did not have those freedoms.

Before he knew what he was doing, he found himself climbing the spiral staircase and emerging onto the platform at the top of the wall. Tierney's eyes were fixed on the orchestra of stars above, and she didn't acknowledge him.

"Your maid said you were up here." He studied her, the way the light reflected off her dark eyes. How her lips curled into the smallest half-smile, like she found him slightly amusing.

Finally, she spoke. "I sent her away so I could be alone."

Alone. "I'll leave you to it then."

"Keir?" She dropped her chin, her eyes tearing from the sky overhead.

"Yes?"

"Stay."

That one word was all he needed to hear. Taking a seat beside her, he tried not to think of how improper this was for the king—to sit so casually on the wall, where anyone could see him. His father had taught him appearance was everything. He had to seem like he cared about everyone in his kingdom. But he truly did care, and he knew those attachments were dangerous.

A sigh echoed from Tierney. "I was just sitting here, wondering if my brother was looking up at the same stars."

"You miss him."

She lifted her eyes to the sky once more. "Of course I do. He's my other half. Without him, I am not whole."

"What makes you think you are not whole?"

She was quiet for a moment, her entire body still. "Can I trust you, Keir? I can't truly tell what kind of fae you are. Sometimes you're ruthless, but others, I think …"

He lifted his hand, using his thumb to press her chin down so her eyes drifted to his. "You can trust me." They were some of the truest words he'd ever said. He wouldn't betray her, not again, not after all the harm he'd already caused.

Her lips parted, and a puff of air escaped. It wasn't until he withdrew his hand she spoke. "Toby, my twin, was born without magic. The only thing he can do is open portals. He's quite a bit better at that than me. But me … I have the power of three kingdoms running through my veins. Yet, I'm at my strongest when Toby lets me channel the power through him. My father and my uncle call him my amplifier. He makes me better, more focused."

"That's—"

"Kind of sad, I know. I can't reach my full potential without his help."

Keir shook his head. He hadn't been thinking it was sad at all. To have that kind of bond with another person, that they made one's magic stronger … "It's amazing."

A small smile appeared on her face, and she looked away so he wouldn't see it. "I think that might be why my power barely works here. I'm too far from Toby, or maybe there's something about the fire plains that severs our connection. Without him, I'm nothing."

Didn't she see it? Even without her magic, she'd begun changing Vondur for the better. She stood strong atop these walls during a siege, inspired his sister to be more than tradition allowed. Taught Keir that being a good king was more important than winning battles that no longer mattered.

"Tierney," he whispered, his fingers flitting under her chin, turning her face. "You could never be nothing. Magic isn't all that you are." This time, he didn't pull his hand back. Instead, he let his fingers trace the curve of her neck, the shell of her ear. Yet, there was still one burning question she hadn't answered since her arrival. "Why have you returned to Vondur?" To the place that held her captive and almost killed her.

Tierney's breath stuttered, and she reached up, covering his hand with hers before pushing it away. She got to her feet and turned to look out across the lonely lands beyond the palace. "Vondur seems different from when I was here last."

He let her deflect his question for the moment and joined her at the parapet. "It is different. We're making progress. My council is working to feed the villages, and we're taking care of those who've lost their loved ones to this war. Eavha's example is making more women reach for their freedom. That one will be slow to change, but it's coming. I made Declan commander of my army."

"Good choice." She nodded.

"He's facing many problems, but I have faith our armies will be prepared for the next battle."

Tierney turned to him, her lips pursed. "Does there have to be another battle?"

"I'm afraid there does. We cannot let Grima take everything we have."

"But what if the Grima queen wanted peace? What if this fight belonged to her mother and your father, and those before them? You two could welcome in a new generation with a treaty."

Something about this wasn't right. His eyes narrowed. "Do you know where the queen has gone?"

Alarm flashed across her face before she hid it. "No. Of course not. I'm only saying what so many of your subjects are already thinking. Both Vondur and Grima. This war isn't theirs. Not anymore."

"For some reason, I don't believe you about the queen."

"Well, you can believe what you want. I don't care." She turned on her heel and marched toward the stairs.

He watched her for a moment before thundering after her, reaching her as she hit the last step inside the tower. He gripped her arm and turned her. She stumbled, falling against him.

"Let me go, Keir." There was no conviction in her words.

Hidden from view of the guards, he backed her up against the wall of the tower, hovering over her. In the shadows, her features grew dark, and he found he missed the light. "Why are you here, Tierney?"

"Please don't ask me that."

"Is it at the request of the enemy queen?" Was she truly a Grima spy now?

"No." The word echoed through the tower.

He bent closer, his face only inches from hers. "Then, tell me why."

Her breath warmed him, and he couldn't have moved if he tried. Her chest rose and fell rapidly against his, reminding him how close they were. It wasn't right, and still, neither of them pushed the other away. He knew what he wanted her to say. That she'd returned because he needed her, because she needed him.

But that was the thing about Tierney. She never needed anyone.

His forehead rested against hers. "Tell me to walk away. Tell me you returned to deliver a message from my enemy." He wasn't even sure that could have stopped him.

Her eyes met his, and she wet her lips. "I can't."

"Can't or won't?"

"Both."

He planted a hand on each side of her head, not letting his lips close that final remaining distance. If he did, nothing would be the same. Kissing Tierney O'Shea would only bring him to ruin.

Yet, he'd never wanted anything more.

"Say something to irritate me," she whispered. "Please."

He chuckled, the sound vibrating through them both. "I'm glad you trusted me tonight." Not with what he'd truly needed to know, what her presence meant. But he suspected the connection with her brother was something she guarded closely. It caused her immeasurable pain to be away from him.

"You're insufferable sometimes, Keir, but I do think you want to be a good man. I knew it even when you had me tied to the back of your horse."

He cringed at the memory. "You had more faith in me than I did."

"Faith is easy." She smiled. "It's only a bit of magic."

"Here in Vondur, not even magic is easy."

Her smile fell. "I—"

"My lady?" Yvonne stopped in the doorway, her mouth dropping open. She had a cloak clutched in her hands.

Tierney pressed both palms to Keir's chest and shoved him back before turning to her maid. "Thank you, Yvonne. I think I will return to my rooms now. His Majesty and I were just discussing Grima."

Keir didn't know why she felt the need to tell her maid this, but he nodded along.

Yvonne pursed her lips. "I'm sure."

To his surprise, Tierney didn't chastise her for her insolence. Instead, she hurried to her side and put an arm around her shoulders. "Come, we can talk in my rooms."

Keir watched them cross the courtyard and enter the palace before scrubbing a hand over his face. Nothing about that woman ever made any sense.

Chapter 14
Tierney

Bronagh had to be around here somewhere. Tierney had barely slept all night after the conversation with Keir, but now he wasn't the royal on her mind.

"Wake up." She kicked the edge of Veren's bed in the identical room next to hers.

He grumbled something unintelligible and rolled over.

"Veren."

Nothing.

Gulliver pushed open Veren's door and poked his head in. "She's not in the hall eating breakfast."

Tierney let out an exasperated huff. "I checked her room in the servants' quarters, and she wasn't there either."

Bronagh hadn't shown up with her usual morning tea—something she was horribly bad at, but she had to do it to keep up appearances.

"Stop tickling me," Veren muttered with a small giggle. He still hadn't opened his eyes. "Oh yes, please keep doing that."

Tierney's eyes widened and met Gulliver's before they both broke down in laughter. It seemed Veren was a flirt even in his sleep. Lenya hadn't changed everything about him.

"Is his tea tray from last night still on the table?"

Gulliver crossed the room. "Yes, but it's cold now. If you're that desperate for tea, I can go and—"

"Just bring me whatever remains in the pot."

Gulliver did as she asked, and Tierney was pleased when she took the pot and it was still mostly full. Not hesitating, she dumped it on Veren's head.

He woke up, sputtering and spitting stale tea from his mouth.

"What in Iskalt's name is wrong with you?" he roared, wiping his eyes.

Tierney handed the pot back to Gulliver. "Bronagh is hiding from me. Get out of bed, Sir Ticklish."

He gave her a confused look as Gulliver folded in on himself in laughter, his tail flicking behind him.

With a roll of her eyes, Tierney grabbed Gulliver's arm and dragged him into the corridor.

Veren threw on a shirt and scrambled after them. "Why exactly is Bron hiding from you?"

Tierney ignored his question, not ready to face what had almost happened. The kiss. She'd come very close to kissing Keir, a man who had held her captive not so long ago, one who did nothing but infuriate her.

Bronagh's enemy.

Tierney had become sort of friends with the Grima queen, definitely allies at least. She could only imagine what went through her mind when she caught Tierney in such a position with her rival. Even if the reason Bronagh was here was to ascertain if she could trust Keir to help save Lenya, it didn't mean he wasn't her enemy.

Gulliver looked sideways at Tierney. He'd always been able to read her, to tell when she was hiding something.

They were passing near the great hall when she heard her name. "Tierney."

"Just keep walking," she said to the others, "and see if he gets amnesia and forgets he saw us."

No such luck. Keir stepped out of the hall, stopping them in their tracks. He looked freshly bathed, with slightly damp hair pushed back away from his face and a pressed red jacket bearing his family crest. Sometimes, it was easy to forget how imposing he could be.

No emotion showed on his face as he pulled his shoulders back and stood ramrod straight. He showed no indication that anything had happened the night before, or almost happened.

"Can I help you, your Majesty?" Tierney lifted her eyes to his. For a long moment, they remained in a silent standoff.

Finally, Keir cleared his throat. "We need to talk."

They did. She still hadn't told Keir about the danger facing all of Lenya, and it was time. Turning to Veren, she sent him a pleading look. "Find B—Yvonne. Tell her I wish to see her."

Veren took off, eager to get out of Keir's presence.

Keir turned on his heel and marched away, probably expecting Tierney just to follow his every move.

Gulliver slid his hand into hers and held her back for a moment. "Please tell me you didn't."

"I don't know what you're talking about." She pulled away from him and started after Keir.

He fell in step beside her, his voice low. "That's why Bron is upset, isn't it?" He scrubbed a hand over his face. "You and Keir, seriously? Tia, you're the Iskaltian princess. Every noble son and daughter of Iskalt is dying to be chosen as your consort. Keir is not one of us."

"I know that." She sighed. Lying to Gulliver always made her feel sick. "Fine, we almost kissed and Bron got a front-row seat."

Gulliver didn't react at first, but she hadn't expected him to. If it was Veren beside her, he'd probably curse and lecture her. Most fae would have, but not her friend.

Instead, he brushed his hand against her arm, a gesture of kindness. "Do you have feelings for him?"

"What?" She reeled back. "Don't be ridiculous."

"You sort of enjoy doing stupid things."

"Falling for that man would be beyond stupid, Gulliver. It was a moment of weakness, okay? Nothing you need to worry about. It's definitely never happening again." As she said the words, she realized Keir had stopped in the doorway of the throne room and heard every one of them.

Face flaming, she walked past him, surprised that for once it wasn't filled with courtiers and servants.

Keir pulled the door shut after them and flipped the latch. "Now," he turned, "it's time you tell me the truth. There's no getting out of it now."

He was right. She couldn't avoid this conversation any longer. "I don't know where to start." She dropped into his throne, throwing one leg over the ornate wooden arm.

A dark scowl crossed Keir's face, but he didn't tell her to move. "I'm listening."

Gulliver hung back by the door, his eyes flicking from Tierney to Keir and back. "Tell him about the fire plains."

Keir's eyes blazed as they focused on her. "What about the fire plains?"

A throbbing started in the front of Tierney's head, but she pushed the pain away, trying not to let it distract her. Rubbing her temples, she sighed. "They're expanding."

Silence. It was so quiet Tierney could hear every intake of breath, every shifting foot.

"Explain." There was no longer any irritation in Keir's voice.

"The fire plains are encroaching on the Grima borders, and we don't think they can be stopped without more magic than what currently exists in Lenya."

By the time Tierney had finished telling Keir about the danger Lenya faced, the dull pain in her head had turned into a searing agony.

Keir had looked skeptical, but she could tell he wanted to believe her, to trust her. The one thing she hadn't told him was about the ship being built in Grima for the sole purpose of crossing the impossible seas. That wasn't her secret, and Bronagh hadn't yet decided to trust him.

When she finally returned to her rooms, Tierney wanted to bury her head under a pillow to block out all light, all noise, and sleep for the next year. But when she opened the door, she found Veren and Bronagh waiting for her.

The queen sat on the settee, her arms crossed over her chest. Her eyes narrowed as they settled on Tierney. "You."

"Me." Tierney closed her eyes against the sun streaming through her window. "Can you yell at me another time? I have a splitting headache."

Bronagh studied her for a moment. "Veren, go to the kitchens and fetch the princess lavender tea."

"Me?" Veren sat up where he'd been lounging on the bed.

Bronagh fixed him with a firm stare. "Yes, you. I have spent days acting as a servant to serve our purposes. The least you can do is fetch some tea. If you do not plan to be useful, why are you here?"

If it wasn't for the headache, Tierney would have laughed. Bronagh was younger than them, but she was every bit the queen, and Veren had never come up against the likes of her.

"They won't have lavender tea," Tierney said. "Ask for gentian tea. It's their specialty. It's pretty awful, but I'm desperate."

He stomped from the room.

Bronagh turned to Tierney. "Lie down. Gulliver, draw the curtains. We do not have time to waste on illness and must have a conversation, but we can make you more comfortable."

Tierney thanked the sweet mercies when the sunlight disappeared behind the thick fabric.

Bronagh fluffed up the pillows Veren had flattened. "Get in bed."

Having no energy to argue, Tierney did as she was told, sighing as her body relaxed into the feather mattress.

To her surprise, Bronagh took a seat on the end of the bed. "I think there is some vital information you failed to tell me before we embarked on this mission."

Tierney closed her eyes. "Last night … it wasn't what it looked like. Keir and I, we're not … he held me captive."

"Yes, I am aware."

"I don't belong here."

"That too is obvious. What is not obvious is what I walked in on. Tierney, I want us to work together to both save Lenya and get you home, but I cannot do that if I don't know everything."

Tierney pushed herself up. "There is nothing to worry about. I have told you everything. You have my word."

Bronagh studied her for a moment longer before issuing one short nod. "Well, then, we have a different conundrum to face. I do not trust this Vondurian king. But we need him, we need his crystals and his cooperation, if we are to make it across the sea."

Tierney nodded, regretting the movement immediately. "I understand, and I know my word is not enough. You must learn how Keir thinks for yourself."

The door opened, interrupting their conversation. Veren walked in, carrying a silver tray laden with teacups, flatbread and peppers, and a pot of tea.

Bronagh's brows drew together. "I only sent you for tea."

"I was hungry." He shrugged as he set the tray down. Both boys dug into the food like wild animals who hadn't been fed in months.

"Watch out for those peppers; the purple ones will rot your insides." Tierney nibbled on a piece of flatbread, not in the mood for the Vondurians' spicy food.

Sighing, Bronagh slid from the bed to pour a cup of heavily honeyed tea. She brought it to Tierney. "Drink this."

She sipped it slowly, cringing at the bitter taste despite the copious amounts of honey. Swallowing, she frowned as an idea formed in her mind. "For you to decide if Grima can trust Keir, you must spend time with him."

"Yes, that is our problem."

"A problem is only an opportunity to be creative. Don't worry, Bron. I've got this."

Gulliver froze with a yellow pepper roll halfway to his mouth. "Oh no. In Iskalt, when she says that, everyone knows to be very afraid."

Tierney drained her tea and sank back against the pillows. Her plan would have to wait until she rested and got rid of this blasted headache.

It was dark by the time she woke again, but Tierney's headache was gone. As were all her companions. Perfect. There was no time to waste if she was going to put her plan into motion.

She had to find a way to procure a certain herb that could make someone very sick. A last resort, for sure, but she wanted it on hand when or if the time came to use it.

Kicking off the blankets, she crawled from her bed, bracing herself for a moment as a wave of dizziness washed over her. It didn't last, and she hurried to find her boots and pulled them on. After lacing them, she used her fingers to tame her hair before giving up and pulling it back into a low tail, searching for anything that could secure it the way human girls did when they didn't want to bother.

A ribbon. That would have to do.

Once she was ready, Tierney rushed into the corridor. At this hour, the kitchens should be deserted, allowing her to search for what she needed.

The kitchens sat in the center of the complex behind the great hall, with the network of corridors and tunnels surrounding them. It wasn't easy to get there without being seen, so Tierney didn't try. She nodded to the few guards at their posts.

A sudden clanging noise reached her ears, faint but present. She turned, trying to find the source of the noise, but there was nothing there. Pausing, she listened again. She could have sworn she heard someone's voice issuing orders.

Her mission momentarily forgotten, she tried the door on her right and found that it led into an ornate sitting room. Red velvet carpets stretched to a wall of windows that looked out onto the palace grounds. Bookshelves towered overhead, full of dusty leather tomes.

To the left, a hearth stood cold in front of two settees with carved backs. But something wasn't right. Next to the hearth, a panel in the wall had been shifted, and it didn't look square.

The sound reached her again, louder this time.

Who would be making such noise in the middle of the night?

Tierney approached the tilted panel, pressing both palms against it. It shifted sideways, revealing an opening to the tunnels. Of course.

As Tierney stepped into the tunnel, she realized what she'd heard were the sounds of a sword fight.

She hurried through the dark tunnel, brushing her hand against the cool stone wall as a guide.

When she finally reached the end, it opened into the giant cavern that held the healing pool. But that wasn't all that was here.

A circle of women cheered and laughed, swords dangling from their fingers as they watched two fae dance around each other, their swords flying through the air.

She stepped closer until she recognized the two at battle. Eavha and Declan.

"Come on, Eavha." Declan grinned, an action Tierney wouldn't have associated with him. "You have more than that."

Eavha ran at him, leaping into the air.

He blocked her, and they went tumbling to the ground in a heap. Eavha didn't move off him, instead looking down at him with a smile stretching her lips. "Be careful what you wish for, Deck. There's always more to me."

He looked like he'd stopped breathing altogether. The other women didn't seem to have noticed as they continued to cheer.

Eavha lifted her gaze, her eyes widening when they landed on Tierney. She scrambled off Declan and got to her feet. "Tia." Pushing through the crowd, she ran toward Tierney. "What—how did you find us? Is Keir with you?" She looked behind Tierney, visibly relaxing when she didn't see anyone else.

"No, it's just me. What is this?"

The women eyed Tierney curiously, and Declan gave her a wary look.

But Eavha smiled. "Training."

"Training?"

She nodded. "You inspired the idea. For too long, the women of this palace, this kingdom, have had to rely on others to protect us. But no more. We deserve to fight for our homes too."

Pride welled within Tierney's soul. She'd inspired maids and cooks and wives to meet in the middle of the night to learn to fight. And it was all Eavha's doing. Tears sprang to her eyes. "Eavha, this is amazing."

"Oh gosh, don't cry." Eavha laughed, pulling her into a hug. "We're trying to be warriors here."

Tierney chuckled against her leather-clad shoulder. "And doing a good job of it, I see. You did very well."

"I have a good teacher." She released Tierney and looked to Declan. His face reddened.

"I'm proud of you."

Eavha gave her a shy smile. "Yeah, well, I'm proud of you too." Her voice dropped. "You did sneak a queen into this palace right under my brother's nose, after all."

Tierney stumbled back. How could she possibly know who Bronagh really was?

CHAPTER 15
KEIR

"Do you think she was telling the truth?" Declan asked from his seat at the council table. He and Eavha had arrived early for the meeting so Keir could tell them what he'd heard.

"I don't know." Keir rested his head in his hands and leaned forward in his seat. "I want to trust her."

"Then do." Eavha leaned back and crossed her arms. "It's not that hard. I didn't trust her once. I told her I wasn't sure I believed her story about Iskalt, and I have regretted it every day since. Tierney deserves our faith, brother."

"But why?" Declan asked, earning him a sharp look from Eavha. "Has she been with the Grima court since she left us? What kind of lies have they filled her head with?"

Eavha slammed a hand on the table. "If you think for one second Tia would fall for any of their lies, then you're even dumber than I thought."

"Eavha, be reasonable."

"Me? I'm the unreasonable one? Tia returned here to warn us, to help us. I don't see how you both can sit there and question that."

"Enough." Keir lifted his head. "My mind is already overwhelmed with questions without you two squabbling. Declan, I don't think we can dismiss everything she's told us. Eavha, we can't just believe it either. We must find out for ourselves."

"How?" The irritation faded from Eavha's face. "The fire plains are expanding, Keir. It might only be into Grima now, but eventually, they'll encroach on Vondur. You won't believe anyone from Grima, so how do you expect to verify Tia's intel?"

Declan met Keir's eyes, getting to the conclusion quicker than Eavha. "Someone will have to go into Grima."

Keir hated the idea of sending one of his fae into enemy territory without an army behind them. If they were found …

"Oh, wow. You're serious." All energy faded from Eavha's voice, and Keir knew exactly how she felt. This wasn't what any of them wanted.

He'd thought of little else since Tierney's revelations. If she was right, if the fire plains were truly expanding, it put all of Lenya at risk. He'd fought for the crown to protect his people, and that meant more than simply fighting the golden warriors of Grima.

"I'll go."

Keir closed his eyes at Declan's declaration. He should have known his friend would volunteer. "Deck—"

"I know what you're going to say." Declan rubbed the back of his neck. "I'm commander of your army; I can't abandon my position. But there have been no battles since you became king, since we stopped seeking them out. Your generals can manage without me for a short while. And even if we were fighting for our lives, this is bigger than that. We must learn the truth of what is happening. For all of Vondur. This war won't mean anything if none of us survive the heat to celebrate the victory."

He was right. Keir knew he was. And if he was being honest with himself, Declan was the best fae to send. There was no one Keir trusted more, no one more capable.

"I don't ..." Keir heaved a sigh. The ball had started rolling down hill, and there was no stopping it. A king must make sacrifices, must send his fae into danger, knowing full well they may never come out. "You're right."

The three of them fell into a full silence, the air thick with things unsaid. It was a while before anyone spoke.

"I'm going with him," Eavha said, her voice unwavering.

"Absolutely not." Keir would not send his sister into enemy territory. Flashes of a familiar battle skipped through his mind as he recalled what his men had done to the Grima queen's sister. Would that be Eavha's fate if she were captured?

"You don't control me."

"Actually, I do. I am the only family you have, but more than that, I am your king. Declan doesn't need to take care of you while he's trying to protect himself." That wasn't the only reason, but he hoped it would be the one to get her to back down.

Eavha shot to her feet, her chair screeching against the floor. "Have you ever thought, your Majesty, that maybe I can take care of myself?" With that, she stomped from the room.

"She can, you know," Declan said, his eyes still on the door Eavha left through.

"I know she probably thinks she can, but this is Grima, Declan. You won't be able to take other soldiers with you for protection because of the attention it would draw. It won't be a simple jaunt across the border. If anything happened to her …" He swallowed. "I have to keep her safe. You and Eavha are the only family I have left."

Declan reached out and put a hand on Keir's shoulder. "I will learn the truth of this and return. You have my word. We won't lose each other yet."

Keir tried to smile, but he couldn't seem to perform the act. "You need to leave immediately. Gather provisions in secret so the council doesn't learn of your mission. We will only involve them when we must."

Declan stood. "Keir—"

"Don't you dare say goodbye."

Declan's lips twitched as he bowed. "Whatever pleases your Majesty."

He was barely out the door before the first council members appeared.

The palace somehow seemed too large without Declan at Keir's side. He'd left the day before, and Eavha had also been avoiding the king. Tierney spent most of her days in the company of her own people, Veren and Gulliver. And that maid of hers from Grima. It made sense. He'd told himself she wasn't Vondurian, but seeing her with her friends made it crystal clear.

She didn't belong here.

Keir had just finished a long meeting that lasted most of the morning when he decided enough was enough. Eavha had to stop pouting. It wasn't right for a princess.

Stopping outside her door, he rapped his knuckles against the solid wood, waiting for her to answer. No answer came, so he knocked again.

"What are you doing?" Tierney walked down the corridor, stopping at his side.

"I need to talk to my sister."

"Me too."

"In private."

"Me too."

He stared at Tierney for a moment, realizing she wasn't going to back down. "I could order you to leave."

"You could try." Her lips stretched into a smile. She was teasing him.

Before he could respond, Eavha's door opened, revealing a nervous-looking maid. "Your Majesty." She dipped into a curtsy.

Keir looked past her into the empty room. "Where's the princess?"

Ariella kept her eyes trained on the floor and bit her lip. "She's … out."

"Out where?"

Tierney sighed. "Obviously somewhere she doesn't want her grumpy brother to know about." She turned to Ariella. "Don't mind his Majesty's mood today. He doesn't like when women don't jump to his every command."

"Not only women," he growled. "I am king. It is my duty to command those under my rule."

"Sure, okay." She rolled her eyes, and Keir wanted to yell at her, to make her realize his power.

And he also wanted to kiss the smirk off her face.

That thought was quickly replaced with another. He knew where his sister had gone. Panic built in his chest, and he released a curse. "Ariella, did your mistress leave the palace?"

"That's a stupid question," Tierney said. "There's nothing out there but trees and—"

"Yes." Ariella still wouldn't look at him. "Your Majesty, she rode out last night."

Keir whipped around so fast he almost knocked Tierney over. After holding her upright, he took off down the hall, heading for the stables. If he left now, he might be able to reach her before she crossed the border into Grima.

"What's going on?" Tierney ran to catch up with him.

"Eavha is in danger."

"What? How could you possibly know that from the conversation we just had with Ariella?"

"I just do."

She grabbed his arm, pulling him to a stop. "Talk to me, Keir." Her voice held none of the mockery it had before. Instead, there was something akin to understanding in the tone.

Keir turned to her, his eyes wild. "I sent Declan to verify your intel about the fire plains. He's crossing into Grima. I think Eavha went after him."

"And you're scared for her."

"Of course I am! She's headed for Grima."

Tierney pursed her lips. "It's not the barbarous place you imagine."

She knew nothing. Leaning toward her, he dropped his voice. "For Vondurians, it is. What do you think they'd do to the enemy princess if they caught her on their lands? Think, Tierney, for once in your life."

Anger rose in her cheeks, flushing them red. She shoved him backward. "And you should trust for once in yours."

"What's that supposed to mean?"

"If you'd trusted me, you wouldn't have had to send anyone to Grima, but no, I'm just a spy in your court."

"Aren't you?"

"Screw you, Keir. I've done nothing but try to save your blasted kingdom."

"I don't have time for this." He turned away, but Tierney's words called him back.

"Don't chase her. She'll only run faster. Trust me, I know from experience."

He stood still, his back to her. "This isn't the same. I am not your father, and Eavha is not you. Grima will kill her. They won't give her the courtesy of making her a prisoner instead."

"Courtesy." Tierney snorted. "Yes, Vondur was so courteous while I was being beaten and almost hanged. You can take your courtesy and shove it. Let your sister make her own decisions. She is not a child you can keep locked away. The harder you try, the more she will yearn for freedom."

Her words rang with truth. If he dragged Eavha back to the palace, he could still lose her. With a sigh, he turned to Tierney. "Like you?"

After a beat, she shook her head. "I was already free. I just didn't realize it until I lost that life."

"Your Majesty." A young boy sprinted across the courtyard, skidding to a halt and bowing. "You're needed in the throne room."

"Thank you." It felt natural when Tierney fell in step beside him, accompanying him on whatever urgent business this was.

They walked into the throne room to find Lord Robert standing near the throne with a bedraggled woman who looked like she might collapse at any moment. Two small children peeked around her legs, a boy and a girl. Each face was blistered red, their clothes singed and hands chapped with burn marks.

Relief flooded the mother's face when she took sight of him. "Your Majesty." She curtsied as low as she could in her weakened state.

"Madam." Keir nodded. "Have you been offered food?"

"It's on its way," Lord Robert answered. "They've traveled a long way and need rest, but you must hear their news first."

Keir lowered himself onto his throne.

Tierney approached the woman, a kind smile on her face. "I'll get you a seat." No one sat in the throne room except the king, despite the chairs lined up against the back wall, but Keir didn't protest. Tierney had noticed the need before he had.

Grateful, the woman lowered herself into the chair Tierney brought and pulled her children close. "We've come from Brenandi, your Majesty."

Keir leaned forward. Brenandi was the closest Vondurian village to the fire plains. "Please, tell me your news."

"Those who were able to get out in time evacuated the village." She stifled a sob. "I'm sorry, sire, it's just … we've lost everything."

An ache threatened to crack open Keir's heart. "Start at the beginning."

She nodded and wiped dirt from her son's cheek. "It started when the water turned bad. Our children grew sick, and we did not know why. Eventually, many of the adults fell ill as well. We lost over half the village to that first plague. And then, the heat came for us. We've always survived in high temperatures, but t-this was different.

Worse. In some places, the air could scorch the breath in your lungs, leave your skin black."

The fire plains. Keir met Tierney's eyes. "Sulfur in the water?"

"Most likely. It happens from time to time for those who live along the borderlands. The expanding heat's just something we've grown to expect when the winds change. But the fires and putrid air." She shuddered at the memory. "By the time we realized what was happening, it was too late for most."

He should have known Tierney would never have lied about such a thing, but instead, his best friend and sister were headed into enemy territory to verify something he now knew to be fact.

The fire plains were coming for them.

And Lenya had so few functioning crystals that they were powerless to stop it.

Magic help them all.

"We're twiddling our thumbs here, Tia." Veren threw himself onto the settee in her room.

"I hate to agree with this one, but I think he's right." Gulliver rummaged through the remains of their tea tray, looking for anything that hadn't been eaten. "We need to decide what's next for us. I, for one, would like to go home with my neck still intact." He stuffed a shriveled grape into his mouth and paced across the room. "Are we going to search for Siobhan or brave the voyage across the stormy seas and hope we find our way home?"

"The ship is ready. We just need to decide when we're leaving," Veren said. "Once Bron has a feel for the king, she will decide what is next for Grima, but for the moment, I feel our fate is tied with hers. She will sail all the way to Iskalt and back if that is the only way to save her kingdom from the spread of the fire. And that might be our only way home."

"I can't think of leaving until I know Lenya will be safe." Tierney twisted her hands in her lap. She desperately wanted to go home—was more than willing to risk the dangerous voyage on Bronagh's ship—but she wanted things settled with these two warring kingdoms before she left.

"The Vondurians will see to their own destruction. One doesn't need to stay here long to see they are a nation of brutes with a thirst for war."

"Veren, that's very narrow-minded of you." Tierney stared out the window at the shimmering horizon where the fire plains made their slow march toward the palace and the people here she cared about. What would happen to Eavha? Ariella? Even Keir and Bronagh?

The door crashed open and a disheveled, soot-covered Bronagh walked into the room. "That blasted king will not stay put long enough for me to observe him." She slammed the door behind her and dropped into the nearest chair. "Did you know when a noblewoman and her maid visit this palace, the castellan can order her maid around?" She dabbed her apron against her forehead. "Veren, please bring me a glass of water if you will. I cannot move another step."

"Of course, your Majesty." Veren shot from his seat to do her bidding.

"Oh, you poor thing." Tierney tried to hide her chuckle. "What did she make you do?"

"I had to clean the fireplaces in the princess' quarters. I don't know how to start a fire, much less clean up after one."

"What did you do with the ashes? Take a bath in them?" Gulliver snickered.

She turned a fierce glare on him. "I flung them out of the window. And I hope they landed on Keir's head!" She snatched the glass of water from Veren and downed it in three gulps. "Is this place always so magic-forsaken hot?" She slumped back, wiping the wilted hair out of her face.

Gulliver and Veren were busy trying not to laugh and being entirely unhelpful. Why was it always up to Tierney to take care of everyone? She moved to the basin in the washroom, longing for her washroom at home with its hot, plentiful water and fluffy towels. Taking a clean face linen, she dipped it in the cool water and went to kneel beside Bronagh.

"Thank you, Tierney." Bronagh sighed as she wiped the cool cloth over her soot-stained face. Bronagh closed her eyes, letting Tierney bathe her face and hands. "We really have to rethink our plans. This isn't working."

"Our plans?" Gulliver mouthed, rolling his eyes at Tierney.

"We're not getting anywhere. I need more time with the king, but he's all over the palace and grounds from sunup to sundown. I don't think the man ever sleeps."

"I'm afraid Veren is right, we are twiddling our thumbs here." Tierney moved to sit on the settee between Gulliver and Veren. "We have to get her some time with Keir. I want to believe he is a good man. As much as he irritates me, I can't shake this feeling that we can trust him to do the right thing in the end. That he would work with us to save all of Lenya and end this stupid war."

"But I have to see these things for myself if I have any hope of gaining my court's support for an endeavor involving the enemy." Bronagh fanned her face with the hem of her apron. "I have to know if he can be trusted. I need to see for myself what kind of man he is. If we're going to deal with the encroaching fire plains, Vondur and Grima need to work together."

"I had hoped he would trust my word about the fire plains." Tierney rubbed her temples, where her head throbbed. "But the first thing he did was send one of his men to verify the information."

"So, while we wait for the king to catch up to the rest of us, let's get Bronagh a front-row seat to a day in the life of King Keir." Gulliver leaned forward, his elbows resting on his knees.

"How?" Bronagh asked. "I'd have to chase him around the palace."

"Who serves the king? Does anyone know?" Gulliver asked, sharing a look with Tierney.

"He has a maid to keep his quarters clean, but he refuses a valet to help him dress. I think her name is Shannon. Why?" Bronagh asked.

"You two look like you're contemplating something nefarious that might get you both locked up in the dungeons."

"We slip her something—and maybe a few of the other maids too just to make it look legitimate." Gulliver shrugged. "Tierney managed to get her hands on a potent herbal blend we can sprinkle over their morning porridge. It'll send them to bed for a day with a wicked upset stomach and lethargy." The corner of Gulliver's mouth turned up. "Then, Tierney can offer a certain stand-in maid for his Majesty's use, and whenever he has need of something—which we'll make sure is quite often—he'll send for Bron."

"That's a ridiculous—" Veren began, but Tierney cut him off.

"It's our last-resort, back-up plan. I think we're there, guys. We need to take action and get back to Grima soon."

"But how did you find this herbal blend?" Bronagh asked. "Are we certain it won't kill the poor maids?"

"I found it in the kitchens with all the medicinal herbs," Tierney said. "It's supposed to help sluggish and sour bowels."

"Do we even know how much to give them?" Veren asked.

"I tried it on a few guards in the dungeon," Gulliver explained. "Turnabout is fair play and all that." He shrugged. "A healthy dose of the herbs in the porridge pot will send the maid staff to bed right away."

"But Bron's a dreadful maid. No offense, your Highness, but you'll likely set him on fire before the day is out, much less brew him a proper cup of tea." Veren wiped a hand across his sweaty brow.

"Surely one of you can teach me how to make a decent pot of tea." Bronagh turned pleading eyes on Tierney.

"Sure, I can brew tea ... from the tray my maid brings to my rooms in Iskalt." Tierney cringed. If she ever got out of this mess, she was going to learn to be more self-sufficient. "But she blends the tea and portions everything out. I wouldn't know where to start or even where those things come from."

"Good grief, you nobles are a helpless lot." Gulliver crossed the room to retrieve the tea tray Bronagh brought Tierney that morning. "Okay, first, let's look at the tea leaves here." He scattered some of the dry tea leaves they hadn't bothered brewing because Bronagh's tea always tasted like mud. "Tell me where you got this blend."

"I saw the other maids scooping tea from several jars, so I took some from each."

Gulliver sifted through the myriad of leaves on the tray. "Next time, use a small scoop of the pale green ones and another of these shriveled looking flowers, with some of this bark looking stuff. Leave the others where you found them. Less is more when it comes to tea blends. And you're serving the king, so bring him lots of honey. Any tea tastes better with honey. Load him up on the savory pastries they serve here, and the little round biscuits and cubes of cheese. Watch the other maids to see how they arrange their trays, and try to mimic what they do. If they use a small vase with flowers, then that's what you do. If they use a large plate, you do too. Several small plates, you get it."

Bronagh nodded. "Sounds easy enough, but when I'm faced with all those different plates and utensils in the kitchens, my mind goes blank. I don't know how the serving staff makes it look so easy."

"Are we really doing this?" Veren ran a hand through his hair. "It's risky. What if the king finds out who she is?"

"He won't even give her a second look." Gulliver seemed so certain of it.

"You're sure?" Tierney had a bad feeling about this. It was bound to turn into a circus act and reveal them all as Grima spies.

"Positive. Kings don't look at servants. Most nobles don't. Especially here. Vondurian men barely recognize the women of the nobility. They have no eyes for those who serve their tea."

"He's right," Bronagh said. "The men in this place have little regard for women beyond those who warm their beds. It's like they believe we are somehow inferior and it's our place to stay out of their way. Did you know I'm not allowed to speak to a man until he gives me permission? It's absurd."

"It's infuriating," Tierney agreed.

Veren groaned. "This is going to be a disaster."

"We have to do something." It was a risk, but if Bronagh was going to get what she came for, they needed to act sooner rather than later. Tierney was running out of time.

Tierney and Veren arrived at the throne room earlier than usual the following morning. Keir spent most mornings with his court, listening to his lord's reports and requests the way Tierney's mother and father would hear directly from their people—no matter their class. In Vondur, it seemed the common folk didn't matter much. At least, not in the eyes of the court. Though, she liked to think Keir would change all that.

Gulliver joined them a few minutes later, giving Tierney a flash of his mischievous smile to let her know he'd accomplished the task. The poor maids were probably already off to their beds.

"Easy as giving me a cupcake and asking me to eat it." Gulliver sidled up to her, offering her his arm. "Shall we take a turn around the room and see if we can run into a maid-less king?"

Tierney tucked her arm around his and nodded. "Let's do just that, though I will never understand this court's obsession with walking around the throne room when there's a perfectly good garden outside. Keep up, Veren; we're going to talk to the king."

"I don't know how you plan to get through the mob around him." Veren walked on her other side, his hands clasped behind him like a soldier.

As they joined other groups walking aimlessly around the room, Tierney kept her eyes on Keir. He seemed bored, like he would rather be anywhere else. She couldn't say she blamed him. Swarms of courtiers vied for Keir's attention, but to Tierney, he looked more like a caged lion than a man who actually wanted the attention he was receiving.

"This is stupid." Tierney tugged Gulliver and Veren along with her. "I'm a princess of Iskalt. If I want to talk to a king, I don't need to play these infernal court games."

"Just don't get us put on the executioner's block this time." Gulliver walked uncertainly with them. "You know how this room makes me nervous."

It was just a few weeks ago she, Gulliver, and Declan stood on the gallows right outside this room. She shuddered to think about that day.

"Your Majesty." Tierney dipped her head into the graceful nod of a crown princess greeting another monarch. Several of the courtiers surrounding Keir gasped at her lack of butt-kissing, as her mother would call it. They still believed her a Grima spy and Gulliver some kind of abomination of dark magic.

"Princess Tierney and Lord Gulliver." Keir returned her nod, ignoring Veren altogether. "We don't usually see you here at court since your return. I'm delighted you've decided to join us." He didn't even sound like himself. She decided she preferred surly, grouchy soldier Keir over this pompous imposter.

Tierney ignored the lords and ladies who refused to move aside for them. She stepped around them, as if they were nothing more than statues. "Your throne room isn't our favorite place, you'll understand." Tierney lowered her gaze.

"Nor is it mine," he murmured under his breath, sounding more like himself. "As a matter of fact, I'd like to escape, and your arrival has given me an idea."

"We'll follow your lead then."

"I'm afraid duty calls, my lords and ladies." Keir beamed a benevolent smile to the crowd of sycophants. "I have an important meeting with the Princess of Iskalt and her noblemen." He offered Tierney his arm and led her to a private chamber where he now met with his council.

Not what she had expected, but they could definitely work with this.

Keir held the door open for her and the others. The room was cozy with plush carpets and heavy oak furniture. Her mom would call it a king's man cave.

"Please have a seat." Keir gestured at the small sitting area under the windows just beyond a huge table.

"I don't suppose we could trouble you for some tea, sire?" Gulliver took a seat in one of the leather chairs.

"I'm sure we can find someone to serve us. I'm afraid a sudden sickness has sent all of our maids to their beds, so I'm fending for myself today. We have a shortage of servants these days, even when they are all well."

"Nonsense, your Majesty." Tierney suppressed a smile. "Please allow me to have my maid, Yvonne, serve you today."

"It's not necessary. I'm a soldier. I've been serving myself since I was a child, and I've never acclimated much to having servants."

"Please, I insist." Tierney stepped to the door to have a footman ring for Yvonne to bring them tea. It seemed like the show was about to start, and she had to make it a good one.

For a reason Keir couldn't begin to fathom, he hated Tierney thinking he couldn't get by for a single day while his maid had taken ill. He wasn't some pampered king who'd never done anything for himself. Life as a soldier was so very different from life among the shimmering, crystal-infused walls of the palace.

He preferred it.

Yet, he smoothed his features, not letting his irritation show. If he had to play the aloof royal with this princess to put distance between them, he would. She'd accused him of not trusting her, but she didn't understand.

Releasing her and letting her travel to Grima under her own control was the ultimate trust. There were so many things she could have told the enemy, and yet, she'd returned.

Tierney's maid, Yvonne, bumped into the table with a curse. Her cheeks flamed in embarrassment. "Your Majesty, I didn't mean to speak with such vulgarity in your presence."

"It's fine." He waved her worry away and focused on looking like nothing bothered him. The truth was, he owed Tierney an apology. Declan and Eavha hadn't yet returned, but he already knew the story Tierney told was true.

The fire plains truly were expanding, and if they didn't stop it, none of this would matter any longer.

Lifting a hand to the carved winged totem hanging at his throat, he felt the weak magic thrum in his veins. What would it be like to have infinite amounts? To be able to use the power for mundane tasks like cleaning the dribbles of tea the maid had spilled on the table or sparring with a partner? He imagined the freedom of not dreading the moment he had to discard one totem and fashion another weaker one.

"So …" Veren drummed his fingers on the table. "It's not that I don't appreciate all of this silence, Keir, but is there a point in you bringing us here?"

Keir's jaw clenched at the man's informality. Something about him had struck him the wrong way.

Before he could answer, Yvonne yelped and lunged toward the table as she fell, her tea tray hitting the edge. It was a disaster he couldn't look away from as tea whipped through the air. He glanced down in horror when it hit his jacket, creating an immediate stain.

No one spoke; no one moved.

And then, Tierney laughed, the sound so out of place in the moment he couldn't help but lift his eyes to hers, couldn't help studying the light on her face. She'd rarely been open around him, happy. She was always too busy arguing.

The corners of his lips turned up.

Yvonne scrambled from the floor. "I'm so sorry. I'm not used to carrying tea trays, and when I tripped, it slipped from my hands."

She kept rambling, but Keir was fixated on one thing. What kind of maid wasn't used to carrying tea trays?

Tierney cleared her throat. "What Yvonne means to say is, her normal duties at the Grima palace don't include serving tea. They do things a bit differently there. Yvonne kept my rooms clean, as well as all other rooms along the corridor. Someone else came along regularly to serve tea."

Something was off in her words. Keir thought he knew her well enough by now to know when she was hiding something. He shook his head, trying to clear it of the distrust that had been ingrained in him.

"Tierney," he said formally, "I owe you an apology."

"Excuse me?" She looked his way in shock. "The great King Keir is apologizing? For what? I mean, there's just so much."

"Do you ever shut up?"

"Not often," Gulliver put in.

Tierney shot him a grin, sticking her tongue out at him in the oddest gesture. Something was seriously strange about this woman.

"It's true," Veren said. "I mean, I've been trying to get her to stop talking since we first courted."

An irrational bolt of rage raced through Keir at that, but the others ignored him.

Tierney scowled at Veren. "Courted is a big word for what we did. I liked you, and you liked my future crown."

Veren frowned. "Not true."

"Sure, okay." Tierney snorted, which caused Gulliver to laugh.

Yvonne hung back by the wall, staying out of the way like the good maid Keir didn't believe she was. But he didn't have time to analyze his suspicions.

"Are all Iskaltians this infuriating?" Keir asked.

Tierney shrugged. "Most of us, yes. You should meet my parents. They're worse than me."

That wasn't possible.

Gulliver lifted a hand. "Um, I'm an infuriating Myrkurian, not an Iskaltian." He coughed. "Just for clarification."

Keir rubbed his face, wondering what he'd gotten himself into the moment he took Tierney captive. His calm king façade slipped, and his back shook in silent laughter.

"Your Majesty?" Yvonne placed a fresh, un-spilled cup of tea in front of him. "Are you okay?"

"Is he seizing?" Tierney yelled. "Someone do something."

Gulliver stood and rounded the table, looking ready to help him.

Keir leaned out of his reach. "Touch me, Gullie, and you'll lose that hand."

That made him back away and reclaim his seat.

Keir's laughter faded, and he shook his head. "I brought you all here so I could apologize. You asked what for, and at first, I thought it was only because I hadn't trusted you about the fire plains, but there is so much more. If it wasn't for me, you may have found each other sooner. You could be back home instead of involved in our fight for survival. For that, I am truly regretful."

Tierney opened her mouth before shutting it without uttering a word.

"Well," Veren said, "that was unexpected."

But it was Yvonne who moved into sight and seemed unable to take her eyes from him. She looked confused, like she was trying to put the pieces of some puzzle together and they didn't quite fit. Her brow furrowed, and she didn't try to hide her curiosity.

There was something about the woman Keir couldn't put his finger on, something that made him think she had a secret buried deep.

"Keir …" Tierney's voice was soft, but she didn't get a chance to complete the thought. The door opened, and the council started filing in.

Lord Garnet took a seat and glanced at Tierney and the others. "Sire, it is time for us to begin. Maybe your friends should wait outside."

He shook his head. "No, they're a part of what I must tell you." It was time. This affected all of Vondur. In the time since Keir learned the truth of the fire plains, he'd contemplated their next moves many times and come up with nothing that would help stave off the coming danger.

"You are my council," he began, "and what I say to you must stay here. There has to be trust between us." He met Tierney's gaze at that.

In turn, each council member nodded their agreement.

"The time has come for us to acknowledge a new danger."

"Has Grima started marching, your Majesty?" Lord Osterian asked. They'd been waiting for Grima's next move, but it hadn't come.

"No, this danger is not Grima." He drew in a long breath. "The fire plains are encroaching on our lands."

A flurry of chatter broke out, but he silenced it with a raised hand. "The deathly heat is expanding. The fae of Brenandi have left their lands."

"We must send someone to find out what's happening." Lord Osterian stood, his eyes panicked. "Are you sure this is true, sire?"

"I have no doubts. The source is …" He looked at Tierney. "A reliable one. General Connel and Princess Eavha have been sent on a mission to gather more information." He wouldn't tell them Eavha disobeyed orders and went on her own. "We will know more when they return."

Talk turned to what actions they could take, but Keir knew only an infusion of magic could help them now—magic they didn't have enough of. He sank into his chair as his lords spoke.

"What if the general and the princess don't return?" one of them asked.

That thought had crossed Keir's mind too many times in the last day. What if he lost them both?

The council meeting lasted long into the night. By the time it was over, Keir was tired and hungry. Yet, he didn't move from his chair. Everyone else left to find their own meals, and still, he sat.

It wasn't until the chair beside him scraped against the floor as someone pulled it out that he realized he wasn't alone.

"Yvonne, would you mind fetching the king something to eat?" Tierney asked as she took the seat.

"Not at all." Yvonne's voice was softer than normal, and she dipped into a small curtsy before hurrying away, leaving Keir and Tierney alone.

"You're a good king."

He lifted his gaze, meeting hers, and a smirk came to his lips. "That wouldn't be a compliment, would it, Princess?"

She rolled her eyes. "You bring out the worst in me. It won't happen again."

His smirk fell, and he leaned back. "Sometimes, it feels as if I'm just guessing at what's best for my kingdom."

"That's because you are."

"I'm not sure if—"

"That wasn't an insult, I swear. For my entire life, I've been raised to one day rule my kingdom. Standing at my father's side, watching him handle the easy tasks and the hard ones. You can never really know what the right thing to do is, but I don't think that matters. What matters is that you try to see what's right."

"And you think I do?" He sighed. "Because there are times I feel too much of my father in me."

"No." Her single word held so much conviction. "Don't ever say that. Your father wanted power. He hoarded magic and executed dissenters. What is this really about, Keir?"

So few people used his name without a formal title in front of it. He was always the king, his Majesty. It was only in small moments with Tierney he was Keir.

"Declan and Eavha …" He swallowed heavily, unable to voice the fears shadowing him.

Warmth enveloped his hand, and he looked down to see Tierney gripping it. "You're scared for them." She smiled sadly. "You can't protect everyone from all things."

"I used to think I could."

"As did I … when I was ten. And then, I became the central figure in a war that nearly destroyed the four kingdoms of my home."

"I've been at war for so long I'm not sure I'd know what peace felt like."

She squeezed his hand, still not letting go. "It's better than you could ever imagine. In Iskalt, the lack of war keeps our fae fed and housed. We have no more destroyed villages. I can walk to the village from the palace without an armed escort."

"Truly?"

"Well, as long as my father doesn't find out. He's a bit … overprotective. But I've spent a lot of time in the village with my friends. Life without war is simpler. You should really try it some time."

He laughed. "Peace sounds so …"

"Peaceful?" She raised a brow. "Just think … Eavha and Declan could get married and have children without sending them off to war. You could—"

"Wait." He narrowed his eyes. "Declan and Eavha are not—"

"In love?" She grinned. "Well, probably not yet. But they will be. Eavha needs to get a bit older for him, but she's already there."

"No."

"Oh, absolutely." She lifted her hand off his and reached toward his face, trying to force his lips into a smile. "Might as well get over it now, Keir. You might think you have control over that girl, but control is an illusion."

"Like your father trying to force you into marriage?"

Her hand dropped, and the smile faded from her lips. "And you see how that turned out. He's in Iskalt, and I'm here."

"I'm glad you're here." The words slipped out before he could stop them.

Tierney was still for a long moment, and he inched closer, unable to resist the draw of her hopeful spirit, her rebellious gaze.

"Keir," she whispered, her breath warm against his lips.

"Yes, Tia?" He wanted nothing more than to close the remaining distance, to give in to whatever this pull was between them.

Her eyes fluttered shut. "We can't do this."

The words were a stream of icy river water showering down on him. Pulling back, the king's mask slipped into place. "Yes, of course.

That was wrong. I'm not sure what got into me. Will you accept my apology?"

"For magic's sake, Keir, you don't have to apologize."

The door opened, and Yvonne entered, carrying a tray laden with breads, cheeses, and fruits. She fumbled with it, finally getting it to the table after kicking the door shut behind her. "I'm sorry that took so long, your Majesty. I had to find someone to show me how to slice the bread."

Keir barely heard her because his eyes were still on Tierney, who'd stood and walked toward the door. Pulling back her shoulders, she yanked it open, not sparing a single glance behind her.

When she was gone, Keir buried his face in his hands.

"May I speak, sire?" Yvonne asked, shifting on her feet.

"Yes." Keir looked at her, seeing a glint of steel in her gaze. This woman had strength.

"Tierney O'Shea will find her way home. I don't believe anyone could stop her. They all will. It is best not to get attached." She dipped into a curtsy and left.

Keir stared after her, wondering what kind of maid had the audacity to speak to a king of such things. The problem was, her words rang with truth.

A truth Keir would force himself to remember.

CHAPTER 18
TIERNEY

"Keep your dagger up." Tierney tapped Margery's wrist until she held her dagger at the correct height. "Relax your hips, and square your shoulders. Be confident."

"Yes, my Lady." Margery gripped her weapon tighter, relaxing her stance.

When Eavha left to follow Declan, Margery—the wife of a minor nobleman—came to find Tierney, asking for her help with the ladies. They needed guidance, Margery claimed.

They needed a miracle. Tierney winced at the way Margery's opponent came at her, wrist limp, her silly jeweled knife clutched in her hand.

"Is that a fork or a knife, Lady Astrid?" Tierney observed the two women sparring.

"It's a breast dagger, Madam," Astrid said, affronted. "I assure you it is very valuable and perfect for a lady's hand."

"The rubies and sapphires certainly are valuable, but a three-inch blade will never cause more than a scratch in a real fight. I suggest you all dispense with the fashionable weapons and use the ones Declan provided for sparring."

"Those are for men, my Lady." Ines wrinkled her delicate nose. "They are far too heavy for us."

Tierney moved to the weapons' table, where Declan had laid out a variety of small swords and daggers, but they were soldiers' weapons. Serviceable. Old. But not pretty. "With practice, they won't be too heavy." She lifted a slim sword with a steel blade and lightweight pommel. She tested the weight of it in her hand.

Moving to another pair of sparring partners, Tierney corrected their stance, showing them how to move on the balls of their feet. "That's better. Yes, just like dancing, it will help tremendously to move on swift feet to avoid your partner's blade."

"Do women really serve in your father's army?" Lady Meghan asked from her seat on the sidelines. Several of the ladies came to watch but were not yet ready to join. Tierney suspected it gave them a thrill to watch the other women dally with swordplay.

"My father's army is made up of men and women in various roles. Some female warriors are officers and some are soldiers, but there is little difference between them on the battlefield. Where I come from, a woman is not limited by the confines of her gender."

"I still can't believe you will inherit your father's throne." Lady Clodagh shook her head. "It just seems so surreal. A woman as king."

"I will rule someday, but I will be a queen. Both of my aunts are queens who rule as well. My mother is a queen who rules beside my father, the king. He includes her in every decision he makes because she is his most trusted advisor."

"What does one call a man who marries a ruling queen?" Lady Margery giggled at the very idea.

"A prince consort. My uncle Myles and uncle Finn are both prince consorts, but they take active roles within their kingdoms."

"Can you even imagine, ladies?" Lady Clodagh fanned her face with an intricately carved fan. Tierney thought it was made of ivory at first, but of course, it was made from a crystal that had long since lost its magic. "A world where we rule our lands and carry our titles while our husbands stand in the shadows? It seems like the stuff of myth, doesn't it?"

"Iskalt is the stuff of fiction, my dear girls." The dowager duchess of … some vast holding or another had become the bane of Tierney's existence. She had a beautiful young granddaughter she intended to marry off to King Keir. She had decided Tierney was a dangerous distraction their king showed far too much interest in.

Even now, she rapped her cane against the stone floor of the chamber they had been using for their clandestine sparring sessions near the king's healing pool. "This is nonsense, and you should all be ashamed of yourselves. Females may rule in Grima, but this is Vondur, and our men are strong and capable. They don't need us getting in the way of a thousand years of tradition." The old crone fairly vibrated with fury. "Prince consorts, indeed," she scoffed. "What foolishness."

"Ah, but traditions are meant to evolve." Tierney lifted her sword and sank into a defensive crouch. Turning in a circle, balanced on one heel, she scanned the room for a sparring partner. "Yvonne is from Grima."

"Yvonne?" the girls whispered in confusion.

"My maid." Tierney beckoned Bronagh forward to choose a weapon from the table.

"I am." Bronagh lifted her chin, selecting a short sword with a wide blade. "And in Grima, if a woman wants to learn to protect herself, it is her right to do so." She gave the weapon a few practice swings. "From the queen right down to the lowliest maid. Women can inherit titles, land, and they can choose whether or not they wish to be married."

"Their fathers don't sell them off to the highest bidder?" Lady Meghan asked.

"She is free to choose her husband. A father provides a dowry for her to set up her household, but it is her money. It never passes on to the husband."

"My father allowed me to choose among a select few suitors he approved," Lady Meghan said. "It was kind of him to choose men close to my age. Years later, when I introduced my wonderful husband to our youngest child after her birth, he claimed she was so beautiful she would fetch the highest bride price in all of Vondur." Her smile faltered. "I know he meant well, but it has never sat well with me. She is a sweet, lovely child. Not a prized pig to be sold at market."

"It is tradition." The old duchess harrumphed, tapping her cane against the stones. "The husband and father know what is best."

"Yvonne, shall we show these ladies how it's done?" Tierney ignored the crotchety old woman, pacing around the center of the room.

"Yes, my Lady." Bronagh slipped off her apron and tossed her weapon from hand to hand to get a feel for it.

They circled each other for a moment, sizing one another up. Tierney knew the Grima queen was skilled with a sword, but she was looking forward to sparring with her to see what she was really made of. Tierney had learned from the greatest sword masters in all the four kingdoms. Few could best her.

Tierney, with her feet firmly planted, made the first advance. Lunging toward Bronagh with her sword lifted high and at an angle to protect her torso, she flicked her wrist, her blade meeting Bronagh's in a crash of steel. Bronagh danced back a few steps, crouching low, her sword even with her shoulders.

The Grima queen was quick with a blade. Together, they danced in a circle around the room. Forward and back, their weapons slicing through the air to meet with a clang. Back and forth they went, but Tierney couldn't gain any ground on her. In one moment, she moved aggressively in an attack, only to find herself retreating again in the next.

Sweat beaded Tierney's brow, and it felt so good to have a real opponent. One who didn't let her win or refuse to fight with their full skill because of who she was.

"What is the meaning of this?"

"Your Majesty." The old duchess stepped forward. "I'm so glad you are here. "These young ladies have lost what little sense they had."

"Keir." Tierney grinned, pushing the sweaty hair back from her face. "Isn't it wonderful what your sister started while I was gone?" Her chest burned with the exertion, but it felt good to have her blood thrumming through her veins.

"This is Eavha's doing then?" Keir stepped into the room, his hands resting at his back with an unreadable expression on his face.

"Before you even ask, I didn't give her any ideas. She started this on her own. "

"And this is …?" A dark brow lifted in question.

"Sparring practice. The young ladies of your court would like to know how to protect themselves." Tierney couldn't wipe the smile off her face. She was so proud of Eavha for doing this all on her own. "Princess Eavha asked Declan to teach them." She pointed to the weapons' table, still working to catch her breath. "Though, they could use smaller weapons sized for a female hand."

"And your maid has been trained well. As well as you have been."

"She's an excellent partner." Tierney gave Bronagh a nod of approval.

"Do they train all the maids in Grima to fight so fiercely?"

"They do, your Majesty," Bronagh replied. "All people of Grima are trained with the sword from an early age. Even women."

"What a strange concept." Keir shook his head.

"You never know when an invading army might arrive to overrun the palace." Bronagh's voice grew hard with scorn.

"That's enough, Yvonne." Tierney shot her a glare.

Bronagh's face flushed with the realization she'd spoken out of turn. "Beg your pardon." She gave the world's worst curtsy. It would be a miracle if they got out of Vondur before Keir figured out he held the Grima queen within his grasp.

"Terribly misguided." The Duchess shook her head, moving to stand beside the king. "I couldn't leave them down here unchaperoned, and I wasn't sure who I should tell, your Majesty. It is difficult to know how to handle such things now that my husband has departed this world."

Keir held up his hand to stop the duchess' dithering.

"A secret circle of Vondurian ladies." He moved around the room, eyeing each woman like an officer surveying his troops. "Ladies proficient with the sword."

"It's not as absurd as you make it sound, Keir." Tierney couldn't stand the tension. This was such a small thing to give these women. Some confidence that if push came to shove, they could protect themselves and their families. Was that too much to ask of this strange kingdom? "I am as proficient with a blade as any soldier in your army. And with a little dedication, the right weapons, and lots of practice, these ladies can be too." Well, they could be better than they currently were.

"It's fun, your Majesty." Lady Margery dipped into a perfect curtsy. "It's good exercise, and if it helps us protect our children, what is the harm?"

"Is that something you ladies fear?" Keir turned to the others. "That there could come a time when there will be no one here to protect you and your children?"

A few heads nodded.

"Your Majesty." Margery stood by meekly with her head lowered, eyes downcast. "Many of our husbands are officers and minor noblemen. They are frequently away. Along with your soldiers. Some of us live in remote areas of the kingdom. We come to court for protection while our husbands are at war. But if I could take my children home, knowing I could protect them, I would much rather be there to see to the estate in my husband's absence."

"I see." Keir turned to Tierney. "You claim you can match any of my men?"

"I can."

Keir moved to the side of the room to inspect the weapons Declan had provided. "These are terribly old. Some are rusted." He shrugged out of his coat. "They will have to be replaced. With smaller weapons, as you said." He drew his sword from his hip.

"What did you say?" Tierney took a step forward. For a moment, it sounded like he would let them continue their practice.

"With Declan away, you'll need a new instructor." He moved to the middle of the room. "But perhaps today, I will be sufficient." He pointed his weapon at Tierney, his mouth tilting up in a wicked grin. "Let's see if you can match *me*, Princess."

Chapter 19
Keir

Tierney stared at Keir as if she hadn't heard a word he said. He knew it was a bad idea the moment it was out of his mouth, but he couldn't take it back now.

Most of the women wouldn't meet his eyes, and he supposed that was Vondur's fault for teaching women subservience was best. Yet, there were two women here who didn't seem to follow those rules.

Tierney stared at him, a wicked gleam entering her gaze.

And behind her, Yvonne, a mere maid, lifted her chin and matched his hard look. He'd suspected it before when she did every part of her job poorly, but this was no maid.

Tierney's voice snapped him back to the challenge at hand. "Are you sure you wish to challenge me, your Majesty?" She stepped closer, her voice dropping. "I won't go easy on you."

Narrowing his eyes, he bent until his lips brushed her ear. "You don't stand a chance, Princess."

A laugh burst out of her, and she stepped back, examining the blade in her hand. With a shrug that seemed to say it was good enough but not perfect, she lifted it. "Let's make a deal, shall we?"

Keir raised his sword, taking up his stance. "What kind of deal?"

"When I win, you agree to train these women until Declan returns. No finding another instructor. It will be you."

"I am a king, Tia." He blew out a frustrated breath. "I do not have the time to train anyone who is not in my army."

"Then, you will let all Vondurian females who wish join your army."

"My men will never allow it."

"Then, I guess you better beat me." The flickering light from a nearby torch cast her face in an orange glow, giving her a deadly look that chilled Keir to the bone. If this was Tierney without magic, he couldn't imagine what kind of force she was with it.

But still, women joining the army would cause men to leave in droves. One day, he hoped Vondur could get there, but today was not that day.

"Fine, if you should best me, I will find the time to train them."

A triumphant gleam entered her eye. "And what do you want on the slim chance you win?"

There was only one thing he truly wanted that she could give. He stepped closer, dipping his head so his lips were only inches from hers. "You." The word was almost a growl.

"Me," she whispered, her mouth popping open in surprise.

His gaze flicked from her lips to her eyes and back again. "I want a taste, Tierney O'Shea. Just one."

The world seemed to still as her entire body went rigid. The only sign of her rapid thoughts was in the heaviness of her breathing. For once, Keir didn't regret letting her know how much he wanted her, how much he thought of closing the distance between them and claiming her in a single kiss. Just one, and then he could shake her from his mind.

Stepping back to give her space, he waited a few agonizing moments.

Finally, Tierney nodded. "I accept." The shock faded from her face, and one corner of her mouth curved up in a slow, delicious arc. "Don't be too nervous. You won't win."

Her words brought a smile to his face. "Big words. We'll see if you can live up to them."

Tierney shot him a wink before bending into a low crouch, her sword at the ready. It was an aggressive kind of stance he'd never seen before, but she looked so at ease with the weapon he realized she'd obviously been trained by a great sword master.

Just as he had. He bent his knees and readied himself the way Daniel taught him before abandoning Keir for the Grima court. That was a long time ago, but he'd never forgotten the lessons.

Never take your eye off the opponent, young prince.

Know where their weapon is at all times.

Do not underestimate a rival.

He'd already failed at that last one. He'd underestimated Tierney the moment she'd shown up during the battle against the golden warriors.

He wouldn't make that mistake again.

A slow murmur came from behind him, and he realized he'd forgotten they weren't alone. But it was no matter. This was between him and Tierney.

She made the first move, which was fine with him. He was a defensive fighter, not an attacker. Her sword crashed against his as she lunged. She pulled away with shocking speed and pivoted on one foot to turn and strike again.

Each blow was stronger than the one before, but Keir fended them off easily, matching her for both strength and speed. Yet, Tierney kept coming. "Nice footwork, Princess." He smirked as he stepped out of her way.

"Oh, just wait." She danced toward him, her sword arcing through the air. He blocked the blow and then turned to meet her next. "I was trained by the O'Shea brothers."

"Your father?" He ducked a blow, not letting her drive him back.

Her breath huffed out. "And my uncle Griff." She jumped so suddenly he didn't see her feet leave the ground and only had a moment to fend off her quick strike, pushing her onto her heels. "Along with the best sword masters of the four kingdoms."

She landed gracefully without missing a step. "My father taught me how to use my size to my advantage." She whirled around, her sword coming from the left and then the right, clashing with his. "He taught me how to make any weapon an extension of myself."

And he'd taught her well. Keir's arms ached as she forced him back a step, taking his ground. The women behind him scrambled out of the way, their eyes on the fight.

Breath burned in his lungs, and he tried to drive her in the other direction. But she didn't give an inch, jumping over his sword when he swept it low and then ducking the next blow.

The weapons weren't blunted, so they had to be conscious of each attack, able to stop before seriously injuring the other. If they had wooden swords, he knew Tierney would have already rapped him over the head with it.

She didn't want to kill him. At least, he didn't think so.

He stepped into her attack, thinking of what a bad idea it would be to win this fight. Nothing good would come from kissing this woman. Yet, he drove forward with all of his might, trying to take that victory.

"And your uncle?" he grunted, remembering she'd said two men taught her to fight. "What did he teach you?"

A grin slid across her face. "Oh, you'll see."

He wasn't sure if he found that answer intriguing or terrifying. Maybe both.

The women cheered, and it took him a moment to realize they wanted Tierney to win, to not only best a man but to beat their king. "It seems you've won over even more fae in my kingdom."

She shrugged. "Only because I challenge how they view their place in this world." She leaped forward, her sword barely missing his side as he jumped.

"You must be beloved in Iskalt."

Darkness crossed her features, and he wasn't sure if it was

because she'd turned out of the torchlight or if it was something else. Her foot connected with his stomach, shoving him into the stone behind him. When had she forced him to the wall?

His totem burned against his neck, begging to be used in the fight. But he refused to draw on it against Tierney.

"Iskalt thinks I'm trouble." She admitted, holding the tip of her sword against his chest. "Do you concede?"

Here in the shadows, her eyes looked almost black. Blond hair had broken free of its braid, hanging in sweaty strands around the pale skin of her face. Red tinted her cheeks from the exertion. She looked like a forest wildling—a creature meant to live freely in the countryside instead of trapped in a castle in a role that was going to destroy the fire inside her.

"Trouble is sometimes what a kingdom needs." Vondur had certainly needed her brand of recklessness.

Her sword dipped the slightest bit, her grip loosening on the hilt. Keir batted it away and stepped around her to take up his stance once again.

Tierney scowled, her eyes narrowing. "You really want to know what Uncle Griff taught me?"

All he could do was nod.

"You asked for it." She walked toward him slowly, her eyelashes fluttering against her cheeks. "Why do you want to kiss me, Keir?"

"Um …" He didn't have an answer for her.

A smirk appeared on her lips. "Is it because I challenge you?" Her tongue poked out to wet her lips. "Or because I make you challenge yourself?" She didn't stop moving until she was within reach of his sword, but he didn't raise it. "Imagine it. A moment just for us. One with no interruptions, no pressing duties." She smiled. "If you want me, your Majesty, come and take me."

There was a dare in her eyes, one Keir couldn't make himself resist as he shifted toward her, his sword still keeping them a few feet apart even though his fingers relaxed.

Tierney moved so quickly he couldn't track her as she ran to the right before turning and heading straight for him. He prepared for an attack, but his mind was no longer in it.

Tierney jumped, landing in a somersault and sweeping his legs out from under him. His back hit the ground with sharp pain, but he didn't have time to evaluate himself because Tierney was there, straddling his waist, her sword at his throat.

She stared at him for a long moment, her chest heaving, before leaning down and bringing her face close to his. "My uncle taught me how to fight dirty." Her lips curved up. "To use every advantage I have. Do you concede now, your Majesty?" The way she used his title sent a shiver through him.

"Yes," he breathed. "I concede."

With a satisfied nod, she climbed off him and stood. Extending a hand down, she grinned. "Maybe next time."

He didn't take her offered hand, and she drew it back seconds before some of the other women mobbed her, uttering soft congratulations and trying not to offend their king.

Smiling in spite of himself, Keir pushed to his feet, stretching to rid himself of the ache in his back.

"Tomorrow," he said to the gathered women. "Sundown." With that, he walked out, not sparing another glance for Tierney.

She was right, of course. One had to use every advantage in battle. He'd just never thought she'd have an advantage over him, that she could throw him off so easily.

He scrubbed a hand over his face as he headed toward the great hall in search of an ale. Finding the women training had been a shock, but he was proud of Eavha for helping them. He only wished she and Declan thought they could tell him about their secret club.

Footsteps sounded behind him, and he turned, expecting to find a guard heading to their evening post.

Instead, Tierney jogged to catch up with him. She stopped a few feet away, looking much less confident than she had during the fight. "Keir …"

He was too tired for guessing games. "What is it?"

"Thank you."

That surprised him, and it must have shown on his face.

"For agreeing to train them. It was important to Eavha."

She didn't say it, but he suspected it was important to her too. Tierney acted as if she cared for little more than returning home, but he knew the truth. She wanted to help his fae.

"That was our deal."

She shrugged. "You're the king. No one would blame you for breaking a deal."

"I would never go back on a promise to my fae, Tierney." Or to her, but he didn't say that last part.

A small smile appeared on her lips. "I'm starting to see that."

CHAPTER 20
SIOBHAN

Siobhan followed Toby and Logan across the castle grounds and down to the lake where the special library was supposed to be located for the moment.

She squinted in the sunlight and saw nothing but snow-covered fields as usual.

"You can't see it yet, Siobhan." Toby laughed, his breath coming out in a white cloud. "My grandfather has to invite us inside." He pointed to two ancient-looking columns buried in the snow. "The village of Aghadoon is just through there. It used to be that only those with the blood of Gelsi royalty could see the village when they weren't inside, but Grandfather and Aunt Neeve found a way to change the magic. Now only those who have been invited may see it once they cross the threshold."

Toby stepped through the columns and disappeared.

"Whoa." Prince Logan stepped back. "Wasn't expecting that."

"Do we wait here?" Siobhan asked.

"I can't remember. It's been a long time since I visited Aghadoon. I was just a kid the last time it was in Eldur."

"You guys coming?" Toby stuck his head out through the

columns. "I promise it's not weird. Well, it is weird, but it's safe." He reached for Logan's hand, pulling him through.

"Anything for Tia." Siobhan sucked in a breath and stepped through the columns. The first oddity she noticed was the absence of snow inside the village. Green grass grew in front of quaint little buildings and houses. It was still cold, but not Iskalt cold. Siobhan shed her gloves and hat, stuffing them into her coat pockets.

"Most of the houses are vacant these days. Just those traveling with the village live here. A few residents stay here while they're researching. And Grandfather Brandon, of course, along with a few of his Gelsi subjects who monitor the library."

Toby led them down a cobblestone street to the center of the village, where a lone building sat. It was larger than the others but still not what Siobhan would call a library.

"This is supposed to house all the histories of magic in the whole world?" She stepped up onto the wooden porch beside Toby and Logan. "It's a shack."

"Ah, but looks can be deceiving, my dear." Prince Brandon stood in the open door of the library, beckoning them to come inside. Siobhan's heart skittered to a stop as she stared at the once king of Fargelsi, father of the current queen.

"I beg your pardon, sire." She sank into a deep curtsy.

"Dispense with the formalities while you are in Aghadoon, young Siobhan. Come inside, and let's see what we can learn of my granddaughter's fate."

"Have you found anything new, Grandfather?" Toby slipped off his coat and hung it on a peg by the door, turning to help Logan out of his coat. They were so cute the way they took care of each other.

"I have, but it's led to more questions than answers, I'm afraid." Brandon moved to the large table at the center of the room. "Make yourselves at home while I bring out my findings. Perhaps you can give Siobhan a quick lesson on how the library functions."

"Will do." Toby pulled a chair out for Logan and one for Siobhan like the perfect gentleman he was.

"Thank you." Siobhan sat down opposite the boys, staring around the musty old building filled with ancient books. "I expected it to be bigger."

"As Grandfather said, looks can be deceiving." Toby shifted through a stack of tomes scattered on the table. "What is physically on the shelves changes based on the researcher's needs. We've yet to catalog everything this library contains, and I doubt we ever will. As the library presents us with what it thinks we need, the contents of the shelves change from one moment to the next."

Siobhan shook her head. "Sometimes, magic is terrifying."

"How so?" Logan tilted his head in question.

"Just the idea that we have to rely on this unknown entity to present us with the knowledge we seek is kind of awful and scary—as a concept, I mean."

"Right you are." Brandon rejoined them, hidden behind a stack of books he carefully set on the table. "It's the unknown of Aghadoon that presents the first problem. Who made the library function this way? And what were they trying to hide within these fathomless walls?"

"Deep questions for another time, Grandfather." Toby lifted a book from the pile. "Tell us what you've discovered."

"These books contain all the references of Lenya that I can find. So far." Brandon moved to sit beside his grandson. "I found a passage here." He flipped to a marked page in a huge leather-bound book with a faded title. He ran his finger down the page. "Here it is; see what you make of it."

"A relic of the old world. From a time long before the four kingdoms formed, an ancient race of fae ruled a land rich and fertile. From their great cities, these fae achieved feats of magic those of the four kingdoms could never fathom. Before its destruction, this land was known as Lenya."

Toby looked up from the book. "Destruction?"

"Keep reading." Brandon gestured to the book.

"The kingdom of Lenya withered and died in a series of natural disasters that resulted in the formation of the Vatlands that encroached upon the land, consuming everything. Ages passed before the Vatlands began to recede and the four kingdoms rose to power, thriving in the lands between the blight that destroyed the once vast and fertile lands of Lenya."

"But if we're living in what once was Lenya, then where is Tierney?" Siobhan leaned forward. "Is there a map of the old Lenya?"

"That is an excellent question, Lady Siobhan." Brandon rose from his seat. "I haven't thought to look for ancient maps. I can't imagine any have survived, nor that they would look the least bit familiar to us, but let's see what we can find." He disappeared among the rows of bookshelves, his footsteps fading unnaturally in the small building.

Toby flipped through the pages of a different book, searching through the sections his grandfather marked for them to study.

"Listen to this." Toby reached for his suitor's hand, as if he drew strength from his presence.

Siobhan watched them wistfully. She wanted what they had. Someday. If they could bring the princess home, maybe she could have that with Tierney.

"Before the ancient civilization of Lenya faded into the ether, a blight spread across the lands. Vast fertile plains burned as temperatures rose, killing thousands who could not escape. Putrid swamps with noxious gasses engulfed villages. Cities and towns sank into the depths of marshlands and swamps, where none survived. The ground shook, breaking the land into deep canyons that flooded with vicious waters. Massive mountains rose so high there was little air left to breathe. Yet, legends have prevailed of a small band of Lenyans who survived."

"If they survived, wouldn't they be among us?" Logan asked, leaning closer to peer over Toby's shoulder.

"No." Toby sat back, his face paling as he met Siobhan's eyes. "There's more.

"Legend claims this band of brave Lenyans found a way to stall the spread of the blight beyond the burning lands, preserving their way of life from ages past."

Toby leaned against his chair, sliding the book forward. "That's where my sister is. I can feel her pulling me toward the fire plains."

"But how can we find a way across?" Siobhan reached for the book, her eyes scanning the pages to read the histories for herself. "And how could we ever know what lies beyond?"

"We probably won't, but this could help." Brandon returned with another enormous book nearly the size of half the table but thin like a portfolio.

"An atlas?" Toby stood to help him with the giant book.

"It's the oldest one I could find on the fly, as your mother would say." Brandon carefully lifted the cover, and Siobhan held her breath. The book seemed so old it might disintegrate before their eyes.

"Lucky for us, the magic of the library keeps these records in whatever condition they were when added to the library. I'd say this one was on death's door when it arrived here."

"It's a map of the four kingdoms." Siobhan moved to stand behind Toby as they all crowded around the large map.

"It even shows Myrkur." Logan pointed to the dark corner on the northwestern side of the map.

"This map predates the Vatlands." Brandon ran a careful hand over the region of Fargelsi. "Before Lake Vilandi formed."

"Look at Eldur." Logan's voice was barely a whisper. "It's as green as Gelsi. And it's bigger."

"Good thinking, Siobhan." Brandon patted her on her shoulder. "You have a mind for problem-solving."

"And here I thought I was just a warrior along the wild borderlands." Her face flushed at the former king's praise.

"Not many fae trapped in the human realm would figure out how to find the rift and travel there all on their own." He gave her another pat on the shoulder.

"Now, if I could just find a way across the fire plains."

At her mention of the Eastern Vatlands, they all turned to the opposite corner of the map.

"That's different." Toby moved to get a closer look. "The fire plains start around here." He pointed to the northeastern corner of the current Eldur lands. "If we go off the size of the known vatlands between Gelsi and Eldur through the marshlands, and the mountains of the Northern Vatlands between Iskalt and Myrkur, then there is no way the Fire Plains could consume a third of this map." He ran a hand over an area the size of Iskalt far to the east.

"It's a plausible theory." Brandon studied the map. "If some portion of Lenyan civilization survived, then it's a safe assumption they were sealed off by the fire plains."

"So, we just need to figure out a way across or around them." Siobhan turned to Logan. "What lies beyond the seas to the east of Eldur?"

"Nothing, I'm afraid. At least nothing Eldurians have discovered. The seas off our coasts are plentiful and smooth sailing for leagues and leagues. But the seas become rocky and dangerous as they turn toward the fire plains. Some say it's as hot as the vatlands there, where the waters churn and bubble and blazing hot steam bursts from the rocks like geysers."

"And what of the Iskalt seas?" Siobhan asked, turning to Toby and Brandon for answers.

"The sea between Iskalt and Eldur is calm and easy sailing," Toby replied. "But the shorelines along the fire plains are impossible to navigate. It's too hot, and the smoke lies thick across the water. I'm not sure what lies beyond the eastern mountains. The frozen tundra in the east is a difficult journey, and then the mountains are as treacherous as the western Vatlands."

"Some have made the journey." Brandon ran a fingertip across Iskalt on the map. "But not much is known of the seas beyond eastern Iskalt. I imagine it is colder than we could fathom."

"So, what you're all saying is no one knows what lies east of Eldur and Iskalt. But if this map is even partially accurate, something is there, and based on Toby's connection with Tia, in all likelihood, she is where we cannot reach her."

"There is more." Brandon returned to his seat, dragging another book from his stack. "The ancient Lenyans were not like us. The histories here speak of them as a superior race of fae. Capable of great feats of magic."

"That does not sound good for Tia." Logan scooted closer to Toby.

"See here." Brandon placed the book on the table, pointing to a faded etching of a king and queen on their thrones. "See how they each clutch a crystal in their hands?"

"What does it mean?" Toby asked, staring at the image.

"Their magic is not like ours. Where the sun gives Logan his day magic and Siobhan receives her night magic from the moon, and I gain my magic from the land itself, Lenyans used carved totems made of a certain kind of crystal that allowed them to touch their magic."

"What kind of crystal?" Siobhan asked, though she couldn't fathom needing to use an object of power to access her magic. To her, reaching for her magic was as effortless as breathing.

"As near as I can tell, it seems like they used what the Myrkurians call fire opals. We have them here in Iskalt, and all across Gelsi and Eldur as well. They are pretty to look at, and they make lovely decorations, but for us, they contain no power." Brandon set a rough-cut stone on the table. A fire opal.

Siobhan picked it up, but it was just a rock like any other. It sparkled with a turquoise core that bled into an orange burst of color that looked like flames. Hence, the Myrkurian name for it.

"This gives them power?" She wrinkled her nose at the concept. "What strange magic."

"It only lasts for a time." Toby read from the book, "*Each totem provides Lenyans with power until it drains from the crystal and another is needed to replace it.* It is this power that allowed them to build cities as grand and populated as modern human cities. I made that last part up, judging by these images. This city here, with huge buildings, reminds me of New York in the human realm. Without the cars." He tapped a finger on a page with another etching.

"You're right. It's a lot like the human cities." Siobhan didn't care for those places when she traveled the human realm. "Too many people." She eyed the etching of busy streets filled with people and large buildings with huge columns and statues that towered above them.

"I think we are dealing with a very different kind of fae." Toby frowned. "If they are so powerful, even Tia might not be able to fend for herself." He gave a shudder, like he dreaded the thought of his powerful sister among such people.

"We have no choice. We have to find a way across the plains." Siobhan studied the map again. "How long does it take to walk across the Southern Vatlands?"

"When one knows the way, it can be done in a little more than a day's walk." Brandon sat back in his chair. "More if the person is uncertain."

"So, we need a way to survive the intense heat of the fire plains for two days. A shield might work to block the heat."

"One would have to sustain it day and night, though," Brandon said.

"A team of Iskaltians and Eldurians could manage it. And maybe a Fargelsian to help along the way." Toby eyed his grandfather.

"Your mother would kill me for even letting you think about it." Brandon shook his head.

"What if we moved the library?" Logan asked. "We could try to move it to the other side, right?"

"We cannot risk the contents of this village." Brandon refused. "If we landed in the middle of the fire plains, all here would be lost."

"So, let's move to the border." Toby looked at the map again. "We can go to this side of the plains and search for a way across. We can use the library to help us find the right magic, and then we'll already be there to act on it. I feel like we're running out of time, Grandfather."

"I can't let you do it, Toby. It's too risky."

"You really think she's there?" A weary voice caught them by surprise.

"Mom." Toby hopped up from the table. "How long have you been listening?"

The queen stood in the open doorway, looking haggard, like she hadn't slept in all the time since her daughter went missing.

"Long enough. Answer my question, Tobias." She moved to sink into a chair at the table.

"She's there. I know it. I can't feel her every day, but when I do—when she feels a strong emotion—I know she's there. She's calling for me. I have to go."

Queen Brea nodded. "The connection you two share has always astounded me. It's like you have your own little language. Logan, dear, could you go fetch the king?"

Logan's throat bobbed as he swallowed. "You want me to go where now?"

"Loch is in with his council. Go tell him we're leaving for the fire plains in an hour, and if he wants to come with us, he better get his butt down here."

"Y-yes, ma'am." Logan stood, and Toby walked with him to the door. "If I don't come back, send out a search party."

"He won't kill the messenger. Just be assertive. He respects that." Toby leaned in to kiss him on the cheek. "Good luck. And remember, he's really not that scary."

"To you maybe." Logan stepped outside, and Siobhan laughed when he took off running as fast as his legs would carry him.

"We're really going?" she asked the queen.

"Yes, and while we're waiting on Loch, catch me up with whatever this map is we're looking at."

Chapter 21

Tierney

I would never go back on a promise to my fae, Tierney.

Those words had stuck in Tierney's head since the moment they dropped from Keir's lips. Because she believed them. Every moment she spent with him only proved one thing: he could be trusted to do what was right.

"How can you not be sure yet?" She paced from one end of her room to the other and back again. "He has shown you nothing that proves he will use the danger to all of Lenya as an excuse to destroy Grima."

Bronagh sat on the settee, bent over with her head in her hands. At that moment, she looked nothing like the queen she was. Each passing day posing as a maid wore on her, Tierney could see it. She needed to be back with her people, to lead them.

But the best way to lead them right now was to discover if they had an ally to stop the destruction.

"I wish I had a totem," Bronagh grumbled.

Tierney stopped moving and planted her hands on her hips. "How would magic help you make this decision?"

"It wouldn't, but feeling the power within me … it makes me feel sane."

A breath puffed past Tierney's lips, and she dropped onto the settee beside Bronagh. "I understand that. I stopped counting how many days it's been since I last had use of my power, and sometimes I wonder if that was the only part of me that ever made sense."

Bronagh lifted her face, turning to eye Tierney. For the moment, they weren't a queen and future queen. Instead, they were very much the young women life hadn't allowed them to be. Unsure. Confused. Conflicted. But young women whose duties included more than raising their children, tending the fields, or even fighting for their kingdoms.

They would never be free from the burdens of the crowns that belonged to them.

"Lenya used to have great power." Bronagh smiled, a sad tilt to the action. Tierney waited, letting her speak, knowing she had to. "In Grima, our elders speak of ancient stories where crystals were in abundance. A Lenyan fae could draw massive amounts of power from their totem all at once because if they depleted it quickly, there were a hundred more to replace it in their possession."

Bronagh sighed, her entire body relaxing into the settee. "Those Lenyans, long ago, assumed the mines would never empty, that we would always have the magic we needed. But now …"

"Now, you must be judicial in your use of the crystals," Tierney finished for her.

"They are only to be used in battle, and even then, one must draw slowly." She turned her entire body to face Tierney. "What I am saying is that we too once defined ourselves by how much power we possessed. And now, we know it is the wielder, not the magic itself that has the true power."

Tierney shook her head. "I have no real power."

"You forget, Tia, I've been forced into the company of the gossiping maids for weeks. I've heard of your accomplishments. Yesterday, I saw my enemy, one who has always seen women as weak and inconsequential, give deference to you."

"To be fair, it was his fae who had those views on women. I'm not so sure about Keir."

"And still, the Vondurian king agreed to take time to train the women of the kingdom." She touched Tierney's hand. "Not all power is magic."

Tierney turned the words over in her mind, knowing they were true but not feeling like it. She'd always defined her worth by what she could do. Took down the prison magic. Intimidated villagers who wronged her or Toby. Emulated anything her father accomplished. She wouldn't have been able to do any of that without magic.

There was a knock on the door, and Bronagh straightened, pulling her hand away moments before Gulliver walked in.

"Where's Veren?" he asked, glancing around the room.

Tierney's brow furrowed. "Since when do you want to be anywhere near Veren?"

"Since he promised to spar with me."

Her shock must have shown on her face because Gulliver scowled. "I can want to learn how to fight better."

"You can want to," Veren said, walking in behind him and throwing an arm over his shoulders, "but it doesn't mean you will."

Tierney crossed her arms. "Why would you go to him instead of me?"

"I feel like I should take offense." Veren kicked off his dusty boots and lounged on the bed.

If the expanding fire plains didn't kill him first, Tierney would. "Off my bed." She stood, crossing her arms as she faced him. "And I don't want Gullie training with you because you'll let him down."

A look of hurt flashed across his face, and he rolled from the bed. "Whatever, Tierney." He stormed from the room, and she turned to the others.

Bronagh pursed her lips. "You're going to be a queen." She stood, smoothing the creases from her soft blue dress as she did. "You should try a little more kindness." She went after Veren, leaving Tierney alone with Gulliver.

He gave her a disappointed look.

"What?" she snapped. "It's Veren."

"Not the same Veren we knew in Iskalt. Come on, Tia, don't tell me you haven't noticed. Something changed in him during his time in Grima. I'm not sure if it was having to fight in battle or not being *the* Veren Rhatigan for the first time in his life, but he's not the guy who used you."

The sad truth was, Tierney had seen that. She knew Veren was trying to be different. But for so long, many of the noble children of Iskalt just wanted to be seen with the princess who destroyed the prison magic, to be associated with her. It made it nearly impossible to trust anyone. Especially someone who'd been vying for her hand in marriage only months ago.

"I suck."

A smile curved his lips. "It's very appropriate to use a human word when you just acted like a human."

"You take that back."

He leaned forward, dropping his voice, a hint of mischief in his gaze. "Human."

That was it. Tierney launched herself at him, and they fell sideways onto the bed in a heap of kicking legs and struggling arms. Managing to pin him, she dug a knee into his stomach. "Tell me I'm not a human."

"But all the human words," he wheezed. "The entitlement, the attitude. Oh, and not to mention your obsession with human things."

"You're the one who wants to court a hamburger. It's odd how in love with an item of food you are."

"Who got us into this mess with their little trip to the human realm?" The teasing note in his voice was the only reason she didn't kill him right then.

Her knee dug in hard. "Call me a fae."

A throat cleared behind them, and they both froze. Tierney

looked over her shoulder, not letting Gulliver free. "Oh, it's the king. Look, Gulliver. He probably thinks we're being intimate."

"Fine," he yelled. "You're a fae!" He shoved her off in disgust. "Don't ever say the word intimate in regard to us again."

A giggle burst out of her, and she was glad there'd never been anything more than a sibling relationship between them.

Keir cleared his throat again. "I'm glad we're clear that you are, in fact, fae." He muttered something under his breath.

"Oh." Gulliver sat up. "I was supposed to tell you the king wanted to speak with you."

Tierney stood to face Keir. "He definitely delivered your message." She sent Gulliver a wink. "I've got your back."

"You know I can hear and see you two, right?" Keir's eyes flicked between them, like he couldn't quite understand anything they did or said.

"Why is he always in such a bad mood?" she asked Gulliver.

Gulliver shrugged. "Maybe they don't let him put honey in his morning porridge."

"Or maybe no one smiled at him yet today." As one, they both turned to Keir, giant grins on their faces.

He stared at them, his expression darkening, before turning on one heel and marching from the room.

Tierney held up a hand, and Gulliver slapped his against it, his tail coming up to hit it too. With another grin, she chased after Keir, falling in step beside him as he hurried down the corridor.

"You wished to speak with me?" she asked. "If it's about training the women, don't think you—"

"It's not about that."

"Then, what—"

"Not here." His eyes darted around the hall, his steps never faltering. With no warning, he grabbed her wrist and pulled her through a doorway, shutting the door.

They descended into darkness, and Tierney backed up, almost knocking over what she thought was a bucket. "Where are we?"

"This is where the maids keep many of their cleaning components."

The king had pulled her into a closet? She didn't know why that made her heart kick up a notch. "And why are we in here?"

"Because there are always fae listening to what I say in this palace, and I do not want us to be overheard."

As her eyes adjusted to the darkness, she realized they were close, too close. Stepping away, she cringed as a broom crashed to the ground. Her butt hit a cold stone wall, and she suddenly had nowhere else to go.

"I need you to be honest with me, Tierney."

"About what?" Her voice was embarrassingly breathy.

"Yvonne."

Tierney's chest seized. This was it, the moment he learned the truth of how they'd deceived him.

"She's not really your maid, is she?" He rubbed his forehead. "I should have known Grima wouldn't provide you with a maid for your return here. It made no sense, but I wanted to believe you."

Words clogged in Tierney's throat, and she tried to force them out. "Yvonne … she's …"

"Your guard," he finished. "It's so obvious. Her skill with the blade, the way she hovers near you whenever she can, how truly terrible she was performing the duties of a maid. Grima has female warriors, but we are not used to that in Vondur, and it blinded me."

Her guard? Breath rushed into Tierney's lungs. Keir deserved the truth, and he'd get it, but not yet. It wasn't her truth to tell, her life to put at risk. She nodded. "My guard. Yes, that's what she is."

He turned away from her, a frustrated huff expanding his cheeks. "You didn't have to lie to me, Tia. I know coming back here must not have felt safe for you. I wouldn't have respected you any less for bringing not only Veren but another guard as well."

"I know." *Think, Tia, think.* "It's just …" Her next words burned like acid in her mouth. "I didn't think I could protect myself surrounded by those who wanted me dead not long ago. I am just one woman after all."

"If meeting you has taught me anything, Princess," he turned to look down at her, "it's that one woman can do anything. But even if you didn't believe that, I'd have protected you."

Tears built in her eyes, and this time, she wasn't playing up a lie. Only she knew the truth. No one could protect her. If they could, she wouldn't be here in Lenya at all.

Keir looked like he had more to say, but his words were cut off by a knock on the door. "Your Majesty? One of the guards said they saw you enter here. Are you in there?"

Tierney wiped her eyes. "It's okay. Go be the king."

He gave her one final look before opening the door. "Just having a meeting." He walked out of the dark closet like it was the most normal thing in the world.

The soldier was smart enough not to comment on it. "Sire, there's a situation."

"What sort of situation?" Keir asked impatiently.

Tierney followed behind them, not leaving unless she was asked. If there was an issue, she wanted to know of it.

"We have news of activity between our troops and the golden warriors."

"A battle?"

"Yes, sire."

No, this wasn't supposed to happen. Prince Donal promised to give Bronagh more time to turn Vondur into allies against the fire plains.

Keir's steps quickened. "Have we won?"

"That's just it, sire." The soldier's own steps faltered. "We do not know."

CHAPTER 22
KEIR

Anger ripped through Keir as he dug his heels into the sides of his horse, urging him to increase their pace. The moment he heard about the battle near the valley, where the largest part of the Vondurian army camped, he'd thought of little except getting there.

He didn't know if the fight was over, if there was a victor, nor how much of his army now lay dead at the feet of the golden warriors.

Tierney thundered up beside him on a giant gray stallion, having refused to remain at the palace. Behind them rode a contingent of guards along with Veren, Gulliver, and Yvonne. If they found themselves riding right into a battle, they'd need all the swords they could get.

Nothing else mattered anymore. None of the lies, nor the secrets he knew Tierney still kept. Not when his fae fought for their lives. And she'd come.

Branches lashed at his face as he barreled into the narrow part of the forest, knowing their destination was just on the other side. Pine needles stabbed his skin, but the scratches barely registered.

All he could hear was the horses, all he could see was the road ahead. Would Grima and Vondur ever see peace? Maybe none of that mattered either. Maybe the fire plains would destroy both kingdoms and wipe this land free of the blood and strife it had seen so much of.

By the time Keir reached the far end of this particular patch of forest, he was ready to fight. He led the riding party up over the crest of a hill, long-dead grass crunching under hooves. They stopped when they reached the top.

A field soaked in blood sat before them.

Bodies clad in red and gold armor were scattered about.

"Draw your weapons," he ordered, pulling his own sword free. The sound of scraping metal came from his right, and he turned.

Tierney's eyes narrowed in determination, as if this was her fight as much as his.

She met his gaze and nodded. He returned the gesture, glad they were on the same side for once.

"On my command." He drew in a long breath. As soon as they dipped into the valley, they would see whatever remained of the army camp. Smoke curled toward the sky, the only sign visible from their vantage point.

After a few beats, he lifted his sword. "Charge." Kicking his horse, he leaned forward. They plummeted down the far side of the hill. Fire. Churning black smoke. The acrid smell of burning flesh.

He didn't slow as he caught sight of the camp that had gone up in flames. A handful of soldiers lay dead among the ruins of tents, sleeping rolls, and cookery. Vondurians.

Beyond the camp, soldiers still struggled against each other, but this was not the kind of fierce battle Keir had expected.

He pulled up on the reins as he made it past the smoldering camp. Groups of men and women were stripped down to their underclothes. They huddled together, ropes securing their wrists and ankles.

Other soldiers patrolled the grounds. One slid his sword through a struggling man, like he was made of nothing but butter and oil. It took a moment for Keir to realize the soldiers rounding up prisoners wore Vondurian colors.

At the far side of the battlefield, fire licked at a pile of golden armor. Vondur had won.

Keir held up a hand to keep his men behind him.

Yvonne rode up next to Tierney and leaned in to speak, loud enough for Keir to hear. "This was not supposed to happen."

He didn't know what she meant, but there was no time to decipher her words because someone screamed, a man. He was one of the prisoners, and he lunged forward as a Vondurian soldier dragged another prisoner away.

The woman didn't fight him, didn't reach back for the man who had reached for her. Instead, there was hopelessness in her eyes. That was when Keir saw it.

A handful of bodies had been meticulously piled rather than scattered like the others. Those soldiers did not die in battle.

He leapt from his horse and opened his mouth to order every one of his soldiers to stand down, but before he could, the tip of a sword pierced the woman's chest. Red bloomed against her white underclothes like a thorny rose. A deadly rose.

No one caught her as she collapsed, her body going still.

The soldier pulled his blade free and gestured for two comrades to put her body with the others.

"Keir." Tierney's voice shook. "They're executing those who surrendered."

This couldn't happen. Not in his kingdom. Not in the Vondur he wanted to create. Storming through the remains of the battle, he sidestepped a dead Vondurian whose eyes were still open to the sky. "Lieutenant," he barked.

The officer turned, looking like he was ready to chastise anyone who addressed him in such a tone. Then, recognition showed on his face. "Your Majesty?"

Keir's jaw clenched as he stopped in front of the man. Tiny drops of blood spotted his cheeks, his uniform. "Report. What happened here?"

The lieutenant looked unsure of himself for only a moment before recovering. "Our camp was attacked by the golden warriors of Grima in broad daylight. Those vermin thought they could take us by surprise."

"Why would Grima attack now?" Yvonne asked. Keir hadn't realized she'd followed him.

The man acted as if he hadn't heard her. "What they didn't know was that our scouts spotted them first. We were lying in wait when they arrived."

Yvonne walked past them to view the prisoners. "I don't understand."

She was from Grima, so Keir tried not to speak ill of her people. "It seems your queen is just as power-hungry as her mother was before her."

Yvonne had her back to him, but he saw her stiffen. She didn't respond.

"How much warning did you have?" Tierney asked.

The lieutenant scowled. "Your Majesty, perhaps I should report to you somewhere more private." Somewhere without women present, he meant.

Tierney rolled her eyes, but Keir's expression didn't change. "What are your men doing with those bodies?" He pointed to the pile that had grown by one with the recently executed woman topping the heap. He already knew the answer, but he wanted to hear it from this soldier's mouth.

Nearby soldiers stood at attention in the presence of their king but did not speak.

"They are enemies of Vondur. The palace dungeons are not large enough to hold every soldier who surrenders, much less feed them."

"You could let them go." Tierney crossed her arms.

He gave her a pitying look. "There's a reason we do not allow women to strategize."

Tierney lunged for him, but Gulliver and Veren held her back.

Keir busied himself viewing the prisoners. Not all were upright; some were quite injured and needed tending. "You're executing them. Even the injured, the women."

The soldier didn't have the decency to look ashamed. "We do what we must."

A familiar face caught Keir's eye, and he walked around the lieutenant to get a closer look. Yvonne had already found him and crouched at his side. The prince of Grima lay on the ground, his head on another prisoner's lap, his skin white as Grima snow. The young man was on death's door.

Donal's eyes fluttered open and fixed on Keir. "We face each other again, Vondurian," he croaked.

Keir's brow creased. "I do not think you are in any shape for a fight."

Donal's laugh turned into a cough. "Are you going to kill me this time?"

Keir looked away, his eyes finding the other prisoners watching them, the same defeat on their faces. The longer he looked at them, the less he saw an enemy. He saw the men and boys of Vondur, pulled from their fields with little choice but to fight for the families they left behind.

When had the common soldier become little more than fodder in this war between crowns?

His eyes drifted back to Donal, a decision made. "No. I'm not going to kill you."

Yvonne's sob echoed in the silence. He wondered if his own people would shed a tear for him like she did for her prince.

Straightening, he looked to his soldiers. "I am proud of your victory today." He paused as they cheered. "But a victory cannot exist without honor. And an honorable kingdom does not execute those who surrender." His eyes scanned the ranks, and he raised his voice. "Vondur does not kill without cause. Our great army is the protector of this kingdom, nothing more.

"We will rebuild your camp and fortify our scouting parties, but these people who fight for the gold crests on their armor are not your enemy when the battle is won. They will be allowed to return home to their families."

He nodded toward the prisoners. "Provision them, and tend to the wounded as you would your own."

Muttering erupted among his men, but he ignored it and turned to Donal. "But not you. You, young prince, are staying with us. Lieutenant?"

The sour man snapped to attention, his face showing none of his true emotions. "Your Majesty?"

"I do not want the prince moved without a healer present. Do you have one among you?"

"Yes, sire."

"Fetch them. And then give the fallen a proper funeral pyre with honor. Both those of Vondur and of Grima."

"You want to … honor fallen enemies, sire?"

"I think it's time we honor all life as precious in Lenya." His men didn't yet know the fire plains would become their greatest enemy, bonding the two foes in their fight for survival.

Once they depleted the crystal reserves, there would be nothing standing between Lenya and the fires that would consume them.

Keir gripped the totem at his neck, begging it to give him strength. He rarely used the power, but its presence bolstered him. After seeing his orders to completion, he climbed back onto his horse, exhaustion weighing him down.

The hairs on the back of his neck prickled like someone had their eyes trained on him. He turned in his saddle only to find Yvonne standing at the side of the stretcher where Donal rested. Her lips were pursed as she studied Keir, her eyes shrewd.

Tierney broke their stare-off as she rode up beside him. "We need to talk."

CHAPTER 23
TIERNEY

Tierney absently handed off her horse to the stable boy, her mind still on the battlefield. She'd experienced battle more times than she could count. Even now, years after the war for Myrkur ended, Tierney would wake up in a cold sweat, haunted by dreams of those days. When she was so wrapped up in her magic, she couldn't focus on her surroundings. But she'd been aware of the war raging around her, trusting in those who fought with her to protect her from harm while she did what no one else could do.

She was ten years old then. And maybe her grandmother Enis, preoccupied as she was with protecting the sacred book of magic, had made sure Tierney never saw the real atrocities of war.

Her thoughts strayed to the battle in Radur City when King Egan claimed the palace for himself, keeping Toby at his side. Even then, when her magic wasn't as sorely needed, she'd never seen anything as … vicious as what she'd witnessed today.

She could still see the Grima soldiers. Men and women who'd surrendered when the battle was lost. Wounded that could have easily survived with the attention of a healer. All murdered. Put down like animals slaughtered for a feast simply to rid the

Vondurian officers of a problem they didn't want to deal with. It came down to logistics. They didn't have room for prisoners of war, so they killed them.

"Tia? Are you okay?" Gulliver's tail wrapped around her wrist, the flat end thumping against her forearm in a soothing gesture.

"I'm fine." She nodded, as if to convince herself.

"Let's go see if Ariella can find us some of that awful tea they drink around here." Gulliver guided her into the palace and toward the east wing where they were staying. Bronagh had gone with her brother. Keir had insisted on bringing Prince Donal back to see the palace healers.

"Where are we going?" Gulliver kept pace with her as she altered their course.

"I need something stronger than tea," Tierney muttered, picking up her pace as they neared the king's rooms. "Keir!" she called, running to catch up with him, dragging Gulliver behind her.

"Tia, you should seek your rooms to rest." He paused in the doorway to his suite, gesturing to his guards to let her pass. "It's been a difficult day."

She brushed past him into his room.

"Don't mind us; I think we're looking for wine." Gulliver, still clutching Tierney's arm, stumbled into the room.

Keir followed, closing the doors behind him.

"There it is." Tierney reached for a glass decanter and three tumblers from the small table under the window. "Wherever there is a king, there is good wine." She lifted the bottle as she moved to sit in a hard wooden chair in front of the cold fireplace. She wondered if there was ever a time the Vondurians needed the fireplaces that seemed to adorn every room in the palace.

"You do know you're a guest in my home? If you wanted wine, you need only ask your maid to fetch it from the cellar." Keir's tone was teasing, but his face said he felt as bad as she did about what they'd witnessed today. He likely felt worse since it happened under his watch.

"Sit." She pointed to the chairs opposite her. "Both of you." She set the glasses on the table and poured two hefty glasses of wine and one half glass, which she handed to Gulliver. Spirits went right to his head every time.

She took her glass and tipped it back, taking a long sip. Wincing, she set it on the table. If this was the wine the king drank, she didn't want to know what everyone else got. It was nothing like the sweet heady fae wines of the four kingdoms. Gelsi wine, in particular, was the finest. She hoped she would get to drink her fill of it someday.

"It has to end, Keir." She took another sip. "Your war is stupid."

"Tell me how you really feel." Keir tipped his glass back and drained it.

"Did he just make a joke?" Gulliver snorted into his glass.

"Probably not on purpose." Tierney wasn't in the mood for jokes. "Your kingdom is suffering. It's time to settle your reign by putting an end to this war before it destroys you all."

"That is easier said than done." He stared over her shoulder and through the window behind her. "It would be my greatest wish to bring an end to this war, but I honestly don't know if it can be done. Maybe it is too far gone."

"You are king." Tierney leaned forward, refilling her glass. It wasn't so bad once one had a warm belly full of it. "You can do anything you want."

"I can, can I?" He turned his focus back on her. "And tell me, Princess Tierney, if there was a finite reserve of power left in your kingdom, and you were down to the last of it, what would you do?"

"I wouldn't fight over scraps with Grima, that is for sure."

"Magic is so overrated." Gulliver's tail swished behind him. "Wine ... is not." He giggled to himself, and then he shot his hand in the air, pointing straight up. "Magic causes more problems than it solves." He hiccuped and reached for the wineskin.

Keir moved it out of his grasp, leaning forward to set his empty tumbler on the table.

"Aw, you're no fun." Gulliver's tail reached over Keir's shoulder to grab the wineskin where it hung on the back of his chair. "I have magic, did you know?" He turned to Keir to distract him while his tail was busy trying to steal the wine he couldn't handle.

"Defensive magic as I recall." Keir had been on the receiving end of Gulliver's brand of magic once before.

"Right you are. I can't use it like other fae use magic. It's just kind of there. Like a second skin that protects me against all you other jerks trying to destroy things with magic you don't understand."

"Is he going to be okay?" Keir watched Gulliver, a smile tugging the corners of his mouth.

"He'll be fine as long as he doesn't drink any more." Tierney snatched the wineskin before Gulliver could get hold of it. "But he is right. Magic is a wonderful tool, but it is not everything. I've recently learned that lesson myself. The hard way. Anyone can survive without magic."

"So, you think my people should give up on our magic? Our way of life?"

"I didn't say that." Tierney still wasn't certain she could trust him with everything she knew. Not yet. "But if it were me, I would look for more."

"More what?"

"Magic."

"And where might I find another source of magic lying around unused?" Keir shook his head irritably.

Tierney tried not to think about the fire opals back home. The ones scattered across the Eldurian deserts like any other rock. The ones big as boulders in Fargelsi. The opal mines in Myrkur, and the whole of Iskalt, where the enormous snow-covered mountains were filled with the kind of crystals that would mean everything to the Lenyans.

"There are other kinds of magic. One needs only to know where to look for it and how to appreciate it for what it is, as much as what it is not."

"Pretty words, Princess." Keir reached for the nearly empty wineskin. "But we've moved far beyond philosophical what-ifs. We need to take action. And soon, or there will be nothing left of Vondur for the fire plains to consume."

Tierney's fist slammed against the table, and Gulliver launched from his chair, ducking behind Keir.

"For fae's sake, Tia. Don't do that." He crept back into his chair. "You know how I get when I've been into my cups." His tail wrapped around his leg, the tip twitching with a nervous tick.

"Sorry." Tierney sat back. "But I need you to listen, Keir. Vondur makes up a small portion of Lenya. There are others to consider."

"I am thinking of all of Lenya. Don't imagine for a moment that what we witnessed today did not affect me. Nothing of the like will happen under my reign ever again."

"Won't it?" Gulliver turned to Keir. "What measures have you taken to see that it's not happening elsewhere as we speak? You threw me into the dungeon upon my arrival, and the only reason I'm sitting here right now is because you've got a thing for ... hic ... hic ... T-ia." His hiccups were getting worse.

"Gullie—"

"No." He pointed a finger at her. "It's my turn to talk." His cat eyes drooped with the effects of the wine, but he clearly had something to say. "Do you even know what prisoners occupy your dungeons, King?"

"It hasn't been a top priority, no."

"Your father filled those reeking cells with innocents. Grima prisoners of war and Vondurians as well. Mostly soldiers who tried to return to their homes when their mothers and sisters, wives and daughters were starving. What have you done about them? Nothing. You let them rot. Yet, you challenged your father to the King's Comhrac to save our necks—and my neck thanks you for it—but the crown fell to you. Be a king, Keir. Be. A. King."

"Gullie is right." Tierney gave her best friend—her completely smashed-on-a-half-glass-of-wine best friend—a rueful smile. "If you truly care for all of Lenya like you say, then it's time to make your peace with the Grima queen and declare to all what kind of king you intend to be."

Keir left Tierney in his rooms so she could deal with a drunken Gulliver. He'd never met a fae who couldn't hold his drink, but he supposed there was a lot he didn't know about the Dark Fae of Myrkur.

There was a lot Keir didn't know about, period. He made his way down from the royal residence to the healer's quarters.

Tierney was right. This war was stupid.

"Your Majesty, a word." Lord Garnet quickened his pace to match Keir's long stride.

"Not now." Keir kept walking, ignoring the man's outrage.

"Your Majesty, I take issue with the crown's purchase of grain from my estates." The man had to run to keep pace with Keir. "The price per barrel has always been upwards of thirty coins. Last week's order yielded half that. I have a family to feed."

Keir stopped, turning on the much smaller man. The king towered over him. "You, a nobleman dripping in gold and jewels, have a family to feed? While half of Vondur starves? Take your sixteen coins per barrel and be happy it's not zero." Something about the look on Keir's face must have told the man he need not push the issue if he wanted to continue drawing breath.

Keir had bigger worries on his mind.

"Your Majesty." A young woman dropped her roll of bandages when he stepped into the infirmary. She was so flustered by his sudden appearance she forgot to bow—something his father would never have allowed.

"I must see the prince."

Stammering, she pointed through a set of double doors.

With a nod, he left her to her work.

"Donal." Keir was surprised to see the young prince sitting up in bed, looking far better than he had on the battlefield, though still quite pale.

"Keir." Donal gave him a curt nod.

"How are you faring?" He moved to sit in an empty chair.

"Better. I thank you for your hospitality … and for not killing me. But why didn't you? I would have if it went the other way. That's twice now you've let me live."

"Let's just say I want something better for the future of my kingdom. And this war isn't it." Keir leaned forward.

"Your Majesty?" A gasp sounded at the door.

"Yvonne?" Keir frowned at Tierney's bodyguard-maid. "Shouldn't you be with your employer?"

Donal looked between the maid and the king, confusion on his face.

"I would dearly love to care for my prince." She dropped into an awkward curtsy. "I've brought Prince Donal a tray from the kitchens."

Keir nodded, thinking she would set the tray on the side table and leave, but she pulled up a chair to sit with him while he ate.

Donal lifted a mug of broth to his mouth, taking a delicate sip of the steaming contents. "You were saying?" He urged the king to go on.

Keir glared at Yvonne. "It can wait."

Donal glanced at the maid. "Anything you have to say can be said in front of … Yvonne. She is a loyal servant."

"Very well." Keir shifted in his seat. "What would it take to bring peace between our kingdoms? I am new to my reign, as your sister is to hers. I do not know yet what manner of queen she will be. But I would like to know if peace negotiations are something she would consider."

Donal nodded, sipping his broth. "My sister was never supposed to be queen. Our eldest sister was the heir. Yet, our kingdom has known nothing but war for more than a generation. My mother was a shrewd woman. After my father died, she ruled as regent, keeping a firm grasp on my sister's throne until she was of age.

"That did not happen. But Mother planned for every possible outcome. In her mind, we were all heirs to the throne. She trained each of her children to step into the role of monarch should we each fall. Bronagh might not have been born to rule like our sister, but she is no less ready for the task."

"Will she consider peace?" Keir grew weary of the prince's prattle.

"Bronagh will do what is best for Grima and her people. She will hear your peace talk—but only if Vondur is willing to compromise."

"I should like to meet this sister of yours." Keir rose from his chair. "I must speak with my council first."

"Let them know Grima will only give so much. Vondur will need to prove they are also willing to concede on the issues."

"I imagine the most successful peace treaties happen when neither side is particularly happy with the outcome." Keir gave the prince a rare smile. "I wish you a quick recovery."

"Keir we need to talk." The door to his bedroom slammed open. "I know it's late, but I've only just gotten away from your sadistic castellan." Yvonne twisted her hands together, pacing across his bed chamber.

Keir sat up against his headboard, setting the reports he'd just been reviewing on the bedside table. Staring at the young sort-of maid, he shook his head. "Have you lost your way to Tierney's rooms?"

"I'm here to see you."

"Did you just use my given name when you barged in here?" Keir slid out of his bed, reaching for the tunic he'd discarded earlier.

"Yes." She stood to her full height. "I am Bronagh, Queen of Grima." She lifted her chin. Her eyes narrowed to slits when Keir laughed in her face.

"I am deadly serious." She moved to sit in front of the fireplace, gesturing for Keir to take the seat opposite her. "Why do you think Donal allowed me to stay during your little chat earlier this evening? He is a prince of Grima; he would never allow a servant to be privy to such a discussion."

Keir wiped his eyes, still laughing as he sat in the leather chair, propping his feet up on the table.

"Queen Bronagh." He shook his head. He was going to murder Tierney. The daft woman brought his greatest enemy into his home. "Explain yourself."

"I do not like this war." She sat primly on the edge of her seat. Even dressed as a maid, now that she'd let go of the act, he could clearly see she was a queen in every way.

"You've been talking to Tierney." Keir ran a weary hand through his messy hair. Being king was harder than it looked. He hadn't had a decent night of rest since he challenged his father to the King's Comhrac.

"I've always thought this war was futile." She seemed to wilt before his eyes.

"Wine?" He stood to cross his room. Someone had already seen to refreshing his wineskin.

"Yes, please." She exhaled, sitting back against the smooth leather of her chair. "Your rooms are rather sparse for a king." She watched him return with fresh glasses and plenty of wine.

Keir groaned as he sat down, pouring them each a full glass. "It is different in Vondur. A prince isn't the king's heir. He's just a pawn. I never expected to be king. It isn't our way." Keir took a sip of wine, observing the Grima queen across from him. She was hardly more than a child, but she was better at this than he was.

"Yes, any man who wants the crown can take it." She took a big gulp from her glass. "As long as he can slaughter his predecessor."

He could hear the disgust in her voice. Staring down at the dark wine in his glass, he thought of the three innocent people with the hangman's noose around their necks that day. That moment haunted him. "I did it to save my best friend. And to save two other innocent lives. That is the only reason I am king now. And it is why I remain in the rooms of my youth. I do not feel like a king."

"I can relate to feeling like … an imposter." Bronagh took another sip of her drink.

"Perhaps, it's time I move to my father's quarters."

"You are more of a king than those who have come before you. I have witnessed it for myself."

"Is that why you are here, masquerading as a maid—a terrible one—among my court?"

"I needed to know if there was any hope of our working together. Tierney said I could trust you, but I needed to see it for myself."

"And what have you decided?" Keir didn't want to think about the part where Tierney had stood up for him. He'd think about that later.

"You have honor. You care for your people, and you want to end this war as much as I do."

Keir lifted his glass. "I'll drink to that."

"I would love nothing more than for us to talk of peace." Bronagh sighed. "But—"

"We have much bigger problems than a war no one wants to fight anymore." Keir leaned back. This was going to be a long night.

"We have all of Lenya to think about." Bronagh reached to refill their glasses. "I'm afraid we will need more wine for this discussion."

"The fire plains are expanding into Vondur lands, as well as Grima."

"It started slow for us, but the expansion is happening faster. We are running out of time in Grima."

"We need stronger magic to slow the spread." Keir took his full glass from the queen and drank deeply, though he couldn't escape this new disaster in the bottom of a glass.

"My thoughts exactly."

"You propose we use the final reserves within the mines to fight the spread?"

"It won't be enough." Bronagh shook her head. "You know as well as I, what we've been mining for the last fifty years are murky stones not half as powerful as the pure crystals of our ancestors."

"What is your plan then?" For clearly, she had a plan.

"When you don't have enough magic to solve a problem, you find more magic."

"Tierney has been a good influence on you." Keir smiled.

"And on you. The crystals are plentiful in Iskalt. We will go there and propose a trade with King Lochlan."

"Excuse me?" Keir blinked rapidly. He must have misheard her.

"It will be a dangerous journey," Bronagh continued, not noticing his surprise at hearing such news. "But we can return with enough magic to push the fire plains back and contain them to their borders. We might even have enough to push them back farther."

They have crystals in Iskalt? Yet, Tierney had never trusted him with this knowledge.

"It is impossible." Keir forced himself to focus on Bronagh's chatter.

"We have built a ship. It was completed just before I arrived here in Vondur. It's the largest ship I have ever seen, but it is capable of crossing the raging seas to the northwest."

"You want to cross the maelstrom? Your ship will never make it." The seas around Lenya were dangerous. To the southwest, no one could pass through the rocky terrain lurking just under the surface.

And to the northwest, the maelstrom waited to drag any ship foolish enough to approach to the bottom of the deep.

"The only other option is through the fire plains, and we don't have enough magic for such a journey." Bronagh's voice was firm and controlled. "The fastest route to Iskalt is across the maelstrom. We have nothing to lose and everything to gain."

"When will you send your men?"

"I mean to go with them as soon as we return to Grima."

"We?"

"Donal will stay behind to rule in my stead with my uncle, but Tierney and Gulliver will want to return to their home. Veren too." Though, the thought of his leaving seemed to sadden her.

"And what part will Vondur play in this adventure of yours?"

"Come with us. Let each monarch of Lenya approach the King of Iskalt as a united nation. We need his help. We are lost without it."

"How do I know you speak the truth?" Keir stared at the girl, wanting to trust her, but a lifetime of hate for Grima was a hard habit to break. "How can I trust this elaborate scheme of yours isn't just a ruse to seize power in Vondur?"

Bronagh leaned forward. "Ask Tierney."

CHAPTER 25
TIERNEY

All Tierney wanted to do was sleep. It was late, and the day wore on her, the images flashing through her mind like a never-ending reminder of the horror she'd seen.

By the time she'd managed to get Gulliver back to her rooms, it was too dark to see much. Someone had lit candles in her sitting room—probably Ariella, the angel—so the moment she stepped inside, the room came to life in the flickering flame.

Now, the candles were down to the nubs, and soon they'd peter out entirely. But she couldn't bring herself to extinguish them.

Gulliver lay sprawled across her bed diagonally, snoring heavily in his drink-induced sleep. Which left her to curl up on the narrow settee, her head resting against the wooden arm.

Head aching, she closed her eyes and rubbed her finger along the totem she'd taken from Keir's rooms. She shouldn't have done it, but it sat there staring at her.

She should've known the only reason it wasn't around his neck was that all magic had left it. Or at least, none of it rose to the surface. She could still feel the burning ember of power at its core, like it would never truly be dead, never truly devoid of what gave it life.

The ache in her head slowly subsided, and she rubbed her temple, where wet hair dampened the skin of her forehead. After she'd washed the remnants of the battlefield from her skin in cold, left-over bathwater, she'd had no energy to do anything except let her body and mind both go still.

Bronagh was nowhere to be found, but Tierney hoped she too had found her bed and escaped into a few moments of blissful peace, free of worrying for her brother.

Tierney turned her mind inward, searching for her absent power. A spark of familiarity, a comforting twinge to tell her she wasn't alone in this body. She'd always seen her magic as its own entity, something most fae didn't agree with. Yes, she worked hard to control it, but the power chose whether or not to obey her. It twisted around her emotions, making it harder to keep them in check.

It was still there, deep inside. She could sense it, even if she couldn't physically feel it or call it forth. "Toby," she whispered into the dark. "I need you."

It took a heroic effort each day not to dwell on the distance between her and her twin, the dangerous path she'd soon embark on to get to him. Was it foolish? Probably. But that didn't mean it was the wrong thing to do.

She pictured the ship sitting in Grima waiting for them. If Keir said no, they didn't have the time to wait for him to come around. They'd already been in Vondur for too long, and it was time to go. Time to try to get home.

Her eyes popped open when a soft tapping sounded at the door. She willed whoever it was to go away, to leave her to her silence.

They didn't listen to the thoughts she sent their way.

With a sigh, she pulled herself off the settee, her bare feet hitting the soft carpet. The floor turned from carpet to stone as she made her way to the door, and the soft slapping of her feet filled the air with its rhythm.

When she pulled the door open, she wasn't surprised to see Keir standing on the threshold, his chest heaving with exertion.

"I—" He sucked in a breath. "Need to speak with you."

Without an invitation, he pushed past her.

"Sure," she muttered, "come on in." Swinging the door shut, she turned to watch him pace the room, stopping when he caught sight of Gulliver in her bed.

"We should go somewhere private to speak." Each word came out as a bite of agitation. She knew he'd been through even more than her in the past hours as he'd watched what his army was capable of, but she wasn't feeling particularly charitable toward any Vondurians at the moment. They truly were the barbarians the Grimans claimed.

"Trust me, Gulliver isn't waking up tonight." When Keir didn't look like he believed her, Tierney walked to the bed. Leaning over, she shoved Gulliver's shoulder. "Wake up, you drunkard." She squeezed his arm and shook.

Nothing.

Turning back to Keir, she found him staring at her in the dim light, his eyes wide. It was then she realized she wore only a nightgown that was much too short for her long legs. Its lacy hem reached mid-way down her thigh. Wet hair hung in tangled ringlets around her face, dampening her shoulders.

Moving to the dressing table, she found a ribbon and secured her hair before pulling a robe off a peg in the armoire and swinging it around her shoulders. "You can stop looking at me like that now."

He cleared his throat. "Like what?"

She rolled her eyes, thankful the semi-darkness hid the action. "Like for once, you've stopped being angry with me."

"I'll never stop being angry with you."

A small smile came to her lips. "Good." She enjoyed arguing with him, enjoyed irritating him to the point his face went red. "Now, what did I do tonight that made you stomp in here like I'd stolen the last french fry?"

"The last what?"

She hid a smile behind her hand. "It's not important."

His scowl told her he didn't like her holding anything back, but they weren't here to discuss the political implications of human food. "I know."

Confusion flashed across her face. "You know?"

He heaved a deep sigh. "Everything."

"Oh."

"Yeah, oh."

One of the candles gave one last flicker before going out entirely. The final one was basically just a nub of a wick in a pool of wax. Tierney focused on it, knowing if she had her power, she could use the Fargelsian fire word and they'd have all the light they needed.

Being stuck in the dark with Keir and his new revelations was not an intriguing prospect. His expression was as dark as their surroundings, little light creeping in.

Tierney backed up until she bumped into the table behind the settee. The nearly untouched tea tray rattled, and a single fragile cup tilted and fell.

Keir snatched it out of the air, reaching around Tierney to set it back on the tray. He was so close she could see the soft whiskers on his chin, where he hadn't shaved in a day or so. Many fae let their facial hair grow, but not Keir.

She wanted to feel the hairs, to touch the tiny bit of imperfection in his otherwise pristine appearance.

His jaw clenched, and she curled her fingers in, reminding herself she didn't get to reach out, to bring him closer.

Because she'd lied to him. About everything. And now, he knew.

The final flame died, throwing them into the black of night, where nothing existed save the tragic shadows haunting their dreams, the nightmares that didn't release them when they opened their eyes.

Silence stretched between them, the only sound their heaving breath.

A curse fell from Keir's lips, and Tierney felt his absence the moment he stepped away, her entire body wilting, as if she'd been trapped against the table and was now free.

Except, this wasn't what freedom felt like. Gnawing guilt wound through her. "Keir," she whispered.

"Quiet."

"But—"

"For once in your life, Tierney, let me think."

She felt a surge of power that didn't come from her, and flames erupted in the unused hearth over the ash-covered logs. Keir stood with his back to her, his fingers clutching a totem that now glowed in a rainbow of colors melding together to look like tiny flaming cracks.

The fae here used their magic so rarely she hadn't examined an activated crystal up close. With magic surging through it, it looked more like the fire opals she was used to. Stepping closer, she peered at it, unable to take her eyes from the fading colors.

"It's beautiful," she whispered, reaching out. "And familiar."

Keir stood still, his statuesque posture a manifestation of his anger. Yet, Tierney didn't stop. She took the totem from his hand, running her fingers over the smooth form. Its power tried to slither into her, but something blocked it, some part of her own magic.

"So, it's true." Keir's voice was low. "You have seen these crystals before coming to Lenya."

Tierney dropped the totem back into his hand and stepped closer to the fire, its heat an uncomfortable companion to the sanity-saving light it provided. "We call them fire opals."

"Yes, I've been told."

"By who?" She stared into the flickering flames, unable to face him as he revealed all her lies. She already knew the answer.

"Bronagh, Queen of Grima."

Her eyes slid shut for a brief moment before she asked, "Have you put Bron in the dungeons?"

When he didn't answer, she dared a look his way.

He stared at her with thinly veiled hurt. "I know the opinion you and your friends have of me, Tia. I know that what I do for my people isn't enough, it will never be enough. But I am not a monster."

"I know that."

"Do you?"

"I told her she could trust you, that you would do what was right, but Bron had to see that for herself."

Some of the tension drained from his shoulders. "Yes, she said as much. And yet, you ask me if I locked her up."

Tierney didn't want to ask again, but she still didn't have an answer.

"For fae's sake, Tierney, she's with her brother." He paused, studying her face. "With the healer … not in the dungeons."

Relief flooded her, followed quickly by shame. She'd told Bronagh to trust him, and yet it seemed like advice she needed herself.

"We have a way to get to Iskalt." Rubbing a hand across her face, she lowered herself to the settee.

"The ship."

Her eyes snapped to him. "Wow, she really has decided to trust you."

He sat beside her, keeping a small distance between them. "Now, I need you to do the same."

Words clogged in Tierney's throat, and she swallowed. "You're right." She pushed out a breath. "No more lies. No more hidden truths or trickery."

"About time."

"Bronagh was right. Iskalt and the kingdoms surrounding it have an abundance of fire opals. They are useless for us, except in Myrkur, where they have a monetary value. In Iskalt, we sometimes use them to adorn furniture, for decoration."

He shook his head in disbelief. "All that power."

"That's the thing; they don't hold power for us." She thought of the way her dormant magic blocked the power from Keir's glowing totem. "Mostly. But for you, they could be everything. There's more than enough of the opals to bring back and keep the fire plains from destroying your kingdoms."

"But to get them, we need to brave the seas."

She nodded. "The Grimians have mastered the art of fishing in the rough waters, but their fishing vessels can't make it far from the coast. Veren—"

A dark look crossed his face.

Tierney sighed. "I know you don't like Veren, most of the time I don't either, but you might want to try, considering he's the reason they even built the ship. It's magnificent. I saw it with my own eyes. Giant sails with pulley systems to bring them in quickly to avoid losing them in a storm.

"A solid hull, impenetrable. We won't sink if we hit the rocks in shallow waters. The ship is built to take on water and shed it quickly. The shipbuilders and Veren have prepared for every possibility. The crossing will be dangerous, but, Keir, I truly think we're going to make it."

"But you might not."

"Well, yes. It is the maelstrom, after all. No one has attempted the crossing and returned to tell the tale. But that doesn't mean we shouldn't try. I'm not sure you understand. I have to do this. Even if the fire plains weren't expanding, Iskalt is my home. My parents and siblings are there. My duty is there. And Toby …" She swallowed a sob. "I just really want to get home. If I die trying to do that, it's still better than sitting here across the fire plains."

She didn't realize his arm was around her until she pressed up against his side, inhaling the sweet oak scent of his soap. Tears stung her eyes, but she brushed them away.

After a few minutes of neither of them saying anything, Tierney whispered, "Keir?"

"Hm?"

"Do you forgive me? You have to forgive me. For the lies, the subterfuge. I promise, I meant no harm to Vondur, but I can't leave with the thought that I've betrayed you, that you hate me. We're never going to see each other again, and if this is our last moment alone together, I want you to know I forgive you for everything you did when I arrived."

He was quiet for a moment. "I do forgive you. But, Tia, we're going to see each other again."

She started to say something, but he shook his head. "Two choices lay before me. I can die here fighting for my kingdom as the fire plains sweep across the land, or I can possibly die trying to save Lenya."

"What are you saying?" She met his dark gaze.

"I'm going with you."

Chapter 26
Tierney

Tension gripped Tierney's neck and shoulders, and her head throbbed as she focused on her plans for the coming journey back to Grima. There was so much to do. She couldn't focus in the quiet corner of the dining hall, where she sat alone, poring over lists. Most everyone had come and gone for the afternoon meal, but Tierney didn't have anywhere to be.

She'd grown restless here in Vondur. Anxious to be on her way and finally taking action against the fire plains and to get herself and her friends back home. After all these months away, both in Vondur and Grima, she'd seen and heard nothing of Siobhan. She could only hope her friend never arrived in Lenya and was safely back home in Iskalt.

"What are you writing?" Gulliver came to sit on the bench beside her. He had an entire pie he'd likely pilfered from the kitchens.

"You have pie." Tierney took the big plate and inhaled the glorious scent of sugared berries. Desserts were rare in Vondur. They seemed to prefer spicy foods and savory snacks over anything sweet.

"Hey, I begged and bribed a kitchen maid to make that for me."

Gulliver tried to snatch it back. "I even picked the berries myself. See!" He thrust out a skinny arm covered in scratches.

"But it's dessert, Gullie." She gave him her best brokenhearted look. "It's even got a crunchy, sugary, flakey, buttery crust on top."

"Fine, you get one piece," Gulliver relented.

"It smells divine." Tierney cut a gigantic piece for herself and slipped it onto the plate from her lunch. "I don't even want to know what you had to do to get her to make this." She shoved a bite into her mouth, savoring the tangy sweetness. "What I wouldn't give for some sweet cream to go on top."

"Who's your best friend?" Gulliver grinned and produced a small clay pitcher of cream from under his shirt.

"Gullie, you're a genius!" She glanced over her shoulder. "I know you stole that, and I don't even care." She drizzled the cream onto her pie. Dairy was in short supply in Vondur, and if they were caught, the castellan would take the cost of it out of their hides.

"When we get back to Iskalt, I'm heading straight to the kitchens, and I'm not coming out till I've had all my favorites. Smoked ham and fluffy white bread."

"With loads of butter and jam." Tierney groaned.

"And cheese. I miss real cheese. The yellow kind, not the white stringy stuff they have here." Gulliver sighed, a look of pure bliss on his face as he ate right from the pie plate.

"I'm sorry, Gullie." Tierney scooped up another bite, swirling it in the sweet cream. "I'm sorry I dragged you here and took you away from your family. And your favorite foods," she teased, elbowing him in the side.

"I'm not." Gulliver's tail draped over her shoulder, patting the side of her face. "If you were here and I was back home, I'd be a wreck. I'm glad to be here with you, Tia. And we're going to get home. Together."

Tierney leaned her head on his shoulder. "Thanks for the pie. It's the best thing I've eaten since we got here."

"Lenya is an interesting place, but they don't know what good food is." Gulliver ran a hand over his flat belly. "I swear I'm wasting away here."

Tierney laughed. "I love you, Gullie."

"I love you too." Gulliver shoveled more pie in his mouth. "I made you something." He leaned back to pull whatever it was from his bag. "I don't know if you've noticed, but the Lenyans have a lot of used-up crystals just lying around. The stones are quite nice for carving."

Gulliver could carve anything if he had a chisel and a good-sized rock, along with some extra time on his hands. Back in Myrkur, he ran a profitable business, taking orders for anything from elaborate knife handles, game pieces, and jewelry to sculptures and priceless works of art.

"To remind you of Lenya." He set a figure on the table between them. A Queen of the Night blossom. The beautiful flower grew near the fire plains.

"Gullie, it's beautiful." She lifted the intricate flower, knowing she would never look at it and not think of Keir.

"Just don't let anyone mistake it for a totem. These people are crazed for more power."

"It's strange how accustomed a fae can become to magic. And then, when it's gone …" She stared at the delicate petals of the flower. "When it's gone, you find you don't miss it as much as you thought you would."

An unholy screech echoed across the dining hall and Tierney covered her ears.

"What is that awful noise?" Gulliver peered over her shoulder into the courtyard below. "It's ruining pie time."

"It's certainly not helping my headache." Tierney finished her last bite, vowing the next dessert she ate would be at home with her family by her side.

"Tia, come look." Gulliver waved her over to the windows. "You're not going to believe this."

Tierney went to have a look. "Is that Keir?"

"Training a bunch of villagers in the courtyard." Gulliver shook his head.

"Female villagers." Tierney laughed. Grabbing her lists, she ran for the stairs down to the courtyard.

Smiling, she approached the group of women. All commoners from the nearby villages. Each woman held a sword or dagger, watching their king as he taught them how to protect themselves.

"What's this?" Tierney caught Keir's gaze. "Did I miss class?"

"Keep practicing ladies; you're doing great." Keir helped one woman adjust her grip on her sword, ignoring the way they laughed when he called them all ladies.

"If I am leaving soon, I want to make sure all Vondurians can protect themselves and their homes. Bronagh and I will be signing a peace treaty this afternoon, but we don't know how our countrymen will react. Anything could happen in my absence. I worry about my people."

"You're a good king, Keir." Tierney watched him as he went around to each sparring pair, helping them correct their stance or the grip on their weapon.

"I sent word to the villages that we would be giving lessons at the palace and all were welcome. Men and women. The villagers aren't comfortable working with the ladies of the court, but they seem comfortable enough with me." He turned, smiling. "Tia, what do you have on your face?" He reached up to rub his thumb over the corner of her mouth.

"Oops." She laughed. "Gulliver talked a maid into baking us a pie." She wiped her mouth with the back of her hand.

"We have pies every night in the dining hall."

"You have meat pies. This was a berry pie. Sweet and juicy and delicious."

"We don't typically have sweets here in Vondur."

"You're going to love the food in Iskalt. And the wine." She gave a little excited hop. "I can't wait to show you my home."

"It's going to be a dangerous journey, but I'm looking forward to seeing your land of ice and snow."

"When will you be ready to leave?" Tierney was dying to get this journey started.

"Soon. Come with me to the peace treaty signing today?"

"Does your council even know about it yet?"

"They do. They aren't happy about trusting Grima, but they are happy to see the end of this war. Most of them anyway."

"Who doesn't want the end of war?"

"There are some who have profited immensely from the war with Grima. But it's time to look to the future. I have no patience for those who insist on keeping the hatred alive. We have bigger problems to worry about now."

Keir returned to his ladies and congratulated them on their progress. "One of my officers will see to your training while I am away. I look forward to seeing your progress when I return." He waved to the women, who all looked like they were thinking they'd be happy to leave their husbands if the king turned an appreciative eye their way.

She followed Keir back into the palace and to the council chamber where they would be making history in just a short time. On their way there, Bronagh and her brother joined them. Donal was still healing but looked better each time Tierney saw him. He would be strong enough for the journey back to Grima, where he would stay and rule in his sister's absence.

Tierney found herself wondering who would care for Vondur while Keir was away risking his life to save them all.

"Are you certain about this, sire?" Lord Robert handed a quill to the king.

"I've never been more certain of anything in my life." Keir took the quill, surveying the treaty that would put an immediate end to the war with Grima. Each sovereign would recall their troops once the treaty was signed.

The treaty also stated that whatever foreign aid they received would be split equally between the kingdoms and their people. Any trade they might negotiate with Iskalt, or the other kingdoms of Tierney's land, would benefit all of Lenya while each kingdom would take equal responsibility to fulfill any trade agreement or debt to the foreign monarchs.

He and Bronagh had worked tirelessly to iron out the details so that neither kingdom had to give up more than they were willing. It had taken some time with his council, but eventually, they reached an agreement.

"All that is left to do now is sign." Queen Bronagh's smile lit up the room. She was a good queen. Strong. And her people loved her. Keir never set out to become king of his people, but he could only hope they would respect him for what he did here today.

The door crashed open, banging against the wall, and several councilmen leaped to their feet.

"It's all true!" Eavha, looking travel-worn and weary, marched across the room to his side. "Everything Princess Tierney said is true. The fire plains are expanding. I've seen it with my own eyes."

"Your Highness, I think we've interrupted something here," Declan murmured behind her. "Perhaps we should come back later?"

"This is too important." She turned to Keir. "The fire plains will sweep across all of Lenya. I fear we do not have enough magic left to stop it."

Her eyes were wild with fright and too little sleep. Once again, he regretted sending Declan on the journey to Grima to confirm what he already knew. Had he known then that his sister would follow his best friend, he wouldn't have sent him.

"We are aware of the grave threat the fire plains pose to us. I thank you and Lord Declan for traveling with such haste, but the burning lands have already expanded into Vondur."

"What can we do, Keir?" She searched his face for answers, but he didn't have the words to say that would make her feel better.

"You're just in time to witness the peace treaty between the Grima queen and King Keir." Tierney, bless her, stepped in to steer Eavha to her side so they could continue.

"Okay. What did I miss?" Eavha whispered, following Tierney to stand behind Bronagh and Keir.

"A lot. I'll catch you up to speed after."

"Shall we continue?" Keir took up the quill and bent over the official treaty document. Taking a breath, he thought of his father, and the burn of the King's Comhrac magic seared his chest. He still owed his father a united Lenya. This treaty was not what the former king meant, but it was a step closer to the kind of future Lenya deserved. Keir didn't hesitate to sign his name for Vondur.

Handing the quill to Bronagh, she stepped forward.

"It gives me hope that we can all be in this room together today, taking great strides toward peace." She gave a nod to Keir and his council before she bent to sign her name with a flourish. "It is a happy coincidence that my brother, Prince Donal, is also here for this historic occasion. I will ask him to sign as a witness for Grima." She turned, handing the quill to Donal.

"It will be my honor." Donal moved to sign under her name.

"I would like to ask my sister to sign as witness as well." Keir reached for Eavha's hand. "No one loves Vondur and its people more than Princess Eavha. As my next of kin, I would ask that she offer her support to this treaty."

"Keir, I ..." She turned to the council with a stern look on her face. "No woman has ever been asked to participate in the governing of Vondur. It would be my honor to sign, but I would like to know what I'm signing." She gave a hesitant smile. "It is a momentous step for women in Vondur. I would do them proud."

"Of course." Keir pulled her to stand at the podium where the treaty sat. He ran through the highlights of the agreement, outlining the terms of their peace to end the war and the terms they negotiated to keep this war from ever happening again.

A tear ran down his sister's face as she bent to sign her name below his. "I never thought I would see the day when this war would end. I miss my father every day. He was a hard man, but he loved me. And in his own way, he loved Vondur. But I believe King Keir is the best thing to happen to our people in many generations. I am so proud of you, brother." She smiled shyly and stepped back from the podium.

Pride swelled within Keir's chest as the council chamber broke into a round of applause. It was finished. The war was finally over.

"Tia!" Eavha jogged to catch up with her in the courtyard. "Where are you going?"

Tierney lifted one shoulder in a shrug. "I'm not really sure. I just needed to clear my head."

After the council meeting, she needed to think. Time was running out for Lenya, and they had to get to Grima, to the ship, as quickly as they could. When she first arrived in Vondur, it had been as a prisoner with no hope of finding her friends, no hope of returning to Iskalt.

Now, she got to stand at the king's side during the most important council meeting he'd probably ever have. Gulliver and Veren were with her once again. And Keir … the man who'd brought her here with ropes tied around her wrists … he was different.

But something was still missing.

"Slow down." Eavha reached for her arm. "Talk to me."

Tierney wasn't one to brood, to keep her feelings to herself. It was why she'd gained a reputation for her bluntness, her ever-present honesty that attached itself to her rebellious ways.

Turning to Eavha, she took her in. The princess hadn't washed or rested since returning home. Her black riding pants, something she'd never have worn all those months ago, were caked with dust from the road. There were dark circles under her eyes, and her hair had a particular dullness that spoke of a long time without a decent bath. "You look tired."

"Thanks for that." Eavha pursed her lips. "You don't look much better yourself."

The two women stared at each other with scrutinizing gazes before the corners of Tierney's lips twitched. Eavha chuckled and wrapped an arm around Tierney's shoulders. "I think we need some tea."

"Or something much stronger."

"Come on." Eavha led her into the palace. The quiet palace. Most servants had tucked in for the night. It wasn't until they'd almost reached their destination that Tierney realized where they were headed.

"Wait." She pulled away. "We can't go in there."

"Relax. He is dead." She said it with cold finality and little emotion in her voice. "He always kept a good supply of wine, and unless the servants have raided it, it should still be there." She pushed open the door to her father's quarters, the king's quarters.

Tierney followed her in, feeling like an intruder in a place she hadn't dared enter. King Turlach had liked fine things. While his fae suffered, he'd adorned his rooms in jewels and crystals that still contained traces of power.

Totems hung on twine behind the dressing table. No one had dared take any since he perished in the Comhrac.

Eavha opened a cherry wood cabinet. "Found it." She pulled out a bottle of wine unlike the others Tierney had seen in Vondur. "It's Grimian wine. The rest of Vondur wasn't allowed to trade with our enemy, but that didn't stop him from doing whatever he liked." She uncorked the wine and took a long pull before passing it to Tierney. "Oh, and I asked all your friends to meet us."

Tierney took a sip, cringing at the intense sweetness. It was better than Vondurian wine but still held no comparison to the reds in Iskalt.

The door pushed open, and Veren sauntered in, looking much less uncomfortable than she had in the old king's rooms. "Wow. Why isn't Keir living here?"

Gulliver shoved past him. "Maybe because his evil dead father did." He shot Eavha a look. "Sorry."

She shrugged. "He made poor choices, and he paid for it with his life. Sometimes, the truth hurts; doesn't mean we can't say it."

Bronagh was the last one to enter.

Eavha's eyes widened, and she dipped into a graceful curtsy. "Your Majesty."

Tierney took a pillow off the settee and threw it at her. "Please don't."

A smile tugged at Bronagh's lips. "Yes, right now, I am just another concerned fae whose life is at risk." She curtsied lower than Eavha had. "Thank you for risking so much to prove the truth of my words to your king."

Eavha blushed furiously. "Oh, it was actually fun. Getting away from the palace with Declan …" She froze. "I mean, um, we were performing our task for the king, nothing else."

Bronagh turned to Tierney. "She babbles like you."

Tierney shot her a playful scowl. "No one can babble as well as me."

Eavha recovered. "Okay, everyone sit. We need to discuss what's wrong with Tierney."

"Many things," Veren said.

Gulliver raised his hand. "How much time do we have?"

"She speaks too many words," Bronagh put in.

Eavha stared at them. "Not what I meant, but okay. Did anyone else notice she left right after the council meeting? She didn't even stick around to gloat about being right."

Tierney took a seat and bent forward, head in her hands. Eavha was right. Something was very wrong.

Gulliver squeezed in beside her, dropping his voice. "Is she right?"

A sigh rattled out of her, and she lifted her eyes to his. "We're leaving Lenya."

"But that's what you want. To return home."

"Of course it is, but don't you realize what it means?" She looked from Gulliver to Veren. Only they would understand. Neither answered, but she saw the realization in their eyes.

"Anyone going to tell us what is going on?" Eavha crossed her arms.

Veren closed his eyes, shame washing over his face. "Siobhan."

"Who is Siobhan?"

"Our friend." Gulliver looked like he wanted to cry. "How could we not think of her?"

Tierney shook her head. "We've been so focused on saving Lenya, on returning to Iskalt." She met Veren's eyes. "Are you positive she isn't in Grima?"

He nodded. "When I first arrived and got to know Donal, he sent messengers to every village searching for all of you."

"We can't leave without her."

"But she isn't here. She isn't anywhere. What if she didn't make it?"

That was a possibility Tierney had tried not to think about. "We can't leave without her."

Gulliver's hand slid into hers. "We have to. Tia, it isn't just us at risk anymore. There's an entire kingdom that could be wiped away."

"Gullie." Tears danced in her eyes. "How am I supposed to return home and say I lost the best of us, that I'm the reason she's gone?"

"We'll come back. Once we get to Toby, he can help you portal back here to look for her."

She rested her head on his shoulder. "Promise?"

"Always." He squeezed her hand.

A tense moment passed, where each fae was scared to speak until Bronagh stepped forward. "I am sorry for your friend."

Tierney took another sip of wine. Gulliver tried to take the bottle, but she hit his hand away. She wasn't making that mistake tonight. "I am too."

"But Gulliver is right. We have bigger issues to face. This peace, for one. I do not know if I can make it hold when my council was not involved in the decision."

"But you're the queen." Tierney didn't understand. In Iskalt, the council advised, but the monarch had the final say.

"Yes, but I am beholden to my people."

"Just say your uncle." Veren met her gaze. "He's the only fae in Grima who might take issue with an end to the war."

Her chest heaved with a sigh. "Yes, my uncle is … difficult. And if I am to sail on this ship, he will be left behind to rule along with Donal, and he must be in agreement. I must have my council finalize the treaty before I can leave."

"We can be your council," Gulliver said, his lips stretching into a smile.

Bronagh's expression softened. "And that is kind of you, but a council must consist of only the Grima born. Even now, my uncle sends my warriors into battles I would not support. He is not easily overcome."

An idea came to Tierney. "Bronagh, does the queen get to decide on a temporary regent in her absence?"

"Of course."

"Then, who says your uncle has to be granted that power?"

"It has always fallen to my uncle to rule in the absence of the queen."

Tierney set the wine bottle on the table and stood. "But there is someone resting in the healer's ward who can stand in your stead, yes?"

Understanding dawned in Bronagh's eyes. "Donal."

The young prince looked much better than he had after the treaty signing. Color had returned to his eager face. He lifted his head when he saw his sister, his eyes lighting up. “Bron.”

She matched his grin. “You look like you’re doing better. I worried the council meeting might have taxed you too much.”

“The healers here have treated me well.”

She set her hand on the bed, and he gripped it. “I need to talk to you.”

His eyes shot to the others in confusion. “Sure.”

Tierney watched the two of them, a longing burning in her chest. Not only for Toby but for all her siblings. Kayleigh and her need to be right, their youngest sister and her endless joy. Her little brothers always getting in trouble with the maids. The way her mom chased them around the palace as they all howled like wolves, scaring the guards and giggling when they jumped.

Her father’s half-scowl, half-smile every time they tried that on him.

“You are my fiercest general, Donal.” Bronagh smiled down at him. “But what if I told you it was time to lay down your sword?”

“I would thank you for preventing more deaths at my hands.” His voice had grown soft, sad.

Bronagh’s shoulders dropped, and she hiccupped back a sob. “I never … Every time I sent you to battle, I didn’t think …”

“We were avenging our family. But we cannot claim vengeance forever. It is a sword that cannot be wielded, only fallen upon.”

She dropped into the chair at his side. “Lenya needs peace.”

“And the treaty will go a long way in bringing that peace.”

“It will.” She drew in a breath. “But I must go away for a while, across the sea to find the one thing that can save us all.”

By his lack of surprise, Tierney knew she’d already told him of her intentions.

“Some might think you will not succeed across the sea, sister, but I know you will. I know it in my bones.”

“Uncle will not agree with us.”

Donal shook his head, and his eyelids fluttered shut. "So you would have me rule in his stead while you are gone?"

"Yes."

"I never wanted to lead the kingdom."

"I know."

None of them got what they wanted. Not Bronagh and Donal, with their lost family. Not Tierney, with her missing friend. Nor Keir, defying everything his kingdom stood for. Yet, they were all willing to fight for a better future.

They had to.

Tierney turned away from the Grimian royal siblings, realizing what they needed now was a few moments to themselves. Gulliver looked at her expectantly, waiting for her to tell him what happened next. Veren made no move to leave Bronagh's side.

Movement in the door caught her eye, and she found Keir watching them. Watching the moment the siblings decided to work together for the peace he'd fought for, risked his standing with his council for.

His eyes met hers, and Tierney's skin heated in a way that had nothing to do with her power and every bit to do with a lack of it. Because it was time to admit she was powerless to save Siobhan, powerless to find a way home that didn't include a high chance of death.

And powerless to resist the feelings swirling inside her chest, clouding everything she thought she knew.

In an instant, she crossed the room. One moment she stood on her own two feet, strong in the face of the destruction this man had wrought on her life, the disaster awaiting her if she gave in.

And the next, she'd stepped onto a dangerous path, one riskier than any maelstrom in the ocean, any height of thrashing waves.

This was Keir, King of Vondur. Her captor. Her liberator.

When his intense dark eyes locked on hers, she couldn't help wanting him, even if just for this single moment.

Tierney's chest collided with his, and she rose up on her toes as he dipped his head. Their lips crashed in a torrent of pain and coming regret. They danced together in a movement of hope and relief.

Keir's hands tangled in her hair, pulling her head back as he dragged her into the hall, away from the eyes of her friends.

Tierney fought him for supremacy, for control, dragging her fingers up his chest until they wrapped around the base of his neck, holding him in place. Pain lanced through her lip as he bit it. She opened for him, allowing him deeper inside her mouth, her soul.

Keir pushed her up against the rough stone of the wall, pressing into her, melding their bodies together with a growl. They were feral animals, whimpering wantons.

When Keir finally pulled away, he rested his forehead against hers, their heaving chests fighting against each other.

"I've wanted to do that for so long." His breath whispered across her lips.

"Then, why didn't you?"

"Because you didn't want it, not yet. I had to wait until I knew you did."

"I'm leaving, Keir. I know you'll be with me at first, but—"

His eyes darkened as he pressed a quick kiss to her lips, quieting her. "For once, there is no future, no tomorrow. This moment is all that exists until the next. A thousand tiny parts of the whole, each one as important as any other."

"No future," she said, knowing how true it could be with the journey they faced.

He shook his head. "No tomorrow."

"Okay," she whispered, drawing him toward her again. "Okay."

CHAPTER 28
KEIR

Keir didn't know what he was doing, only that he'd wanted this for too long. He'd wanted to look sideways at Tierney and not have to hide it when she met his gaze. He'd wanted to taste the curve of her lips, feel the softness of her skin as he traced a hand along the dip of her neck.

So few things about this woman were soft, fragile. Her strength intrigued him, excited him. But for the first time, she let a small vulnerability shine out of her, and it was beautiful.

Every day of his life was spent acting like an unbothered and aloof king, the man the kingdom could count on to protect them from the ravages of war. Here, now, he was just Keir Dagnan, just a man who knew whatever this feeling for Tierney was, it couldn't last. Their paths would diverge once they saved Lenya—if they survived the journey.

Tierney turned to him, a smile stretching all the way to her eyes. "You know, I might actually miss Vondur."

Keir found his lips tilting into a half-smile. "Lies." He pressed a kiss to the corner of her mouth and backed her into the one room he'd never be comfortable in. "All lies."

"Maybe." She turned away from him to cross his father's quarters and push her way into the tunnels. There was one place she'd said she wanted to visit before leaving.

Their footsteps echoed off the stone floor, the sparkling walls. When they reached the cavern, it hummed with the energy of magic traces, just enough to lend power to the water.

Tierney lifted her eyes to the ceiling, illuminated by torches hanging along the walls. This cavern meant so many things. A place of healing, both of body and spirit. A place of training those who were not supposed to train.

"You know," Tierney said, her voice barely above a whisper, "when Eavha and Declan brought me here, it was the first time I felt any kind of wonder at being in a kingdom most people in Iskalt had never even heard of." A contented sigh parted her lips. "Before that, all I felt was fear and anger."

Fear and anger. Because of him.

"Tia." He stepped up to her side. "I—"

"If you apologize to me right now, Keir Dagnan, I'm going to stomp on your foot."

"Stomp on my foot?" His laugh echoed through the cavern. "You're supposed to be a fierce warrior, and the best you can do is stomp on my foot?"

She bit back a smile. "I never said it was all I'd do, but it would be the first thing. Stomp on your foot so you can't get away, and—"

"How hard are you planning to stomp? It wouldn't exactly hinder me."

She continued without missing a beat, "And then, I'd do something to distract you."

"Oh?" He liked the lightness she infused into him. "Like what?"

Tierney stepped close, and his breath stuttered. She pressed herself flush against him, rising on her toes. Her words vibrated against his lips. "This distracting enough?"

When he didn't respond, she grinned, pulled a dagger from a sheathe in his belt, and whirled around to press the tip into his back.

"I'm at your mercy now, Princess. What would you have me do?"

"I am a lady, your Majesty. I do not appreciate the lurid tone."

"I'm lurid?"

"Yes, it is very … lurid."

"Why, my Lady, you do have a way with words." He wasn't sure what had gotten into him. Flirting was a new action, but it was a lot more fun than brooding.

"Shut up."

"Has anyone ever told you how irritating you are when you use your human phrases?"

"Has anyone ever told you how irritating you are all the time?" There was more laughter than bite to her words. She pulled the knife away, and he turned to face her, taking the knife and sliding it into its sheath.

They stared at each other for a long moment before he stepped forward. She backed up until she hit the stone wall and lifted innocent eyes to his. Except, they were anything but innocent. She knew exactly what she did to him.

"We might die on this journey." He pressed closer.

"I thought we were pretending the future didn't exist."

His lips hovered inches from hers. "We were wrong. Tomorrow always lies in wait, preparing to take everything from us. It is why we must hold on to today."

They collided in a heat of kisses, soft touches, and ragged breath. If this was all they had, he'd make it count, memorizing every gasp, the way her fingers curled into the collar of his shirt before sliding into his hair.

Keir hadn't forgotten what awaited Tierney in Iskalt. Pressure to marry a nobleman, a life that didn't involve the king of a far-off kingdom. And he knew she hadn't forgotten either.

But all of that seemed like a distant moment, one that didn't yet exist.

Tomorrow, he would prepare to leave his kingdom in the hands of his sister, someone who'd struggle and fight for every bit of power she could take simply because she'd been born a woman.

He would prepare to travel into the kingdom of a new ally, one that didn't yet know of the peace treaty their queen signed, the piece of parchment that transformed them from generational enemy to ally, foe to friend, with the single stroke of a pen.

Keir leaned away from Tierney, breaking their kiss. Tonight, they both needed peace to face the storm raging on the horizon. He threaded their fingers together and tugged. "Come on."

They crossed the cavern to where the healing waters stretched to the far wall. To the simple observer, they looked like nothing out of the ordinary—a simple, yet expansive, bath, but to touch the water was to know differently.

Lowering himself to the stone, he pulled Tierney down at his side and dipped his feet into the water. Just underneath the surface, it swirled and bubbled around his ankles, reacting to his presence.

Tierney followed his lead and sighed. "I would never leave this cavern if I had a choice."

Keir leaned back on his elbows. "Do you have healing magic in Iskalt?" He still knew so little of their power.

Tierney was quiet for a moment. "There are stories, rumors, that my mother once used her magic to heal my father. But it is not commonly done. Our healers can speed up the process in a way, but we believe a body must have time to heal itself."

"And the mind? Does your power give it peace?" When he sat at the healing pools with steam filtering through the air, he was able to ignore what ailed him, let his thoughts rest.

Tierney smiled, and she looked down at her hands. "We carry the power within us at all times. Sometimes, it can make me feel out of control, like I can't grasp my emotions, can't control my actions. And other times, it is like a constant companion and I am never alone."

She sounded sad, lost, and he wanted to reach out to her, but all he could do was watch her expressions shift. "Except here."

She hesitated a moment before nodding. "Here, I have been very much alone." A breath quivered coming out of her. "It is not only the power. My brother and I … we're connected. He's a part of my magic. When I use it, I can feel him with me. Even after all this time in Vondur apart from him, I'm not sure I know who I am without that tie."

"You're a future queen."

A harsh laugh burst out of her. "Whether I want to be or not."

"You're a warrior."

That made her smile. "I've been trained to be nothing else."

"You kiss like the world is ending."

She looked down at him, a smirk flashing across her face. "It just might be."

Keir pushed off his elbows to sit up and bumped her shoulder with his. "Are you afraid?"

"Yes," she said, not hesitating.

"Of the journey?"

She nodded. "But more than that, I'm afraid we're leaving Siobhan behind in a foreign kingdom. I'm afraid kissing you was a mistake." She turned, her eyes meeting his. "I'm afraid we will fail, and I'll let everyone down."

He had no answers for her. Her final two fears were also his. So, instead of words, he pulled her into a hug, reluctant king to future queen. What he didn't do was promise they'd succeed, because it would have been a false vow. But they would try, they'd give everything they had to their kingdoms, risk their lives.

He only hoped it would be enough.

Keir left Tierney at the door to her rooms with a long look. When he turned away, he slid his mask back into place and became the king again. It was late, but he knew where Declan would be.

Since they were boys, Declan's sleep was troubled upon returning from a journey. No matter how exhausted and road-weary he was, sleep eluded him. And he'd never been one to sit in his rooms when he could be out under the open sky.

Keir nodded to the night guards as he entered the courtyard. Above, a full moon lit the sky, casting a silver glow over the palace walls. The crystal-infused walls reflected it back, sparkling.

Stars sprinkled the clear sky, creating a beauty only found in the heavens above Vondur. Maybe, once this war with the fire plains was finished and his people truly had peace, they could bring some of that beauty back to Lenya, rebuilding long defeated cities, villages that had lost too much.

He found Declan atop the walls staring out over the barren land between the castle and the forest.

"I shouldn't be surprised you knew I'd be here." Declan didn't turn to look at him.

Keir stepped up beside him. "You never did enjoy being confined by the palace walls."

"Some of us didn't grow up here." Declan had been raised in a nearby village, but he'd joined the army when he was not even ten, and the only boy young enough and green enough to spar with him was Keir in the years before his father became king. He hadn't been a prince then, but his father's status as a noble meant he'd spent his formative years at the palace.

"Did you fare well on the journey?"

Declan snorted. "You forget, Keir, I know you as well as you know me. I gave my report already, you did not come here to ask about my journey."

He was right. "Eavha would not like me speaking with you."

"I'm not sure I like it either."

Keir shook his head. "I must leave. There is no way around it. It is not guaranteed I will return, but even if I do, my sister will rule in my stead."

"A wise decision."

"But she will need protection."

Declan turned his head slightly to look at Keir out of the corner of his eye. "Do you really think you need to ask?"

"I know she is learning to fight, but that will not help her with those who do not wish to listen to a woman. Having my commander in her corner will convince a lot of fae."

"Again, Keir, I do not have a choice but to stand with her."

"There's always a choice."

A look crossed his face that Keir couldn't quite decipher. "Not when it comes to her. If anything should happen to Eavha, I ..." He rubbed the back of his neck and looked away.

Keir studied him for a long moment before clapping a hand on his shoulder. "You're a good man. The status of your birth cannot change that. Do not let it stand in the way of what you truly want."

Declan cleared his throat uncomfortably. "Sometimes, Keir, I think you were not made for the kingdom of Vondur."

"Sometimes, I agree with you." When his father was king, he'd always felt so out of place being made to do things he knew weren't right. "There's one other thing."

"I won't let your castle burn to the ground. Anything you ask of me is something I would do without hesitation."

Keir drew in a breath. "There is a woman called Siobhan who will most likely claim to be from Iskalt. Tierney thinks she must be in Vondur or Grima. I need you to send men to find her. Bring her to the palace and keep her safe. If we survive the journey, we will return and she can go home to her fae."

"Anything you ask of me, Keir, I will do."

Leaving Vondur in his sister's hands took no thought at all. His kingdom would be safe. But saying goodbye to Eavha, to Declan, the only two fae he'd ever truly loved, would be the most difficult thing of all.

CHAPTER 29
TIERNEY

Tierney paced the length of her room, searching for the last of her things. During her time in Lenya, she'd managed to amass a hodgepodge of possessions she didn't want to leave behind. Keir had given her several histories on Lenya that would be great additions to the Aghadoon library. And she planned to give him a set of volumes on the histories of the four kingdoms in return.

Securing the lid on a jar of dried Queen of the Night blossoms, she tucked them into her bag. She would share them with her mother and sisters. Tierney had no doubt all the ladies at court would be eager to purchase their own once they heard about the lovely scented flowers.

Thoughts of trade between the kingdoms filled her mind as she packed. She could see a bright future for the six kingdoms. Once they traveled the impenetrable seas, found their way into Iskalt over the mountains, and crossed the frozen tundra of eastern Iskalt. And then, dealt with the issue of the expanding fire plains. Easy stuff.

But later, when all of their problems were solved, she was confident Toby's O'Shea magic would allow him to portal to Lenya. He would have to help her create a portal here since one could only portal to a place they had visited before. But Toby was more than capable of helping her do it right. And then, he could travel here himself, bringing all the Lenyans home.

The thought made her sad. But they would see each other often as the four kingdoms brought Grima and Vondur into the fold.

It would be a whole new world for everyone.

The portrait on the wall rattled, but Tierney was used to Eavha coming and going whenever she wanted.

"Don't you know you can use the actual door to my rooms now?" Tierney folded her jeans and the t-shirt she wore upon her arrival in Lenya. It felt like a lifetime ago now. So much had happened.

"The tunnels are faster." Eavha pushed through the hidden door. "You have to talk to Keir," she blurted, looking agitated.

"What's he done this time?" Tierney turned to retrieve Gulliver's Queen of the Night blossom carving from the bedside table. Wrapping it in her spare travel tunic, she bundled it into their bag, hoping it would survive the long journey home in one piece. She hoped they all made it there in one piece.

"He's refusing to let me go to Iskalt."

Tierney sighed, turning to face her dearest friend in this kingdom. "He's right, Eavha." She sat on the edge of her bed, patting the space beside her.

"I can make the journey. I am strong. You have to tell him it's not too dangerous for me."

"Oh, Eavha. You're one of the strongest women I've ever met. That's why you need to stay here." Tierney cupped the girl's cheek. "You remind me so much of my sisters. Strong-willed and spirited. Don't ever change."

Eavha moved back, pushing Tierney's hand away. "Don't you dare say goodbye, Tierney O'Shea. I am coming with you."

"Don't you realize how much Keir needs you here? Not to keep you safe but to keep Vondur safe in his absence."

Eavha's lower lip trembled. "I don't want to say goodbye."

"Neither do I. But I know—right here," she placed a hand over her heart, "I will see you again."

"What am I going to do without you?" Eavha took her hand, moving closer to her side.

"Declan is going to need you. He is a good leader, but he commands Keir's army. The council needs a royal to guide them. Not because those of us born to play the roles of kings, queens, and princesses are somehow better than others but because it's our duty to serve our people. You represent Keir's interests. His vision for Vondur. The council will follow your lead."

"They don't respect me. That Keir let me sign the peace treaty was a huge step forward for Vondurian women, but the council won't allow me to rule while the king is absent."

"Don't give them a choice." Tierney took both of the young princess' hands in hers. "You walk into that chamber like you own it and don't take no for an answer. They will respect you."

"It's a big job." She sighed, her shoulders drooping.

"Your brother knows you can do this. Otherwise, he would have put someone else in charge."

"You sound like Keir." Eavha's nose wrinkled. "I don't think I like it when you two are on the same side."

Tierney laughed, pulling Eavha into a hug. "I am going to miss you so much."

Eavha leaned her head on Tierney's shoulder. "Me too."

"I look forward to the day when my brother opens the first portal into Vondur and I get to bring you to Iskalt to meet my family. My sisters are going to love you. I have a brother just a year younger than you, and he's going to fall hopelessly in love with you."

Eavha blushed. "I think I'm spoken for already."

"I should hope so. All that time you traveled with Declan, just the two of you. I shudder to think he didn't get it through his thick head that he's in love with you."

"He thinks he isn't good enough for a princess."

"Men are idiots, Eavha." Tierney shook her head. "It takes them far too long to listen to us and realize we've been right all along. He will come around."

"Sometimes, I wish I wasn't a princess. It would make life a lot easier."

"Tell me about it. Wishing I wasn't a princess is what landed me here in the first place."

"Well, I am glad you hated being a princess because you've changed our lives, Tia. I don't know where we would be without you."

"Can the girl power meeting be over now?" Gulliver stuck his head into the room. "I've lost my good boots, and I'm pretty sure they're in here."

"Come in, Gullie." Tierney rolled her eyes. "You better be finished packing by now. We leave at first light, and we're supposed to be in the great hall right now. Tonight's dinner is a celebration, and we don't want to be late."

"Keir's had the cooks making all sorts of special dishes just for you two." Eavha wiped her eyes and fixed her dress. "It's going to be a feast of all your favorites. They even managed to find a few pigs to roast since Lord Gulliver has been lamenting our lack of ham since his arrival."

"Ham? There's ham?" Gulliver snatched his boots from the settee, where he'd left them, and shoved them onto his bare feet. "Let's not keep them waiting."

"The court?" Eavha frowned. "They wouldn't dare begin without the guests of honor."

"He means the hams." Tierney laughed as they moved into the hall and she closed the door behind her.

It was a feast. The cooks had outdone themselves with dishes that were somewhat similar to the foods they missed from home. The ham was delicious. And the desserts were even better. Someone made Gulliver his own cake with buttercream frosting. He was in heaven.

Tierney sat at the high table with all her friends and the king. Even Bronagh was given a seat of honor at the king's left. She and Veren were carrying on a private discussion, but Keir was quiet.

"Nervous about crossing the border, your Majesty?" She turned to get his attention.

"What?" He shook his head, as if he wasn't aware of his surroundings.

"You looked like you were a million miles away just then."

"I was." He smiled. "I'm not so worried about traveling to Grima. It's the sea voyage I'm not looking forward to. I've never been on a ship before."

"Really?"

"Vondur borders the fire plains. We have very little coastline where Grima is almost all coastline. We do have a port city on the far side of the kingdom, for small fishing vessels. They don't go far out. I've been there many times, but never on a ship."

"I hope you don't get seasick."

"Seasick. Is that a thing?" Keir frowned.

"It's definitely a thing," Gulliver interjected. "I used to get seasick a lot when I was a kid, but I grew out of it the more I traveled with Griff. He's my adoptive father—a Prince of Iskalt."

"Wait. King Lochlan's brother is your father?" Keir asked Gulliver.

"Yes. But Griff is super low key compared to Loch"

"Everything makes so much more sense now. You two really are like siblings." Keir looked from Tierney to Gulliver.

"Haven't we said that like a hundred times?" Gulliver shook his head, returning to his third plate of ham and roasted potatoes.

"We've been best friends since we were ten years old." Tierney smiled at the memory of her first meeting with the Dark Fae. She and Toby were ice skating on the lake just down from the castle when Uncle Griffin and Aunt Riona arrived from Myrkur with a skinny little boy with half a tail and a big appetite. His tail grew back. His appetite hadn't changed at all.

That was the day when Tierney decided they would be friends.

"No, Eavha. Don't ask me again." Keir took a long sip from his wine glass, as if fortifying himself for another argument with his sister. "You're not going."

"Keir I—" Eavha tried to interject, leaning across the table to get his attention.

"I'm serious." Keir spoke softly. "I need you here to keep the council in line. Keeping you safe is just a secondary advantage."

Eavha smiled, shaking her head. "I can see right through that reasoning, Keir Dagnan, but fine. I will stay. That wasn't what I was going to ask though."

"Oh, what do you need then?" His tone said he would give her anything her heart desired if she would just stay home and stop arguing with him about it.

Eavha cupped her hands around her mouth. "A crystal," she whispered. "I know they're in short supply, but I've been practicing, and I think it would be helpful to have the extra power just in case."

"Yes, of course. Didn't I give you one from the king's reserve?"

"I gave it to Declan while we were traveling. We ran into some issues ..." Her voice trailed off, and she dropped her gaze to her plate

"I will have one delivered to your rooms this evening. If you have need of anything else, Eavha, you only have to ask. Even when I am gone, Lord Robert will be available to assist you with whatever you need. I trust him above all others on my council, second only to you."

"Just return home in one piece." She reached for his hand across the table, turning her gaze on Tierney. "Watch out for this one for me?"

"It would be my honor to protect your king, Princess Eavha." Tierney gave her a formal nod of agreement.

"You two think you're so funny." Keir's face flushed, and he gave them a crooked grin. "I can take care of myself. I am a master swordsman, after all."

"But you tend not to make the best first impression." Tierney arched a brow at him.

"And you're kind of growly and mean when you're uncertain of your surroundings," Eavha added. "You need to be on your best behavior when you meet King Lochlan and Queen Brea."

"Okay, you two, enough teaming up on me. We have an early morning tomorrow, and I have a last-minute meeting with my council before we leave at first light. I think it's time we all retire. Gulliver is going to fall into a deep food sleep soon, so we should probably get him upstairs. He didn't have any wine, did he?"

"Look at that." Gulliver grinned. "Keir's developed a sense of humor. Who would have thought?"

Keir was the first to laugh, and the others couldn't resist joining him. Tierney's cheeks hurt from smiling. She was going to miss this so much. As heir to the Iskalt throne, she'd spent most of her life believing others wanted to be her friend only because she was a princess. That was why she and Gulliver had remained such close friends all these years. She trusted in his genuine friendship and that he wanted nothing else from her. She could only say that about a few other people in her life. Most of them royals as well. Now, she could add a few more names to that short list of friends. She just hoped they would remain friends always. Even from a distance.

CHAPTER 30
TIERNEY

Tierney barely slept her last night in the Vondur palace. Thoughts of home filled her mind with hope for the long journey ahead. It would be dangerous, but if sheer willpower alone was enough to get them through it, they would arrive in Iskalt in no time at all.

But thoughts of home weren't the only reason Tierney couldn't sleep. It was also the long road to Grima. The nights she would sleep under the stars. The long voyage across the seas, with nothing to do but spend time with Keir. Uninterrupted, idle time with the handsome king.

The king she should not fall for. She would rule Iskalt one day. She must marry someone who could be at her side, a nobleman or woman who did not have their own kingdom to rule. But that did not mean she couldn't enjoy kissing him while she had the chance.

"What has you smiling like Kayleigh in love with the latest pretty courtier?" Gulliver stuffed his saddlebags with extra food he'd pilfered from the kitchens after a bit of flirting. The kitchen maids here would be sad to see Gulliver go.

"Oh, hush." Tierney tightened her saddle and draped her bag over the horse's flanks. "I'm just excited to be going home, Gullie. It's finally happening."

Gulliver pulled himself up into the saddle and munched on a piece of fruit. Shaking his head, he scowled at her. "I will not be sad to leave this place and never see it again for the rest of my days."

"Won't you miss the people we've met here, though? We could come for visits once Toby creates a portal here."

"Portals go both ways." Gulliver waved his fruit in the air, pointing to the dusty road that led toward the fire plains. "They can come visit me in Myrkur."

Tierney laughed. She supposed if she'd spent their first weeks in Vondur in the dungeons the way he had, she probably wouldn't want to come back here either. She pulled herself up into her own saddle, smoothing a hand over her mount's soft black mane to soothe the nervous mare.

"I'm anxious to see my little sisters. Just don't ever tell them I said that." Gulliver tossed the remnants of his fruit into the bushes surrounding the stables. Gulliver's little sisters idolized their big brother. They also liked pulling his tail and pelting him with pebbles as they flew over his head. The girls were only six and eight years old, but it was no secret to anyone that Gulliver adored them.

"What are we waiting for?" He glanced around at the growing party of soldiers accompanying his Majesty to Grima. Veren and Bronagh were helping Donal onto a litter that would transport him home to Lenya. The prince was well on the mend, but still not up to sitting in a saddle for hours at a time. Tierney couldn't imagine any form of transportation would be comfortable for the young prince.

"I think we're just waiting on Keir." Tierney looked around for the man who stood head and shoulders above his soldiers. "And I expect Eavha will show up to say a last goodbye at some point."

"It's going to be hard for her to let you go, Tia," Gulliver said, leading his horse beside hers as they joined the gathering line of travelers ready to depart. "You're her hero."

"I'm no one's hero." Tierney sighed, thinking of all her mistakes that had led them here.

"You've given her confidence she probably never would have exerted without your influence. You've shown the women here how to stand tall. You've shown the men here that they need to let them."

Tierney laughed. "A select few of them, I suppose." Movement at the rear of the palace caught her gaze. Keir, Declan, and Eavha headed toward the stables, where their mounts waited.

"Is she coming with us after all?" Bronagh asked as she and Veren joined the queue, with Donal resting in the litter hitched to Veren's horse.

"Tia!" Eavha scrambled onto her horse and trotted across the stable yard to join them. "Declan and I thought we would ride out with you this morning just for a little way."

It would just prolong their goodbyes, but Tierney was happy to have a few last moments with the princess.

"How was your council meeting this morning, Keir?" Tierney asked as the king joined them and gave the order to move out.

"Good, good." He nodded, not meeting her gaze. "They wanted me to send a delegate in my place, believing the journey too dangerous for their king, but I convinced them otherwise."

There was something he wasn't saying, but Tierney knew she couldn't be privy to all the king's conversations with his council. As long as he was coming with her to Iskalt, that was all that mattered.

"It will be a quick ride to the east road," Keir turned his attention to his sister, giving her a stern look. "Declan and I will ride ahead with the soldiers and leave you two to enjoy your remaining time together." Sitting tall in his saddle, Keir urged his horse into a trot and moved to the front of the line, without a word, Declan followed.

"He is worried." Eavha watched him go. "So much rides on the success of your journey."

"We will make it to Iskalt in time to stop the spread of the fire plains. I can feel it in my bones." She would risk it all to see her family again, but it wasn't just Tierney on this journey. She had others to think about too.

"I was serious when I asked you to protect him." Eavha turned in her saddle. "My brother will sacrifice his life to reach Iskalt. Not only for Lenya but for you as well. I hope you find your way home, Tia, but please keep him safe. I need my brother to return whole."

Tierney reached for Eavha's hand. "I promise I will do all in my power to send your brother home safely." As much as it would hurt to see him leave, his place was with his people. They needed their reluctant king because he was the best thing to happen to Vondur in generations.

As they neared the road that would take them toward the Grima border, Tierney grew sad. She didn't want to say goodbye to the girl who'd become as close as a sister to her throughout her time in Lenya.

"I'm going to miss you." Eavha sniffed her own tears back. "All of you." She turned to Gulliver and Bronagh.

Keir and Declan brought the short line of travelers to a halt and dismounted to say their last goodbyes. Tierney took Eavha into her arms, hugging her tight and resting her chin on the princess' head.

"The council has their instructions." Keir spoke softly to Declan as they walked to the rear of the line. "I leave it to you and Eavha to keep them on course."

"We will handle everything while you're gone, your Majesty." Declan gave a formal bow before he stood tall and held out his hand to Keir. "Be safe, brother."

Keir pulled him into a hug, slapping him on the back. "Take care of my sister."

"I'm pretty sure that's going to go the other way." Declan laughed, moving to stand with Eavha.

Tierney gave Eavha one last squeeze and pulled her to arm's length. "Stay strong. You've got fire in your blood. Use it."

"I will." Eavha flung her arms around Tierney one last time, tears rolling down her cheeks. She buried her head against Declan's chest. He held her close, murmuring comforting words to her as Tierney mounted her horse and prepared to ride away.

Keir guided his mount beside hers and gave the signal to march on. Tierney couldn't see through the veil of tears clouding her eyes, but she followed.

"We're doing the right thing, Tia." Keir reached for her hand, and she grasped hold of it like a lifeline.

"Why does the right thing always hurt a little too much?" She sniffed, refusing to look back because she'd just left a piece of herself behind in Vondur forever. She would miss Eavha like she'd missed her own sisters.

Just before sunset, they reached a forest of the massive trees Tierney had seen on her first trip to the Vondur palace. Back then, she hadn't dared ask questions about their surroundings.

"What makes your trees grow so huge?" Tierney asked, admiring the deep red tones of the tree bark.

"Don't you have ancient forests like this in Iskalt?" Keir asked. They'd ridden side by side through most of the day, talking like neither would have dared the first time they made this journey together.

"In Iskalt, we have snow, ice, and fir trees covered in snow and ice. They grow tall, yes, but nothing as large as these."

"Our history is veiled in shadows. Lenyans have been in these lands since the beginning of time itself. In ages past, when magic was in abundance, I imagine these forests grew tall and strong because it was in the very soil. I've read accounts of a time when our crystals littered the grounds and one had only to pick them up to have all the magic they needed. I can't fathom such a world."

"It is like that in Eldur and Fargelsi. Your crystals can be found anywhere. In Iskalt, they lie in abundance under the snow and within the mountains. And in Myrkur, there are many fire opal mines already."

"Will there be enough to share?" Keir frowned, seeming unable to comprehend just how many crystals she would be able to give him upon their arrival to her homelands.

"Plenty for all of Lenya, and still more for Myrkurians. They use the opals for trade. The other kingdoms use them because they are pretty. We won't miss what isn't much use to us and so vital for our new friends and allies."

Keir shook his head with a smile. "I still find it hard to believe such a place exists."

"You will see it for yourself soon."

"But first we must travel to the Grima palace. A place that will not likely welcome me with open arms."

Tierney and Keir followed the soldiers leading them along the dusty roads through the forests they began to leave behind. Smoky skies opened up before them across a wide-open terrain of stunted shrubs and yellowed grasslands.

"You will arrive at the palace with their queen as your ally." Tierney pulled a scarf over her face to shield her from the smoke. "They will accept you." Tierney frowned as they left the road, crossing the dry grasslands to higher ground. "Are we stopping already? There is still daylight left."

"The sun has set, Tia." Keir smiled. "You are seeing the lights of the burning plains. We could travel for another hour or two by the light of the plains, but that would put us closer to wolfhound territory at their peak hunting hours."

"Looks like a lovely place for a camp." She grinned, nudging her horse up the incline to the flat-topped butte, where they could better see their surroundings.

"There is a campsite here we frequent when traveling this way. It won't take long before we have a fire and hot food."

"And the first of many hard beds on the ground." Tierney rubbed her lower back, eager to get out of the saddle and walk around, stretching her legs.

In no time at all, Tierney sat beside Gulliver on an aged log that had seen many a campfire, stuffing her face with the roasted game and hard bread. On the trip to Vondur, she'd lamented the bland food they had on the trail. Now, after months of spicy foods, it was heaven.

"Hungry?" Keir laughed as he sat on the ground beside her.

Tierney wiped meat juice off her chin and went back for her last bite. "Starving."

"I'm going back for seconds." Gulliver left them by the low burning fire to join the soldiers still carving up the pair of fianna they'd hunted before they made camp. They were smoking a portion of the meat to bring with them. The rest, they would have for breakfast.

"No surprise there." Keir stirred the dying embers with a charred branch, coaxing the coals back to life.

Tierney slipped from her seat on the log to sit beside him on the ground.

"We made good progress today." Keir sat back, leaning against the log and draping his arm around her.

She scooted closer to his side, happy the others had made themselves scarce. Donal was exhausted from the trek and was already asleep. Bronagh had gone with Gulliver and was now making her own bed under the stars. The young queen had come a long way since she left the comfort of her palace.

"How long until we arrive at the border?" Tierney stared up at the stars shining bright overhead. She wondered if they were the same stars that shone down on Iskalt.

"If we ride hard tomorrow, we should reach the border by nightfall." Keir ran a hand over her hair, and his touch sent a shiver through her. "And another few days to reach the palace."

"And then, we set sail." She sighed, smiling to herself. For at least a few days, she could snuggle next to Keir under the stars and dream about home.

Chapter 31

Tierney

"Do we even know if we're on the right road at this point?" Tierney squinted, trying to see through the haze of smoke. But the acrid air just made her eyes water and burn.

"We're nearing the palace." Bronagh adjusted the scrap of fabric she'd torn from her dress to cover her face. Sooty tears leaked from her red rimmed eyes. "We should reach the village soon. The fresh sea breezes should clear away this smoke and we'll be able to breathe easier."

Tierney shared a worried look with Keir. If the smoke from the fire plains had reached the main road to the Grima palace, what might they find when they arrived?

Far to the east, churning black smoke billowed along the horizon above the intense flames of the encroaching fire plains. Tierney didn't want to know what homes and villages once occupied the lands along the road they now followed. The thought of what those poor people were going through was just too much. Her palms itched with the faint stirrings of magic inside her. Magic that still lay dormant.

"You can't dwell on what-ifs, Tia." Gulliver rode quietly beside her.

"I don't know what you mean." She tore her gaze away from the fires and focused on what little of the road she could spot. It was like traveling through the worst blizzard she could remember back home. They couldn't see beyond their horses' next steps. And given the rapid expansion of the vatlands, it left her on high alert for dangers they couldn't sense.

"Yes, you do." He pulled his hood low over his eyes to protect them from the sting of the smoke. "You're thinking if you had your magic, you could do something to protect these people. But you don't have your magic, so it isn't healthy to think of things that might have been."

"If you tell me to focus on the solution and not the problem, I'm going to scream."

"I didn't say it."

"You were thinking it."

"So were you, or you wouldn't have said it."

"You two bicker like an old married couple." Keir shook his head at them.

"You take that back, Keir Dagnan!" Tierney growled at him.

"That was so rude, even for you." Gulliver gave him a disgusted look.

"I've found it best to just ignore their odd little relationship." Veren's voice was muffled through the many layers of his face coverings. He'd claimed the smoke would do untold damage to his skin if he wasn't extremely careful.

"Is that ..." Bronagh pointed ahead. "What's burning?" She turned to her brother riding along in his litter beside her.

Donal propped himself up to get a better look. "It looks like the stairway from the palace to the village is burning."

"The stairs are cut right into the mountain. It's all stone." Bronagh squinted to get a better look.

"Can stone burn?" Gulliver asked.

"It's … glowing," Keir said. "Like metal under a blacksmith's hammer."

"Have the plains reached this far already?" Bronagh sucked in a breath as she dug her heels into her horse's sides.

Tierney urged her mount to follow as they rushed headlong down the road through the thick churning smoke.

"Tia, wait!" Keir called behind her, but she wouldn't leave Bronagh to this discovery all on her own.

As they neared the village, the smoke thinned and the fresh sea air filled Tierney's lungs. The charred smell of recently dead things still stung her nose, but the unmistakable ocean air cleared her mind.

"It's gone." Bronagh pulled her horse to a stop at the edge of the village. At least, what was left of it. "Where is everyone?"

Tierney's gaze followed the orange glow of the stairway that led up to the queen's palace among the mountains above.

"It's burning!" Veren shouted in alarm.

"No." Tierney frowned up at the palace and the mountain it sat on. "It's … melting." The rambling roof of the mountain fortress oozed toward the ground, the walls collapsing in on themselves. The mountain itself, once whitecapped with snow, now seemed to slump in defeat. "I didn't know stone *could* melt." She turned, catching Veren's horrified expression.

"The docks!" Veren kicked his mare into a gallop, circling the heat radiating from the ruined village. Tierney and the others followed.

The foul ruins belched sulfurous clouds of putrid smoke, and Tierney clutched her face covering against her nose. Dead and rotting gulls lay scattered along the rocky shores, where they fell from the skies in their retreat. Dead fish and charred seaweed churned in the shallows, steam billowing up from the boiling surf.

They made their way across the rocky shoals around the village and down to the docks. Tierney came to a dead halt beside Veren. She let out a strangled sob, her hand covering her mouth. Soul shattering fear shot through her, piercing her heart and stealing her breath.

Veren sat silently atop his horse, his face gone white with shock. "We've lost, Tia."

"No." She stubbornly shook her head, refusing to accept the defeat staring her in the face. "We will find another way. We will see our home again."

Keir guided his horse to stand beside hers, his shoulders slumped and his eyes smoldering like the fires they had no chance against.

"We will die along with every single Lenyan before that happens." Veren turned toward her. "We don't have time to build another ship."

Tierney watched the white smoke billowing into the air above the ship that should have saved them all. The fire still smoldered in places, long after it had consumed the massive vessel and reduced it to nothing more than a mountain of charred wood and ash sitting atop the water.

The warmth of Keir's hand closing around hers surprised her, but it gave her strength too. Gripping his hand, she took a deep breath. "I will never stop fighting for Lenya and the hope of returning to my home someday. And neither will you." Tierney released Keir's hand and guided her horse back toward the village, determined to have enough hope for them all.

Epilogue

Toby

"Toby, what's wrong?" Logan reached across the library table for his hand. "You've gone white as the Iskalt snow."

Coughing, Toby gripped his intended's hand. He couldn't catch his breath. "Something's wrong." He launched from his chair and out the front door of the library just in time to lose his breakfast over the porch railing.

"Are you sick?" Logan came up behind him, checking his forehead for a fever. "You've been working too hard, and this desert heat isn't helping."

"It's not me." Toby shook his head, sucking in a deep breath and wrinkling his nose. "Can't you smell that? Ugh, it's awful." He waved a hand in front of his face. "It's like dead fish … and sulfur."

"I don't smell anything. Are you sure you're not having an apoplexy?"

"No, I'm not having a stroke." Toby took the steps down to the street and turned toward the exit of Aghadoon. He needed to see the fire plains.

"What's happening?" His mom stood from her rocking chair on the porch of the house the king and queen were staying in.

"Have you found something, Toby?" His dad came to join them, his mom following close behind.

Toby shook his head, still trying to rid himself of that putrid smell.

Logan murmured behind him with Toby's mother as he darted through the ancient pillars and into the desert sands of Eldur.

For weeks, they had studied everything the library had revealed to them concerning the kingdom of Lenya and the birth of the vatlands. And still, they had no way of reaching his sister across the burning lands. Nothing they tried seemed to work. Magic was failing them.

"She's scared." Toby stopped when the intense heat of the fire plains became too much for him to bear.

"Come back away from the edge, Toby," his mother begged. "It's too hot."

"Tia needs me." He took another step toward his twin. "She's scared." He turned toward his parents, surprised to see Logan standing beside him, clutching his hand.

Sweat beaded Logan's brow, but it evaporated before he could wipe it away. His sun-browned face blistered in the shimmering heat of his homeland. Prince of Eldur and raised among the desert sands, the fire plains were even too much for him.

"Go, it's too dangerous." Toby squeezed his hand.

Logan shook his head. "I go where you go."

Turning back toward his sister, Toby sighed. "She's running out of time."

The story continues in
Fae's Return: Queens of the Fae Book Nine.
Turn the page to dive in.

Queens of the Fae
Book Nine

Fae's Return

Melissa A. Craven
M. Lynn

MYRKUR KINGDOM
NORTHERN VATLANDS
FARGELSI KINGDOM
LOCH VILLANDI
SOUTHERN VATLANDS
ELDUR KIN
DRAGUR FOREST
VINDUR CITY
ELDUR
LOCH LANGT

NORTH EASTERN KATLANDS
NGDOM
HUNTING LODGE
VALE OF STORMS
FIRE PLAINS
LENYA
GRIMA KINGDOM
MINES
THE BURNING SEA
VONDUR KINGDOM
CITY
THE ROCKY SEAS OF LENYA
THE GRIMA SHOALS

CHAPTER I
TIERNEY

Life wasn't always fair. There was no way to change the unchangeable, no way to alter a future that was set in stone.

These were the thoughts on Tierney O'Shea's mind as she sat in the mouth of a cave with the giant network of mountain caverns the people of Grima had built over the centuries at her back. Her legs dangled off the edge of a steep drop-off. One wrong move and she'd crash against the rocks below, tumbling toward the sheer fall into the turbulent seas.

Somewhere in the distance was a fishing village, where Grimian people bundled in furs to brave the rocky seas, never venturing close enough to the Vale of Storms to even catch a glimpse of the churning maelstrom beyond that dangerous corridor. There was a point out there, far beyond the white caps. A point no fae could survive traveling past.

Yet, they'd planned to.

A chill raced up Tierney's spine, and she pulled the fur Bronagh had given her tighter around her shoulders. The wind up here was unrelenting in its iciness. Yet, to Tierney, it felt good. The cold. The snow-topped mountains. The ice hanging from her eyelashes.

It felt like home.

She closed her eyes, picturing the white fields of Iskalt, the frozen lakes, and the cold stone palace. Home was just a far-off fantasy now during the day, and a haunted nightmare every time she tried to sleep.

Their one chance of reaching those jagged shores was reduced to ash, burned up by the heat of the fire plains. Soon, they'd expand across all of Lenya.

Soon, there would be nothing left of her or the people she'd come to love here.

The ship had been a desperate attempt to reach Iskalt, a dangerous journey that would have provided one last chance to return home and save a kingdom. But for all she knew, if they'd boarded the ship built to brave the maelstrom, they'd have still ended up at the bottom of the endless depths.

A sigh escaped her lips, her breath releasing in a fog in front of her face.

She could already see signs of the encroaching fire plains in the distance. No one knew how long it would take the unseen force to reach this far up into the mountains, but a trickle of water ran the length of the stone beside her. She dipped one finger into the dampness, feeling the melting ice for herself.

"You shouldn't sit so close to the edge." Keir's gruff voice shouldn't have surprised her. He was always telling her what to do, what not to do.

"If you do not wish to see me fall, go back inside to warm yourself by your precious hearth." He'd hardly left the fires since their arrival the week before. Unlike her, he hadn't been bred to withstand the cold, to brave icy winds and damp feet.

"Are you going to jump?"

She snorted a laugh, the harsh sound foreign to her ears. That wasn't how she laughed. There was no joy in it. "Does it matter?"

"No."

One corner of her mouth curved up. "Well, hate to disappoint, but I have no plans of tumbling to my death."

"Shame."

"Jerk."

"Yes." He lowered himself to sit on the bare stone a considerable distance back from Tierney and her daring ledge.

They'd barely spoken since their way to Iskalt was destroyed.

"I could really use some magic right about now." She scooted back and pulled her knees in to hug them to her chest.

"Is the great Iskalt princess cold? I thought ice ran in your veins."

Tierney shot him a scowl. "I'm not cold. But I am hungry. Do they ever eat anything here besides fish?"

"Grima is a fishing kingdom."

"Yes, but can't they also be something else? We're in the mountains. I'm sure there is plenty to hunt."

He frowned. "Sometimes, I forget how little you know of Lenya."

"Oh please then, inform me, great wise one." Tierney wasn't in the mood for lessons from Keir. She wasn't in the mood for anything from him. They stood on unstable ground, both trying to forget everything that happened to them back in Vondur.

Keir let out a huff of exasperation, a sound she'd realized he reserved only for her. Something about that forced her to hide a smile.

"There used to be crystal mines in the mountains," Keir said. "They were probably the deepest and most prosperous in all of Lenya. That wealth, that magic, is how they were able to build such intricate networks of caves without our knowing. I'm guessing this is where they came after we captured their palace."

"What does this have to do with food?"

"A few years ago, my father mounted an expedition to destroy the mountain mines. If he couldn't abscond with the crystals, he didn't want Grima to have them."

"But … by then, he must have known Lenya was running low, that one day magic would disappear from the kingdom altogether."

Keir nodded. "He led one battle at a time. I did not accompany this unit of men, but the story when they returned was that the mines were gone, and …"

"And what?"

"The best way to beat an army is to cut off their food supply."

"No." She could tell exactly where this was going.

"There is a river that runs down the mountain, providing water to every spring, every lake. My father used a totem to infuse poison into the very land around it so it would leech into the water continuously."

"But the Grimians have magic too."

"To my knowledge, they never figured out what the source of the poison was. But it destroyed the animal population."

Tierney released her knees, resting back on her hands and staring out into the sea. "But the river runs to the sea, and the fish—"

"I do not know exactly, but we always suspect the water dispersing prevented high enough concentrations to affect the sea."

Tierney closed her eyes, saying a silent prayer for the vast amount of creatures killed by that vile man. It was worse than she'd imagined. "How can the Grimian people stand to work with Vondurians, even if it means saving their kingdom?"

Keir didn't respond to that.

Tierney knew being here wasn't easy for him. The Grimians stayed mostly away from him, casting suspicious looks. He was unwelcomed, unwanted. And yet, he was still here. For now. Soon, he'd return to his palace to prepare his fae for what was coming.

And Tierney wouldn't go with him. She'd already made that decision. Her place was not in Vondur.

"Wait." She turned to meet his gaze. "If the mountain water is poisoned with magic, how then do these caverns survive?"

He pushed to his feet and turned.

"You're just going to leave when I asked you a question?"

He looked back at her and quirked a brow. "Are you coming?"

"Oh." She scrambled to her feet. "I guess. Following you into the depths of a cave beats jumping."

"I'm flattered." His mouth flattened into a thin line.

Tierney couldn't resist a smile as she followed. Whatever happened between them, whatever they'd never be to each other, having him here, for the time being, was still a comfort.

Fresh, icy air quickly turned to a damp cold that sank into her bones, the kind of cold she rarely even felt in Iskalt. No velvet carpets spanned the stone floor to provide the illusion of warmth; no colorful tapestries adorned the walls.

Only a few torches hung along the walls when they passed what was called the gathering space. It was the one cavern big enough for meetings and announcements. Now, only a few servants rushed through it to get from one section of the caverns to another.

Keir took one of the torches off the wall and led Tierney into a part of the caves she hadn't yet explored. All light faded until only their torch illuminated the way.

Before long, she heard the distinct sound of water hitting stone. The walls grew bright as they neared the noise, almost sparkling like ... Her eyes widened. Like crystals were infused right into the stone.

As soon as Tierney stepped through the low archway, she felt it. The magic. A rushing stream flowed from a gap in the wall, hitting a pile of rocks before tumbling into a pool of water.

"Keir," Tierney whispered.

"I know," he said. "I was surprised when I found it. The water is like our healing pools, with crystals embedded in the stone beneath. I think that's what keeps it free of the poison."

Tierney stepped to the edge and bent to dip her hands into the water, feeling the power snake up her skin. She closed her eyes, remembering what it was like to have full control over this kind of magic, how empowering it was. How strong it made her feel.

"Be careful," Keir warned as her toes rocked on the edge.

Tierney didn't open her eyes, but her lips curled into a smile. "Careful is the opposite of what we need. Don't you ever just want to feel it, Keir?"

"Feel what?"

"The magic."

"I do." She could picture his brow furrowing in confusion and agitation.

"No." She rotated her hand, not wanting to ever leave this behind. "You use your magic when you need to. It's a battle weapon for you. But sometimes, you have to just feel it, to let it live inside you."

"You speak of it as if it's a living thing."

"Isn't it?" Maybe his power was different since it came from an object outside of himself, but she didn't think so. "When you use your power, do you feel invincible?"

"Invincibility is a dangerous concept in war."

She shook her head and opened her eyes to see her hand dipping in and out of the crystal-clear water. "War is not all of life, Keir. There are things beyond the battlefield that can cause us greater pain."

"Tell that to those who never leave that battlefield."

She did not want to discuss the tragedies of war with a king who knew nothing else, but she would have rather died fighting for Iskalt than live in exile far away from the land she loved.

Keir didn't speak to Tierney again before he left her in the peace of a magic she could touch but not control. Maybe this was a lesson, the greatest of her life. For so long, she'd trained to always have a handle on the power inside her, to not let it take control of her.

But magic was to be respected, revered. Not used as revenge against her brothers, as a way to get what she wanted. In Lenya, they could only use it when it mattered most. Yet, in Iskalt, it was incorporated into every area of life.

Was that wrong?

She was still sitting in the room with the strange underground spring when Gulliver skidded in, his tail flicking in excitement. "Good; Keir said I'd find you here."

Tierney shot to her feet. "Has something happened? What's wrong?"

The smile on his face allayed her fear. "Nothing is wrong, Tia."

"Then, what is it? Spit it out."

"Eavha. She's here."

"What?" Tierney started toward the door. "Keir left her in charge of Vondur. What in the name of magic would she be doing in the Grima mountains?"

"Maybe she came to finally make Keir go home. Wouldn't that be great?"

Tierney couldn't help laughing at Gulliver's eagerness to be rid of the grumpy king. "We can hope." Something heavy settled in her stomach, as cold as these stone walls.

Gulliver continued chatting, but as they reached the gathering space, Tierney left him behind to seek out a certain disobedient princess.

She found Eavha standing with her brother, waiting for Bronagh's arrival.

"What's going on?" Tierney asked.

Eavha grinned when she saw her. "I never thought I'd see you again." She yanked Tierney into a hug.

Tierney patted her back and pulled away. "Okay, but will someone please explain why you're here?"

"We received word about what happened to your ship," she said.

Keir nodded. "I had Bronagh send a messenger on our way here."

Eavha continued, "I know my brother, so I knew he wouldn't come home quite yet, not until he figured out a way to try to save both Vondur and Grima. I want to help."

"But you're supposed to be leading Vondur."

"I told her not to come," Declan grumbled nearby. "But does she ever listen to me?"

Eavha rolled her eyes. "I left Lord Robert in charge. He'll do better than me anyway. Acting as the queen was sort of constricting."

Tierney couldn't fault her for that. She worried she'd feel the same when her father's crown fell to her.

Fae flooded the room, dressed in the furs they'd worn since arriving at the caves. Tierney didn't miss the way they eyed the Vondurians—Eavha, Declan, and their guards. She didn't miss the tension pulled taut across the crowd.

Grima and Vondur were enemies, fighting for generations. Now, suddenly, they were supposed to work together to fight a new enemy, one that had no beating heart.

"I don't like this," Gulliver whispered.

Tierney didn't either. How long would the truce last? It didn't matter if Keir and Bronagh had developed a tentative trust when their people only knew one another across a bloody battlefield.

"Vermin," a Grimian soldier spat.

Eavha turned on her heel, her eyes finding the man. She was about to open her mouth when Tierney clamped a hand down on her arm. "Don't. That's Captain Norix."

"And why should he be allowed to speak to me in such a way?" Said like a princess who'd only truly known a life of ease.

Tierney had been in war. She saw what it did to fae, no matter their side. "He lost three sons and a brother to the battles with Vondur."

Eavha's entire body froze and, when she turned to Tierney, there were tears in her eyes. "I ... that's so sad."

"That's war," Keir said. "War is sad."

An older gentleman walked toward them with the grace of a much younger man. Tierney hadn't yet met the Grimian swordmaster, but she'd heard stories of the Vondurian warrior who had switched his allegiance. He'd seen what Tierney saw. The Vondurians fought for supremacy. The Grimians fought to survive.

"Your Majesty." Daniel bowed to Keir. "I only just arrived with a fresh wave of troops and was surprised to hear you'd come." There was a question in his gaze.

Keir looked like he wanted to run away right then, like facing the man who'd taught him how to be the warrior he'd become was too much.

"Daniel." Declan stepped forward. "It is good to be on the same side once again."

The swordmaster's weathered face stretched into a grin. "Declan. Boy, you've grown."

"General, now."

"General? Well, I always knew the status of your birth wouldn't hold you back. I'm glad your king here saw the same as me."

His king. A deliberate separation from Vondur. Daniel was making it known Keir was not his sovereign.

Murmuring surrounded them among the crowd waiting for the king. Most of them were soldiers, men and women who'd followed Bronagh from the palace, waiting for their next move. There were also servants, cooks, and a few children.

And none of them liked their revered swordmaster conversing with the enemy.

Enough was enough. Tierney grabbed Eavha's hand. "We're going to see what's taking Bronagh so long." She ignored the gasps at her informality.

Keir stepped forward. "Maybe I should—"

"No." Tierney pinned him with a look. "You stay right there." She yanked on Eavha's arm.

As they walked away, she heard Keir's voice. "I'm still a king, right?"

"Tierney, wait."

Tierney turned so fast Eavha crashed into her. "Are you going to tell me why you're really here? Your brother might buy the whole seeking adventure thing, but I know there's more."

"There's no—"

"Don't lie to me, Eavha Dagnan."

Eavha sighed. "Fine. When we received the messenger who told us you and Keir were here, Declan and I got worried."

"He didn't really try to stop you, did he?"

"Do you think he'd actually believe he could?"

"Good point." One bright spot of staying in Lenya … not losing Eavha. It didn't make up for missing Toby, but it soothed some of the burn.

"We brought our best warriors with us as guards."

Tierney still didn't understand, and it must have shown on her face.

"Tia, my brother, the king of Vondur, is in a Grimian stronghold with few fae who would support him should they need to. He is vulnerable and alone among the enemy."

"Grima is not—"

"They have always been our enemy. I want this truce to hold too, but I do not trust them. Certainly not with my brother's life."

"So, you came to protect him." The picture cleared, and Tierney couldn't say it didn't warm her a bit.

"Yes. At least, we brought him more guards, but they wouldn't have gained entrance without my presence."

Tierney leaned back against the wall. "What will Bron think of you bringing armed fae into the caverns?"

Another voice joined them. "Bron will think the princess was being smart." Tierney turned to find the queen herself walking toward them. "My fae do not trust Vondur. Nothing I have done or said has changed their opinions. I do not want anyone getting ideas about restarting this war. Protecting Keir is the best way to prevent that."

"My thoughts exactly," Eavha agreed.

Tierney wanted to believe that if she was stuck in Lenya, at least she could live with the Grimian people. She could make a home with Gullie. But if they hurt Keir, no matter how much he aggravated her, that was something she wasn't sure she could move past. After everything that happened, he'd become a sort of friend, one she too wanted to protect.

Bronagh turned to Tierney, echoing her thoughts. "I don't think he's safe here. And with your association, neither are you."

Chapter 2
Keir

Keir followed Daniel and Veren from the caves down to the docks along the craggy shoreline of Grima. Their situation was nothing short of catastrophic. It was barely perceptible, but the fire plains expanded more each day. At this rate, there would be nothing left of Lenya soon.

"Stop it. You're stuck on the worst-case scenario." Declan elbowed him as they walked down the endless steps, with their confusing switchbacks and tiered offshoots to different parts of the village. He feared he would never find his way back to the caves without a Grimian escort.

"We are living in the worst-case scenario, aren't we?" Keir's shoulders and spine tensed at the reminder of their predicament. Even now, this bountiful village that lay along the busy wharf would cease to be in a few short months. How long could they keep moving out of the burning path that would lay waste to every corner of Lenya? How long before there was nowhere left to flee?

"There's always a way out." Declan gave him a pat on the back and an uplifting smile. But that was Declan. He was always the more optimistic one. "We just have to find a new plan."

"The docks are where everything in Grima happens," Veren

explained, an impatient look on his face as he waved them forward. "We will find a solution to our problem. Keep an open mind and it will come to us."

"Here?" Keir frowned at their surroundings. Fishermen were coming in with the late afternoon tide, hauling their nets in behind them. The catch seemed to be failing more and more every day as the boats headed out farther into the most dangerous parts of the seas in search of fish to feed their families and those displaced from the palace.

That had been a blow Keir had not bounced back from yet. No one had. They'd had such high expectations of sailing the great ship the queen had commissioned. The one Keir never got to see. Now, only the charred remains sat in the cove they could no longer access, just a half-day's ride up the coast. There, the waters still churned with the heat of the fire plains, chasing all the fish from the shores into the cooler waters of the deep sea.

That ship was supposed to save them all. And it had taken them months to build it. Months they no longer had. They couldn't wait for another to be built. Which meant they might not be able to reach Iskalt by sea. They might have to find a way across the plains. Perhaps around them, where the temperatures weren't as intense. But could they sustain the putrid air and harsh temperatures for long lengths of time?

"The people of Grima live along the coastlines, where the air is clear of the smoke from the fire plains and life is much easier than in Vondur." Veren marched along the boardwalk, waving to captains and first mates from various ships he seemed to recognize by name. "We've been able to trade easily with those in the west. They send us fresh produce, and we send fish and shellfish. But it's getting harder now as crops are failing and the catch is drying up. If food shortages continue, we'll starve before the plains reach us."

"You have trade vessels?" Keir asked. "With large cargo holds?" He'd only ever seen small fishing boats in Grima. Not that he was ever in a position to pay much attention to such things when inside their borderlands.

"We do, your Majesty." Daniel walked beside Veren, his hands clasped behind his back. "Coastal trade has been our livelihood for many generations. We even have flat-bottomed vessels that sail up the rivers inland to deliver supplies to the estates in rural areas. We trade with them for grains and sugar."

"I suppose it is easier when you have safe sea routes to navigate from one side of Grima to the other." In Vondur, they had no such routes, and trade caravans over land never fared as well in the face of thieves and highwaymen eager to plunder what they could. It was always harder in Vondur, where the land was unforgiving. They survived on the things they could produce at hand. If they couldn't grow it or make it, they often did without.

Keir watched the sailors unload their cargo holds, which seemed to yield very little these days. He imagined another time when this harbor would have been prosperous with trade. He wanted to give that back to them. And to his own fae. Perhaps when this was all over, they could open up trade routes between Grima and Vondur. That was a future he would love to see.

Though, Keir didn't imagine he would ever get to experience such a thing.

Several young children ran past, hurrying along to the docks to greet an incoming ship.

"Papa!" a little boy screamed, waving scrawny arms in the air as his older sister tried to keep him from falling into the harbor.

"Mind your sister!" a voice echoed across the water.

Keir smiled when he saw a man not much older than himself, standing at the ship's bow as it sailed closer to the docks. The man waved at his children, clearly eager to get his feet back on land so he could hold his family.

They were just fae. Like those who lived throughout Vondur in the villages and towns he knew so well. For many years, he'd fought in a war against the brutal Grimian soldiers. He'd seen slaughter and bloodshed. Warriors to a man. But they weren't the lifeblood of Grima. These fae were. Just as the common folk of Vondur were the lifeblood of his kingdom.

They were all Lenyans. That was all that mattered anymore, and he had to do something to save them from the fiery end they all faced.

"Captain Michel!" Veren called as they approached one of the largest ships currently docked at the far side of the harbor, where the waters ran deeper.

"Ahoy there, Master Veren." A weathered and wrinkled face peered down at them. "How's that fine ship of our lady queen's coming?" The old man scaled down the side of the ship like a wiry young sailor.

"You haven't heard then?" Veren's voice dropped to a funerary tone. Of everyone, Veren had taken the loss of the ship the hardest. He'd worked with the queen's finest builders to bring that vessel to life. All for naught.

"No." Captain Michel's eyes widened in surprise. "Caught by the fires?"

"I'm afraid so."

"She was a fine ship, Master Veren. But she was too big to make it across the Vale of Storms."

"Too big?" Keir stepped forward. This was the first negative account he'd heard of Veren's perfect ship.

"Aye, sir." He turned adoring eyes on his own vessel. "The Wind Runner is light and fast. She rides high in the water and takes a beating from the torrential rains and surging seas. Even when she's weighed down with a full cargo in her belly, she holds steady through any storm. I've taken her out farther than any other captain in this harbor. She handles the rocky seas to the south without incident. I've brought in some of the largest hauls of the most beautiful fresh red sea bass you've ever seen. They only swim around the Grima Shoals. Got a king's ransom for that haul, you better believe it." His eyes shone with delight at having the rapt attention of a new audience.

"The Queen's Maiden was equipped with oversized sails that could capture the winds and keep us moving through a gale," Veren argued. "She was bigger and heavier to keep us grounded in rough seas."

Captain Michel shook his head. "Any shipbuilder would tell you such." He tapped his nose. "But a captain spends his life on the seas. He knows things. Things a builder will never understand about the wiles of the waters."

Keir smiled, the first semblance of hope flickering in his chest. "Captain Michel." He clapped the man on the back. "What do you say to an ale?"

"I'd say lead the way, sir." The captain swept his hat off his balding head, running his hands through what little hair he had left.

"What are you up to, Keir?" Veren walked behind him toward the tavern on the wharf. "The old coot's full of stories, but that's all it is. Tall tales and boasting."

"I have some questions for him." Keir shrugged. "We still need to find a way across the sea or around the plains, but before we do that, I'd like to know more about our options. And now that we don't have the ship built for the voyage, it's going to be a lot more dangerous."

Declan held the door open for them as they entered the musty old tavern that looked to have been there since the beginning of time itself.

Daniel and Declan found a corner table and ordered them each a tankard of ale from the pretty barmaid.

"Captain Michel." Keir sat down at the sticky table, grateful for the dark corner where they could talk freely. "I'd like to ask your honest opinion." He leaned forward, forearms resting on the splintered wood. "What would it take to navigate the Vale of Storms? To cross the maelstrom and reach the shores of whatever lies beyond?"

The captain's face paled. "What did you say your name was again?"

"Keir Dagnan." He didn't see any reason to lie to the man when asking such an important question.

The captain nodded, looking like someone had walked over his grave. "I see. We must be in dire straits indeed if the King of Vondur sits across from me asking for advice." He moved aside for the barmaid to set his tankard in front of him. Taking a long drink, he wiped the back of his hand over his mouth.

"Can I get you, gentleman, anything from the kitchen?" the barmaid asked, making eyes at Veren.

"No thank you, but I imagine we will need a second round before long." Declan slipped her a coin and sent her on her way.

"Surely there must be another way." Captain Michel took another long swig.

Keir tested the ale for himself. He expected a dreadful sour stout, but it was delicious and refreshing. It seemed everything in Grima was of better quality. Even in a wharf-side tavern full of dirty old sailors who just might hold the answers to the questions plaguing Keir's mind.

"If there was, I would not be here." Keir raised his tankard. "I would know your opinion on the voyage we must make if we are to save Lenya." By now, all Lenyans were aware of the ever-encroaching burning lands that had turned their fresh water rancid, stolen their lands, homes, and whatever security they might have possessed in this war-torn land.

Captain Michel nodded, staring at the contents of his tankard. "It's a foolhardy journey. But a ship like the Wind Runner could do it." He finally spoke, all boasting gone from his voice. "She would have to be outfitted for it. Larger sails, taller, stronger mast. Empty hold, packed with sandbags secured to the port and starboard sides to keep her from rolling. She needs a good, strong crew with experience, quick minds, and sharp wit."

"Michel, you bloody fool, you cannot pass over the Vale of Storms with an empty hold." A wizened old man with a long, braided beard slapped him on the back. "You need to weigh her down." He pulled up a chair and joined them without invitation, a pipe clutched between his yellow-stained teeth. "Let her ride low in the water. She'll have better balance, see." His eyes sparkled with interest at the very idea of sailing across the maelstrom most would avoid at all costs.

Michel shook his head. "Hyde, you old charlatan, she'll roll for certain if she's weighed down too much."

"Not if her crew knows how to handle her." Hyde turned his attention to Veren. "You let her have her head as the winds pick up, gather her speed, like so." His hand moved across the table, mimicking the movement of their theoretical ship. "Keep her on the outer edge of the vortex, moving fast with the wind in her sails. No fear. You cannot hesitate when you're on the cusp." His toothy grin lit up his weathered face. "Ride the edge as long as you can, and when the winds turn, you start to break away, let her momentum push you out of the eddy little by little." He gave a loud clap of his hands. "And when you break free, she'll have carried you to the other side, bound for lands unheard of outside the old storybooks."

"You're both dodgy old fools." Another captain approached, clutching his tankard of ale. "It's impossible. The vale will carry you down to the bottom of the sea, and then we'll all be lost to the fire plains." He grabbed his hat off his head. "Begging your pardon, sirs, but you'd be better off circling the Rocky Seas to the south to reach the other side of the plains. It's a far stretch and slow going, but with the right flat-bottomed ship, it could be done. Successfully so, if you don't mind me saying."

It seemed Veren had told anyone who would listen about the great ship that would save them all. Now that it was gone, they all had an opinion. And Keir wanted to hear every last one.

"Wouldn't she break up if she hit the wrong shoal?" Keir tilted back in his chair, eager to hear his answer. The Rocky Seas were dangerous but not quite as terrifying as the Vale of Storms.

"Not if you're running with an experienced crew who knows how to navigate a small vessel through the narrow passes." The man leaned against the filthy wall, his eyes intent on solving this conundrum. "It's dead stressful out there, but you likely won't drown so much as have to turn back and look for a better pathway a time or two."

"The lads don't have time for that, McCoy." Hyde waved the barmaid over for another round. "The vale is deadly but fast. It's your best bet for reaching help in time for it to actually arrive before we're all fried to a crisp."

"And if they die before they pass through the vale, then we all die. The shoals are the safest route." McCoy turned to Veren. "My crew has gone as far as anyone living. The fishing there is plentiful, and the weather is fine. We've mapped out the best routes."

"And what happens when we try to go farther than you have?" Declan asked. "What sends you back home when you've gone as far as you can?"

"Aye, we'd have to find a new route around the far reaches of the shoals. We've run into nothing but sandbars and coral reefs we've not yet ventured past. We haven't had reason enough to find a way, but it's there."

"Sandbars?" Hyde frowned, turning to share a look with another captain who'd pulled up a chair in the crowded corner Keir thought would have been a private place to discuss the matter.

"Aye, you could move across the sandbars with the right equipment and crew. Can a man stand on them and keep his head above water?"

"The last time we sailed that far, it was only ankle deep."

"Ropes and pulleys would get you across with a flat-bottomed boat. Especially if she was small and lightweight." Keir didn't even recognize where some of these opinions were coming from, so many had joined the lively discussion.

"It's not far from land." McCoy sighed. "It's possible the temperatures have risen; it was already hot with steam rising and geysers spewing from between rocks. We'd have to plot a new path farther from the shores." He stroked his beard thoughtfully. "I still say it's the best option for actually reaching your destination, but maybe not the fastest if time is of the essence."

"You could be out there wandering around for months while the rest of the world burns," Michel muttered, clearly unhappy the others had butted into their conversation.

"It is an impossible choice to make," Veren finally spoke. "Either way could yield success, or we could all die in the attempt. What matters now is that we make a decision and see it through." He stared at Keir across the table.

"He is right. We must make an informed decision and give it our all." The captains all launched into another round of debate on which was the best route and how it could be done.

"You don't think we can trust any of this conjecture, do you?" Declan leaned in. "They've traveled these sea routes all their lives, and I know they have much wisdom to offer, but this is a life-or-death voyage, Keir. We need this to work."

"It will." Keir lifted his tankard, draining its contents with a smile on his face.

"What am I missing?" Declan scowled. "You look too happy to have heard the same conversations I'm hearing."

"The point, Declan, isn't in deciding which one is right. They all are."

"How many of those ales have you had?"

"Listen to what they aren't saying." Keir grinned.

"What do you mean?"

"All these men." Keir gestured at the room filled with captains and their crew, all discussing the dangerous journey they would soon make. Because they would be going. Soon. "Not one of them has said it isn't possible."

CHAPTER 3
TIERNEY

"Absolutely not." Bronagh paced the length of her less-than-elegant room in the caverns. It wasn't exactly fit for a queen, but nothing about this place was. "It can't be done."

Tierney sat quietly on the stone floor at the edge of the hearth, basking in the warmth from the ever-present fire. For once, she didn't voice an opinion. She wasn't sure she had one yet.

Keir let out a huff of exasperation as he faced off with the Grimian queen. "I think you're wrong."

"And you know so much about the Vale of Storms? Tell me, Vondurian, have you ever set foot on a ship?"

"That's not the point."

"Actually," Veren put in, "that's exactly the point. I agree with Bron on this one. Those old coots are just looking for a grand adventure, but they'll end up with a lung full of briny water and fish pecking out their eyes at the bottom of the sea."

"Nice visual," Tierney muttered.

Veren shot her a wink, looking for just a moment like the charming snake of a boy she'd known in Iskalt. It brought her a strange bit of comfort.

Bronagh drew in a breath, as if calming herself. When she spoke, her tone was measured, careful. "When we began construction on the ship meant for this purpose, we consulted every shipbuilder in Grima. There were five of them, and they were all in agreement on what was needed to cross this particular sea."

"And how would they know?" Tierney hadn't realized she'd spoken until every eye fell on her. "I mean, don't get me wrong, I think what Keir is saying is completely insane, but no one has survived the maelstrom, right?"

"Not that we know of." Bronagh nodded.

"This captain…"

"Michel," Declan supplied.

Tierney continued. "Captain Michel, he's come close."

"As close as anyone living." Keir lowered himself to the settee, his eyes on Tierney.

"So he says." Veren shook his head.

"Hush," Eavha snapped at him. "Tierney is working through something here; let her think."

She was grateful for Eavha's faith in her, faith in the knowledge Tierney would have all the answers. But the truth was, she was as lost as ever. Was this her way to return home? Or just another way to die?

They all sat around the queen's rooms. Bronagh still on her feet, Veren at her side. Eavha and Declan sat together across the hearth from Tierney, their shoulders brushing. Gulliver was silent beside Keir on the settee.

Gulliver met Tierney's eyes in a silent argument.

Don't, he seemed to say.

I think we might have to.

Tia, this isn't one of your adventures. It's dangerous.

She sighed and shot him a look that said, *Everything we do here is dangerous. I don't want to die by the heat of the fire plains.*

Wouldn't that be the cruelest fate of all? The ice princess, who'd always fought for her independence, burning from the inside out as she yearned for her family and the protection she'd always scorned.

Tearing her eyes from Gulliver, she inched away from the hearth, no longer finding comfort in its warmth. When she glanced around the room, she found Eavha watching her with worry in her eyes, Veren studying her.

And Keir, his gaze was the worst. Imploring. Seeking. He needed her to be on his side in this, not to win but to give his fae a chance. There was desperation there.

"Well, we might die," she said.

"Precisely." Bronagh crossed her arms over her chest. "The seas are unforgiving. Without the proper ship—"

Tierney cut her off. "But won't we die if we do nothing at all?"

The queen closed her mouth, and a heaviness settled over the room. These were their choices, and each looked as bad as any other.

Bronagh pinched the bridge of her nose. "I need to think. Can you all please leave?"

Tierney picked herself up from the floor and followed the others out into the hall. She slipped her arm through Gulliver's and pulled him to catch up with Keir. "My room." The words were barely a breath, but she knew he'd heard them by the way he stiffened and issued one abrupt nod.

The hour grew late as they navigated the network of caves, and only a few fae remained awake, mostly guards going about their duty. It didn't slip Tierney's notice that the guard rotations doubled in size the day Eavha and Declan arrived with a host of Vondurians. The entire place felt ready to explode into battle.

Tierney yanked Gulliver into her room, shutting the door behind them. They'd left Keir to talk to Declan and Eavha for a moment, but he'd arrive soon. "We need to leave this place." She flopped onto the bed she shared with Eavha and groaned.

Gulliver perched on the corner of the hard mattress. "At least they keep the fires burning." He gestured to the hearth. "I've lived in worse places."

Sometimes, Tierney forgot Gulliver grew up in the prison realm before the magic barrier came down. He'd been born to a life of drudgery and starvation in a place where a hearth would have been life's grandest luxury.

Tierney lifted her head. "I miss home."

Gulliver's face fell. "Yeah, I miss my dad."

"We've been treated well in Grima, but I think our time here is over. Not only ours … if we don't get the Vondurians out of here, I'm afraid of what will happen."

He didn't speak for a long moment. "We've heard stories of the NAME sea, Tia. Do you really think we can cross it?"

She sat up, reaching for his hand. "Since when has there ever been anything we can't do?"

He gave her a squeeze, his tail lifting to tap her wrist. "Now, you're that ten-year-old girl again."

"With one major difference."

He didn't need to ask her what that was. "Your magic."

She sighed. "I need my brother, Gulliver. I need to return to him. I never fully understood it before. We knew he amplified my power, but now I think he *is* my power. Just like the totems are for Lenyans. It doesn't work without him. I will do anything, face any risk, to return to him." And not just for her magic.

A knock at the door interrupted them before Eavha barged in. "You don't have to knock, Keir. It's my room too since we're all packed into these caverns."

Keir and Declan followed her in.

To Tierney's surprise, it was Gulliver who spoke first. "Okay, Mr. Majesty, we're in." He met Tierney's gaze, but this time there was no argument between them, only gratitude. His eyes told her he'd do anything to get them back home too.

"In?" Declan looked confused.

Keir nodded, his expression matching Tierney's determination. The two of them weren't so different. Maybe that was why there was a tension between them, a rage right underneath the surface. It wasn't for each other, but only their circumstances.

This time, they were on the same side.

"No." Eavha gasped. "Tierney, it's a death sentence."

"But what if it's not?" And as they'd said before, staying was also a death sentence.

A smile curved one side of Keir's mouth. "Yes, what if it's not?"

The hike down from the caverns wasn't easy on a normal day, but this morning, the narrow stone steps were slick with rain—an icy blast that soaked through Tierney's clothes, chilling her to the bone. She didn't think she'd ever been so cold, even in Iskalt.

What she wouldn't give for a warm fire in her mother's rooms, a fur wrapped around her shoulders, and one of her mother's human hot chocolates.

Instead, she was traipsing through the mountains of a foreign kingdom.

From her favorite vantage point high in the caves, she hadn't been able to view the nearest fishing village, but Keir told her it wasn't far once they reached the bottom of the pass. The treacherous climb was the reason Grimians were mostly safe in their caverns.

Tierney hardly slept the night before. She tossed and turned in bed until Eavha finally hit her over the head with a pillow and told her to stop. After that, Tierney found her way to the library, if one could call it such. It looked almost like a war room, with maps lining the walls and a few bookcases holding precious leather tomes, the few that were saved from the palace.

One of the maps showed the expanse of the Vale of Storms with an unnamed land across it that she guessed was Iskalt. It showed the swirling maelstrom, the rough waters. But she wondered how accurate it could have been when no one was known to have traveled that route.

Her foot slipped, and a yelp escaped her, but a firm grip on her arm kept her upright. Keir.

It was only the two of them this morning. They'd left before the rest of the palace woke, before Bronagh could convince them it was a bad idea.

Keir's grip didn't loosen, and Tierney looked back at him.

He released her immediately with a gruff, "Be careful."

Tierney's breath was shallow the rest of the descent. When she hit the bottom, air rushed into her lungs, and she wanted to kiss the ground underneath her feet.

Glancing up, she saw how far they'd come, how far back up they'd have to climb. A lump lodged in her throat. She could do it. Why were there so many ways to die?

Keir wiped rain out of his eyes. "Come on. The village isn't far."

Drops of water dripped from her lips as she blew out a breath and followed him.

By the time they reached the village, her entire body was stiff with cold. She heard the docks before she saw them. Fishermen yelled to each other from the riggings as they prepared to head out for the day. Weather didn't stop them.

Most of the sails hadn't yet been raised, creating an eerie feeling. She'd never been around ships without the constant flapping of canvas in the wind.

"Veren said most of the captains breakfasted at the Lucky Goose while their fae prepare their ships."

"By breakfast, you mean—"

"Ale, most likely."

She rolled her eyes. "Of course."

"Maybe cider on a day like today."

"What ever happened to fae drinking water?"

Keir flashed her an uncharacteristic grin. "Says the woman who likes her wine."

She shrugged. It was true. "Iskaltian wine, though. Not your Vondurian swill."

He ignored her comment. "Ale and cider can be easier to come by in these parts than water fit for drinking. It's less likely to make one sick."

Behind the docks were a line of warehouses and taverns. Beyond that, ramshackle houses leaned together, as if they'd fall without holding each other up.

It wasn't hard to find the Lucky Goose. A wooden sign swung as rain pelted it above a half-open door. Chatter spilled out as they neared. Tierney wasn't sure what she expected to find this early in the morning, but it wasn't a tavern full of loud men and women chatting animatedly and laughing.

As if sensing her surprise, Keir leaned in. "Those who work on boats are a different sort."

They stepped in out of the rain. No one paid attention to the newcomers or the puddles dripping at their feet. It was so very different from back home. When she walked into a tavern near the Iskalt palace, everyone knew.

"He's in the back." Keir wound around tables to a bald man who looked like he'd been sucked into the maelstrom and spit right back out.

"Captain." Keir gave a respectful tilt of his head.

The man looked up, surprise etched into his face. "Why, if it isn't the enemy king. What can I do you for, young man?"

Keir slid into a seat opposite him. "First, you can keep it under wraps who I am."

The man mimed locking his lips and throwing away the key.

"This is Tia." Keir gestured for her to sit in another empty chair. "Tia, meet Captain Michel."

"Pleasure, Tia." He pretended to remove a cap that wasn't on his head.

Tierney liked the man already, but it didn't escape her notice that Keir failed to tell him just who Tierney was. She could use that to her advantage.

"Captain," Tierney rested her hands on the table, "Keir tells me you've come closer to the maelstrom than anyone in Grima."

"Grima or Vondur." He grinned, his vanity successfully stroked. "No one dares stray as far from shore as my ship can handle."

"And why is that?"

"Because I built her for speed but also stability. The trick is not to spend longer than one needs in rough waters. Get in, get your fish, get out."

"And the maelstrom?"

His brow furrowed. "Well, not even I have ventured that far, but we have stories. Waves so big it's like trying to sail up a waterfall, wind so harsh it'll rip a sail right to shreds, if the hull hasn't splintered and dashed to the bottom of the sea first. I would love to see it just once in my life." He sighed, a wistful smile on his face.

This was the moment. Tierney met Keir's gaze, and he gave her a nod. She leaned forward. "What if you could?"

Time froze as the captain stared at her. And stared some more. Red crept into his cheeks. "All of this …" His breath stuttered on the way out. "All these questions … You're not asking me to …"

"Sail through the maelstrom?" Tierney said. "Yes, we are."

Captain Michel shot to his feet. "Are you insane?" His words were so loud all nearby chatter stopped, all eyes turned on them. "All this talk … It was a fantasy, not supposed to be real. You can't possibly think there's a fae in Grima who'd risk it." He stormed toward the door.

Tierney and Keir jumped up to follow him. This wasn't exactly going as planned.

As they ran into the rain, a barmaid yelled at Captain Michel that he didn't pay.

"Put it on my account," he hollered back, his steps never faltering.

For an old man, he sure was fast. He reached a boat slip and hauled himself onto a ship that looked just as weathered and tested as him. A handful of sailors shouted greetings.

Tierney knew enough not to board a boat she wasn't invited onto. She stood on the dock and yelled to him. "Is it possible?"

He stopped, the rain bouncing off his head. "I don't know."

"Coming aboard!" A woman pushed by Tierney and Keir, bounding with shocking agility onto the ship. She pressed a kiss to the old man's cheek, and Tierney could barely catch their conversation.

"I heard you caused a commotion in the Goose."

"That was my fault," Tierney called.

The woman turned to her, and Tierney saw just how young she was. She couldn't have been more than eleven or twelve. Not a woman, just a tall willowy girl. "And who are you?"

Tierney was tired of trying to convince fae to save their kingdom without them knowing the full truth. "My name is Tierney O'Shea. I'm a princess from the kingdom on the other side of that maelstrom. And I want to sail through it to get home, but also because if we don't, all of Lenya could be lost."

Keir cursed under his breath, but the captain and the girl looked on with wide eyes.

Tierney cleared her throat. "But you can call me Tia."

"Well," the girl started, "you should probably come aboard."

"Imogen." There was a warning in the captain's voice.

"Da, we owe it to Mama." She twisted a wet lock of blazing red hair around one finger.

The captain closed his eyes for a brief moment. "Fine. We'll listen to you."

Tierney took that as an invitation and climbed aboard. Keir followed her, still not saying a word. It was probably for the best. A few sailors gave them quizzical looks, but Tierney ignored them as she followed Imogen down a set of narrow stairs to where a handful of rooms branched off. They turned left into a kitchen of sorts with long wooden benches.

A young man glanced up from where he'd been messing with the stove. The captain waved a hand, and he scurried out.

"I'd offer you some tea, but this can't take long because we need to head out soon." He lowered himself to one of the benches.

Tierney sidled up next to Imogen. "You mentioned your mother?"

The young woman nodded, wet stringy hair clinging to her cheeks. "This is about the fire plains, isn't it?"

"Imogen, don't," her father pleaded.

Tierney turned to face the girl, taking in her ruddy skin, the way her eyes held no fear. "It is. If we do not act, they will destroy Lenya."

"I knew it." Imogen didn't look pleased with herself. "What other reason would someone risk crossing the vale?"

To get home. But Tierney didn't say that.

Imogen glanced at her father almost in apology. "The fire plains destroyed our village a few days' ride from here. Da was out on the ship. First came the sickness from contaminated water. When the heat came, Mama was too sick to go, but she told me to run."

Tierney's heart ached for this family, for all the families destroyed by the fire plains. She bent so she was at eye level with the girl. "Across the sea is my kingdom. It's called Iskalt. There, we have all the magic needed to drive the fire plains back, to make sure that doesn't happen to anyone else. But we need to get there."

Imogen turned to her father. "Since I was little, you've dreamed of going farther and farther, of discovering what lay on the other side."

"It can't be done." Captain Michel rubbed his face.

"I thought you said you didn't know if it could." Keir shifted his feet, staring down at the man.

Tierney watched them both. "Just because something has never occurred doesn't mean it can't."

Captain Michel looked helplessly from Keir to Tierney to his daughter.

Imogen sat beside him. "Da, what if we could have saved her? Would you have thought it too impossible to try then?"

A beat of stillness passed before his shoulders dropped. "No, I'd have done anything to save your mother."

"Then, let's try to save other mothers, children, our way of life.

There is a reason this princess and her guard have walked into our lives."

Tierney almost laughed at Keir being called a guard.

"Honey," Captain Michel said, "that man is a king."

Her brows shot to her hairline. "We've been chosen to help, to escort the likes of kings and princesses across the sea, a sea that is our home. You are the best captain in Grima. They need you."

Captain Michel looked at his daughter, pride shining in his eyes, before meeting Tierney's gaze. "My daughter wants to help, and who am I to stop her?" He stood. "I will not force my men to go on such a perilous journey. Volunteers only. Which means, every person on this ship will have to work."

Tierney nodded, a smile coming to her lips. She couldn't wait to see Veren mopping the deck or cleaning the lav. But more than that, it felt real.

They might never make it, but at least now they had a chance.

Chapter 4
KEIR

"Stop pacing, Keir." Tierney sat perched on the edge of a flat-topped boulder. The vast cavern was empty for the moment, but it would soon be filled with Lenyans, come to hear the bad news that would confirm all the rumors told in hushed whispers in the corners of taverns and the marketplace.

"We're going to instill panic and chaos if we don't handle this right." Keir leaned against the stone wall beside Tierney. He didn't like the idea of telling the locals about their plans. At least, not all at once.

"We will give them the truth. It's the least they deserve." Bronagh sat in a straight-back chair at the front of the cavern. She made the derelict piece of furniture look like a throne. That was something he would never have. King, he may be, but royal, he was not.

"She's right." Tierney tapped her foot impatiently. "They aren't going to like it."

"They aren't going to trust it," Veren added.

"But they need honesty from their leaders." Gulliver sighed.

"The people will come around." Captain Michel twisted his hat in his lap. He seemed unable to fathom how he'd ended up in this situation. Already, his men were outfitting his ship with everything they would need to make the voyage. He was still quietly looking for volunteers, but after today, Keir imagined he would have more than he needed. Fae were bravest when their lives and the lives of their families were on the line.

Bronagh's people from the palace began to arrive, filing into the room and taking their seats. The Vondurians arrived next, each giving their king a formal bow. They wanted everyone here to know they answered to Keir and Keir alone.

The air in the room was tense. As if at any moment a battle would break out and nothing would stop it.

Keir was so tired of it all. So tired of a war he didn't want Lenya to keep fighting. Tierney was right. They had much bigger problems now.

As the villagers, fishermen, and merchants began to make their way into the back of the cavern, Keir, Tierney, and Bronagh stood together at the front of the room.

They'd rehearsed this part. The people needed to see them as a united front. Neither Bronagh nor Keir should be seen as the 'leader' of this venture.

"Welcome," they said in unison.

"Today, we are not Grima versus Vondur," Bronagh began.

"But Lenyans." Keir stood proudly beside the young queen. "United against the threat that stands on our doorstep."

Whispers erupted all around, and Keir held his hand up for silence.

"It is true," Bronagh said, her voice ringing across the cavern like a bell. "The rumors you've heard, they're all true."

"The fire at the palace?" a lady from Bronagh's court asked.

"Not an accident." Bronagh clasped her hands in front of her, stiff as a soldier beside her. "The fire plains are expanding, sweeping across Lenya, and we are powerless to stop them."

Gasps of surprise and sobs of protest rang out.

"It begins with the water turning foul," Keir explained. "It will make some too sick to leave their beds. Then, the temperatures rise, the air turns putrid, and the earth begins to shake. The ground becomes so hot that fires spring from nothing to burn the land and whatever lies in its path."

"We need magic. Magic will save us!" the villagers cried out, begging for an easy solution.

"Even if we emptied the mines, gathered Vondurian and Grimian reserves, and used every drop of magic we have left in Lenya, it will not be enough." Bronagh reached out a hand as if to soothe her people. "I would gladly sacrifice what magic we have left and live without it if it meant we could save you all. But our magic is weak. It is not enough. We need help."

"Magic has caused us nothing but heartache," Keir continued. "And in the end, it will fail us when we need it most."

"What can be done?"

"Will we be left to die?"

"Why have you brought us here?"

The questions and the fear that drove them tore at Keir's heart. He hadn't let himself feel it for a long time, but he loved his people and this land. He would do everything in his power to save them. Or die trying.

"There is a way to stop the spread of the fire plains." Tierney's voice rose above the din. "That is why we have called you here today." She stepped forward to stand among them. "My name is Tierney O'Shea, and I am not of Lenya. I am princess and heir of Iskalt, a kingdom of ice and snow that lies far beyond the borders of your world. Months ago, a magical ... experiment gone awry brought me and three of my friends here by mistake. In Iskalt, we have great magic. But unlike here in Lenya, our magic is infinite. I am too far from home to use my magic here, but we have access to crystals there. More than you could imagine and—"

"You expect us to believe this?"

"You would share your crystals?"

"What would your people want in return?"

"No one gives away magic for free."

"What will it cost us?"

Tierney raised her hand for silence. She had that same royal quality that Bronagh had. The thing that made all fae respect her and show her deference. The room quieted, and Tierney smiled.

"I come from the four kingdoms. Iskalt is just one of those kingdoms with lands far beyond what you can imagine. We do not use the crystals for magic. We don't need them. To us, they are beautiful stones we use for decoration and nothing more."

"We must find a way to reach Iskalt." Keir stepped forward to join Tierney. "It is our best chance of survival."

"My father, King Lochlan of Iskalt, will gladly come to your aid. My mother is sister to the Queen of Eldur, which lies on the other side of the fire plains to the west. Her other sister is Queen of Fargelsi, a land so green and fertile it's hard to imagine." Tierney turned to Gulliver. "And my dearest friend in the world is of Myrkur, where the Dark Fae live. His father, my uncle, works closely with King Hector of Myrkur, where they already mine crystals to use for trade. My family are all kind, benevolent rulers who have fought hard to attain the peace we have enjoyed for more than half my life. I speak for them all when I say we will never allow the fire plains to destroy Lenya. As long as it is within our power to do so, we will help you defeat this threat and give all Lenyans access to magic no fae should ever do without."

Astonished faces stared back at them. Keir wasn't sure if they were stunned or if they just didn't believe them.

"It can't be done."

"There are no other lands beyond Lenya."

"The seas are too treacherous."

"It is true." Keir's voice rose above the din. "We must first find a way to cross the Vale of Storms to reach Princess Tierney's homeland."

"It is impossible."

"It's too risky."

"What other option do we have?"

"We have no other option." Bronagh joined Tierney and Keir. "The seas to the south are too shallow and rocky to safely navigate. To the north, they are equally treacherous."

"The maelstrom is impossible to sail across."

"So it has been said," Keir replied. "We've all heard the stories of the dangerous seas. We have always been locked inside the borders of Lenya, believing there was nothing beyond our world. But we have never before had such motivation to risk breaking through those borders to see what lies beyond our knowledge. We have nothing to lose and everything to gain."

"If we do nothing, we will all perish in the fires." Bronagh stood taller, her gaze never wavering.

"Who will make this journey?" A man Keir recognized from the docks clutched his hat in his hand.

"We will. I will travel with King Keir of Vondur and Princess Tierney of Iskalt. Together, we will take the risk for you. I will be leaving Prince Donal in command during my absence."

"And I have left my sister and my council in charge of Vondur." Keir nodded to Eavha, sitting among the crowd with Declan and Gulliver. "By now, you have all learned of the treaty that has brought an end to the war between our kingdoms. We cannot afford to be divided any longer. From this day forward, we fight for all of Lenya."

"How do we know you all aren't just abandoning us to our deaths?" A bold man of Bronagh's court stood among the villagers in the back, looking as weary and worn as the hardest working Grimians.

"Lord Branigan." Bronagh nodded. "You will just have to trust us. We will be asking for seasoned sailors to volunteer to join us. To my knowledge, you have years and years of experience sailing the Grimian seas as a merchant sailor. You are welcome to join us as we risk our lives to pass through the Vale of Storms and around the maelstrom. As we speak, the Wind Runner is being outfitted for our voyage. We will set sail for the shores of Iskalt as soon as she is seaworthy."

Lord Branigan lowered his gaze. "Forgive me, your Majesty. I only worry for my family."

"As do we all." Keir gazed across the audience, trying to give them a sense of peace about this venture. "You all have families you care for. Please know that Queen Bronagh and I care for our people as dearly as you care for your own families. We will not fail you, nor betray you."

"You have our word as your monarchs. We will die before we abandon you all to the fires." Bronagh gave them a look that said they were done here. "We leave in three days' time. May the magic of our ancestors protect you all until we return." She marched from the cavern, her head held high as her people stood to watch her go. Captain Michel and Veren followed her, urging the court to return to their temporary homes.

"Vondurians, you are dismissed." Keir couldn't be seen following the queen, so a military dismissal would have to do. As they all filed from the room, Keir turned to Tierney. He wanted to reach for her hand, but with so many eyes on them, he wasn't sure it was a good idea. His people needed to see him as a king working with the other monarchs, not beholden to them in any way. That was the surest way of losing their support.

"Keir, you can't go." Eavha waited until the room had emptied before she blurted the words, her tears not far behind. Keir had never been able to stand strong in the face of her sadness. "It's too dangerous." She flung her arms around him. "You are all I have left. I cannot lose you."

Her shoulders shook as Keir tried to comfort her. "It's all right, Eavha." He pulled back to search her face. "I am king. It is my responsibility to see Vondur through this."

"Why can't we just take whatever magic we have left and use it to save as many as we can? We could stop the expansion from spreading any farther, couldn't we? We won't have magic anymore, but at least we will have each other."

"And what would you say to all the men and women and their families who couldn't be saved? And what if our magic isn't enough to stop it? Eavha, you know we need help. Not just access to more crystals but real help. Tierney's people have a kind of magic we don't. Not only that, they have information we don't. We won't find the answers to Lenya's problems in Lenya. I have to go."

"I wish you could just be my brother." She sniffed her tears back, stepping into the circle of his arms to lay her head on his shoulder.

"What kind of king would I be if I let anyone else do this?"

"It would make you like Father." She sighed. "And you've always had too much of our mother in you to be anything like him." She gave another sniff and nodded. "Very well." She straightened the collar of his shirt. "You have to promise to return. All of you." She turned to glare at each of them. "Sail through that storm and bring the magic back to Lenya. I will accept nothing less than success. Let's go, Declan. Gullie. We have preparations to make." She pivoted on her heel and stomped from the cavern.

"That girl would make a fine queen someday." Tierney came to stand beside him when they were the only two left. "It's too bad she loves Declan or I'd introduce her to my cousin. He's heir to Fargelsi, and in a few years he's going to be in the same predicament I've been in."

"Which is what?" Keir asked in an amused tone.

"In the four kingdoms, an heir must marry another royal or the highest of their noble houses. All the royals are related or close enough to be considered family, even if the blood ties aren't there. It diminishes the pool of eligible consorts tremendously. My father was desperate to find the right match for me."

"That's what sent you running to the human realm, is it not?" Keir asked.

"It seemed like the end of my world at the time." Tierney laughed.

"My father and his stupid list." She shook her head. "I guess I'd forgotten what real problems were then."

"And now?" Keir arched a brow at her.

"May the magic help us through this." She let out a long breath. "Because we have real problems running out of our ears."

Chapter 5
Tierney

"Be safe." It wasn't the first time Eavha muttered the words, and Tierney had no response. This wasn't a journey where safe was a possibility. They had to be daring, bold, brave. Safe could get them killed, or worse. It could lead them to failure, and a return to face the fae they let down.

So, instead of issuing false promises, Tierney hugged Eavha with all her might, wishing for another life in which they didn't have to part. She wanted to take the princess to Iskalt with her, to introduce her to a world of peace, where children were allowed to play and young women danced and sparred, and laughed.

Pulling back, she gave Eavha one last look before turning to board the Wind Runner. A handful of sailors who'd volunteered for the journey prepared to set sail. It wasn't enough. One didn't have to be a seafarer to know that.

But she was grateful for every one of them.

"Look out below!" a voice called moments before Imogen dropped onto the deck, landing in a crouch and straightening in one smooth movement. Tierney lifted her eyes to the rigging above, wondering where the girl had come from.

Imogen grinned. "Just making repairs."

Great, they hadn't even set sail and the ship already needed repairs. Imogen intrigued Tierney. She'd recently lost her mother, and yet it didn't seem to have dimmed her spirit. Unlike her father, whose trepidation was obvious, the coming adventure put a spark of excitement into her.

"Something wrong?" Tierney asked.

Imogen shrugged. "We'll be fine."

In Tierney's experience, "we'll be fine" was more a statement of hope than a point of fact.

Imogen left to join her father on the starboard side, and Tierney stepped up to the worn wooden rail circling the deck. Her eyes scanned the Grima coastline, wondering if this was the last time she'd set eyes on Lenya. It was a place of great pain for her but also one of discovery. She was a captive, a refugee, and now, possibly, their salvation.

It wasn't the first time she considered maybe her portal brought her here for a reason. Maybe she was supposed to help Lenya.

Yet, it was also a place of shame.

Veren stepped up beside her, and Gulliver joined her on the other side.

"Siobhan could still be out there." It wasn't fair that the three of them had found each other and she hadn't.

Gulliver's tail wrapped around her back. "If she is, Declan's fae will find her."

Veren, standing perfectly still, surprised her when he spoke. "Is anyone else … sad? To be leaving."

"No," Gulliver and Tierney said at the same time.

"Not all of us were kept in luxury since day one." Gulliver looked down at his hands, and Tierney wondered if the scars of the Vondurian dungeons would ever go away.

"I know." Veren sighed. "It's just …" He glanced back over his shoulder to where Bronagh was boarding the ship.

Tierney hadn't understood, but she did now. Reaching out, she lay her hand over Veren's. "She's with you now."

"And if we survive this, she will return home."

Tierney had no words of comfort for him because right then she caught sight of Keir in an intense conversation with his sister down on the docks. They looked to be arguing before he pulled her into a hug and held on like he didn't want to let go.

Releasing her abruptly, he clapped Declan on the shoulder, muttered a few words, and bound up the rope ladder and onto the ship. Tierney left Gulliver and Veren to approach Keir. "Everything okay?"

His brow furrowed. "We're about to embark on a journey no one has conquered before. Our ship looks like it has seen better days, and I have to share a room down below with Veren and Gulliver."

"So … yes?"

He gave her a reluctant smile, and she prided herself on pulling it out of him.

"But really, I meant with Eavha."

His smile dropped. "Just Vondurian business."

She wanted to press, but his expression closed off, and she knew she'd get nothing else.

"Everyone aboard?" Captain Michel yelled. "We need to set sail if we don't want to miss the tide."

Tierney searched their group. Veren and Gulliver were where she left them. Bronagh stood nearby, gazing across what was left of her kingdom. A few of her fae, guards mostly, took up position on either side of her, their golden armor glinting in the early morning sun.

A handful of Vondurians sat on crates near the door to the stairwell.

And then, there were the sailors, the fae who belonged on this ship.

Seemingly satisfied, Captain Michel gave the order to untie the ropes anchoring them to the dock.

The ship bobbed in the rippling water as a cool breeze skated across the surface.

"Oars," the captain yelled.

His fae took up position and long wooden oars protruded from the ship, dipping into the water. And then, they were moving. There was no more second-guessing, no turning back.

Tierney walked toward the Grimian queen, the one who'd been against this risky journey. She'd eventually realized they had no other choices before them. Bronagh was a brave woman. Despite her fears, she'd agreed to set sail.

One of the golden warriors moved aside for Tierney to stand next to Bronagh and watch Grima disappear. Neither of them spoke for a long moment.

Finally, Bronagh's voice filled the silence. "I sure hope you're right about what's on the other side of this sea."

Tierney drew in a briny breath, letting it settle in her lungs before exhaling. "Me too."

The first day at sea was a deception, one they'd expected. Calm waters greeted their journey, and as the winds picked up offshore, the captain ordered his fae to unfurl the giant canvas sails. They stored their oars and got to work directing the ship and keeping it steady.

The sails looked like a patchwork of tears, sewn together with odd colored canvas. Yet, they managed to propel the ship forward under the afternoon sun.

Out on the water, the temperature dropped. By nightfall, Tierney could hardly stand it. The only thing worse was going into the warmth down below that smelled like sweaty bodies and rotting sewage.

The ship was surprisingly large, with three cabins other than the main hold. One belonged to the captain and his daughter. The officer's cabin had been given to Keir, but Tierney and Bronagh convinced him to share it with Veren and Gulliver. And the third was for Bronagh and Tierney.

The soldiers and sailors slept in hammocks in the cramped crew quarters.

Tierney sat on near the ship's bow, surrounded only by stars. Noise came from the quarterdeck, where sailors gathered, but Tierney tuned them out, lifting her face to the sky.

"I'm coming home, Tobes," she whispered into the night, wishing a breeze could carry her words. "I'm going to make it." Through the maelstrom and across the uncrossable sea.

She closed her eyes, leaning her head back against the wall, and feeling the night. Not merely hearing it or smelling it. Waves lapped against the ship. Cool, salty air, the freshest she'd ever experienced. Her magic settled within her, content and calm on the sea. Soon, she'd have control of it again.

Getting to her feet, she stepped to the rail and peered down at the dark water, the silver light of the moon casting it with an iridescent glow. In two days' time, they would reach the first of the rough seas at the entrance to the Vale of Storms. Five days later, if their calculations were correct, the maelstrom.

And no one knew how long it would take to reach Iskalt should they survive that.

Tierney yawned, her chin lifting. If she was going to have any energy to face the coming days, she needed rest.

The smell hit her the moment she opened the door leading to the narrow wooden stairs. Stale air pushed out at her, and she had to fight the urge to stop breathing altogether.

Descending the creaky stairs, she headed toward the berth that promised her rest, but a sound coming from Keir's room had her turning. It was ... laughter.

The door was already ajar, and she pushed it open, stopping at the sight before her. A card game. Keir sat on the edge of the bed, bending over a small table. Veren perched in a shoddy chair, balancing on two legs. Gulliver was on the floor, cards clutched in his hands.

Veren and Gulliver shared a grin as Keir placed a new card down.

"I can beat that." Gulliver slammed his hand down on the table, his cards face up.

Veren let out a hoot. "How's it feel, your Majesty?"

"To lose at a game I've never played before?" Keir lifted a brow.

Tierney stepped into the room, but no one paid her any mind until she spoke. "Since when are you all friends?"

"We aren't." Keir frowned.

"Gross." Veren crossed his arms.

"Since we proved the king here has a vulnerability after all." Gulliver was the only honest one.

"Yeah?" She had to hear about that. "What is it?"

"Cards." Gulliver grinned. "He's actually terrible. He didn't even know that the Eldurian crown beat the Fargelsi flame."

"I hardly know what Fargelsi or Eldur even are." Exasperation rang in Keir's voice.

"A little tip," Veren said, "Fargelsi flames are the weakest of the four flames. Everything beats it."

"Wait." Tierney peered closer. "Who had a Kingdoms deck?"

"I made one," Gulliver said. "I found some Grimian game while we were there and needed a reminder of home."

Kingdoms was a popular gambling game in Iskalt, not fit for a princess. Yet, she'd loved it. Her friends from the village let her join their games as long as no one found out. And when she was with Gulliver and Griff, they played all the time.

"Can I play?"

Gulliver and Veren let out simultaneous groans.

"Why can't she play?" Keir asked.

It was Gulliver who answered. "Because she's a freak."

"Hey." She wasn't a freak.

Veren nodded in agreement. "She can't lose. I don't know how, but Tia wins. Always."

"That can't be true." Keir looked from them to her. "There's too much luck involved."

"I don't always win." Tierney hugged her arms over her chest, trying to remember the last time she'd lost the game. She'd won many sweets over the years, the only thing her friends had to gamble with. But she'd always brought them pastries from the palace.

"Fine." Gulliver sighed.

Veren picked up the deck and shuffled rapidly, his fingers nimble. "Guess his royal Majesty has to see for himself."

Tierney sat beside Gulliver and met Keir's eyes, a challenge in their depths. He wanted to beat her. Tough luck, buddy.

Her tongue poked out to wet her lips as Veren dealt eight cards. Keir's gaze followed the movement, settling on her mouth. Did he want to kiss her as much as she wanted him to? Everything that happened to them in Vondur seemed like some distant past. It was a new world now.

Vondur and Grima were behind them. They wouldn't reach Iskalt for a long while. No kingdoms were keeping them apart out here, only their egos.

"Are you two going to stare at each other all night or play?" Veren asked.

Tierney's face heated as she realized they were waiting for her to pick up her cards. As soon as she did, she suppressed a grin. This was going to be fun.

Four games later and Tierney still hadn't lost.

"I give up." Keir threw his cards on the table.

"Told you." Gulliver leaned back on his elbows. "She's a freak."

"Or I'm just exceedingly talented." Tierney sent them a wink. The exhaustion she'd felt was gone now, and she wanted to move. Standing, she started toward the door.

"Where are you going?" Gulliver asked.

"Up top. I can't stand another minute in this horrid room with you lot." Really, she'd have stood a lot worse with them. She didn't know when she'd started counting Veren as a friend again, but even his presence brought her comfort now.

It wasn't until she escaped into the fresh air that she realized she wasn't alone. Keir followed her silently, as if it was the most normal thing in the world. He stumbled as the boat swayed.

Tierney laughed, rolling her eyes. "We've been on the boat all day. Still not used to it?"

"Vondurians aren't meant for the sea."

"Neither are Iskaltians. We're more suited to frozen tundra where we wrestle bears and fight wolves."

His eyes widened. "Truly?"

"No." She chuckled. "The frozen tundra part is true, but the other is just what some fae think of us."

"I have no doubt you could take down a bear."

"Well, thank you for your faith in me." She peered over the edge. "What about creatures of the sea? In Lake Villandi, we have the Asrai, and they can be vicious, but I've heard stories of animals with razor-sharp teeth who can survive in the sea."

"I try not to think about it."

She turned to him. "Why? Is there something the great warrior king is afraid of?"

He met her gaze, hesitating for a beat before lowering his voice. "There are some things."

Somehow, Tierney knew he didn't mean whatever swam in the depths. Her gaze held his like a magic force kept her right where she was. His totem shone like a beacon where it hung from his neck, but the longer she watched him, the more it dulled.

"Keir." She reached out to touch the crystal, the back of her fingertips brushing his chest. "When?"

"Yesterday." He put his hand over hers. "I felt the moment the last of the magic drained from it."

"Why didn't you ask Bronagh for another?" In Vondur, he wouldn't have had to ask.

"Tia, did you notice how almost no one in Grima used magic. I can't remember seeing it there once."

Tierney thought over her time there. Keir was right. "They've depleted their crystals entirely."

"Not exactly. They do have precious few, but they do not use them unless necessary. And Vondur, I didn't want to take a crystal that might be needed to save fae from the fire plains while we're away."

He had no magic. Without a crystal, there was none inside of him. She hadn't noticed Bronagh with a totem either, which meant there wasn't a single bit of magic on this ship.

"Why do you still wear a depleted totem?" she asked, drawing her hand away.

"Because it is a reminder. Even without magic, we still have power." The words were for her and her alone because she understood all too well.

She hadn't realized she'd stepped so close to him until she turned and her shoulder brushed his chest. "Why did you do it, Keir? Why did you save me those months ago in Vondur?" She'd never truly been able to answer that question. He killed his father, risked his life. For her. For Declan and Gulliver too, but not only them.

Keir turned, peering out at the calm water. A breeze blew the hair back from his forehead. "My fae needed a king with their best interests at heart."

"But you never wanted that to be you."

A breath rattled past his lips. "Tierney—"

"Say it, Keir."

He pushed a hand through his hair and closed his eyes. "My father was an evil man. I'd known that for a long time, but it wasn't until you … what he did to you. I hated myself for the role I played. It gave me the courage to act."

"Why?"

"What do you want from me, Princess?" He turned hard eyes on her, his lips dangerously close to the side of her head. "I gave you your answer."

"Not the full of it." She faced him, the mist from his breath skating over her cheeks.

His eyes searched hers, looking for his own answers and most likely finding none. Tierney didn't even have answers for herself. "I couldn't bear the sight of you hanging," he whispered. "I think it would have ripped me right open."

Tierney would shred just as thoroughly should anything happen to him. She hadn't planned on it, hadn't wanted it, but whatever this was sitting between them in choked silence wouldn't go away.

Reaching out, she gripped his arm, telling him it was okay to feel things. He didn't have to be stoic and hide his emotions all the time. He could be a king and still be afraid.

Afraid of losing her.

Afraid of losing himself.

Afraid of failing the one position he'd never aspired to.

"Goodnight, Keir." Tierney gave him a soft smile before turning and leaving him up on deck.

By the time she lay her head down beside Bronagh's, wrapped in furs and burrowed into the hard bed, sleep dragged her into its depths like the sea coming to claim her as its own.

Chapter 6
Tierney

By the second day, they'd left the calm seas far behind. Even Tierney had trouble keeping her feet firmly planted beneath her, and she had some experience sailing the rough waters of Loch Villandi.

The hour was early, but she couldn't take another minute in the narrow chamber she shared with Bronagh.

"Careful, Tia." Gulliver reached out to take her hand as she stumbled up the last step and onto the rolling deck. His tail snaked around her middle, anchoring her to him and the ship the hopes of two kingdoms rested on.

"Need fresh air." She blew a damp strand of hair out of her face.

"It's only going to get worse, isn't it?" Gulliver clutched her hand, staring out across the surging waves that crashed against the hull, spraying a fine mist of seawater over everything. Pretty soon, they would all forget what it felt like to be warm and dry.

"Much worse." Tierney sucked in a deep breath of sea air. With a new stench of decaying fish on the wind, it wasn't exactly fresh, but at least it wasn't stale human bodies and vomit filling her nose.

"How's his Majesty fairing this morning?" Amusement filled Gulliver's tone.

It turned out the King of Vondur did not have his sea legs yet. The minute the calm waters diminished behind them, Keir's stomach began to heave and roll with the waves, and no amount of staring at the horizon helped.

"He hasn't stopped vomiting yet. I fear he's in his bed for the duration."

"I will not stay in my bed a moment … longer." Keir staggered across the deck, his face as pale as the Iskalt snows, his dark hair hanging in limp curls around his face. "I just need to walk around a bit." He sucked in a breath and let out a strangled groan.

"He's going to blow." Gulliver moved them aside, turning Keir toward the ship railing. "Best get it out."

Keir lunged for the portside, emptying the meager contents of his stomach over the railing. Tierney wanted to go to him, but the captain had warned them all to keep to the center of the ship when on deck.

"Your Majesty." A sailor approached him with eyes full of sympathy. "You'll feel better if you stay below deck with a cup of tea and a biscuit or two. Keep something in your stomach and in a day or so, you'll be right as rain." He clapped Keir on the back and went about his duties.

They all had duties to see to. Gulliver was quite good at climbing up into the rigging to help handle the sails and cables. Tierney didn't like the thought of him up there when the seas were so unpredictable, but they all had to pull their weight onboard.

Tierney was responsible for running messages from the captain to the crew, and she helped mend the sails when needed.

Bronagh handled the cleaning below deck and filled in wherever an extra pair of hands was needed. And Veren was assisting the captain with navigation and keeping watch with the other sailors.

Keir wasn't up to helping anyone yet.

Tierney let out a breath when Keir finally backed away from the railing. She didn't like seeing him so close to the edge when he wasn't at his strongest.

"I'm not going to fall overboard if that's why your face looks like that." Keir wiped his mouth with the back of his hand.

"I wish there was something to help you with the seasickness." Tierney reached out a hand to keep him steady.

"I'm afraid nothing will help except maybe a knife to the gut." He closed his eyes and leaned into her. "I pray the Iskalt shores are closer than we think."

"I'm on duty soon." Gulliver gave Tierney a worried look. "We should get him back inside."

"I'll make my way below deck in a moment." Keir opened his eyes, lifting them to the heavens.

"Just be careful. Both of you." Gulliver left them for his short morning shift among the rigging.

"I've never seen such a strange sky." Keir took in another deep breath, a hint of color returning to his cheeks.

"The air is thick, and the salt burns your lungs." Tierney looked up into the angry green clouds churning overhead. "It's an eerie sight." She gave a shiver that had nothing to do with the chill in the air.

"It's better here at the center of the ship." Keir rested back against a stack of barrels containing a good portion of their fresh water. "I can almost feel normal right here."

The ship dipped over a big wave, and Keir groaned. "That didn't last long."

"Your color is fading again." Tierney took him by the arm. "Let's get you back down to your room. You need a cup of strong hot ginger root tea. It will help ease the nausea."

"I don't like your ginger root." Keir scowled, putting some of his weight on her as they made their way across the deck.

"Have you tried the pressure points I told you about?"

"What I need is a totem with magic I can use to find my equilibrium."

"Stubborn man." Tierney helped him move down the steep steps into the berth he shared with Veren and Gulliver. Both were working their shifts with the crew. "It will be nice and quiet in your room. Maybe you can finally get some rest."

"I don't want to rest. I want to do my part."

"Well, get some rest and give your body time to adjust, and maybe you can." She shoved through the narrow door into the larger room. "Sit." She pushed him down onto the edge of the bed. "Press here." She lifted his left hand and showed him how to press down on his wrist in just the right spot to relieve nausea. "Do that until I get back with your tea."

"Fine." He sat sulking.

Tierney pulled her woolen shawl close around her shoulders as she made her way to the galley, where the cook kept a pot of boiling water on when he was able. Tea was the one thing they had plenty of. It warmed the body and filled the belly.

"How's his Majesty this morning?" Darby shuffled around his small galley kitchen, stirring a pot of porridge and reaching for a wooden mug from his cabinet.

"Still struggling with nausea." Tierney pulled down the tin of freshly grated ginger root mixed with shaved citrus rind and a dried flower she couldn't identify. It smelled wonderful. Mild and calming.

"Make him drink this tea." Darby filled the mug with hot water. "And give him these to gnaw on." He set a tin of dry biscuits on a tray. "If he can keep them down, we'll get him some porridge with a bit of honey."

"Thank you." Tierney lifted the tray.

"Well, now, wait just a minute." He pulled down another mug. "You look like you could use a good cuppa too." He gathered several tins and added a pinch from each to a linen tea bag. "Good strong black tea with some lavender and lemon verbena and a smidge of honey. That will calm you right up and give you some energy for the rest of the day." He poured hot water over the little bag of tea leaves. "And a spot of porridge for you too. We all need to eat to keep our strength on this voyage." He winked.

The weathered old man set her to rights and sent her on her way.

She balanced the tray as she made her way carefully to Keir's room. He lay back on his bed, his fingers still pressed to his wrist, fast asleep.

She set the food on the bedside table, and his eyes snapped open. "I don't know what kind of witchery this is," he lifted his hands, "but it's working."

"I asked around and the old sailors swear by it." Tierney pressed the mug of tea into his hands. "Drink that and try to eat at least two of these." She opened the tin of unappetizing lumps that looked more like rocks than any biscuit she'd ever seen.

"Darby says you get to eat porridge if you can keep that down."

Tierney sat in the only chair in the room and stirred her porridge.

Keir scrunched up his nose as she took a bite. "I don't know if I want that."

"It's rather like eating paste. It doesn't taste bad. Though it doesn't taste like anything, really."

"I've had worse." He sipped the tea. Taking a biscuit from the tin, he nibbled on the edge of it. "Way better than the hardtack soldiers eat on the trail."

The ship continued to roll beneath them, but for the moment, Keir seemed to be feeling better.

"I don't know if it's better or worse down here where I can't see the sky." He leaned back against his headboard, gripping the warm mug between his hands.

"It won't be long before we reach the maelstrom, and then we won't have time to think about our stomachs."

"How long do you think it will take to go around it?"

Tierney shrugged. "I hope it's quick and the swift currents take us where we want to go."

"Tell me about Iskalt. What will we see first?"

She smiled, sitting back and putting her feet up on the edge of his bed. "The first things you'll see are the ice floes. They will look like land, at first, from a distance. Then, as we approach, we'll see patches of snow-covered ice floating on the sea. Once we see that, it won't be long until we reach the fjords."

"I don't know what that is." Keir smiled. "But it sounds wonderfully exotic."

"Exotic is not the right word for Iskalt." Tierney laughed. "The fjords are these massive sheer cliffs that extend out into the sea like the fingers of a giant's hands. The sea flows between them like rivers heading inland."

"And do people live on these fjords?"

"No. It's far too cold, and there isn't much land that isn't steep and rocky and covered in ice. But it's so beautiful with the afternoon sun glinting against the cliffs."

Her heart ached with longing for her homeland. She would never again take it for granted. She might never reach home, but she would give anything for one last sight of Iskalt before she died trying to reach it.

"And after we see these fjords, what comes next?" Keir reached for another biscuit, breaking it apart to eat small bites.

"I don't know, actually. I believe we will reach the far eastern shores of Iskalt first. The Northeastern Vatlands should be there, though I've never seen them myself."

"What is a vatland?"

Tierney sipped her soothing tea, grateful to Darby for the aromatic blend. "It's what we call places like the fire plains. They're rural areas between the kingdoms where the terrain is harsh and the climate intolerable. In Iskalt, we have the Northern Vatlands to the west separating Iskalt from Myrkur. It's a rough journey through the wild mountain terrain there, but there is one mountain pass we use most frequently to reach the shores of Loch Villandi. The Northeastern Vatlands are also a mountain range, but they're impossible to navigate. The far reaches of eastern Iskalt are wild and uninhabited. From Lake Fryst to the Northeastern Vatlands, it is nothing but frozen tundra. Cold beyond the likes of anything you can imagine. Along the edge of the tundra, the vast mountain range of the vatlands rises to impossible heights. It is said the mountains are so high one can't even breathe the air at the top. Beyond those mountains, there is nothing. Nothing but the maelstrom and Lenya."

"And where do you think we will make landfall?" Keir leaned forward, hanging on her every word, his seasickness all but forgotten.

"I hope we will make it to the other side of the storm to find the seas that flow between Iskalt and Eldur. One side borders the fire plains and the other the impenetrable mountains of the Northeastern Vatlands. If we can sail through those waters, then we are home free. We can then make our way across land."

"We are pinning everything on this voyage. I hope you are right about what we can expect on the other side."

"It's a gamble for sure, but it's all we had left."

Keri nodded. "What kind of reception will we receive when we arrive?"

Tierney couldn't help the smile that spread across her face. "When we reach Iskalt, I'll arrange for a messenger to travel ahead to give my parents the news of our arrival. I imagine they will ride out to meet us. Mother will be beside herself after all these months. She won't be able to sit still. Neither will Father for that matter. Then, they'll ride the rest of the way home with us and there will be chaos when my brothers and sisters realize I'm home.

"Father will want to hear every last detail of what happened … twice. He will have many questions for you and Bronagh. It might feel like he's interrogating you, but he means well. He'll be on edge when he realizes he's hosting two unknown monarchs from kingdoms he's never heard of."

"Your father sounds … stern."

"He is. They call him the ice king for a reason, but he's very sweet and loving to those who know him best."

"What will he think of me?" Keir drained the last of his tea and eased back onto his bed.

"He will wait to form an opinion of you until after he's questioned you. He'll want to know all about Vondur and Grima."

"You must have had a terrible time with your suitors and such a protective father."

"Oh, you have no idea." Tierney laughed. "When I was fourteen, I went with Father to one of his noble's estates. We were there to tour their land and discuss a potential contract between the crown and the duke who lived there. They produced the finest leather and furs in all of Iskalt. The duke's son was just a year or two younger than me. He was a brat." Her face fell. "It was hard for me then, before I came into the full use of my magic. I was the Iskalt heir, but I had Fargelsian magic. Others my age had no magic to speak of. Not until they were older. I hardly remember a time when I didn't have magic thrumming through my veins." Her fingertips rubbed together.

"Other children thought me strange. The duke's son made fun of me. I can't even remember what he said, but my father heard it. I ran to my rooms in tears. Father came to find me and told me I was perfect just the way I was. I dried my eyes, and we returned to the main hall for the evening meal.

"The duke was horrified and insisted he would punish his son for his insolence, but Father told him he would handle the punishment. He made the boy approach each nobleman in attendance that night—my father right there beside him the whole time—and confess to what he had done. He had to ask each nobleman to absolve him for his transgressions, and at the end of the night, my father made him publicly apologize to me. I've never seen him since." Tierney shook her head with a frown. "It is odd that he wasn't on Father's list of suitors."

She sat forward suddenly and laughed. "Oh my goodness! I've never seen that boy at court. Ever." She smacked a palm over her face. "My father banned him from court that day. I don't know why I never thought of it before. He never said a word to me about it, but it's something he would do."

"You are not making me eager to meet your father." Keir yawned, his eyes drooping with fatigue. "Maybe I should ingratiate myself to your mother instead."

"She's a tough one too. But she will like you." Tierney sat on the side of the bed, tucking the blankets around Keir. "You should get some rest while you can."

The ship gave another heave, and Tierney held onto the bedpost with an iron grip. A gust of wind rushed through the lower deck, snuffing out the candles in the room, leaving them in the darkness of the eerie day under the cold green skies.

Keir was fast asleep.

Her hand froze, hovering just over the dim crystal he wore around his neck.

It felt different. She couldn't resist touching it, running a pale finger over the smooth surface. The magic flickered inside the crystal. Just a flutter, gentle like the touch of a feather, but it was there. And it was different. There was not enough power left inside the crystal to be useful, but she could still feel it deep within the totem.

Keir said it was useless. He felt nothing from the empty vessel. The magic of Lenya was a strange thing Tierney wasn't sure she would ever understand.

But how might the two types of magic interact? They were vastly different sources of power, and she wondered if they would come together to entwine, or if they would repel each other.

Tia.

A bolt of energy shot through her, and she leaped to her feet, running down the hall and up the steps into a torrential downpour. "Toby!" she screamed into the wind. "I'm coming!" She clutched a hand over the heart thumping in her chest. She could feel him. It was faint, but it was there. Her brother, her twin, was still right there with her. And he knew she was trying to find her way home.

If Keir had to stay down here breathing this foul air for one moment longer, he was going to march right up those stairs and jump off the side of the ship, hoping to swim all the way to Iskalt.

Who would willingly subject themselves to a ship's constant turmoil when they didn't have a kingdom to save?

"Keir." Imogen rushed toward him as soon as she saw him in the hall. "Are you sure you should be out of bed?"

With such cramped quarters, those on the ship had gotten to know each other quite well, and all formality had flown right over the side of the wretched vessel. Even Bronagh's soldiers had taken to calling her by her given name. It was as if, out here, they were all equals.

"I'm fine, just …" He drew in a struggling breath. "Need sky." To see it, to smell it. The rains had finally stopped, the drumming against his skull coming to a blissful halt.

Imogen pursed her lips. "Tia was clear. You aren't allowed to leave your quarters."

Of course she'd given that command. She was the most stubborn, irritating, capable, beautiful fae he'd ever known. Wow, the sickness had addled his brain. "Tia is not your king."

Imogen crossed her arms, her young face twisting into a smirk. "And neither are you. I am Grimian. I recognize no king of Vondur."

Keir let out a groan. "Are you going to help me or watch as I try to climb those steps, tumble back down, and break my neck?"

She cast a dubious glance from him to the steps before sighing. "Fine. But if Tia asks, you threatened me."

His lips twitched. The girl was scared of Tierney. He knew the feeling.

Imogen ushered him toward the stairs, one arm around his waist. "I hope you don't mind me saying, Keir, but you reek."

"You don't exactly smell pleasant yourself." They'd all been stuck on this boat for days, sweating in the damp, muggy air. It made him long for the cold of the Grima mountains or the ice he knew was coming for them in Iskalt.

At the top of the stairs, Imogen opened the door and blessed sunlight poured in, a welcome change from the past few dark and stormy days. Keir gulped fresh air, his feet stumbling as Imogen released him.

"Imogen," Captain Michel called. "I need you up fixing the sails."

Not wanting to slow down as they approached the maelstrom, they hadn't lowered the sails for repairs. It was only during the worst of the storms they'd drawn them in. But now, to fix any damage caused by the howling winds, it meant climbing into the highest reaches.

Keir's gaze followed Imogen as she made her way up the ropes, her agility astounding.

"She's incredible, isn't she?" Bronagh asked from beside him.

The two royals hadn't spoken much since boarding the ship. The truce still sat uneasily between them, the trust fragile. Their entire lives, they'd been taught to hate each other, to only view the other as an enemy to be destroyed.

"When did the storm end?" Keir asked, still not looking at her.

"In the night. It was the strangest thing. The storm raged over the seas. I was watching it with Tierney from a doorway. And then, suddenly, it stopped."

"Like someone had turned off a switch." Tierney joined them, her eyes roving the calm waters before them. When Keir and Bronagh shot each other confused looks, Tierney groaned. "Oh, for magic's sake. A switch is how the humans turn electricity on and off."

"Electricity ..." Keir never understood what she was talking about, but her knowledge of the human world always intrigued him.

She rolled her eyes. "They don't use torches and candles and oil lamps for light. It's this ... okay, let's just say it's like magic. Imagine you had a glass ball and you put a crystal in it and told the crystal to provide light to read a boring document or something. Then, the light shone through that glass."

Bronagh clasped her hands together. "But why do we need the glass when the crystal could provide enough light on its own?"

Tierney scrubbed a hand across her face. "You know what, sometimes I just have to remember fae won't believe in human magic unless they see it for themselves."

"I wasn't aware humans had magic." Keir had pictured them as docile creatures without true power.

"Well, they don't call it that. It's technology. Anyway, what I was saying is, the storm just suddenly stopped, and the waters calmed in an instant. It was unnatural."

Keir leaned against the rail, trying to keep himself upright. He was no longer nauseated, but the weakness remained. And that's when he noticed it. It wasn't just the water that barely even showed the ripples in the boat's wake. The sounds ... "Do you hear that?"

Bronagh cocked her head. "Just the wind."

There was enough of a wind to keep them moving, but that was it. "Where are all the birds?" Before the storm, they'd seen many of them.

"We're probably too far from land for birds." Not even Tierney sounded sure of her words.

"That's true," Captain Michel said from behind them. "But it is not the only truth."

The three of them turned, taking in the man who'd gotten them here. He held his cap in his hands, wringing it between his fingers. Nerves flitted across his face.

"Everything okay, Captain?" Tierney glanced at Keir in concern.

She was right. The man looked stressed, almost scared.

Captain Michel looked out at the horizon. "I think we've reached the sea of glass."

When none of them spoke, he explained, "It's called that because all turmoil disappears here, all waves, storms. The water looks smooth as glass, the winds calm, and the sky a bright reflection. It was just a rumor … I've never heard of anyone making it so far beyond the Vale of Storms."

This was it. They'd gone farther than any other. "And what comes after this sea of glass?" Keir met the man's gaze.

The captain swallowed, his face darkening. "The maelstrom."

Bronagh sucked in a breath. Tierney stilled completely. The sea of glass was the calm before the storm, the last bit of peace any of them might see.

He didn't want to ask his next question, but it couldn't be helped. "When do you expect to reach the maelstrom?"

"We can't know for sure, as our maps and calculations are mere guesses."

"Captain."

"Tomorrow."

Tomorrow. One day. One day left to play cards with the men who'd only just become his friends in a way, one day left to drink tea with common fae he'd never imagined getting to know.

One more day to feel the energy crackling between him and Tierney.

"Captain, may I have a word?" Keir mustered all his strength to stand up straight, to not let his weakness show.

The old man nodded and led Keir farther along the bow of the ship. When they stopped a far enough distance not to be overheard, Keir turned to him. "What do we need to do to secure the ship?"

Captain Michel trained experienced eyes on him. "Young man, my seamen have been preparing for this since the day we left port. Every bit of the hull has been repaired and reinforced. Anything on deck is strapped down to avoid projectiles damaging the mast."

"Or killing us."

"You will weather the maelstrom down below and allow my crew to keep you safe."

"If there are tasks to be done—"

"I will have my fae do them. This mission you embark on cannot be carried out by just any fae. If my kingdom is to have any chance at surviving what is to come, we need you and our queen to reach these foreign shores intact. I don't need you decapitated by a severed rope."

Could a rope really do that?

As if reading his mind, Captain Michel went on, "We're going to have ropes snap in the kinds of winds we've never imagined. If you don't think they'll be flying through the air fast enough to cleave your head right from your body, then you're dumber than you look."

"I get your point." Keir's jaw clenched. "We have to stay safe."

"There is no safe in the maelstrom. If the winds up top don't kill you, you'll probably drown when the hull splits. If luck is on our side, and that's a giant if, a few of us might make it out. But I don't have time to coddle anyone's pride. When I tell you to stay below, you will."

Keir wasn't stupid. He saw the sense in the captain's words, even if he didn't like feeling useless with a battle coming. But this wasn't a battle he could fight with sword and shield.

Only luck.

By the time night descended, an air of apprehension settled over the entire crew and passengers of the Wind Runner. No one knew exactly what kind of monster headed straight for them.

It was too dark down below, too full of worry and fear. One by one, they filed onto the deck and sat with their backs resting against a stack of crates that had been strapped and triple strapped to the deck.

Keir sat in the center with Tierney on his left, their shoulders pressed together. Gulliver sat on her other side, his hand entwined in Tierney's. To his right, Bronagh and Veren leaned on each other, neither seeming to notice the intimacy of the position. Maybe it didn't matter any longer. None of the proprieties, the expectations of society.

Tomorrow would be bigger than any of them, bigger than the role they played within their kingdoms. Here, under a clear sky full of false hope and distant stars, there were two royal leaders from warring lands, the heir to a fabled kingdom's throne, a nobleman turned soldier, and the adopted son of a prince. They weren't ordinary fae, and this wasn't an ordinary task, yet their titles wouldn't help them now.

This night, everyone was powerless.

They sat silently together, soaking in the remaining moments of stillness.

Gulliver leaned closer to Tierney. "I love you," he whispered. The words tore at Keir's heart because they were so close to everything he hadn't been able to say to the fae in his life, everything he wanted to say now.

Tierney's lips curved into a smile, the fear leaving her eyes for a beat. "I love you too." She leaned her head on his shoulder. "I'm sorry you're here."

Gulliver smoothed a hand over her hair. "I've told you before it isn't your fault. Whatever happens, never blame yourself. Even if we die tomorrow, I'm glad I ended up in Lenya with you, that you weren't alone."

"Not me," Veren put in. "I could be back in my bed in Iskalt right now."

They all chuckled because if it wasn't for this journey, even Keir knew Veren wouldn't have regretted anything. He barely knew the man, and yet, he'd watched him change, just as Tierney had.

His father used to say suffering made one stronger, but he had it wrong. It wasn't the suffering that made a fae stronger, better. It was the desire to end suffering, to fight for something greater than one's self.

Keir settled his head back against the edge of the wooden crate, but he froze when Tierney jerked up.

"Toby," she said.

Gulliver reached for her. "What's wrong?"

She lurched to her feet. "I can … I … Toby? Are you there?" She walked toward the afterdeck.

Gulliver moved to stand, but Keir yanked him back down. "I'll go." He pushed to his feet and followed Tierney to the rail. She looked off into the darkness, her mind in another place. "What happened back there?"

She jumped at the sound of his voice and turned. Moonlight bathed her face, reflecting off her dark irises as she drew in a deep breath. "My brother … I felt him."

"Felt him?"

"I've told you about how he's connected to my magic. I lost that connection in Lenya. That's why my magic doesn't work. I'm too far away from Toby." She shook her head, her eyes still holding a faraway look as she clenched her fists in frustration. "It's never made any sense. There have been so many times when Toby has gone to the human realm with Father and it never affected my magic. But somehow it seems as though whatever separates Lenya from the Four Kingdoms is much greater … or more powerful than the veil between the human and fae realms. The closer we sail to Iskalt, the stronger the feeling becomes. It's not all there, but there are moments when I can sense him with me, feel his hand in mine. You probably think I'm losing my mind."

Keir shook his head. He'd seen enough unexplainable things recently that he believed in every possibility. A princess appearing out of the sky from a mythical kingdom. Stagnant fire plains moving and growing like they were alive.

"Your totem," she said. "Do you still have it?"

Keir drew it out from beneath his shirt. "It's useless." Without magic, it had no power, but he'd kept it anyway for the sheer comfort wearing it brought him.

Tierney reached for it, her fingers grazing his chest right over his heart. The vessel kicked up a notch, reacting to her nearness.

"It's stronger."

"What?"

"The connection with my brother. When I'm near the crystal, I can feel him more intensely. It's like the power inside it touches mine."

"But there is no more power."

"That's not true." How was this possible? "It's just a flicker, not enough for you to draw out, but it's still there. I think you've been wrong all along. No crystal ever completely loses its magic; you just lose the ability to use it."

Studying her for a moment, Keir slipped the leather strap over his head. His chest instantly felt naked without it, somehow more vulnerable. "If it makes you feel closer to your brother, you should wear it."

It might not help her magic, but maybe it could give her some peace if tomorrow happened to be their end.

Tierney took it, tears filling her eyes. "Keir," she whispered. "I can't. It's yours."

He closed her fist around the totem, not wanting her to realize what it meant to him to go into tomorrow without it. Even if it couldn't protect him, it provided him with an inner strength to get through anything. "Yes, you can."

"Thank you." She slipped it over her neck, closing her eyes. "If I never make it back, at least I can sense him with me when it ends." When she opened her eyes, tears spilled over her perfect cheeks. She stepped forward, wrapping her arms around him and burying her face in his chest. "You're not the horrid man you try to appear, Keir Dagnan."

It took him a moment to make himself move, but he wrapped his arms around her, closing his eyes and soaking in her nearness, the way his body thrummed with energy.

He wasn't sure how long they embraced or why neither of them pulled back, but a slight rocking of the boat jostled them apart. Tierney leaned over the side. "It seems we've reached the end of the sea of glass."

The eerie stillness was gone, and the wind picked up. The water underneath the ship undulated slowly, just small waves. By morning, there'd be nothing small about them. This was only the beginning.

Tierney's hand slid into Keir's, her grip tightening. "When we get through this, I'll be almost home."

Home. Her kingdom, not his. Yet, the truth of the last thing he'd done before leaving Lenya sat heavily on his heart. He hadn't yet told Tierney of those final conversations.

"I should have helped you return from the moment my men found you on the battlefield." Instead, he'd tied her up and taken her to his father. "Tierney—"

She turned so quickly her chest bumped his. And then, she kissed him. This wasn't like the kisses back in Vondur, frantic and needy. This time, they were slow, methodical, memorizing every moment. Kissing Tierney had never been about getting something or even giving it; it was about living, about being.

For so long, he'd obeyed orders, done his duty, and failed to consider what life could truly be like. Like a kiss, feather-soft and so calming he could forget the storm coming for them, forget that soon they might be torn apart.

Forget that they'd been trained as royals never expecting choices, true decisions in their lives.

Tierney gripped the hem of his shirt, yanking him closer. The totem she now wore around her neck brushed his chest, sending adrenaline racing through his veins.

By the time Tierney pulled away, they were both breathing heavily.

Keir touched his lips. "What was that for?"

A sad smile tilted the edges of her mouth. "Tonight may be our last, Keir. For once, I didn't want to deny myself what I needed."

"And that was to kiss me?"

She brushed up against him again, her breath whispering over his lips. "If you wish, I can stop."

"Tierney, I could live a thousand lives and never wish for your kiss to end. Even if tomorrow is the end of our world, you broke mine long ago."

That brought a grin to her lips that threatened to stop his heart completely. "Well, my family has always said I'm trouble. Breaking worlds is in my nature."

"Do you ever stop talking?"

"Not when I'm annoying you. It's my job to—"

He swallowed her words in a kiss so bright it stole the stars from the sky. And all at once, that broken world started to look a lot more whole.

"Promise me," he whispered against her lips, desperate to have some kind of hope.

"Anything."

"Promise me you'll still be here to irritate me after tomorrow. That we'll make it through this. No heroics, no added dangers. We stay below and survive the maelstrom."

Tierney didn't answer him as she pressed her face into his shoulder, hiding the knowledge in her eyes. But he knew what they'd say.

She was a hero, someone who would always risk her life and walk right into danger. There was no promise she could make beyond tomorrow that wouldn't be a lie.

Chapter 8

KEIR

She won again. Keir tossed his cards down. "I'm out. I know when I'm beat." He reached for the wineskin at his belt. It was full of water. Staying hydrated seemed to help his seasickness almost as much as Tierney's wrist trick had.

That and the smooth sailing they'd had for most of the day crossing the sea of glass. They'd left the calm waters behind, and the ship rocked gently in the rising swells as they continued on their northeast heading.

"I told you not to let her play." Gulliver shuffled the cards and stuffed them back in the box he'd carved for them. He was a talented fae, and not just because he was a brilliant craftsman. He had a myriad of other skills. Some not exactly above board for the adopted son of a prince.

"I can't help it if I have good luck, boys." Tierney scooped up her winnings—a handful of coppers and a few trinkets she'd collected off them throughout the evening.

"If only her luck would see us through the maelstrom." Veren lifted his own wineskin and drank deeply.

"I'll drink to that." Gulliver reached for Veren's, but Tierney slapped his hand away.

"Now is not the time, Gullie."

"Right, right." He shoved his hands into his pockets. "But when we get home, I'm nicking the biggest bottle of wine in the Iskalt palace, and you can't stop me." He shot her a glare.

"Steal two, and I'll join you." Tierney grinned. "But I won't be the one to put you to bed when you're too drunk to walk in a straight line."

"It's a date."

"Just think of it, Gullie. A few days from now, we could be at the palace in our old rooms with all of our family and all our things."

"I thought Gullie lived in Myrkur," Bronagh said, leaning back against the crates, where they sat in the fresh air, soaking up their last moments of peace.

"I do, but my father is an O'Shea. He can create portals like Tia is ... supposed to be able to do, but she's rather awful at it." Gulliver shrugged. "I spent a lot of time at the Iskalt palace growing up."

"You have your own rooms there?" Keir asked, astonished. He supposed it was normal in their world for the ward of an Iskalt prince to have the rights of a natural-born son, but it was not so in Vondur. A man like Gulliver would be lucky if his adopted father was able to give him a name, much less a fortune and status.

"Why? Is that weird?" Gulliver shared a look with Tierney. "My best friend is the princess, and she's sort of my ... sister-cousin."

"Wait, she's what?" Bronagh snorted a laugh.

"Was I not supposed to say that?" Gulliver glanced at Tierney, his brow lifting.

"What he means is, his adopted father is actually my natural father. Mine and Toby's, of course. It's a really ... really long story." Tierney laughed. "But a good one with a great ending. If we make it through tomorrow, I'll tell you all about it."

"Is it ... not something your people know?" Keir asked, though Veren seemed to know all about this shocking revelation.

"Oh, everyone knows." Tierney waved a hand as if it was nothing. "Uncle Griff and my mom were married for a time, but she was really in love with my dad. And he's been my true father. We're just alike, though he likes to insist that I'm exactly like my mother."

"Tia's a perfect blend of Loch and Brea." Gulliver smiled. "The only thing she got from Griff is her strawberry blond hair. He has auburn hair and Loch has white-blond hair. She has her mother's face and eyes, so really, she's a bit like all three of them rolled into one troublesome package."

"And it worked out well for Gullie to get a father all to himself." Tierney leaned against him. "At least until Griff married Aunt Riona and they had Gullie's little sisters."

"I miss the little beasts, flying around like a couple of winged pests." Gulliver shook his head.

"Your sisters ... have wings?" Bronagh asked, a note of uncertainty in her voice.

"Their mom's Dark Fae like me. A slyph—a rare one too. They both inherited her wings and tattoos."

"I would like to visit your land one day, Gullie." Keir clapped him on the back. "It sounds fascinating."

"Myrkur isn't much, but it's got one thing going for it Lenya does not." Gulliver stretched his legs out in front of him. "No bloody fire plains."

"I'll drink to that." Keir threw his head back and laughed. "We'll raise a glass of this fancy Iskalt wine I keep hearing so much about and toast to the death of the fire plains."

"Here, here." Veren laughed. "I never thought I would miss the snow and ice of Iskalt, but if I never feel the heat of the burning lands again, it will be too soon."

For a brief moment, they were all smiles. Just a group of friends who had nothing in common but the circumstance that had brought them together. Keir had never seen anything more beautiful than Tierney's face under the light of the stars as she laughed and joked with Gulliver about his sisters. Keir joined in their laughter at the look on Bronagh's face when Veren described what ogres were. He wasn't so sure he believed there were actual sentient creatures that looked more like talking, mossy boulders than fae, but he really hoped they would survive this journey so he could find out for himself.

"It is time, your Majesties." Captain Michel came to break up their gathering. "We've entered the currents of the maelstrom. We will reach the edge of the storm within the hour, and we'll be in the thick of it by dawn. Best get below deck now."

"The wind will pick up soon." Imogen bounced along the ship railing, peering into the darkness like she could already see the great maelstrom waiting to devour them. "We'll get our first look at her just before the sun comes up. I bet she's a magnificent sight."

Keir wished he could look at what they faced the way Imogen did. Like it was a great adventure just waiting around the corner, and not the cause of their imminent deaths.

Bronagh was the first to her feet. "May the magic be with you and your crew, Captain." She pulled him into an awkward hug. The weathered old man flushed with pleasure, patting her shoulder gently. "It has been my greatest honor to serve you, your Majesty." He stooped into a courtly bow.

"May this be the first of many ways you will serve the people of Lenya." Bronagh squeezed his hand and made her way below deck with Veren.

"I am happy to help if you need an extra pair of hands and a mighty quick tail." Gulliver stood before the captain. "I know your crew is all seasoned sailors, but if you need me, I'll come."

"Thank you, Lord Gulliver. You're a fine lad and a good sailor." The captain clapped him on the shoulder. "But I think your princess is going to need you more."

Gulliver nodded, taking Tierney's hand.

"You have no idea, Captain Michel, what it means that you were willing to make this journey with us." Tierney choked back tears. "Please don't die." She flung her arms around the old captain, giving him a fierce hug before she turned and ran from the upper deck with Gulliver on her heels.

"Captain." Keir nodded. "The fate of all of Lenya rests in your capable hands, sir. All of our families are counting on this voyage to reach its destination."

Michel nodded, his hands shaking as he reached to wipe the beads of sweat from his brow. "I will do my best, your Majesty." He gave a proper bow, something no Grimian would ever give a Vondurian royal.

"You have my gratitude and my deepest respect, sir." Keir returned the bow. "May the winds be in our favor this day." He turned and left the old captain standing alone on deck. It was going to be a very long night … for all of them.

Keir wished something—or someone—would knock him over the head so it would all be over when he woke up. It didn't take long for the seas to turn violent as they neared the massive storm. And along with the dips and rolling of the ship, Keir's seasickness returned in full force.

They'd all agreed to stay together in the berth Tierney shared with Bronagh. It was the smallest of the cabins, but it rested closer to the center of the ship than the one he shared with Veren and Gulliver. Still, they could hear the roar of the waves, the torrential downpour, and the shouts of the crew. Thunder crashed overhead so loud it drowned everything out for a moment before sound came flooding back in.

Keir pressed the sensitive point on his wrist, begging for the room to stop spinning. There was nothing left in his stomach to heave up, but it didn't seem to know that.

They all sat on the floor between the two small beds. Bronagh and Tierney clutched each other, and Gulliver's tail wound around Tierney's waist, anchoring her to his side. Truth be told, Keir wished he could hold on to her like that.

"How far into it do you think we are?" Veren asked. He'd asked the same question at least a dozen times already.

"The tug of the current is strong." Tierney chewed her bottom lip. "I can feel it in my bones. I think we must be right on the edge of the storm." The ship trembled beneath them, and the crash of thunder sounded like cannon fire, making them all wince.

"And if the boat starts to tilt hard one way or the other, it likely means we've lost control." Bronagh rested her head against the bunk behind her. "Do you think we'll fall into the center of the maelstrom, or will the ship just break apart?"

"Don't dwell on such things, Bron," Veren whispered. "We will be all right." But from the look on Veren's face, he didn't believe his own words.

"Why is it so bloody hot in here?" Gulliver wiped the sweat running down his face. "It must be a thousand degrees."

"We're nearing the fire plains." Tierney's face brightened.

"Why do you look so happy about that?" Bronagh groaned, fanning her face with her hand.

"Not your fire plains. Mine." Tierney beamed. "Don't you see? We're nearing the Four Kingdoms!"

"I hope we are, otherwise we're going to be cooked alive right here in this room." Keir ran a hand through his sweaty hair. The temperature had risen steadily since they sought their safety below deck. It was that putrid kind of hot that couldn't be anything but the fire plains.

Keir pulled his knees toward his chest. He was a soldier. It was unnatural to sit where it was safe, waiting for the storm to pass while others saw to the danger. It went against everything inside him.

"I feel it too." Veren nodded at him. "The maddening uselessness, but there is nothing out there to swing a sword at, Keir."

"Nothing but the wind." He sighed. "I still feel like I'm sitting out the biggest battle of my life."

"It's not our battle to fight. Not today." Veren turned his attention back to Bronagh sitting directly across from him, as if staring at her would keep her safe from the storm raging just beyond the ship's hull. One wrong move and it could break apart, sending them all to the bottom of the sea.

"Drowning is supposed to be a peaceful way to go." Gulliver laid his head on Tierney's shoulder.

"Hush, Gullie. We have to stay positive." Tierney bit down on her thumbnail, worrying it between her teeth.

The ship chose that moment to let loose a groan like the aged beams might splinter and crack any second.

Bronagh cried out as the boat listed sharply to the side, tossing them around the room like they weighed nothing. Keir rolled toward the door, landing on his back as something crashed and the light from the lantern guttered out leaving them in darkness.

"Ouch." Tierney cried. "Gullie your tail—"

The room tilted again, and Keir feared they were about to capsize.

He landed hard on his shoulder, and something soft and warm tumbled on top of him.

"Oh, sorry." Tierney's breath was hot in his face. "Who have I landed on?" she whispered, her hands braced against his chest.

Keir wasn't sure what came over him. Maybe it was the thought of dying, but he needed to taste her lips one more time. He found her mouth in the darkness, her lips soft and inviting against his.

"Oh." Tierney pulled back for a moment. "Keir," she breathed his name, and her lips claimed his again. "I think we must be dying." A salty tear splashed his cheek.

"Just a bit of a rough patch." Keir wiped the tears from her face. "We'll see it through."

"Well, the lantern's useless." Gulliver's tail made a swishing sound. "Everyone okay?"

"Fine." Bronagh sounded breathless as she sat up.

"Felt like we nearly lost it there for a minute." Veren sounded a bit breathless himself, and Keir wasn't so sure it was from the circumstances.

"We must be nearly through." Tierney sat beside Keir where they had landed near the door. She crept closer to him, and he wrapped his arm around her. If they tumbled again, he would be ready.

"Tia, you okay?" Gulliver sank down beside them. "I lost you." He groped for her hand in the darkness.

Keir lifted his hand from Tierney's shoulders as Gulliver's tail wrapped around her again. "I'll keep a better hold on you next time."

"I'm okay, Gullie." She tucked herself against Keir, grasping her best friend's hand. "We're all okay." She rocked side to side slowly, muttering to herself.

Just as Keir's heart finally found a regular rhythm again, cries rang out along the deck and the ship began to groan and creak loudly. Tierney grasped his arm, her grip like a vise.

"Toby," she whimpered, clutching the totem Keir had given her. "I'm not going to make it home."

Keir gripped her on one side as Gulliver held her tightly on the other.

"You tell him we're going to be fine, Tia." Gulliver's voice was firm. "We will get through this."

"Does it feel cold to anyone else?" Bronagh asked. "Or am I in shock?"

"It's cold." Tierney shivered. "That can't be a natural shift in temperature."

"Are we on the other side?" Gulliver asked. "It almost feels like Iskalt cold."

"How can it be hotter than an inferno one moment and cold as ice the next?" Veren's voice shook.

Even Keir felt it. The sweat from earlier had soaked his clothes, and now his back was like a sheet of ice. He couldn't imagine what it must be like on deck.

The wind howled, and the ship trembled. Keir resisted the urge to fling open the door and run up the steps to the open deck to demand a progress report.

Really, he just wanted to see the stars one last time. To meet his death head-on rather than cowering below deck, waiting for death to find him.

A loud snap echoed in the silence, and the ship roiled.

Ice cold water flooded into the room. Tierney and Bronagh shrieked as they all scrambled to move away from the rising water.

"We're sinking!" Veren shouted. "We have to do something, Keir."

Clutching for the totem he always wore at his neck, he cursed himself when it wasn't there.

"We've failed everyone." Bronagh sobbed, turning to Veren for comfort.

The water flooded in quickly.

Another great shudder ran through the ship, and the hull split right before their eyes. Water rushed into the room just as lightning streaked across the strip of sky he could now see past splintered wood.

It seemed he would get to see the stars one last time after all.

Veren shoved Bronagh behind him, his eyes wild with fright and indecision. There was nothing they could do. The sea would have them soon.

The gap in the hull widened.

"Toby!" Tierney screamed as chunks of ice and snow streamed into the room. Keir could see more heading their way. Larger chunks of ice. Tierney had mentioned them before. The icy floes. The first signs of Iskalt.

"Tia." Keir slipped, nearly losing his grip on her. "I'm sorry, Tia. I'm so sorry for everything." But she didn't hear him. She was somewhere else, trying to reach her twin in her last moments.

Keir positioned her behind him. "Keep your grip on her, Gullie." He blocked them with his body and held onto the carved post of the bed, bracing himself for the inevitable. Tierney's fingers clawed at his arm, searching for a hand. He gripped hers, giving it a reassuring squeeze.

A massive wave crashed through the gap in the hull, bathing them in icy seawater. Something cold and hard crashed into Keir's head, and his grip slipped. The current pulled him toward the open sea. His head throbbed, and his stomach churned.

"Keir!" Tierney screamed. Her hand slid out of his.

The ship tilted at a sharp angle, and Keir stared into the maw of the maelstrom.

He caught sight of Tierney before he was swept overboard. Her eyes lit with fire and ice. Something warm and familiar shot right through him, but the waves crashed over his head and darkness took him.

Chapter 9
Tierney

It started with a bone deep chill that soaked into Tierney's skin. It gave way to a scorching heat that flooded her veins.

And then, she felt him again, seeking, searching. Toby knew she was here. The cries of her friends faded away, and all she could feel was power, pure and familiar.

Just off the barren shores of Iskalt, Tierney's magic had returned.

The blinding pain snaking up her leg shocked her back to the present, to the chaos erupting all around her. Bronagh and Gulliver clutched each other as they clung to the bed that had started to shift, groaning as it moved toward the gaping hole in the side of the ship.

Veren held onto the wall as water poured into the room, shouting into the dark abyss. It took Tierney a moment to realize what he was looking for. Keir was gone, swept away with the raging sea.

The door splintered inward as another rush of water entered from the hallway moments before Imogen ran in. "Is everyone okay?" she yelled above the roaring of the storm.

Tierney didn't have an answer. She was frozen in place, her magic taking hold of her, warming her, controlling her. *Save yourself,* it seemed to whisper. She couldn't save everyone. Not Keir. Not Gulliver or Bron.

"Keir is in the water," Veren hollered.

Panic crossed Imogen's face. "He isn't the only one. We lost most of our sailors when the boat capsized. By the time it righted itself, it was just me and Da. You have to get up top. It isn't safe down here anymore."

Nowhere was safe.

Tierney wrestled frantically with her power, out of practice and weak. She tore its restraints from her limbs, propelling herself into motion. Gulliver yelled after her, but she didn't turn back before diving through the rift and plunging into the icy sea.

Saltwater stung her eyes, but she kept them open, using all her strength to draw power into every corner of her body, warming her limbs in the freezing ocean depths. Keir would have no such protection. She kicked deeper, her lungs crying out for oxygen.

If only her magic had the power to help her breathe.

The darkness of the water stole her sight, forcing Tierney to shoot up, gasping as her head breached the surface. A giant wave headed for her, and she looked up just in time for it to crest over her head, sending her tumbling underwater. For a moment, she didn't know which way was up, and then she saw the moonlight reflecting on the surface.

Swimming for the light, she reached it and caught sight of the ship, broken and sinking. It tilted on its side. The mast had long since snapped off and now floated among the waves. Someone clung to it, and she didn't know if it was one of the sailors or the man she searched desperately for.

Maybe it didn't matter. She could save someone.

Her arms ached but she forced them to cut through the water as waves tried to drag her under. Tierney had never been a strong swimmer, but this time, she had her magic to bolster her, lending her the kind of will she hadn't felt in months.

The thought that Toby was close enough for her magic to return kept her going, kept her from giving in to the pain and exhaustion eager to drag her into the depths. She refused to stop now.

Tierney reached the floating mast. It had broken in half, and the longer of the two pieces blocked her from her destination. She hauled herself over it on her belly and flopped back into the water.

Keir didn't move from where his body draped across the second wooden pole, his face in the water.

No, he had to be okay.

Tierney lifted his face, placing one hand on each cheek and instructing her magic to warm him. Color returned to his skin almost instantly, but still, he didn't move. She had to get him back to the ship. It might be sinking, but it was the only choice.

Drawing in a fortifying breath, Tierney slid him from the mast, doing her best to keep his head above water.

"I know you're stronger than this," she screamed, the words meant for the power inside her that still seemed hesitant to heed her command. "Please help me!" It had been so long since she used magic she'd forgotten how difficult she'd once found it to control.

But it wasn't working. Tierney treaded water, sinking lower and lower as her legs tired and her sodden clothes weighed her down. Keir slipped from her grasp, but she reached down and pulled him up again, not willing to concede the futility of it all.

"We are not going to die out here," she said, knowing Keir couldn't hear her. "I promise you that." Before, she'd refused to make promises, but right now, it was all she had. That and a magic with untold power that wouldn't cooperate.

It had to do more than warm her.

A wave dragged her under, and she tightened her hold on Keir, wrapping her arms around his middle.

She broke the surface with a roar. "I am Tierney O'Shea, and we are partners. When I call, you come."

Power flooded her veins, a power that didn't completely belong to her. She felt her brother lending his strength as he'd done so many times as her amplifier.

Someone threw a net over the side of the tilting ship, and then

Veren and Gulliver were there, peering out at the sea, their eyes searching. Tierney only had to get to them.

The pain faded from her limbs, the ache disappeared from her lungs, and she shot toward the net with a series of giant kicks, not letting another wave take hold.

Reaching up desperately, her fingers found the thick net, and she didn't wait for them to pull her up. Using her magic for strength, she started to climb, dragging Keir with her.

She reached the halfway point, and the net moved, the boys pulling it in the rest of the way with the help of the few remaining soldiers. Keir's body tumbled through the gap made by a broken rail, and Tierney threw herself onto the deck beside him, her chest heaving.

When Keir still didn't move, she rolled toward him. "Not today, your Majesty." Lifting one hand, she curled her fingers into a fist, bringing it down with force to try to push the water from his lungs.

It didn't work.

The deck pitched, and she slid, her feet finding purchase on a trunk that had wedged itself into the second gap in the rail. Others held on to whatever they could find, but Keir ... his body hit hers like a sack of grain.

"Tia, you still there?" Gulliver yelled.

"Yeah, you okay?" There was no room for fear, not when the world around them had disintegrated into madness.

"As good as a human who's just been hit by one of their metal monsters."

"Cars, Gullie. You should know that by now." She pushed Keir onto his back again.

"Really not the time."

Biting her lip, Tierney searched Keir's face for any sign of life. She couldn't tell the tears from the rain on her face as a new wave crashed over the side of the ship and it righted itself, the bow still sinking lower in the water.

"Keir," she cried, brushing the sopping hair back from his face.

"Please wake up." She'd heard stories of her mother saving her father long ago using her magic unknowingly. The power flooded into his heart and jolted his body into healing.

Determined to try, she placed both hands on his chest.

"What are you doing?" Bronagh crawled toward her.

"Whatever I have to." She closed her eyes against the rain and howling wind, against the imminent death and hopelessness. *Toby, I need you.* Searching inside herself, she felt her Iskaltian magic rise, strengthened by the moon. It was soon joined by her brother's presence, which in itself lent her more power.

It flooded down her arms into her hands, and she let it free to snake through Keir, to do what no natural thing could.

In the distance, she heard her friends calling to her, telling her to take hold of something. She felt the boat move beneath her with a resounding crack. And still, she focused.

Nothing.

Keir didn't wake; he didn't move. Even as she pushed water from his lungs, warming him from the inside out, he remained still. Her chest ached where that knowledge lived, and she started to pull back, letting the scene around her rush in.

Gulliver now clung to the rail, his body hanging over the side as he screamed for help. Imogen had a hold of one of his arms and Veren the other.

The captain continued steering the broken ship, yelling into the wind.

And Bronagh tugged on Tierney's arm. "We're all going to need to jump."

She couldn't be serious. "What?"

"The ship is sinking. We need to get away from it before it pulls us under."

Tierney caught sight of a guard dressed in his golden Grima armor—a bad choice for a storm—as his grip slipped and was lost to the sea.

She scrambled to her feet and ran to help Imogen and Veren pull Gulliver onto the ship.

Peering into the water, she caught sight of a large broken piece of the hull floating atop the waves. Bronagh was right. They had to jump into the icy waters of the fjords and hope they made it to shore before the seas claimed them.

"Captain," she screamed. "We have to go."

He shook his head. "I won't leave my ship."

"Da." Imogen tried to run up to the bridge, but Veren held her back.

"Get her out of here." Captain Michel couldn't meet his daughter's eyes. "Please, majesties. Make the world a safe haven for my daughter."

Tierney looked from the sobbing Imogen to Veren who still held her. Her gaze slid to where Gulliver gasped on his knees beside a comatose Keir. And finally, it landed on Bronagh. They still had a chance to save Lenya, no matter how small. "We will."

Tierney shook off her fears and took actions. "Gulliver, help me with Keir." She couldn't leave him behind. Gulliver pushed wearily to his feet and helped her pull Keir up between them. "Everyone off this ship if you want to live." There was no time to soften her words, not now. Only time for the truth. The captain was right. Now wasn't about saving their own lives, but about salvaging their last chance to bring Lenya back from the brink of destruction.

Veren pulled Imogen to the gap in the rail. She'd stopped fighting him and cast one more desolate look at her father. He lifted a hand toward her, and then Veren pulled her with him as they jumped. Bronagh went next, disappearing over the side.

Tierney and Gulliver dragged Keir to the gap, but as they reached it, the deck tilted and they tumbled off the edge. A scream lodged in her throat seconds before she hit the water.

The blast of cold had her moving quickly to grab hold of Keir. Gulliver swam toward her, his tail working just as hard as his arms and legs. Together, they breached the surface and made their way to the floating side of the hull. The others reached it before them.

A crack rent the air, and they looked back just in time to see the deck split in two as the aft reared up.

"No," Imogen screamed for her father.

Tierney pulled half her body onto the wood. "Grab hold of me." No one moved. She tugged Keir up with her. "Now!" Hands reached for her, clutching her arms, her shoulders. She sent her magic into each of them, keeping them warm as freezing water crashed over their heads.

It was the only way she knew how to give them a chance.

Tierney's eyes fluttered open as she felt solid ground beneath her. The ground was cold, but it was land. The shocking memory of the previous night jolted her awake. She lay on a snow-covered beach, water and chunks of ice rushing in with the tide. Iskalt. It had to be.

And then, she remembered everything. "Keir." Her eyes searched the beach. Gulliver lay pressed against her, her magic keeping him warm. But the others were nowhere to be found.

Boots crunched in the snow, and Tierney shifted to look behind her where Veren walked toward her up the beach. "I was just returning to get you two. I helped the others into the cover of the forest. We have a fire going to keep us warm."

The woods. Tierney surveyed the landscape, her mind reeling with too much information at once. Behind them were dense forests leading to a range of majestic mountains, their peaks unreachable by even the strongest of Iskalt warriors. "We're …"

"In Iskalt." Veren nodded with a grin. "We made it."

Not all of them. The agony of their losses lanced through her. Keir was gone. Had they lost his body to the sea? She wanted to cry, to give herself a moment to break down, but that wasn't her. Keir wouldn't want her to fall apart now, not when they were so close to saving his kingdom.

"I'm guessing we're not far from the Northeastern Vatlands."

Tierney tried to place them on a map in her mind. Her father had made her learn every inch of Iskalt during her studies. "We need to find a way through the mountains."

"Why don't you wake Gullie and come to the fire. You must be exhausted from keeping us warm all night."

"Is your …"

He nodded, knowing what she wanted to ask. Veren now had full use of his magic too as long as the moon was in the sky. It was most likely how he'd started the fire.

Tierney pushed herself up onto her aching legs and nudged Gulliver with her foot.

He grumbled and rolled over, his body shaking from the cold without her there to warm him.

"Wake up."

Gulliver groaned as his eyes opened. "What happened?"

"We made it through an unsurvivable storm, lost our ship and way too many fae, but we're here. We're home."

"Home." He said the word like it was foreign to him and got to his feet.

Veren clapped them each on the shoulder. "Come on."

They trudged up the beach, crossing into the canopy of trees, a carpet of pine needles soft beneath their feet. Tierney's entire body ached like she'd just gone five rounds against the prison magic. But no amount of exhaustion could shake the triumph of her homecoming.

The first person she saw was Imogen. She'd curled in on herself near the fire, tears streaking her face. Tierney's heart broke for the girl who'd now lost both parents to tragic circumstances. She leaned down when she reached her. "Your father was a hero." Without him, they'd never have made it.

She didn't respond, didn't move.

Bronagh sat across the fire, her expression sad. They'd survived, but the cost of the journey was high.

And next to her, resting his back against a tree … Tierney stopped, her breath stuttering in her chest. Keir's eyes were closed, but his chest rose and fell with slow breaths.

"How?" she whispered.

Veren shrugged. "We aren't sure. Maybe it was your magic or simply time. He woke up on the beach, same as us. He wanted me to get you to the fire first, but I knew you could stay warm on your own."

Her steps faltered, and she stared at him, taking in the way his hair stuck up in every direction, the cut on his cheek. He was still beautiful, even if a bit rough. His eyes slid open, latching onto hers.

Gulliver trudged past her to edge closer to the fire, his tail hanging limp and frosty.

Flames flickered in Keir's dark gaze, and she stepped toward him, each movement slow, tentative.

He lifted his chin to track her with his eyes. "I heard you jumped in after me." His voice was harsh, raspy, as if he'd injured some integral part of his throat.

Tierney lifted one corner of her mouth. "Someone had to save you."

He arched a brow. "Do I have to thank someone who speaks with their ego?"

She lowered herself to the ground beside him and nodded. "Yes. You very much have to thank me. And then, you have to do it again."

He tried to lean in, but when she noticed he didn't have the strength, she brushed her lips against his.

"Is that thank you enough?" he whispered.

"Absolutely not." This time, she let the kiss linger. He tasted of saltwater and life. Her forehead rested against his, and she breathed him in, unable to truly believe he was here in front of her. That they'd made it to Iskalt, even if they'd ended up in the far Eastern Vatlands, away from anything resembling civilization.

Veren sat down. "As nauseating as you two are, I think it's time we talk about what happens next."

He was right. They didn't have much time to linger. Tierney's stomach gave a fierce grumble. "We're going to need to find some food."

"That shouldn't be a problem now that we have our magic. Tierney, you and I will need to hunt."

Hunt. Her eyes widened. The mountains. She knew exactly where they could go. "There's a hunting lodge near Lake Fryst, just beyond the vatlands. My father rarely uses it, but if we can make it there, we can take the time to recover before setting out for the long journey to the palace."

"It's still going to be a tough journey to reach Lake Fryst." Veren looked into the fire for a moment, lost in thought before he finally nodded. "But it's our best chance. None of us are fit for a long journey across the wilds of Iskalt. We need at least a day of rest here before we set out."

Several days on foot with clothes not fit for the Iskalt snows, and their trunks at the bottom of the sea. Just perfect.

At least she had her magic. With that, she was confident she'd get them all home safely to see their families again.

Chapter 10
KEIR

Keir had never known such cold.

He would rather face the maelstrom a thousand times over if it meant he could get out of this frozen mountain pass with its drifting snow he could barely move through and the sheer cliffs that rose so high on either side of the trail they blocked out the sky.

They'd been climbing for days, huddled close to Tierney and Veren to absorb whatever warmth they could give them with their strange magic.

He still couldn't get over how easily magic came to her now. From within. Without the benefit of a totem to harness it. It wasn't natural.

They began their descent that morning, and already they were making much better time than they had on the upward climb.

"We may reach the valley tomorrow." Tierney shivered under the too thin layers of her shawl.

"I like the sound of a valley." Bronagh's teeth chattered.

"Don't get too excited. It's a frozen valley." Gulliver huddled beside her. "Nothing but snow and more snow."

"At least it will be flat." Tierney's eyes flickered with magic in a way Keir found fascinating.

That was a startling development Keir hadn't expected. It was a little unnerving to look into her eyes and see such power shining within their depths. It was astounding that she and Veren could use their magic to keep them all from freezing to death and still have enough energy left over to climb a mountain. Granted, they both slept like the dead whenever they made camp.

"We have to hunt tonight, Veren." Tierney trudged through the snow, her breath puffing out in white clouds. "We need a good meal if we're all going to make it to the hunting lodge in one piece. Do you think we'll reach the forests before nightfall?"

"I will hunt for something, no matter if we reach the forests or not," Veren said. "Then, you can rest."

"I can hunt." Keir kept his eyes on the ground, making sure his frozen foot had solid purchase before taking another labored step through the thigh-deep snow.

"We don't have proper weapons." Veren panted as he helped Bronagh through the snowdrifts. "The only things to hunt in these mountains are the rare small stag or mountain goat you can find down among the forests. They're hard to find and too fast for anything but magic to bring them down."

Imogen nearly toppled over, and Veren tried to catch her, but he was weak from using too much magic in the pre dawn hours. Keir managed to grab her around the waist and settled her back on her feet.

"Thank you." The captain's daughter had grown quiet on their journey through the mountain pass.

"It will be nice to have something more than shriveled berries and nuts for supper." The Grima queen's voice was muffled by the extra layer of fabric she wore draped around her neck and covering her mouth. All three women had created scarves and mittens from scraps of fabric they'd torn from their underthings.

"I will need help with the butchering." Veren sucked in a shallow breath. It was difficult to fill their lungs at this altitude. "I'm not sure I can manage that and the hunting without dropping wherever I stand."

"I'll go with you. We'll haul the kill back to camp between us." Keir rubbed his hands together to keep the blood flowing. "I'll do the butchering while you rest."

"Toby," Tierney muttered.

She said his name often.

"Can you sense where he is?" Gulliver asked.

"Toby?" She turned glassy eyes on Gulliver. "Oh, yes." She shook her head, something she did when returning from wherever she went when she searched for her twin. "We are out of practice. It's strange." She looked up at the cloudy sky that blocked out the sun and left them trembling in their frozen boots.

"He knows I am trying to make my way home, but I don't think he can tell where we are yet. We are still too far apart. It almost feels like ... he's not in Iskalt."

"Of course he's not." Gulliver snorted. He walked with his arms tucked inside his tunic and his tail wrapped around his waist. "Toby is more sensitive than Tia. He's probably known for a while now where we were. My guess is he's either in Eldur, searching for a way across the fire plains, or he's in Gelsi with Brandon, scouring the Aghadoon library for answers. The one thing I know for certain is Toby is ten steps ahead of everyone else, and considering he's the smartest of us all, he probably started heading right for us the moment he sensed our return."

"I think he just said you're thick-headed." Keir wanted to laugh, but it was too cold.

"Oh, no, he's right." Tierney suppressed a giggle. "Toby is the level-headed one with a sensitive spirit. If he'd been with us from the beginning, we would have been home ages ago—even without the benefit of his stronger O'Shea magic."

"I am anxious to meet this brother of yours." Keir measured his steps to Tierney's shorter stride. The day grew late, and she would be weary by the time they made camp. "Does he look like you?"

"He has darker hair and coloring, and he's much taller than me. He's gentle and kind." A beautiful smile played around her lips. She loved her brother very much. "Honestly, he's nothing like me. Or if he is, he is the best parts of me compounded a hundred times."

"Then, I shall like him immensely."

Keir sat by the fire, alone in the growing darkness. He'd never been so tired in his life. Weary to the bone, starving and freezing, he took it upon himself to see to their dinner while the others rested in their makeshift shelter.

They'd reached the shelter of the forests just before nightfall. It was a welcome change, where the snow wasn't quite knee-deep below the canopy of fir trees. Iskalt trees looked a little weak and stunted to Keir, but he was used to the massive ancient forests of Vondur.

While Keir and Veren hunted, the others had gathered bundles of fir branches they propped against a craggy cliff to create a lean-to structure large enough for all six of them. They would sleep easy tonight, gathered together in the warmth of Tierney and Veren's magic.

He could use a little of that right about now. He held his hands out to the fire.

"Smells wonderful." Tierney came to join him. "Is it done yet?"

"I think the strange creature might be ready." He turned the spit over the fire, checking the meat one last time.

"You don't have goats in Lenya?"

"We do, but they are small and annoying. Not much use for anything. This animal is huge in comparison."

"Mountain goats are a bit larger, but I'm hungry enough to eat this poor fella all by myself." Tierney tugged her shawl around her shoulders.

"We'll have to wait for it to cool off a bit."

"Let me handle that." She reached for the spit, pulling the creature from the fire with her bare hands.

"Watch out; it's hot." He lunged after her.

"Magic." She waved her fingertips at him, her eyes swirling.

Keir shook his head with a laugh. "I'll never get used to someone using their magic for trivial things. It seems like such a waste."

"Our magic comes from within. There is no limitation for us except for the time of day—for most, at least. So, I'm going to use mine to block the heat of this scalding hot meat so I can get it in my stomach." She tore off a big piece and passed it from hand to hand for a moment before she held it out to Keir.

"It's ready." She smiled, taking a big piece for herself. She made no hesitations, sinking her teeth into her dinner with a groan of pleasure.

"Yes, dinner is ready." Gulliver came to sit with them, helping himself to the basic fare. "Delicious." He nodded eagerly. "Oh, how I've missed you, dear succulent, juicy meat." He held up his haunch of goat. "Thanks for this, Keir." He turned to Tierney. "And thanks for the dome of heat. This is the first time I've been warm in days."

"I'm just harnessing the heat of the fire so it stays with us longer." Tierney shrugged. "We haven't had a fire big enough to do that with yet."

"Dome of heat?" Keir wasn't sure what that meant, but it had grown a lot warmer since Tierney came to sit with him.

"My magic pulls the heat in close to us, trapping it so we stay warm. If we keep the fire smoldering tonight, I should be able to pull the heat into the lean-to."

"Oh my goodness, it's so warm over here," Bronagh exclaimed as she entered the circle.

The others made their way over one at a time until they all sat around the blazing fire, stuffing their faces in silence.

It was the best thing Keir had ever eaten. Rich and flavorful, the roasted goat warmed his stomach and re-energized him.

"Did you do something extra with your magic?" He took another bite. Something about it seemed off. He'd eaten much of the roasted game on the trail, and it never fortified him quite like this.

"Maybe." Tierney gave him a mischievous smile. "I figured we could all use a little zing in our steps for tomorrow."

"You should conserve your energy. You're pushing yourself too hard."

"My magic?" She grinned, reaching for his hand. "I don't think you realize just how different my magic is from what you're used to in Lenya. I have done far more than keep a few people warm all day and night and make their food taste better. I'll be fine."

"Then, why do you collapse at the end of each day like you can't keep your eyes open?"

"Why?" She looked around at their surroundings. "Did you forget I'm a princess? I don't do hikes through snowy mountain passes. I do horses and sleigh rides with fur blankets and hot drinks. And for the last months, I've lived in a world where it's sweltering hot all the time. I'm just exhausted from all the physical stuff, Keir. My magic doesn't drain me like that, not unless I use way more than this. Please don't worry about me."

Veren came back from a trip into the woods, searching for some sort of plant he thought might grow near here.

"Look what I found!" He held up a fistful of an ugly-looking, shriveled green flower.

"Oh, is that what I think it is?" Tierney's eyes lit up with excitement.

"What is it?" Bronagh asked as Veren set a large nutshell packed with snow on the rocks closest to the fire.

"Mountain jasmine." As the snow melted, he crushed a handful of the leaves and added it to the water to steep.

Cupping his hands around the makeshift teacup, he heated the water with his magic. Taking a sip, he passed it to Bronagh.

"Oh, that smells lovely." She took a sip for herself and passed it to Imogen. "It's sweet and minty."

Veren went to work on the second cup of tea as they finished the first one. It felt good to drink something warm and sweet after days of drinking ice-cold water from melted snow.

"With a good night's rest, we'll be ready for the hike down to the valley in the morning." Tierney's eyes shone brightly in the firelight. "We'll be safe at my father's lodge soon if I don't get us lost. I think the hardest part of our journey is behind us now. Pretty soon, we'll be wrapped up in diplomatic meetings, and we'll have help heading to Lenya quicker than we can blink."

Something about that statement left Keir feeling almost sad. Out here on the trail, they were just a couple of weary travelers. Their needs were basic. Food. Shelter. Water. Fire. Companionship.

Once they reached the lodge, he was no longer just Keir. And she wouldn't be just Tierney. He would be representing Vondur, and Tierney would return to her role as the heir of Iskalt. Nothing would be simple for them anymore.

Keir wasn't sure Tierney knew what a valley was. This frozen wasteland, with its fierce winds and unforgiving, bitter cold, was like no valley he'd ever experienced before.

Nothing stood between them and the elements but Tierney's magical warmth. They made minimal progress across the frozen tundra. Huddled together, they moved slowly through what Keir could only describe as a howling blizzard.

He couldn't see anything but the person to his left and his right. They held hands so they wouldn't lose each other. But the wind made it impossible to speak.

Now and then, Veren brought them to a halt while he figured out which direction to follow. The first night on the open tundra, they had no fire, but Tierney created a bubble of warmth where they could rest without the snowfall and wind. They ate the rest of the roasted goat and slept fitfully before heading out at dawn for more of the same.

They were all running low on strength, and no matter what Tierney claimed, using her magic round the clock was taking its toll on her. If they didn't reach the hunting lodge soon, she was going to collapse.

Keir held onto her hand, her fingertips nearly fused to his in the icy temperatures.

Bronagh struggled to put one foot in front of the other as Veren coaxed her along. And poor Imogen clung to Gulliver's hand, shivering despite all Tierney did to keep them warm.

They were like sitting ducks out in the open like this. Keir wanted to ask if they should be worried about wolves when he heard barking and howling in the distance.

In their exhaustion, the last thing they could handle was a pack of wolves preying on the weak and injured. They wouldn't make it through the night.

Keir vowed he would keep watch all night if he had to. This close to their destination, they couldn't fail now.

"Toby!" Tierney cried, charging through the snow with renewed energy. "I'm here! I'm here!" She sobbed as she tumbled to the ground.

"Tia!" Keir rushed to her side, trying to pull her back to her feet. "We have to keep going." He tugged on her arm but didn't have the strength to pick her up. "Like you said, the hard part is behind us. This is just a walk across a field, right?"

She pointed into the white blur of the blizzard before them. "I'm here!" she cried out again.

Two bundled figures emerged from the snow.

"Who is that?" Was he seeing things?

"It's him." Tierney sank back down to her knees and fell into the snow.

Chapter II
Tierney

Strong arms lifted Tierney out of the snow, and for a moment, she wondered if she was dreaming. She'd imagined this for so long it didn't seem real.

"Dad." Tears froze on her face as her magic slipped, letting the cold permeate her skin.

Lochlan O'Shea stared down at her with glassy eyes and pulled her closer to his chest. "I've got you. I'm here."

"We need to get them to the lodge." Her mom's voice was like a soft blanket settling over her. She ran a hand over Tierney's hair.

"Guys." Toby walked forward. "Stop staring at her and get moving. They're probably waiting anxiously."

They? Who else was here? Tierney couldn't get the words past her lips. If she tried, she'd start sobbing right here in front of all the people she'd just led through the frozen tundra.

"It's just a little farther," her mom said to the others. "Come, we'll do introductions once we reach shelter." She wrapped an arm around Gulliver and leaned in. "We've missed you, kiddo."

Her parents would never stop thinking of her, Toby, and Gulliver as kids, but right now, that knowledge warmed Tierney. They were kids, barely out of their childhood, not ready to traverse wild seas or unknown kingdoms. And yet, they had.

Her father didn't set her down, opting to carry her across deep drifts, bundled close to his snow-dusted coat, held safe in his strong arms. Her father, the man she'd run from. The one who'd tried to force her into a marriage she wasn't ready for. He was also the best man she knew.

He'd been wrong, but her actions weren't exactly the right ones either.

She felt pressure on her hand as a mitten slid over her frozen fingers. Lifting her head, she met Toby's gaze. Her brother, the one who'd led her home. She never wanted to be so far from him again. Not only because it meant going without her magic, but it wasn't until that moment as he walked beside her that she felt whole again.

A sigh of relief rushed through her when the hunting lodge came into view, a white-capped wooden monstrosity set along the rocky shores of Lake Fryst. She would never understand her father's and uncle's love for the cold of the far reaches of Iskalt. If she never traveled this far east again, it would be too soon.

The door of the lodge burst open, and there was Uncle Griff. Aunt Riona rushed out after him, her wings shooting her into the air as she crossed the snow.

Keir startled back with a curse as Bronagh gasped. Imogen just stared, her eyes wide.

Gulliver took off into a half-run, half-stumble. Riona collided with him, lifting him into the air in a hug and turning to reach for Griffin, who'd also started across the snow, though at a much slower pace.

The three of them clung to each other much the same way Tierney wanted to do with her family, but she couldn't make herself move, exhaustion weighing her down.

"Get him inside, Griff," Lochlan barked. "They started to freeze the moment Tia stopped using her magic to warm them."

Griffin scowled at him. "And Brea didn't step in?" He pulled Gulliver protectively closer.

"I'm kind of a mess right now, Griff." Brea sniffed and blubbered as she ushered them all toward the lodge.

Listening to her parents and uncle argue made Tierney smile. Toby caught sight of her and matched the expression. This was their family; this was home. The two brothers loved each other, but sometimes they also wanted to kill each other.

The moment they stepped into the lodge, Lochlan set Tierney down. She wobbled and righted herself before launching into her mom's arms.

Brea sniffled. "My girl," she cried. "I can't believe you're home."

"Mom, you're hogging her." Toby pulled Tierney away, wrapping long arms around her. She buried her face in his chest, finally letting a few sobs break through. Her power thrummed with approval, finally finding its other half. "See what happens when you go off to have a birthday party in the human realm without me," he muttered into her hair.

Tierney laughed, but it sounded more like a sob. "Never again." She looked up, meeting his glassy eyes. "You know it wasn't planned, right? It just sort of happened. I'd never leave you behind."

"Yeah." He squeezed her tighter. "I know." Leading her over to the fire roaring in the giant hearth, Toby sat Tierney down and wrapped her in a thick fur.

For a moment, she'd forgotten it wasn't just the two of them, but then Imogen sat beside her and burrowed under her fur, snuggling into her. "Oh, these are my friends." Tierney looked up at the two foreign royals then at Imogen. "I'll explain later, but for now, know they saved our lives."

"No one saved my life." Veren sat on the floor near the hearth, getting as close to the flames as possible.

Gulliver laughed, the sound musical after so many teeth-chattering days with nothing to smile about. "Except Bron." He gestured to Bronagh, the queen who'd allowed Veren to join her court.

Veren shared a smile with Bronagh but didn't respond.

Keir stood back from the others, watching silently, observing.

Uncle Griff walked out of the kitchen with a tray stacked high with bowls. "Who wants something hot to eat?"

"Oh, definitely me." Gulliver reached for a bowl. "What did you make, Dad?"

"What else would he make?" Her uncle wasn't exactly the best cook in the world, but there was one dish he excelled at, one she'd never imagined she'd eat again. "At least, I hope he didn't try anything else."

"Har har." Griffin rolled his eyes. "Yes, it's turkey soup."

"Turkey?" Keir stepped forward. "We have such an animal, but they'd never survive the cold of this place."

Veren dug into his soup with a sigh. "Are there any biscuits?"

"Yes." Riona carried out a plate. "And don't worry, Tia, I made these." She shot her a wink.

Tierney caught Keir's eye. "The wild northern turkeys adapt to their climate. They aren't plentiful here, but they are sometimes seen. My mother is the only one in the family who can ever catch them."

"Not true," her father said.

"Very true." Her mother laughed. "Though, I don't like to harm anything. I rarely go hunting, but if my hubby begs, I'll trap something for him. Just to get him to be quiet." She patted Lochlan's cheek.

"Hubby?" Imogen looked up at Tierney, confused.

"Our queen," Veren started, his mouth full, "was raised human. She says the oddest things."

Imogen's eyes went wide.

Tierney accepted a bowl of soup, not letting it cool or even using her power to do it before digging in. Soft noodles, thick chunks of turkey. It was heaven. Someone handed her a biscuit, and she dipped it in, moaning when she bit off the softened part. There was nothing better.

She watched Keir accept a bowl and sit with supreme satisfaction. He'd barely looked at her since her family found them, but that wasn't her concern at the moment. Not when Toby wedged in between her and the arm of the settee.

"Mom, stop staring at me." While Keir wouldn't look at her, her mother hadn't stopped. "You're being a creep."

Her mother laughed, her eyes tearing up again. "It's just … I'd started to think I'd never be able to creep you out again."

She was so weird, but a weird Tierney hadn't wanted to live the rest of her life without. Tears gathered in her eyes once more, spilling down her cheeks. She'd thought none of these fae would ever stand before her again, would ever make her cry or laugh so hard it hurt.

Once she finished her soup, Griffin took her bowl, and she leaned her head on Toby's shoulder. "I'm surprised it's just you guys." The rest of her siblings would have clamored to come, no matter how young they were. Then, there were Uncle Myles and Aunt Neeve, Alona and Finn, Hector, the Myrkurian king who acted like another uncle, and every single one of her cousins.

"Trust me, it was a hard fight to get them all to back off. We didn't want to overwhelm you. Plus, we were going through a portal and didn't think bringing an army of fae to the human world was the best idea."

The mention of a portal made Tierney's insides clench, her stomach curdling.

Toby, reading her as always, took her hand. "Don't worry, we aren't making you travel home that way. We brought a sled and dogs."

Her face brightened. She'd only visited Lake Fryst a few times but she'd never had the opportunity to travel by dogsled. It wasn't needed when the O'Shea's had portals. Other Iskaltians used them to traverse the tundra all the time.

The chatter continued as the others finished eating, not touching on anything important. Tierney didn't tell her parents who Keir and Bronagh were, not yet. That time would come.

No one asked about Siobhan, and she knew they probably assumed something happened to her if she wasn't here with them. How would Tierney tell them she'd never found her friend? How would she face Siobhan's father?

"Okay," her mother said, sitting on the other side of Imogen. "It's time we learn who your friends are, Tierney."

Tierney wasn't ready for the truth. For them to know there was yet another kingdom to save, that the fire plains could endanger Eldur and eventually Iskalt.

So, she went with a version of the truth. "This is Imogen." She hugged the young girl to her side. "The bravest sailor I've ever met. Her father was the captain of the ship that got us here."

Her mother was astute enough not to ask what happened to him. "Well, Imogen, it is a pleasure to meet such a brave sea woman. I, myself, am quite accomplished on the water."

Tierney rolled her eyes. "You went on a ship once, Mom. And that was like a hundred years ago."

Her mother gave her a playful scowl. "It's nice to have you back, Tia, if only so none of us can have our egos inflate too large."

Tierney stuck out her tongue before continuing. "That's Bronagh. She's … a good friend." She sent Bronagh a smile.

A laugh bubbled out of her when she caught her father scowling at Keir but not letting anyone see. "That's Keir Dagnan. He's …" She didn't know what he was. "A good man."

Lochlan stood and extended a hand. "Thank you for bringing my daughter home safely."

Tierney met her mom's eyes, and they both rolled them simultaneously. Her dad was so predictable. Women fought in his army, yet when it came to his daughters, he was a big old fogey.

"Uh, Dad." Toby laughed. "Pretty sure Tierney didn't need anyone to get her here. Seriously, you're so dense."

Lochlan let go of Keir's hand and looked from his daughter to his wife. "I didn't mean … sometimes, you O'Shea women …" He shook his head.

To Tierney's surprise, Keir spoke up. "In my kingdom, our customs do not favor women. But your daughter opened my eyes to how wrong we have been, and how capable women truly are. She didn't need me to save her, sir. She saved all of us."

Tierney's cheeks warmed as she waited for her father to correct Keir. The king wasn't a sir, but Keir was also a king and wouldn't bow as her father probably expected.

Yet, to her surprise, her father let it go and looked at her with pride in his eyes instead.

Veren had inched closer to the fire, looking into the flickering flames. "Just so you know, your Majesty, I'm not marrying your daughter."

Tierney choked on a laugh. Keir sent Veren a dark glare.

Veren continued, "I thought we should get that cleared up first thing. I've spent enough time with her recently, and I'm not going to live with her for the rest of my life."

Toby and Tierney both burst out laughing.

"As if I'd marry you." Tierney shook her head, just glad to be home.

They weren't traveling home by portal. That news had been more welcome than any other. Griffin and Riona would go on ahead while the others stayed at the lodge for a day to recuperate. Her father argued they should wait longer so everyone regained their strength, but Tierney knew they didn't have time to wait when the people of Lenya were counting on them. Who knew how far the fire plains had expanded in their absence? Were Eavha and Declan okay?

They were leaving in only a few hours, but Tierney couldn't sleep. She sat in the sitting room alone in front of the fire, staring into it and remembering everyone left behind. She pulled the fur blanket up to her chin, her magic resting peacefully inside her.

Footsteps sounded on the wooden floor, and she looked up to find Toby approaching her. "Couldn't sleep?" he asked.

She shook her head.

"Me neither." He sat on the floor in front of the hearth, looking up at her. "My mind just wouldn't stop whirring, thinking about the fact that you're finally home."

"Aren't I usually the one who overthinks everything?"

A wry smile spread across his face. "Guess I needed to make up for your absence. I knew where you were. All this time, I've known you were across the fire plains, and I couldn't get to you. We're supposed to save each other, and you were out of my reach."

Tierney slid to the floor and pulled the blanket around them both. "I was so scared without you." She'd tried to hide it, even from herself. A beat passed between them. "I didn't have my magic."

His eyes snapped to hers. "What?"

"There is something about the fire plains that kept us from our magic, but it was more for me. I was too far from Iskalt, from you. I could feel my magic just under the surface, but it couldn't come when I called. I couldn't feel you."

"I'm sorry you went through that." Toby had never had magic except for the connection between them that amplified her power. That and the portal magic he gained through their O'Shea heritage.

"Is that how you always feel? Powerless? Helpless? Like there's something inside you, some strength that you can't bring to the surface?"

"Not really." He shrugged. "But I've never known what it is to have power other than opening portals. This … emptiness is the only thing I've ever felt."

Toby leaned his head against hers as they faced the flames.

"What was it like?" Toby asked. "Across the fire planes."

"Terrifying." It was the first word that came to mind. "At first, all I could think about was returning home. We were all separated coming out of the portal, and I didn't know where the others were. I was so alone and without magic."

He squeezed her tighter to his side.

"But then ... it got better. I found Gullie, and our circumstances changed." She wasn't yet ready to tell him about Keir holding her prisoner or his father almost killing her. "Eventually, it felt like this grand adventure. Lenya isn't like here. They're struggling. Their magic is dying, and they've been at war for generations. After a while, I knew I could make a difference. It's been so long since I felt ... useful in that way."

"Since the prison realm?"

She nodded.

He pushed out a breath. "Me too."

"I'm just glad to be back."

"And these fae who've returned with you?"

"They need us, Tobes." It was all she needed to say. He understood.

"Then, we'll do whatever it is we can to help them."

"I love you."

He sent her a knowing smile. "If you love me, you'll tell me what the deal is with this Keir dude."

"Dad wouldn't like you saying dude." He always joked his fae children were too human. Their mom had made sure of it.

"Don't change the subject."

"I really don't know what you're talking about."

"Really?" He nudged her. "That's what you're going with?"

"You're nosey."

"We never keep anything from each other. I mean, the first time I kissed Logan, you knew before Darra even did."

"Because Darra would have told Alona." Logan's sister was one of Tierney's best friends, but her favorite pastime was getting her older brother in trouble. It had taken their parents a little while to stop thinking of Logan and Toby as cousins. There was no blood relation, after all.

"No, it's because you would have guessed it anyway. Just like I know there's something about Keir you aren't saying. The way you two kept avoiding each other's gazes with Dad between you ... it was pretty epic."

"Shut up."

"Tell me."

"No."

"Tierney ..."

"Don't you dare." She knew what was coming.

He lunged sideways, his fingers digging into her sides to pin her to the ground. The blanket dropped away as the two of them wrestled. Tierney brought her knee up into his stomach and twisted.

Toby was daring but he'd never been able to beat her in a fight.

She scrambled away from him and reached for the iron fire poker next to the hearth. Toby ran for a broom leaning against the kitchen doorway. He returned and took up his stance.

"You can't keep anything from me." He jumped, bringing his broom down like a quarterstaff.

She blocked it with the poker-sword. "Try me." A grin spread across her face. Now, she felt like she was truly back where she belonged.

Toby ran at her, and she jumped away, leaping up onto the settee and over the back, landing in a crouch. Toby tried the same move, tumbling as he hit the floor.

Tierney was on him before he could catch his balance, sweeping his feet out from under him. He landed on his butt, and she pushed him back, arcing the poker. He blocked it with a grin.

"You've been practicing." She laughed.

"Can't have you beating me forever."

"What is the meaning of this?" Their dad's heavy footsteps crossed the room.

Tierney and Toby looked at each other, suppressing grins.

"You should probably let your brother up, honey." Their mom bit back a laugh, her cheeks puffed up with effort.

More entered the room, finding the twins still in their fighting stances with poker and broom.

Gulliver shrugged and went back to his room, used to their antics. Veren followed him, mumbling something about blasted royals waking him up.

Keir only stared, one eyebrow raised.

Someone gripped the back of Tierney's shirt, hauling her up.

"Let me go, Uncle Griff."

He clicked his tongue. "Tia, how many times have I told you that when you pull a dirty trick, don't let them get their weapon up in time to stop you?"

Lochlan groaned. "Letting you spend time with my daughter was the worst mistake I ever made."

"I don't know." Brea lifted one shoulder. "I quite enjoy watching her beat her brother."

"Mom," Toby groaned. "Thanks for playing favorites."

Her face turned serious. "I love all my children equally." She held a hand down. "But you know, girl power and all that. Plus, it's especially entertaining as long as you don't kill each other."

Lochlan turned with a grunt to return to bed.

Griffin scrubbed a hand over his face. "Please don't wake me up again. We have a long journey ahead of us."

"Griff." Brea shook her head. "You're traveling by portal. The rest of us don't have that luxury."

They returned to their rooms to sleep, and Tierney started toward the one she shared with Bronagh.

"I will get it out of you," Toby called.

"Go on. It's fun when you try, baby brother."

"Only by a few minutes!"

She sank into her bed, smiling at how normal the evening felt.

Chapter 12
Keir

They arrived back at the palace after five days on the sled, five nights of making camp, and staying warm with fires and magic. Keir couldn't take his eyes from the spires stretching toward the sky, the ornate balconies glittering with marble and some kind of dark gemstone.

It was grander than anything he'd ever seen in Lenya. The Vondurian palace was a fortress, meant to protect the people in a time of war. Nothing about this place said war, not the charming villages they passed by nor the cheerful peace of the snowy fields.

"It looks the same," Tierney whispered beside him. "Like time has just frozen in place."

"Time always marches on, Princess." Keir had taken on a more formal tone since Tierney decided not to tell her parents who he was. She had to have her reasons, and he would follow her lead. But it meant keeping his distance from her and from her brother's curious gaze.

They were twins who looked nothing alike at first glance. But the closer he studied them, the more he realized they had the same delicate cheekbones, the same curve of their eyes. And their smiles … while Toby's didn't hold nearly as much mirth in his, there was something secretive in the way he grinned that reminded Keir of Tierney.

Like he knew more than he revealed. It was as if he could see things that hadn't been said. The way Keir felt for Tierney, for one.

The guards near the front door snapped to attention. They didn't wear their battle armor for their post, and that told Keir they didn't have to be prepared to march against an enemy at any given moment.

Both of the guards smiled as the group approached on foot, having left the dogs in the village with their handler.

"Princess," the one on the right started, a young man with a too familiar look of genuine affection. "Welcome home."

"Caleb." Tierney ran toward them and hugged the guard, an improper gesture for a princess. She then hugged the other, a much older woman. "Clodagh."

"Princess." Clodagh had tears in her eyes. "We've been so worried about you."

Keir waited for someone to tell them it wasn't right to act so familiar with a member of the royal family. But he'd learned on the journey that few fae told Tierney what to do.

Caleb bowed to the king. "They're waiting for you, sire."

"Thank you, Caleb." King Lochlan patted the man's shoulder as he passed. "Tell Kala we're wishing her well with the pregnancy."

"I will. Thank you, your Majesty."

They walked under a grand archway into an even grander entryway. The moment they passed through the doors, the cold disappeared. Keir found an explanation in the hearth nearby, not wanting to think deeper about the immense magic these fae held.

Next to them, Lenya was little more than a cow pasture full of fae who'd been killing each other for too long. Why would the kings and queens of these great realms want to help them?

As if she could sense his thoughts, Tierney's hand slid into his, squeezing before letting go. It was like she was telling him to trust her.

That was something, he'd come to realize, that had been inevitable.

Brea walked past them and turned to face the group. "I gave Griff instructions to have rooms made up for you all, but before we can be allowed to rest, I'm afraid there are fae waiting on us."

Tierney groaned. "Don't tell me you've called a council meeting right when I've returned. Can't I have a day before jumping back into heir duties?"

Brea wrapped an arm around her shoulders and pulled her along. "Do you have so little faith in me?" She leaned in, dropping her voice, but not low enough Keir couldn't hear. "Your father suggested it, but I wouldn't let him."

"It would have been protocol," Lochlan grumbled.

"Last time we were missing, they showed up without being summoned," Toby said.

Bronagh looked from Toby to Tierney. "Do royal children go missing quite frequently here?"

"You'd be surprised." Gulliver laughed.

Tierney scowled. "Toby and I just went to visit our cousins in Fargelsi. I left a note, so technically we weren't missing."

"Except, the note ended up getting lost underneath a bed." Brea shook her head. "And they were gone for two months that just happened to coincide with the Fargelsian Festival of Lights."

"Our aunt is the Queen of Fargelsi," Tierney explained. "It was all blown way out of proportion."

Keir barely followed the conversation as they walked through the palace. What he wanted was a bath and a good night's rest in a soft bed. The latter being something he hadn't experienced since leaving Vondur.

All he knew was, it sounded like Tierney's life had been so different from his. He'd spent his youth training for battle and then fighting in them, not enjoying ceremonies or parties. There were no relatives to visit, no loving family except his sister.

Servants bowed as they passed, issuing well wishes to Tierney and Gulliver. The palace hummed with life at their return, as if everyone down to the lowliest servant had mourned their absence.

"Veren, your father has been summoned and should arrive shortly." Brea sent him a kind smile. "He has been beside himself."

"Losing one's heir does that." Veren didn't look particularly happy at the prospect of a reunion.

The halls quieted as they passed a pair of guards into a more secluded corridor. Tapestries adorned the walls, dressing them in bright colors that added to the warmth.

They stopped outside a set of ornate wooden doors.

"Why would the council be in the residence?" Gulliver asked.

A smile slipped across Tierney's face. "Because they didn't call the council." She shoved open the doors to reveal a massive sitting room brimming with fae.

Griff and Riona were there, but Tierney also seemed to recognize others.

A man ran for them first, sweeping Tierney into a tight hug. "My favorite O'Shea girl is back."

"After all our friendship," Brea shook her head, "you love my daughter more than me."

Tierney pulled back. "Mom, Uncle Myles is my friend now. I thought you'd gotten over that when I was like ten."

A tall woman with skin much darker than Tierney's joined them. "Myles, she won't disappear if you let her go."

"Aunt Neeve." Tierney hugged her.

It seemed everyone Tierney ever met was here. Her younger siblings circled her, clamoring for attention.

And then, she screamed.

A dark-skinned girl with long curly hair and bright eyes crossed the room, tears rolling down her cheeks. Tierney ran for her, joined soon by Gulliver. The three of them cried together, clutching each other like they couldn't bear letting go.

"You're alive," Tierney cried.

"You're back," the girl said.

Veren stepped up beside Keir. "Siobhan," he explained.

Relief flooded through him. For months, he'd watched Tierney disappear periodically into grief and guilt at her friend's disappearance, at the fact that she couldn't find her. This reunion meant everything to Tierney.

The door burst open behind them, and a guard ushered in a frazzled man with pale skin and a mop of blond hair. "Veren." He rushed forward and yanked Veren into a hug.

"Father." Veren's voice held a familiarity but also something more. When Keir glimpsed the tears on his face, he understood. Relief.

It wasn't until that moment he realized that no matter how much Keir had wanted Tierney to stay forever in Vondur, she'd never belonged there, and she never would.

None of them were meant to stay. He caught sight of Bronagh watching Veren, the same realization on her face. The three outsiders stood together, watching a family embrace their returned adventurers. Keir, Bronagh, and Imogen had a kingdom to save, a kingdom that belonged to them in a world very different from this one.

Keir stood in the room the queen had set aside for him, staring into the looking glass. A maid had left fresh clothes for him when she came to draw a bath—a fur-lined doublet and thick woolen trousers. Despite the always present hearths in every room, the place still chilled him, with its cold stone floors and marble-lined hallways.

Iskalt embraced its status as the ice kingdom, and he supposed those living here were quite used to it.

He was thankful he didn't have to share a room because it gave him time to think about what needed to be said to convince the fae of this kingdom to help his.

First, he had to admit who he truly was. Not a mere sailor or someone sent to protect Tierney. A king come to beg for the assistance his people needed.

He turned to survey the table in front of the settee, its dark top gleaming like amber in the light of the fire. He'd felt the power since the moment he set foot inside the room. It wasn't only here. This palace was rimmed in a power stronger than any he'd ever experienced. If he crossed the room and laid a hand on the table, he knew what he'd sense thrumming beneath the surface.

Magic. His kind of magic.

How was it possible?

A knock sounded on his door, and he tore his eyes from the table to open it. Tierney smiled at him from the other side, and he was so mesmerized he didn't see her brother with her.

Toby pushed past her into the room. "You can stop staring at each other now." Another boy followed him in. "I know everything."

Tierney shot him an annoyed look as she closed the door behind him. Toby gestured to the boy with him. "This is Logan." He took Logan's hand, and the two made themselves comfortable on the settee.

"Like you and Logan don't constantly make eyes at each other." Tierney crossed her arms. "And you don't know anything."

"I know he's a king."

They all stopped.

Toby was the only one who kept speaking. "Gulliver told me."

Tierney groaned and flopped onto the settee, resting her feet across Logan's lap. "Of course he did. Gullie is a terrible secret keeper when it comes to you."

"Only because he assumed I already knew. But this time, you didn't tell me." He sounded hurt.

"It was my fault." Keir wanted to make him feel better. For Tierney. "I asked her not to tell anyone yet."

"Bull." Tierney shook her head.

"Where?" Keir searched the room for a bull's head or a painting, something that would explain anything that was going on and what it had to do with him.

Toby started laughing. "Oh, he's adorable."

"I know." Tierney giggled. "You should have seen when I explained electricity to him."

"I'm right here." Keir crossed his arms and leaned against the wall next to the hearth.

Tierney sent him a rebellious smile. "I meant, Keir didn't make the decision. I did. The truth is, he's come here for a reason, but there was no point in discussing it and having Dad distrust him even more before we were back at the palace where we could do something about it. You, Toby, have a little habit of telling Mom everything. And you know she can't keep secrets from Dad."

Toby huffed but didn't respond.

Keir had the distinct impression he'd walked into a dynamic more complicated than he could've imagined. In his family, Eavha and him only trusted each other. There were no other factors at play.

"What are you all doing in my rooms anyway? I could have been resting or bathing."

"Are you trying to tell me you haven't been ready for hours?" Tierney raised a brow.

Okay, fine, she had him. He'd gotten a bit of rest, but he couldn't just sit here when he needed to advocate for his kingdom. "When do I get to speak with your parents?"

She stood and crossed to him, taking his hand in both of hers. Her voice was soft when she spoke. "At dinner, I promise. We won't waste time now that we're here. We're supping in private with Bronagh and my parents. Not even Toby gets to be there."

Toby scowled at that, but Tierney ignored him. "They're going to help, Keir."

"I wish I could be as certain."

She looked up at him, so much sincerity in her eyes. "If you can't trust them, trust me. I know they will help, but should they not, I will. Believe in me, okay?"

He lifted a hand to her cheek, wondering how he'd gotten to this point, where he knew without a doubt that every one of her words was genuine, every one a promise she wouldn't break. Maybe it was when she'd saved him from the icy waters or even before that when she'd kissed him for the first time.

"I do," he whispered. "I believe in you."

The smile that graced her lips brought a light to her eyes he couldn't look away from. It was then, with her brother looking on and Tierney's words still ringing in his mind, he realized the truth.

He was in love with her.

And he still couldn't have her.

"Well, enjoy dinner." Toby stood. "We're going to go."

Logan lingered for a moment, watching them. "You look happy, Tierney. It's good to see."

When they were finally alone for the first time since the night before the storm let loose on the ship, Keir couldn't think of what else to say.

"Your palace is beautiful." He cringed at how bland the words were.

She chuckled and stepped away from him. "Thanks." Walking to the table near the looking glass, she lifted the crystal flagon and poured two cups of deep red wine.

Nearing him again, she held one out. "You'll never want Vondurian wine again."

He lifted it from her fingers and tilted it against his lips. It struck his throat, and he started sputtering as the strong, yet sweet liquid slid over his taste buds.

Tierney laughed. "It's much stronger than anything in your kingdom."

"Just a bit," he wheezed, catching his breath. Strong but also strangely delicious. The flavors burst across his tongue like nothing he'd ever experienced before. Suddenly, every other wine he'd ever tasted paled in comparison.

Tierney lifted on her toes and fit her lips to his. She tasted of sweet wine.

"Mmm," she murmured. "Delicious." With a smile, she stepped back and drank her wine. Keir wished she'd come close again, that she'd kiss him as she had in Grima or Vondur. But there'd been something hesitant in both of them since reaching the Iskalt shores.

They both knew their time was limited.

"So." Keir cleared his throat. "Your father ... tell me more about him." They'd been on the road for days, and he'd barely said two words to Keir.

Tierney hid a smile with her wine glass. "Well, he's ... difficult. He loves me very much, and he's a great king, truly the best, but we clash sometimes because we're both too stubborn."

"Oh no, don't tell me he's exactly like you." He wasn't sure if he could handle two of them.

"Sort of. I get my rebelliousness from Mom, but Dad and I share a ... profound belief in our own intelligence, as my mother says."

"Is that just a queenly way to say you both think you're always right?"

"Definitely not." By the way she turned away, he wasn't sure he believed her.

She stopped, still not facing him. "I am, though."

"You are what?"

She grinned over her shoulder. "Always right."

If she truly was like her father, he wasn't sure how he'd get through this night.

"Come on." She drained the rest of her wine. "We should get to dinner, but first, you'll need to finish that."

He lifted the wineglass. "I think I should have a clear head."

"Well, if you want to have supper with my parents on only a few sips of wine, it's your funeral. Me, I'd rather have a bit of courage in me."

He didn't want to ask what he needed courage for.

Chapter 13
Tierney

Tierney and Keir were the first to arrive in the dining hall.

"Why such a big room for one table?" Keir moved to stand in front of the enormous fireplace at the front of the room. The poor man was always cold.

Tierney gazed around the familiar room, trying to see it for the first time through Keir's eyes. A long table sat on an ivory and blue rug under an enormous chandelier made of powerful crystals.

She cringed at the sight of so much power used for simple adornment. What must Keir think of them? She turned her back, moving to the buffet table to pour them each a glass of wine.

"It used to be a dining hall for the full court." Brea entered the room, dressed in her preferred tunic and trousers. She rarely wore queenly attire when it was just the family and a few guests. "When the twins were small, after I first came to Iskalt as queen, I couldn't handle the intensity of having the court present at every meal."

Brea stepped up beside Keir, admiring the family portraits that sat along the mantle. A human custom she insisted on keeping.

"I didn't want my kids to have to grow up behaving like perfect little princes and princesses all the time. I wanted them to enjoy the occasional food fight and laughter around the dinner table. So, I banned the court from the dining hall. We hold frequent dinners in a more formal setting where the court joins us."

"Food fights?" Keir turned toward the queen, his back straight as a rod and his hands clasped behind his back like a soldier.

Tierney lingered by the buffet table to watch them.

"Well, we had four kids under the age of ten, so tantrums often ended up with flinging mashed potatoes and vegetables they didn't want to eat." Brea shrugged. "When you have kids, you'll know what I mean." She clapped him on the shoulder and joined Tierney at the buffet.

Brea made a show of pouring her own glass of wine and muttered out the side of her mouth, "You're related to all the royals—or as close to related as you can get. So, what does my daughter do? She goes and finds herself a handsome king—don't be mad at Toby for telling me—from a fabled land and brings him home to dinner." She turned, leaning against the table. "And he is handsome, isn't he?" She elbowed her daughter.

"Mom," Tierney hissed, hoping Keir hadn't heard her. "He is a king. He has his own kingdom to rule. It's not like that."

"It looks like that." Brea gave her a knowing grin. "If you remember, I was supposed to be the heir of Eldur, and you see how that worked out."

"Stop it." Tierney's face flushed scarlet.

"Well, does he have a younger brother?" Brea raised her brows, all innocence.

"Why, are you leaving Dad for a younger model?"

"Of course not, but we're going to be right back here with Kayleigh in a few years, and if the man has a brother, then they need to meet."

"Seriously?" Tierney rolled her eyes.

"Hey, I have a lot of royal children to marry off, and there's a serious lack of suitable candidates available. Excuse a mom for thinking ahead."

"He has a sister, Eavha. I would steal her here in a heartbeat, but she's head over heels for the commander of Keir's army." Tierney let her thoughts wander to how Eavha might be doing without Keir. The girl was brave and noble. She would inspire her people to stay together until help arrived.

"We have to send help to Lenya, Mom. As soon as possible."

"We will. After we hash it all out tonight. We have a lot to discuss." Brea's head tilted to the side. "Darling, why is that man staring at my chandelier like he wants to put it in his pocket and take it home? Gullie made that for me. And that makes it priceless."

"Oh." Tierney laughed. "We have so much to talk about."

She left her mother's side and went to join Keir at the fireplace.

"Drink this and stop staring at the priceless crystals." She shoved a wine glass in his hand.

"You know, this beautiful work of art contains enough power to restore my kingdom to what it once was. Between that and the table in my room, the entirety of Lenya could thrive for a generation."

"You don't need tables and chandeliers to do that." She took his hand, giving it a gentle squeeze. "We will send help soon."

Keir gazed around the opulent room. "I'm afraid I have nothing to offer in trade for the crystals we need to save my people."

"I don't know what you mean about crystals." Brea took her seat near the head of the table. "But if your people are hurting and we can help, I am certain something can be arranged. It doesn't need to be an equal trade."

Love for her mother bloomed inside Tierney's chest. She didn't even know how dire the situation was in Lenya, yet she was already offering to help.

"I missed you so much." Tierney leaned over the back of Brea's chair and hugged her. "You have no idea how many times I needed my mother."

Brea took Tierney's hand and pulled her into the seat beside her, gesturing for Keir to take the chair opposite her. "Can we just call the time of death right now? Your jaunt to Lenya when you meant to come home has to be the final nail in the coffin of your

O'Shea magic, Tia. I shudder to think where you might end up next time."

"I won't be using my portal magic without supervision ever again. I'm fully prepared to admit to anyone who will listen that I am no good at it."

"Do my ears deceive me or did the great Tierney O'Shea just admit she wasn't good at something involving magic?" Lochlan entered the room, a smile on his face. "Things have certainly changed during your time away." He dropped a kiss on her head and moved to his seat at the head of the table.

"Very funny." Tierney rolled her eyes. "You make it sound like I was on a holiday."

Lochlan's smile faded. "I can't imagine what you've been through. I'm just so glad to have you home safe."

"I hope we aren't late." Bronagh approached the table, every bit the queen she was. Veren followed her at a distance. Pausing to give his king and queen a proper greeting.

"Your Majesties, I hope I am not imposing. Queen Bronagh has asked me to join her in an advisory capacity this evening."

"Of course, please join us." Brea gave them a warm welcome.

"When we first arrived in Lenya, we were all separated," Tierney began. "I crossed paths with Keir almost immediately, but it wasn't until much later I discovered Veren had fallen in with the Grimian army and Queen Bronagh. Veren has become a close advisor to the queen."

"Well done, Veren." Lochlan gave him a nod of approval. "You've represented Iskalt with honor."

"Thank you, your Majesty." Veren took the vacant seat beside Tierney and across from Bronagh.

A host of servants came in to serve the first course, and Tierney laughed when she saw what was on the menu. Her absolute favorite human meal. "Spaghetti and meatballs!" She beamed a smile at Keir. "You're in for a treat, but you should know nothing will be spicy like the Lenyans prefer."

"Oh." Brea's face fell. "I didn't realize. I thought comfort food was the best way to go tonight."

"I'm sure this … spaghetti dish will be delicious." Keir rushed to put her at ease.

"The food, you would love it, but Dad would starve. It's so spicy." Tierney laughed. It felt so good to be home again, but she already missed Lenya more than she thought she would.

After the servants left them for their meal, Lochlan lifted his wine glass. "I'd like to make a toast. To the safe return of my eldest daughter and the new friends she's brought with her."

"Here, here." Brea lifted her glass, and Tierney followed suit, not sure the Lenyans knew what a toast was.

"My people need help," Keir blurted, his stony soldier's face firmly in place. "I appreciate the warm welcome and the lovely dinner, but I worry for my people. My sister back home. My best friend. They are all in danger."

"We have a lot of ground to cover before we're all caught up." Tierney caught his gaze. "Both Keir and Bronagh have made enormous sacrifices to be here. Without them, we would have never made it home. For that alone, I feel Iskalt owes them a debt of gratitude, and I would ask our king to provide them with the one thing they need more than any other. A small thing we have in great supply."

"And what is that?" Lochlan asked, taking a bite of his spaghetti and gesturing for the others to do the same.

"Magic." Tierney stabbed a cheese-slathered meatball with her fork. "Lots of it."

"Magic welders?" Brea frowned. "We do have plenty of those, but I thought your people had their own kind of magic." She turned to Keir in confusion.

"We do, madame," Bronagh began.

"Oh, please, call me Brea. Let's dispense with all the formalities this evening, shall we?"

"Of course, Brea." Bronagh nodded, examining her dish of

noodles and red sauce. "In Lenya, we have great magic, but we must have a totem … a vessel used to harness the magic from within. It's a certain kind of crystal of which we are in short supply." She lifted her eyes to the chandelier shining down on them. "Even as I sit here, I can feel the immense power of the crystal used to create this lovely light. It is enough to save my people—at least, it contains more power than any crystal I have ever seen in my lifetime." Her voice came out breathless and eager. "Such a vessel could change our lives."

"The mines once produced enough crystal for all Lenyans to access their magic," Keir continued. "But over the last many generations, the mines have failed, and there is little enough for the nobility and military officers to use for only the direst of circumstances."

"Our kingdoms have been at war for generations," Bronagh added. "We've fought for control of the last remaining mine and the reserves set aside by our grandparents." She shared a glance with Keir. "The Vondurian king and I have come to our roles only recently, and we have agreed the fighting must end."

"And no sooner had we signed a milestone peace treaty between our kingdoms than we were faced with an even bigger problem." Keir leaned back, uninterested in his meal.

"The expansion of the fire plains?" Lochlan sighed.

"You know?" Tierney gaped at her father. "How?"

"Much has happened here since you left, Tia," Brea said. "All the vatlands are expanding. On all sides. You must have noticed how much worse the northeastern mountains were than what has been recorded. The storms raging through the mountains and across the tundra have progressively expanded. The blizzard has reached the lodge. It won't be long before our home there is completely snowed in. And if it keeps moving at the same rate, all of Iskalt will drown in a sea of snow and ice.

"It's the same in the Northern Vatlands too, along the border with Myrkur. We've had reports of avalanches and earthquakes. That is why Siobhan and her father are here. Their estate has been destroyed. An earthquake shifted the lands where the manor house rested on the cliffside. Their home was dashed to rubble in a rockslide. Even the mountains themselves seem to be expanding, like they're growing right from the ground. Myrkur is experiencing the same from their side."

"And the Southern Vatlands between Eldur and Fargelsi have been expanding as well," Lochlan continued. "We don't know what started it, but we've been hard at work trying to find a solution. Half of southern Gelsi is gone. Almost the entirety of the Dragur Forest is marshland now.

"It's even worse in Eldur. It's coming at them from both sides. To the northeast, the fire plains drift across the desert, but to the southwest, the marshlands have engulfed the Teotann Oasis and nearly swallowed Loch Langt."

Tierney's eyes burned with unshed tears. "So, we're all in this together then." She took a deep breath, trying to wrap her mind around the enormity of the problem they now faced. It wasn't just a threat to Lenya anymore. It was a threat to all fae.

"Lenya is small." Bronagh picked at her meal. "I never truly realized just how small until Lochlan showed us a map of the four kingdoms this afternoon. I used to think Grima was huge, dwarfing the size of Vondur, but we are nothing compared to the might of Iskalt and your allies."

"Do not sell yourself short, Bronagh." Brea reached across the table to take her hand. "We owe our might to the lineage of Lenya. Your people once occupied all of the fae world in ancient times. Toby and my father, Brandon, have been researching in the Aghadoon library. They've recovered a great deal of lost history, but we still have not solved the problem. I fear if we don't soon, we will run out of time."

"Have you been able to slow the expansion at all?" Tierney asked.

"Some." Lochlan set his fork aside. "It's taken a great deal of magic to stall the spread, but we can teach you what we know."

"I think we should make that a priority and send someone to

Lenya immediately through a portal with enough crystals to help them." Tierney turned toward her father, waiting expectantly.

"I'll check with the palace craftsmen to see what we have on hand. But you will need to be the one to open the portal. You're the only O'Shea who has been there. Are you prepared for the possibility that you might not be able to do it?"

Tierney shook her head. "No. I have to do it. But I will need Toby's guidance."

"Very well. We will put everything we have into that tomorrow. Who will return to Lenya with these crystals?"

"I would like to." Bronagh was the first to speak up. "I would very much like to return to my people to let them know what's happening."

"I will go with you, your Majesty," Veren volunteered.

Bronagh reached for his hand. "Stay. Your father and your family just got you back. I don't want to take you from them again so soon. We will see each other again."

"I don't like the idea of the queen traveling through a portal alone. Not when she isn't familiar with such magic."

"He means he's worried I'll send her to some other lost kingdom we know nothing about." Not that Tierney could blame him.

"Perhaps Imogen could accompany Bron back to Lenya," Keir suggested. "I should think she would like to tell her family about her father's brave sacrifice."

"I'm not sure she has any other family," Tierney said. "I believe she's very worried about what will become of her."

"I will see she has everything she could ever need." Bronagh lifted her chin. "It's the least we can do for the captain."

"Then, that matter is settled." Brea sipped her wine. "I will work with Bron in the morning to show her what little we've been able to accomplish to stall the spread, and then when night falls, Tierney and Toby will open a portal."

"Must it wait for night?" Bronagh asked. "I am very anxious to return."

"I am afraid in Iskalt, most matters of magic must wait for nightfall," Lochlan explained. "Where your magic is powered by these crystal vessels, ours is fueled by the moon. My wife has Eldurian magic, which is ruled by the sun. She will be able to assist you until a portal can be opened."

"I see." Bronagh nodded. "It seems we are not so different after all then."

"That's right." Tierney gave her a sad smile. "We are all fae."

"We are all fae." Bronagh reached for her glass. "That sounds like a wonderful toast."

"Here, here." Lochlan lifted his wine. "To the six kingdoms of the fae."

Smiling, they each drank their wine and returned to their meal.

"Once we have dealt with all immediate threats, Keir and Bron," Lochlan began, "we will have to draw up a treaty between our lands. Just something to note the assistance Iskalt and the other kingdoms will offer Lenya in the form of the crystals you need, and an agreement that your magic will never be turned against us."

"Dad!" Tierney couldn't believe him. "Is that necessary to discuss at the dinner table?"

"I don't know your friends, Tia. I must think of Iskalt." Lochlan refilled his plate. He seemed to be the only one with an appetite.

"You think I don't consider Iskalt? Of course, we need to settle an agreement in writing, but Keir and Bron have come a long way—a journey that should have gotten us all killed were it not for the courage of Captain Michel and his crew, who all died, by the way. Matters of diplomacy can wait."

"None of you would have been in such trouble if you hadn't run away from home."

"And what was I running away from?" Tierney crossed her arms over her chest. "You remember your stupid list?" She scowled at him.

"Iskalt must be secured for the next generation." Lochlan shot back.

"And I will secure it. In my own time. I'm not marrying anyone from that list, and I'm not having babies any time soon, so just go feed that list of yours to the goats because I don't want to see it again."

"It's okay," Keir tried to interject.

"Let them argue." Brea passed him the breadbasket. "It's their favorite pastime. You should try a spaghetti sandwich with garlic bread. It's my favorite." She pulled two pieces of garlic bread from the basket and piled spaghetti and meatballs onto one piece, smashing the second piece on top.

Keir helped himself to the breadbasket. His appetite seemed to have returned. "I expected as much," he interrupted, bringing Lochlan and Tierney's bickering to an end. "To be honest, I thought your king might demand a price we could not pay for access to the magic we so desperately need. If a peace treaty between our kingdoms is all he requires, I am more than happy to speak for Vondur that no fae of my kingdom will ever turn their magic on Iskalt or any of the four kingdoms unless it is a life-or-death situation in which they believe they are protecting themselves from harm."

"I have no qualms signing such a treaty," Bronagh echoed Keir's thoughts. "I know my council will fall over themselves to sign any treaty that might restore magic to our kingdom."

"We must speak to Queen Alona of Eldur and Queen Neeve of Fargelsi, as well as King Hector of Myrkur," Lochlan said, "but I see no reason why the four kingdoms couldn't all set up a system of trade for crystals."

"We have nothing of value to trade." Keir frowned.

"That's not exactly true." Tierney leaned forward. "The Queen of the Night blossoms would be a good trade. The ladies of the courts across the four kingdoms would pay a high price for such a lovely perfume."

"Well, I suppose we could also trade Gentian tea." Keir nodded.

"No. We don't want that stuff here." Tierney shook her head, thinking of the first time she'd tasted the bitter tea. "But your red peppers and Grima's hot chocolate drink would be perfect for trade."

"Chocolate?" Brea turned to Tierney. "Did I hear something about chocolate?"

"It's not exactly the same, Mom. But it's the closest thing to it I've ever tasted. It's sweet and creamy, and it smells like heaven in a cup."

"Iskalt will trade crystals for your chocolate drink." Brea beamed a smile at the Grima queen.

"I feel like all the chocoah in Grima couldn't equal what you propose to give us in return." Bronagh shook her head in wonder. "Chocoah for crystals." She threw her head back and laughed. "My brother will find that quite amusing."

"You have a brother?" Brea leaned forward. "Older or younger?"

"Younger." Bronagh smiled. "Donal is fourteen, though he thinks he's forty since he's been leading my army, fighting battles with enemy kings, and nearly getting himself killed."

"I have a daughter about his age. Maybe on your next visit, you can bring Donal with you."

"That would be wonderful; thank you for the invitation."

"Watch out, Bron. Mom is matchmaking," Tierney whisper-shouted across the table.

"I also have a nephew about your age." Brea ignored her daughter. "But I think Veren might have something to say about that." She winked at the young nobleman.

"You're so embarrassing." Tierney rolled her eyes, but she was so happy to be home she didn't care if her mother tried to set up marriages for all her children with the Vondurian and Grimian royals and nobles.

"Sue me. I'm a mother and I want my kids to be happy. Toby will marry Prince Logan someday, and I want all my babies, and my nieces and nephews, to experience that kind of love for themselves. You know, after we save the world again."

Tierney sighed. One of these days, she wanted a little peace and quiet where the world no longer needed saving every time she turned around.

Chapter 14
Keir

What a strange place. Keir stood on one of the upper balconies of the palace, gazing down at the snowy field stretching all the way to the nearest village. If he craned his neck, he could see a frozen lake, where a group of children pushed a black ball around with sticks, yelling at each other and falling all over the ice.

Other children ran through ankle-deep snow, chasing each other, their laughter reaching the balcony. He didn't understand what they were doing. It certainly wasn't the type of work children in Vondur performed. They typically worked with their parents in the fields or in the shops and many smithies, making items to provision the army. Once they reached an age, the boys left their homes behind to fight for their kingdom.

It had been the way of things for as long as he could remember.

"I was you once," a voice sounded behind him.

Keir turned to find the king in the doorway. There were no guards following him, and he wore no protection, having no obvious worries of someone aiming an arrow at him should he stand in the open too long.

Lochlan walked farther out onto the balcony. "My home was in danger, but the danger was within. I resided in a different kingdom, and all I could do was watch my people suffer."

"What did you do?" Keir asked.

Lochlan gave him a tight smile. "I fought. Now, my fae know peace." His eyes drifted to the yelling children. "They can play because we refused to give up on them. How long have you worn the crown?"

"Not long."

Lochlan nodded, as if he'd expected that answer. "Well, a good king always puts his kingdom before himself, always strives for peace."

"Peace. It's such a foreign concept. Lenya has been at war for so long no one alive remembers a time when the fighting didn't overwhelm our lands. Grima and Vondur have a tentative alliance now, but it is new."

"One thing I have learned in my many years upon the throne is that an army may fight, but if given the choice, they will trade their swords for plows, their horses for oxen. Give them that choice, Keir, and never take it away. They will love you for it."

Maybe they would have, but Keir would never get the chance to know. "And if fighting is the only option?"

"Ah." Lochlan nodded. "You wish you were able to return with Bronagh." He studied Keir for a moment. "Come, we have much to discuss."

Lochlan led him in out of the frigid temperatures, but the chill didn't leave him. It was a constant reminder that he was in this frozen kingdom while his fae suffered the effects of scorching heat.

They walked through the palace, across velvet carpets, to a sitting chamber with two settees facing each other in front of a roaring fire set back in the marble hearth.

A servant followed them in and bowed. "Sire, I have sent for tea."

"Thank you," Lochlan said absently. "I do not need anything further."

The man bowed again and backed out, shutting the doors and trapping Keir with Tierney's father, a man who'd intimidated him before they'd even met.

Tierney idolized the man. That much had been clear since she was Keir's prisoner in Vondur. But it was more than that. She loved him. Disappointing him hurt her. It was the kind of dynamic Keir never had with his own father. He couldn't imagine his father searching for him if he'd gone missing or worrying for him every day like it was clear Lochlan had done.

There were deep lines of exhaustion in the face of the Iskalt king. As if these last months still weighed him down.

"Please," he said, "sit."

Keir lowered himself to the settee, and Lochlan took the seat across from him. They didn't speak, the silence stretching between them. A knock sounded on the door before a young woman entered, carrying a silver tray laden with a pot of tea, two cups, and a plate of what looked like biscuits. Sort of.

She set the tray on the table between the settees and left.

Lochlan leaned forward, pouring tea into the two cups. "Milk?"

"Please." Keir picked up one of the biscuits and smelled it. There were dark spots across the top, and it reeked of sugar.

"Cookies," Lochlan explained. "My wife insists on making them herself with ingredients she gets from the human realm. I believe she calls them oatmeal. She tells me it's like porridge baked in the oven."

Keir set it down without taking a bite.

Lochlan chewed on one of his own. "They're actually quite good. The dark bits are chewy and sweet. I forget what she told me they're called, but the children adore them."

"Is being wed to someone so connected to the human realm odd?" Keir asked, truly interested. Tierney was strange in her human sayings, but he'd sensed it was nothing compared to her mother.

"Young man, marriage itself is odd."

Keir laughed at that. "You seem to have a wonderful family."

A fond smile spread across the dour king's face. "They age me to no end, and sometimes I feel as if I will never be free of rebellious women and the boys who can't resist them, but then I remember I am one of those boys. My family is more than I ever imagined it could be. There was a time I didn't believe in much, not even in myself."

Keir had a hard time imagining that. This man, who seemed to know all, to wear his crown as if he was meant to. He was so sure of his actions. "You hide it well."

"The secret is to find one person who sees your vulnerabilities. If they allow you to have your doubts, to voice your questions, with the rest of the world, pretending becomes second nature. As long as that one person lets the act fall, it will not become who you are."

One person. Keir saw her so clearly in his head. Tierney saw who he really was, not the man raised by a cruel father or the one who kept her prisoner. She looked past everything he'd done, everything he tried to pretend he was.

"Ah," Lochlan said. "I thought so."

"Sir?"

"You've already found that person."

He had. The way Lochlan looked at him, a calculating gleam in his eyes, had Keir wanting to stand and run from the room. Instead, he sipped his tea and crossed one leg over the other.

Lochlan nodded, his face growing serious. A crease formed in his forehead, and blue sparked in his eyes. He blinked, and it was gone. "I am sorry. I don't know if anyone has explained our magic to you, but strong emotions draw it forth, and it isn't always easy to hide when it rises."

"Was there something I said that angered you?" The last thing he wanted was to get on this man's bad side. He needed him to help Lenya.

Lochlan sighed. "No. I was thinking of my daughter, and she always sparks such a reaction in me. Tierney is stubborn. I'm sure you've noticed."

Keir's lips twitched. "Maybe a time or two." What would Lochlan say if he knew Keir had held his daughter captive? Would he still be a welcome guest, a potential ally?

"But she is strong, stronger than any fae I have ever met. Ruling Iskalt is an honor, one Tierney earned when she was ten." He paused. "If I'd had crowned her then, the Iskaltians would have accepted her. At ten, I had never faced hardship. But she saved four kingdoms."

"Tierney is unlike anyone I've ever met."

"Keir, are you in love with my daughter?"

"Yes." He didn't hesitate. It was a conclusion he'd come to on the ship when they first sailed into the maelstrom. He hadn't wanted to love her, to need her. For so long, Tierney was a temptation, a fae he couldn't resist. He hadn't known it then, but they were connected.

"Hm." Lochlan stood and walked toward the hearth, staring into the flames. "I know what some think of me, but I have my reasons for wanting Tierney to marry. I'm not a cruel father, but if she is going to be queen, she needs someone to temper her, to calm her rash actions and weather her storm."

It was the perfect analogy. Tierney was a storm that had ripped through his life, wreaking havoc. But in the aftermath, there was peace.

Lochlan turned. "Do you wish to marry my daughter?"

Keir couldn't breathe. He couldn't summon words or pick out a single thought swirling through his mind.

"She refuses all the nobles of Iskalt," Lochlan went on, seemingly oblivious to the crisis inside Keir. "She needs a powerful ally, one who will always support her should anyone try to take her throne." He took his seat again. "My parents lost the Iskaltian throne when my father died, and it plunged our family into years of betrayal and took a war to win it back. My brother and I were raised in foreign courts. I do not want my people to ever go through such unrest again."

It made so much sense now why Lochlan was so desperate to secure the throne for generations to come. He was scared. History did not predict the future, but it could inform it.

"I would like to add a marriage to the treaty between our kingdoms." Lochlan steepled his fingers. "Lenya will receive access to all fire opal resources in the four kingdoms, but to secure our alliance, you will marry my daughter."

He didn't know. Keir held a giant secret, but if he was going to consider such a deal, if he truly wanted to marry Tierney, Lochlan had to know. He cleared his throat, coughing into his fist. "I ..." He drew in a breath. "There is something you must know before making such a deal, something no one knows other than my sister and my most trusted council member."

Lochlan waited, not saying a word.

Keir just had to get it out, to voice the very thing he'd been afraid of, the one act that made him a poor king. "I abdicated the throne."

Silence. It stretched like a violent sea preluding the storm.

Keir pictured Eavha's face when he'd told her what he planned. She hadn't agreed with him, but she'd signed the documents as a witness in front of Lord Robert.

He'd never wished to be a king. Keir only wanted peace for his kingdom, and he achieved that. Once he stopped the fire plains, they needed someone who could rule out of duty, love. Not a man who'd gained his crown through his father's spilled blood.

Keir stared down at his hands, as if he could still feel the warm blood from not only his father but all the nobles who issued the King's Comhrac. Vondur deserved a fresh start.

Finally, Lochlan spoke. "Tell me, Keir, did you give up your crown out of a sense of fear or a true love for your fae?"

"I do not fear duty. I was not the ruler my fae deserved."

Understanding entered Lochlan's gaze. "Believe it or not, I do know what you speak of."

Keir didn't get how Lochlan could possibly understand, but he didn't question it. "Now that you know the truth, do you still wish for me to marry your daughter?"

Lochlan hesitated for a moment. "I do not care if you wear a crown, only that you're able to support hers."

"I will support her with everything I have. But you must know, whether Tierney and I marry is not up to you, and it is not up to me. She has a mind of her own, and she will make her own decisions."

A smile flashed across his face before it was gone. "Then, we have a deal."

"No." Hadn't he heard him? "Not yet."

Lochlan stood, extending a hand. "I am glad we could reach an agreement."

Keir didn't take the hand as he got to his feet. "There is no agreement."

Lochlan nodded. "You may leave now." He put a hand on his back and ushered him to the door.

Keir turned when he stepped into the corridor. "There's no deal."

The Iskaltian king only nodded and shut the door, leaving Keir to wonder what in the world just happened. Had he agreed to be married?

There was someone he needed to find. It took him the better part of an hour to seek Gulliver. He sat in a library with his father, a map spread out before them.

"So, Lenya is here?" Griff pointed to a blank part of the map across the fire plains, his eyes bright.

Gulliver leaned his chair back, balancing on two legs. His tail rose and flicked his father's hand. "I already told you that."

"Gullie, you've been to a land no one else even knew about. Forgive me for being curious."

Gulliver rolled his eyes to Keir. "Curious is an understatement. Obsessed is more accurate."

"King Keir." Griff shot to his feet. "You can help us. I want to know everything there is to know about Lenya."

Gulliver groaned. "You don't have to talk to him. He's just being obnoxious. I've already told him about Vondur and Grima."

"Yes, but their magic works from fire opals? It's fascinating."

"We do not call them opals," Keir explained. "But yes, they allow us to harness the power."

"Amazing."

"Ask me about the dungeons while you're at it, Dad." Gulliver scrubbed a hand across his face. "Would you like to know what I named the rats?"

Griff's mouth opened and shut, and guilt curled in Keir's gut. He waited for Gulliver to tell his father who'd kept him prisoner, but those words never came.

"Fair enough." Griffin sighed. "You don't want to talk about it. I'm sure Keir didn't seek you out to listen to you being mean to your old man."

Gulliver shook his head, a hint of a smile appearing on his lips. "Did you need me for something, Keir?"

Keir hesitated before walking forward and taking the empty seat at their table. "There's something I wanted to talk to you about."

Gulliver lifted a brow.

"Oh, do go on." Griff grinned. "This sounds interesting."

Keir swallowed heavily. He had to force the words out. Here went nothing. "The king has asked me to marry Tia."

Gulliver and his father stared at each other before bursting out in laughter.

"Lochlan will never learn." Griffin laughed.

Gulliver wiped away fake tears. "I hope for magic's sake you said no."

"I did … but he didn't seem to hear me."

"Classic Loch." Griff lifted his eyes to the ceiling. "Everyone is either in agreement with him or simply wrong. Does he not realize his daughter ran away the last time he tried to marry her off?"

"I'm not going with her this time." Gulliver crossed his arms, still laughing.

"There is a difference now though." Griffin's laughter died away. "Tierney might say yes."

Keir's chest inflated with hope, but it slowly faded when Gulliver shook his head. "You have no idea. Keir and Tierney had this weird toxic thing going on, but they hate each other most of the time."

"So did your mother and I."

"Ew, gross. I don't want to imagine you two being as sickening as Keir and Tierney have been, even if I was around for a lot of it. I blocked it out."

"When hate turns to love, son, it can be the most wonderful, passionate—"

"Don't say passionate."

"—relationship."

Gulliver rested his face in his hands, his palms muffling his voice. "Why did you come to me, Keir? Was it for my blessing?"

Keir wasn't really sure. "I ..."

"The only blessing that matters is Tierney's, and if she finds out her father is playing with her life again, I guarantee it won't be pretty."

"I'm in love with her." There was desperation in his voice. Ever since Lochlan asked the question, all Keir could think about was spending the rest of his life fighting with Tierney, loving her.

"And that's great, but she won't play a part in any scheme. For the record, I believe you love her, and yet you still don't get it. You were raised in a kingdom where women had no control over their lives, no respect. You have come a long way, but the next lesson you must learn is that Tierney won't marry you just because she loves you—if she does. That isn't enough. You need to prove you respect her as much as you love her."

"And if I do that?"

"Well, she'll still probably say no."

CHAPTER 15
TIERNEY

"There you are." Tierney wandered into the library, where Keir poured over a map of the four kingdoms.

"Your world is so vast I can hardly fathom it." Keir didn't look up from his scrutiny of the fire plains along the Eldur border. "Did you know there's an active volcano in Eldur that wasn't part of the fire plains until recently?"

"Yes. It's called Eldfal, and my mother was about my age last time it erupted, but it wasn't a natural event, so I'm not sure it counts." She moved to stand beside him. Hanging over his shoulder, she blew a warm breath in his ear to catch his attention.

"What?" Keir reached for his ear. "Oh, hi." He grinned up at her ruefully. "I was doing it again, wasn't I?"

"Fangirling over the four kingdoms? Yes." He was obsessed. And even if he wouldn't admit it, he idolized her father. The two men had become fast friends.

"I don't know what that means. But your world is so exciting."

"And the most you have seen of it since we arrived is this library and the palace." She grabbed his hand, tugging him away from the library table.

"You're up to something." He resisted for only a moment before he followed her from the library.

"I wouldn't be Tia O'Shea if I wasn't up to something."

"Where are we going?"

"You want to see Iskalt while you have the chance, don't you?" She turned, walking backward down the hall as she pulled him along. "Or would you rather pour over books about Iskalt instead of visiting the nearest village with me?"

"Let's go." He laid a hand at her back, and they hurried down the hall.

Gathering their cloaks, they ventured out into the stable yard across the palace grounds.

"Is it always this cold?" Keir tucked his face into the warm woolen scarf he wore around his face and neck.

Tierney laughed, her eyes bright in the clear afternoon sunshine. "It's a bit colder than normal but hardly noticeable for most of us used to the weather here." She waved at the stable hand when he emerged with two fine geldings. A chestnut and a dark roan.

"Thank you, Stephan." Tierney took the reins. "How is your mother doing? She was ill before I left, wasn't she?"

"Aye, your Majesty." The boy beamed a worshipful smile for the princess. "She is doing much better, thank you."

"Tell your mother I'll be along to visit as soon as I can." Tierney mounted her horse.

"I will. It's wonderful to have you home again, Princess." Stephan bowed, turning to hand the reins of the other horse to Keir before he trotted off back to the stables.

"You visit your stable hands' mothers often?" Keir arched a brow at her.

"As often as I can." Tierney made a soothing sound to her horse to ease his nervous shifting. "You coming?" She glanced over her shoulder at him.

"Shouldn't we wait for the others?" Keir climbed atop a horse.

"What others? It's just you and me today."

He trotted up beside her, giving his horse a gentle pat. "We're going into the village; you'll need a guard at least."

"I've never taken a guard with me into the village." She nudged her mount into a trot. "It's perfectly safe. You'll see."

They rode along the winding path that led from the rear of the palace down to the lake, where children played on the ice.

"I've watched them from the windows and balconies, and I still can't fathom what they are playing." Keir watched them battle across the ice for possession of the puck.

"It's only the best game in the entire world." Tierney's eyes sparkled in the sunlight as she watched the children. "It's called hockey. It's a human sport, but I grew up playing it with Gullie and Toby and all our friends in the village.

"Once my mother introduced the sport, Iskaltians took to it like they invented it themselves. I haven't played in ages, but I'll teach you before you leave for Vondur." A pang of something she didn't want to identify shot through her, and she rushed on. "There's almost always a game happening here at the palace. Father gave his permission ages ago for the village children to use the lake whenever they liked." Tierney missed those days sometimes. She had some of her fondest memories right here.

"Does the snow ever melt away?"

"Never. There are times of the year when the snows are infrequent, but there is always a blanket of crisp white dust covering the world." She waved to a group of girls walking along the wide path.

"Your Majesty." They all smiled, dipping into awkward curtsies.

"The village school is just over there." Tierney pointed across the expanse of snow-covered fields to a stone building that looked like it had been there for centuries. "I used to beg my father to let me go to school with the other children, but I had magic as a young child. Erratic magic, and I was prone to using it when I wasn't supposed to."

"Why does that not surprise me?" Keir chuckled. "Your children don't have magic?"

"In Eldur and Iskalt, we inherit the use of our magic when we come of age. I've only had my Eldurian and Iskaltian magic for a little more than four years, but I've had Gelsi magic my whole life."

"And it's unusual for a fae to have all three types of magic?" Keir asked.

"I'm the only one." She shrugged. "My mother has Gelsi and Eldurian magic. For a long time, it wasn't common for fae of one kingdom to interact with those of another, much less join in marriage. It's much more common now. My mother thinks in a few more generations, everyone will be like me but with Dark Fae features, and we'll all just be fae without any differences at all."

"Princess Tierney! Welcome home!" A cheery woman crossed the street into the village proper, waving frantically.

"Mrs. Fintan, how are you?" Tierney called. "Is Eloise in town today?"

"She's working at the general store; she would love it if you popped in to say hello."

"I'll do that." Tierney led them along a cobblestone street lined with fir trees and people coming and going about their business. It was a prosperous village, but most of Iskalt was like that under King Lochlan's rule.

"Do you know everyone by name?" Keir asked after she nodded to another passerby.

"I've lived here all my life, and I'm positive I spent more time in the village than at home."

Keir glanced around the town square, a slight frown on his face.

"What's the matter?" She rode close beside him.

"You have … everything here. There's a mill and a smithy. You have stores and pubs, and I don't even know what most of these businesses are. It's … wonderful. Eavha would fall in love with your village if she could be here."

"I hope she will come for a visit someday soon." Tierney turned them down a side street, pointing out the various businesses. "That's a bookstore. And there's an apothecary at the end of the street. They have everything you could ever need and then some. Then, there's a tea shop and something my mom calls a restaurant, where they serve the best beef strudel you have ever tasted."

"Is it like a tavern?" he asked.

"No, the tavern and the best pub is back the way we came. Gallagher's only serves food and watered wine. No ale, and he doesn't put up travelers for the night. Mom says that's a lot like human restaurants, where people go for a meal."

"And where are we going?" Keir leaned forward, all eyes for the cooper's yard, where all sorts of wares were for sale and in various stages of construction. "Surely you have somewhere you're taking me?"

"Sweeny's Pub. It's just down this street."

"But you said the best pub is back the way we came. Are you taking me to a substandard place?"

"Sweeny's is my favorite because they have good cider and plenty of snacks, but they also have more privacy. And we have things to discuss, you and I."

"We do?" The color faded from Keir's bright red face.

"You haven't forgotten that pesky little problem we nearly shipwrecked ourselves trying to get here to solve." Tierney narrowed her eyes at him. He was staring and acting odder than usual.

A smile quirked his lips, and he laughed. "We did shipwreck ourselves if you remember correctly."

"I've blocked it out. That was not a fun time." Tierney tried to bite back her laughter. She was so grateful to be here with Keir right now after all they overcame to reach Iskalt. She guided them down a narrow alley until they reached an unassuming stone structure with a simple wooden sign overhead proclaiming it as Sweeny's Pub.

"Does your father know you frequent the local pubs?" Keir slipped from his mount, looping the reins over the hitching post.

"Oh, he gave up trying to keep me away from Sweeny's a long time ago." She dismounted and headed for the carved wooden door.

A bell rang overhead when she walked inside, blinking in the dim light until her eyes adjusted.

"There's my favorite princess." A big burly man with a balding head charged out from behind the bar, sweeping Tierney up in a bear hug. He whirled her around before he set her on her feet. "You can't be leaving for unexpected trips to lands unknown without telling me first." He stood back with his hands on his hips. "It near broke my heart to see your mother, our dear queen herself, so heartbroken at your absence."

"I'm sorry, Sweeny. It won't happen again. I'm swearing off the O'Shea magic for good. I'll leave portals to my brother." Tierney shrugged out of her cloak, leaving it to hang on the hook by the fire to dry with the others.

Keir followed her lead, his jaw dropping when yet another commoner cried out her pleasure that their favorite princess had come home at last. "Dear child!" A plump woman in a long woolen skirt scurried out of the kitchen, wiping her hands on her apron. "Poor old Sweeny was crushed when we found out you were lost. I prayed for your soul every morning and here you are, safely returned." She took Tierney in her arms.

"And I'm so happy to be back." Tierney let the woman mother her, returning her embrace like she wasn't the heir to the throne but just another villager.

"Your poor father." She clucked, fussing over Tierney's cold hands, leading her to warm up beside the fire. "Our king just wasn't the same without you by his side." She turned to Keir. "Ever since she were a little girl, she was always right beside him. Two peas in a pod those two." She left Tierney by the fire, turning her attention on Keir.

"Come, come. Any friend of our Princess Tia is a friend of ours. Come warm yourself by the fire. Frank, get them some hot cider." She turned back to Tierney. "You'll be wanting your favorites then? Cheese curds and freshly baked pretzels?"

Tierney groaned. "Mrs. Sweeny, you have no idea how many

nights I dreamed of your pretzels and cheese curds with a hot cider to warm my belly."

"Have a seat, lassie." Mr. Sweeny shooed his wife off to the kitchens. "She'll be flapping her jaws at you till tomorrow morning if you're not careful."

"I missed you." Tierney lunged at the old man, wrapping her arms around his barrel-sized chest. "Now, it feels like my homecoming is complete." Tierney grabbed Keir's hand and led him to a corner table, where two hot ciders waited for them.

"You come here often?" Keir sat across from her.

"The Sweeneys are like my adoptive Iskaltian grandparents." Tierney took a sip of her drink and exhaled, a dreamy smile on her face. "My grandfather Brandon lives in Gelsi, and my grandmother Faolan lives in Myrkur with her wife, Shauna. They've only been married for a few years though. My grandmother Tierney was killed in a war before I was born, and my father's father was killed when he was just a child—and we don't talk about Dad's mother much—so the Sweenys are my surrogate grandparents."

"Here you go." Mrs. Sweeny set two baskets on the table. "You just let me know if you need anything else."

"Thanks, Mrs. S, you always have the best snacks." Tierney picked up a twisted piece of brown bread and broke it in half.

Mrs. Sweeny chuckled as she walked away. "Just like her mother."

"This will hit the spot." Tierney passed half of the bread to Keir.

"What is it?" He gave it a sniff and frowned. "Is this salt?" He flicked a piece of the rock salt off the bread.

"That's the best part." Tierney dipped the twist into a brownish yellow substance and took a big bite. "Just try it." She rolled her eyes at him.

Keir dipped his twist and took a bite. His eyebrows shot up as he chewed. "That's delicious. It's not like our bread at all."

"It's a pretzel. It's not bread like you're thinking. It's more of a snack that pairs well with ale or cider. We wouldn't serve it with a meal."

"You have spicy things." He pointed at the mustard. "It's more tangy than hot, but it's flavorful."

"Because we don't have to singe our mouths to taste our food." Tierney reached for the basket of cheese curds. "Try these. You'll thank me later."

Keir took a lump from the basket and dipped it in the brown substance served with it. Taking a bite, something gooey rushed out and juices ran down his fingers.

"Yeah, you kind of just need to go for it and eat the whole thing." She giggled, popping one of the curds into her mouth.

He grinned, cleaning his fingers. "I see why you were never a fan of our hard cheese."

"It's just wrong."

"See, I told you they would be here." Toby dropped into the seat beside his sister, and Logan pulled out the last chair.

"Do you mind if we join you?"

"Of course not." Tierney slapped her brother's hand away from the basket of pretzels. "Order your own. I've been deprived for months and months."

"No worries, dearies," Mrs. Sweeny called from the bar. "I'll have another round headed your way in a moment."

"Thanks, Mrs. S!" Toby called back.

"What are you doing here?" Tierney nudged her brother playfully.

"We have things to talk about." Toby pulled a map from his bag, spreading it across the table. "I sketched this from a map Grandfather found in the library."

Tierney leaned in, scrunching her nose up at the map. "It looks like the four kingdoms but bigger."

"It predates the Vatlands. This is a map of the original Lenya."

Keir leaned in to get a better look.

"Your people once ruled over all of the fae world long before our people even existed."

"What do you know?" Tierney turned to her brother.

"The Lenya of ancient times was destroyed by the formation of the vatlands. Your people managed to survive, but you were sealed off by the fire plains. There is a record we found that speculates your ancestors found a way to stop the spread of the fire plains.

"Over time, they receded. Grandfather believes the vatlands have expanded and receded at least one other time after that first instance. We have to find a way to destroy them, or it will happen all over again. Except, this time, it's possible none of us will survive."

Tierney reached for Keir's hand. "We have to find a solution. You need your magic. We have to get you a crystal so you can practice. It's been too long since any of you have been able to wield more than the simplest of magic."

"I thought of that." Logan rummaged through his pockets. "I went to the palace carpenter this morning and asked if he had any fire opals lying around. He gave me this one. I don't know if it's big enough for what you need, but it's a place to start until we can get more." Logan set the fire opal on the table. It was shaped like an icicle.

Keir just stared at it. "Your crystals are different from ours. The color is strange."

"Is it not the right kind?" Logan asked. "I can ask for another."

"No, it's powerful," Keir whispered, still not touching the crystal. "Ours are milky white, with streaks of clear blue and orange. I think they're weaker stones. We've been scraping the mines for what's left for generations. I think your fire opals must be purer."

"Can you sense how much power this holds?" Tierney ran a fingertip down the length of the fire opal.

Keir swallowed, his throat bobbing with the motion. "I think this totem is stronger than anything of its size I've ever seen in Lenya. I'm afraid to touch it."

"We're going to need all hands on deck to drive the fire plains back." Toby gave him a gentle nudge. "That means we're going to need everyone performing their best. You need practice, Keir."

"You're right. I ... don't even know what I'm capable of with this much magic. It feels … wrong to use such a thing for practice. Like a waste."

"You need to get over that because there are a million more where this one came from." Logan slid it closer to Keir. "This is the first of many. As we speak, King Loch is ordering a second trunk of crystals just for your use during your time here in the four kingdoms."

"Start with something small." Tierney squeezed his hand, and she blew out the candle at the center of the table. "Just light the candle."

Keir nodded, wrapping his fingers around the fire opal. He sucked in a breath, his eyes closing. A look of wonder fell across his face, and Tierney wanted to kiss him. To feel for herself all that he was feeling right now.

Keir lifted the opal. Opening his eyes, he muttered under his breath, and the candle flickered to life again. A storm blazed in his eyes as he took another breath and dropped the crystal.

"How did it feel?" Tierney whispered.

"Like I could lay waste to the entire world with just this one totem. It's like nothing I've ever known."

Toby grinned. "The vatlands don't stand a chance against all of us together."

Chapter 16
Keir

"I should be going with her." Keir paced the length of the throne room, waiting.

"We've been over this." Tierney lounged on her father's throne, and he couldn't help remembering the way she'd sat on the throne of Vondur the same way. Back then, it annoyed him. Now, she looked like she belonged there. "You can't both return to Lenya when we still need to figure out how to drive the vatlands back."

Keir stopped walking and turned to her. "What if all it takes is magic?"

Throwing one leg over the ornate golden arm of the throne, Tierney sighed. "Nothing is ever as simple as just needing magic. It isn't a cure-all for the world."

"But—"

"No, Keir. Stop. Bronagh will be fine. We'll figure out how to help her from here, and then you can return home for good and forget about all of us."

He didn't understand the bitterness in her tone, but when she mentioned him going home for good, something clenched inside him. Her father hadn't told her of their conversation, and it was clear both Gulliver and Griffin had kept silent as well.

"Tierney, I—" The double doors opening interrupted him.

Lochlan walked in with Toby, stopping when he caught sight of his daughter. He pointed one long finger at her. "Up."

She heaved herself off of his throne, muttering "It's just a chair."

Lochlan rubbed his eyes, as if the mere sight of her exhausted him. He took his seat as the queen breezed into the room with Bronagh, Imogen, and Veren. "Oh, good. You're all here. Let's get this started, shall we?"

Tierney hugged her arms across her chest, not meeting anyone's eyes. She hadn't spoken to him of her portals, but he knew fear when he saw it. The last time she opened one, she'd ended up a prisoner.

"Oh, and Tierney?" Her mom wrapped an arm around her shoulders. "You will also be going through."

"What?" Her eyes rounded, and Keir wanted to drag her away from this place, from anything that could hurt her.

"Told you she wouldn't like it, Mom." Toby rolled his eyes.

Lochlan leaned back on his throne. "Eldur and Fargelsi are trying to push back the swamplands. If we are to overcome the fire plains, attempting a less dangerous path first is wise. You and I will observe what they are doing and try to find a solution."

It was wise. Keir didn't relish the idea of stepping through one of the O'Shea portals either, but he'd do just about anything to help his kingdom.

The doors opened again, and two guards walked in, a giant wooden trunk between them. "Everything is prepared, your Majesty," one of them said.

Lochlan nodded to them. "Thank you. You may leave that here."

"Are those the crystals?" Bronagh asked, fiddling with the latch on the trunk. She managed to get the top open and revealed what must have been hundreds of small, fiery stones with colorful veins of magic running through them. It was … Keir had no words.

The room thrummed with power, and he soaked it in, letting it set every nerve ending on high alert. It wasn't until Lochlan stood and clapped his hands that he snapped out of it. "All right, dusk has fallen, and there is no use waiting now. Toby will open the portal to the human realm as he is best at bringing fae with him. Once we are there, we must hurry before dawn breaks. Then, Tia will help Toby open a portal to Lenya, but she won't go into it with them. After that is open, we can leave for Fargelsi."

It sounded complicated; most things in this kingdom seemed overly complex to Keir. But he'd learned in his short time that the king was trustworthy, and he'd never do anything to put his children in jeopardy.

Lochlan walked toward them, pressing a kiss to the side of his wife's head before turning to his daughter. "Are you ready for this?"

Tierney hesitated for a moment before dragging her eyes up. Her jaw clenched. "Yeah. Yes. I'm ready."

"That's my girl. Okay, everyone needs to have a hand on Tobias. Veren, Brea, you should both stand back."

Veren was already across the room, staying as far from the portal as physically possible.

Stepping up beside Tierney, Keir put a hand on Toby's arm next to hers, their pinkies brushing together. Lochlan, Bronagh, and Imogen joined them, and Toby closed his eyes, resting a hand on the trunk.

Keir didn't see it coming. A burst of light erupted in front of his face. Someone pulled him forward, and his stomach dropped as he fell through open sky, landing on the soft earth, his arm bent in an awkward angle. Pain twisted through him, and groaning surrounded him.

"Thanks for that landing, Tobes." Tierney scowled as she pushed herself to her feet.

"Everyone hurry." Lochlan looked to the sky.

They'd left Iskalt at dusk, but here, in what Keir presumed was the human realm, the early light of dawn peeked over the horizon. He barely got a chance to glance around before Lochlan started issuing orders.

"We probably only have a few more minutes before the Iskalt

power rests. Tierney, take your brother's hand. Picture Lenya; hold it in your heart. He will direct the magic."

Tierney shook her head and took a step back. "We've never done it this way before."

"Yeah, Dad, how do we know it'll work?" Toby looked more skeptical than scared, unlike his sister.

"It's a theory, but you need to try before we lose the moon altogether."

A breeze rustled the grass at Keir's feet, and he had no time to take in the human realm, to see anything other than Toby reaching out a hand to Tierney. They could do this. He knew it, but Tierney didn't.

Tears danced in her eyes. "I can't."

"You have to." Her father softened his voice. "Do we let our fears determine what we accomplish?"

She drew in a long breath. "But what if—"

"We have no use for what-ifs, Tia." He put a hand on her shoulder. "Only what is."

As hard as the Iskaltian king could be, Keir wanted to be a man like him, one who believed in the fae around him, who inspired them to greatness. A good leader didn't only help his fae; they motivated their fae to help each other.

After what felt like an eternity of waiting, Tierney nodded. "No what-ifs." She set her hand in Toby's, reaching the other out for Bronagh, who had Imogen on her other side. Toby gripped the handle of the wooden box of crystals. One moment they stood before him, and the next, it was only Tierney, a look of shock on her face.

"Did they get through?" Lochlan asked.

"I-I think so."

They wouldn't know until Toby returned, but there wasn't time to wait.

"Okay," the king said, holding out his hands. "Now, it's our turn."

In stunned silence, Keir grabbed hold of him and waited for the stomach-churning feeling he'd experienced only minutes before.

And then, he was falling again. This time, he landed in a thick patch of mossy forest. Tierney collided with him as she hit the ground, her knee digging into his gut.

But the warmth. It thawed out the chill—a persistent presence since the moment they washed up on the Iskaltian shore. Instead, a wave of heat enveloped them.

Tierney shrugged out of her fur-lined cloak. "I hate Eldur," she grumbled. "Always so dang hot."

Lochlan's lips hooked into a smile. "Try growing up here."

There was a story there, but no time to ask it because the snap of a stick told them someone was near. Keir immediately rose into a crouch, hand on the dagger at his waist. In Vondur, one must always prepare for an attack.

"What's he doing?" Lochlan asked.

Tierney shrugged. "Being weird."

A man stepped into view, a long sword hanging off his belt. He rested a hand on the hilt lazily. The intruder had an opposing frame, with a full beard and flashing eyes.

He stopped when he saw them. "Thought I heard trespassers back here. What's your business in Eldur?"

Keir would protect Tierney with his life. Today had been such a strange day, a fight would only cap it off.

Lochlan rose to his full height. "I speak of my business only to the queen. Do you realize to whom you speak?"

"Someone who thinks too highly of their own influence."

Tierney smirked. "I've been telling him that my entire life, so you're a little late."

The man approached Tierney, and Keir moved to stand between them.

"Boy," their attacker growled. "If you know what's good for you, you'll step out of the way." He looked over Keir's shoulder. "Really,

Tia? I thought you'd have better sense than to travel in the company of someone who'd try to start a fight he can't win."

Keir's spine stiffened when Tierney laughed.

"For the record, Uncle Finn, the only person who can best Keir in a duel is me." She ducked around Keir and wrapped the man—Finn—in a hug.

Shame washed over Keir. This man was the King of Eldur, and he'd wanted to fight him right here in his own forest.

"This is Keir," Lochlan said, walking past the man. "Don't scare him off, Finn. I like this one."

Finn turned to follow him. "Of the two of us, I think I'm less likely to send one of Tia's suitors running in the opposite direction."

Lochlan only grunted in response.

"He's not a suitor," Tierney said. "He's a king." Neither of those statements were true, but she didn't yet know.

Lochlan caught his eye, giving an encouraging nod. He just had to keep going, to figure out how to save Lenya, and then he could figure everything else out after.

They entered a clearing where sand and dirt mixed on the forest floor, as if the area couldn't decide whether it was a desert or a woodland. An army of fae occupied the space, some using their magic to push at an invisible foe.

"We're waiting for Neeve to arrive," Finn explained. "She sent word that she was a day's ride out. That was two days ago."

"The swamplands can be unpredictable." Lochlan rubbed the back of his neck. "If they had to travel around a bog or fight one of the creatures residing here, a small delay isn't something to worry over."

"Uncle Finn?" Tierney stared at the ground before surveying the surrounding area. "These aren't the vatlands. Dad would never have brought us so close."

"They are now. Until a few weeks ago, the ground we walk on was desert. It becomes more unstable by the day. We must be vigilant and on guard for quicksand as it changes."

"Tia!" A girl who couldn't have been more than a few years younger than Tierney ran toward them, giving Tierney a tight hug. "When my mom told me you'd returned, I wanted to go to Iskalt right away, but they needed me here."

"This is more important than me, but it's good to see you, Darra." Tierney released her. "What progress have you made?"

"Very little." As the girl reported to Tierney, Keir walked farther into the clearing. The ground underneath his feet was soft, saturated. Water seeped up through the grass and sand with each step he took.

For a moment, he watched the magic wielders work. They'd all been right. He may have wanted to go to Lenya, but being here would provide more aid than he could there.

The sound of many hooves pounding the dirt preceded horses thundering into the clearing. Keir turned to watch an impossibly tall woman jump from her saddle. She moved with the grace of someone who'd spent their entire life trying not to be seen. That must mean this was Neeve, the maid turned queen.

There were no excited greetings or introductions, only mild hellos before she got down to business. "The marsh is almost to the palace grounds." She gave a weary sigh. "If we do not stop its further movement, I do not know what will happen."

A hand slipped into Keir's, and he squeezed, knowing Tierney needed the strength as much as he did.

Finn scrubbed a hand over his beard. "We've been at this for the last two months now, and it's only grown. I don't know what more we can attempt."

"There's always more," Tierney put in.

"Our fae are tired." Darra sighed. "We cannot keep operating as we have been. When nothing works, we must change our tactics."

"What did you have in mind?" Lochlan looked willing to take the young woman's advice, and it reminded Keir of Eavha and how often he'd brushed her aside. He vowed never to do that again.

"Tia is here now. No one has a power like hers. Maybe she should try."

Tierney shook her head. "This isn't the prison magic, Darra. It's ancient and more powerful than we could ever imagine. The magic of the vatlands has created swamps, frozen mountains, fiery wastelands, and even a maelstrom in the center of the ocean. They're designed to keep us all apart, every kingdom."

"Yes, but you have the magic of three kingdoms in your blood." Even her father was looking at her like this idea might work.

"It's not that easy. I have the three, but that does not mean they are equal within me. My Fargelsian training has been in depth and I have the most experience with it. My Iskaltian magic is nearly equal, but my Eldurian magic is a distant third—and I've been without all of it for many months now. I can only attempt the simplest acts and this is not simple."

Neeve rubbed her forehead. "She's right. But we can't stop trying. It has been a long day and evening is nearly upon us. I'll have my fae begin shortly with some of the more complex Fargelsian spells and Tia can join with the other Iskaltians as best she can. We need all sides of magic working together in this."

Finn, Lochlan, and Darra followed her to where the other fae gathered near a fire that lit up the night.

Tierney didn't move to join them, her voice soft in the dark. "I feel like I'm letting them down."

"Tierney, look at me," Keir said.

She lifted her eyes, locking them on his.

"You aren't letting anyone down. No one knows your magic better than you."

"That's the thing, Keir. Ever since we've returned, I feel like I don't know it at all. I worked for years to control the power and never fully grasped that control in the way others do. But being without it for all those months …" She shrugged helplessly. "It's like a muscle memory has been lost."

"You'll get it back."

"I hope so."

He pulled her into a hug, and she rested her head against his chest.

"I want to do whatever is necessary to help your kingdom."

"I know you do."

"But I'm afraid of unleashing multiple sides of my power at once. What if I make it worse?"

"Can it be worse than threatening to destroy all fae life?"

She let loose a muffled laugh. "Probably not. Maybe we should just all evacuate to the human realm."

His nose scrunched. "I've heard your stories, your weird sayings. I think I'll take my chances with the fire plains."

She pressed a kiss to the side of his chin. "And if we can't stop them?"

"We never stop fighting."

They stood that way for a while, watching the Fargelsians work under the light of the moon. The Eldurians retreated to their tents to await the return of their magic with the sun.

Keir didn't sleep that night. Instead, he lay awake imagining a different world in which the vatlands never separated the kingdoms, never left Lenya on their own to become a warring land split in two. He could have grown up with prosperous villages, a father who loved him, the ability to keep his family safe.

In that world, there were no Comhracs, no battles with gold-clad warriors. Children didn't die of starvation. Mothers didn't live in fear.

Maybe, just maybe, it was the kind of world they could create one day. But first, they had to figure out how to have a future at all.

He crept from his tent as the sun rose to find the Eldurian contingent preparing to get back to work. Finn and Darra argued over something while Neeve looked on.

Lochlan sat on his own, a tin cup of tea in one hand.

Tierney wandered into the clearing, her mind clearly occupied.

"Everything okay?" Keir fell into step beside her.

"No."

"Care to tell me what's wrong?"

"Quicksand." She pointed through the trees. "Almost fell in it. The vatlands moved last night. They got too close to camp."

Something had to be done. If they couldn't solve the problem of the swampland, Lenya had no hope of holding off the fire plains.

Tierney joined the others and explained what she'd found. They jumped into action.

There wasn't much Keir could do but watch the efficient way the two kingdoms worked together now that the sun was out. He'd never seen such an alliance, but the Queen of Fargelsi and the King of Eldur stood side by side, their magic pooling in their fingertips as they tried to push the powerful vatlands back to where they belonged.

But where was that? The vatlands existed long before any of them were born, but they weren't natural to this world. For the first time, Keir wondered if simply stopping the spread wasn't enough.

Could they destroy them altogether?

"Lochlan," Finn yelled, "get your kingly butt over here."

Keir followed Lochlan and Tierney to where Finn was bent over, examining something on the ground. He pressed a hand to the soil, where only a few blades of grass poked through.

"Keep going," Finn yelled as his magic soaked into the ground. "I think it's working."

Neeve lowered herself to her knees to imitate Finn's actions, her eyes widening. The movement was small, slow, a tiny trickle of water pulling back through the ground. They all saw it.

Whatever they'd done, however this happened, Keir needed to learn everything.

Because for the first time, he saw the faint lines of hope in the form of receding water, drying land emerging from the murk of the swamp.

CHAPTER 17
BRONAGH

Bronagh's stomach sank to her toes as a light erupted around her. She clutched the trunk handle as if her life depended on it. Because it did. And not just her life. The lives of all her fae rested on this one chance to return to Lenya with enough magic to protect them from the immediate threat of the fire plains.

Without warning, the ground rushed up to greet them, but a small tug somewhere around her navel slowed her descent, and her feet touched the ground gently.

"That wasn't so bad." Toby glanced around, as if he magically transported himself to new lands every day. "It's rather hot here, isn't it?" He fanned his face with his free hand. The other held the trunk suspended between them.

"I don't think she's breathing." Imogen lunged for Bronagh. "Your Majesty, are you all right?"

Bronagh couldn't seem to remember how her lungs worked, and it took her a moment to suck in a breath.

"There it is; she's fine." Toby patted her shoulder in a soothing gesture. "It's never a fun way to travel if you're not used to it." He eyed the bleak countryside. "Any idea if we're where we're supposed to be?"

"We aren't in Grima, that's for sure." Imogen wrinkled her nose. "It don't smell right, does it, your Majesty?"

Bronagh shook her head. "Vondur." She pointed across the dry, cracked ground, where a well-traveled road stretched into the distance. Turning, she squinted into the bright afternoon sunlight. It was disconcerting to leave one place at dawn and arrive at another in the blink of an eye to find it nearly dusk with a blazing hot sun. "That way." She pointed to a hillside, where the road disappeared. "The palace is just beyond the crossroads."

"Do you think they'll receive us, Majesty?" Imogen bounded beside her queen, eager to help carry the trunk, but Bronagh wouldn't let it out of her sight.

"We have a peace treaty with Vondur now." Bronagh picked up her pace. "They will honor it." At least, she hoped. They had much bigger worries than an age-old war no one wanted to fight anymore.

Dust kicked up just beyond the hill. "Let's hurry." Toby matched Bronagh's pace. "Maybe we can hitch a ride."

Bronagh smiled at the strange saying. "You're not at all like your sister in so many ways, but in others, you're the same."

"Mom says I'm her quiet, even-tempered child." Toby shrugged. "I think that's Mom talk for I'm her favorite."

A troop of scouts trotted along the road, kicking up more dust. Bronagh was sweating and eager to get out of the baking hot sun. The ground crunched beneath her feet, and she swore the bottoms of her shoes were melting.

"Hail there!" a soldier called out to them. "Do you seek refuge from the burning lands?"

Bronagh shielded her eyes from the sun as she looked up to see a mixture of Vondurian and Grimian uniforms. She smiled at the sight. "I am Bronagh Agnew, Queen of Grima. I have returned from Iskalt with Prince Tobias O'Shea. We must speak with Princess Eavha Dagnan right away."

"Your Majesty, you made it!" A young officer slid from his mount. "We've been worried sick for your return." He led his horse across the hard ground to her side. “Please, take my mount. I will carry your trunk.”

“I would keep it with me if you please.” She passed the trunk off to Toby and pulled herself up into the saddle. “I’ll tie the trunk to the back of my saddle, but could my companions also have a horse?”

“I’ll ride with Imogen.” Toby smiled and thanked a soldier for lending him his horse.

He pulled Imogen up to sit behind him, and Bronagh led the way down the worn road to the crumbling castle, where she hoped they could all work together to defeat the fire plains before it was too late.

“Bron? Is that you?” A shriek of excitement echoed from the ramparts, where a leather-clad Eavha leaned over the parapet to get a better look. Her pet rested on her haunches beside her.

“We have returned.” Bronagh beamed at the young girl. “And what a tale I have to tell you!”

“Who is that with you? Is it Tia?” Eavha gasped and ran across the wall to the tower steps that led to the courtyard.

“Well, I can’t wait to tell my sister someone thinks she looks like me.” Toby ran a soothing hand over his horse’s mane and urged her into a trot.

“Eavha is more exuberant than observant.” Bronagh laughed. “But she grows on you. She also adores your sister.”

“And she has a very large cat chasing her.” Toby’s eyes shot up as they entered the courtyard and the princess came darting down the stairs to meet them.

“Sheba, don’t freak out our guests.” Eavha made the big cat sit before she came to greet them.

“I have so much to tell you.” Bronagh slipped from her mount, reaching back to release the trunk from its binding.

“Did you find it? Is my brother okay?”

“Iskalt? Yes. And it’s beautiful. Keir is still there with Tierney and the rest of her family.”

"They'll be in Fargelsi by now." Toby dismounted and turned to greet Eavha. "Hi there, I'm Tia's twin brother."

"Toby?" Eavha's jaw dropped open, and she lunged at him, wrapping her arms around him. "I didn't think I'd ever get to meet you."

"It's a pleasure, Princess Eavha." He released her and gave her a small bow. "I won't be with you long. I'll need to return to my family once the moon rises."

"The moon?" She turned questioning eyes on Bronagh.

Bronagh just shrugged. "Let's go inside, and I'll tell you everything."

"We don't have the luxury of time, I'm afraid." Eavha looped her arm through Toby's and the other through Bronagh's. Imogen followed them with the chest of priceless crystals. "The fire plains are upon us, and we're losing the battle. Most of Lenya is lost, and we're surrounded now.

"How many have we lost?" Bronagh was afraid to hear the answer.

"Too many to count." Eavha guided them into the palace and straight to the throne room, where most of the Vondurian court were in attendance.

"Leave us," Eavha called to the room. "I will be in the council chambers with Queen Bronagh and Prince Tobias." She marched across the room, careless of the whispering.

Bronagh sent Imogen with a maid to get settled comfortably and have a proper meal. She was clear that the girl must be cared for as if she were a princess herself. As far as Bronagh was concerned, the girl would never want for anything the rest of her life ... however long that might be.

When they were alone in the small hall behind the throne room, Eavha threw her hands up in the air. "I hope you have the answers to all our problems in that powerful trunk of yours because just the feel of it is terrifying."

Bronagh flipped the latch and opened the trunk filled with the most potently powerful crystals anyone in Lenya had ever seen.

"Oh my." Eavha sank into the nearest chair. "I've never felt so much power from one little box." She clutched the totem around her neck. "I wouldn't even know what to do with them."

"We're going to have to figure it out. It isn't just about Lenya and the fire plains anymore. It's happening on the other side too. They call places like the fire plains vatlands. And they're all expanding."

"My family and the royals from each of the four kingdoms are hard at work searching for a solution." Toby reached for a crystal from the trunk. "Our magic is different. We don't need such vessels to reach it, but none of that matters. Iskalt, Fargelsi, Eldur, and Myrkur are all your allies now." He handed Eavha the crystal, but she shrank back from it.

"I couldn't ... it's too much. I wouldn't know what to do with it."

Toby smiled, placing the crystal back into the box. "We will work together to find a solution. But I must leave you tonight. Now that I have visited Lenya for myself, I will return once we have more news."

"I have some news myself. I fear you'll never believe me." Eavha eyed the crystals, moving to sit at the large wooden table near the windows. "You'll want to sit down for this." She set a key on the table. It was an old-fashioned kind of key made of silver and set with blue sapphires.

"Keir gave me this key before he left. It unlocks a small chamber in the king's rooms. It contains all the knowledge of ancient Lenya."

"Like a library?" Toby leaned forward. "We have lots of experience with ancient libraries."

"Not a library. A book. A journal really." Eavha's brow furrowed. "A journal of all the kings of Vondur, all the way back to the very first one. But it goes back even further than Vondur. It has histories of every ruler of ancient Lenya. I've studied the book night and day, looking for answers, and I thought I found it. This has all happened before. I think it's how our kingdoms came to be isolated from yours."

Toby nodded. "We've found similar histories."

"There was one line I read." Eavha leaned forward. "It spoke of how the fire plains came to be and how they were controlled. When our people retreated to this side of the plains, they were fleeing in much the same way we are now. But they were able to stop the spread."

"How?" Toby and Bronagh both hung on her every word.

"There was a spell of some sort, but it was in a language I didn't recognize."

"May I see this book?" Toby asked.

"That's just it." Eavha shook her head. "It disappeared."

"Someone stole it?" Bronagh asked.

"No. It vanished. Right from my hands, like magic. Like real, honest-to-goodness magic. One moment it was there, and the next it was gone. I know I can't expect you to believe such a thing, but—"

Bronagh held her hand up to stop her. "I've seen enough strange things since I left Lenya. I believe you."

"What are we going to do, Bron?"

"We're going to use these crystals and put our best soldiers and magic wielders to the test. We'll do the best we can with what we've got."

"And I will be in touch with more news as soon as I'm able." Toby took Bronagh's and Eavha's hands in his. "We are all in this together."

CHAPTER 18
TIERNEY

It took nearly two days to leave Fargelsi and portal back to the human realm, wait for night, and return to Eldur, where the sun was just setting when they made camp along the banks of Sol Loch. Normally one of Tierney's favorite places to visit, with its warm sulfur springs and hot mud baths, it was now in danger of being consumed by the fire plains. Already, the vast lake was evaporating in the intense heat.

They waited impatiently for the sun to rise so they could get to work. Neeve accompanied them to Eldur to help push the fire plains back in the same way her people were doing along the Gelsi-Eldur border dealing with the marshlands. It was slow going, but it was working.

Uncle Finn and his Eldurian magic wielders were well-rested and ready to get to work. Tierney was anxious to do her part, bringing as much Gelsi magic as she could contribute alongside her aunt and the handful of fae she'd brought with her. Even Brea was prepared to aid with either side of her magic wherever it was needed.

"This is exhausting." Keir paced across the cracked desert clearing. They were camped as close as they could get to the plains without risking their tents to fires. "Does it not drive you mad to wait for the sun and the moon to use your magic?"

"Not any more than it would drive me mad to need a vessel to use my magic. Just think of it like the sun acts as a totem for all of Eldur. They have to await its arrival to be able to reach their power."

"I'm just anxious to see this work."

"It started working for Gelsi, it will work here." Tierney pointed to the horizon. "Look, they're gathering already. Come on."

Sweat poured down Tierney's face as they crossed the desert sands, trying to ignore the way her shoes felt like tiny ovens strapped to her feet.

Dozens of Eldurians knelt in the sand, waiting for their magic to rise with the sun. The Gelsi fae were already at work, their hands reaching into the hot desert earth, letting their magic trickle into the ground, soon to meet with Eldurian power. Together, the two kingdoms would heal the fire plains, pushing them back within their borders.

Part of Tierney wished they could push them all the way to Lenya. She wanted a world where her friends weren't so isolated.

"Ready for this?" Tierney's mother said as she and aunt Alona came to join them.

"We've got this." She squeezed her aunt's hand. Alona would wait with Keir, Uncle Myles, and Lochlan while everyone else went to work.

Sinking her fingers into the hot sand, Tierney called on her Fargelsi magic, murmuring the words Aunt Neeve had taught her.

Laekena pao sem brennte hefur verio.

The ground heated as Eldurian fire magic poured in to join the Gelsi magic. Tierney held her breath, waiting for some sign that the plains were receding. For the sand to cool and moisture to return to the air. Something.

"It's not working," she whispered to her mother.

"Keep trying." Brea pushed her hands deeper into the ground, the Gelsi spell falling from her lips.

An hour later and nothing had changed. Neeve sat back on her heels. "I am afraid we are wasting our energy."

"Why would it work in Gelsi but not in Eldur?" Tierney frowned, dusting the sand from her blistered hands. "It doesn't make any sense."

"We will just have to try something else." Brea stood and brushed the sand from her leggings. "We have enough magic wielders here that we are bound to come up with a solution."

But Tierney didn't miss the shadow of worry that filled her mother's eyes. "We can't leave them trapped in Lenya much longer, Mom. If we can't find a solution …" Her eyes filled with tears as she thought of the danger Eavha and all her people could be in right this moment.

"If all else fails, we will bring them here. We will not let them suffer. We just need more time." Brea ran a hand through her sweaty hair. "The one thing we don't have enough of."

The wind kicked up, and sand whirled around them.

"Something's happening." Tierney looked around, hoping for a miracle, but she knew what this was. "Keir! Over here!" she called, waving him frantically over to her side.

"Your grandfather really shouldn't be driving that thing. He's never been very good at it." Brea ducked her head and held on to Tierney.

"What's happening?" Keir reached her side, draping an arm around her as if to protect her from some strange foe.

"It's okay, Keir," Tierney shouted over the roar of the wind.

Golden light sparked above them, and the Library of Aghadoon appeared, settling into the landscape like it always belonged there.

"He must be out of sorts if he forgot to hide the village." Brea shook her head with a smile. "I think you need to help Keir out. I'm not sure he's breathing."

Tierney reached for his arm. "It's fine; everything is fine. It's just my grandfather."

Keir gaped at the sight of the normally concealed village. He pointed at the buildings, blinking his eyes as if to clear the vision from his sight.

"Did that ... just drop out of the sky?"

"There's no place like home." Brea snickered, and Uncle Myles threw his head back and laughed. Everyone else just shook their heads at whatever human nonsense they were talking about.

"You know, sometimes I hate living among the fae." Brea shook her head. "No one ever gets my jokes."

"Begone, my pretty!" Myles cackled in a creepy voice as he advanced on Brea, hunched over with his hands raised like claws. "Before someone drops a house on you!"

It was Brea's turn to laugh.

"Just ignore them." Tierney sighed. "My guess is they're shouting movie quotes at each other. Let's just pretend whatever they're doing didn't just happen."

"What about that?" Keir pointed at the village. "How did that place just fall out of the sky?"

"It's a really long story." She linked her arm around Keir's. "The short version is this is the village of Aghadoon. It contains a very powerful library with all the histories of the fae. My grandfather Brandon—former King of Fargelsi—is the custodian of the library. If he's gone to the trouble of moving the village, then he's likely found something important."

"Okay, but I want the long version of this story at some point. Libraries don't just fly around, Tia."

"Here, they do." She tugged him toward the crumbling columns that marked the entrance into the village. Brandon was already making his way down from the library.

"Hi, Dad, what have you found?" Brea walked to greet him. He carried a large leather-bound book, thick with handwritten pages. He held it open to a specific spot.

"It's not a solution, but it's important." Brandon paused to drop a kiss on Brea's forehead. "Sorry for the sloppy arrival. I was in a hurry." He thrust the book out in front of him. "The vatlands aren't natural."

Tierney had never seen her grandfather so rattled. "What do you mean?" She moved to stand behind her mother, peering over her shoulder to see the book.

"It seems there was an ancient war among the original Lenyans who ruled these lands before us. There were many kingdoms at that time, and they were at constant war with each other for one reason or another. They couldn't negotiate peace, so they agreed to live separately. They created the vatlands as physical boundaries to separate their kingdoms and bring an end to the conflict. For ages and ages, it worked and there were no more wars. But then, the vatlands began to expand as they are now."

"What did they do?" Tierney stepped closer, her heart in her throat as she hoped for some clue that would lead them to the answer.

"They died," Brandon said flatly. "Except for a small group, who somehow survived."

"Doesn't that book tell you how they survived?" Her voice cracked. They needed answers, not more dead ends.

"Not that I have found , but we're still looking."

"We are running out of time, Grandfather."

"May I ask where you found this book?" Keir's face had gone pale with shock.

"The library here is a mystical place. I'm not sure I can explain where it came from, but it showed up while I was searching for information on your homeland."

"That is my father's book. How could you possibly have a book that sits in my father's rooms in the palace of Vondur? I gave my sister access to that very book before I left, hoping she would find some source of information in it."

"Are you certain it's the same book?" Tierney sniffed back her tears.

"May I?" Keir reached for the book, and Brandon let him take it.

Flipping through the pages, Keir stopped on a page toward the back. "It's the same. This is my father's handwriting. I don't understand how you have it. Can your flying library reach Vondur?"

"The library houses all the knowledge of the fae worlds." Brandon scratched his head. "That doesn't mean every book and scroll is physically there at all times. The magic of the library shows us what we need based on the subjects we are searching for. It's possible the magic somehow acquired this book ... or perhaps an identical copy of it simply because we needed this information."

"That is a conversation for another time." Tierney pulled their attention back to the important discussion. "The fact is, we need to study this book. It has to be what Keir's father mentioned when he told me he had access to great knowledge of the histories of all the realms. At the time, it seemed like he knew a lot more than he was saying. This book might be the clue to what we're looking for."

"Why is it always a magic book we have to decipher to figure out how to save the world?" Brea muttered.

"There is one other thing." Brandon's voice grew soft. "There was a treaty the ancients created when they set the vatlands in place." He glanced at Brea, taking a deep breath before he continued. "The vatlands were meant to be stationary as long as the terms of the treaty were honored. It seems when Tierney crossed into Lenya, taking the magic of *three* kingdoms with her into a land that had no such magic, she broke the treaty. The magic saw her arrival as an invasion of three kingdoms against one, and it triggered the consequences the ancients set in place. They wanted the treaty to last, and so they made the consequences of breaking it so dire no one ever dared risk it."

"But how can that be?" Brea asked. "Tia has traveled across vatlands before. We all have."

Brandon shook his head. "When she was a child with Gelsi magic, yes, but since she came of age and inherited the magic of Eldur and Iskalt just a few short years ago, has she made such a journey?"

"Anytime we've visited Gelsi, Eldur, or Myrkur in recent years, we've traveled through portals." Brea's shoulders slumped.

"So, you're saying it's my fault." Tierney took a step back. "All of it." A vital piece of her soul shattered inside her, and she couldn't see past the veil of tears clouding her eyes. "The expanding fire plains that have killed thousands. It's because of me and my stupid, childish impulsive behavior."

"Tia." Brea took a step toward her daughter.

Tierney shook her head. "No." She turned and walked away from their sympathetic eyes.

"Any luck?" Keir asked Brea as she approached.

The queen gave a sad sigh and shook her head. "She won't talk to me. I'm the only one in this entire realm who could understand the power inside her, how it's shaping her reactions, her emotions, but I can't help her if she won't allow me to."

"You mean she's even more upset because of the magic?"

"In a way. If we do not control it, it amplifies our emotions. The news is horrible, but it is not her fault. She didn't know the consequences of such an action. Yet, there's so much turmoil inside her I'm not sure she'll be able to see that."

"Let me try, Mom." Toby walked toward them through the dark. He'd only arrived a few minutes before, returning from Lenya.

His mom placed a hand on his shoulder. "Honey, I think the best thing we can do for her right now is give her peace."

"But—"

"Come, let's get you fed. From what Tia tells me, I'm sure you didn't enjoy the food in Lenya with all of its spices." She looked at Keir. "He's always had a bit of a weak stomach when it comes to spice, like my husband."

"Mom." Toby groaned.

Keir was torn between following Toby to get a report on Lenya and seeking out Tierney. The latter won out. Once Toby and Brea were safely occupied and not watching, he walked off into the dark. Pulling a crystal from his pocket, he used it to light his path.

He found Tierney sitting on a sandstone boulder at the edges of Sol Loc, where the water had receded from the banks. She had her knees pulled up to her chest and her chin resting on them. For a moment, she didn't look like the version of Tierney he knew—the warrior, the fierce princess.

Instead, she was just a girl, one who'd received the worst news of her life.

"If you knew me at all, you'd know I want to be alone," she said without turning to look at him.

Keir stepped forward, stopping at her side. "It's a good thing I don't know you at all then." He lifted a brow and looked down at her. It was a lie. He'd started wondering if he knew Tierney O'Shea better than anyone else in her life. For one, when she said to leave her alone, he refused to allow her to wallow.

They both stared at the shrinking lake as the silence stretched between them. Finally, when Tierney spoke, her voice wavered like she was trying not to cry. "Do you hate me, Keir?"

"No," he answered quickly.

"You should. Your fae are dead because of me. Your lands …" Her breath stuttered as it pushed past her lips.

Keir didn't move. "My fae are dead because our ancestors decided magic was the only way to peace."

"Isn't it?"

"Come on. I know you better than that. There's always another way." She'd spent months in Lenya with no magic and managed to bring peace to his kingdom for the first time in many years.

At first, he thought she might consider his words, but she shook her head. "Peace has no meaning if there isn't anyone left to enjoy it."

"Tierney O'Shea, are you giving up?"

Her head jerked up, and her eyes snapped to his. "No."

"Really? Because it sounds an awful lot like you are. We're still trying to pull back the fire plains, and I'm not ready to call it a failure yet. I refuse to believe we came this far only to be stopped by a little magic."

"A little magic." She snorted. "You mean all the power of our ancients? They were strong enough to divide the kingdoms, to place the vatlands between us."

"And you're stronger." He lowered himself to the boulder at her side. "*We're* stronger."

"You sound like my Uncle Myles with his undying hope. Stop it. It's not natural for you."

Keir bumped her shoulder. "Maybe I'm tired of fearing the worst. Maybe I'm tired of focusing on what's wrong and want to make things right."

Tierney glanced away into the dark. "That doesn't change what I did."

"No, what your magic did. Aren't you the one who says it's like its own being? That you can't always control it?"

"Yes, but—"

"No, listen. You made a giant mistake. I won't say you didn't. But you didn't set off to hurt anyone." He pictured his kingdom, how both Vondur and Grima now worked together. If they managed to succeed in fighting off the fire plains, a new day would dawn for all of Lenya.

Tears streaked down Tierney's cheeks, and she didn't wipe them away. "But I did. I hurt so many fae."

Every sob that echoed out of her further cracked his heart. He wasn't sure when her feelings had become his, but he couldn't stand how broken she looked. Wrapping both arms around her, he held her against him.

Tierney clutched his tunic, crying into it, her back shaking. "I don't know how to get past this."

"You keep fighting."

"What if I don't know how?"

Keir smoothed the hair back from her face and pressed a kiss to her forehead, closing his eyes. "You will." He had more faith in her than he'd ever had in anyone else. Trust didn't come easy to men like him, but he knew Tierney's heart. He knew every intention she'd had was of the purest sort.

They sat together for a while, neither of them feeling the need to speak. Tomorrow, they would go back to battling the fire plains, but tonight, it was just the two of them and the dark.

After a while, Tierney's breathing evened out into sleep. She leaned most of her weight on Keir, and he smiled into her hair. In sleep, she wasn't sad or fierce, irritating or stubborn. She was just Tierney, free from the masks she wore.

Keir gathered her into his arms and stood. Her head lolled onto his shoulder, her breath warming his neck. The night was hot, his skin sticky with sweat, and yet he didn't want to let her go. Not now, not ever.

Carrying her through camp, he greeted Brea and Toby with nods. Toby tried to follow him, but Brea held him back.

Keir ducked into Tierney's tent and lowered her slowly to the bedroll. She murmured something unintelligible, and he smiled. It was so rare he saw her with her defenses down. He could have watched her all night.

On his knees, Keir bent forward, pressing his nose, his lips to the spot right above the corner of her left eye. "I'm not giving up on you, Tierney," he whispered. "Please don't give up on yourself."

Most of the camp was quiet as Keir emerged from the tent. The Iskaltian magic wielders were working at the border of the fire plains while the Eldurians rested. Tierney would be vexed she fell asleep instead of helping, but he didn't have the heart to wake her.

A single figure sat by the fire, more for light than warmth in this hot climate. Keir had no desire to be close to anything that would add to the heat, but he found himself walking in that direction regardless.

Brandon O'Rourke looked up as he neared. "Ah, our Lenyan friend. I was wondering when I'd finally get to speak with you." He gestured to the space next to him. "It's a little crowded out here, but I've made room for you."

Keir glanced around the empty area before lowering himself to the ground. "You're the one who … er … flew the village here."

"Yes, yes. Normally, I would be among my books right about now." He gestured to where the village rose out of the dark. "But I came to speak with my daughter and then was hoping to speak with you."

"Me?"

"Oh, yes. Lenya is fascinating to me. We did not know of its true existence until the library decided to show us the right materials. You use fire opals as magical totems, correct?"

Keir only understood about half of what the man said. He pulled out his crystal. "We don't call them opals, but yes, they allow us to harness the power."

Brandon shook his head, his eyes wide. "Truly amazing. And here we thought the human realm was our most incredible discovery. You sailed here through the stormy seas, I'm told."

Keir nodded. "They call it the maelstrom and told us it was impassable. It probably would have been had it not been for Tia's magic returning."

"The maelstrom. Brilliant." He stared into the flames, and Keir could practically see his mind turning. "Where would you say this maelstrom was?"

"Far out at sea."

"Yes, I know that, but did it come upon you while you passed the fire plains?"

"Actually, it was after we got around them, but not long after."

He smiled, as if he'd known that would be the answer. "I have some theories, young king. I think the maelstrom occurs when the sea and the air around it shifts so suddenly from the extreme heat of the fire plains to the icy blasts of the mountain vatlands. It's an unnatural phenomenon."

"Wait, so you're saying it's all a part of this magic as well?"

"In an indirect way, yes."

That meant … "If we succeed in pulling back the fire plains, the maelstrom—"

"Might disappear. But like I said, it is only a theory."

The implications of such a theory were endless. If Lenya was no longer limited in their use of the seas, it changed everything from fishing capabilities to trade.

A snore came from Tierney's tent, and Keir looked back over his shoulder.

Brandon followed his gaze. "Is my granddaughter well? I probably shouldn't have revealed what I'd found."

Keir couldn't fault the man for bringing them any and all information he found on the vatlands. "No, she would have wanted to know." He sighed. "She blames herself for all of this, you know."

Brandon was quiet for a moment. "Every action we take has consequences. The severity of those consequences comes down to luck." He paused. "The O'Shea portal magic is both the most powerful and most unknown magic in the fae realm. Tierney has never had much control over it, and her actions were rash and irresponsible."

Keir was about to defend her when Brandon continued.

"But that girl has done more for the four kingdoms than any other living fae. She was a child when she started correcting our mistakes from long ago, righting our wrongs. Now, it is time for us to do the same for her.

"No one is ever blameless. And no one is ever entirely at fault." He pushed to his feet. "I think I'll return to my bed in the village. When Tierney wakes up, tell her she is welcome to an actual room, though I doubt she'll take me up on it. Stubborn as her mother, that one." He smiled. "But stubbornness is what saves us all."

He walked off, leaving Keir alone with the night and his thoughts. For so long, he'd blamed his father for problems in Vondur, he'd blamed himself.

No one is ever blameless, young king. And no one is ever entirely at fault.

They would fix this mistake made by their ancestors long ago. They would defeat the vatlands. And then, maybe everything they'd done would be worth it.

Maybe there would be fae left to enjoy the well-earned peace.

CHAPTER 20
BRONAGH

Bronagh stared across the wasteland at the remnants of the newest village to succumb to the fire plains. Where wooden houses once stood, only ashy ground remained. Stone pillars and fences bore the mark of fire, black scorching up their once smooth surfaces. In the center of the village was a well, now nothing more than a circle of stones, the ground beneath them sucked dry.

And it was so close. Too close.

The children and feeble of Grima were safely tucked into the mountain fortress, the network of caves that had hidden Grimians for generations.

As the fire plains expanded up into the mountains, though, even that wasn't safe.

The line between Grima and Vondur was blurred, the borders overtaken by bubbling geysers erupting from the ground, hot steam pouring into the atmosphere.

Now, there was no division, no two kingdoms against each other. Only one.

"We don't have long." Eavha stepped up beside Bronagh, Sheba shadowing her as always. The huge cat intimidated Bronagh, but there was also a strange comfort in the protection she provided, though not even her long teeth and razor claws could fight their enemy now.

"Are you afraid, Eavha?" For their fae, for their kingdom, and the future they wouldn't have.

Eavha lifted her chin. "You cannot have courage without first experiencing fear."

"And it's going to take every ounce of our courage to overcome this now."

Donal joined them, his arms crossed over his chest. He was too young for this, they both were, but circumstances forced them into roles they had to embrace. "When the Iskaltian prince returns, can't he just usher our fae to safety through that … portal he opened?"

Bronagh shook her head. "We will succumb to the fire plains before they do, but they are not immune. Each of their vatlands is expanding, covering more ground and encroaching on their villages."

"Vatlands." Her uncle crossed his arms where he stood a few paces away. "Magic without totems. Are we sure we wish to put our faith in such notions?"

"Keir is there. He is of Lenya."

"He is of Vondur." A scowl flashed across her uncle's face. Old ideas were hard to overcome.

Eavha turned to face him, her cheeks flushing red. "And what is wrong with Vondur, Grimian?"

Uncle Cormac started to respond, but Bronagh cut him off. "Not now. There is no time for this." She turned and walked back to where their party gathered. Sweat dripped down the small of her back, and it would only get worse.

The air hung heavy with the scent of sulfur and the intense heat. "Declan, bring the crystals." She'd tasked the general with protecting them on the journey. Eavha trusted him, and that was enough for her.

Declan lugged the trunk forward and set it on the ground. He popped the latch, and when he opened it, a collective gasp wound through the group.

Here, on the edges of the fire plains, the best warriors of all of Vondur and Grima stood together, red and gold, friend and foe. These were the fae trained to use totems to their greatest potential. One day, she hoped the magic could be accessible to all Lenyans.

Imogen crouched next to the trunk and pulled out a crystal, lobbing it toward the nearest soldier. He plucked it out of the air, and she threw another one, never missing.

"What you hold are the fire opals of the kingdoms on the far side of the fire plains. They may be our only hope of holding them back. We must work in shifts to have totem wielders awake at all times. This will not be easy, and it may not be short. Our fae are counting on our ability to stop the spread." She had no delusions that they'd be able to push the fire plains back, but they may just be able to slow its progression until Keir learned of another solution.

"Is everyone ready?" When a few soldiers murmured in assent, she nodded to Declan. "Your men are up first."

"Yes, your Majesty." Declan was good at taking orders, at playing the role of king's general. In her case, at the moment, he was the queen's general. She hoped Keir wouldn't mind if she stole him.

Declan approached the place where the air seemed to shimmer and move. Sweat broke out across his face. Bronagh joined him, clenching her jaw against the intense heat.

As Declan's men lined up, they lifted their totems.

"Now," Bronagh yelled.

Light exploded from the opal, and Bronagh's feet lifted as the force of the power threw her backward. She hit the ground and stared up into dark skies. Despite the early hour, rain clouds blocked the sun from view. She couldn't help thinking how fitting it was as she tried to breathe.

"Bron." Eavha bent over her. "Are you alive?"

A laugh burst out of Bronagh, and she stopped when pain lanced through her. "Yes." She rolled onto her side and pushed herself up.

"I'm fine." Around her, most of Declan's men picked themselves up off the ground.

Declan surveyed them with a dazed look. He was the only fae still standing.

"That was ..." Bronagh shook her head. She'd never felt such power. It called to her, wanting her to let its full force free. These fire opals were not the weak crystals the fae of Lenya were used to.

She stared at the opal lying in the grass beside her.

"It's moving," Declan yelled. "Everyone get back." He jumped just in time to see the ground where he'd been standing die, green grass going black before crumbling into dust.

The Lenyans scrambled away from the heat, urging their horses closer to the forest at their backs.

No, this wasn't happening. Bronagh stilled and focused on the crystal in her hand. "Eavha," she called. Eavha, Declan, and Donal ran toward her. "We have to slow it down."

Her uncle joined them, an opal clutched in his palm. "Let the magic inside you, let it filter through you. Gain control through your will."

Bronagh closed her eyes, slowing her heartbeat and sending all her energy into the stone. Magic curled around her fingertips, arcing up over her arm and engulfing her in a wave of power unlike anything she'd ever experienced. Was this how Tierney felt every day of her life?

It was exhilarating to be this strong.

She gripped the opal tighter in her fist, imagining she held the magic in the palm of her hand. This time, when she let it free, it had a leash around its neck.

A blast of golden power hit the hazy edges of the heat. A geyser of steam extinguished as the others joined her.

"I think it's slowing down," Declan yelled above the roaring in Bronagh's ears.

Energy leached out of Bronagh until it was all she could do to hold herself up. They'd done it. They'd slowed the spread. At least for the moment.

The crystals worked, but they weren't enough.

If they were going to reclaim Lenya's scorched plains, it was going to take a lot more power than they possessed.

Chapter 21

Tierney

"I swear, all we're doing is making it angry." Tierney tucked her face under the scrap of fabric she'd wrapped around her head to shield herself from the sand storm. Each grain of sand felt like tiny hot needles stabbing into her flesh.

She mopped the sweat from her brow and searched the sea of dirty faces around her. "We're throwing everything we have at this, hoping something will stick. We need to work smarter."

"I think we're all tired and we might need a break." Brea stretched her back and groaned. "This old lady needs a glass of wine and a bath. A cold one." She wiped the sweat from her face with the back of her hand.

Tierney paced back to the campsite, flinging herself down on the ground in the shade of a lone tree. She saved the more comfortable seats for her parents, aunts, and uncles. They were old, after all.

"Aunt Neeve?" Tierney waited for her aunt to sit as the other royals made their way back into camp. "I don't understand how this is working in Fargelsi and not here."

"I don't either, love, but I received a report this morning that it continues to work. They've managed to push the marshlands back toward their borders. It will take time, but I believe we can eventually heal the entire marsh. We have fae working from both sides now. The Dragur Forest is nearly free of the effects already."

Tierney was thrilled for Gelsi and Eldur. It was a relief to know something was working somewhere. It was getting worse everywhere else. Ice storms were raging across Iskalt. If they didn't get results here in the fire plains soon, they were going to have to join the magic wielders back home to see if they could make progress there. For now, it was safe to say Iskaltians knew how to handle a blizzard.

"Tell me again how it worked."

"Darling, let your aunt Neeve have a rest." Brea fanned her face with a palm frond. "We need our wits about us if we're going to figure this out."

"That's just it, Mom. I feel like it's right there, just out of my reach. I can feel it, like my magic knows the answer and it's just waiting for me to catch up." Tierney worried her bottom lip, chapped from the hot desert winds racing across the plains.

"Is it something in your magic specifically?" Keir came to sit in the shade with them.

"No. Yes. Maybe? I don't know." She threw her hands up, wishing the answer would just fall out of the sky.

"Maybe your young man is onto something," Neeve said, and Tierney chose to ignore her aunt's nosey insinuations.

"Like what?"

"It wasn't exactly a specific Gelsi spell that worked. It was more a request to heal the land. But it didn't work until we joined with the Eldurians, like we needed the right blend of magic we just happened to stumble upon."

"Oh!" Tierney sat up straight, trying to force her mind down the right path to the answer that continued to elude her.

"What is it, Tia?" Her father was the one to catch on to her excitement.

"I need a map! Does anyone have one?"

"Yes, we all carry maps of the world in our pockets when we're on an emergency expedition to save Eldur and Lenya." Brea's dry humor rolled right off Tierney's back.

"I have one." Keir fished through his bag. "Well, a sketch of one I made from a map I found in the library at the palace. Not your magical flying library." He passed her a journal opened to the center page.

"Perfect, you already added Lenya." Tierney's eyes darted across the pages, her mind working faster than she could articulate her thoughts. "May I draw on this?" She glanced at Keir.

"Well, yes, but don't ruin it." He handed her a quill and ink. "I'd like to replicate it for our records once I return."

Tierney sketched a line where the original fire plains should be within their boundaries along Eldur and Lenya. "If you had to guess, where would you think the maelstrom would fall on this map?" She held it out for Keir to see.

"Somewhere in here." He pointed to the narrowest part of the sea separating Lenya from the far reaches of Iskalt. "Your grandfather and I were just talking about this the other day. He believes the maelstrom occurs because it resides between fierce opposing temperatures."

Tierney nodded. "That makes sense." She sketched a quick spiral shape where the sea narrowed. From there, she drew a line to represent the Northwestern Vatlands.

"Look at this, everyone." She held up the map, using the feathered quill to point to the fire plains. "What if all of this is one big vatland? The fire plains, the maelstrom, and the impenetrable mountains?"

"That is possible." Lochlan studied the map. "What are you thinking, Tia? If we can find the right magic, we can heal all three areas? That still doesn't solve our current dilemma."

"Look here." Tierney scrambled across the sand to sit at her father's side. "It's working in the marshlands." She pointed to the map. "With Gelsi and Eldurian magic." She pointed to either side of the marshlands.

Lochlan's eyes widened in surprise. "My daughter's a genius." He scanned the map.

"Sure, she's your daughter when she's a smarty pants, but she's mine when she opens portals to lands that shouldn't exist," Brea muttered.

"It's the borders." Lochlan dropped the journal, beaming at his daughter. "It takes the magic of the lands on either side of the vatlands."

"So, the fire plains need the magic of Eldur, Lenya, and Iskalt." Tierney returned her father's smile.

"Then, we have a lot of work to do because I'm the only Lenyan on this side of the world." Keir stuffed his journal and quill back into his bag.

"We have about an hour until dusk. This is only going to work for a short period, so we're going to have to make the most of the time we've got." Brea set off to tell the others. They would need all hands on deck to try this.

"It puts a damper on things when you've got to wait for the sun and moon to get things done." Keir shook his head as everyone scattered to deliver the good news.

"I think this is going to work, Keir." Tierney wrapped her arms around his waist and laid her head on his chest. "We're going to fix this so you and your people won't be so isolated. Think of what that will mean for Vondur and Grima."

"If it works." Keir let out a nervous breath. "Do you think I can do it? The part where I have to perform powerful magic for Lenya when the most complex thing I've ever done with magic is restore my energy during a long battle."

"We'll help you." She laid her hand over his, a crystal clutched in his fist. "But the magic itself will guide you. You just have to listen and trust in it."

Keir nodded. "All we can do is try."

As dusk fell, every Eldurian, Iskaltian, and Keir lined up along the border of the fire plains, as close as they could get to it without burning. Even in the fading light, the air shimmered with heat.

"What do we do?" Keir whispered, leaning close to Tierney. "I mean, how do we know how to direct the magic?"

"Start by embracing your power. Let it flow from the crystal into you, and then direct it into the earth like the Gelsi magic wielders do."

Keir nodded. "I sure hope this works." He sank to his knees, waiting for the signal to start.

"Begin!" Lochlan's voice, magically amplified, echoed across the camp.

Streaks of every color of magic lit up the sky and ground as each person added their magic to the attempt.

"Now you, Keir." Tierney held her hands steady as her Iskaltian magic joined the others. It was a wonderous sight, and it reminded her of another time, long ago, when all fae had united as one to fight a common foe.

It brought tears to her eyes to think of how much she loved these people. All of them willing to help each other or die trying.

Keir's magic hummed like a live creature in his hands. It was beautiful, like a song in its musical quality. She watched as he clutched the powerful opal now pulsing with a fiery light. Sinking his hands into the sand, he released his magic, guiding it into the land that needed healing.

Tierney held her breath, waiting for something to happen.

"It's not working." Keir groaned.

"Give it a little longer." Myles paced behind them, his human eyes on the shimmering wall of heat. "These things take time and patience."

"Myles, look!" Neeve pointed to the sky.

Tierney looked up, keeping her magic steady. The boundary of the fire plains shone with an iridescence, like a rainbow of colors reflected back at them. Gasps of surprise echoed around them as the wall began to collapse, shrinking from the magic of the united kingdoms.

"It's so beautiful," Tierney murmured, sniffing back her tears.

"The colors are pretty," Keir said, "but why the tears?"

Tierney shook her head. "It's not the colors. It's the people. The unity. It's the most amazing thing I've ever witnessed, and this is the second time in my life I've seen it. I feel so lucky to be part of it. Then and now."

"Forward!" Lochlan called. "Careful now, we don't want the boundary to snap back in place as we move. Keir, be very careful as you move forward. Don't break your connection with the magic."

Lochlan paced behind the row of magic wielders, barking orders. "Someone get the boy another crystal. He's going to need it as a backup."

"There has to be enough magic in this one crystal to get us all the way to Lenya." Keir lifted his hand from the sand, carefully moving forward a few steps at a time.

"This is powerful magic, Keir. It will go quickly." Tierney stepped forward, keeping her magic steady as she moved.

"What do we do when the Eldurian magic fades?" someone called out. "Will it bounce back?"

"We have no way of knowing." Lochlan paced, kicking up sand in his urgency now that they were making progress. "Eldurians, give us a shout when you're nearing the end of your power."

The dusk stayed with them long enough to move the boundary back at least a league. As the Eldurians pulled away when their magic faded, everyone held their breath, prepared to run if the boundary wasn't stable.

A cheer went down the line when Keir, as the last magic wielder, stepped away and the boundary settled exactly where they'd pushed it.

Exhaustion swept through Tierney, and her arms felt like dead weights, but she was happier than she could ever remember being. "It worked!" She cheered with the others. "Can you believe it, Keir?"

"I just wish we could keep working at it." He stared behind them. The fire plains shimmered and glowed in the darkness as they made their way back to camp. "It could take months of this to reach Lenya."

"We'll be ready at dawn." She took his hand. "And we'll keep working at it until there is nothing left but scorched earth."

Every fae that worked the boundary had blisters and burns from the blackened charred ground that now lay cooling in the evening breeze.

"Isn't it wonderful, Tia?" Toby and Logan joined them, strolling hand in hand in the moonlight.

"It's exhausting work, but look at how far we reached?" Logan beamed at them. "At this rate, we'll be walking to Lenya in a few days."

"We have no idea how far it is," Keir said.

"Think positive." Logan shrugged. "This was just the first day. We've figured out what we need to do now. I'll wager we reach twice as far at dawn."

"I'll take that wager." Keir grinned, slapping Logan on the back. "I bet we'll reach three leagues by the time Tia's moon magic wanes."

"Dude, she has Eldur magic too. She can't even tell when the switch happens." Toby's teasing voice made Tierney smile. She liked seeing them all get along so well.

"Then, we'll base it on your father's magic," Keir decided.

"You're on." Logan lifted a brow. "What are we betting?"

"Loser has to wake Tia up before dawn every day for a week." Toby snickered. "She's vicious in the mornings. She's been known to give a few magical black eyes and fat lips when she doesn't want to get up."

"Very funny, Tobes." Tierney stuck her tongue out at her brother.

"Oh, I don't know, I think she'd be nice if I were the one waking her up." Keir grinned down at her, taking her hand in his.

"So, what you're saying is, you're going to lose." Toby nudged Keir.

"Could be well worth it." Keir shrugged, and Tierney's cheeks flushed.

"Awe, they're so cute," Logan whisper-shouted. "Do you think they'll ever figure out they're nuts about each other?"

"Poor Keir is in for a long wait. Tierney's always been the stubborn one." Toby shook his head in mock sympathy.

CHAPTER 22
KEIR

It took them just two days to push the fire plains back to their original borders, moving their camp as they went. Everyone was hot, sweaty, and dirty, but in good spirits.

They received word that the blizzard had receded into the mountains in Iskalt, and Myrkurians and Iskaltians were working together to drive the snows from the Northwestern Vatlands back into the mountains. For the Myrkurians, it seemed to be the willing act of assisting their Iskaltian neighbors with the task that fulfilled their requirement. King Hector led a team of ogres carrying magic wielders into the mountains to places they couldn't have reached otherwise, and the Slyph took to the skies to survey the progress.

They were going to defeat the vatlands and the ancient magic that caused them in the first place. The magic was exhausting, but they worked during the short windows of dusk and dawn, leaving them the better parts of the day and night to rest.

Keir emerged from his tent, pulling the fresh tunic away from his body. Even as the sun began to set, it was hot, and the charred ground burned through the soles of his boots.

The shimmering wall of heat danced across the clearing of the blackened ground. He'd grown used to the temperatures but already reached for his wineskin filled with cool water. Tierney showed him how to protect his water supply so it wouldn't boil and evaporate while he worked.

Kneeling on the hot ground, he waited for the sting of it to leave him, using a bit of magic from his totem to protect his skin from blistering.

"I wonder what Lenya will be like when the fire plains are gone." Tierney approached him, knowing he was always the first to arrive at the border, and among the last to leave.

Keir stared at the horizon, trying to see what it might become in time. "I think it will be a lot like Eldur in Vondur, and a little more like Iskalt in Grima."

"Sounds like the best of both worlds." She sank to the ground beside him. "You ready?"

"Almost." He pulled on the magic of his second totem. He'd had a hard time accepting the second one when the first one went dark. He still felt like it was a reckless use of so much magic, and probably would always feel that way. Logically, he knew he could easily find another one from the supply they brought with them or even one of the rough natural fire opals littering the ground back at their original campsite. But Keir would always fear for the future of his people. They needed to be responsible with their magic so they never again faced a world where fae fought over a few scraps of power because their ancestors were greedy.

"Let's do this." It was a bit early to get started, but Tierney had both sun and moon magic, and Keir liked to call on his magic when no one was looking. He still struggled to harness such enormous power and liked to have a firm grasp of it before the others arrived. It wasn't vanity on his part so much as extreme performance anxiety. These people understood their magic in a way Keir didn't.

Tierney leaned forward, and together they pressed their hands against the scorched ground. Little by little, as they had pushed the borders back, the scarred and broken ground began to heal. New grass and thorny shrubs were already peeking through the ground behind them. In a few short months from now, Keir wondered if any of them would be able to tell the fire plains ever existed.

He closed his eyes as both sides of Tierney's magic enveloped him. If he were honest with himself, this was the true reason he liked to begin early. When it was just the two of them, Tierney's magic filled him. He was in awe of her power.

He took a ragged breath as her power joined his. There was something intimate about the way they worked together this way. But if he thought a single pure fire opal held more magic than he'd ever sensed in one vessel, it was nothing on Tierney herself.

"It's okay." Tierney shifted away from him.

"What do you mean?"

"Lots of people get nervous around my magic." She shrugged, staring at her hands pressed against the ground. "But I promise there is nothing to fear from me. We're in this together, Keir."

She thought he was afraid of her? It struck him then, not only just how powerful Tierney O'Shea was but also how lonely it must have been for her.

Keir smiled. "Your magic is fierce, but I can't imagine you any other way." He bumped her shoulder. "I could never fear you. I trust you too much for that."

Tierney's smile rivaled the sunset, and Keir wanted to be the one to make her smile like that every single day.

"Let's take back the fire plains."

"You doubled down on your bet with Toby and Logan, didn't you?"

"They're determined to put me on wake-up Tia duty. I'm starting to think they have ulterior motives."

"Those two are always up to something."

As the others began to arrive and cast their magic against the fire plains, they moved forward until they were slowly walking toward their first major obstacle. A lava pool.

Up until now, they'd only recovered flat barren plains. The wall of heat moved in a straight line with them, from the Sea of Iskalt to

Radur Bay to the south. Once they hit the lava pools and the active volcano, they were going to have to be more careful.

Lochlan and Toby strolled together behind the magic wielders, the king stepping in for anyone who grew tired and needed a break.

"Steady everyone, we're approaching the lava pool." Lochlan and Toby helped each fae position themselves far enough away from the small pool so they could easily continue on.

"Be careful, everyone," Keir called, eyeing the spotters he'd suggested Lochlan appoint. "I've seen these pools spew lava like geysers."

"Remember to test your footing," Lochlan called out. They weren't certain how steady the ground would be around the pools.

"Remember to breathe too, Tia." Keir put himself between her and the bubbling pool of angry lava.

He took a step forward, and his foot started to sink into the sand. He wasn't the only one who took several quick steps back. He waited for the spotters to tell him where to move before he proceeded.

Within a few moments, they uncovered more than half of the pool, giving it a wide berth on both sides.

"Something's happening," Tierney shouted. "The magic is wavering!"

"Hold steady, everyone." Lochlan joined his daughter, adding his magic to the mix.

Everyone held their breath as the lava pool bubbled and the wall of heat pushed against them.

"Be ready to run to me if this fails." Lochlan moved to join Finn and Brea to create a heat shield that would protect them if their magic failed.

"I think it's collapsing, Dad." Tierney pushed forward, letting both sides of her magic guide the others.

With a rush of blistering hot wind, the wall bulged and collapsed. Tierney ducked, and Keir covered her with his body as they all ran for Lochlan and the heat shield.

Keir waited for the fire plains to burn them to ash where they stood, but it never came.

"Look," Toby cried. "I think you did it! The fire plains are gone."

Keir stood up, releasing Tierney from his grip. Together, they all stared at the ruins before them. Lava pools were already cooling. The ground still trembled, but only smoke and steam billowed up into the sky from settling volcanoes. It was a valley. And it was clear as far as they could see.

"Have we reached Lenya?" Logan stood to his full height, craning his neck to see through the dissipating smoke.

"Not yet." Keir wished he could get a clear picture of what lay ahead of them. "I think there's another lava pool at the end of the valley." He shielded his eyes from the blazing sunset. "But I think we just took down a giant portion of the plains in one fell swoop."

Cheers went up as they continued forward. Crossing the now open valley took most of the little time they had left before dusk turned to night. They arrived at another lava pool with hardly an hour left to work before the Eldurians had to stop.

"How much farther do you think?" Tierney approached the fiery line of the new border. The land itself was burning here, but they just might make another big push tonight.

This time, when they pressed against the larger lava pool, they were prepared for the push back. It seemed the fire plains would not give up their hold without a fight.

"Press on, boys." Logan took a step forward, urging his Eldurian comrades to follow.

Keir wanted to caution him not to stray too close to the lava pool, but his words caught in his throat as the ground beneath him began to shake and the rancid hot winds broke free to crash over them once again. Everyone stopped to watch in awe as another huge section of the fire plains failed, collapsing farther this time.

Smoke belched from the lava pool, and a loud sound like cannon fire accompanied the tremors.

"Fall back! To me, to me!" Lochlan cried as billowing black smoke rushed across the field.

Tierney stumbled toward Keir, and he grabbed her hand, pulling her toward her father. "Logan," she shouted, coughing on the churning smoke.

"It's going to erupt, Tia. We have to move." Keir's feet sank into sand so hot it melted right through his boots to scorch his feet.

Flaming stones rained down like pieces of the sky falling from the heavens, and heat shields went up all around them.

"Logan!" Toby screamed, running toward the lava pool.

"No!" Tierney stopped him, wrapping her arms around him. "Help me, Keir!"

Keir grabbed onto Toby, refusing to let him go as Tierney flung a heat shield over them.

Logan stood just a few paces away, swaying on his feet. A streak of blood and soot ran down his face. Toby screamed, struggling against them as Logan stumbled to his knees.

"He's gone, Toby." Tierney clutched his head to her shoulder. "Don't look. Don't look." She shielded his eyes, her tears streaming down her face.

Logan slid forward, a hand stretched out toward Toby as he fell face-first into the charred sand. A molten red stone glowed against the back of his head where it had struck him and caved in his skull. Keir held onto Tierney and Toby as they all slid to the ground, their sobs breaking his own heart for the gentle young man he'd hardly known.

"Toby," Tierney whispered. "Shhh, Toby. I'm so sorry." She rocked him gently. "I'm so sorry."

"We need to move, Tia." Keir set his own heat shield in place, just in case hers slipped. Lava rocks still rained down around them, and any one of them could face the same end Logan just experienced.

"We have to get him." Toby pushed to his feet. "I have to bring his body back to camp. He is the heir of Eldur. I will not let him burn up out there. We will take him back to his people."

"We'll go together." Keir stood, helping Tierney up. Together, the three of them walked across the burning ground, safe for the moment under the protection of their combined magic.

Toby gathered Logan into his arms, struggling under his weight, but he refused help. Tierney and Keir walked silently beside the heartbroken prince of Iskalt.

"Logan!" A woman's blood-curdling scream met them as they left the burning lands behind.

"Aunt Alona, I'm so sorry!" Tierney stepped toward the Queen of Eldur, her husband just managing to hold her up. Princess Darra knelt on the ground at her mother's feet, sobbing her brother's name.

Death was a part of Keir's life. But this grief? This raw, overwhelming grief was not something he'd ever witnessed before. In Vondur, the endless years of war had hardened them. Death was expected. Some even embraced it.

But this? This was something he couldn't watch. Their grief was so painful and personal. Keir shouldn't be here to witness it.

Toby laid Logan on the ground at his parents' feet. Tears streaked the soot covering his face. This was heartbreak in its rawest moments.

"Stay with Alona and Finn," Tierney whispered. "Stay and mourn your loss." She pressed a kiss to Toby's forehead.

"No. We need to keep moving." Toby stood, a wild look in his eye. "He will not die in vain."

"We've lost the daylight, brother." Tierney wrapped an arm around his shoulders. "Stay with Darra. She will need you."

"Darra," Finn whispered, sinking to his knees beside his daughter. "You must leave and return to the palace, sweetheart."

"No. I'm staying here with Toby and Logan."

"You are the only heir now." Alona's hands shook. "This place is too dangerous."

"Griffin!" Tierney shouted as her uncle came running from the fire plains. She grabbed his arm and pulled him in, whispering in his ear. "Take Darra and Toby to the farmhouse with Alona and Finn. They need a quiet place to mourn. I'll see to Logan's body."

"They won't go." Griffin gave her a heavy look. "You know what you're asking, right?"

Tierney nodded. "They can blame me for it later."

Griffin nodded, and in a flash of violet light, the grieving family vanished through a portal to the human world. Keir would never get used to seeing that.

"Can you help me with him?" Tierney sniffed back her tears. "We need to get his body to camp and send him with an escort home to the Radur City palace."

Keir lifted Logan into his arms, following Tierney to camp as she called out orders to fall back from the unstable border. They would be at it again at dawn. Hopefully, they would reach Lenya soon. Or whatever was left of it.

Chapter 23
Bronagh

There was nowhere left to go except up.

The fire plains surrounded the fae of Lenya who'd come to fight, Vondur and Grima forces pushed together to become one. At their backs was the last remaining way into the mountains, little more than a goat path. Most of the fae from the villages hid in those passes, waiting for the fire plains to claim them.

Bronagh once thought she could save them all.

"Magic wielders, don't break formation," she yelled. "Next wave!"

Fresh totem wielders stepped to the front, if anyone could be called fresh at this point. She'd lost count of the days they'd spent losing ground, expending every last ounce of energy, of magic.

The store of crystals she'd brought from Iskalt was almost depleted.

Eavha bent over to catch her breath, getting her first break in hours. She looked as they all did: tired, weary, ready to see what they'd refused to recognize.

They'd lost.

"Bron, we should get everyone into the mountains."

Declan stood at her side, his shoulders wilting in defeat. Yet, his words spoke of what they all wished was possible. "There's still a chance. We can keep fighting it."

"It's over, Deck."

Bronagh watched them glare at each other before crouching down to where her brother practically collapsed on the ground, his chest heaving.

"It isn't over until there's no more breath in our bodies." Declan was stubborn, and they'd needed that before. But now, Bronagh wasn't sure what they needed.

Eavha plopped herself on the ground with a weary sigh. "We've lost. At least if we escape into the mountains, we can stop fighting long enough to enjoy our final days."

"No."

"Declan."

He knelt beside her. Bronagh felt like an intruder hearing their private moment, but she was too tired to move, too tired to do much of anything.

"I won't stop trying to save us." Declan's jaw clenched.

Eavha looked up into his eyes. "Why? Why can't you just give in and come with me?"

"Because I love you too much to just let you die."

Love. It had never been a foreign concept to Bronagh. Her mother and sister, despite their faults, had loved the family. Donal was the most important fae in the world to her. Even their uncle loved them very much, though his actions might not always show it.

But the kind of love she witnessed between the Vondurian princess and the general ... there was only one man who'd ever made her feel an inkling of what they had. One man who came into her life such a short time ago, yet she could hardly remember a time without him.

If these fire plains overcame them, she'd never get to tell Veren how she felt. She wouldn't get to ask him to give up his kingdom to help her put Lenya back together.

There would be no Lenya anymore.

"Bron." Donal lifted his head. "Eavha is right. We should get into the mountains."

She shifted her gaze to the sheer cliffs above her head, to the single narrow path winding around to the far side of the mountain. They wouldn't be able to reach the Grimian caves where her fae awaited word of their success, but if they made it up into the highest passes, it might give them an extra week, maybe two.

Sweat dripped down her back. The heat intensified with each day, each hour. Yesterday, two Vondurian soldiers were killed by steam erupting from the unstable ground.

"Sister." Donal pushed himself up. "You're the queen. It's your decision. Do we keep going until the remaining crystals empty of power?" There was no judgment in his tone, and she knew he'd accept whatever she decided.

She looked from Donal to Eavha and Declan, who were peering at her with more trust than any Vondurian should. Then, there was her uncle, yelling orders to the magic wielders, trying to keep the plains at bay. Her golden warriors, their armor shed in this heat. The Vondurians, who put aside their animosity and obeyed her command.

Something soft nudged her shoulder, and she lifted a hand to find Sheba beside her, the giant cat giving her an understanding look. She should be terrified down at eye level with a beast who could rip her throat out. Instead, it gave her clarity.

The fire plains were a predator like no other. They would give no quarter, had no master. Unlike Sheba, who did little more than intimidate Eavha's foes, they wanted to destroy.

And they'd get their wish.

"We have to make it into the mountains." It wouldn't save them, but they'd have a week, maybe more, to say goodbye to each other, to Lenya.

Donal nodded and took off to talk to their uncle. A few moments later, the command rang out. "If you are not currently wielding a totem, make for the mountains."

Activity surrounded her, soldiers gathering their few remaining possessions, hurrying to be the first up to those ominous cliffs.

"You two should leave with the first wave." Declan gestured to Eavha and Bronagh.

Bronagh shook her head. "I stay until my last fae has made it."

Eavha linked her arm with Bronagh's, tears streaking down her dusty face. "I'm with her." Her voice didn't waver.

Declan rolled his eyes to the roiling red sky, where plumes of smoke and ash rose among the clouds. He muttered something Bronagh only heard parts of, the words "stubborn" and "cursed" reaching her ears.

Sheba growled, and Declan put his hands up in front of his chest. "Eavha, tell Sheba to back down."

"She has a will of her own. I'm not her boss." With that, Eavha dragged Bronagh to the line of magic wielders. Her uncle pressed crystals into their hands.

All they had to do was give their fae enough time to get away, then they'd make a run for it.

Magic bloomed in her, weaker than it had been before. "This crystal is almost dead." She reached out to her uncle. "Can you hand me another?"

He shot her a panicked look. "There are no more."

If there'd been any last shred of hope, it was gone now. "Well, then, I guess this is it."

"Your Majesty," Declan yelled, "look."

Bronagh peered into the fire plains, seeing only billowing smoke and spewing lava. The air shimmered with heat. Then, it was there. Movement at the farthest point where the plains curved around a row of giant blackened boulders toward the volcano.

"What is that?" Eavha stepped closer, but Declan yanked her back.

A girl walked out into the open, looking like she'd stepped right through the burning heat. Behind her, a line of fae appeared, each directing magic down into the very earth.

"Is that ..." Eavha gasped. "It's Tia."

Bronagh peered closer, her broken heart melding together with a new hope. "They've done it," she whispered to herself.

The Lenyans who'd started toward the mountains stopped what they were doing, and a cheer rose up.

Tears stung Bronagh's eyes, drying as they sizzled on her cheeks. They really did it. She caught sight of Keir, of Toby.

And Veren.

A giant grin spread across his face, but he didn't lose focus on the magic.

The other fae were strangers, but they'd come to save Lenya, to save all their realms.

Shouting erupted among the newcomers, but Bronagh couldn't hear their words. Fae scrambled backward to where King Lochlan beckoned them. The ground shook, the fire plains moving once again.

"Everyone back!" Bronagh yelled, stumbling away from the wall of heat.

When she regained her footing and searched out the fae on the other side, her eyes caught on Veren still running to the protection of whatever his king offered.

His mouth opened in shock, and if Bronagh had been closer, she knew she'd have heard him scream. That look wasn't one she'd ever forget. He dodged a geyser of steam, but it wasn't enough. As the fire plains bounced toward him, he stumbled, reaching for someone to help him.

Tierney sprinted forward, gripping his hand and dragging him to her father, but even from this distance, Bronagh could see.

Veren Rhatigan wasn't moving.

"No," she whispered, blinking back tears. Moments ago she'd prepared for the fire plains to steal the lives of everyone in Lenya, but now when there was finally hope ... she couldn't comprehend what was happening.

"Sister." Donal's arms came around her, but she hardly noticed he was there.

Veren. She saw the day he'd appeared at court, already a trusted friend of her brother's. The way he'd embraced Grimian ways and never stopped searching for his missing friends.

Her entire body shook until a voice boomed through the light of dawn. "We need help." It was Tierney.

Bronagh pulled away from her brother. Despite the fissure straight down the center of her heart, she was the queen, and it was time to save her kingdom.

"We need help." It was the only thing Tierney knew to do. She couldn't stop staring at the charred remains of Veren's body, the bottom half completely black from being caught in the shifting fire plains.

But it wasn't time to mourn. Not yet. Keir's crystal had no more magic. As soon as they caught sight of the Lenyans, it brought them a renewed sense of purpose. None were so determined as Veren.

Ducking underneath her father's heat shield, she knew it couldn't last much longer as the fire plains grew closer again. Dawn was almost through, and if they didn't end this now, they might never succeed.

"Aimpliu," she whispered to herself so she could continue. The Fargelsian spell allowed her voice to carry. "Bronagh, listen to me. There's not much time. We must break through now or not at all. We need every bit of magic your fae have left, even just the smallest traces in the stones. Dig deep to bring it out. This will take all of us. Channel it into the earth. We're coming for you."

She had no way of knowing if Bronagh understood, only that the Lenyans were backed up to the mountains making their final stand.

It would be a final stand for all of them.

"I need Eldurians and Iskaltians at the front, those not too exhausted to give everything they have left." She issued the commands like she was in charge here. Not her father, not King Keir. And her father didn't intercede. Instead, he ushered his fae to obey her.

Tierney lined up with them, waiting for her father to drop the remnants of his heat shield. "I know you're tired," she said to those around her. "I know Lenya is not your kingdom. We have lost friends over the last days." Her eyes flicked to Siobhan, who understood what Veren's loss meant. "But what we have not lost is our resolve.

"We have one more chance to right the wrongs of our ancestors, to become the alliance of kingdoms we were meant to be. Those fae across from us are no different from your neighbors, your friends, and your family. Seek out whatever you have left, let your magic guide you, and become a hero today."

Her father stepped up beside her, his hands raised. "I'm proud of you, Tia."

She glanced over her shoulder to where Keir paced, unable to help without his magic. He met her gaze, giving her a nod of thanks.

If the Lenyans had no more power, if they weren't prepared, all of them were doomed. Yet, she readied herself anyway. Not a single one of her fae, Eldurian or Iskaltian, gave up, gave in. She'd never been more proud.

A smile curved her lips. "Let's do this."

Heat rushed in as her father dropped the shield. Her Iskaltian magic weakened, telling her there wasn't much time left. She dug into her Eldurian side, channeling every bit of energy she could into the ground.

The fire plains seemed to shake and inch back. Tierney stepped forward, gritting her teeth against what felt like flames licking up her arms. "Geyser," Brea yelled. A handful of Eldurians scrambled out of the way.

Molten lava burped from the ground in front of them, but as soon as the plains receded past it, it hardened. Not much farther now.

It was working. Bronagh had heard her.

After days and days of this, pain and exhaustion wound through her limbs. Her body wilted, but she remained upright. When she stumbled, strong hands caught her from behind.

"Keep going, Tierney," Keir whispered.

For him, she would. For Lenya. She caught sight of Eavha, totem in her palm, and pushed harder. Beside the Vondurian princess, Declan directed power into the ground. They were both okay. That knowledge gave her a renewed energy.

The fire plains bent and wavered from the Lenyan side, and the magic wielders there advanced. Tierney could almost reach out and touch her friends now. Just one more push.

"For Logan," she gritted out. "For Veren." With one final heave of power, the sky cracked in a roaring thunder and rain exploded from the clouds. They stood there in shock for a moment, rain drenching their rapidly cooling skin, a balm to their scorched palms.

Tierney took off running, crossing the remaining feet to launch herself at Bronagh and Eavha, catching them both against her in a hug. Relief breathed new life into her, gave her the will to remain standing.

Keir joined them, sweeping his sister into his arms, tears dancing in his eyes.

Around them, Eldurians, Iskaltians, Vondurians, and Grimians celebrated. Some fell to their knees; others stared up into the sun breaking through the rain clouds.

Tierney opened her mouth, catching drops of water on her parched tongue. Nothing had ever tasted so good.

Keir caught her around the waist, and they fell against each other, holding each other up. He bent to kiss the side of her sweaty face as the rain washed the soot away.

Bronagh backed away from them, turning to walk toward the charred mess of ground that was once the fire plains.

"I have to go after her." Tierney patted Keir's chest. "Stay here with Eavha and celebrate."

She took off after the queen. Bronagh kept going, passing craters that once bubbled with lava, cracks widened by steam breaking free. She didn't stop until she reached where they'd left Veren's body, his top half still looking like the arrogant, charming boy Tierney hated and appreciated for most of her life. He'd challenged her, made her see truths she'd wanted to deny.

And when it came down to it, he'd fought to survive right alongside her, for her. Their experiences bonded them, made them—dare she say it—friends.

Bronagh kneeled beside him, a hand on his chest. Tierney approached slowly, her heart aching because a part of her still thought this was entirely her fault.

She lowered herself to the ground beside Bronagh, surprised at how cool it was. Rain gathered in her hair, dripping down her face, but she didn't shield her eyes. Instead, she looked down into Veren's face.

"I always thought he was handsome," she started, emotion clogging her throat. "When I was younger, I fancied myself in love with him."

Bronagh sniffled. "He told me the story. He hated how he'd used you, felt great shame for it."

That made Tierney smile. "He changed a lot when he came here." She brushed sopping hair out of his face. "I think it was your influence."

Bronagh shook her head. "No, that was all him. He changed me too. Before Veren arrived in Grima, my life had no color. Every part of me was a formal, bland girl who did what she was told. It wasn't who I wanted to be, but it was who I thought I was allowed to be since I was never supposed to be queen."

Her chin dropped to her chest. "But then, this warrior walks in, and it … it's hard to explain. He brought me to life."

"You were in love with him." Tierney had suspected as much, but the confirmation speared through her in a jolt of pain.

Bronagh wiped her face before her tears were replaced with rain. "No. I am in love with him. Death does not cause it to cease."

She thought of Toby, how no news of this victory would soothe his grief. Of Finn and Alona, having lost their only son and heir. Imogen, now an orphan. There was too much loss in this battle, and the only foe had been magic itself. Magic had created the vatlands. It had separated the kingdoms and nearly destroyed them.

Tierney looked down at her hands, now washed clean by the rain. "And it saved them."

Bronagh's body shook with tears, and Tierney pulled her into a hug, letting her sink into her.

"Your Majesty," a small voice said.

Tierney looked up into the young face of Imogen, the girl with nothing left. Like so many others.

Imogen kneeled on the ground next to Bronagh, and the queen tilted into her embrace.

Tierney pushed to her feet, knowing the two of them likely needed each other more than they needed her. She walked back toward the joy that was hard to feel. Even in accomplishment, the costs seemed too high.

CHAPTER 25
KEIR

The palace of Vondur was scarred beyond measure. Not even the crystals infused in the walls had saved it from the fire plains. Keir picked through the blackened ruins, reminders of the life he'd lived before. He wasn't the only fae mourning what was lost. Most of the villages of Vondur and Grima would need to be rebuilt, brought back from destruction.

Friends were gone.

He hadn't known Logan well or even Veren, but their losses sat heavily on his mind, as did the losses of so many men, women, and children of his realm.

"We were here just days ago." Eavha walked up behind him, her voice wavering. "I was sitting right in this room."

They stood in the throne room, where marks of the fire stretched up the walls and the furniture had turned to ash. "We've lost everything."

"Not everything." Eavha slid her arm into his. "We saved our fae, and that's what truly matters."

She was right. Homes and possessions weren't the true value of Vondur. Those who occupied the homes were. In the two days since they'd destroyed the fire plains, fae trickled out of the mountains. In the weeks and months to come, more of them would return home to build new lives.

"We're going to have to rebuild." His mind worked through so many plans. The palace could be even grander than it was before now that they had a practically unlimited supply of magic. The war with Grima was through, meaning he could create more of a home than a fortress meant to withstand battle.

"Keir." Eavha stepped away from him as she sighed. "We need to talk."

"Nothing good ever begins with that phrase." He crouched down to brush ash from a painting that had somehow survived the heat. It was protected by glass made from crystal and depicted their father sitting atop his horse prepared to ride into battle.

"All the documents in the palace have been destroyed." She paused. "Including the ones only Lord Robert and I knew about."

Keir didn't have to ask what she meant, but he didn't have an answer for her unasked question.

"Talk to me, brother."

He closed his eyes for a brief moment and stood, turning away from his father's portrait, the image of the man he'd never wanted to be, the one he was scared of becoming. "I never wanted this." He gestured around the room, not exactly meaning the destruction.

"I know." She did. More than anything, more than anyone. Eavha had always known. "But I don't want it either. You left me in charge against my will, and that's not me. I don't want to be a leader. I want adventure, to explore this new world that has opened to us. The crown was never meant to fit my head."

"Nor mine." Both children of a king who wanted nothing but power, both wishing it hadn't fallen to them.

"Yes, but I'm not the one who called for the Comhrac."

"If I hadn't, we'd all be dead by now." His father never would have allowed a mission to seek Iskalt.

"I know. I didn't mean you were wrong." She touched his arm. "But the duty fell to you. Vondur needs you."

Did they?

Eavha gave him a tight smile. "Think carefully of your next decision. It will define our kingdom." With that, she turned and left him in the throne room that had never felt so empty, so forsaken.

He walked from the room, down the hall where tapestries once adorned the walls and now lay scattered along the floor, ashes under his feet. When he entered the courtyard, his eyes went past where the heavy wooden gate once stood to the top of the wall and the two figures sitting there.

Toby had returned the day after the final fight with the fire plains, but he'd barely spoken to anyone except Tierney. Even his parents couldn't get anything out of him. They would have to return to Iskalt soon, but for now, they camped outside the gates of the palace, offering any assistance to his fae they could.

He'd forever be grateful to them.

Declan walked toward him, a grim expression on his face. It had been there since they first discussed how much work there was to be done. "The King of Iskalt would like to speak with you."

"Are you his messenger boy now?" Keir attempted the joke, but they'd all found it hard to smile once their relief and celebration died down and reality set in. They may have succeeded in saving their fae, but the work had just begun.

Keir followed Declan from the palace to a sea of tents that housed what was left of Vondur and the contingents from Eldur, Iskalt, and Grima. Bronagh planned to leave within hours, but the rest would stay for a few days longer at least.

He found Lochlan seated next to his wife, along with Finn and Alona of Eldur and Bronagh. Deep circles lined Finn's eyes, as if he hadn't slept since his son died. Alona's face was stoic, her jaw clenched, her brows drawn tightly together.

Lochlan nodded to Keir as he entered their circle around the fire. Since the destruction of the plains, a chill wound through Vondur for the first time. "Have a seat, Keir."

It would always strike him as odd, the familiarity the royals had with each other. If the Fargelsians were here, he knew they'd call everyone by their given names as well. Keir sat next to Bronagh on the ground. None of them seemed uncomfortable by the lack of accommodations. Another surprise. If anyone had asked his father to sit on the ground, even in an army camp, he'd have thrown a fit.

"We have suffered too many losses." Brea looked at Alona in sympathy and reached out to grip Finn's hand next to her. "Precious losses we can never get back, but each of us here also has a duty."

Finn swallowed heavily. "We will return to Eldur and begin mining for more opals. We'll send word to Hector in Myrkur to do the same. Lenya will need them for rebuilding."

Bronagh attempted to offer him a smile, but it never quite reached her eyes. "Thank you. Lenya will forever be in your debt."

"We do not do debts." Lochlan leaned forward, looking at them each in turn. "When our worlds are threatened, we come to the aid of our allies without expectation of payment. We are all fae, and fae take care of each other."

Brea sent her husband the most glorious smile.

Lochlan continued, "Iskalt may soon see a major change, one I've been waiting for, but whatever we look like, we will be your allies."

"That's ..." Keir cleared his throat. "We are eternally grateful." If Tierney had never accidentally portalled to Lenya, he never would have found the other fae kingdoms.

Bronagh lifted her chin to speak, her voice clear. "Grima and Vondur will no longer war with one another. We will be as one in Lenya, tied together by our common heritage." She looked to Keir. "We've never been different, after all. We're all of Lenya, all after the same thing. We want to survive, to thrive. And our fae finally get to experience peace with full bellies and safe homes. No more lost family to battle. No more grief."

Keir's eyes drifted to the walls, where he knew Tierney and Toby were hidden. No more grief. No more loss. Thrive.

He looked to Lochlan, one of the few fae aware of the documents that were destroyed in the palace by the fire plains, and the king gave him a subtle nod.

"Tradition in Vondur does not pass the crown from father to son. For so long, bloodshed and death won the throne. Cruelty and war kept it. If we are to enter peace, we cannot have a king who did not come to power through such peace."

No one seemed to understand, but only Bronagh spoke. "Keir, if you're talking about holding some kind of election for the throne, I'm not sure now is the time. Our fae are displaced. We have so much work to do."

Keir shook his head. He knew this was the right thing, but it was difficult to get the words out. "You said Lenya is to become one. I do not think we can accomplish such a feat as separate kingdoms."

"What—"

"You, Bron. You should rule the Vondurian fae." It seemed so simple now, such an obvious decision. He never should have expected Eavha to want the throne. "Vondur and Grima cannot thrive unless it is done together."

Lochlan gave him an approving smile, and he knew he'd said the right thing, the kingly thing.

"Only a true king gives up his power when he knows it will better serve his kingdom," Brea said the words to Keir, but her eyes flicked to her husband and softened.

Bronagh was silent for a moment before turning to Keir and meeting his gaze. "I, Bronagh Agnew, queen of Grima, promise to count all Lenyans as my own. There will be no more division under me, no more war. All of Lenya will prosper."

As Keir heard the sincerity in her words, he knew he'd done the right thing, the only thing.

Darkness enveloped the world by the time Keir walked toward the palace. He would never sleep within its walls again, but he couldn't find his bed without walking through one more time.

Movement across the courtyard caught his eye. He'd thought everyone was back at camp, but a small glow illuminated that perfect smile.

"Thought I'd see you here." Tierney walked toward him, the light emanating from her palm growing larger.

"Comes in handy." He gestured to her magic.

"Oh." She closed her palm, and the light winked out. "Just a Fargelsian spell. It draws starlight from the sky."

"You're incredible." The words tumbled past his lips before he realized it, but they were true. This woman was fascinating, stubborn, strong, and beautiful.

He could barely see her in the dark, but the soft smile that curved her lips was unmistakable. "Today has been a long day."

"How is Toby?"

Her shoulders sagged. "He loved Logan. The two of them … I think they've been in love since before any of us knew what love truly was. I miss Logan too, but my heart is shattered for my brother. Through our connection, I can feel a part of his pain, but it's more than that. Looking at him … I don't know if he'll ever recover from this."

"I'm sorry." It was the only thing he could think to say. He was sorry for what happened to Logan, sorry that her people had to sacrifice themselves for his.

To his surprise, she stepped closer and wound her arms around his waist, pressing the side of her head to his chest. Neither of them spoke as he held her to him, not wanting to let go.

He rested his chin on her head, closing his eyes. "I'm giving up my throne."

She stepped back so suddenly his arms reached for her. "You can't do that."

"It's my throne." He crossed his arms. "I can do whatever I want."

Her eyes narrowed, and he recognized it as her fighting stance. "Keir, Vondur needs you."

"No, Vondur needs a united Lenya. Bronagh is going to rule both kingdoms."

She opened her mouth to speak before shutting it, unable to refute his claim. Finally, her voice came out small. "Did you do this out of some misguided allegiance to me? Keir, just because I helped save Lenya doesn't mean you owe me anything. What we have is—"

"Love." He stepped toward her. "What we have is love." His hand lifted to caress her cheek, and she didn't pull away. He'd have sworn she wasn't breathing if he didn't feel a small puff of air leave her mouth. "I love you, Tierney, and I know you feel the same."

"You don't know anything," she whispered.

"I know I have no misguided allegiances because of what happened in the fire plains." His eyes met her gaze in challenge. "I abdicated before we boarded the ship bound for Iskalt."

Her mouth popped open, and he wrapped his hand around the back of her head, digging his fingers into her hair. "You …"

"I fell in love with you the first time I kissed you." He leaned in. "I tried to stop it, to remind myself we were from different worlds and that one day we'd go our separate ways. But what if we didn't have to?"

"What are you saying?"

"I don't want to be apart from you, Tierney O'Shea." His lips were only a breath away from hers now. "I couldn't bear it."

Her kiss was soft at first, testing, tasting. His lips traveled from the corner of her mouth, arching over her cheek to the sensitive spot below her ear. "I love you," he whispered, trailing kisses down her neck. "I love it when you argue with me." He kissed the underside of her jaw. "I love it when you best me in sparring or with magic. You're so much more than I ever imagined, so much more than I deserve."

Tierney put a finger under his chin and brought his face up so their eyes met. "There is nothing you don't deserve, Keir." She pressed her lips to his, and this time, there was nothing soft about it. Her body molded to his in the dark, seeking out connection wherever it could find it.

"I love you too," she whispered against his lips.

In the coming days and weeks, he knew he'd wonder if it was right to leave Vondur, to make a new home in Iskalt. But he'd never question this, her. Tierney O'Shea saved his kingdom, saved his life, and she saved his soul.

Chapter 26
Tierney

"It's good to see you back home and settled again." Siobhan reclined against the lumpy old sofa in the library. "I just wish Veren could have made it back." She played with the fringe on the pillow in her lap. "I can't shake this feeling of overwhelming guilt that I wasn't there for all of you. Maybe he would have made it if I'd done my part."

"His death was an accident." Tierney plopped onto the sofa beside Siobhan, weary down to her bones. "It's not anyone's fault, but I feel the same guilt."

"Must be a survivor's thing." Siobhan sighed. "I just wonder how different things might have gone if I'd ended up in Grima with him from the beginning. Having an extra Iskaltian there might have made the difference. With Logan and with Veren. We might have made that final push a bit faster."

Tierney choked on her tears. She'd shed too many in recent days. Instead, she reached for Siobhan's hand. "If it's anyone's fault, it's mine for screwing up the portal in the first place."

"Then the whole of Lenya would have suffered." Siobhan reminded her.

"How about we just blame fate for being cruel?"

"Deal." Siobhan squeezed her hand.

"Well, I, for one, am glad we're back in Iskalt." Gulliver rummaged around in his bag, placing several new figurines on the mantle over the enormous fireplace. He'd returned from Lenya with a bag full of new carvings and spent crystals he planned to turn into something beautiful. Tierney had no doubt they'd be just as stunning as the queen of the night blossom he'd carved for her. It lay next to her bed now. A constant reminder of her time on the other side of the fae world.

"But I can't wait to get home-home soon." Gulliver adjusted a series of fiery flames he'd carved from the brightest orange crystals he could find. A reminder of the fire plains that were no more. "I miss Myrkur."

"You can't go home yet." Tierney glanced out the window and caught sight of three odd specks of white in the sky. "There's too much work to do between Lenya and the four kingdoms."

"I guess we're the five kingdoms now, aren't we?" Siobhan said softy, staring out the window as the bird-like specks drew closer to the palace.

"Exactly. And we will have so much work to do to bring Lenya up to speed with the rest of us. Trade agreements and the like. Father will need you and I to act as liaisons since we know the Lenyans so well. I imagine we will be needed for a delegation trip soon"

Gulliver turned to face her, hands on hips and his tail lashing behind him. "I am not going back to that awful place, and you can't make me! And I will not think of Vondur or that crappy dungeon ever again."

"Relax." Tierney pulled him down on the settee beside her, sharing a secretive smile with Siobhan. "It's not like anyone will ever mistake you for a—"

"Mongrel? Freak of nature?" Gulliver supplied, his cheeks bright with color.

"I was going to say a nobody." Tierney rolled her eyes. "Everyone in Lenya knows of the great Lord Gulliver O'Shea of Myrkur by now. And it won't be long before they're introduced to other Dark Fae."

"I don't think you understand what I'm saying, Tia." Gulliver crossed his arms over his narrow chest. "I am not, nor will I ever, return to the palace in Vondur. Period. I don't care if my life depends on it; I'm not going. I am going home to see my sisters. I miss them, but don't you ever tell either of them I said that or I'll deny it."

"Gulliver O'Shea," a familiar stern voice sounded at the front of the library. "I know the princess is your best friend, but you should have more respect." Riona stepped around a tall bookshelf, and Gulliver froze.

"Mom? I thought you went home already."

The room exploded into shrieks of "Gullie!" as two small, very loud balls of energy flew into the library, swarming around Gulliver's head. One of them pulled his tail, and the other wrapped her silvery-white wings around his middle.

"Niamh and Nora, what have I told you girls about flying inside? It's rude. And for heaven's sake, let your brother have some breathing room."

"It's okay, Mom." Gulliver hugged Niamh, the older of the two siblings, ignoring the way Nora fluttered around him, her wings flapping in his face.

"What did you bring us?" the girls demanded.

"You do realize I wasn't on a pleasure trip, don't you?" He eyed his sisters in mock seriousness.

"You still brought us something. We know you did."

"Girls, calm down or we will go straight back to Myrkur this instant." Riona elbowed her way into the fray, yanking Gulliver roughly into her arms. "I haven't had nearly enough hugs since you returned." She clutched him tightly in her arms. "Every time I think about what you got yourself into, I want to break things."

"It wasn't actually my doing, you know," he muttered into her shoulder.

"I know. I was talking to your princess friend here." She managed to take her glare down a notch or two for Tierney's sake.

"You have no idea how sorry I am, Aunt Riona." Tierney's shoulders slumped as she avoided her aunt's silent reprimand.

"Good luck with your sisters." Riona patted Gulliver on the back. "I made a special trip to bring them here because they missed you so much. We flew the whole way back, and I was hoping it would tire them out, but you see how that's worked out." Riona moved to sit beside Tierney, folding her into her arms. "I was scared for you too, silly girl."

Niamh and Nora hurled questions at Gulliver faster than Tierney could keep up with the tiny Dark Fae girls. The smile on her best friend's face was worth the headache that was sure to strike any moment from the level of shrieking the girls were doing.

Tierney sank into the comfort of her aunt's embrace, feeling like the ten-year-old version of herself who fought in the war for Myrkur's freedom right alongside Riona.

"I ran into your father on the way in." Riona finally pulled back. "He's looking for you. That's as good an excuse as you'll get to escape the madness of Niamh and Nora."

"I'll walk you out." Siobhan leapt from the sofa, and the two women left Gulliver to his chaotic family reunion.

Tierney found her father in his study, the doors to the moonlit courtyard flung open to let the cool evening breeze in. She had missed the ice and snow of Iskalt. The temperatures were milder this time of year but still far colder than any she'd experienced since leaving Iskalt.

"You called for me?" Tierney sat on the chair beside her father's desk. It was her chair. Had been since she was old enough to crawl up in it on her own. It was where she had learned how to become the heir of Iskalt.

Lochlan sat back in his chair, turning to face her. "I'm proud of you, Tierney O'Shea." A hint of a smile tugged at his stern features. This was King Lochlan, not just her dad.

"I kind of made a mess of things."

"But you fixed it. And you did a beautiful job of bringing Lenya into the fold of the now five kingdoms. You're ready."

"Ready for what?" A twinge of uneasiness crept up her spine.

"To rule."

"Oh no, I'm not." She shook her head furiously. "Not even a little bit. Are you daft, old man?"

Lochlan chuckled at her reaction. "You know how I became King of Iskalt. I fought to take our kingdom away from my uncle, who had brought us to near ruin with his greed for power."

"Don't remind me of Uncle Callum." Tierney shivered, thinking of her kidnapper from another lifetime.

"It was my duty to our people to rid them of a cruel ruler and to give them an heir capable of leading them into a bright future. That was my job, and it's done."

"Are you dying?" she blurted, her eyes wide with fear. That was the only thing she could think of that would have her father talking about such things. And she was prepared to drag him to the Vondur palace this instant for a dunk in the healing pools to cure him.

"No. I'm perfectly healthy, but I've always known my time as king would be brief. I grew up in Eldur, unsure of my future. You have grown up knowing you would one day rule. You and I have worked together, right here, side by side as it should be. It was the way my father would have groomed me to take his place had he lived."

"If you're not dying, why are we having this conversation?" Her hands twisted in her lap as she tried not to sound as panicked as she felt.

"The fae world is changing, Tia. It's growing and evolving. And I believe Iskalt needs you more than it needs me. You are ready to be queen. You are so strong and wise. A little reckless, but you wouldn't be your mother's daughter if you weren't." Humor danced in his eyes along with something else she wasn't certain she'd ever seen there before. The respect of one monarch for another.

Tierney dragged in a steadying breath. "Are you … abdicating?"

"Yes. I have done all I can do for Iskalt, and I don't want to spend the rest of my life under a crown that doesn't need me anymore. And I don't want to watch you waste your best days as a bored princess when you can bring the fire of youth and passion to our people who love you."

"But, Dad. No." Tierney clutched her hands in her lap to keep them still, staring into the fathomless blue eyes of the one man she respected more than any other. "You are a wonderful king. I cannot hope to follow in your footsteps. Not yet. Not for a long, long time."

"Sweetheart, that's just it. I don't want you to follow in my footsteps. I want you to forge your own path. You are the future of Iskalt. You have always been the future. I have just been holding the crown for you until you were ready. The woman I saw down there fighting the fire plains and leading the fae to victory was every inch a queen. A queen I would be proud to serve."

"Are you sure you aren't … old and addled? Because you aren't making any sense."

"I am not old or addled." His mouth narrowed into a thin line. "But I am determined. You are ready, and it's time to pass the torch to you. I will always be here to guide and advise you, but I am stepping down."

Tierney looked into his eyes and saw his resolve. Eventually, she nodded. "I'm scared."

"Don't be. I'll always be here to catch you if you fall."

Tierney lunged from her seat and threw her arms around her father. "I have to admit one thing, though. You were right."

Lochlan leaned back to study her face. "About what?"

"I need to get married. If you're going to abdicate, the kingdom will feel more settled if I am married when that happens. Our people need to see me as an adult, rather than the little princess they've watched grow up."

"My thoughts exactly." Lochlan crossed his arms over his chest. "And who do you have in mind for the role of husband?"

"You let me handle the whole husband thing." Tierney rose from her seat.

"Have you talked to Keir about this?"

"Not yet, but he'll get over it."

Tierney scoured the castle and the grounds, looking for Keir, but he was nowhere to be found.

Bursting through the doors of her least favorite pub in the village, she was well on her way to angry. Had the blasted fae gone back home without telling her? If he had, he had better not get too comfortable.

"Your Highness?" The man behind the counter dipped into a stiff bow. "What can I do for you?"

Tierney's gaze swept the nearly empty room, dim and dingy, with only a few patrons tucked away in secluded corners. Her shoulders slumped in defeat when there was no sign of Keir's imposing figure anywhere. This was the last place she could think of to look for him. "A glass of your best Gelsi red." She sank down onto a barstool at the counter.

"Are you sure, Highness?" He gave her a wary look. "The stuff is potent, you know."

"I do, and I am certain." She sighed, trying to hang on to her anger so the tears wouldn't come. "Where in the fracking five kingdoms could he be?" she muttered to herself.

"Here you are, Princess." The man set a glass of her favorite red wine in front of her and she took a long draught. It wasn't sweet and refreshing like the Gelsi berry wine she couldn't drink if she wanted to access her magic. This was crisp and tart, and it went right to her head the way even a sip of the weakest Vondurian wine made Gulliver a drunken fool.

"Should I send to the castle for someone, Princess?" The bartender gave her a strange look.

"No, I'm fine." She took another sip from her glass, letting the magical intoxication wash over her. "I'm going to be just fine, I promise." She hiccupped and ran a hand through her wind-swept hair. A few scattered leaves fell out, and she scowled at them, wondering how she'd managed to get leaves in her hair. She must look a sight.

"Did … did you know you're crying, your Highness?" The kind man gave her a linen handkerchief.

"No, I'm not." She sniffed. "It's the cold." She dabbed at her face. "I'll have another please." She drained the rest of her wine and set the glass on the counter.

"How about an ale instead?" A shadow loomed over her. "I hear the red stuff is pretty potent."

"That's the point," she muttered, frowning at the bartender when he set two mugs of ale in front of her.

Tierney squinted up at the newcomer, her vision only slightly blurry at the edges. "Keir!" Her insides warmed at the sight of him. "I found you!"

"I think I'm the one who found you." He settled down beside her. "Do you know how long I've been looking for you?"

"No, I've been looking for you." She scowled at him.

"I know. Everyone in the five kingdoms has seen you today but me." He took a long draught of ale. "I've been ten steps behind you all day," he explained at her look of confusion. "A metaphor for life with Tierney O'Shea if I've ever heard one."

"I know why I'm looking for you, but why have you been looking for me?" She sipped slowly on the ale, her mind still a little fuzzy from the heady wine.

"Um, you go first." He set his mug down, avoiding her gaze.

"Nu-uh, you go."

"You're impossible. You know that, don't you?"

"I've been told." Her mouth thinned into a tight smile.

"But," they both said at the same time, laughing as the tension eased between them.

"But," Tierney continued, "for a little while there, I thought you might have left for Lenya without saying goodbye."

"I'd never do that, Tia." Keir leaned in closer. "Saying goodbye to you would kill me."

"Good." She nodded, propping her elbows onto the bar and leaning in close. "Because I want you to stay."

"Stay?" He tilted his head in question.

"Yes. I think you should be my co-ruler. I'm a princess and heir to Iskalt, so it's kind of up to me to make these decisions since most men wouldn't think of proposing to a woman like me. But I don't want a king consort for a spouse. I don't want my husband to be bored waiting in the wings for me to finish my job every day because my job is never finished—even as a princess, my work keeps me busy all the time. Now that … well, let's not give the village too much to gossip about, but let's just say … I'm going to be a lot busier soon," she whispered softly. "And whoever I marry, I want them to be part of my life in every way. And that means I need someone to rule with me. Maybe not in name. Not at first, anyway. The council would have an epic meltdown if I even mentioned it, but in the years to come, I want my husband to be as much a ruler of Iskalt as me. That's sort of how my parents did it, and it worked for them." Tierney paused to suck in a breath, and Keir leaned in to kiss her, his lips warm and soft against hers only for a brief moment.

"There, that shut you up." His warm breath brushed against her cheek. "Now, in all that absolute babble, I heard something about husbands and consorts in there. Was that Tierney for 'will you marry me'?"

"Yes, Keir! Yes, I will marry you!" Tierney flung her arms around his neck and kissed him.

"Wait. Wait a second." He pulled back. "In the years to come, I foresee the retelling of this moment going in the direction of pure fiction. For the record, I did not ask you; you asked me."

"I did not." Tierney's eyes widened innocently as a smile tugged at the corner of her mouth.

"Did too." Keir rolled his eyes.

"Did not." Tierney stuck her tongue out at him.

"Ah-hem." The bartender cleared his throat. "As a man married to the same woman for forty years, son, it'll be in your best interest to let her have this one." He gave them a toothy grin and refilled their mugs. "And may I be the first to offer my congratulations, your Highnesses." He swept into a courtly bow and left them to their celebrations.

"*Forty* years." Keir's eyes widened as he caught her gaze. "You think we'll make it that long?"

"Absolutely. Now, what was it you wanted to tell me?"

"Oh, it was nothing." He reached for his tankard of ale.

"You ran all over the palace and the village looking for me all day to tell me nothing?"

"Fine." He sighed. "I was looking for you so *I* could propose." He fished around in his pocket for something. "In Vondur, we have a tradition." He took her hand and slipped something around her wrist. "It's tradition for the future husband to give his future wife a gift that once belonged to his mother."

Tierney pulled her hand back to study the beautiful bracelet made of tiny silver vines tipped with lovely blue stones that seemed to glow with magic.

"It's beautiful, Keir. But how did you have this with you?"

"I brought it with me from home. I knew I'd work up the nerve eventually."

"You managed to hold on to it from Vondur all the way here? Through fires and storms and a shipwreck?"

"And don't forget the trek across a frozen wasteland."

Tierney gazed into his eyes, lifting her hand to touch his cheek. "I love you, Keir Dagnan."

"I love you too." His eyes burned into hers, and her cheeks warmed.

Clearing her throat, Tierney lifted her drink to tap against his. "And that is how we will remember the proposal."

Epilogue

GULLIVER

Six months later

Gulliver paced the hallway outside the queen's council room, trying not to stare at the intricately carved wooden doors depicting the history of Iskalt. It was only Tierney on the other side of that imposing door. Yes, she was a queen now. A queen who summoned him from Myrkur just weeks after his return from an extended stay in Iskalt during her coronation celebrations. But she was still his best friend, right? Did queens get to have best friends?

The doors opened and advisors and representatives from Lenya filed out of the room one by one, scurrying off in a dozen different directions like their lives depended on it. Most of them looked pretty agitated.

Gulliver's tail twitched behind him, and he took a few steps toward the doors, debating whether or not he was allowed to just walk in.

"Why is this so weird?" he muttered under his breath.

"Gullie? Is that you?" Tierney's head popped out into the hallway, and she was all smiles for him, like nothing had changed. "Get in here." She pushed the door open and shooed him over to the huge table where Keir looked at home.

Gulliver eyed the vacant throne at the apex of the room.

"I can't make myself do it yet." She plopped down into one of the seats at the table. "To me, that's my father's chair, and I get freaked out every time I try to approach the throne. It's still too weird." Keir put a hand on her arm, and she visibly relaxed, before he took his seat next to her.

Gulliver let out an easy breath. This was definitely still the Tia he'd always known, just with a calming presence at her side now. It was weird to think that the man who agitated her also soothed her.

"Well, sit down already." She shoved a chair toward him with her foot.

"Why did you summon me with the official-looking queenly parchment and wax seals? I thought I was being arrested when the guard showed up to deliver it."

"I haven't had to summon anyone yet, and I wanted to try it." She gave him her most impish smile.

Keir shook his head with a wry grin. "Why do we like her?"

"Love." She pouted. "You both love me."

"You wanted to try it?" Gulliver scowled at her, still stuck on that point. "Do you know how long the trip from Myrkur is? My saddle sores have sores, Tia!"

"Ew, I don't need to know that."

Gulliver shook his head and stood. "If you don't actually need anything, I'm going to go to the kitchens to get some snacks, and then I'm taking a nap. When the moon rises, I'm going to go find Toby to open a portal for me so I can get back home to my family."

"Sit." Tierney's face changed in an instant from his best friend in the world to a proper ice queen.

He dropped back into the chair without thinking.

"I do need you, Gullie. I called you here for a reason, but you have to swear not to tell another soul. Not yet."

"What's wrong now? Have you discovered another kingdom on the brink of war and destruction? Because if you have, I think I'd rather sit this one out if you don't mind."

"Not quite." She scooted her chair closer, until their knees were touching. "About a month ago, I received a top-secret disturbing report from my father—you know, Mom and Dad are on an extended trip right now. Mom thought it was best to get him out of my hair while I establish my authority as queen."

"And her authority as wife." Keir grinned at her and she rolled her eyes.

"Gulliver doesn't need to know that."

He definitely didn't. Gulliver could imagine it would be difficult for Tierney to take over when her predecessor was still very much respected and loved throughout the kingdom. Worse still with her father breathing down her neck. It was no secret that Lochlan O'Shea was happy to abdicate to his more-than-capable daughter, but at the same time, he wasn't the sort to step back and keep his opinions to himself. In the first weeks after her coronation, Lochlan about drove her insane.

"What did he have to say that involves me?"

"This is like code red stuff, Gullie. You cannot tell *anyone*." Tierney looked over her shoulder to make sure the doors were shut and they were alone.

"What's code red mean?" They both ignored Keir.

"Then, how about you don't tell me? I think I'd prefer that option." Gulliver tried to stand up, but she shoved him back down. "Seriously, Tia?"

Tierney ignored him, dropping her voice to a whisper. "Dad says this could be super dangerous."

"Okay. But what has that got to do with me?"

"You're the only one I can trust with this, Gul. We have to act quickly and quietly."

"Yep. Sure. Sounds good. You let me know how that works out."

"Gulliver." She sounded a little too much like her mother when she said his name like that.

"*Tierney*." He tilted his head to the side. "What have you gotten me into this time?"

The story continues in
Fae's Envoy: Queens of the Fae Book Ten

FAE'S ENVOY

QUEENS OF THE FAE BOOK 10

With a sentient tail and cat-like eyes, Gulliver O'Shea has always been different, and everyone can see it. Except for his best friend, the queen of Iskalt. She treats him like he matters. So, when she says jump, he flies. And when she asks him to travel through a portal to a strange human city and gather information on a dangerous group attacking fae, he… reluctantly realizes he has no choice.

He just didn't expect he would have to bring along a sullen Toby—lost after the death of his intended—or that New Orleans would be so much more frightening than the small human farm he was used to visiting.

Gulliver's obsession with everything human brings him face to face with a girl unlike any he's ever met before. Sophie-Ann Devereaux. She's kind and clumsy and… sick. So sick he knows her frail human body won't last much longer.

The closer he gets to the humans behind the fae attacks, the more he realizes what he's done. He's failed Tia. Lost his mission. Become as useless as he always feared he was. Because the waitress, the one fading from this world, isn't just a random human girl. Her father is the man Gullie was sent to find. Together with his second in command, they intend to erase the fae from their world. And they'll resort to any means necessary to see it done.

From an accidental carjacking to an unhealthy obsession with beignets and cute human girls with blue hair, Gulliver embarks on an adventure of a lifetime in Fae's Envoy.

ABOUT MELISSA A. CRAVEN

Melissa A. Craven is an Amazon bestselling author of Young Adult Contemporary Fiction and YA Fantasy (her Contemporary fans will know her as Ann Maree Craven). Her books focus on strong female protagonists who aren't always perfect, but they find their inner strength along the way. Melissa's novels appeal to audiences of all ages and fans of almost any genre. She believes in stories that make you think and she loves playing with foreshadowing, leaving clues and hints for the careful reader.

Melissa draws inspiration from her background in architecture and interior design to help her with the small details in world building and scene settings. (Her degree in fine art also comes in handy.) She is a diehard introvert with a wicked sense of humor and a tendency for hermit-like behavior. (Seriously, she gets cranky if she has to put on anything other than yoga pants and t-shirts!)

Melissa enjoys editing almost as much as she enjoys writing, which makes her an absolute weirdo among her peers. Her favorite pastime is sitting on her porch when the weather is nice with her two dogs, Fynlee and Nahla, reading from her massive TBR pile and dreaming up new stories.

Visit Melissa at Melissaacraven.com for more information about her newest series and discover exclusive content.

Join Melissa and Michelle's Facebook Group: Search for Melissa and Michelle's Fantasy Book Warriors

Follow Michelle and Melissa on TikTok at @ATaleOfTwoAuthors

ABOUT M. LYNN

Michelle MacQueen is a USA Today bestselling author of love. Yes, love. Whether it be YA romance, NA romance, or fantasy romance (Under M. Lynn), she loves to make readers swoon.

The great loves of her life to this point are two tiny blond creatures who call her "aunt" and proclaim her books to be "boring books" for their lack of pictures. Yet, somehow, she still manages to love them more than chocolate.

When she's not sharing her inexhaustible wisdom with her niece and nephew, Michelle is usually lounging in her ridiculously large bean bag chair creating worlds and characters that remind her to smile every day - even when a feisty five-year-old is telling her just how much she doesn't know.

See more from M. Lynn and sign up
to receive updates and deals!
michellelynnauthor.com

Join Melissa and Michelle's Facebook Group: Search for Melissa and Michelle's Fantasy Book Warriors

Follow Michelle and Melissa on TikTok @ATaleOfTwoAuthors

Want More From Brea's World?

Don't miss the free prequel, Fae's Dilemma available at

BookHip.com/VJMXVGD

www.ingramcontent.com/pod-product-compliance
Lightning Source LLC
Chambersburg PA
CBHW020243030826
48979CB00030B/2539/J

* 9 7 8 1 9 7 0 0 5 2 2 4 4 *